FAIRYDALE

VERONICA LANCET

VERONICA LANCET

Fairydale

Edited by: Alex M.

Beta Read by: Oana D, Jennifer SF, Saba A, Samantha R.

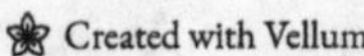

PREFACE

Dear Reader,

Fairydale is a mix of gothic, horror, fantasy, and paranormal fiction with a dash of history, but at its core it's simply a love story. It's quite possibly my favorite story that I've written, and I hope you will enjoy it as much as I did writing it.

Before proceeding, there are a few disclaimers to address.

If you're looking for a typical romance book, this isn't it.

This is a long journey (and by that, I mean almost 1000 pages), so if you're not a fan of complex narrative threads, lengthy books or extreme slow burns, then this will **not** be the book for you.

This is also **not** the book to skim, or you may find yourself lost in a sea of information, which is, at times, purposefully misleading. The plot is complicated, featuring a large cast of characters, and three different timelines.

Though the story contains alternating historical timelines, due to the nature of the topic at hand, this does not attempt to be a piece of authentic historical fiction. I've tried to make those sections as digestible as possible while still keeping some historical realism.

The story can get quite dark and emotional at times, so I urge you to check the content warnings carefully before proceeding.

I hope you enjoy it and *please* do not spoil the story for others!

Content Warnings: blood (gore), blood play & period play, death, derogatory terms, discrimination, drugs, graphic torture, graphic violence, graphic sexual situations (humanoid & non-humanoid), inces-

tuous situations, infertility, kidnapping, murder, rape, weapons, PTSD, suicide.

Prologue

The sun was setting and Lizette still could not bring herself to go back home. Not when her family would take one look at her and guess what had happened.

It hadn't been her fault—she was aware of that much. But she didn't think her family would agree. Certainly not her mother, who could barely stand the sight of her most days. If she knew, she would only have one more reason to hate her—potentially one more reason to send her away.

She was alone in the forest at night, a rather dangerous place to be in if you were female, but Lizette had already suffered the worst a woman could suffer. Even now, that place between her legs would not stop bleeding, no matter how much she tried to wipe it away with the material of her tattered sweater.

As she made her way towards the waterfall deep in the forest, her only thought was to wash away any trace of him off her body.

The sound of the water slowly reached her ears. Her cheeks were red, her tears already dried up. Yet as she came upon the waterfall, she couldn't help herself from crying anew.

She gently removed her clothing, careful of her wounds which still pained her a great deal. Neatly folding her dress on the ground, she neared the river bank as she dipped her toes into the water. The first chill caught her unawares, but then that's what she got for attempting to bathe in a river at the beginning of December.

Yet she still had one hidden weapon in her arsenal.

Rubbing her palms together, she willed the heat from her body to spread to the water in the river, making it the temperature she desired.

Lizette might not be as powerful as her mother, but she did have this one ability she was proud of—the ability to heat things up. Unfortunately, even that hadn't been enough to stop his attack.

When the water had warmed enough, Lizette submerged her entire body, scrubbing at her skin and wishing she could remove her memories as easily as she could his scent.

She spent moments on end in the river, dreading the fact that she would have to face reality when she was done.

Slowly, she got out of the water and for a moment simply stood on the river bank next to her dress, unable to bring herself to put on the garment again. Luckily, due to her ability, she could keep herself warm without the need for clothing.

Yet as she stood there contemplating her life, she noted a colorful butterfly flying close to the surface of the water.

She didn't know how any butterfly could survive a winter there, but she was too taken by the beautiful scene to question such a sighting.

The butterfly seemed to have a clear purpose as it headed straight for her, batting its brilliantly blue wings as it stopped right in front of her eyes. Before she realized what it meant to do, it went lower, settling on her lower stomach.

"What are you doing?"

She found the strength to smile anew as she thought herself so lucky that the beautiful butterfly had come to her.

"Of course you wouldn't answer back," she chided herself as she released a weary sigh.

As she stared at the butterfly, it suddenly turned with its head towards her, almost as if it understood her. Yet that was not the strangest thing.

In the blink of an eye, the butterfly slowly melted into her skin until nothing remained of its beautiful form.

Startled, Lizette stood up. She was afraid she might have harmed it with her abilities.

One day, she would realize that she hadn't killed the butterfly.

She'd given it life.

Part One

Chapter One

August 1955. Boston, Massachusetts

"Miss O'Sullivan, Miss O'Sullivan!

Turning my head in the direction of the voice calling my name, my mouth tugs up in a wide grin as I notice Stevie, one of my pupils, rush towards me.

"It's for you, Miss O'Sullivan!" He stops by my side, huffing out a breath as he extends a thick brown envelope. "Mrs. Jennings said it's for you."

My brows furrow in confusion. But as I accept the envelope, I confirm that it has my name scribbled at the top in immaculate penmanship.

Miss Darcy O'Sullivan.

More odd is the fact that there is no sender, nor a return address.

"Thank you, Stevie. Why don't you go back to the others. Lunch will be served soon," I smile at him as I ruffle his thick locks.

His lips spread into a huge smile as he grabs my waist in a tight hug, whispering a muffled *I love you, Miss O'Sullivan*, before he dashes away, his cheeks already tinged with red.

Shaking my head at his little stunt, I place the envelope under my arm as I head back to my room in the staff quarters.

Saint Russell Boarding School is one of the top boarding schools in the country, and though a requirement of my position had been to live on its premises, I'd been more than happy to do so considering the generous remuneration.

Reaching the hallway, I walk down to the third door before I knock carefully three times.

I share my room with Allison, another teacher who'd joined at the same time I did. I'd been extremely lucky to share the room with only one other person.

As a young child, I'd always slept in the same room with my mother, and after her death when I was ten years old, I was entrusted to an orphanage. There, the rooms could have eight or ten people at a time. Compared to that, the lodgings at Saint Russell are spectacular.

"Come in," Allison calls out in a groggy voice.

I push the door open, and Allison shuffles in her bed in an attempt to get up.

"No," I immediately call out. "Don't move on my account."

"It seems that every day you see me only in bed," Allison adds dryly, her mouth quirking up.

"It's not your fault you caught the flu. In fact," I say as I put the envelope on my bed before going over to hers. Placing my hand on her forehead, I brush it across her skin, checking her temperature.

"You're not boiling anymore," I say, noting her chapped lips. Turning to the bed table, I pour her some water and hand her the glass. "Now you just need to hydrate yourself and you'll be as good as new."

"What would I do without you?" She smiles, shaking her head. "You should have applied for the nurse position, not the English teacher one. Everyone knows by now that you have a healing touch."

"You know I couldn't have," I flush lightly at her praise. "I didn't have the qualifications for that."

I'd been lucky enough that the sisters at the orphanage I grew up in had sponsored my training as a teacher, and upon finishing my course, they'd successfully placed me with Saint Russell.

Without them I would have never gotten where I am today and I am eternally grateful for everything they've done for me—particularly Sister Mary and Sister Anne. From the beginning they'd been my biggest champions, helping me succeed when the odds had been stacked against me.

"I can't imagine anyone being better than you. My fever didn't go down with all the medicine the doctor gave me, but it went away after that tea you made."

"Just lucky, I guess," I smile, smoothing her blanket around the edges.

I'd always been drawn to medicine and the art of healing, and at one point I might have entertained the thought of pursuing a career in it. But I couldn't have refused the sisters' offer knowing how hard they had looked out for me over the years. So I'd simply continued with teaching. As much as I enjoy preparing teas and tinctures, I love spending time with the kids and teaching them about the wonders of literature.

Any way I look at it, I can't help but feel like I've been continuously blessed with good fortune.

"What's that?" Allison points to the envelope.

"Oh, I forgot about it. I got mail," I quip enthusiastically. Except for the sisters, I don't have anyone who would send me anything, so my best estimate is that it's a package from them.

"I'm jealous. Those nuns of yours treat you better than my own mother treats me," Allison grumbles, but I know it's not with ill intent.

Sister Mary always sends me fabrics to make myself some clothes, while Sister Anne makes sure to send me a new book every month. It's their way of letting me know I'm always in their thoughts. In return, I make sure to send them tinctures I make with local plants.

"They are lovely, aren't they?" I sigh absentmindedly. Despite being orphaned so young, I consider myself incredibly lucky. I have a job and people who care about me. I have a roof over my head, a place to sleep and warm food in my belly. Regardless of how you look at my situation, it's far above average—certainly more than a lot of people can boast about.

Perhaps that is why I am reluctant to confess that there is something missing.

I love and am loved in return, yet there is a gaping hole in my heart that seemingly bleeds invisible blood.

It's something I've lived with my entire life—this sense of missing something integral to my being. But it's also something I've never admitted to anyone else. To do so would make me seem ungrateful, and that is the last thing I am.

I am just...restless.

Straining a smile, I take a seat on my bed as I open a drawer and rummage for a paper cutter. Carefully slicing the top of the envelope, I sneak my hand inside to pull the contents.

My eyes widen as I spot three different smaller envelopes—one very thick, and two other slim ones—together with a jewelry case.

"Is it the nuns?" Allison probes.

I shake my head slowly, blinking as I take in the contents. Once more, I turn the envelope around searching for the sender but there is none. Even the smaller ones are blank.

"Who is it then?"

"I don't know," I answer softly.

Curiosity gets the best of me as I open the thick envelope first, a gasp making its way past my lips as I see the green hue of the notes. And upon pulling them out, I'm shocked to see wads of cash unlike I've ever beheld in my life.

"Darcy, that's..."

"Who would send me so much money?" I whisper. My body is frozen in shock as I can't take my eyes off the money.

Allison is quicker than me as she comes to my side, taking a seat on the bed and counting the money.

"It's one thousand," she whispers, the awe in her voice mirroring my own. "One thousand dollars, Darcy. It's a quarter of what we make in a year."

"But how..."

"Check the letters," she points to the other two.

Using the paper cutter, I open the first envelope, fishing a neatly folded letter out of it and what looks to be a train ticket.

"So? What does it say?" Allison asks impatiently as my eyes scan the contents of the letter.

"It's from Mr. Vaughan. A lawyer," I mutter, unable to believe my eyes. "He claims he's writing on behalf of my biological father, Leo Pierce, who..." I swallow uncomfortably. "Recently passed away."

"Your biological father?" She frowns.

I'd already told her that I never knew who my father was. My mother had never revealed that information, and on the off-chance I asked about him, she would tell me he wasn't a good man.

"There's more," I whisper as I wet my lips. "He requests my presence at Leo Pierce's funeral, which will take place in three days, and for the reading of the will since I am included in it. But for that he wants me to come to my father's hometown—Fairydale."

"Fairydale," she frowns. "I've never heard of it."

"Apparently it's somewhere in Massachusetts," I say as I look at the train ticket.

It's labeled Boston-Fairydale, with a flexible date range of August 28th to August 31st.

"And he gave you a thousand dollars for what? It doesn't make sense," she comments.

"He says it's to make sure I have everything I need until I reach Fairydale."

And that's not everything.

Mr. Vaughan relates that I have other family members—two half-siblings. But going by their ages...

I barely stifle the gasp at the realization that not only am I illegitimate, but also most likely the product of an affair. And his wife will be there.

No, I couldn't possibly go knowing I would be unwelcome.

But as I read on, Mr. Vaughan assures me of the opposite.

"*The family wishes to make your acquaintance as soon as possible*," I read out loud.

"So you're going?" Allison asks, startling me from my daze. "You need to. If he gave you a thousand dollars for everything you need, then who knows what's in that will."

"I don't know..." I murmur, uncertainty clawing at me.

Once I finish the letter, I read it again. Something uncomfortable tugs at my chest, but I do not know what.

A thousand questions go through my mind at once.

Why now?

My father never bothered to contact me while he was still alive, so why would he go through the trouble of leaving me anything in his will?

But more than anything, how did this Mr. Vaughan track me to Saint Russell? How could he have known where I live unless...

"He must have known all along where I was," I whisper, blinking to chase away the sudden moisture coating my lashes.

My father, this Leo Pierce, must have known where I was all this time. And even knowing that, he left me to be raised by strangers, all alone in the world.

The realization leaves me reeling.

Instead of joy at finding out I have additional family, or that I may stand to inherit some good money, all I feel is unease.

Yet once that train of thought starts, nothing can stop it.

The money for my teaching course. My placement at Saint Russell. Was it all a farce, too? Were the sisters in on this as well?

I'd always wondered why me. Why was it that only I had been blessed to have so many things paid for when others could only dream of the same.

At the time, I'd thought I showed most promise, and it had been an entirely merit-based process. Now...the doubts are clamoring.

Allison takes the letter from my hand, quickly reading it from beginning to end.

"He's saying it's *mandatory* for you to go for the reading of the will," she points to the word mandatory in the letter—a word I'd skipped over as I was digesting everything.

"And if I don't?"

"Maybe they won't be able to read it? What if it's a condition for everyone to be there before they read it?"

"You're right," I sigh.

But before I can make a decision, I turn my attention to the other envelope and the jewelry case.

"Don't tell me they sent you some expensive jewelry, too?" Allison groans. "Your father must have been rich as hell."

I don't reply as I carefully open the box, almost afraid of what the contents would reveal.

And just as I'd suspected, it's something that must be worth a fortune.

It's a swan brooch encrusted with diamonds—or at least what I assume to be diamonds. The back is entirely made of gold, while the white front must be some type of porcelain.

As my fingers brush over the smooth, luxuriant surface, a shiver of awareness travels down my back—almost as if I'd done the exact thing countless times before.

Both Allison and I are staring in awe at the little accessory, knowing we'd probably never seen anything as fine in our lives.

But as the shock soon wears off, a disappointment unlike any other settles in my bones.

Though I'd gotten wonderful opportunities throughout my life, I'd always felt as if I had worked for them. Yes, luck had factored in the equation, but I'd also done everything in my power to be deserving of my good fortune.

The letter from Mr. Vaughan, the monetary gift and now this priceless brooch I am staring at are telling me all the previous *luck* had been nothing more than calculated interventions.

"Open the letter," Allison places the small envelope in my hands.

With shaky fingers, I slice through the paper, in the process cutting myself.

"Ah," I startle as a drop of blood falls onto the white of the paper. Bringing my finger to my mouth, I suck on the small cut.

"You're emotional. It's normal," Allison assures me. "Let me help," she says as she takes out a square black carton and a key. My name is written in gold lettering on one side of the carton, while on the other it's an address—*12 Astor Place.*

"What's this?" My friend frowns. "A key to what?" she blinks.

"I honestly don't know, Allison. I can't make sense of any of this," I say honestly.

My heart is beating loudly in my chest, my head swarming with confusion the more I think of all the implications.

Today I found out I had a father. Today I also found out I *lost* a father.

And while neither seem to affect me much, the idea that Leo Pierce must have known about me—must have been keeping *track* of me—is unnerving.

"Why would he not take me in?" I voice out my utmost concern. "If he knew where I was—what I was doing—why not reach out? Why do I find out about him now, when he's already dead?"

Allison is silent for a moment, merely regarding me intently.

Though I'm not yet crying, frustration, anguish and pain must all be etched on my features.

"You can only find out why by going there."

I bring my teeth over my lower lip as I turn my gaze to everything I'd received—the information that had just turned my life upside down. At this point, money is the last of my worries, even though I've just been gifted one thousand dollars as if it was pocket change. I'm simply terrified of the truth, and how that would change everything I've known so far about my life.

"I don't know," I shake my head.

The truth is that I am scared about what I could find out. Yet if I don't go...the doubts will keep clawing at me.

Taking a deep breath, I gather all the files to put them back in the envelope, unwittingly smearing some blood from my finger on the black carton. I wipe it as best as I can before placing everything in my nightstand.

"I can't make such a decision now," I tell Allison. "I'm too conflicted," I purse my lips.

"Take your time, but I don't think you can take too long," she tells me carefully, and I know her words to be true.

Because if I *must* be present, my sense of responsibility tells me I can't *not* go.

I make Allison another cup of my special brew before I excuse myself, telling her I need some time to think things through.

My schedule is done for the day so I can go to my usual spot on the roof of Albert Hall. Only faculty have the keys to the roof, but no one ever goes there.

Dropping by the dining hall first to pack some food, I then sneak to the back stairs, making my way to the roof. Immediately, the fragrant, warm summer wind brushes against my face, lulling me into a deceptive sense of comfort.

Taking a seat on the ground, I rest my back against the wall and release a tired breath.

Though my body is relaxed at being in a familiar environment, my mind is continuously at war.

Why only now?

Why had Leo Pierce never reached before? Surely if he left me something in his will, then he must have held *some* affection for me.

The answer, though, is staring me right in the face—or, as much as I can make sense of it.

He was a married man when he took up with my mother and got her pregnant. At the time, he must have felt embarrassed by the fact, so he'd hidden it. Only in death did he have the courage to admit to the world that he had another child—one he'd never once looked in the eye. In the end, this only amounts to a dying man's regret.

Yet regardless of my feelings on the matter, it seems it's imperative I go—for the other members of the family who might be waiting for me to wrap things up, and also for my own state of mind.

I know myself.

Eventually, the what ifs would get to me, eroding at my subconscious until they'd bleed into my consciousness and never let me go. The more I'd try to bury this matter, the more it would try to resurface.

Then there's the curiosity.

I have...siblings.

Bringing my finger to my lips, I absentmindedly trail my tongue around the cut in an attempt to soothe the light sting.

Mr. Vaughan had mentioned two half-siblings—a brother, August, and a sister, Grace.

It's hard to believe that there are other people out there who share the same blood—the idea almost surreal.

Though I'd had some friends at the orphanage, jealousy and distance had ultimately cut all ties. I no longer kept in contact with anyone, and I'd be lying if that hadn't hurt me.

Allison had been a godsend, and in her I'd found a good friend.

Still, August and Grace are my siblings. My only living relatives.

Could I go on my entire life without knowing them? Maybe I could have, before I was aware of their existence. But now that I know, I can't simply ignore that too.

The more I dwell on it, the more my mind is made up.

I need to go to Fairydale. But I also need to make sure the claims in these letters are legitimate, and for that I need to have a discussion with Sister Mary and Sister Anne.

The following day, I start putting my affairs in order so I may leave soon.

I speak with the headmistress and she grants me a one month leave —with deducted pay, of course. Then I pack some of my clothes and necessities in a small suitcase.

Though the train ticket I'd gotten had been from Boston to Fairydale, I'm going to take a small detour by going to the orphanage in Worcester first to have a conversation with the sisters. If they confirm the information in the letters is accurate, I will travel straight to Fairydale via Boston. It might be a longer journey, but I'd rather be safe. I've read of a number of inheritance scams in the newspaper, and though I doubt scammers would give me one thousand dollars upfront, the reality is that I am an unmarried woman with no immediate family, which could make me an ideal target.

"You're awfully brave to do this," Allison comments as she watches me fold my clothes in my suitcase. "But smart to check with the nuns too. I would have jumped at the first chance of some extra money," she states candidly.

"It is a lot of money," I nod, thinking the contents of the will must involve much more than I'd already been given. "But I've never been concerned about that. I am comfortable as I am," I shrug slightly. "I like my job, and I don't have any personal expenses that would necessitate a lot of money."

"Maybe because it's all you've ever known," Allison points out. "Think about all the things you could buy—the dresses, the purses, the *shoes,*" she exclaims dreamily. "Or think about the trips you could make. Didn't you say you'd like to visit Europe one day?"

I nod.

I've been dying to visit England since the first time I read Jane Eyre. But I've also been aware all along what a foolish dream that is.

I am a teacher. And while I might have a comfortable yearly wage, it's nowhere near what one would need to afford an overseas trip.

"You might be able to if they give you a lot of money," Allison giggles. "You could go to London. See those fancy palaces. Maybe fall in love with an Englishman," she winks at me.

I blush, looking away as I feel myself redden from head to toe.

Allison has a beau she visits on the weekends. He's a banker at the Bank of Boston, in his late twenties, and thoroughly set for success. They've been talking about marriage for a while, and Allison is convinced he is going to propose soon.

Through her, though, I've gotten to experience vicariously what it means to be in love and have a relationship. And despite my protests at times, she'd even shared details about their intimate life.

To my virgin ears it had all sounded so scandalous, yet I couldn't help but feel the allure of it—of finding that one person you could share all of yourself with.

Although I am content with my life as it is, I have to admit that I've always dreamed of meeting my own prince charming. Maybe some charming Mr. Rochester or a brooding Heathcliff. Yet despite that, I've never made an effort to date.

I've been to some social events, and I've even been asked out by some handsome gentlemen. Every time, for some unknown reason, I turned them down.

Here I am, twenty-four and I have never been on a date.

But even if I were to come into some money, would my life change so drastically?

Would I finally have the courage to go out into the world and do the things I've always wanted to do? Somehow, I doubt that.

Still, at least I'll have the option.

"Maybe," I mumble. "Money can certainly buy a lot of things."

But there's the unspoken. Can it really buy happiness?

I know Allison would answer positively in a second, and objectively, I should agree. But there's something niggling at my conscience. The same restlessness I've always encountered makes me think there's something more. A freedom unlike any other that has nothing to do with the material, maybe not even the corporeal.

Somewhere in the world, there's a certain happiness that calls to me—something ineffable that speaks to my soul rather than my mind. Perhaps I do not know what it is now, but there's something within me that tells me I will—when I am ready, I will.

"I hope you won't forget about me if you suddenly become a millionaire," Allison jokes, and I shake my head in amusement.

"His family lives in a town called Fairydale. I doubt that's a popular destination for millionaires," I say as I fold a couple of clean shirts.

On a whim, we'd spread a map and tried to pinpoint Fairydale. It's a historic town in north-eastern Massachusetts, about an hour east of Ipswich, but we couldn't find much information about it.

"Besides, I will have to split the money with his other children, who are probably more deserving than I am based on the fact that they are legitimate and..."

"Stop right there," Allison suddenly stands up, before sitting down again as a wave of dizziness assaults her.

I make to move to her side but she puts her hand up, stopping me. "Why would you be less deserving? If anything, he should give you more because he was never there for you. At least his other children got to spend time with him. What did you get?"

I purse my lips.

Her words have merit. But there's a discomfort inside of me every time I think about the money—almost as if it isn't mine to take, regardless of whether it's been given to me. It's the same discomfort I feel every time I think about the thousand dollars I'd placed at the bottom of my suitcase.

"Do you think they will hate me?" I ask on a whisper.

How could they not, though? I was the product of an affair, and I was coming to their home to take some of their money. Regardless of the fact that Mr. Vaughan had assured me the family knew of my existence and desired to get to know me, I'm still a little wary about it.

"Who knows," Allison shrugs. "They might, or they might not. You're going there to find out."

I chuckle nervously. Sometimes her honesty hurts. I'm already taking the risk of a lifetime by going to a foreign location. I don't want to think that I might end up the most hated person in that town.

"All done," I take a deep breath when my suitcase is closed.

I don't own many items, but because I'm meeting these people for the first time, I want to make a good impression. As such, I've packed up only the more qualitative pieces of clothing I own—a couple of shirts and a pair of trousers, a skirt, two dresses, a nightgown and some underthings.

The following day, I break my fast with Allison before I leave for the train station.

"Be careful. Give me a call if you're able to," she says as she wraps her arms around me in a warm hug.

"Of course. Who else would I tell anything to, if not you?" I smile, kissing her cheek.

"Safe travels, Darcy. I know you'll find what you're looking for."

Waving goodbye, I get on the train. The journey to Worcester takes close to two hours. I'd already phoned Sister Mary and Sister Anne to let them know I was coming, and they'd promised they would be waiting at the station for me.

Sure enough, the moment I get off the train, they are there, looking as bright and beautiful as ever.

"My dear Darcy," Sister Anne exclaims as she draws me into a big hug. "I didn't think we'd see you so soon."

"Thank you so much for waiting for me."

"Nonsense. We see each other so rarely now, of course we'd come for our favorite girl," Sister Mary said.

Giving them a sweet smile, we start chatting as we make our way to the main street to hail a cab, which I insist on paying for. They are a little peeved at me, but soon our interactions go back to normal as they tell me about their newcomers and that they'd used some donations to build another wing in the dormitory, which they offer to show to me as soon as we get to the orphanage.

It's only a few hours later that we close ourselves in their office to have the *serious* talk I'd requested. And as we take our seats at the small table, I belatedly recognize the worry marring their faces and the fact that all this idle chat had been nothing but stalling.

"We know why you're here," Sister Anne says without preliminaries.

My eyes widen as I slide my gaze from one woman to another.

With their lips pursed, their features stern, they look guilty.

"How..." I whisper.

Sister Mary rises from her chair, going to one of her cabinets and removing a small box from a hidden compartment.

Bringing the box in front of me, she opens it, presenting the contents to me.

I freeze as I spot an exact replica of the swan brooch I'd received in the mail from Mr. Vaughan.

But more than anything, I feel myself growing cold as all the pieces fall into place, this one piece of jewelry the confirmation I needed.

"You knew who my father was," I whisper, slowly looking up.

Sister Mary purses her lips, but eventually gives me a light nod.

"Your mother knew she was dying when she asked us to take care of you," she starts, taking her seat across from me once more. "She was sick and penniless and she didn't know what else to do. All she had left was that brooch, part of an identical set from what I gathered later on. She didn't say much about your father at the time. She didn't even mention he might be an option for your custody so we didn't pry."

"After she died, we were to sell the brooch and use the funds to provide for you and your education," Sister Anne continued. "Knowing it could fetch a pretty dollar, I went to get the brooch appraised by a professional, and while we were waiting for an answer from the jeweler we got an anonymous message inquiring where we had gotten the brooch from. We corresponded back and forth for a while before a lawyer, Mr. Vaughan, appeared to personally look at the brooch. It was then that he showed us the twin brooch and recounted that they were custom made and the only one who could have had the second one was your mother. When we told him about Lisette and you, he was shocked."

"From what we gathered, your mother left your father while she was still pregnant and he couldn't find her," Sister Mary adds.

I blink, slowly taking in the information. My mother had run away from my father?

There are vague memories in which she'd remind me my father was a bad man, but she'd never told me why. And I never asked for more. Sensing her discomfort with the subject, I'd simply acted as if I didn't have a father—and never wanted one either.

Could it be that she didn't know he was married? That she found out after the affair had already been consummated? It would make sense why she'd brand him as a bad man for stepping out on his vows and potentially deceiving her in the process.

As soon as that train of thought surfaces, a calm settles over me.

I may not have too many memories of my mother, but she was a fine woman who did her best to raise me despite her circumstances. She'd been unmarried and on the verge of poverty and still, she'd managed to give me love and a safe environment to grow up in. I'm happy there is a high possibility she didn't willingly participate in the affair—or, at least did not know it *was* an affair.

"That doesn't explain why he never came for me," I speak slowly, doing my best to remain rational despite my emotions running high. To say the last couple of days have been a whirlpool of emotions would be an understatement.

Sister Mary and Sister Anne share a knowing look before Sister Anne speaks.

"He was married and already had a family. He thought you would be better off with us," she explains, though I fail to see the logic of it.

Who could possibly be better off at an orphanage over a family? Despite my luck at having found the two sisters, I know my case is a fortunate one. Most orphanages are devoid of love and warmth or any semblance of a familial feeling.

"He did promise to provide for you, and he made several donations to the orphanage as well as continuous payments for your personal needs and education," Sister Mary confirms what I'd been suspecting all along—that nothing was earned.

"Everything?" I ask in a soft voice.

They nod.

"He wanted you to have the best despite not being able to be there for you," she gives me a sad smile. "And he did hope that you could meet at some point when you grew up."

"Not anymore," I add, and their expressions don't change.

They know.

"We received a letter from his lawyer that he'd passed, and that you were included in his will. Mr. Vaughan knew it might come as a shock to you, so he sent you the brooch as proof."

I nod slowly.

Everything seems to fit in place well—*too* well. And though there are no holes in the narrative that I can immediately identify, there's something too coincidental about this scenario for my liking.

Sister Mary and Sister Anne had raised me to be judicious and always question everything. Despite that, they are now looking me in the eye and expecting me to believe everything.

If he hoped he might meet me as an adult, then why did he never communicate after I turned eighteen? Or after I got my teaching position? There were many opportunities for him to reach out, just as there were many years of me being *grown up.*

Somehow, I can't wrap my mind around the explanation.

Just as doubts start drowning me, I shake myself.

These are my mentors—my surrogate mothers. I can't just doubt them. If they say that's how it happened, then it must be how it happened.

"You must go, dear Darcy," Sister Mary takes my hands in hers. "I'm terribly sorry you had to find out like this and that you won't get to meet your father. But at least you can meet your other family?" she adds on a hopeful tone.

"Did you ever meet him?"

"No," she sighs. "We met Mr. Vaughan, and we corresponded with your father but we never personally met."

"I see," I slowly nod, forcing a smile. "If you assure me that it's the right thing to do, then I'm going."

"Wonderful," both sisters exclaim in unison.

"One other thing," I remember to inquire. "Do you know anything about Fairydale, his hometown? It's farther than I've ever traveled and..."

"It's just a town. Don't worry too much," Sister Mary interrupts, waving her hand dismissively. "From what I gathered, it is a haven for rich people who want to spend some time away from civilization. And you know those rich people. They value their privacy," she adds, almost jokingly.

"Indeed," I reply dryly.

"But if you encounter any hardship, you know we're one phone call away, dear," Sister Anne adds, giving the other nun a harsh look.

I force a smile, refraining from adding that I doubt a small town would have many functional telephones.

We spend the rest of the day chatting, and they offer me a place to sleep for the night before catching the first train in the morning.

It seems that I am bound for Fairydale, after all.

And as I board the train the following day, I try to cheer myself up on my new adventure and put my doubts aside.

Allison was right. I need to look at the bright side. Most likely I will be coming into some money—a sizable amount according to the nuns—and I will also get to meet my half-siblings.

What could possibly go wrong in a town that rhymes with fairytale?

Chapter Two

Two hours after I leave the orphanage, I am back in Boston as I wait for the connection to Fairydale via Ipswich. Taking advantage of the hour I have until the next departure, I buy some food since the journey is set to be some five hours.

When I board the train, I take my seat and remove a book from my purse—Jane Austen's Northanger Abbey. It's my first time embarking on such a long journey, so I'd brought along snacks and entertainment to keep me occupied.

But a couple hours later and no matter how much I tell myself I can hold it in, my bladder is demanding instant relief. Certainly, as I watch the hands of my wristwatch move at a snail's pace, my anxiety skyrockets until all I can hear is the sound of water trickling down...

Releasing a sigh, I tuck my things to the side as I take some tissues from my purse before going in search of the restroom.

The train's facilities are not exactly sanitary, but I make do. The floor is rattling under my feet from the moving train, the clattering noise clogging my ears and making this not the most comfortable experience.

After I flush, I move to the sink, washing my hands and watching my reflection in the mirror.

The pale skin under my eyes has a blue-ish hue, and you can tell I've barely slept a wink in the past couple of days.

Not only have I been worried about this journey into the unknown, but I've also been plagued by thoughts about my father—my other family. I want to know them, but at the same time I'm afraid of doing so —scared they are not going to like me.

Wetting my hands, I bring them to my face to freshen up.

Right at that moment, the confined space of the restroom becomes draped in darkness as the train passes through a tunnel. The terrain becomes uneven, making the train rattle even more.

I grab the handle on the wall in an effort to stabilize myself, waiting for the train to get out of the tunnel before I attempt to leave. Holding tight, I squeeze my eyes shut as a screeching noise from the rails erupts in the air, the sound as grating as nails on chalkboard.

Despite the overstimulation of my senses, the feeling of something brushing against my neck is unmistakable, as is the soft, warm air that fans my skin. My breathing intensifies, my body wound tight as I swallow hard.

What starts as the gentlest touch becomes increasingly bolder until I feel a slight pressure right under my pulse point.

My eyes snap open.

Two beams of light stream through the tiny window of the restroom, the rest of the space bathed in darkness.

For a second—one brief second—I almost swear I can make out an outline in the mirror. Yet as I blink once more it's gone.

It's gone, and light inundates the room once more as the train makes it out of the tunnel.

The mirror is fogged from my erratic breath, but as I look around, it's to find myself completely alone.

"Goodness," I exhale, feeling silly for getting so shaken by a simple play of shadows and my overactive imagination.

Regaining my composure, I smooth my palms over my skirt before I open the door and return to my seat.

It must be the nerves. And the fact that I'm being *daring* for the first time in my life.

Smiling to myself, I pick up the book, losing myself in the story once more. Alas, it seems that Catherine's rubbing off on me with her silly notions.

I'm so immersed in the story that I barely realize when the train stops, the Ipswich station announced.

Putting the book aside, I look around, noting that everyone is getting up to leave. I frown, but I don't find it strange since Ipswich is the biggest town on the map in the area. I doubt Fairydale is the final destination for many people.

Shrugging, I bring my attention back to the book.

"Ma'am?" A voice starts me not one minute later. Lifting my gaze, it's to find the conductor before me.

"Yes?" I ask, forcing my lips in a smile as is polite, though all I want to do is snap at the man for interrupting me right when General Tinley was about to consent to Catherine and Henry's marriage.

"You need to get off. This is the final station," he says in a curt tone.

"What?" I frown. "That can't be. I'm going to Fairydale," I explain as I rummage through my purse for my ticket. Taking it out, I hand it to him.

"See?" I point to the itinerary.

"I'm sorry but there must have been a mistake," he blinks as he reads my ticket. "There is no railway that passes through Fairydale. Whoever issued this ticket must have made a mistake," he says, scratching the back of his head.

"How can that be when the ticket examiner checked it?" I ask, outraged.

"He must have misread the destination. I'm sorry, ma'am, but this is the end of the line."

That can't be. The ticket examiner took his time looking at my ticket. I'm sure he couldn't have missed the name Fairydale in bold letters. But say he *had* misread it, why would Mr. Vaughan send me a faulty ticket? If he is from Fairydale himself, then he should know there is no railway in the vicinity of the town.

"What am I to do then? I need to get to Fairydale."

"I can't help you with that ma'am. You could try to find a coach or a driver heading in that direction. Though I should warn you," he stops, pursing his lips.

I lift my brows in question.

"There aren't many people going to Fairydale these days. And I would encourage you to reconsider, too."

"Whyever not?" I inquire, taken aback by his words.

"I'm guessing you haven't heard about the Joker of Ipswich?"

I frown, shaking my head.

"He was a murderer who liked to mutilate his victims. All women," he nods to me in a low voice, pausing as if he's waiting to see my shocked reaction. When I don't give him that, looking at him expectantly instead, he clears his throat and continues. "He was found a couple years back living in Fairydale with a dozen or so corpses in his house."

Although what he's saying is terrible, I don't see why that would turn Fairydale into an undesirable destination, and I pose the same question to him.

"But if he's been caught, then why would people avoid Fairydale?"

"You see, ma'am, he's not the first criminal to be caught in that town. It's like a magnet for bad people," he shakes his head. "You won't find too many people who'd want to go there."

Sister Mary had said it was a haven for millionaires. The conductor is now telling me it's a haven for criminals. Then again, who said the two don't necessarily overlap?

"I see," I reply, keeping my features blank.

Dear God, but what have I gotten myself into?

"Thank you," I nod, putting my items in my purse before rising and taking my suitcase from the overhead compartment.

"Wish you luck ma'am, but if I were you, I'd avoid that place. Especially if you're alone..." he trailed off, but the implication was clear.

"I'll take that under advisement. Have a good day," I incline my head before I make my way through the rows of seats. Stepping out of the train, I take a moment to look around and plan for my next steps. All the while, alarm bells won't stop ringing inside my head, the light scare from the bathroom making my pulse speed up.

This is what I get for trying to be daring for the first time in my life. I should have stayed behind, comfortable in my—maybe *too*—cozy life. All the money in the world is not worth the stress of being alone in a foreign place.

As an unaccompanied woman.

Haven't I read enough stories of young women gone missing? Or heard on the radio about the latest disappearances? The last thing I need is to become an additional statistic, since I doubt anyone would have much incentive in locating an orphan with no living relatives.

The cautious, sensible side of me keeps telling me to purchase another ticket and go back to Boston—back to my *non* dangerous life.

But there's also another part of me—one I've been stifling all my life. The one that craves adventure, family, and a sense of belonging. A part of me that seeks a purpose I know fully well I will not find in the halls of Saint Russell.

I may be proud of my job and derive satisfaction from being good at it, but it's not who I am. It's not my identity. Or, at least, not my *entire* identity.

I've read and dreamed about adventure, yet I've never once tried to embark on one for myself. For God's sake, Worcester to Boston is the farthest I've traveled before. Not to mention that all my travels have been strictly business-related. I've never taken a trip for myself. And considering I've been employed for more than a year now, with my own wages, I could have easily done that.

Yet I hadn't.

I'd stayed in my little bubble, content to watch the world from afar, read and hear about it from other people, but I've never dared to do anything on my own.

That restlessness that's been hiding away my entire life decides to poke its head right at that moment, propelling me further. One foot in front of the other, I march forward, energized with new confidence and determined to find someone who might tell me how to get to Fairydale.

Instead of poor orphaned Darcy, I'm going to be brave *heiress* Darcy.

Yet as soon as that thought crosses my mind, I find myself reeling when someone bumps into me. Before I can regain my balance, my suitcase is wrenched from my hands.

I'm slow to react and by the time I try to grab my suitcase back, a man with shaggy hair and red eyes gives me a disgusted look, spitting me in the face and pushing me so hard I fall on my back.

Breathing hard, I watch with wide eyes as he's running away with my suitcase and I'm unable to do anything to stop him. People all around the station are watching, but no one is batting an eye. Some pitiful glances, a few head shakes, but no one even inquires if I am alright.

Blinking back tears of frustration and embarrassment, I attempt to stand up, wobbling a little in the process. My back hurts, and my elbows sting from the contact with the pavement as I'd used them to cushion my fall. When I inspect them, I see skin peeling and a hint of blood.

"Drat it," I mumble, sniffling harshly and biting back a curse that would make the nuns swoon from the blasphemy of it.

At least he didn't take my purse. It's the only thing I can tell myself as I rummage for a napkin to wipe the gross saliva off my skin. Yet even that positive thought doesn't take long as I realize most of my money was at the bottom of the suitcase. Not to mention my clothes, all items I loved and had saved up for months to purchase.

Tears coat my lashes just as my anger mounts.

"Ugh," I grind my teeth, about to kick at the building in front of me but stopping myself at the last second as I realize I would only be hurting myself more.

Not only did I just find out there is no train to Fairydale, but now I've also been robbed.

What. A. Marvelous. Start.

I have less than fifty dollars in my purse, and as I look around, I breathe out in relief when my fingers brush against the small jewelry case.

I still have the brooch.

Yet how can I rejoice at such a small thing when I lost almost all my possessions?

If a moment ago my spirits were soaring, now they plummet to such horrifying depths I don't know how I'm not devolving into a crying mess right at this very moment. It must be all the people watching... I've already become the center of attention as I see a few women giggle in a corner while other men are whistling at me and making indecent offers.

If this is how people behave here... Then I'm scared to think that Fairydale will be any better. But I'm not going to let that stop me now that I've decided I'm going to push through.

Gritting my teeth, I push my chin up high as I stride inside the train station, heading straight for the information kiosk.

"Excuse me," I knock on the window. A bored woman loudly chewing gum raises a brow at me.

Flustered, I swallow hard as I try to maintain my composure.

"Could you please tell me how I can get to Fairydale?" I use my most people-friendly voice in hopes I can get some useful information.

But even that isn't enough as the woman looks me up and down, her lip twitching in annoyance.

"Unless you have a car, honey, no," she answers, the words rolling off her tongue with off-putting ease.

Just as I'm about to ask another question, she turns with her back to me, effectively ignoring me.

I blink in surprise. Surely, this isn't how she treats other people when it's her job to answer questions.

"Excuse me," I clear my throat as I speak louder.

She half-turns, giving me a *what more* type of look.

"How can I find a car?"

"Honey," she emphasizes the word. "Does this look like a rental place?"

My lips part in shock at her tone.

"You might have better luck at the main road," she says before she ignores me again.

Realizing I won't get anything out of her, I look around, following the signs and exiting at the main road.

Fifty dollars should get me to Fairydale and still be enough for a ride back in case things don't work out. That doesn't ease my frustration at losing over nine hundred dollars, or my most beloved clothes.

Just like that. Gone in the blink of an eye.

Moisture accumulates at the corners of my eyes, and I bring my hand up to wipe the tears away. The last thing I need now is to succumb to my increasingly erratic mood, or show weakness when it's clear that everyone is desensitized to felonies in this area.

Taking a deep breath, I trudge my way to the main road, thinking to find a cab driver willing to take me into Fairydale. It might run more expensive but I'd be more comfortable than hitchhiking a ride from a random driver.

A long—and rather empty—road stretches in front of me. The sun is high up in the sky, the heat almost unbearable.

I bring my napkin to my forehead as I wipe a few drops of sweat.

I'm wearing a navy blue shirt and a long black skirt, and I know I will boil in these clothes if I have to walk around in this heat to find a cab.

Yet just as I start walking down the street, the shrieking sound of an engine blasts through the air. Not one second later, a black Bentley Continental stops right in front of me. I may not be very knowledgeable when it comes to cars, but I do know this one—and the fact that it's an extremely expensive brand, usually only seen in movies or on billboards.

I watch curiously as a man in a four-piece suit climbs out of the car. He looks to be in his early fifties, gray hair peppered around his temples.

"Miss Darcy O'Sullivan?" He inquires, taking a step towards me.

Instinctively, I take a step back as my brows furrow in confusion.

How could he know who I am?

"Who are you?" I snap, my gaze already taking in my surroundings as an escape plan forms in my mind. If he takes one more step towards me, or tries to grab me, I'll scream. I'll bash him over the head with my purse, maybe kick him between the legs and then I'll run as fast as I can.

Nodding to myself, I assume a ready-to-fight stance as I give him a suspicious glare.

"My apologies," the man says, smiling. "I'm Mordechai Vaughan, Mr. Pierce's lawyer. I sent you the letter regarding his passing?"

His tone is soft, almost as if he's trying to lull me into trusting him. But it does the opposite, because what kind of devilish coincidence is this?

The ticket he sent had a flexible date. He couldn't have known what day and hour I would arrive—if at all.

"Prove it," I dare him.

He smiles slowly.

"Of course. Besides the letter, I also sent you a swan brooch and a key," he says, confirming the contents of the envelope he sent.

"Fine," I huff. "Let's say you *are* Mr. Vaughan. How did you know *when* to come for me? How come you're here right on time?" I ask, watching him through narrowed eyes.

He doesn't miss a beat, his facial expressions the same all throughout. He's sporting a laid-back, easy smile.

"Sister Anne rang me. She was worried about you," he replies. "That I got here right on time is a mere coincidence," he chuckles. "I thought I'd be late."

I nod slowly. Though his explanation makes sense, I can't help but feel like something isn't right.

Yes, Sister Anne *would* have rang him to make sure I arrived alright, and she would have probably pestered him to come get me. But that doesn't explain the other issue.

"There's no railway going through Fairydale," I state in a deadpan voice. "Why was the ticket issued *to* Fairydale?"

"Oh, was it really?" He looks genuinely surprised. "Must have been a printing mistake. I asked my assistant to get you a ticket to Fairydale. I didn't mean one *straight* to the town," he chuckles. "Everyone knows there's no train station in Fairydale."

"Right," I mumble, still assessing him.

He says all the right things, with all the right facial cues. But do I trust the man?

"Fair enough. But one more thing before I get in the car with you," I say with as much confidence as I can muster.

"Yes?"

"May I see your official ID. To make sure you are who you say you are."

"Of course," he readily agrees, moving forward just as his hand goes to the inside of his coat. For a second, the thought that he might be pulling out a gun on me crosses my mind, and my eyes widen as a million scenarios build up in my head—including the urge to duck and dash.

But as he withdraws a fancy leather wallet, sliding his driver's license from the first slot and handing it to me, I realize Catherine Moreland has nothing on me.

I'm going crazy.

Scanning the contents, I swallow my embarrassment.

The picture matches. The name does, too. As does the Fairydale address.

"If there is anything else I can do to put your mind at ease..."

"No." My lips tug up in a strained smile. "That would be enough, thank you."

"Great. We can get going then. The family can't wait to meet you, Miss O'Sullivan."

"You can call me Darcy," I murmur as I slide in the backseat of the car.

He doesn't bat an eye at my choice as he gets into the driver's seat and starts the engine.

"I couldn't help but notice you didn't bring any luggage?" He asks a couple minutes later, seemingly trying to make conversation.

Still smarting from my previous experience, I groan out loud at his question.

He raises a brow at me, which I notice in the rearview mirror.

"I got robbed," I sigh. "Someone stole my suitcase when I got off the train."

"Oh no," he suddenly stops the car. "We should get back then, see if we can get it back."

"No," I shake my head. "The man is long gone. We would never get it back. Besides, you were saying everything is time-sensitive."

"Are you sure? I can make some inquiries..."

"I'll be fine," I force a smile. "There must be a clothing shop in Fairydale for me to buy something to wear, right?"

"Of course. You'll see that our small town has everything you need," he gives me a warm smile and as he brings up Fairydale his entire countenance transforms.

If before he'd seem a little stiff and polite, now he is more animated.

"Can you tell me more about it? What's it like?"

"Fairydale? The best place you'll visit," he praises enthusiastically.

"You've lived there long?"

"All my life," he nods. "It's small and quiet, all surrounded by a historical atmosphere unmatched anywhere else. In my opinion, of course," he adds as he sees me frown.

"Someone mentioned some criminals?" I probe carefully, but he doesn't seem to mind.

"Oh, that Joker stuff?" he chuckles. "They finally caught the bastard, forgive my language. That he happened to be in Fairydale at that point is a mere coincidence. He wasn't a local. We are a very tightly knit community where everyone knows everyone. He'd only been renting a place for a few months before they found him."

"That is a little more reassuring," I give him a genuine smile for the first time as I breathe out relieved.

"Don't mind the gossip. Fairydale's bad reputation is only because of all the arrests happening around. But I always counter it with the fact that at least we have arrests. It means our sheriff is doing his job. What about other places? They boast zero crime not because it's not happening, but because it goes undetected."

"You're right about that," I find myself nodding.

"I bet you'll love it. Everyone is looking forward to meeting you."

"Including the family?" I ask softly, hugging my arms around myself in a protective gesture.

"Of course they do," he assures me. "August, your half-brother, has been overseeing everything with me, and I know for a fact he's wanted to meet you for a long time."

That surprises me.

"Have they known long about me?"

For the first time, he hesitates, pursing his lips as he takes a deep breath.

"August knew. Grace and Vicky only found out after Leo died."

I don't reply. If they only found out recently, then I'm sure they can't be very thrilled to have a stranger come and claim some of their money.

Mr. Vaughan continues to speak, singing more praises to the town and assuring me I'll have a lot to do during my visit.

"I know it can't compare to a place like Boston, but our little town has its attractions. We are right by a natural reservation, and there's a wonderful waterfall by the river. The town itself has many historic buildings. At least fifty percent of them are from the eighteenth century."

"Really? That's impressive," I exclaim, excited to visit those.

I've always been passionate about old architecture and well, old things in general.

"The Hales own a manor to rival a castle. It's up on the hill, you won't miss it when we enter the town. But there's the Old Church that was built during the seventeenth century—the oldest one in the town and one of the oldest surviving churches in the country. It's not open for the public, but it makes for a striking sight."

I lean forward, enthralled by that piece of information. When I'd heard that Fairydale was a historic town I'd grown excited at the prospect of visiting some real life ruins. Boston boasts a lot of historic buildings, too, but there's a significant difference between urban architecture and rural one.

"That sounds so exciting. I can't wait to see them," I quip, my lips tugging up.

"I gather you like that sort of thing?"

I nod enthusiastically.

"I teach English, but I've always had a soft spot for history," I tell him.

"Any period in particular?"

"Hmm," I tap my finger against my chin as I muse. "Early nineteenth century. And I suppose Ancient Mediterranean History? Although I doubt I'll be able to visit Italy or Greece any time soon," I chuckle.

"Why not? You never know where life will take you," he remarks with a knowing smile.

"You're right," I shrug. "I shouldn't limit myself."

"That's a good mentality. But if you love the early eighteen hundreds, then you might be interested in the plague cemetery at the outskirts of Fairydale. It has some of the most ornate tombs I've ever seen," he whistles.

"Plague cemetery?" I repeat, frowning.

"A plague hit Fairydale in eighteen-five and wiped out the entire population. Most people who live there right now are descendants of the families that moved in after the plague."

"That sounds fascinating," I nod, sneaking a glance at my wrist watch and marveling at how quickly the time had passed. We've been on the road for almost an hour now, but it feels as if only ten minutes have passed.

"And there it is," he points out at the sign up ahead.

Welcome to Fairydale. Founded in 1805.

"Why is it named Fairydale?" I ask. I'd been wondering that from the beginning.

Mr. Vaughan laughs.

"It's quite the tale. The mansion on the hill I mentioned? One of the founders of the town built it for his wife. She was nicknamed the *fairy* by the locals, so the name of the town stuck."

"He built her a mansion?" I smile. "That's quite romantic."

He nods thoughtfully.

"It was. Even now the town celebrates them during the Fairy Festival. That's every 1st of October."

I'm about to say something when the car breezes past the *Welcome to Fairydale* sign.

Turning to the window to watch the scenery, I'm struck by the unexpected gathering of clouds marring the sky. Whereas a second ago the sky was sunny and clear, now it's gray and downcast.

A sudden rumble in the sky makes me jump in my seat, just before a flash of electricity bleeds into the blackening sky. Like a tree branch descending from heaven, the bluish-white light covers everything in the horizon.

One strike. Two strikes. One after another, like a celestial swan dance, the flickers of electricity move sinuously into the sky, the entire display antithetically bright despite the gloomy background.

"Damn it," Mr. Vaughan curses as he bangs on the steering wheel, and for a second his expression shifts, no longer the easy-going smile from before, now a snarl pulls his features tightly together. When he notices my startled expression something flashes across his face before he's back to normal, his lips drawn up into a big smile.

"Just a little thunder storm, Miss Darcy. We're close to the ocean so we get a lot of these storms all year round."

I fall back in my seat, staring in shock at the rearview mirror and the sinister expression I'd seen on his face. But my attention is soon taken over by the brewing storm again as thunder cracks into the sky like a finely tuned whip.

There's a certain melodic quality to the sounds of nature, and despite knowing every loud bang should come across as cacophonous to my ears, the opposite happens. I feel lulled into a sense of comfort—of belonging. Noises erupt around me, yet all I feel is silence.

The wind is ravaging the fields, the grass almost flattened from the force of it. Not a while later and torrid rain accompanies the crushing thunder and blinding lighting. The window of the car is immediately blurred by dripping raindrops, the tapping sounds echoing inside the car.

Just as the rain continues to rage on, the wind intensifies, carrying with it debris and carelessly throwing it around.

Mr. Vaughan suddenly pulls the brakes when a couple sheets of paper cover his entire front view. He's holding the steering wheel in a death grip as his features tense and relax.

Seeing my previous reaction to his outburst, he's controlling himself.

"It's just a storm," I feel compelled to say in an attempt to diffuse the tension.

"Yes, of course," he comments, almost mechanically.

Activating the windshield cleaners, Mr. Vaughan tries to remove the paper, but it's not budging.

"I think it's stuck to the windshield," I add softly. The sheets are too wet and have likely adhered to the glass. "We might have to go out there and remove them."

He purses his lips, his gaze flickering in the back to me. For a moment, I wonder if he's going to ask me to go out, but as he mumbles something under his breath, he kicks the door open, exiting into the storm.

The moment the door is open, the howling of the wind intensifies. Mr. Vaughan has a hard time keeping himself upright as he battles the force of the storm. He takes one step forward and two back.

It feels like an eternity before he makes it to the front of the car, his hands grasping at the white pieces of paper. But no matter how much he tries to pry them off with his nails, he isn't making any progress.

When minutes on end pass and he doesn't succeed, I take pity on him and decide to go out and help him. After all, two people should certainly be more efficient than one. And with him looking so wet and thoroughly disgruntled, I can't help but feel bad for him.

Pushing my door open, I swing my legs off the seat before jumping out. I expect to feel the cold rain on my skin—I'm actively preparing for it—but as I stand tall in the rain, I feel anything but cold, or wet, or battered by the merciless wind.

At the moment, I blame the phenomenon on my warped perception and my single-minded focus to get this done so we can proceed further. Making my way to Mr. Vaughan, I offer to help.

"Let me try? I have longer nails," I wave my nicely manicured hands. Allison and I go monthly to a salon to get our nails done. My position doesn't allow for extravagance, so I always get a basic French manicure.

He suddenly turns, his brows furrowing as if he hadn't expected me to come out. But as he looks me up and down, he blinks in confusion.

When he doesn't reply, I simply move to his side, leaning forward to reach for the windshield as I easily pick one sheet after another.

"There, they're coming off," I smile back at Mr. Vaughan.

He doesn't share my amusement, though. A few steps away from me, his hair is all wet, as is his suit and he's staring at me as if he's seen an apparition.

"Is there something wrong?" I ask, baffled when he simply pins me with a harsh glare, the corners of his mouth down-turned, half-way into a scowl that he's barely holding back.

"Mr. Vaughan?" I move after I've picked up all the sheets of paper. Seeing him frozen to the spot, his expression so chilling, I fear something must have happened so I reach for him.

"Are you alright?" I barely get to his side as he recoils from my touch, taking a step back and sneering at me.

My eyes widen, and a flare of panic erupts in my chest.

"I'm quite alright," he gruffly states, his countenance changing just as he goes back to the car.

I climb back in as well, a little rattled by his behavior.

Closing the door, Mr. Vaughan doesn't even glance back at me as he starts the car once more. Yet as I look down at the damp sheets of paper in my hands, I'm surprised to see letters strewn haphazardly on the pages. Each sheet has different letters, and shuffling them around, I manage to assemble them together into a sentence.

"Miss Darcy," Mr. Vaughan suddenly calls my name.

My head whips up, my gaze connecting with his in the rearview mirror. His lips are pulled into a twisted smile that doesn't quite reach his eyes.

"Yes?" I flutter my lashes in confusion.

"You're not wet," he states in a deadpan voice, a heaviness underlying his words.

I slowly bring my eyes to my body, patting my clothes and my hair and realizing that, indeed, I am not wet.

"It must have been the direction of the wind," I murmur, barely fighting the shock of the discovery. Yet the excuse sounds ludicrous even to my own ears.

"It must," he agrees, though his expression belies his words.

My mouth pulls into a tremulous smile, unsure what else to add since it feels like my own brain is playing tricks on me. But then I stare back to my lap, and to the sheets of paper I'd arranged that spell out three words.

Don't. Trust. Them.

Looking back up, I'm startled to see Mr. Vaughan watching me covertly, his attention fully on me instead of the road. Caught, he gives me a friendly smile, but one I'm not sure I fully believe anymore.

Dear God, what did I get myself into?

Chapter Three

The storm persists, the sound of the marauding rain hitting the car windows becoming more and more pronounced.

Mr. Vaughan doesn't try to engage me further in conversation, and I'm grateful for the small respite. I'm still restless from his earlier hints of micro-aggression and I don't know what to make of him, or of the situation overall. Though Mr. Vaughan had seemed cordial enough at first, I can't help but feel there's something lurking beneath his easy smiles.

The sheets of paper with their odd message did little to calm my increasing anxiety, and I find myself nervous of what is to come.

Luckily, we soon enter a populated area as houses appear on both sides of the road—small, nondescript buildings. And after a while, the houses become bigger and more ostentatious before we reach an area that has some of the most beautiful homes I've ever seen.

Oddly enough, the moment the architectural scenery shifts, the storm seems to abate. The clouds slowly dissipate, the rain becoming sparser and sparser until it stops altogether. By the time we round a corner, the sun is shining brightly in the sky, as if there had been no storm in the first place.

"We're here," he announces curtly as he stops the car in front of a four-story house. "This is the Pierce house," he tells me as he instructs me to get out of the car.

Taking a deep breath, I push the door open, following Mr. Vaughan down the small alleyway to the main entrance of the house.

He knocks, and within a few seconds someone answers the door.

"Mordechai, darling, you're all wet," a woman exclaims sweetly, barely stopping herself from jumping in his arms.

"Vicky, " Mr. Vaughan greets her, a different cadence to his voice. "We got caught in a storm on the Fringes," he gives her a little summary of what happened, half-turning towards me.

It's at that moment that Vicky—who I presume to be my late father's wife—looks past Mr. Vaughan and notices me. Her lips pull into a thin line as her eyes move over my form, appraising me from head to toe.

"Miss Darcy O'Sullivan, I assume," she murmurs, her voice dropping an octave.

I force a smile.

"Pleased to meet you," I take a step forward, extending my hand to her.

Her smile is equally as strained as she reluctantly takes my hand in a half-hearted shake.

"She's not wet," she whispers, her gaze finding Mr. Vaughan.

"So she isn't," he replies tersely, and I get the sensation that there's a hidden meaning to their exchange.

I don't get to dwell on that, though, as I'm ushered inside the house and to a large living room. Another man and a girl I assume to be around my age are already there, almost as if they'd been waiting for us.

"Miss Darcy, this is August, and his sister Grace," Mr. Vaughan states in a bored tone as he motions towards the two.

"Welcome to Fairydale," the young man gives me a hesitant smile. He has black hair and dark blue eyes, both features quite similar to my own, and I can't help but wonder if it's something we both inherited from our father.

I have yet to see a picture of Leo Pierce, but I remember my mother and we'd looked nothing alike. She'd had strawberry blonde hair that had a reddish hue in the summer, and pale, gray eyes—entirely unlike my dark hair and deep blue eyes.

"Pleased to meet you," I shake August's hand before I try to do the same with Grace. She's around my height, her hair a dark brown while her eyes are a light green.

Her upper lip twitches as she meets my gaze, and releasing a loud huff, she turns, snubbing my salute.

"I expected something different," she adds dryly, barely looking at me. "Didn't you say she was a city girl? Then why is she so...boring?"

I blink, taken aback by her words.

I'm not the only one struck speechless by her rude comments, as her mother gasps, while Mr. Vaughan mumbles something about minding her manners.

"Well, I expected Fairydale to be more...happy. We don't always get what we want," I reply immediately, a little more sarcastic than intended.

I'm already in a foreign land, surrounded by strangers. I can't let them see me as weak or they will attempt to take advantage of me. Especially since a feeling of unease had settled in the pit of my stomach the moment we'd entered Fairydale.

Her eyes widen at my retort, and she looks about to give me one of her own, but whatever she sees behind me—likely in her mother's expression—makes her stop right as she's about to open her mouth.

I wonder if her dislike of me has anything to do with the will. No one would like it if they had to suddenly split their assets with a stranger. Based on the reception so far, no one seems too thrilled to see me, regardless of what Mr. Vaughan had told me before.

"Grace, you should apologize to Darcy," Mrs. Pierce lightly admonishes her daughter.

"It's fine," I intervene. "I know I'm not very fashionable," I add with a small smile. "I'm a teacher, not a billboard model."

To an extent, her comment has its merit since both my hair and clothes, unlike hers, don't follow the latest fashion. Her hair is cut short and fashioned in a Grace Kelly style whereas mine is long and plaited in a simple braid that goes down my back. Her clothes are richly patterned, while mine are a monotonous color. But that is because I've never had an incentive to follow modern fashion. I don't go out. I teach, and then I go back to my books. Why would I put in so much effort in a style that no one saw?

That doesn't mean I don't appreciate fashion. I just don't have the circumstances to allow myself to indulge in it.

Grace's mutinous expression hasn't subsided, and I have no doubt she doesn't want anything to do with me.

"You're so gracious, dear," Mrs. Pierce comes to my side, grasping my arm. A current of electricity courses through me—an uncomfortable pricking sensation that makes me wince.

Without even thinking, I wrench my arm out of her grasp.

"Sorry, I'm a little sweaty from the journey. If you could direct me to a shop so I can buy some clothes for my stay, that would be lovely."

"Miss Darcy had her luggage stolen at the train station and needs some new clothes," Mr. Vaughan explains.

"Nonsense," Mrs. Pierce interjects, her expression animated. "Grace can lend you some of hers, can't you dear? You two look to be the same size." Her tone is sweet, yet there's an unmistakable command to it as she gives Grace a hard look.

The girl hesitates before she nods.

I glance between the two of them, certain there are some unspoken cues I cannot understand because Grace seems entirely put off by that yet she's completely subservient to her mother's wishes.

"I'd rather buy new ones," I smile. Of course I am not comfortable borrowing *anything* from the girl shooting me daggers with her eyes.

"Don't worry about it, dear," Mrs. Pierce touches my arm again and it takes everything in me not to flinch. "You can buy new stuff later. For now, let Grace lend you some."

A little more back and forth and I realize she won't take no for an answer so I agree to borrow a few pieces until I can buy some.

"Why don't you go upstairs so Miss Darcy can change and then we can all have dinner together. I'm sure you're famished after such a long journey, aren't you dear?"

"Indeed," I muster a reply. Her exceedingly jovial tone is not only grating, but comes across as entirely artificial.

Following Grace upstairs, my eyes are drawn to the beauty of their home. The wealth is evident, from the size of the house, to the materials used and the furniture.

She pushes a door open on the third floor, reluctantly inviting me inside.

"Thank you," I murmur, though she doesn't reply.

Her room is enormous, and probably three times the size of the room I share with Allison at Saint Russell's. And she has it all to herself... I blink, taking in my surroundings and noting there's an ensuite bathroom as well as a sitting room right by the sleeping area. It's the type of bedroom I'd only seen in magazines, and seldom in movies.

As I gawk at the beauty that is her room, Grace goes to her closet, rummaging for a short while before removing a few pieces—two dresses, a matching set of a blouse and a pair of trousers and something to sleep in.

"That's too much," I protest. I won't take more than a day's worth of clothes since I plan to get my own as soon as I get to a store.

"If I don't give you proper options my mother will have my ass," she says in a deadpan voice, pushing the clothes towards me.

I nod slowly.

"You can go there to freshen up and change," she motions to the ensuite bathroom.

I give her my thanks and I head inside.

Taking my clothes off, I wash myself lightly before I put on one of the dresses Grace gave me—a floral white one with a cinched waist. The fit is fantastic, as is the soft material. I spend a couple of minutes simply watching myself in the wall-sized mirror and marveling at the way the dress flatters my body.

Depending on the allotment of the will, maybe I'll be able to buy myself some similar ones in the future.

My cheeks redden at the thought. As Allison rightly said, once I have the money I'll be able to do anything I want. The thought of that kind of financial freedom is the only thing spurring me further despite the unease I still feel at being here.

Already, I am quite disillusioned with my half-siblings as neither seems too thrilled about my presence. August had been more circumspect, but I could sense his hesitance too. Grace may have been rude, but she'd hinted at what everyone was thinking.

I'm not welcome.

Taking a deep breath, I go back to the room to find a scowling Grace tapping her foot impatiently.

"Took you long enough," she mumbles, her eyes skittering over my body before she's out of the door.

Pursing my lips, I follow her downstairs to the dining room where everyone is already seated.

It doesn't escape me to notice that Mr. Vaughan is sitting at the end of the table—where the head of the family should have been. And though Leo Pierce had died, shouldn't that role befall to August?

Odd. But then so is his interaction with Vicky Pierce, their body language too familiar for a simple employer-employee relationship.

Alas, it is not my business to speculate on their personal relationship. I'm here for the reading of the will after which I will return home.

Plastering a smile on my face, I take a seat at the table, right between August and Vicky Pierce.

It doesn't take long for two servants to bring the food, placing an appetizer in front of me.

"Tell us more about you, Darcy," Mrs. Pierce speaks first.

"There's nothing much to tell," I say as I give them a short summary of what I do and what my credentials are. I don't go into further detail than what is already on paper and they are undoubtedly familiar with.

"I must say. It was a shock to hear that my dear Leo had another child," she sighs.

"You mean that he cheated on you?" Grace brazenly asks.

"Grace!" Both August and Mrs. Pierce intoned at the same time.

"You know it wasn't like that. We were separated at the time, and he moved to Boston while I stayed here," she says as she wipes the corners of her mouth in a delicate manner. "I can't condemn him for finding someone else when we didn't think we were going to get back together."

Mrs. Pierce goes on to relate what had happened during that time, and as I glance around the table, no one seems to truly pay attention as she prattles on—almost as if this was a rehearsed speech prepared only for my sake.

"Please don't think I hold anything against you, Darcy. You're a part of Leo just like my August and Grace. And we're very happy to have you here," she reaches to touch my hand at the same time I pick up my glass of water.

"Thank you," I murmur, taking a sip and slowly leaning away from her.

I don't know what it is about her, but I've never had such an adverse reaction to someone before. She seems nice—if not a little fake—but she strikes me as a regular trophy wife, not an axe murderer.

"I have one question," I turn towards Mr. Vaughan. "What was the cause of death? Your letter didn't mention why he died."

Everyone is quiet, the only sound in the room is the heavy breathing that echoes in the spacious room.

"A heart attack," Mrs. Pierce says at the same time as Mr. Vaugh responds with, "Brain damage."

More silence.

Glancing around, my eyes flutter in confusion.

From the corner of my eye, I spot August tightly holding on to the knife, almost bending the tip. Mrs. Pierce's lips are pressed into a tight line, while Mr. Vaughan narrows his eyes at me.

"It was both a heart attack and brain damage," he speaks slowly, almost as if he's imparting the information to everyone present. "He had a heart attack after which we tried to resuscitate. We got a pulse but he'd been too long without oxygen to his brain so he was declared brain dead."

Nodding slowly, I bring the glass to my lips, taking a sip of water as I covertly watch the four strangers around the table. In what I think is an unprecedented moment, their eyes are set on each other, their expressions naked, malice and greed dripping from them. As if I'd been dumped in a forest teeming with wolves fighting for dominance, for the first time I'm struck by a thought. Whatever the contents of the will, I'm not the only enemy in the house.

Almost as if recognizing the mounting tension at the table, Mrs. Pierce diffuses the situation by shifting the conversation to the late Leo Pierce and sharing some anecdotes of him.

Soon, the dinner is finished, and Mr. Vaughan lets me know that he will drive me to my house.

"My house?" I exclaim, taken aback.

"The key I sent you, Miss Darcy. It belongs to a property north of here that Leo owned. Vicky and I have prepared it for you since we didn't want you to feel uncomfortable living with strangers," he explains. "You'll have the privacy you need since the following days could prove to be rather demanding," he says as he details the upcoming schedule. Tomorrow is the funeral while the reading of the will would take place the day after tomorrow.

"Oh, thank you. That is very thoughtful of you," I thank both Mr. Vaughan and Mrs. Pierce. And after saying goodbye, I find myself once more in the back of the car as Mr. Vaughan drives towards the destination—12 Astor Place.

It's soon evident that by the northern part of the town, he meant at the other end.

We drive for close to ten minutes, and for a small town, that is a *long* distance.

Despite the darkening sky, the more we drive, the clearer the view of the famous Fairydale hill is, as is the view of the majestic Hale manor Mr. Vaughan had mentioned.

He hadn't been lying when he'd described the manor resembling a castle. Though built in a neoclassical style, its grandeur and sheer size make it qualify for the title.

Even from afar, its imposing built and the accompanying scenery make for a striking picture. As we approach further, sparks of excitement spread through my body, my belly tightening with anticipation.

Besides the tourist attractions in Boston, I haven't seen many historical buildings. I certainly haven't visited any in depth. But hopefully, before my sojourn here ends, I will be able to visit the grounds of the manor.

I'm so enraptured by the sight of the manor as night falls, that I barely register the car coming to a stop.

"We're here," Mr. Vaughan suddenly mentions.

Shaking myself back to the present, I slowly get out of the car. I take in my surroundings, goosebumps appearing all over my skin at the bleakness of the location. Hale manor might seem like the cradle of sophistication up on its lonely hill, but here it's anything but that.

There are only two buildings as far as I can see—12 Astor Place, and another building across the street. Other than that, a field stretches on both sides of the make-shift road.

It's not even paved.

Good Lord, but I'd been so focused on admiring the manor that I hadn't realized we'd left the more civilized area. This is right at the outskirts of the town.

"This is rather far from town, isn't it?" I ask hesitantly.

"Not at all." Mr. Vaughan comes by my side, his features stern. "The town is fifteen minutes of walking in that direction," he points towards the direction we'd come from. "That's the Hale manor, and there's a cliff that leads to the ocean."

I purse my lips in consternation.

"And that?"

I turn to point at the building on the other side of the road. Different in architecture, its sharp angles, pointed arches and stained glass suggests a gothic style.

"That's the Old Church. Don't worry about it. It's locked. No one uses it anymore, but no one wants to repurpose it either. It dates to the seventeenth century," he adds and I remember him telling me about it.

I nod absentmindedly, though inside, I can't help but be put off by the entire thing.

"Is there no other place in *town* I can sleep at for a couple nights?"

Though the house in front of me is lovely, the fact that I'm so far away from town *and* across the street from an old church that looks more creepy than beautiful despite its assuredly fascinating history doesn't make me look forward to my stay here. A shiver travels down my back the more I think of it.

The Hale manor doesn't look as close either, despite the optical illusion given by its location. And that situates me...in the middle of nowhere. In a foreign town. Surrounded by strangers.

No. Not a good idea. And I tell Mr. Vaughan exactly that.

"I can't possibly stay here alone."

"This is the house your father wanted you to have, Miss Darcy. It's not a coincidence that I gave you the key. It will be yours in a few days' time."

I blink, not expecting to hear that.

"Are you sure?"

He nods.

"I've been Leo's man of affairs for decades. He wanted you to have a place to stay here in Fairydale since it's your home, too."

He smiles then—a rehearsed smile that doesn't reach his eyes. Instead, his gaze is on me, waiting for me to agree with him.

"Is there no hostel?" I rephrase, though the chances of a town this small having a hostel are slim at best.

Why can't he understand that the area is creepy? That I'm a single woman in the middle of a field. How could I possibly accept to stay here when I doubt there isn't even a telephone for miles?

Given the position of the house, I'm most certain a pastor must have lived here with his family in the past—when the Old Church was still operational. And I don't think I want to sleep in a house that...

"What are you so scared of, Miss Darcy?" He interrupts my thoughts, asking me in a gravelly voice—one that makes the hairs on my body stand up.

Instinctively, I take a step back as I hug my arms to my chest.

"I'll be alone," I grumble. "What if someone tries to break in?

What if..."

He puts a hand up, interrupting me.

"So you're concerned about safety?"

I nod fervently.

"Come," he says in a tone bordering on exasperation as he tells me to give him the key. I do so and I watch as he opens the door, the floors immediately creaking under his weight.

I visibly wince at the sound. Saint Russell's may have been an older building, too, but at least there I'd been surrounded by people.

Flicking the light in the hallway, Mr. Vaughan beckons me inside.

The interior is more modern than the outside, but it's clear no one's lived in the house for years—maybe decades.

"Look," he points to the door and the many locks on the wall. "If you secure it, no one will be able to come inside. Besides, despite those nasty rumors about crime, Fairydale is a very peaceful town. Our residents have never been accused of anything. It's the outsiders that get in trouble with the law," he explains matter-of-factly, but there's a small twitch in his cheek as he regards me.

"I see," I reply softly.

What else can I say? That I will not, under any circumstance, sleep in this place? I could try, but everything about his countenance tells me he isn't amenable to arranging anything else for me. And that means it's either this place, or...nothing.

"The house has a living room downstairs and two bedrooms upstairs. You can choose the one you like the most. The water is clean and potable, and there is gas and some canned food in the cupboards. Vicky made sure to stock up the kitchen for you."

My eyes widen in surprise at hearing that.

"Thank you," I murmur, now feeling a little ashamed about my earlier outburst. The last thing I want them to think of me is that I'm a spoiled brat that's only after the money—which, admittedly, the latter part is true. However, they have received me well, and have gone through a lot of trouble to ensure my stay here would be comfortable. I'm not about to turn up my nose at that.

"The funeral starts at noon tomorrow. I will come get you at eleven thirty. Good night."

He doesn't wait for me to respond before he's out the door, leaving me alone in this ancient—*fine, not as ancient as the church across the road*—house.

The door closes with a thud, and I hurry to latch every lock in place.

Only when I'm sure that the door is thoroughly locked do I move, going to the windows to ensure they are also closed shut.

Still, the fact that no one can come in doesn't seem to calm my nerves. My heart is beating loudly in my chest.

"You can do this, Darcy," I tell myself in an attempt to cheer myself up. "Think about the money. And the things you can do with it. A vacation in England, or France, or even a cruise on the Mediterranean. You'll visit the Versailles, sunbathe in Capri and amble around the Acropolis."

The more I imagine the future, the more determined I am.

If this is the only way I can get that money, I'll do it.

Nodding to myself, I feel some of the earlier unease leave me as I take a few long, deep breaths. When I have myself under control with my determination soaring, I decide to check the house out. After all, according to Mr. Vaughan this is to be mine—officially mine.

I roll my eyes at that thought. It's unlikely I'll ever come to Fairydale after the division of assets.

The first room I enter is the kitchen. Dropping the bag with the clothes I'd borrowed from Grace on a chair, I inspect the cupboards, confirming that there is plenty of food—certainly *not* for one person staying for a few days. All the compartments are full, almost as if someone had planned for the apocalypse.

Chuckling to myself, I move to check the fridge and opening it, I find fresh produce, meat and vegetables.

Vicky really thought of everything, didn't she?

A little hungry since I hadn't eaten much at the Pierce house, I make myself a small sandwich before I set out to explore the rest of the house. Going to the staircase, I find the light switch on the wall, flicking it and the one on the hallway when I reach the second floor. With the house bathed in light, I feel more confident. There are three doors on the second floor—one that leads to a bathroom and the other two which lead to bedrooms.

I check out each bedroom in part, settling on the one closer to the bathroom since I'll likely be scared to walk the longer distance at night.

There is a double bed in the middle of the room, a big closet and a desk by the window. The sheets on the bed are clean, an odd, floral scent clinging to the material.

Despite the not so ideal circumstances, my lips tug up in a smile, and before I can help myself, I jump on the bed, a giggle escaping me when it bounces with me.

It's the first time I'll have such a big bed to myself, and giddiness suffuses me at that thought. Rolling around in bed, I giggle more as I feel the soft sheets against my skin.

Yes, this is the beginning of something new. And after all the weirdness of today, I feel good about the future. I can feel it, somewhere deep within me, that this experience will change my entire life.

A little more rolling against the fresh linens before I decide I should take a shower and call it a day. After all, I'm sure tomorrow will be busy.

Getting out of bed, I take out the nightgown Grace had loaned me and I go to the bathroom.

Just like the kitchen, the bathroom has soap, shampoo, towels and toilet paper. Glad that I'll be able to thoroughly scrub all the grease from the travel, I close the door to the bathroom, locking it just in case, before I shed all my clothes and pin my hair up.

Moving to the tub, I turn on the water, adjusting the temperature. When I'm satisfied with the warmth, I get inside, pulling the curtain and making myself comfortable.

The tub continues to fill with water as I soak in its warmth. Leaning back, I release a weary sigh as I close my eyes and let the stress melt away.

How long has it been since I've had a proper bath?

Though Saint Russell has good sanitary conditions, it doesn't have a tub. We have to shower quickly as per allotted quota of hot water. I've never had the chance to relax like this.

The only times I've had a proper, relaxing bath had been when Sister Anne and Sister Mary had allowed me to use their quarters.

Thoroughly soaked in, I reach for the soap. But just as my fingers brush against it, a shadow moves in the corner of my eye, right behind the curtain. Startled, I whip my head around, instinctively backing away.

Nothing.

There's nothing.

Just to be sure, I wrench the curtain aside, revealing the same thing.

Nothing.

Breathing hard, my pulse skyrockets the more I stare at the white curtain, certain I'd seen something move.

"I'm going crazy," I mumble to myself.

It must be all those books I've been reading and the fact that I'm alone in a strange environment. Catherine's silly notions come to mind, and I mentally berate myself for acting like her.

"There's no such thing as ghosts," I say out loud, almost as I'm willing it to be true. But ghosts do not exist. Everything is in my mind and in the fanciful notions years of gothic literature have created.

There is no crazy woman living in the attic, just as there is no Rebeca to haunt me.

Even though the rational part of my brain believes that, there's also the other part—the superstitious one that sees everything as an omen. And since arriving in Fairydale, I've had plenty of them...

"No," I shake my head, my lips tight in a tense line. "I won't go down that road again."

It had happened to me once before, right after my mother had died.

I'd been new to the orphanage and quite honestly, petrified. I couldn't sleep at night, and at some point I started seeing a shadowy figure watching over me while I slept.

That had lasted for almost a year. At first, I'd told the nuns, only to be assured there was no one there—that the other girls sleeping in the same room could not see anything.

After I'd been properly admonished for inventing ghost stories to scare everyone else, I'd stopped talking about it, until eventually, the shadowy figure had disappeared.

Now, it feels like a distant memory. But back then it had been terrifying. Just as much as the fact that no one had believed me, instead making fun of me and calling me crazy.

Yet the odd thing hadn't been the fact that I'd seen such an apparition—for I am sure there had *been* something. It had been that though I'd been scared because it was something unnatural, the entity itself had not felt threatening. In fact, sometimes it seemed as though it had been looking over me while I slept.

To this day, I've had a hunch that it might have been my mother trying to help me cope with her death—in her own, ghostly way.

Maybe it's silly. Maybe I'm too much like Catherine. But I prefer to believe that rather than think I was crazy—that I'm *still* crazy.

Getting out of the tub, I dry myself with a towel before I put on the nightgown. All the while, though I can see I am alone in the bathroom, I can't shake this feeling that someone is watching me. The sensation has me turning around a couple of times, confirming that there is no one around.

Huffing out a breath, I go back to the room, getting under the clean sheets and forcing myself to go to sleep.

Yet a couple hours later and I'm still twisting and turning, sleep proving to be elusive. One glance at my watch and I note it's close to midnight.

"Drat it," I curse softly.

Lying flat on my back, I stare at the ceiling, wondering if counting sheep would help.

Ready to give up, I start.

"One sheep, two sheep, three..." I trail off when a cacophonous sound blasts through the air.

Sitting up straight, my eyes widen, all my fatigue gone in the blink of an eye.

The first note is a deep bass one, followed by a succession of softer notes.

Music.

It's music.

At this hour.

In the middle of nowhere.

But as I keep on listening, I recognize the quality of the sound as belonging to an organ. And who else would have an organ but...the Old Church.

I swallow hard.

Mr. Vaughan said no one uses it, and considering the remote location, who could it be at this hour? Someone playing a prank? That's the most likely scenario.

And as soon as that thought crosses my mind so does something else. What if...

What if this is all an elaborate scheme to get me to run off and relinquish my hold on my inheritance? What if the Pierces know this house will be passed down to me and want to prevent that?

I would have felt bad accusing them in my mind had I not seen the way they behaved at dinner, and the hidden glances they shot each other when they thought I wasn't watching.

A quiet resolution settles over me as I jump out of bed, quickly taking off my nightgown and putting on one of the day dresses. After I put on my shoes, I leave the room, my stride determined as I go down the stairs.

If they want to play with me, it's high time they realized I'm not a weakling, nor am I someone they can bully.

Removing all the locks on the door, I exit the house, crossing the road to the Old Church.

The music is still blasting in the air, the stillness of the night making it seem even louder. Yet as I stop in front of the church's entrance, the music changes. This time, I recognize the melody as Bach's Toccata, the sound hauntingly beautiful and evoking.

I freeze, my skin erupting in goosebumps as my hand hovers over the door's rusty knob.

The sound bursts through the night, surrounding me in a protective cocoon until all I want is to preserve the melody and let it play *ad infinitum.*

Yet the idea that this could be a senseless prank incites my temper again.

My hands clench into fists and before I change my mind, I stride forward, wrenching the door open. To my surprise, it gives way easily.

Shouldn't it have been locked?

That only solidifies my decision to march forward. If it's not locked, then surely someone must have opened it.

There is a small arcade at the entrance of the church.

Everything is bathed in darkness, the only light that of the moon as it filters through the richly colored stained glass. The atmosphere is eerily intoxicating, especially with the music echoing in the background.

"Is there someone there?" I ask, though my voice can't cut over the loud music.

One foot in front of the other, I move forward until I reach the nave of the church. On each side, there's an aisle. Though the church didn't look too big from the outside, the inside with its high vaults makes it look enormous.

For a town church, it's certainly *too* big, and it makes me wonder who would have built it—a wealthy patron?

There is a small gallery on each side of the church, behind which there are sets of stained glass, all capturing the moonlight perfectly and reflecting it along the nave.

At the far end of the church is the choir, and as I take a few more steps, I spot the organ in the corner, oriented with the back towards the aisles.

The music is still playing, the same melody on repeat. But when I reach the middle of the nave, it suddenly stops.

My eyes widen, and thinking the culprit saw me inside and is ready to make his escape, I dash towards the choir.

In just a few seconds I'm right by the organ. A little out of breath, I turn the corner.

"Got you..." I trail off when I see there is absolutely no one.

What's more, the fallboard is covering the keys, a thick, even layer of dust settled on top of it—a sign that no one had touched it in a *long* time.

"What the..." I whisper, unnerved.

But I don't have time to dwell on it as something moves in my field of vision right before the sound of punctured steps echoes in the church.

"Wait!" I call out, convinced there *was* someone inside.

I chase the sound until I reach the main entrance again. The door is closed shut, and as I open it, the creaking noise makes it clear no one had gone out.

What the...

My heart is beating loudly in my chest, my thoughts racing at the speed of light.

Who was it?

Who the hell was it?

I'm past caring that I'm cursing in the House of the Lord—even if it's not out loud. I'm past caring about anything but the fact that I've never felt greater fear before.

If it was indeed a prank, then well done. I am well and thoroughly terrified.

The sheer oddity of the situation coupled with my increasing anxiety propels me to leave the church.

I look around left and right as I step onto the small pathway leading back to the road. But I am so focused on avoiding any no-good-doer that I don't realize when I walk straight into a solid wall.

"Whaaaat," I yelp, jumping back a step and ready to scream so loud the entire town would hear me.

"Easy," a man's harsh voice penetrates my mental fog.

But it's too late, as my self-preservation has kicked in, together with the moves I'd learned from *Seven Samurai.* My fist flies towards the man's face before I can stop it.

On the bright side, if it makes contact, then it's likely *not* a ghost.

Alas, it does *not* make contact with his face. But not because he's not corporeal, but because his own hand closes over my clenched fist before it can reach its destination.

My mouth drops open in shock, and flabbergasted, I can only stare at him.

"You're not a ghost," I state, quite foolishly.

His mouth curves up in a smile that threatens to make my insides explode—from fear or fascination, I don't know.

He's probably a foot taller than I am, but even in the darkness of the night I can make out his features—his dark hair and eerily light eyes. So light, in fact, that they seem to glow white in the moonlight. He's built like a tank, all muscle and hard edges—no wonder it felt like I had hit a wall.

"Who are you?" I whisper. My fist is still in his hand, and a shiver of awareness travels down my back as his touch registers on my body.

Before I can think it through, I pull back, keeping my eyes still on him.

"Not a ghost?" He tilts his head, studying me with a lopsided smile that must work wonders on the female population.

"Well," I clear my throat, chasing away all remnants of fear—for now. Pushing one finger against his—*very, very, hard*—abdominals, I nod to myself. "Clearly not a ghost."

He's still smirking at me, his gaze indulgent, as is his half-smile.

Not wanting to look like a besotted fool—though it is my first time seeing such a fine male specimen—I push my chin up and regard him with a pointed brow.

"Who are you and what are you doing here at night? Alone?" I narrow my eyes at that.

Yes, he might not be a ghost, but he could still be a criminal. And I have no way of defending myself.

Alarm bells go off in my head, just as I look around for a potential weapon.

"You can bash me over the head with that metal bar," he states, his voice a deep drawl that makes love to my ears—*makes love to my ears?* Since when did I become so poetic? I may be an English teacher, but I've never had a gift for words.

You didn't find the perfect muse before.

Straightening my back, I ignore my inner voice as I grab the bar he pointed to.

"I will if you don't identify yourself," I say firmly, proud of myself for not stumbling over my words—not even once.

He chuckles at that. And before I know it, he's in front of me. So close I can smell him—a smokey, arcane scent that I can't pin down.

"You're interesting," he notes in the same thick voice.

I gulp down.

"I'll be even more interesting when I *do* bash your brains," I proclaim with all the confidence I can muster. He might be a handsome devil, but beauty is a cover for many dark things. After all, Lucifer was at one point the epitome of perfection.

The stranger smiles again, this time more pronounced.

Leaning forward until he's on eye level with me, his breath fans across my lips, his gaze never leaving mine.

"Hale," he states. "Caleb Hale."

I stare at him for what feels like an eternity before I realize he just told me his name.

He's a Hale. A Hale... That means he's...

"You live there?" I ask, pointing towards the grand manor house.

"Indeed," he drawls, a wolfish grin on his face. "And I assume you're the new troublemaker in town."

I frown at his choice of words.

"Troublemaker?"

"Troublemaker. I.e. one that stirs trouble," he says, reciting the definition to me.

"I didn't ask what it was. I asked you why," I grit my teeth, snapping at him for the first time just as I raise the metal bar in his direction. If there is one thing I cannot stand, it's when men take jabs at my intelligence.

"And the kitten has claws," he laughs, leaning back. "You'll find out soon enough, Darcy O'Sullivan. In any event, pleased to meet you."

Easily removing the metal bar from my hand, he thrusts it aside, grabbing my hand in his and shaking it. I cannot move as I simply stare at him and the way his proximity unnerves me unlike anything else.

"Welcome back to Fairydale."

Chapter Four

His voice echoes in my ears as I dash across the road, getting inside the house and closing the door, making sure all the locks are latched in place.

My breathing is erratic as I run up the stairs to the bedroom, closing that door and locking it, too. And still, I don't feel safe.

My entire body is primed for fight, almost as if it knows my life is in danger before my mind can rationalize it. Yet I can't ignore the conflicting feelings taking shape inside of me—horror, fear...*longing*?

I gulp down, discomfort settling deep in my stomach.

And before I can help myself, my feet take me to the big window facing the Old Church.

Pulling the curtain aside, I peek outside.

My mouth forms an o as I come face to face with him.

Caleb Hale.

He's in the middle of the road, his face tipped upwards, his eyes on my window—*on me.*

My eyes flutter in shock, and though the moonbeams are the only source of light, I can almost swear I note another smirk on his face.

He's just standing there. Watching me. Knowing *I* am watching.

Slowly, he brings his hand to his forehead in a mock salute. All the while, the same smile remains in place—one that is both chilling and alluring. Then, just like that, he turns and leaves, walking up the road towards the manor house.

My heart is in my throat as I finally duck—a few moments too late. Yet as I'd met his gaze, it had been almost as if I were caught in a spell.

One that kept me rooted to the spot and unable to do anything but focus my attention on him.

And that is the crux of the matter. There *is* something oddly appealing about him. Something magnetic, raw, and unrestrained. Enough so that even when my doubts were overflowing my mind, he held a certain power over me, befuddling me with his slow, deliberate movements and secretive smiles.

Now, as moments pass, my mind, too, becomes clearer.

Clear enough that a myriad of questions assails me.

What the hell happened at the Old Church? Had it been Caleb who'd been playing the organ? There had been someone else in the church with me, of that I am sure. And with Caleb's appearance there not a moment later, it stands to reason that it could have been him.

Maybe it *was* a prank after all.

Perhaps there is a secret door out of the church and he'd used it to spook me.

Well...spook me he did. I'm still shivering from the encounter.

Not only had his appearance been fortuitous, but there had been something about his manner—beyond his, admittedly, good looks.

Alas, I don't want to dwell on that anymore. Not when it might become the source of my nightmares later tonight.

Making sure the window is latched too, I pull the curtains to ensure no one can peek inside before I change once more into the nightgown. This time, as I lay in bed, I will myself to think only of the good times ahead.

April 1789. Haversham House, Kent.

Mama and papa are arguing again.

Usually, they are rarely in the same place to be able to get on each other's nerves. But since we've arrived at Haversham, they haven't stopped arguing. It's to the extent that their voices echo in the entire house when it happens.

"My Lady, you should have been abed by now," Mary, my lady's maid chides when she sees me at the top of the stairs.

"How can I?" I whisper. "No one will be able to sleep until they resolve their issue."

Mary purses her lips.

"I'm afraid it shan't be too soon," she says, the corners of her mouth tipping up.

I let out a giggle.

The servants, too, know how difficult my parents can get, and they do everything in their power to avoid getting on their bad side.

Their marriage had not been one of choice, but rather one of obligation. From what I'd gathered from gossip, papa had gotten mama pregnant and he'd been forced to wed her. Back then, he'd only been a third son, unlikely to ever inherit, and he'd been adamant that he would never marry. Nevertheless, my grandfather had made sure he got to the altar and said his vows. That he'd never respected them...well, that is another matter altogether.

Most people think that because I am young, I do not understand what's happening around me. But it's because they never mind me much that they don't realize I notice more than most.

A few years after my birth, papa had become the first in line for the succession of the marquisate, and with his father's poor health, it hadn't been long before he'd become the Marquis of Haversham.

I can't say for sure if the infidelities began around that time, or maybe not one moment after he'd married my mother. At this point, it's common knowledge that the Marquis has his pick of mistresses, sometimes not even bothering to hide the fact by inviting them to events and flaunting them in front of my mother.

That has been one of their main conflicts over the years.

My mother may have been in love with him at some point, but she'd been quickly cured of the notion when she'd seen his true nature. Every time he took a new lover, he not only embarrassed her publicly, but he also made her the talk of town.

Mary tries to persuade me to return to my chamber when I suddenly hear my name.

"Leave Elizabeth out of this," mama yells.

Shaking my head at Mary, I tiptoe my way down the stairs and towards papa's study. Not wanting to leave me alone in case I got caught, Mary trails quietly behind me.

The door to the study is slightly ajar, the light inside the room shining bright despite the late hour of the night. My mother is the only one visible from the angle of the door, and I cannot help but notice her tense countenance, and the lines that mar her face.

"She's going to be presented at court in less than a month. If you do that... You're ruining her future," Fiona, the Marchioness of Haversham says through gritted teeth.

"Ruining her future?" My father, William, repeats angrily. "I'm ensuring her future! Do you think anyone else is going to marry her? She's bloody daft, Fiona!"

I barely stifle a gasp at his words. It's not the first time I've been referred to as such, but I'd never heard the word come out of papa's mouth. And despite our strained relationship, it hurts.

"She's not daft and you know it," Fiona points her finger at him. "She's just...different."

"If it weren't for the extra wages we pay our staff, everyone would have already known how *different* she is—that she spends her time talking to animals like a bloody bedlamite."

"And that's why you've decided Clifford will do? He's forty to her seventeen. For goodness sake, he's a swine!"

"But he's a rich swine, Fiona," William sighed impatiently. "He's already seen her and he is willing to accept her. He only wants an heir and a spare and he won't bother her again."

"You mean he'll lock her somewhere in the country like you planned to do with me."

"Don't bring your own frustrations into this. Elizabeth would have had to marry at some point. I've merely secured her a match sooner," he states matter-of-factly.

I'm frozen by the door, the topic of the conversation slowly sinking in.

My father wants to marry me off. To Lord Clifford.

"So God help me, William, if you go through with this... If you dare give my precious daughter to that pox-ridden bastard, I'll gut you. I'll bloody gut you myself, even if they hang me."

My father's nostrils flare in anger, and as he takes a step towards mother I fear he's going to strike her. Instead of cowering, she regards him squarely in the eye, daring him to do it.

I blink in shock at the scene in front of me.

Just as he raises his hand against her, he suddenly strikes the shelf next to her.

"She's marrying Clifford and it's final. He's coming at the end of the weekend for the ball. There will be a two week courtship after which the bans will be read. This is final, Fiona. Don't you think to disobey me on this or you'll regret this."

"How can I regret anything more than having married *you*?"

William lets out a dry laugh.

"Let's see if you're still as determined when Richard comes home from Eton."

He's in my direct field of view, and there's no mistaking the pure evil radiating from him as he smiles down at my mother.

Despite her stubbornness and determination, if he's threatening her with Richard... I don't know if she'll be so eager to rally for me anymore.

Having heard everything I needed to, I silently trudge my way back to my bedroom.

I'd always known my father would have the last say in my marriage. But I'd never thought things would progress so quickly—and so unpleasantly.

He won't let me make my debut at court because he thinks I will embarrass him. Instead, he'll just wash his hands off me at the first opportunity.

That night, I wish I could cry. But the tears won't come.

THE FIRST DAY of the house party is in full swing after everyone had arrived earlier in the afternoon. Though I am not allowed at the nightly festivities since I have not made my official debut yet, my father had instructed me that I am to allow Lord Clifford to spend time with me during the day.

I hadn't argued with him, simply because I know no good could come out of a conflict. Especially since I've seen the toll the entire situation has taken on my mother.

She may not know I listened in to the conversation, but I can note the weariness on her face, as well as the fact that Dorothy, her lady's maid, had sent for laudanum and a combination of herbs best used for sleep remedies.

Mama hasn't been sleeping, and I am certain it's because of the entire Lord Clifford debacle.

"Please reconsider, My Lady," Mary tries to reason with me as I dress in the darkest clothes I own so I can be as inconspicuous as possible.

"I need to see with my own two eyes, Mary. I want to see this Lord Clifford and why my mother is so anxious at the thought of me marrying him."

I don't tell her that I'm equally as terrified. Mama wouldn't be so vehemently against the marriage if she didn't know there was something wrong with him. From what I recall, Lord Clifford had visited Haversham a few times to meet with my father, but I'd only seen him from afar and I'd never taken notice of it—I'd never had reason too.

And quite frankly... I don't want to marry *anyone*.

I'm content by myself, and with my animals. So what if everyone thinks I'm daft. If I had only one cottage by the woods, I would lead a peaceful existence, grateful to be left alone by everyone.

"But if you're caught..."

"I won't be," I assure her. "Please don't worry. If anyone checks on me, please tell them I'm asleep," I instruct her, motioning to the pillows I'd piled under the sheet to make it look like a human form.

When Mary at last agrees to help me, I use the servants' door to sneak out of my room, going out the stairs and then exiting the house and heading to the main lawn.

The ball is in two days, but every night there is a soiree for the guests.

Mary, who'd been watching for the guests, had already spotted Lord Clifford and had described him to me as well as what he is wearing for this evening—a deep plum-colored vest that should help me identify him easier.

As I'd told her, I only want to see with my own eyes the man I'm supposed to marry. Maybe it's my innate curiosity, or maybe there's something more to it—the last push I need to think about before doing something drastic. So drastic, in fact, that I would be ruined in the eyes of society.

A garden stretches in front of the double doors that lead to the drawing room where most people are already gathered. Luckily, my father pays his gardener a pretty sum to keep the trees in perfect condition—and oddly looking shapes. As I move, they give me cover, helping me go undetected.

There is little light, though.

The garden path is set ablaze by a multitude of candles, as is the inside of the house. The rest, though, is bathed in darkness.

Reaching my desired spot, I have an unobstructed view of the drawing room. My eyes search for the plum-colored vest, and though at first I cannot spot him, a few minutes later Lord Clifford appears within my field of view.

He's...just as Mary had described. Greasy graying hair, and a visage that has multiple skin lesions. Although I cannot make out everything in great detail since I'm at least a dozen paces away from the glass doors, the redness is evident against the white of his skin.

I gulp down, pain erupting in my throat as if I'd swallowed pieces of glass.

My mother's words echo in my ears.

Pox-ridden.

I may be innocent, but with father's blatant affairs and his sometimes penchant for light-skirts, I'd heard the term pox more than enough to know it's something you get from dallying with doxies.

Bile rises up my throat, and I barely stop myself from casting my accounts at that very moment.

That is supposed to be my husband? The husband who will have full rights over my person, over my body? Who will...touch me?

Shaking my head vehemently, I step back.

My curiosity has been well assuaged, and I don't know if it's a good thing or a bad one. All I know is that I'd rather be dead than allow that man to lay one single finger on me.

I'm close to the servants' entrance when I hear a soft meow.

Turning, I spot a little ball of fur nestling next to one of father's odious trees.

"What do we have here?" I murmur, my escape briefly forgotten.

Dropping to my knees, I pat my hands on my thighs as I beckon the little cat to me. At first, he releases another meow, his eyes flashing red. But eventually he decides to trust me, taking a few steps until he reaches my side.

I don't make to touch him yet, giving him time to smell me and get used to my presence.

He's all black with a small tuft of white hair on the top of his head —the only recognizable thing about him in the darkness of the night.

My lips tip up in a smile when he brushes his head against my knee.

Another meow and I know it's his way of letting me know I can touch him.

Bringing my hand to his small head, I pat him slowly.

"You're such a pretty little thing," I whisper, already thinking how I could keep him.

My father *hates* animals, and he's prohibited me time and time again from spending time with them. He's afraid someone is going to see me interact with them and come to the same conclusion he had—that I'm daft because I speak to the animals as if I'm waiting for them to answer back.

"But you understand what I'm saying, don't you? You may not answer me, but if you could, you would tell me that you like my touch, isn't that right?" I coo in a soft voice, getting a meow as a reply.

"He's wondering if you have any food." A manly voice startles me. My eyes go wide as I lose my balance and fall on my bottom.

"Who is there? Show yourself!" I demand immediately just as fear blooms in my chest at the thought that news of this escapade will reach my father's ears.

A figure draped in shadows appears from behind one of the trees. At first, I can't make out who it is, or what he looks like. But as he takes another step, my mouth parts in awe.

"My apologies, My Lady," he gives me a formal bow, yet I can't seem to react.

Not when my eyes are affixed to his form and the oddest visage I've ever seen. Yet it's not odd in a bad way, merely in an unusual, *unique* and fascinating way.

He's dressed all in black, eschewing any color that others would have been eager for. But it all contrasts with his hair—the whitest shade of blonde

I've ever seen and longer than the current fashion allows. I can't quite make out the shade of his eyes from this distance, but they look to be a light blue.

The more I regard him, the more handsome he becomes right under my gaze.

"Who are you?" I ask on a whisper, barely able to get my bearings together.

Though I'm not wearing a corset, my breathing feels as constricted as if I wore the tightest contraption. My pulse is racing and I can feel the heat climb up my cheeks, undoubtedly painting them the deepest red. And for that, I am thankful for the cover of the night—otherwise this stranger would see just how flustered I am in his presence.

"I should go," I suddenly murmur. "It's not proper to be alone with a gentleman," I make the excuse as I get to my feet. Yet I can't find it in me to leave Mr. Meow behind, so I tuck him in the crook of my elbow, turning to leave.

"How do you know?" he suddenly asks, stepping closer.

I stop in my tracks.

"That I'm a gentleman," he continues, a hint of a smile in his voice.

I half-turn, the corner of my mouth tugging up.

"Then all the more reason why it wouldn't be proper to be alone with you."

"Hmm... And are you proper all the time?"

I blink, confused by his question.

At the same time, Mr. Meow starts struggling in my arms, lodging his claws in my arm.

Giving a small yelp, I release him, watching as he races away into the dark of the night.

"It's all your fault," I level him with a harsh stare, taking one step towards him. "You scared Mr. Meow," I accuse.

Though if I'm perfectly honest, this is merely the best excuse I could come up with to get closer—see him from up close. And just as I'd imagined, his features are...otherworldly.

Chiseled cheekbones, straight patrician nose, and those light blue eyes that regard me as if he could see right into my soul.

"Mr. Meow?" He raises a brow, a lock of white hair falling on his forehead. It's then that I realize several things. His hair isn't powdered, nor is he wearing a wig. No, his hair *is* white, despite the fact that he doesn't look a day over thirty.

When I don't reply, he chuckles.

"I think that's my cue that you're not all proper, are you? No one cavorting with stray cats in the middle of the night can be very proper," he murmurs with amusement, his eyes never leaving mine.

"What is it to you if I am proper or not? You still have not answered my question. Who are you?"

"Who do you want me to be, chérie? Tell me and maybe I'll make that true," he drawls, his hand coming up to my face but hovering over my skin instead of touching me.

"You're being rather presumptuous, *mon cher*," I fire back, narrowing my eyes at him.

He could very well be a rogue out for a tryst in the gardens, and instead of his intended he came across me.

"You're wrong," he suddenly says, just as one cold finger touches my chin, tipping it up so I look him in the eye. "I'm not here for anyone else," he smiles, showing white, even—predatory—teeth.

"How... How did you know?"

"You called for me," he leans forward, whispering in my ear. "Your soul called for me. So make your wish. What is it you want, Lizzie mine?"

My lips part in shock. Though he'd called me chérie before, *this* term of endearment seems so much more intimate. So much more...alluring.

"What are you talking about?" I clear my throat, trying my best not to succumb to the spellbinding effect his deep, rusty voice has on my senses.

"You call and I come," he continues, his breath caressing my ear, its warmth seeping in my skin. Yet he doesn't touch me further. His body doesn't meet mine, though this madness inside of me wishes it would do so.

"You're mad," I accuse lightly, though I seem to be the one suffering from the malady.

"Are we not all a little mad, Lizzie mine?" He draws back, a gentle smile on his face—one that's shadowed by great sadness. "But what if my madness recognizes yours?" he asks, stunning me into silence.

For what feels like an eternity, my eyes are lost in his, my breath coming out in short spurts and meeting his in the middle. There's an intense feeling of déjà-vu that washes over me, almost as if this meeting had taken place a thousand times before—always at a standstill; always an eternity apart.

Yet the spell is soon broken as a loud cry erupts in the stillness of the night, followed by more noises as the guests from the party flood into the garden. Knowing it would be disastrous were I to be found with a stranger, I step back, giving him a small head shake.

"I don't know what you're talking about."

One step. Two. I try to put distance between us yet I can't seem to turn away, walking backwards because something within me cannot stand the thought of not seeing him again.

He merely smiles, watching me until I wrench the door to the servants' quarters open and dash inside, heading straight for the stairs leading to my room.

Only when his gaze is no longer on me do I release a harsh breath, my body trembling, my heart almost bursting in my chest.

"Who was he?" I whisper to myself, barely paying attention to where I'm going. I've never in my life met someone who affected me so—who made me want to run away from him *and* towards him at the same time.

Yet I trust my instincts. And this duality in my heart is enough to make me keep my distance—if I ever see him again that it.

But why do I feel so sad at the thought of *never* seeing him again?

Shaking myself, I try to make my way up the stairs though the light is out. The servants must all be working to ensure the event goes smoothly and likely they forgot to light the candles on this staircase. One hand on the wall, I walk slowly, feeling my way in the darkness.

Just as I reach the landing of the first floor, I find myself flat on my front, a hand pulling at my ankle.

"Let go," I kick with my free foot, turning in an attempt to gain more balance.

"You fucking whore!" The words, so full of vitriol, catch me by surprise. "I was promised a virgin bride, not one who spread her legs for anyone," he spits at me, pulling me towards him just as his hand comes down on my cheek, the slap leaving me reeling. "You think I didn't see you spying outside? What, were you looking for a fucking? I'll give you a bloody fucking."

Despite the darkness, I realize this must be Lord Clifford, and dread fills me to the brim.

I keep pushing against him, hitting and kicking, and trying my best to escape his hold. When nothing works, I attempt to scream for help, but he doesn't let me get more than a few sounds out before his putrid hand is on top of my mouth, muffling the sounds.

Pinning me to the ground, his other hand is roving down my body, searching for the hem of my dress and attempting to push it up.

Panic unlike any other suffuses my being, tears stabbing at my eyes. No matter how much I struggle, nothing seems to work.

Nothing at all.

And at this rate...

No.

He can't touch me. He can't...

Help.

One echoed word, just as one tear flows down my cheek.

One moment Lord Clifford is wrestling with my dress, the next he stills on top of me, a spurt of thick, viscous liquid coating my entire face and bodice.

Not a second later, a spark of light flares to life, illuminating the entire corridor.

Blinking, I can barely move as I come face to face with Lord Clifford's rotten expression—now forever frozen in place. There's a gaping wound on his neck, one that keeps spurting out blood.

It's at that moment that I realize the liquid on my face is...blood.

And Lord Clifford is dead.

Gasping, I look up—shocked, or maybe not—to see the stranger from outside. He has a small candle in his right hand, his left one dripping with Lord Clifford's blood—yet there's no weapon in sight.

How had he...

I stare at him and I cannot seem to find my voice. Maybe I'd screamed too much, though none had been heard. Or maybe...maybe he did hear.

"Can you be quiet?" He asks in a severe tone.

I don't know how I find the strength to nod, Perhaps I am still in shock.

Or, perhaps, this is all a nightmare and I'm yet to wake up.

"Come," he says as he pulls the dead body off me, flinging it aside and giving me his hand—his ungloved hand.

"Hurry," he snaps, impatiently tugging me to his arms, lifting me off the ground and holding me close to his chest. Without my saying anything, he expertly maneuvers us around the servants' stairs until he reaches my room. How he knew which door led to my room, I do not know. Nor do I ask. I am beyond logical connections at this point, though I have no doubt that will come later—in the future when I will have time to reflect over everything more at length.

Closing the door behind us, he places me on the bed before he locks both doors.

I'm barely aware of what's happening around, but suddenly I feel a wet cloth against my cheek, slowly wiping the blood away.

"Are you alright?" he asks—the man with the white hair and blue, blue eyes.

I blink, fighting back tears. Dear God, I was about to be raped.

If not for this man in front of me, I *would* have been raped.

"Thank you," I whisper, my voice ragged from so much screaming.

I don't know how he knew to come, and honestly, I no longer care.

I'm only happy that he did—that he saved me.

"Thank you," I repeat as I cover his hand with mine, stopping his movements.

There's worry in his eyes—so much worry for a strange girl. Yet as he looks at me like that—as if my pain was his pain—maybe I'm not a strange girl to him at all. Maybe...

"You never have to thank me for anything, Lizzie mine," he shakes his head lightly. "I should have come earlier. I *would* have come earlier, but..."

"You came at the right moment," I interrupt. "You saved me and that's all that matters," I say as a sob breaks through my seemingly strong façade.

"Shhh," he whispers, pulling me in his embrace and slowly rocking with me. "I'll always save you, Lizzie mine," he speaks in my hair, holding me so tightly to his chest I fear I won't be able to breathe again.

But I don't protest.

Instead, I bask in that closeness and the fact that his body heat has a marvelous effect on me—lulling me into a sense of comfort and security unlike I've ever known.

If before I felt slightly apprehensive about him, now all I want is to melt in his embrace, merge my skin with his so I'm never without him again—never without the safety of his arms.

When I've calmed some more, he resumes his ministrations, cleaning the blood off my body and instructing me to get rid of the clothes.

"We can't leave any evidence behind," he says as he removes his vest.

When he sees my reluctance, he arranges a divider for me to afford me some privacy.

I do as he asks, quickly shedding the soiled garments and donning my nightgown instead. When I hand him the clothes, he stuffs them in a makeshift bag.

"Will you at least tell me your name?" I ask, suddenly afraid I won't see him again.

He gives me a lopsided smile.

"This isn't the last you'll see of me," he tells me, not for the first time seemingly reading my mind.

I nod slowly, yet I can't seem to wrench my gaze from him.

Why did I ever think him dangerous? Staring at him like this, all I want is to go to his side, take his hand in mine and ask him to never let go.

In a flash, he's before me.

"That time will come," he murmurs, his knuckles caressing my cheek. "Soon, Lizzie mine. Soon, you'll be *all* mine."

Wetting my lips, I find myself lost in the depth of emotion I witness in his eyes. Once more, the question is on the tip of my tongue. Yet no sooner do I think of it than he speaks.

"Amon. Amon d'Artan," he answers the unspoken question, his voice a soft caress.

A smile tugs at my lips. Yet as I blink, it's to find him gone.

Like he was never there...

My eyes widen as I look around the room.

"Amon?" I call out, yet the only reply is the slight echo of the room.

The doors are still locked. The windows are untouched.

It's like he vanished into thin air.

I don't get to ponder it further as a loud commotion coming from outside claims my attention. Wrapping a robe around me, I open the door, noticing a flurry of servants rushing up and down the stairs. A few seconds later, I spot Mary.

"My Lady!" she cries out, rushing to my side.

I blink in confusion, and for a moment I'm scared they found Lord Clifford's body and they're coming for me—that I'll hang for murder and...

"He's dead," she announces, and I freeze on the spot.

"Your father's dead," she bemoans, recounting how they'd found him collapsed in his study. A heart ailment, they believe.

She prattles on, and I merely nod along, only one question in my mind.

Amon... Did he...

AUGUST 1955. FAIRYDALE, MASSACHUSETTS.

I shoot upright in bed, sweat dripping down my face as my chest constricts, my breathing harsh and out of control. Wildly looking around, it feels as if the walls of the room are closing in on me, suffocating me.

The dream... It felt so real. From the clothing, to the architecture and people's speech—*my* speech.

My heart is beating wildly in my chest as I try to make sense of it.

Never in my life had I been so immersed in a dream—so fully in tune with every little detail.

Wiping the sweat off my face, I look down to my hands, almost expecting to see blood on them. Even now, I can feel the warmth of the blood on my skin, *his* gentle touch as he wiped it away.

Amon...

How in God's name could I have conjured up someone like him?

Someone so...odd yet familiar. Someone who inspires both fear in me, and a sense of security the likes I've never experienced before.

All my life I've relied solely on myself, knowing that although I have people who love me in my life, I can only count on myself when it matters most. I've always thought that by being strong, I could be impervious to loneliness. And despite having a part of me that longed for something—an ineffable something—I'd tried to push it aside, afraid of disappointment.

Yet his embrace...his arms around my body had been like an arrow to the heart, targeting my one weakness and exploiting it. Because it hadn't been just one hug. It had been warmth, and gentleness coupled with a scorching heat that made me think of only one thing.

Home.

His embrace had felt like home.

But the issue is... I've never had a home before.

Closing my eyes, I try to recreate his image from before. But now that I am awake, his features are shadowy, almost blurred out. Despite that, the feeling remains—everything he arose in me with one touch, and one action.

My skin tingles with awareness and heat travels up my neck.

I dreamed of a man. Clearly, a very attractive man.

One who didn't seem immune to me either.

My eyes squeeze shut with embarrassment just as I find the strength to get out of bed, going to the bathroom to do my morning ablutions and prepare for the day.

As I wash my face, I watch my reflection in the mirror, tracing my features and wondering what he would have seen in me.

Dark hair, pale skin and dark blue eyes.

I'm passably pretty, but not the type that inspires unquenchable lust in men.

But then, just like a bolt of lightning hitting me, I recall my encounter with Caleb Hale the night before. As if everything falls into place, I can't help but wonder if my dream hadn't been a reaction to that. To the fact that I'd found the man more attractive than any other man I've ever seen in my life. And deep down, though I've been reluctant to admit it to myself, the truth is that he'd made quite an impression on me.

He *rattled* me. And that uneasiness I felt? It was purely my physical reaction to him.

At the same time, though, the two men could not be any different. Whereas with Caleb I'd felt a predominant sense of unease, with Amon I'd found the greatest peace...

"Get your bearings together, Darcy," I mumble as I slap my cheeks a couple of times.

I'm not here to engage in any affairs of the heart—or any other type. My time in Fairydale is limited, and I need to remember my purpose. I can't let any pretty face sway me from that. Especially one that called me a troublemaker and behaved entirely too forward with me—something that makes me wonder if the entire town had found out about my arrival.

More than anything, it tells me I need to have my guard up. I've already witnessed the hidden animosity of the Pierces, and I imagine they won't be the only ones to have an adverse reaction to a stranger in their town.

Finishing up my routine, I dress and prepare for the funeral. Grace had lent me a black dress as well, and that should work just fine.

I look at my wristwatch, noting there is still some time before Mr. Vaughan will come pick me up. And as my curiosity is getting the best of me, I decide to check the Old Church once more.

Getting out of the house, I lock it before I cross the road.

In daylight, the church doesn't look as ominous as before, and I can better admire the architecture and the colored glass.

I go straight to the entrance, but as I attempt to open the door, it won't budge.

Frowning, I try again. And again. But it's all to no avail.

It's locked.

"It wasn't locked last night," I blink in confusion. Looking around, I shrug my purse on my shoulder as I walk around the church, looking to see if there's any hidden entrance Caleb might have used to play a prank on me.

Yet after two full circles around the building, there's absolutely no other entrance.

Baffled, I can only stare at the old edifice, not for the first time feeling as if my mind is playing tricks on me.

"Am I going crazy?" I murmur softly to myself.

I remember clearly what happened last night. The door had been open and someone had been playing Bach on the organ. Then I'd heard some steps, after which I'd come across Caleb.

Deep in thought, I'm startled by a meowing sound coming from the back of the church. A few steps, and I'm face to face with a cat—a black cat with a tuft of white hair.

I freeze on the spot as my mind goes back to my dream and the little creature I'd seen there. It's nearly identical.

Before I can get closer to it, however, Mr. Vaughan's voice resounds in the air.

"Miss Darcy! What the hell are you doing there?" He asks as he strides towards me.

"I heard a cat and..."

"What cat?" he demands when he reaches my side, but as I point to the little ball of black fur, I realize it's already gone.

"It must have run away," I whisper in dismay.

"Let's go, we need to get to the funeral on time."

"Wait! Who has the key to the church?" I suddenly ask.

"The key to the church?" He frowns. "There's no key to the church."

"What do you mean?"

"The church has been sealed shut since the plague. The only way to open it is to blow up the door," he explains, his tone almost put off by my question.

"But... Are you certain? I heard the organ playing last night and when I came to check..."

He releases an exasperated sigh as he marches over to the door, his hand on the handle as he tries to wrench it open with all his strength.

Just like before, it doesn't budge.

"But... It can't be," I mumble, staring at the sealed door in shock.

"You must have dreamed about it, Miss Darcy," he says gruffly, not looking at me.

"That's not true!" I protest. How dare he tell me I dreamed it when I saw it with my own eyes—when I *heard* the melody with my own ears.

"Caleb Hale was there, too. He can confirm it," I declare proudly, pushing my chin up.

But his reaction is not what I expected.

His lips spread into an insidious grin before he laughs out loud.

"Caleb Hale?" his amusement doubles, especially as my brows shoot up in confusion.

"He ain't right in the head, Miss Darcy. He's been that way since he came back from the war in Korea. My advice, stay the hell away from him. He's bad news."

But...

He turns his back to me, walking towards the car parked by the side of the road, thereby ending the discussion.

And I'm left more confused than ever.

Chapter Five

"There will be other townsfolk at the funeral, too," Mr. Vaughan mentions on the drive towards the cemetery. "I would encourage you not to be too friendly. Some don't take well to outsiders."

"So I'm supposed to ignore everyone?" I ask, confused.

"Precisely. The less people you interact with, the easier it's going to be for you. Especially the Hales. I'd advise you to stay far away from them."

"But you said only Caleb has...issues. Why the others, too?"

His mouth tightens in a flat line, and I note the severity of his expression in the rearview mirror.

"They were business rivals of your father. The Pierces and Hales have been at each other's throats for generations," he pauses, looking back at me. "I wouldn't put it past them to try to use you to get back at the Pierces."

I nod slowly, though the doubts still remain, as does a sense that nothing is what it seems—especially when it comes to the Pierces and Mr. Vaughan.

"Anyone else I should not speak to?" I inquire sarcastically.

"As a matter of fact, yes," he responds, surprising me. "The Baileys are friendly with the Hales," he gives me a list of everyone I should not interact with, topping it off with another warning about Caleb Hale.

I almost roll my eyes at him, but then he goes to add something else.

"One more thing. Don't go around telling people silly stories about the church. The last thing we want is for people to question your judgment," he grumbles away, but all I can think is that he purposefully placed me in a house in the middle of nowhere, across the street from a church where supposedly the bodies of the plague victims had been dumped.

A shiver goes down my back.

Did I really imagine everything? No. I refuse to believe that.

And regardless of Mr. Vaughan's warnings about Caleb Hale, I *will* question him. At least he should be able to tell me I'm not going crazy —if he's not as crazy as I am that is.

Mr. Vaughan continues to lecture me about the do's and don'ts of the town, almost as if my very presence threatens Fairydale's entire fabric of existence.

By the time we reach the cemetery, all I want is to go back and sleep the day away—maybe dream some more of Amon. If only he could save me from this dreaded day just as he saved me from that creepy man... Alas, I can almost imagine him appearing in a flash before me, as he'd done in my dream, and teleport me from the funeral.

A small chuckle escapes me at the thought, and Mr. Vaughan gives me a harsh glare.

"You're not to laugh at the funeral, either. That would be in poor taste, you understand," he tells me in a serious tone.

"Of course," I clear my throat, getting out of the car and turning my attention to the matter at hand.

This is the worst of it. After the funeral is done, I'll only have to stay for the reading of the will and then I will be able to leave.

Home...

A shiver travels down my back at the thought, because, really, where is home?

Yet I can't ponder that as Mr. Vaughan leads me through the gates of the cemetery towards the back where a small chapel lies.

There are nondescript tombs left and right, and I try to ignore the fact that we're among so many dead.

It's daylight. There is no such thing as ghosts.

Don't be Catherine, Darcy!

Yet the more time I spend in this town, the more I start behaving like her, finding something suspicious in every little action—something *otherworldly* suspicious.

Even after what happened in my childhood, I've never been a great believer in the supernatural. How could I when we live in an age of scientific advancement—when a man-made creation can wipe an entire city, if not a country, off the map?

As we reach the chapel, I note that everyone is already there.

The closed casket is in front of the chapel, the priest walking around it.

The Pierce family is by the casket. August is in the middle while his mother and sister are by his side.

On both the left and right side there are people that I haven't seen before. But it strikes me as odd that they are separated in such a way, and I ask Mr. Vaughan about it.

He doesn't look too happy with me at the moment, the man who'd picked me up the other day from the train station all but gone. Progressively, his countenance has become worse and worse, to the point that he doesn't even try to smile at me. All his expressions are severe, like the one he's sporting now.

"It doesn't matter now, does it? Like I said, some families have conflicts with others. Just stay by our side and everything will be fine," he says, his tone telling me this is the end of the discussion.

Sighing, I follow him as he all but positions me right next to the family. Grace gives me the same belligerent look. August has a tight smile on his face while Vicky barely acknowledges my presence.

She's looking at me intently, her gaze boring a hole through me. But as I catch her staring, she surprises me with a wide, almost inviting, smile.

Glancing around, I make a quick inventory of the people present, unwilling to admit my disappointment when I don't see Caleb anywhere.

On the left side there are about twenty people, some younger, some older. On the right side, however, there are only four people—a girl who looks to be my age accompanied by a man and a woman who I presume to be her parents, and another elderly lady.

"If everyone is here, can we commence?" The priest asks, looking at Mr. Vaughan for confirmation, which strikes me as odd. Why wouldn't he inquire with the family of the deceased?

Mr. Vaughan nods, and the priest starts with his brief ceremony. For a moment, I think he's going to open the casket for viewing, but I breathe out relieved when he doesn't.

I didn't know what he looked like alive, I'm not sure I want to know what he looks like in death. Certainly, I wouldn't want *that* to be the defining image I have of him.

When the priest is done with his little eulogy, he asks the family members to come and say a few words in honor of the deceased.

There's a small podium right behind the casket, and Vicky is the first one to go up and make a little speech about her history with Leo Pierce. August is next, followed by Grace, and they all detail what a loving father and extraordinary human being he was.

"One that abandoned his child," I mutter under my breath, and Mr. Vaughan is quick to give me a reproachful look.

"We also have someone else here today with us," Grace suddenly says before she's about to end her speech. Her gaze lands on me and a smirk pulls at her lips. "My father had another daughter that he never told us about, but that he decided to include in his will. Darcy, why don't you say a few words to the man who's going to fund your life from now on?"

My eyes widen at the direct appellation as heat travels up my neck.

Suddenly, all eyes are on me, my name on everyone's lips as whispers resound in the quiet cemetery.

Vicky gives Grace a harsh look while Mr. Vaughan goes to her side, undoubtedly reprimanding her for putting the spotlight on me. Another person seems to join them, a man I'd previously seen sitting on the left side. He's older than Mr. Vaughan, his countenance polished, his looks distinguished. As he addresses Vicky and Mr. Vaughan, both of them immediately stop to listen, denoting him as someone with authority where they are concerned.

At that moment, I hope someone will say that it's not necessary for me to speak. But between the argument the Pierces are having amongst themselves and the intense looks I'm getting from all the other attendees, the priest is forced to invite me to the podium to speak.

It's not as if I'm a stranger to public speaking. I am a teacher, for God's sake—I've given my fair share of lectures. But what can I possibly say about a man I'd never met? One I didn't even know existed until a couple days ago when I received the letter about his demise? A man who fathered me but was never a father to me?

As my feet carry me to the podium, everyone's eyes are riveted to me —everyone *but* Vicky and Mr. Vaughan whose glares are enough to send me running.

Grasping the wooden edges of the podium stand, I take a deep breath as I say a couple of platitudes—just enough to give the public what they want.

"As Vicky and August have already said, Leo Pierce was a great man," I plaster a smile on myself even as I feel the lie burn on my tongue.

Forgive me, God. I'm standing next to your House and I'm spouting lies.

Clearing my throat, I take a deep breath as I continue.

"He was such a great man he left me to grow up in an orphanage."

My eyes widen just as I slap a hand over my mouth. Gasps erupt everywhere, with the people on the left side staring at me as if I'd killed their cat.

Yet for some reason, I can't seem to stop myself as the words pour out of me.

"In fact, I've never met the man. How can I say anything good about him? I know you're not supposed to speak ill of the dead and all that, but how can I sing him praises when he never once showed his face? When he never once tried to contact me," a dry laugh escapes me.

"Enough, Darcy," Mr. Vaughan says through gritted teeth.

"Sorry, I laughed," I shrug, giggling some more.

What the hell is happening to me?

"But really, if he was such a family man, the best father you could have ever had, why was he not a father to me too?" I ask pointedly as I look at the Pierces.

At some point, though, I must have leaned in too much. The podium wobbles, and as I try to stabilize it, I only manage to push it further until it hits the edge.

When had I leaned in so much?

Maybe my speech had been a little too passionate. There's that moment when I know something bad will happen, the creaking already foreboding, but the clicking sound of wood snapping against wood proves to be my doom.

No sooner were the *truths* about my father out of my mouth than I am already falling—together with the podium stand.

And it's not a pretty fall. Not when the stand had been placed right behind the slightly elevated *closed* casket.

No sound comes out of my mouth—though I could have sworn I screamed bloody murder—as the stand tilts to such an angle, it crashes straight into the casket, denting the expensive wood right in the middle.

Oh, dear God, please save me from this ignominy!

A small yelp escapes me as I hold closely on to the podium. But though I feel the impact, there's no pain—not even one little scratch.

My eyes are closed in shame, and the gasps I'd heard during my speech have now turned into wails and curses—all probably directed at me.

I open one eye, furtively looking around. And it's just as I'd imagined.

Mayhem.

But people aren't looking at me. They're looking to my right. To...

Slowly, I turn my head, my entire body freezing in place as I realize the podium hadn't just dented the casket. It had broken the hinges of the lid, sending the small piece of wood flying and revealing the dead body.

I blink in shock.

The body that...isn't so dead.

He's not, right?

I stare at him just as he stares back at me, and I doubt dead people can open their eyes just as I doubt the mortician would *not* have closed his eyes.

He's *staring* at me, and his nostrils flare.

Come on, dead people don't breathe!

"You're not dead," I whisper, feeling myself sway lightly even though I'm glued to the flat wood.

He doesn't reply. Instead, he yells loudly.

"Mordechai!"

Dead people definitely do *not* speak—or yell.

"You're not dead," I repeat like a broken record.

Mr. Vaughan is by the casket in a second, hauling me up none too gently. If the fall hadn't hurt my limbs, his impossibly tight hold certainly does.

"Mr. Pierce," he exclaims, wonder tinging his voice.

But as I raise my gaze to his face, I realize his eyes don't share the same surprise. Almost as if...he'd known about it?

"This is a miracle! A miracle I'm telling you," he calls out. At the same time, Vicky comes running to the casket, tears streaming down her face as she embraces her husband.

I retreat by the sidelines, gawking at the show before me like everyone else around.

Yet why does it feel like I'm the only one *not* in on the joke?

Why does it feel as if this is one elaborate prank?

I'm losing my mind.

Either that, or *they* are making me lose my mind.

Nonetheless, now that Mr. Pierce is clearly alive and well, and quite possibly shooting me daggers with his eyes at the moment, I can finally bid adieu to Fairydale and forget about this absolutely *horrendous* experience.

Mr. Vaughan is helping Mr. Pierce rise from his casket, Vicky and Grace fawning over him while August is trying to convince them to give him some space. Then there's the older gentleman from before, and he's watching the entire debacle with his brows pinched, his mouth set in a grim line.

"A miracle!" Both Vicky and Grace continue to exclaim, and looking around, everyone is playing along *but* the four people on the right who are regarding Mr. Pierce suspiciously.

"I can walk by myself, woman," Mr. Pierce grits out, pushing Vicky off him and showing that he is, indeed, *not* the great man everyone was eulogizing him to be—certainly not the most polite one either.

A scowl is etched on his features, and as his gaze settles on me once more, his anger becomes more pronounced.

Taking a step towards me, he points his finger to my face.

"You," he sneers. "You goddamn hussy," he spits out, the insult making me reel in shock. "Just like your fucking mother and your entire fucking family. I'll fucking show you..." he takes another step, his stride determined as he advances towards me.

What the...

Instead of thanking me for waking him from the dead—though I somehow doubt he was too dead in the first place—he's threatening me?

My mouth hangs open in shock, and I can barely find my words to rebuke his claims.

How dare he insult me like that? A *hussy*?

I've never so much as held a man's hand—well, fine, *except* Amon's, but that was in my dream so it doesn't count—and he dares call me a hussy? For what? For accidentally revealing his ruse to the world?

A myriad of questions are going through my mind. If he's not dead, there's no will, right? And if there's no will, then why did they invite me to Fairydale?

As he comes even closer, my bravado makes its appearance—after all, I won't just sit here and let him call me names when it's he who is the charlatan.

"How dare you," I raise my voice, my fists clenched and ready to act.

This isn't a father who'd watched over his daughter and wanted the best for her, hoping to one day meet her. Malice drips from him, his eyes full of hate as he settles them on me.

This man doesn't love me. He abhors me. And I have no idea *why*.

"You should have stayed dead, old man," I tell him squarely. "At least then I wouldn't know what I was missing out on," I huff out loud.

Everyone is gathered around us in a circle, all watching the spectacle but none daring to intervene.

He's a couple of feet away from me, but as he takes another step, he suddenly stops.

His eyes widen as he blinks repeatedly. His lips part and a strangled noise erupts from his throat. Clutching his hands to his neck, he's struggling to say something, almost as if he's suffocating.

Instinctively I take a step back as he falls to his knees, the whites of his eyes turning black right before my eyes.

"What..." I whisper, unable to believe my eyes.

Hunched over, he starts dry heaving until something seems to be coming out of his mouth. Something...

Everyone gasps as he proceeds to vomit his organs. One by one, he spills them onto the ground, some liquified, some semi-solid.

He retches until he's thrown up everything within him.

Until he's dead.

Again.

Yet this time it seems it's not enough.

One second his face is frozen in time, with all the pain, shock, and agony. The next, his entire body is enveloped by black flames that swallow him whole.

No one moves.

Everyone watches with morbid curiosity. From the beginning, no one tried to lend him a hand.

Seconds on end, the fires rage and rage, covering every inch of his skin. Then, like nothing had existed in the first place, the fire stops, his remains turning into fine dust taken by the light summer breeze.

What the hell...

Am I going crazy, or did everyone else see the same thing I saw?

As I lift my gaze towards the Pierce family, I'm surprised to see there's no shock. Only anger. Raw, palpable anger.

And it's all directed at *me.*

"Witch," Vicky steps forward. "You're a fucking witch. Just like your mother. Just like your entire..."

She doesn't finish her soliloquy as Mr. Vaughan reaches for her, restraining her in his arms and whispering something in her ear.

Her mouth tightens, but she nods.

"This isn't the last you'll hear of me. *Witch,*" she repeats, spitting at my feet. I jump back, though I can't possibly let this rest.

"I'll see you at the reading of the will," I chirp, waving cheerfully as Mr. Vaughan leads Vicky and Grace away from the death scene.

The rest of the people disperse too, but not before throwing the same word around.

Witch.

Great. Now not only am I the outsider in this town. But I'm also a witch?

I roll my eyes at the insanity, and though I've just witnessed the most grotesque show of my life, I can't find it in me to be sorry.

Yes, I am shocked. But sorry? No.

"I hope I'm still getting the money now," I mumble sarcastically.

Yet for all my outward jolly attitude, inside my mind is clouded by doubts and confusion.

Hadn't Vicky said she didn't know who my mother was? Then why pick on her to insult me—almost as if it was personal? And what about the family both she and Mr. Pierce were talking about?

What else do they know and I don't?

And most importantly, why am I here?

When most of the crowd has moved on, I let out a relieved sigh. But

I soon realize that Mr. Vaughan, who'd brought me to the cemetery, had left with the Pierces, thereby leaving me...stranded here.

From what I'd seen, the cemetery is located at the opposite end of town, and walking on foot to the house would probably take me an hour—at best.

My shoulders slump, and just as I try to cheer myself on, someone calls me from behind.

"Miss O'Sullivan?"

Startled, I turn and come face to face with the people who'd been sitting on the right, a good distance away from the others.

"Yes?" I blink, for a moment ready to hear more accusations or insults.

"We wanted to take a moment to introduce ourselves and maybe offer some help," the man says.

"I'm Katrina Hale," the younger girl thrusts her hand at me, her eyes sparkling with mischief.

"Darcy," I shake her hand.

"I am Connor Hale and this is my wife, Thomasa," Connor introduces his wife. "And that over there is my aunt, Rhiannon Hale."

"Pleased to meet you," I greet them, my eyes going to Rhiannon, the elderly woman who is currently hunched over what little remains of Leo Pierce.

Getting to her feet, her movements are brisk for someone her age as she comes over to our side.

She doesn't speak as she simply shakes her head at Connor.

"This is Darcy O'Sullivan," he points to me, redirecting the old woman's attention.

"Oh, Darcy," her lips tug into a welcoming smile. "Welcome to Fairydale, my dear. I'm sorry you had to witness such a spectacle. I promise we don't always...self-combust."

I still for a moment as it dawns on me she's joking. Releasing a chuckle, I nod.

"I gathered you're not a fan of the Pierces, are you?"

"We can't say we are," she laughs. "But who would miss the funeral of the thorn in their," she pauses, her eyes glinting playfully, "bottom," she amends, though I have no doubt she was about to use another word.

I give her a tight smile.

"Katrina, why don't you show Darcy around town. Get her more familiar with the surroundings," Rhiannon suddenly suggests, all but pushing Katrina towards me.

"That won't be necessary," I put my hands up. "I don't plan on staying much longer. Tomorrow is the reading of the will and after that I'm going back home," I explain. "I would, however, appreciate it if you could give me a lift to the house I'm staying at? It's on the way to your house."

"Is it?" Rhiannon muses in a knowing tone.

"Nonsense," Connor interjects. "Regardless of whether you leave tomorrow or not, you should still get the full Fairydale experience. Don't let this little horrific event mar your opinion of our little town."

"Exactly," his wife joins in. "There are a number of things you can see and do around here."

All of them start talking at the same time, extolling the virtues of the town and telling me I'm missing out on a lot of great experiences by limiting myself.

"I guess I do need some new clothes if you could show me a shop?" I suggest.

After today, I don't think I want to wear any of the clothes Grace had loaned me. In fact, aside from the reading of the will, I don't want to have anything else to do with them.

"Wonderful!" Rhiannon exclaims, and based on their dynamics, I realize she's not only the matriarch, but the true head of the family.

We walk over to their car, Connor and Thomasa taking the front seats while I'm crammed with Katrina and Rhiannon in the back.

They continue chatting on the drive to the town's central square, each instructing Katrina to take me to see this and that. When we finally reach the destination, Katrina and I get out of the car, but Rhiannon doesn't miss the chance to ask me to have dinner with them tomorrow night, after the reading of the will.

She's looking at me so expectantly that she's making it hard to say no. So I reluctantly agree. Besides, when else will I have the opportunity to see that manor of theirs up-close?

They drive off, and only Katrina and I are left. So I turn to her and pose the question that's been on my mind from the beginning.

"If you're not on good terms with the Pierces, then why are you nice to me?"

She laughs.

"After that speech, I think it's safe to say you're not on very good terms with the Pierces either, are you?"

"I don't think I ever was," I murmur.

"Vicky Pierce is notorious in our town for her attitude. She can smile sweetly at you while cursing you and all your past generations," she cracks a smile.

"I kind of gathered that," I add dryly, thinking of my previous interactions with her.

"Let's go to the shops so you can pick up a few clothes, and then let's have lunch, shall we?" She asks enthusiastically.

"I am quite famished," I admit.

I haven't eaten anything since the night before, and truthfully, now that I know the true nature of the Pierces, I am a little hesitant to eat any of the things they've left for me in the house.

"Perfect!" She exclaims, taking my arm and leading me towards a street that has a lot of colorful shops.

"These are the stores. There are a few more in other parts of town, but these ones have the trendiest clothes," she tells me as we stop in front of a store with a blue façade.

There are a couple of mannequins in the window, the style of clothing agreeable. So we go inside.

I browse their selection of dresses for a few minutes and I'm pleased with their offerings and the prices. These clothes are certainly cheaper than in Boston. I don't go too crazy though, only buying a few day dresses, some new underthings and a nightgown. In the end, I can't pass on buying a nice, slightly more expensive dress for the dinner at the Hale manor—of course, *not* in the hopes that I will see a certain someone.

Once I've paid for everything, Katrina is once more leading me down the street until we reach a diner.

"This is the most popular diner in Fairydale," she says as we go inside.

The diner isn't very busy, only a couple of people inside. But the moment we step inside, their attention is riveted on us, their expressions ranging from cynical to downright dislike.

"Don't worry about it," Katrina shrugs. "It's not about you. My family isn't the most welcome in town."

"But aren't you one of the founding families?" I frown.

We take our seats at the end of the diner, putting as much distance between us and the other customers. Still, the nasty glances don't stop, now coupled with rather loud gossip and bad-mouthing. And of course, it doesn't escape me when I hear the word *witch.*

A waitress wearing a tight smile on her face takes our orders. I go for a roast beef while Katrina orders a chicken casserole.

When the waitress is out of hearing distance, Katrina finally turns to me.

"We are," she sighs. "But Nicholson rules the town. Together with Pierce and Vaughan, he's the authority around here. Compared to them, we are quite the pariahs," she smiles sadly. "Most people ignore us, but there are some that make their distaste known," she nods towards some men leering at us.

"Nicholson? I don't think I've met any from that family."

"You saw him. The old man in the gray suit from the funeral," her lips curl in distaste. "He's the Nicholson patriarch, and the *most* influential person around here."

Recalling the way Vicky and Mr. Vaughan had both reacted to him, it suddenly makes sense. They had both deferred to him as if his word was law.

"Mr. Vaughan told me of a conflict with the Hales, and he mentioned something about Bailey?"

She nods.

"The Baileys are the only ones who haven't snubbed us. They don't always acknowledge us, though. But they are at least friendlier than anyone else in town."

"When did this start? I don't understand why you'd stay here if everyone is so against your family," I add.

I'd seen the way they were apart from everyone at the funeral, and thinking back, I could note how the others had glared at them with animosity. The reaction of the people at the diner alone is telling, but to hear that almost *everyone* behaves like that? I don't know if I could live in a place where everyone hated me.

"When did it start?" she smiles, shaking her head. "It's been like this for decades. Of course, I only know the stories from my grandmother. The Hale family settled in Fairydale immediately after the plague, soon followed by Nicholson and then Pierce and Vaughan. It's my understanding that the first conflict was over the manor and the accompanying lands. Before the plague, they used to belong to the Creed family, but everyone perished from the illness."

I listen attentively, surprised to hear there was another owner of the manor, and I can't help but wonder if the Creeds were the ones who named the town Fairydale.

Katrina takes a sip of water before continuing.

"The Hales had claim to it through Lydia Hale, the daughter of the original owners. Nicholson claimed it should have been passed down to him because he was the son of Abel Creed. But because he was illegitimate, he couldn't prove anything. Since then, they've done everything in their power to discredit us in hopes we will leave Fairydale and abandon the house. And that brings me to your other question. Why stay? Because it's our legacy and our duty to stay in Fairydale," she gives me a warm smile.

"That's quite a tumultuous history."

"And it's just the tip of the iceberg," she groans. "When they couldn't win fairly, they resorted to dirty tricks, and they've managed to convince almost everyone that we're somehow cursed and bring bad luck." Katrina shakes her head at the absurdity of it.

"But how could anyone believe that? We live in the twentieth century. Everyone knows there's no such thing as curses," I immediately add, though the words don't feel as secure on my lips after a couple of days in Fairdale. Particularly not after witnessing Leo Pierce's wretched demise. Not only had he purged himself from inside out, but he'd also combusted right in front of us before turning into dust.

Though I tried not to give that incident too much thought, I can't help but replay it in my head, marveling every time at the impossibility of the situation.

"This isn't Boston, Darcy. People here believe what they see. If the moon suddenly turns red, it's a bad omen. It's the same if the river changes color, or if animals suddenly die. Every little thing can be suspicious to someone who is looking for it. Just like everything can seem a coincidence to someone who isn't."

I nod slowly, a shiver going down my back at all this talk of witchcraft. Still, I try to ignore the odd little things that have been happening to me since I arrived in this town. I don't know if I'm yet ready to attribute that to witchcraft.

"What do you think happened to Mr. Pierce then? Wasn't that a little...surreal?"

She purses her lips, the topic clearly not a welcome one.

"I don't know. They've been crying wolf about us for so long, I wouldn't be surprised if it was *them* who engaged in God knows what. And maybe," she pauses, bringing her eyes to mine as she regards me intently. "Maybe it was well-deserved."

I blink, surprised by the conviction in her tone.

"I still don't understand why call me here if he wasn't dead. Why go through all the trouble..."

"Perhaps they needed something from you," she suddenly adds. "Something you, and *only* you can provide."

"But what?" I ask exasperated. I'd been trying to find an explanation for everything that's been happening, yet I keep coming empty-handed. No matter how you look at my situation, things don't fit. And I know they will not fit until I have all the information in my hands. Because as it stands...I'm reluctant to admit that I'm fully in the dark.

Katrina shrugs carelessly.

"Who knows. They are a weird bunch," she adds, but something about the way she's speaking suggests she knows more than she's letting on.

The food is served and the conversation moves to a lighter subject as Katrina describes all the spots I should visit in Fairydale before I decide to leave—the waterfall and the river, the fairy hill, and of course, the Hale manor.

"We have some amazing galleries from our ancestors, as well as sculptures and priceless artifacts from the entire world. The Creeds were collectors and everything was intact when my family moved into the manor."

"Like a museum," I add in awe.

"Just like a museum."

"I would love to visit." I tell her sincerely. We may not have spent too much time together so far but she's been more welcoming than anyone, and her kindness doesn't seem dependent on anything—as it was the case with Mr. Vaughan and the Pierces.

"There's something else I'm curious about," I make the courage to say as a blush stains my cheeks. I can't *not* ask her about her brother and what Mr. Vaughan had said.

Is he dangerous? Is he...trustworthy?

I know war can cause trauma, and I've seen plenty of people retreat within themselves after the experience—with some turning particularly violent.

Is he like that, too?

Despite telling myself that I should forget about him altogether, I haven't been able to. He made a strong impression on me, the likes of which I've never experienced. Certainly more than any other man I've met before.

And given the fact that he'd even influenced my dreams...I think it's fair to want to know more about the man.

But just as I'm about to ask her about him, she suddenly stands up, her eyes growing serious.

"I'll be right back," she says as she takes off her napkin and places it on the table. "I just need to take care of something," she mumbles as she all but dashes through the aisles, exiting the diner.

What...

Blinking in shock, I look at the empty seat in front of me before I bring my gaze to my food and I release a weary sigh.

Just when I think I find a normal person in Fairydale and this happens...

I take a sip of water before I signal the waitress for the check. After I pay, I finish my food and prepare to leave since I don't think Katrina will return anytime soon.

Getting up from the table, I smooth my hands over the black dress I'm wearing and grab my shopping bags—a little too excited to wear my *own* clothes and not Grace's hand-me-downs.

I blank my expression as I pass by the other tables. More people had trickled in, and judging by their sneers, they've heard about the disaster from the funeral.

The whispers don't fail to register, and out of nowhere, I feel a harsh sting on my bottom, followed by whistles.

"Nice piece of ass, *witch*," a man laughs, quickly joined by everyone else in the diner.

Even the waitress is looking at me as if I *deserved* that.

Gritting my teeth, I realize I can't make a scene or they will all band on me together. Already my skin is crawling from the lascivious gazes I'm getting.

I release a loud huff, straightening my spine as I half turn and hit his hand aside with my shopping bag.

"Ops," I feign a smile. "Careful before I put a hex on you," I look him dead in the eye before I invent a few words in a non-existent language while pointing my finger at him.

"*Ashlyndl Bdl Gol*. Ha," I nod to myself, bringing my finger to my lips and blowing on it as if it were a gun.

If I had any doubts that these people actually believed in this witchcraft nonsense, I am now fully convinced as the man blanches right before my eyes, his breathing growing harsher as panic overtakes him.

I don't stick around to see what happens, but I do hear the terror in his voice as he yells to the entire diner.

"I've been cursed."

Just one more reason to cut my Fairydale visit short. Now I probably won't be able to show my face at the diner without getting doused in holy water and beaten with crucifixes—is that even how you harm a witch?

Chuckling at my own silliness, I barely get to exit the diner as a car skids right in front of me, the noise making me jump back.

"Dear God," I mutter, my eyes going wide.

The door opens, and inside I spot none other than *him*.

Caleb Hale.

Chapter Six

He has a cigarette in his mouth, Ray Bans perched on his nose, and a dress shirt that's been turned into a leisure outfit—the buttons on his neck popped open, his tie missing, and the sleeves of the shirt folded around his elbows. As I lean in, I can see the veins on his arms and the pure bulging muscles.

"Hop in," he commands in that deep voice of his that my ears have not yet forgotten.

For a moment, I find myself trapped in the allure of his presence—so much so that I forget all about my abhorrence of being told what to do. Even more so when I find myself sliding in the passenger seat, closing the door and buckling my seat belt.

The interior is as luxurious as the exterior—all leather—and I'm reminded that the Hales are obviously as well off as the Pierces, if not more.

"Where are we going?" I ask just as my mental fog lifts and I realize I got into a car with a stranger—putting myself in an incredibly vulnerable position.

"Secret," he winks at me, a dimple appearing in his cheek.

"It's not funny," I mumble, doing my best to not get caught up in his dazzling looks.

"I'm not going to murder you and hide your body, Darcy," he half-turns, amusement dripping from his voice. "If that had been my purpose, I would have had plenty of opportunities last night, wouldn't you say?"

I don't answer—mostly because he is correct. It would have been entirely easy for him to do anything to me the night before. And with that house being in the middle of nowhere, no one would have been wiser about it.

But even now, having just become the hottest topic in town—and not in a positive light—I doubt anyone would care if I disappeared.

"Stop worrying that pretty head of yours," he continues as he sees my pinched brows and pursed lips.

My lashes flutter in surprise as I latch on to his words, wanting to be sure he said what I think he said...

"You think I'm pretty?" I blurt out, my cheeks turning a deep shade of red.

"I didn't peg you for the type to fish for compliments, Darcy darlin'," he drawls, turning to me just as his sunglasses fall down his nose, his gaze connecting with mine.

I freeze.

His eyes... I could have sworn they were a light color the night before. But now?

They're black. Pitch black.

"You're staring," he suddenly says, raising a brow.

"And you're not paying attention to the road," I snap, caught red-handed.

His chuckle fills the air just as heat travels up my neck.

"You're safe with me. Safer than with anyone else," he tells me in a self-assured tone. One that would be cocky on anyone but him, since as he says the words I *believe* them.

Weird? *Extremely*.

Not for the first time I have to wonder what it is about him that affects me so. He'd not only prompted my fantastical dream, but also a profound loneliness—that part I'd buried long ago that only wanted to belong.

Somehow, with one—*no doubt inconsequential for him*—meeting, this man triggered that restlessness I've always kept just beneath the surface. Whereas before I've merely been alive, he makes me want to *live.*

The question remains.

Why? Why now? Why him?

"You heard about that?" I ask dryly, not wanting to dwell too much on what the mere sound of his voice does to my senses.

"Who hasn't? By this time everyone knows of the blue-eyed witch who made Leo Pierce self-combust," he laughs.

"And do you believe them? Maybe I really did it—curse him until he became nothing more than dust in the air."

He doesn't answer for a moment, his gaze focused on the road.

"You don't have it in you," he suddenly says. "You could never execute someone, could you?" he muses, posing a question for which he already has an answer.

"Who knows," I shrug. "Maybe under certain conditions I could."

He huffs at that, the corners of his mouth pulling up in a knowing smile.

"I'm sure you could," he adds sarcastically.

"Why do I feel like that is a challenge?" I narrow my eyes at him.

"Not entirely a challenge as much as..." he pauses, his eyes back on mine. "I'd be curious to see how far you can go now," he gives me an intense look, my gaze dropping to his lips just as he says my name in the most emphatical way. "Darcy."

"Now?" I frown.

He merely smiles.

"In the future," he amends, flinging his cigarette out the window.

"Right, I'll make sure to *actually* bash you over the head with a metal bar next time you catch me unawares at night," I mumble under my breath.

Yet everything I say seems to amuse him further. His lips are stretched in a perpetual smile and I swear his attention is more on me than it is on the road.

Not that I mind it.

But I'm not sure what to make of him yet, and though his presence makes my knees weak, I need to tread carefully.

"Caleb, you were there last night," I start, biting my lip in apprehension. "The door to the Old Church was open, wasn't it?" I ask as I turn to him.

His brows shoot up.

"What? Of course not," he answers immediately. "That place has been sealed since the plague. No one's been inside."

"But..." I'm about to protest, but then I remember Mr. Vaughan's reaction. The last thing I want is for people to think me mad, so I keep it to myself. Maybe it *was* all a dream...

"You weren't there today," I clear my throat as I change the subject. "At the funeral."

"I wasn't," he states.

"Why?"

"I'm surprised Mordechai didn't warn you away from me," he notes, successfully dodging the question.

"He did. But I can make my own decisions."

"Well, there you have it. If I had shown up, there would have been two funerals instead of one. Leo's and..."

"Mr. Vaughan's?" I ask, chuckling.

"Indeed. He would have had a heart attack seeing me anywhere in his vicinity."

"Why is he so against you?"

He sighs.

"You probably noticed that he's quite close with Vicky Pierce," he starts and I nod. "They've been *close* for over two decades. It's an open secret."

My eyes widen with realization. I'd suspected it, but to have it confirmed?

"When you say two decades, you mean..." I trail off. He wouldn't have specified the length of time if he hadn't been alluding to something. And considering Grace is around twenty years old.

"I see you did the math."

"So Grace is his daughter," I say slowly, and Caleb nods. "But why..."

"Grace has always had a crush on me," he states matter of factly, but that one sentence is enough to open a chasm inside my chest.

Seriously, Darcy? He's a stranger!

"Let me guess. You rejected her?" I offer, hoping to God my tone doesn't sound so...wishful.

"Yes," he laughs, but all I feel is a strong sense of relief that fills me to the brim.

Maybe I *am* mad—or something akin to that—for I cannot comprehend what is happening to me and why this man makes me feel so confused yet at the same time so secure.

"She didn't take it well," he continues. "And since our families aren't on good terms, Mordechai decided to declare open season on me for making his little *angel* cry."

"He told me you weren't well from the war," I probe carefully, biting my lip as I watch his reaction from the corner of my eye.

He doesn't get to reply, though, as he finally pulls into a small driveway.

I'd been so focused on our conversation that I hadn't paid much attention to where we were going. Looking around, I note that we're no longer in the town. There is a forest to my right, and what looks like an open field across the road.

"Are you sure you *really* didn't take me here to murder me and hide my body?" I joke, turning to look at him and waiting for a witty reply.

Instead, I find him resting his forehead on the steering wheel, his breathing labored.

He stays like that for a moment before he turns, sweat trickling down his temples, his face paler than before.

"Caleb?" I ask as I reach out, my hand touching his for the first time.

My mouth parts in a small o. Our gazes connect just as my skin rests on top of his.

He's cold. So, so cold.

"You're not well," I say, immediately placing the back of my hand to his forehead.

"Just a trifle," he strains to smile, yet I don't find any of this funny.

He must have been feeling off for a while. That's why his answers were so sluggish. So...

"You need a medic," I tell him when I note his forehead is as cold as the rest of his body. "What if you have the flu? Or worse," I babble, immediately worried.

"There," he nods behind me to what looks to be a small cabin. "Help me get there."

I'm about to protest—that he should drive to see a medic while he's still able. But one look at him and I know I won't be able to convince him.

"No medic could treat this, Darcy," he says in a soft voice. "I just need a moment—rest a little."

"But..."

"Please," he releases a harsh breath just as blood starts dripping from his nose.

My heart is in my throat as I quickly get out of the car and go to his side, opening the door and already finding him swaying on his feet as he tries to stand up.

"What the hell is wrong with you, Caleb?" I mutter, my own limbs growing colder from the panic growing inside of me.

"Language, Darcy darlin'," he chuckles but ends up coughing instead. Coughing...blood.

"How can you be amused when you..." I bite my lip, willing my mind to *not* go there.

He places his arm over my shoulder as I do my best to help him move towards the cabin. His harsh breath is in my ear and I know this is no ploy to get me along in a secluded location. He's *really* ill.

And I don't know how to help him.

With great difficulty, I manage to get him to the front of the cabin. He pushes the door open, pointing towards a bed in the back of the room. We stagger together and he collapses on the bed, his hand going to his chest almost as if he's having a heart attack.

"Caleb? What's wrong?" I ask as I kneel by the bed.

Removing a handkerchief from my purse, I bring it to his face, dabbing at the blood from his nose and around his mouth.

He wraps his big hand around my wrist, stopping me. And as he turns his head, his eyes open in my direction, emitting such a blinding light I'm forced to snap my own eyes shut.

"Caleb?" I ask again, squinting.

He's looking at me but it's like he isn't seeing me. His eyes are completely white, his irises losing all their color.

"Caleb," I repeat, worry mounting inside of me.

As if reacting to my voice, he blinks, and when he opens his eyes again, they are back to the same color as before.

I exhale in relief, but that doesn't remove the anxiety I feel at seeing him in such a poor condition.

"Tell me how I can help," I urge in a low voice, palming his face between my hands.

He looks disoriented, his pupils going in and out of focus as he simply stares at me.

Shaking his head slightly, he covers my hand with his, holding tight just as he leans into me.

"I won't die," he coughs. "I just need...some...rest," he says right before he becomes limp in my arms, his eyes closing.

Panic unlike any other takes hold of me as I shake him, calling his name and pleading with him to react. Yet he doesn't.

He's...out.

Bringing my finger under his nose, I feel for his breath, calming a little as I confirm he's not dead.

Wiping the rest of the blood off him, I do my best to make him comfortable on the bed while I take in the small cabin and explore its contents—all in hope I may find something to help him.

Dear God, but we're God knows where. Caleb is sick. I don't know how to drive. There's absolutely no way to contact anyone in town. And he *desperately* needs a medic.

As I look around, I notice various weapons on the wall, as well as littering every corner of the room. It dawns on me that it's a hunting cabin.

But if that's so, then it should also have some medical supplies.

The space is crammed, and soon I'm ransacking every little crevice, finding some canned food, ammunition, some old magazines and eventually a small box with a red cross on it. Opening it, I can't find anything but some bandages and disinfectant, both not useful in this instance.

Releasing a sigh of frustration, I gaze back at him to find even more blood pouring out of his nose, which makes my worry skyrocket. After I clean him up, I check my wristwatch, noting it's late afternoon. It will get dark soon, too.

Biting my lips in consternation, I decide that instead of wasting time and praying for him to wake up, I could go into the forest and look for some plants to help.

I may not be a professional, but I can recognize most medicinal plants. And if I can help him in any way...

Taking only my purse with me, I follow a beaten path deep in the forest, keeping myself alert to memorize my surroundings so I can find my way back.

I wander for what feels like forever when I finally spot something—red clover. A few paces over and I find even more treats—basil and horseradish. All good for cold or the flu, though I fear Caleb might suffer from a worse ailment. I pick some of each, placing them carefully in a napkin and depositing them in my purse.

Suddenly, I'm glad he picked me up when he did. I may not have much worldly experience, but medicinal teas and concoctions are my specialty. If this helps him, even a little, then I'll be more at peace.

As I catch sight of another plant, then another, I wander aimlessly while tucking away all types of leaves, roots and anything I think might help.

I'd carefully checked the entire place and unfortunately, I hadn't been able to find many cooking tools aside from an old iron pot. But given that the cabin does not have any appliances, nor electricity, I won't be able to use it regularly.

On my way back, I also grab a few pieces of wood for a fire, since I will need somewhere to boil the plants and make the tea.

The trek back doesn't take long, and I'm thankful I haven't lost my way.

As soon as I get back, I check on Caleb again, noting he hasn't woken up, his skin completely damp. Going to his side, I wipe some of the sweat away, my lips set in a thin line as helplessness overtakes me.

He must have known he was ill. Then why in God's name had he brought us here instead of to a medic's office?

"You can't die on me," I whisper, barely stifling the urge to shake him awake and make him promise me that. "I'm not going to let you die."

Yet the issue is that I don't know what he's suffering from. My teas help with colds and respiratory ailments, but if he has neither, then I fear it is all for naught. But I can't lose hope now.

Steeling myself against those intrusive thoughts, I wet a rag, placing it over his forehead while I go outside and try my best at lighting a fire.

I've done it a couple of times in my childhood, but it's never an easy walk in the park.

It takes me maybe five attempts before the flame sparks to life, growing bigger and bigger as I add more wood and flammable material.

After I arrange some stones in the shape of a funnel, I finally place the water-filled pot on top of it.

I leave the door open to the cabin so I can see if Caleb stirs, and I glance at him every now and then.

Sighing when I note no movements, I gather my dress around my legs as I lower myself to the ground, getting into a comfortable position as I go through the plants I'd collected.

After I inspect them, I clean them and drop them in the boiling water.

The infusion duration matters, and because some of these plants have an extremely bitter taste, I need to monitor the boiling time carefully.

When I'm done, I struggle a little to pour the liquid in a mug without burning myself. I fill two cups to the brim and I turn to the cabin.

My eyes widen as I see Caleb awake.

He's sitting on the edge of the bed, his eyes fixed on me.

From that distance, I once more get the impression that he has the lightest eyes humanly possible. But as I put one foot in front of the other, reaching his side, I realize it must all be the play of the dimming afternoon light.

His eyes are black. Just like before.

He doesn't make to move as his gaze follows every move I make, the intense way he's looking at me sending a shiver down my back and making me wonder if I did something wrong.

"How are you feeling?" I ask, plastering a smile on my face.

He doesn't return it, all amusement from before seemingly gone. Instead, there's only this nerve-wrecking intensity that has me squirming on the spot.

Placing one mug on a table, I take the other to him.

"This should help you feel better," I add as I extend the tea to him, a little nervous when he doesn't say anything.

He's simply watching me like a predator would his prey.

Yet before I know it, his hand is on mine, squeezing tightly and making me yelp in surprise. My eyes widen as the liquid teeters in the mug and I do my best to stay still and not spill it—on him or on myself.

"Caleb?" I ask tentatively. "What's wrong," I whisper, seeking his gaze in an effort to understand what's happening.

He doesn't answer.

Abruptly tugging me to him, I don't know what I'm more shocked about, the fact that no drop of tea ever spills on my skin—or *anywhere*—or that I'm so close to his face I can feel his breath on my lips.

"The tea," he rasps roughly, his voice thick and harsh—almost as if he hasn't used it in an eternity.

"Yes, I made you tea," I say softly.

I don't know what's happening to him, if this is a symptom of his illness or the onset of delirium. But as I take in his features, taut and vibrating with unreleased energy, I can't spot any of the previous signs of sickness. He's no longer pale or sweating. In fact, his skin looks golden and healthy, a natural glow to his cheeks that makes him look even more striking than before.

"The tea," he repeats in the same unyielding tone, his nostrils flaring. "Have you made it for someone else?"

"What?" I blurt out, taken aback. "I made it for you, of course," I immediately say.

His eyes narrow, his lush mouth tightening as if he's barely holding himself back.

"The tea." This time his voice has an exasperated quality to it. "Have you *ever* made it for another man?" He asks just as his hold on me tightens, pulling me closer.

"What are you talking about?" I whisper and as I stare into his eyes, I could swear they flicker red.

What in God's name is happening?

"It's a simple question, *Darcy*," he grits out. "Have you, or have you not made this for another man?"

A sliver of fear washes through me, but I push it down.

Slowly, I shake my head, the word *no* on my lips the softest whisper.

"Good," he purrs, leaning in and brushing his lips against my ear. "You are not to *ever* make it for someone else."

It takes me a moment to digest his words—the fact that he's prohibiting something when he has absolutely no rights over my person.

"You have no right..."

Just as I'm about to state my rebuke, his finger is on my lips, pushing against them and effectively silencing me.

"Right..." he chuckles, leaning back and giving me a scathing look. "Careful, Darcy darlin'. Careful with what you say," he enunciates each word, the message clear.

I gulp down, warring with myself. I could nod and follow his cue, or I could argue, as is my instinct. Yet it doesn't escape me the fact that he's fully recovered, strength radiating from him. Or that we're alone in the woods—which, I only have myself to blame for.

Choosing self-preservation, I slowly give him my nod of acquiescence.

His face breaks into a smile.

"You're not showing me those sharp claws of yours?" He raises a brow. "Pity," he chuckles, taking the mug from my hand and bringing it to his lips.

As he removes his hold on me, I take a step back, watching him with trepidation—as if one wrong step could prove my doom.

He sips the tea, yet he doesn't look away.

"Only for me, isn't it, Darcy?" He raises the mug, an arrogant expression on his face as he all but dares me to contradict him.

Putting on a tremulous smile, I nod.

"Only for you, Caleb."

Yet this one interaction is enough to put a damper on my growing attraction to him. He might be handsome, but behind that perfect facade lurks something—something dark and sinister.

How could I have compared him with the person in my dream? Amon had been the true definition of a gentleman, despite disavowing the term. Though he'd killed someone to save me, his presence brought me a sense of security unlike any other.

Caleb, on the other hand...

He scares me. And it's not only in the way his smoldering gaze makes me fuzzy on the inside, but also in the way his intensity is terrifying me and making me fear for my safety.

Going out and pretending I'm tending to the fire, I try to ignore his presence as I think of a plan of escape.

God, but I need to get out of Fairydale as soon as possible.

"You're no fun, Darcy darlin'," his voice echoes behind me.

I don't need to turn to know he's leaning against the door of the cabin, his eyes on me.

Fear courses through my veins, but I can't let it show. Not if I want to get away with both my life and my virtue intact.

With the same smile plastered on my face, I address him in the softest tone.

"We should head back. It's starting to get dark."

Dusk is already on us, orange beams against the dark blue background.

He merely raises a brow at me.

"So we should," he says slowly, and I'm taken aback by his easy acquiesce.

"Let me get my purse and..." I don't get to finish my sentence and rain starts pouring down, extinguishing the fire and soaking me to the skin.

It all happens in a matter of seconds.

One moment I'm looking at him, hopeful I'll get back to Fairydale by nightfall, the next he's before me, one with the rain.

I blink, not understanding what's happening and how the weather could change like this—in the blink of an eye. The sky had been clear, no cloud in sight.

"You're getting wet, Darcy" he drawls, yet he seems unbothered by the cold drops hitting his skin.

"And you'll get sick again," I say as I regain my wits about me. "We need to leave now."

I all but grab his hand to steer him towards the car when he surprises me by swooping me up in his arms and carrying me back to the cabin.

"Caleb..." I gasp. "What are you doing?" I push at his shoulders, but he won't budge, his body so hard it's as if it were made of stone.

As he enters the cabin, he closes the door behind him with his foot, striding to the bed and depositing me on top of it.

"There," he smiles, wet tendrils of hair sticking to his forehead, drops of water dripping down his perfect features. "You can't be outside now," he says, his tone gentler than before.

"We need to go back," I tell him emphatically. "I can't stay the night out with...a man."

My cheeks heat at the mention and he smirks.

"Then you shouldn't have gotten in my car in the first place, isn't that right, Darcy?"

I blink in confusion just as he leans in front of me, his knees hitting the ground just as he removes a dry towel out of nowhere and starts drying my arms.

"That's not how good girls behave, isn't it? Getting into strange men's cars..." he trails off as he gives me an amused look.

"I..."

"But you're not a good girl. You're a very, very bad girl, aren't you, Darcy darlin'?"

"Stop calling me that," I mutter as I remove my hand from his grasp, wishing I could get as far away from him as possible.

He tips his head up, a sinister smile playing at his lips right as he sets his eyes on me—red, *red* eyes. But it's only for a second before they're back to their original black depths.

Once more, I have to wonder if my mind is playing tricks on me.

"I don't like what you're insinuating, Caleb," I push against him.

"Why?" His grasp becomes firmer, his lips pressed into a tight line. "How many other men's cars have you climbed in? How many, Darcy?" He demands in a harsh tone—one that scares me to my bones.

Though I try to put some distance between us, he won't let me.

"How. Many?" The same intensity from before appears in his face and fear pools in my stomach.

"None," I whisper, hoping this would help me get out of this increasingly dangerous situation.

It doesn't.

Not when he smirks at me like that. Not when his hand curves along my neck, grabbing my nape and pulling me towards him.

So close... So close I think he's going to force a kiss on me—or more.

I barely keep myself from trembling as I flatten my lips in a sign of rebellion.

"Don't, please," I whisper, turning my gaze to his so he can see the sincerity of my plea.

"Hmm," he muses, a low vibration in his throat that makes my body hum with unreleased tension. "I wonder, Darcy darlin'," he starts, amusement in his tone and it's clear he's using that term of endearment mockingly. "How many men have tasted your lips?"

My eyes flutter in shock at his question, and I quickly shake my head—though his hold doesn't allow for much movement.

His brow goes up in question.

"No one. Please let me go," I whisper, my palms on his shoulders as I push lightly. "I'm not like that, please."

It takes everything in me not to cry, or beg him to let me go—but I don't know how he would react to that.

He's already so unpredictable—so brash. I can't take any chances with his mood changes.

Yet now I berate myself for not listening to Mr. Vaughan. He may not be on my side, but he was right that Caleb isn't right in the head. He can't possibly be...

My answer seems to appease him, a genuine smile appearing on his lips and lighting up his features.

"That's right," he grins, showing white, even teeth. "You're only going to be bad for me, aren't you?"

His question throws me off, and I can only stare at him in disbelief. He's not going to attempt something with me, is he? He's not going to try to...

I don't get to dwell on that thought as he leans in, bringing his nose to my face—breathing me in. He nuzzles his face along my cheek, skin on skin.

A shudder goes down my body, yet I keep myself as still as possible.

"You smell so good. Just like I knew you would," he whispers, his warm breath on my skin. "Been waiting too long," he murmurs just before I feel the swipe of his tongue over my cheek.

I'm one second away from hyperventilating—low tremors starting from my extremities and traveling all the way to my core.

Think, Darcy!

"We should go now," I manage to get the words out in an even tone.

To my surprise, he draws back, tilting his head as he regards me with an unnatural glint in his eyes—something wild and untamed.

His hair damp, rain clinging to his skin and clothes, he looks like a savage ready to make me his meal. Yet there's something more. It's in the way he's looking at me as if he can't understand me—as if human mores are beyond his comprehension.

"I'll go check the car," he suddenly says, getting to his feet and leaving the cabin.

My heart is almost bursting out of my chest, and I recognize the onset of a headache. Every cell in my body is humming with terror—and not the type I'd experienced when I heard the organ and no one was playing. No, this is something else. Something primal that makes me fear not only for my life, but for my immortal soul.

Despite that, I can't let myself succumb to fear. Not until I'm out of this terrible situation and as far away from Caleb Hale as possible.

Yet it's not a few seconds later that he's back.

"There seems to be a problem with the car," he says, not even a twitch as he lies to my face.

Of course the car wouldn't start. Isn't that the best scenario for him?

"Why don't you try to see what's wrong?" I ask sweetly, smiling up at him.

If I take the offensive, then he's likely to become more vicious as well.

He nods thoughtfully.

"Let me get some tools."

He goes to one of the boxes in the corner—boxes I'd well rummaged before—and removes a tool box, taking it with him outside.

Yet because I'd ransacked the entire place before, I know there are no car tools in there, just some rusty pieces of metal. He most definitely knows it, too, and is just pretending to try to fix it to bide his time until it becomes pitch black outside.

Shuffling from the bed, I look out the window and note it's still raining.

Still, I can't possibly stay inside with this madman. Not when it's clear his intentions are not in the least honorable.

As I ease the door open, I peek outside and find him under the car's hood.

That's my moment!

Taking advantage of his lack of attention, I dash into the rain, running as far away from the cabin as I can. At this point, it doesn't matter if it's storming outside, or if it's about to get dark—or if there are wild animals lying in wait.

Any fate is better than whatever Caleb has in store for me.

"Darcy!" His voice echoes through the woods.

Not even a few minutes and he already noticed my absence.

Damn it!

I run faster, jumping over a log, and doing my best to keep my balance as the ground becomes muddier and muddier. Fear propels me further, giving me strength even when I feel like my body is about to give up on me.

"Darcy, stop!" Caleb yells after me, his voice closer and closer.

I keep running.

"Stop, damn it! You'll hurt yourself!"

His voice barely reaches me when I trip on a boulder, my arms flailing in vain. In just a matter of seconds I'm on the ground, the impact making me reel—yet there's no pain.

Then why are my lids so heavy?

Why...

Chapter Seven

My eyes snap open as morning light filters through the window. As I look around, it takes me a moment to recognize my surroundings before everything that had happened the night before comes to me.

Caleb.

His odd behavior. Him chasing me in the rain...

Gasping, I stand up—a little too suddenly—and my head feels like it's about to burst. Bringing my hand to my forehead, I note there's a bandage in place.

Immediately, I shoot out of bed, finding my purse and removing a small hand mirror from inside. Taking in my appearance, I note the shadows under my eyes and a splotchy red spot over white gauze.

I fell.

When he was chasing me, I fell.

Looking around, I exhale in relief when I don't see Caleb around, and as soon as I'm able to get to my feet I go to the door and latch the lock in place.

Dear God, what happened?

One glance at my wristwatch and I note it's eight in the morning.

I spent the entire night here. With him. And I was out of it for the entire time...

As things start to become clearer, I realize I'm also not wearing the same dress as before. My gaze dips down at the beige gown I'm garbed in—one of the dresses I'd bought yesterday. Yet as I move, more things hurt, including...

Panic takes hold of me.

Without a second thought, I slip the dress over my head, intent on inspecting my body.

Tears prick at my eyes as I move my hands down my ribcage, wincing at the contact with my tender flesh. There are bruises everywhere.

But that's not the worst.

I swallow hard as I take in my naked body and the fact that I'm not wearing my underthings. I'm completely bare under the dress.

What makes me want to bawl my eyes out, though, is the fact that there is crusted blood all over my inner thigh, starting from the junction of my legs and drying in trickles to my knee.

There are gashes and scratches all over my legs—all indicating a struggle.

He... Did he...

A loud wail erupts from my throat as I fall down to the floor, my entire body shaking, my mind slipping from me.

I don't know how long I stay on the floor, crying and sobbing from the depths of my soul. But after some time, I realize I can't possibly linger here any longer in case Caleb returns—in case he tries to hurt me again.

There is a small grace in the fact that I cannot remember what he did to me. But the evidence is clear as day.

He...raped me.

A knot forms in my throat as I acknowledge that fact to myself, yet I have to be strong.

I'm still alive, right?

Finding some water, I wet a towel and I try to clean myself as best as I can before I slip the dress back on, getting my purse and shopping bag before I leave the cabin.

Yet as I open the door, a loud meow draws my attention to the ground, to a black cat with a small patch of white hair.

"You..." I blink. "Is it you, Mr. Meow?" I ask just as I realize how silly I am. Of course it can't be Mr. Meow. But he is cute enough to make me momentarily forget my plight.

Leaning down, I beckon him closer, surprised when he lets me pet him and take him in my arms.

"Come with me?" I ask, though I know far too well he cannot answer back. Still, he nuzzles his furry cheek against mine and I take it as a sign of assent. "Good boy," I chuckle, despite the tears still running down my cheeks.

I hug the little furry creature to my chest as I trudge my way back to the village.

And as I continue to cry while walking, the cat meows gently in my ear. If it had been another human I'm quite sure it would have been a word of comfort.

"Thank you," I sniffle. "I'm a mess today." I admit and he snuggles closer.

"I'm sure you don't want to hear about my problems... But I just want to leave this damn town and forget it ever existed—forget everyone in it existed, too."

"Meow," he releases a soft sound as he licks my cheek.

"I could take you with me. I'm sure I could convince Allison to let me keep you. Would you like that?"

"Meeeeow."

I chuckle, though my face is still frozen with pain.

"I'll take that as a categorical yes."

In spite of the language barrier, I'm thankful for his presence. Talking with him despite getting no reply is helping me to stop thinking about what happened.

At the fact that Caleb...

It's all my damn fault for getting in his car. For trusting him when I should have never done that. And now... Another pained cry escapes my lips when I think about what he did—what he stole from me. I barely manage to put one foot in front of the other as pain unlike any other takes root in my heart.

How could he? How could he do that to me?

I'd always imagined I would one day fall in love with someone, and then I'd share everything that I am with him—body and soul. Yet now there's a hollowness inside my heart when I think of someone violating my body in that manner—taking what wasn't his to take, only mine to give.

My stomach rebels at the very thought, and I feel ill for ever thinking him attractive, for dreaming what it might be like if he touched me. But not like that. Not without my permission, and certainly not against my wishes.

"Meow," Mr. Meow licks my face again.

"You're a very nice cat, Mr. Meow," I coo as I give him a light pat.

In an attempt to forget my sorrows, I tell Mr. Meow about my life back home, about my job and my friends, about the nuns who raised me.

Recalling happy memories makes me push aside the bad ones.

After what feels like an eternity, I finally make it back to the town, but because I can't quite recall where the Pierce house is, I spend another hour wandering from house to house.

When I finally locate it, I knock at the door.

"If they yell, don't be too scared. Vicky tends to do that sometimes," I tell Mr. Meow.

But just as the door opens, he jumps from my arms, running in the bushes.

I'm about to turn to go after him when Vicky calls my name.

"And the hussy is here."

I blink.

"Hussy?" I croak.

"You think we wouldn't know you didn't spend the night at Astor Place?" she sneers. "Who knows who the hell you slimed about with and now I have to welcome you into my home," she sneers before she spits at my feet.

I jump a step back, confused about her attitude. That doesn't mean I'm going to let her cast aspersions on my character.

"You're wrong," I push my chin up. And though I hate to lie, this instance will have to be an exception. "I slept at Astor Place. I just got home late after the Hales invited me to dinner."

Her face screws in disgust, but as she mules over my words, she doesn't try to contradict me. After all, she won't be able to confirm that with the Hales due to their enmity.

"Step aside, Mrs. Pierce. I am here for the reading of the will and I will leave afterwards," I tell her squarely.

For a moment she doesn't seem like she will comply, but Mr. Vaughan's car stops in front of the car. As he gets out of it and comes towards us, she simply huffs her nose in the air and enters the house.

"Good morning, Miss Darcy," Mr. Vaughan greets, his voice tinged with suspicion. "I dropped by your house to pick you up but you were not there."

"I walked," I shrug.

"Nasty wound on your head," he suddenly mentions.

"That," I unconsciously touch the bandage. "It's just a little slip."

"If you say so," he shrugs, his eyes boring into me. "After you," he motions to the door, and I take a step inside.

All eyes are on me, the tension palpable.

They don't have to say it out loud for me to realize they somehow blame me for Mr. Pierce's death, though whose fault is it that he wasn't dead in the first place?

If you ask me, I just righted a wrong.

"Right," Mr. Vaughan mutters. "Let's get this over with," he says as he takes a seat on the armchair in the living room. I sit myself on the opposite end while the family is close to him.

Grace is regarding me with pure contempt, and now even August looks as if he hates me.

Of course, Vicky doesn't make it a secret that she hates me, one jibe after another coming my way.

Hussy.

Witch.

Bastard.

Well, I guess the third does fit.

"As all of you can attest, this document is sealed," he removes a manila folder from his bag and shows us the official seal. "I will now open it and read it for everyone present."

Mr. Vaughan then proceeds to read everything from the beginning.

When it comes to the split of the assets, I am surprised to see just how wealthy Leo Pierce was. He left his son the majority of the stakes in a shipping company, with a few split between Vicky and Grace. Aside from that, Vicky gets the main house as well as a few properties that Mr. Vaughan enumerates. Grace, on the other hand, doesn't get anything more. Her eyes go wide when she realizes that was it for her. But if she is, in fact, not Leo Pierce's daughter, than I'd say he was already generous enough to leave her anything.

My name is mentioned next.

"To my daughter Darcy O'Sullivan, I leave the house at 12 Astor place and the sum of one million dollars."

I blink repeatedly, unable to believe my ears.

One million dollars? That is a sum I would have never even dreamed about.

My mouth drops open in shock. But Mr. Vaughan is not done.

"With the condition that she resides in Fairydale for a total of two full months," Mr. Vaughan pauses. "Today is September first. You will need to reside in Fairydale until November first to get the allotted sum of money."

"But... There was no condition for them..." I point to the others.

"Leo must have wished for you to get to know the family better," Mr. Vaughan makes the excuse, but I can't wrap my head around it—around anything really.

"Why did he pretend to be dead?" I suddenly ask.

"What? The gall on you, you little hussy," Vicky bursts out. "How dare you besmirch my husband's name after what you did to him."

"I did nothing and you all know it," I rise to my feet, instinctively grabbing my purse and bag. "And he *was* pretending. Let's not call it otherwise. What I don't understand is why," I say exasperated as I look around me. "Why get me to come to Fairydale, and why make me stay another two months? Why was it so important for me to come here?"

"Leo just wanted..."

"Oh please, spare me that rehearsed speech," I roll my eyes. "He did not care about me one whit. So that begs the question. Why reach out at all? Just what do you want from me?"

Everyone is staring at me with unabashed disdain—so much so that I'm done with this.

Turning, I head straight for the exit, opening the door and squinting as a ray of sun hits my retina. I barely take a few steps outside when Mr. Vaughan comes after me.

"Miss Darcy! If you leave Fairydale at any point before the two months are up, then you are forfeiting your inheritance. *All* of it," he tells me in a condescending tone.

"So? What is it to you? Why would you want me to stay when I can see that you dislike me. You, Vicky and everyone in that goddamn house."

I don't swear. In fact, due to my upbringing at the orphanage under the tutelage of the nuns, I've always tried to avoid doing it. But in moments when my temper is tested—like now—the bad words simply come out.

Vicky doesn't tarry in joining us, too, followed by Grace and August.

"Let her, Mordechai. Let her leave. Let her lose the money. I don't want to see her face again in our town!" Vicky rages, and before I know it, she throws a bucket of water at me. "We want nothing to do with easy women around here."

My eyes widen at the sudden insult, but really I should accept nothing else coming from her. Despite her initial welcome, she must have taken an immediate dislike of me for the mere fact that I am written in that will while her daughter is not.

"Easy? Me? How about you look in the mirror first, Vicky dear. Your daughter doesn't look much like Mr. Pierce, does she? Why, her eyes are the same shade as Mr. Vaughan's."

Her face drops, while Mr. Vaughan's lips are pressed into a thin line.

"Mom!" Grace yells, clearly unaware of her true parentage. "Is that true? Tell me it's not true."

"Darling, I..." she stammers for a moment, truly at a loss of words, before she turns once more towards me, her features filled with vitriol.

One moment she's a foot away from me, the next she has her hands in my hair, pulling with all her strength.

I yelp in pain, but as I push against her, nothing works.

"I should also add that by leaving, the money will go to Vicky and her daughter," Mr. Vaughan adds from the sidelines in a bored tone, doing nothing to stop the catfight.

As soon as his words register, I realize what it means for this hateful woman and her brood. And though I was reluctant to part with the money in the first place, now I get to be petty too.

"Don't worry," I say between gasps as I'm wrestling with Vicky. "I'm not going anywhere. The money and the house are mine," I add emphatically, and Vicky snaps.

"You damn hussy," she screams, about to launch herself at me once more.

But before she can do that, strong arms pull me closer, easily disentangling Vicky from my side and pushing her away—hard enough that she falls to the ground.

What...

"That's enough," his voice booms, and everyone suddenly stills.

"Hale," Mr. Vaughan intones in an annoyed voice, while Grace yelps, "Caleb!"

Slowly turning my head, I look up and come face to face with my biggest nightmare.

"Let go of me," I sneer, ready to go into full attack mode.

"Shh," he leans to whisper in my ear. "Sheathe your claws for now, Darcy darlin'. We have a show to put on."

No sooner did he say that than he redirects his attention to Mr. Vaughan.

"I heard the terms of the will, Mordechai. Darcy will not leave Fairydale. As a matter of fact, she's been invited to stay with my family for the duration of the visit, and as such she will have witnesses for the entirety of the specified duration."

My head hurts as he speaks.

Stay with the family?

He means... He means me saying at the Hale manor? Where he lives? Where he could have access to me as he pleases?

No. Categorically no.

But as I try to speak, I find that I cannot.

I open my mouth, yet no sound comes out.

Panicking, I look around to see that they are deep in an argument, and in a matter of seconds Mr. Vaughan has a gun out, threatening Caleb to get off his property or he would kill him.

There are also screams.

Grace is crying.

Vicky is yelling.

August is also pointing a gun.

This is hell on earth.

Yet just as I think it will all blow up, Caleb swoops me up in his arms, taking me away.

It's only when we're a distance away from the Pierce house that I seemingly can move and talk again.

"Let me go," I grit out.

Surprisingly, he puts me down.

Stepping away, his intense stare is on me as he peruses me from head to toe.

"You weren't at the cabin when I came back," his tone is even, his words punctured.

He's not happy with me.

A shiver of fear goes down my back as I instinctively try to put more distance between us.

"You think I would have stuck around after what you did to me?" I ask, tears stabbing at my eyes again.

Seeing him like this, all perfectly put together, with his perfect face and perfect everything, and my heart breaks in my chest that he can act like nothing happened when *everything* happened.

"What are you talking about?" he frowns.

"Don't you dare pretend you don't know," I accuse, raising my hand to wipe a tear from my cheek. "Don't you dare, Caleb Hale! I'm going to the sheriff. I'll tell him everything and..."

"What, Darcy? What the hell are you talking about?" he repeats, and the question is like an arrow to my heart.

"You raped me," I hiss. "You raped me, Caleb, and you dare ask me what happened?"

He looks as if struck by lightning.

"What did you say?" he asks, this time his tone gentler, yet nonetheless holding the same firm quality to it.

"You know exactly what I mean. I saw the evidence—the blood," I whimper at the memory, and pain assails me once more.

"Darcy," he takes a step towards me, but I put my hand up to keep him from encroaching my personal space. "Darlin', I never did that," he says in the softest voice. "I never raped you. You can't possibly believe..."

"There was blood," I croak. "You know I've never been with a man before. You know that." The more I speak of it, the more the tears won't stop.

"There was blood," he agrees. "From your wounds. You fell on a bed of rocks, Darcy. You hurt yourself all over," he explains as he tries to come closer again.

I shake my head.

"You undressed me. You took everything off..."

"Yes." There it is, the admission. "You were soaking wet. I couldn't let you catch a chill. And that's why I know all the places you injured yourself."

"But the blood..."

"There was a small gash on your upper thigh. You can confirm its existence. It probably continued to bleed even after I put you to bed."

What... No... There's no way.

"I don't believe you."

"Darcy," he takes a deep breath. "Aside from the blood, do you feel sore between your legs?"

My brows pinch together at his question, and I slowly shake my head.

"Do you feel any pain at all there," he continues, and once more, I shake my head. "Then there you have it, darlin'. Nothing happened. I promise you," he adds poignantly, and God, but I almost believe him.

My cheeks heat as he explains that for the amount of blood I'd seen, I would have had to tear down there pretty badly, and that would have resulted in intense pain. I don't know how he knows all of that, but I have to admit that aside from the visible injuries, nothing else hurts—certainly *not* the area between my legs.

Now I feel foolish for jumping to conclusions, but after his previous behavior, how could I not?

"Then what about before that? When you..."

"When I..." He raises a brow.

"You were asking me all those inappropriate questions, telling me I was your bad girl and..."

"Darcy," he says my name as if horrified. "Darlin', I think we need to get you to a medic as fast as we can. I didn't think you hit your head that bad but... That never happened."

"What? What are you talking about? You said that. You insinuated I was easy. That I..."

"I never did any of that, darlin'," he sighs, exasperated. "It started raining when we reached the cabin. When you got out of the car you tripped and fell on the bed of rocks right next to it. You were out of it the entire afternoon."

Blinking, I can't believe what he's saying. I *know* what happened.

"That's not true. You were sick and I helped you to the cabin. Then I went to pick some plants to make you tea and... Your eyes. They were *red!*"

"Red eyes?" A look of horror flashes across his face. "Darcy darlin', you're worrying me. That never happened."

"What?" I ask in shock.

What does he mean it never happened? I remember it clearly.

"I was never sick. And you never went to pick out plants. Please, think about it."

No, that can't be...

I stare at him in befuddlement as I replay every event from the day before. His words ring in my ear...the way he'd behaved... I can't possibly have imagined all of it.

Yet as I think back to this morning, I admit to myself that there was no trace of the fire I'd built, not even ash left behind. I hadn't noticed that then as I was in a hurry to leave.

At the same time I have a hard time grasping how this could have all been a product of my imagination. Because...how?

A whimper escapes me.

Dear God... Can he be right? Is this all in my head? Was it another dream?

"Darcy..." he calls my name with such heartfelt longing that I can't help but raise my gaze to his, finding only sincerity.

There are no signs of deception. Only worry. And that makes me more confused than ever.

"Can I come closer," he asks, and God, it's like he's an entirely different person than the one from yesterday—*the one from my dream?*

I give him a brisk nod and he wastes no time in pulling me to his chest, hugging me tightly.

"I'm so sorry I left this morning, but I had to get to town and get more supplies. You have no idea how scared I was when I found you gone. But please believe me that nothing like that happened. I would never touch you without your permission, you know that?" he murmurs, drawing back to see my expression.

Do I? Do I know that?

"I don't know you, Caleb," I speak slowly, the information from before slowly settling in. "That means I also don't trust you. I realize now it was a mistake to get in your car yesterday, and it's a mistake to be with you alone..."

"Don't. Oh, darlin', don't say that. I want us to get to know each other. It's why I promised I'd vouch for you with Mordechai. I *want* you near," he declares.

Biting my lip, I regard him quietly for a moment.

"I don't know," I whisper.

How can one go from hating someone so much one moment, to finding out the hate was based on nothing? How can I react to that?

This morning I was ruing the day I ever set eyes on him, but now his soft words and gentle looks make me reconsider everything.

"I won't rush you with anything. Just let me take care of you," he whispers as he slowly pats my hair. "I don't have any nefarious intentions with you, Darcy. On the contrary. My intentions are all honorable."

"What do you mean?" I suddenly pull back, frowning.

"Exactly what you think I mean," he smiles.

I'm struck speechless. I stare at him and I cannot comprehend anything.

Is he handsome? Yes. Is he entirely dreamy? Also yes. But there's also something else about him—the same sinister energy I felt in my dreams, I still feel now.

But maybe it's just this town messing with my head. That and the fact that with each passing day I turn more and more like Catherine.

I wonder what's next. Ghosts? Demons? *Zombies*?

"We could get to know each other," I finally relent.

If it was all a dream, then it's not fair to keep him accountable for something that's solely a product of my imagination. Yet that doesn't erase the fact that I'm wary about him—about everything he makes me feel.

Perhaps that's the issue. I've never felt like this before, so I'm unsure whether this fluttering in my stomach is because I'm drawn to him, or because he instills in me terror unlike I've ever known.

He gives me the biggest grin.

"But," I put a finger up. "I'm not moving into the Hale house. I'm staying at Astor Place," I tell him firmly. "You will take me on dates, in *public*. And I don't know what you may think of me, but I'm not modern like other girls. I will not sleep with you, or anyone else, until marriage."

An amused look crosses his face at my list of demands, but he doesn't protest any.

"Anything else?" he chuckles.

"As a matter of fact, yes. I want a notarized statement about your finances. If you say you are serious about me, then I must be certain it is not because of my inheritance."

At that, he laughs.

"Ah, Darcy darlin', you're a gem."

I narrow my eyes on him.

"Of course. You'll have your statement. I can vouch that I am not penniless, nor am I a fortune hunter. I happen to have quite a sizable net worth."

"Well," I push my chin up, "you better."

Still laughing, he tugs me closer, his arms coming around me as he keeps me fitted to his body.

Despite everything that happened, my own body reacts to the nearness, my heart skipping a beat just as my stomach does some odd somersaults.

"Why don't I take you on a date now, then?" he murmurs in my ear.

My cheeks heat up and I nod.

"But first, we're visiting the medic."

I don't protest as he leads me to his car, taking me to the medic's office. After all, I am worried about it as well.

How could I have made up entire interactions in my head? How could I have come up with such scenarios?

The office ends up being a short distance away, and luckily, the primary physician is Emmet Bailey, a friend of the Hales, which allows me to go in without an appointment.

"The wound looks good," he notes as he examines my head injury. "You did well to clean it and dress it, Caleb."

"Could I have hallucinated because of it?"

He nods.

"It's highly probable. But I don't think there should be more reason to worry. I'll dress the wound again and prescribe you some medication in case you get a headache," he goes on to show me how to dress the wound by myself after I take a shower, and advises me to visit again if I have problems with hallucinations again.

Caleb is leaning against the wall, intently watching Dr. Bailey's every move. Tension radiates from him, and even Dr. Bailey can feel it, every now and then glancing at him for approval before touching me. And every time, Caleb barely gives him a strained nod, as if that small acquiesce costs him everything.

"Let's tend the other injuries," he says, asking me to show him the gash on my thigh.

"That will be enough for today, Emmet," he interjects in a thick voice. "I'm sure Darcy can do that herself."

A look of confusion crosses Dr. Bailey's face for a moment before he takes a step back, his hands in the air in a gesture of surrender.

"Of course," he readily acquiesces, adding a few more bandages to my package.

Not a few minutes later and we're out of the office. Caleb has a tight expression on his face, his fists clenched by his side and I can't figure out what set him off.

"What's wrong?" I grab his shirt, stopping him. "Did something happen?"

Turning, he takes a deep breath, his eyes glinting dangerously as he regards me.

"I don't like other men's hands on you, Darcy," he drawls. "I thought I could bear it for your sake. But all I could think of was him touching your pretty face and your delicate neck and I was close to losing it," he exhales. "I'm still close to losing it," he admits as he brings his gaze to mine, showing me all the turmoil hiding there.

"It was just a checkup, Caleb," I add softly, patting him lightly on the shoulder. "Dr. Bailey was just doing his job."

"Because I didn't do *mine,*" he rasps.

I frown.

"I didn't protect you. I'm sorry about that, precious," he whispers, cupping my face between his big hands and leaning in to place a kiss right next to my injury.

"It happens," I laugh nervously, though my skin tingles from where it met his lips.

"It shouldn't. Not to you. Not now, nor ever," he says vehemently. "You're mine to take care of, Darcy darlin'. You get that?"

My lashes flutter in confusion.

He hasn't even taken me on a date and he's already claiming me as his?

"It's too early for that, Caleb," I force a smile on my face as I draw back.

He narrows his eyes at me.

"I don't think you understand me, Darcy," he punctuates each word. "You belong to me," he growls. "I might go slow for you, but don't imagine for one moment that you're not mine."

Pursing my lips, I don't know how to reply. I know that if I protest he's going to turn even more overbearing. Instead, I merely give him a tentative smile.

Caleb Hale is an enigma I can't solve.

Add in the fact that I'm having trouble differentiating reality from hallucination, and I simply don't know how to read him or his intentions.

As we get in the car, he suggests we go to one of the less popular diners in town for lunch—and our first official date.

I agree, though after the last time at the diner, I'm not too thrilled to come face to face with the townsfolk who'd decided I must be the Devil's disciple.

"You're quiet," Caleb notes as he drives. "Does your wound still pain you?"

I shake my head.

"Still ruminating over what happened yesterday," I admit.

"I thought we moved past that."

"We did but," I take a deep breath. "I fear something's wrong with me, Caleb," I confess. "It's not the first time this has happened—these hallucinations..."

"What do you mean?" he turns to me, frowning.

"Ever since I came here. Weird things have been happening around me. And I don't know if they're all in my mind or..." I bite my lip in apprehension. "But everyone saw how Leo Pierce died, and that wasn't normal. I just no longer know what is real and what is not..."

"Darcy," my name on his lips is like a tender caress.

Slowing the car down, he stops it by the side of the road so he can give me his full attention.

"There's nothing wrong with you," he takes my hand in his, massaging my pulse point with his thumb. "You're in a new place, and people have behaved horribly towards you. It's normal to be a little stressed."

"You think it's stress?" I ask on a whisper.

"I think you're overwhelmed. Maybe Leo's death affected you more than you realized?" he offers, a tight smile on his face.

"How could someone just burst into flames?" I mumble, the memory from the day before still fresh in my mind. "But more than anything, why aren't people more concerned about it?" I ask the question that had plagued me from the beginning.

Aside from a few insults from the Pierces, no one had seemed too surprised—not only at his sudden resurrection, but also the manner of his subsequent death. No one had tried to step in to help either, merely watching his death from the sidelines. As if it was, indeed, a regular occurrence.

Then there were those interactions at the diner—they had been bawdy and tawdry in the beginning but the moment I hinted at *actually* being a witch, everyone had been terrified.

"Fairydale people aren't strangers to odd deaths. Just as they aren't strangers with the more...occult ways of life."

"What do you mean?" I frown.

"It's not something I can explain. It's something you'll have to witness by yourself," he chuckles.

"Well, I'm not sure I want to," I grumble, already dreading the two months I'd promised to stay.

"You should never worry about anything while you're here, Darcy darlin'," he murmurs. "There may be forces beyond our understanding. There may be black and white, dark and light, evil and good. There may be opposites... But you, you'll forever be safe in the gray."

I wet my lips, regarding him intently as I try to decipher his words. "Are you saying there *is* something evil in this town?"

His lip curls up in a smug smile.

"Is there?" he muses knowingly. "If there is, I'll make sure it never touches you," he winks at me playfully, and a blush suffuses my cheeks. "Now let's get you some food. I wouldn't be much of a boyfriend if I let my darlin' go hungry, would I?"

"Hey," I jab my elbow in his side. "Who said you're my boyfriend? I haven't agreed to anything," I fight the smile on my lips.

"Oh but you will, Darcy darlin'," he chuckles as he starts the engine. "You will."

The journey to the town square is filled with teasing and laughter, and I slowly let my guard down, forgetting my previous reservations about Caleb.

He's handsome, charming, and has a silver tongue. And though I feel myself succumbing deeper and deeper under his spell, I don't forget the fact that he never answered my initial question about Leo's death, or its reception.

Just how odd are the deaths in Fairydale?

When we get to the square, we slow down as we notice a crowd of people in front of the Fairydale monument.

"What's happening?" I ask as I try to get a better view.

He shrugs.

"We can take a look. The diner is in that direction anyway."

Parking the car a distance away, he comes to my side to open my door as he takes my hand in his. Not for the first time, a wave of pure electricity travels down my back from the touch of his skin on mine.

He feels it, too, going by the way his gaze flickers as he looks me in the eye.

For a moment, neither speaks as his fingers curl around my hand before sliding towards my wrist, holding lightly and bringing it to his mouth.

Still holding me captive with his gaze, he slowly—ever so slowly—parts his lips over my pulse point, giving me a short but sensuous kiss.

I am so attuned to his every move that the prolonged contact of his lips on top of my skin is making me pant, my breath coming out in short, shallow spurts, my brain disconnecting from reality.

Yet just as I find myself caught in his spell, I'm once more startled by a change in scenery.

It only lasts for a second, but everything decays around us, turning black and bleak. Darkness suffuses my field of view, the color of his eyes morphing before my very gaze. From the previous impenetrable black, they turn a phosphorescent blue before red—*blood*—bleeds out of them.

I blink, and everything is back to normal.

His lips are still on my flesh just as his gaze dips to my mouth, making me curious what it would feel like if...

Heat travels up my cheeks and I eventually avert my eyes. But not before I notice the look of pure hunger that overtakes his features.

"Shall we?" He arranges my hand in the crook of his elbow as he leads me towards the crowd.

I strain a smile, hoping to look unaffected when I'm anything but.

Never in my life have I felt so conflicted about something, and it's more than just me feeling out of my element under male attention. It's the pure fact that Caleb Hale is like a drug to my senses, tantalizing and dazzling me until I lose track of everything around me.

And if I give in—if I embrace this newly found addiction—I fear I might never be the same.

My thoughts are interrupted by the spectacle surrounding the monument. People are yelling and cursing, their voices getting louder and louder until it's hard to ignore the words tossed around.

Dead.

Murder.

Killer.

Caleb frowns, and taking my hand, he tugs me closer to his side. "Stay close to me," he whispers.

A few more steps and we have a front row at the carnage.

My hand flies to my mouth as a gasp escapes me.

The monument, an angel with spread wings, is fully coated in blood.

Blood that's dripping from the three people defiled on top of the statue.

But the worst? I recognize each and every one of them.

"Caleb... What the hell is this?" I ask in a tremulous voice.

"You shouldn't look," he purses his lips, moving in an attempt to shield me.

"No, don't," I stop him. "I know them. All three," I barely manage the words out loud.

The first one is Vicky. Her organs have been emptied from her chest cavity, and instead she's been stuffed with newspaper clippings—all of them containing unfavorable terms.

Crook. Thief. Adulteress.

Every clipping is depicting one sin she's allegedly guilty of.

I swallow down, the sight pitiful as it is horrifying.

Her face is forever frozen in pain, her mouth open, her eyes wide, and I wonder if the killer tortured her before killing her.

For all her nasty behavior towards me, I would have never wished something like this upon anyone.

Yet it gets worse.

The next man is stuck on the angel wing, the stone passing right through his gut.

I know him, too. I recognize him as the man who'd pinched my bottom at the diner the day before.

But if these two had been coincidences, both residents of Fairydale, the third one can't possibly be.

He's at the feet of the angel, his head in his lap after a very clean decapitation. Yet I remember his features perfectly—the dirty hair and bloodshot eyes.

He's the man who stole my luggage at the Ipswich station.

Despite not wanting to let my mind wander to the worst scenario, it's simply impossible.

These three people all have something in common.

And that's...*me*.

The other townsfolk are all crossing themselves and saying the Hail Mary, with some brave ones stepping forward to help the sheriff remove the bodies from the statue.

They successfully do so with Vicky's body and the second man. But when they reach the third, they stop for a moment as they don't recognize him. And since he's not a local, they set about searching his pockets for any form of identification.

"What's that?" One of the men asks as something falls out of his front pocket.

"It's a notebook," the sheriff frowns, picking it up. The moment it's in his hands, I know exactly what it is—my journal.

"Darcy O'Sullivan," he reads the name on the first page.

I freeze. Caleb's hold tightens on me, as he can undoubtedly recognize what will follow.

"Isn't that the new girl in town?"

"Pierce's illegitimate girl."

"Fuck me! It's the girl that made him catch fire!" Another exclaims.

"She didn't do it," someone yelled, while another man said I did.

"You need to question her, sheriff!"

"We need to leave," Caleb whispers in my ear, slowly moving me away from the crowd in an effort to be undetected.

The voices get louder and louder until suddenly they stop.

"That's her!" A man yells, and turning, I note they're all pointing their fingers at me.

"Quickly! Stop her!" They all scream in a chorus, hurrying to catch up with us.

Caleb is right ahead of them as he pulls me into his arms, running with me at full speed. His physical condition is flawless, and it only takes a few seconds to reach the car.

Swinging the door open, he lowers me inside while he dashes to the other side and getting into the driver's seat.

"Hold on, darlin'. We're about to go at full speed."

He starts the engine, swiftly changing gears and driving the car in the opposite direction as a mob of people run towards us.

My entire body is shaking at this point, both from the shock of seeing the slaughtered bodies, and from the reactions of the people—all blaming me.

Yet despite *knowing* I had nothing to do with it—not personally, in any event—I can't help but feel that they all died because of me.

Somehow, I am the link.

But *how*?

As we pass by the monument again, I'm struck by something else. Right next to the bodies is the same old man I'd seen at the funeral. The one who'd been conversing with Vicky and Mr. Vaughan. And despite their previous chummy interaction, he's sitting by the body with complete disinterest.

He's holding a cane in his right hand, and something on top of the handle shines bright in the sunlight—almost blinding me in the process.

When I finally manage to blink away the painful light, my eyes meet his.

His mouth curves upwards in a smug expression, his lips moving slowly as he's miming a word.

"*Soon*," I spell out the word.

What the hell is that supposed to mean?

Chapter Eight

By the time Caleb pulls up to Astor Place, I'm still shaken from what happened. So much so that I only want to close myself in my bedroom, away from everyone around me.

Yet more than anything, I resent the fact that I agreed to remain in Fairydale. Why in God's name did I have to accept the clause?

Because you're petty. And because it's one million dollars.

The pettiness is technically out the window since Vicky is no longer a contender. But it's one million dollars.

One. Million. Dollars.

What fool would give that up? And for two months of living in this godforsaken place.

Although this morning I would have said that I could bear to stay two months, now I'm not sure anymore.

Odd deaths? Just how many odd deaths can be in a small town?

Add to that the many unusual things that have been happening around me, and I'm either truly losing my mind, or there is something really off about Fairydale.

What had Caleb said, that the town is acquainted with the occult?

A shiver goes down my back at the thought. Yet I can't not consider the possibility.

Not anymore.

"I don't feel comfortable leaving you here, Darcy. You should come stay with us," Caleb says as he helps me out of the car.

I shake my head.

"I told you I won't. I'll be fine here. If the sheriff calls on me for a statement, then I will go. But I didn't do anything, so why would I hide?"

"I'm not saying you did anything. I *know* you didn't. But they don't. You saw how those people reacted..."

"I'm aware. But that doesn't mean I have to hide like I'm *guilty*," I sigh.

"Let me stay over at least," he suggests, and my brows shoot up in surprise.

"You know I can't do that," I tell him softly, fighting the blush going up my cheeks. "It wouldn't be proper. And I don't want to feed the gossips even more. I have to stay here for two more months."

He purses his lips, clearly not pleased with my decision.

"I'll sleep in another bedroom," he probes further, but I remain firm in my decision.

"I'm already embarrassed that you had to take care of me last night. That you..." I pause, undoubtedly red from head to toe. "That you undressed me," I add on a whisper.

A knowing smirk flashes across his face.

"If it makes you feel better about that, Darcy darlin'," he says as he takes a step forward, his hand slowly trailing down my face. "I tried to preserve your modesty."

"You...did?" I blink in surprise.

He nods slowly, his lips tugging up.

"I did my best to not make you uncomfortable," he whispers as he leans forward. "Although I have to admit. The temptation was...agonizing."

"Well," I clear my throat, my entire body humming with awareness, "I'm glad you were so circumspect," I say as I swallow hard.

"For now," he murmurs, wickedly winking at me.

"What?" I squeak.

"You make it very hard for me to be a gentleman, Darcy. But that's what you want, do you not? A proper, virtuous, *boring* gentleman."

"Doesn't everyone want that?" I counter in a soft voice—one that doesn't seem convincing even to my ears.

"That's what you *think* you want, darlin'," he drawls, his voice a combination of decadence wrapped in seduction. "But I know what you *need.*"

My pulse accelerates from his nearness and intense perusal.

"And what is that?" I ask slowly, fighting to keep my voice unaffected.

"You need a bad man, not a gentleman," he rasps as his gaze connects with mine. "You need corruption and sin, Darcy darlin'. You need someone to worship your innocence and despoil it at the same time."

I stare at him, unable to find a proper reply. Not when despite the alarm bells sounding in my head, my body is aflame at his nearness, growing hotter with every spoken word—every threat that sounds like a slow seduction.

"Despoil? You make it sound so...violent," I laugh nervously. "We're not in the middle ages anymore," I mumble quietly.

"No. Pity we're not," he replies in a serious tone.

Suddenly, he leans in, his lips brushing against my earlobe.

"Violence and sex are inevitably interlinked. They have the same urgency. The same impetus to drive forward," he murmurs softly. "The same desire to plunder and possess."

"I... I wouldn't know," I gulp down, feeling myself in entirely foreign territory.

"But you will," he says as he draws back.

I expect to see amusement in his features at making me flustered, but instead all I see is a frightening intensity that leaves me breathless and wanting.

"Good night, Darcy darlin'. Dream of me," he brings my hand to his lips, kissing it like he did before, all the while not taking his eyes off me.

His lips curl up when he senses my erratic pulse, but he doesn't comment further. He simply urges me on, getting in his car only when I'm inside the house with the locks in place.

Just like the first day, I hurry to my bedroom window, pulling the curtain aside and watching his car disappear up the hill.

My heart is still beating loudly in my chest, and as I bring my hands to my cheeks it's to feel them hot to the touch.

"Drat it," I mumble, heading to the bathroom to splash myself with some cold water.

Yet as I turn the faucet off, I hear a very familiar sound.

"Meow!"

Following the meows, I come face to face with Mr. Meow. Right in my house.

He's on my kitchen table, casually licking his paw and giving me a satisfied look.

"How did you get here?" I ask, startled to find him here.

"Meow..." he comes closer, nuzzling his cheeks against my waist.

It's then that I remember the first time I'd seen him had been by the Old Church. Maybe that's the area he frequents since he doesn't seem to have an owner.

But what was he doing around the cabin then? That's at the outskirts of Fairydale, quite a distance from here.

My thoughts are a whirlpool of confusion, but as I gaze into his big eyes, I can't find it in me to toss him out.

Didn't I want to keep him before?

He must be pretty smart since he found me first.

My lips tug up in a smile as I grab him, tugging him to my chest.

"Well, it's good that you're here, Mr. Meow. I'm going to feed you and take care of you from now on," I tell him gently as I go to the cupboards, removing a few cans of food and heating them up.

Some, I choose specifically for him, and some for myself since I didn't get to eat earlier.

When the food is ready, I go against dining etiquette and allow Mr. Meow to eat at the table with me. In fact, I'm surprised by how well behaved he is. He doesn't even try to sneak his snout into my plate, keeping strictly to his own serving.

"That's a good boy, aren't you?" I smile as I pat him on the patch of white hair.

Turning, he licks his lips, giving me a loud meow to suggest that he enjoys that gesture. So I repeat it.

What I expected to be a lonely meal turns into quite an animated one. Maybe I can't exactly understand what Mr. Meow is saying to me, but his body language is quite clear. He leans into me when he likes something and shies away from my touch when he doesn't.

He's smart like that.

When we're both done, I clean the plates and place them up to dry. Then I take him in my arms and head upstairs to the bedroom.

Taking some paper and a pencil from my purse, I make a list of things I must do now that I'm going to spend the next two months in Fairydale.

The first thing is to find a telephone and call the school, Allison and the nuns. I wouldn't want them to worry about me.

I doubt the school will want to keep me with such an extended vacation, and if they decide to let me go then I will agree with their decision.

For God's sake, it's one million dollars. At the end of it all, I don't even know what I'll do with that type of money.

Maybe buy a house and settle somewhere, get a part-time job and invest the rest?

Hmm... The choices are infinite. One thing is for sure, though. I'll need to be careful with the money. I've seen cases where people lost the money as easily as they got it.

After I've made a to-do list, I chat a little with Mr. Meow—though he can only meow his reply. And as nightfall is upon us, I start preparing for bed.

I carefully take off my bandage, inspecting my wound.

To my surprise, I don't see any of the skin abrasions the doctor had described. In fact, as I stare at the mirror, I have to wonder if the light isn't faulty because I can't see anything.

My skin is as unblemished as it was before.

Frowning, I take my dress off, inspecting the other places on my body—finding them equally as pristine.

No wonder my rib cage had stopped hurting after some time. As I look at it now, I can't find any bruise—not one discoloration.

Even the gash on my thigh is gone, the skin absolutely flawless.

"What..." I mutter to myself.

Was it all in my head?

But it can't be. Caleb himself saw the injuries, and Dr. Bailey treated my head wound. He inspected and dressed it.

That was only *hours* ago.

How in God's name are all my injuries gone now?

Thinking a relaxing bath would help, I run some hot water and get in the tub to soak my body.

Yet it's all in vain.

My muscles are still tense, my mind rattled by all the events that had happened to this point.

I have absolutely ***no*** injuries! And this morning my body was teeming with gashes, scratches and bruises.

Maybe it wouldn't have been so worrisome if it had been an isolated incident—*though let's face it, it's absolutely unusual*—but combined with everything that's been happening, and I can't help but feel I'm missing something.

Closing my eyes, I take a deep breath as I go back to the beginning in an attempt to understand what's happening.

The first red flag is that I'd been called to Fairydale under the assumption that my biological father was dead, but he was only pretending. No matter how much I think of it, it has to have been a premeditated act.

The question is why...

Then there are the sadistic murders. First Mr. Pierce. Then Vicky and the two men.

I'd already established that *I* was the link, but not *why.*

And the answer comes easily. All of them, at one point or another, had tried to harm me.

Mr. Pierce had threatened me, as had Vicky—on top of attacking me. One of the men had stolen my luggage while the other had leered at me and pinched my bottom.

All four of them had done something against me.

But if it's clearly not me who is doing this in some twisted game of revenge, then someone out there is.

Who?

The only person I know in Fairydale that I am on good terms with is Caleb. And he had been with me at the medic's office.

But what about before?

I blink, the thought suddenly crossing my mind.

There's no telling for how long those bodies were hung there.

Caleb had arrived at the Pierce House right after the will reading, but where had he been before that?

Suddenly, I'm scared to entertain that thought. Surely, he's not capable of something that heinous...

But Mr. Vaughan had said he'd been in the war, and I'm certain he'd had to do...things there.

There is also the matter of yesterday—or what I remember as yesterday.

Despite him being on his best behavior today—playful, flirty, and seemingly having my best interests at heart—I can't stop thinking about the other side of him... The one he says was only a product of my imagination.

But how could I possibly imagine him behaving in such a manner? How could I entertain the thought that a man could treat me like that?

Something doesn't fit...

Yes, he appeals to me on a deeper level. But he also scares me all the same.

"Meow..."

Mr. Meow pushes the bathroom door open with his head, sneaking inside and coming to the edge of the tub.

"Do you want a bath as well?" I smile, banishing all doubts.

Leaning over the tub, I grab Mr. Meow and I bring him inside, wetting him just a little before he releases a startled meow and jumps on me.

Luckily, his claws are sheathed, so he doesn't end up hurting me. He's just holding on to my neck with his little paws, his body fitted to my torso.

"A little water won't harm you," I chuckle.

A few moments in his presence and I already feel invigorated.

Bit by bit, I manage to submerge him in the water, cleaning him and rubbing his belly as he likes it.

When the water grows cold, I take him in my arms and we both get out. I dry him first before I dry myself and put on my nightgown.

"It's not too late but I'm exhausted," I murmur as I lay a kiss on his forehead. "Shall we go to sleep?"

With a meow of confirmation, I take him with me in bed, snuggling with him as I drift into sleep.

JUNE 1890. ESSEX, GREAT BRITAIN.

"You just got out of mourning, mama. We shouldn't go to a house party and pretend everything is alright," I try to convince my mother as our carriage rattles into the majestic estate of the Duke of Essex. "It's not proper."

"After all the ignominies your late father made me suffer over the years, this is not in the least improper, dear. I'm going to that house party and I'm going to have fun for once without looking over my shoulder. It's already been a year, and considering Haversham's reputation, no one will blame me," she huffs her nose in the air, snapping her fan at me and thereby closing this discussion.

I release a weary sigh as I burrow myself in the velvet cushion of the carriage.

After my father's sudden death, we've had to forgo the London season due to mourning. And though the requisite period has technically passed, I still think it's too early to show our faces in society—particularly after the nasty rumors that my mother had a hand in father's death.

My older sister is already married and settled at her own home, so now it's only my mother, my brother and me. And with my mother's tyrannical bent, even though the title came down to my brother, she is in charge of everything.

"And here we are. Our new chance at life," my mother breathes out in awe as the opulent estate comes into view.

"Maybe yours," I grumble under my breath.

It's not that I don't love my mother—I do. She's been my champion growing up, trying to make everyone see past my eccentricities and accept me for who I was. But she's also an extremely strong willed woman who is used to getting her own way.

Even during her marriage with my father, though she abhorred the public humiliation, she was happy to be left alone to her devices as the mistress of the manor. She took her duties seriously and made Haversham the most profitable it had ever been. The staff liked her, the villagers *loved* her and she was seen as something of a fairy godmother to all her acquaintances.

"Elizabeth!" She gasps, horrified. "This *is* your true chance at making a proper match. Not the ones your father would have chosen for you," she chides. "He only cared about his own interests, not your wellbeing. But don't worry. With me by your side, I'll make sure you have only the *best* suitors," she nods to herself, pleased with her reasoning.

I force a smile, barely stifling the urge to roll my eyes at her.

She'd done this with my sister, and though she'd matched her with a wealthy viscount, I doubt my sister is very happy. At least that is the impression I get every time I see her and she complains to mother that her husband is still visiting her bed despite having given him two sons.

My mother, of course, had told her to listen to her husband and given her some type of potion to make the entire situation more bearable.

I'd eavesdropped on their conversation, of course, since mother would never allow me to know things that pertain to married life yet—ironic considering I will experience it at some point, too.

Yet seeing the wretched state of my sister doesn't give me a lot of confidence in what mothers consider a good and proper match. She might have my interests at heart, but ultimately, she holds her own even closer to her heart.

The carriage draws to a halt, and when our door is opened, my mother is the first to get out, with me next.

"Can you believe we'll be here for the next fortnight? No more exile, Elizabeth," she tips her chin up, her eyes closed as an expression of pure happiness descends upon her face.

"Of course mother," I nod, going along with her.

For her it might be a fortnight of fun, but for me it will be one of wasting my time in the nursery. Father died right as I was about to make my debut, and we entered mourning immediately after. As such, I have not made my official entrance into society, and though I am allowed to attend the daytime events, the same cannot be said about the soirees or the balls that are the highlight of the Duke of Essex's house parties.

We're soon greeted by the hosts before we're led to our rooms. Oddly enough, we're separated, my mother having a room in the east wing, while I am in the west.

Mary trails behind me as we head to the room, one of the footmen walking alongside her as he's carrying my luggage.

Leaving the bags in the room, Mary tips the man as she shoos him out of the room.

"Come on, he's probably ill from the confines of the trunk," I say frantically as I take one of the smaller bags, laying it flat on the floor as I unlock it.

Not a second later and Mr. Meow makes his appearance, thrusting his head forward just as he emits a loud meow when he sees me.

"I'm so sorry, Mr. Meow. You know how mama gets when she sees you."

How I've managed to hide him for close to a year, I don't know. Since finding him in the backyard, I couldn't find it in me to part with him, so I'd stolen him into my room, giving him food and taking care of his needs.

In the time we've spent together he's become my greatest friend, always there for me, always ready to give me an understanding meow or a comforting pat.

Maybe our languages are not compatible, but I feel as though we understand each other better than if we spoke words.

He jumps on me, thoroughly licking my face and I know he's not upset about being confined in such a small place.

"I have a treat for you," I whisper as I remove a small piece of food from the inside of my dress, holding it to Mr. Meow's face.

His eyes go wide before he leans forward, wolfing the piece of ham in one go.

"I'll steal more from the kitchens for you," I promise him, finally putting him down.

In the same trunk, I'd packed him a small cushion on which he can sleep—although he always ends up in bed with me—as well as a necklace I'd had custom made for him. Removing the necklace from the silk pouch, I'm once more reminded I'd used all my pin money to commission the engraving. Yet as I place it around his neck, I can't find it in me to regret it.

A white leather strap—to complement his patch of white hair—goes around his neck, with a small silver pendant hanging from it, which has an engraving on it.

Lizzie's Mr. Meow.

A wide grin pulls at my lips as I look at him.

"Oh my, but aren't you dashing now Mr. Meow?" I ask playfully.

Like the smart cat he is, he walks straight to the wall-sized mirror on the other side of the room, stopping to admire his reflection.

Until Mr. Meow, I'd never realized that cats can recognize their own reflection, much less look for it of their own volition. It all proves that my Mr. Meow is no ordinary cat.

"You like it, don't you?" I move to his side, dropping to my haunches in front of the mirror.

I swear I detect a nod before he jumps up at me, giving me another lick.

"You're officially mine," I tell him proudly, taking him in my arms and patting him on the head.

For the next few hours, I get ready to meet the guests, taking a bath and dressing up to perfection as mother instructed.

Though she hasn't specifically said so to me, I am aware that this house party will be a perfect opportunity for her to scout a potential husband for me. In fact, if she manages to marry me off before I'm due for my season, she won't have to act the matronly chaperone and she can go on her marry way and do things as a widow that she was never permitted to do while married.

Despite knowing her wishes fully well, I can't get on board with her idea.

I am aware I must at one point get married. But how can I when I am still hung up on one person?

Amon d'Artan.

It's been more than a year since I last saw him, and though I doubt I'll *ever* see him again, I can't help the way my heart skips a beat as I remember his sharp features, or his naturally white hair.

It hadn't been only his looks that had forever seared themselves in my heart. It had been his act of kindness, and the way he'd tended to me after a vicious attack.

He's been kind, sweet, and ever so gentle.

Despite the fact that he disavowed the term as applying to his person, he'd shown me kindness and consideration—more so than the distinguished gentlemen of the ton who only see me as a broodmare.

But then there was his appellation for me—*Lizzie mine.*

I still dream about it, and sometimes, in the silence of the night, I could swear I hear him whisper that in my ear.

A year has passed, and he is still always on my mind.

"There you go, My Lady," Mary's voice startles me from my thoughts.

I give her a nod as I examine myself in the mirror. She'd done my hair in a simple style with a few curls down my side.

Rising from the chair, I pat my hands down my gown, smoothing out the wrinkles before I ultimately don my gloves.

If there is one thing I am happy about for having missed my debut the year before, it's the change in fashion. No longer the big hoops, heavy wigs and ostentatious styles of dress, now everything is minimalistic; simple but elegant.

It certainly aids movement more than the odious contraptions I was supposed to wear before.

"Thank you, Mary. Now wish me luck," I smile at her before I'm out the door.

A servant soon intercepts me, leading me to the drawing room where I'm supposed to meet my mother and Her Grace, the host. It is my understanding that Her Grace has decided some outdoor games would be the best way to get everyone familiar with each other, though I doubt the option is still on the table considering the gathering of clouds I spot out the window.

"There she is," Fiona, my mother, rises to come greet me.

Placing her arm around my back, she pushes me forward.

"Please allow me to introduce you to my daughter, Lady Elizabeth Montford," she adds in a buoyant tone, going around the room and doing the introductions with everyone present.

"Pleased to meet you, Your Grace," I curtsy to the Duchess before I do my best to politely interact with everyone.

It's only after a lengthy series of inane small talk that I am allowed to take a seat.

"There's only one person missing," the Duchess suddenly says. "Oh, there he is. And right on time," she brings her hands together in a clap just as thunder resounds in the sky. "Good thing we have the Dowager Duchess," she adds lightly. "At her age, she can feel the storm brewing in her bones," she laughs, prompting everyone else to do so as well.

Straining a smile, I look around the room until my eyes suddenly meet...his.

"This is Amon d'Artan, Marquis d'Ombre," the Duchess starts, "a relative of my husbands. He has decided to make England his home permanently after what happened in France last year."

"Good afternoon," he nods to everyone. "Of course I couldn't stay," he flashes the Duchess a smile. "I predict it's going to get quite nasty. Better run while I can," he winks at her.

The Duchess blushes profusely, and I can't help but feel a stab of jealousy in my gut.

What follows next are the same inane introductions as before, and when it's my turn, I give him a small smile and a curtsy.

"Pleased to meet you, Lady Elizabeth," he drawls, his voice making the hairs on my body stand to attention. Yet I can't tell whether he recognizes me or not.

No, what I'm feeling is purely a result of his presence and of his utterly ethereal looks.

Just as I remember him, he has long white hair, currently tied to his back. His eyes are the lightest blue I've ever seen, and at times I get the impression they are glowing—an unnatural light that makes him seem as otherworldly as I remember.

Sadly, I'm not the only one noticing this.

Every woman in the room, married, unmarried, or widowed, nearly swoons when he directs his attention to them.

Already, one second in his presence and I know everyone is scheming on how to get him to the altar—if he's not already married.

My eyes widen at that thought, but just as if he could read my mind, Amon brings his hand to his temple, showcasing an empty ring finger.

I swallow uncomfortably at the glee that erupts in my chest when I realize he is unattached.

When the storm shows no sign of abating, the Duchess declares we must all gather for tea and cakes.

No sooner does she place the order than a sea of servants enter the room with a variety of cakes, sandwiches, and most importantly tea.

It becomes immediately apparent that the Duchess has thought about everything, with several spare plans to use in case the former fails.

As the staff arranges the mini-buffet around the room, everyone starts to mingle and interact with one another.

Seeing that my mother is involved in quite the animated conversation with a General, I leave her side, going to peruse the selection of food.

"Are you a fan of sweet, or savory, Lady Elizabeth?"

I don't have to look to know who is speaking to me, my heart already jumping in my chest from his deep rumble.

"Both," I answer in a soft voice. "I find that they complement each other, wouldn't you say so, My Lord?"

Coming closer than it is proper, his breath is on my cheek as he whispers.

"Have you missed me, Lizzie mine?"

The words have their intended effect on me as I become short of breath and rather dizzy, but I cannot allow him to see that.

"Whyever should I miss you, My Lord?" I half-turn, giving him a small smile. "We don't have that type of acquaintance where I'm allowed to miss you, do we?" I murmur.

His mouth is set in a grim line as he regards me mutinously, clearly not pleased with my words.

"Perchance I haven't proven that to you, and I accept it as my fault."

"Proven what, My Lord? You'll have to be more clear," I smile.

"That you're mine, Lady Elizabeth," he adds with a mischievous smile. "But I'm sure I'll enjoy proving it to you."

"Hmm," I turn from him. "You speak pretty words to a lady you've only met once before. How am I to know this is not your *modus operandi*? That you're not charming every lady you meet the same way?"

"You wound me, Lady Elizabeth," he brings his hand to his heart. "Alas, you would be wrong to make such an assumption," he says in a playful voice before dipping his head lower, his mouth close to my ear as he continues, "There is only one woman I wish to claim, Lizzie mine. Past. Present. Future—and for an eternity to come."

"Why now? Why seek me out after so long?" I demand on a whisper, unable to hide the disappointment in my voice.

"It wasn't my intention to do that," he sighs. "Things...have kept me away. Abroad," he clarifies, moving closer. "I would have come sooner for you had I been able to."

Deep down, all I want is to believe him. Even realizing how foolish it is to yearn for someone as much as I have him, I cannot stop myself.

One meeting and he imprinted himself on me.

"You made me no promises," I shrug, the words burning on my tongue.

"The blood I spilled for you was promise enough," he murmurs. "The blood I would spill again, and again. Just to keep you safe. Happy. *Mine.*"

I swallow hard, his voice sending shivers down my back just as his hand accidentally brushes against my gloved one. Despite the lack of skin to skin contact, the surge of electricity is immediate. So much so that I can't help but turn to look at him, my eyes on his, my breath coming out in tandem with his.

For a moment, one short moment, everything stills.

There's no one else in the room but he and I, lost in each other's gazes and the timelessness of time. The air hums with energy, the storm raging outside only serving to emphasize the precarious storm taking shape within my breast.

He's close, yet he's so far away, and though I know I shouldn't, all I want is to reach out.

"Elizabeth!"

The spell is broken as my mother reaches my side, giving Amon a deadly look before all but dragging me away from the buffet table.

"Don't talk to him again," she orders me. "I don't want to see you *ever* talk to him again."

My eyes widen with shock at her vehemence. I've never seen her act like this with anyone before.

"Why?" I frown. "He's a friend of Her Grace's."

"He's bad news, Elizabeth. He's the *worst* news and I prohibit you from talking to him again," she grits her teeth. And as she glances back at where Amon is sitting, casually looking at me with unabashed hunger, my mother becomes even more erratic. "Go to your room. Don't come out tomorrow either. I'll arrange something with Her Grace..." she drones on, but I easily find myself gazing back at Amon and his knowing smile.

Winking at me, he turns to leave the room. True to his word, he doesn't engage with anyone else.

"Are you listening, Elizabeth?" My mother snaps.

"Of course," I nod. "You said to not talk to him again."

"Exactly. It's for your own good dear. He's not for you," she gives me a tight smile before she sends me back to my room.

Crossing the corridor to my room, I barely realize when a door to my right opens, a hand curling around my wrist and tugging me inside.

I'm about to scream when I come face to face with Amon.

"What..."

"There's a ball two nights from now," he whispers, and in this position I have to crane my neck to look at him. "Come."

"I can't," I sigh. "I'm not allowed, and my mother would never let me," I explain, disappointed at the missed opportunity.

Despite being a little wary of Amon due to his previous disappearance and my mother's warning, I can't ignore this want inside my chest—this inexplicable desire to be near him, always with him.

For a year he has persisted in my thoughts, with just one interaction irrevocably claiming my heart—though I am reluctant to admit as much.

I want to dance with him, touch him, feel his breath on top of my skin and hear his voice rumble in my ear.

I just...want.

"And you'll have it, Lizzie mine. You'll have all of it," he says, his words cryptic. "It will be a masquerade. I've persuaded the Duchess to throw one. That means you will be able to attend and no one shall be the wiser."

"But how? I don't have anything to wear and..."

"You will. I've sent for a package to be delivered to your room. In it you shall find everything you might need," he smiles, his eyes roving over my face as if it's been eons since he's last seen me.

"Why?" I ask softly. "Why me? Why are you doing this?"

Why now?

His smile deepens.

"Precisely because you're you. And because that makes you *mine*."

I barely get to process his words and I'm back on the corridor, moving towards my room.

Yet despite all the confusion, there's a giddiness that overtakes me as I'm finally alone in the confines of my room.

Amon d'Artan is back.

ALTHOUGH I'D SUSPECTED my mother had simply warned me off Amon because he is reputed to be quite the rogue, I'm surprised to see how vehement she is that I stay away from him.

Barely one day has passed since she issued the first warning, and now she's back to reiterate it—this time calling me to her chambers for an important discussion.

"I don't understand you, *mama*. I'm sure the Marquis would have no interest in me."

"I saw how he was looking at you," she hisses. "You don't know him, or his kind, my dear child," she sighs when she sees my perplexed expression. "All my life, I've tried to protect you and your siblings from this side of the world."

I shake my head.

"What side of the world?" I frown, not understanding her.

She waves her hand, dismissing the topic.

"It's not important now. But I need you to keep your distance from that man. This is for your own good, dear."

"But how? If you don't tell me, then I won't know how to protect myself."

"Come here," she says, tugging me into her arms and giving me a heartfelt hug. "You're special, Elizabeth. More so than you'll ever know. And because of that, I must do everything in my power to protect you. Do you understand me?"

I nod slowly.

"Promise me you won't seek him out," she whispers against my hair.

"I promise," I reply, the lie making me physically ill.

My mother has never been so decisive about something, and though the logical part of me knows I should heed her warning, the fickle, romantic side of me has already decided I will not.

Not when Amon isn't just the reprehensible rogue my mother portrays him to be.

He is my savior. The man who's haunted my dreams—during the night *and* daytime.

As such, when the night of the masquerade arrives, I proceed with my plan.

"Are you sure, My Lady?" Mary asks as she regards me with worry in her eyes.

"You can retire, Mary. I just have a slight headache. It should be fine once I go to sleep," I tell her, feigning a tired voice.

"If at any point during the night you feel ill, please call on me and I'll fetch the physician."

"Of course. Good night, Mary."

She lingers for a moment longer before she sighs and leaves the room.

I wait a few more minutes and I jump out of bed. Lowering myself to my knees, I grab on to the big box I'd hidden under the bed, sliding it towards me.

My lips tremble with excitement as I take the top off, revealing a glamorous black dress accompanied by a simple lace mask featuring a black feather.

I first put on the dress, marveling at how easy it is to do it by myself.

In fact, I have to wonder if Amon took that into consideration when he picked it...

As soon as that thought arises, it dawns on me that he must have planned this for far longer than he let on—otherwise how would he have had a dress on such a short notice? And one that seems to have been made for me, too.

Despite the fact that my first instinct should be to be suspicious, I can't help but feel flattered. The fact that he'd thought of this in advance must mean that his words *were* true. He was biding his time...

A blush appears on my cheeks.

It seems that our fateful meeting a year ago hadn't been one sided. Maybe he had been equally affected by the moment—equally fascinated by me as I'd been by him.

Fanning myself, I realize I need to get to work on my hair if I am to make it to the party on time. It always happens that the moment I think of him I lose track of time, just as I lose myself in the maze that is my imagination of him.

Given that Mary isn't here tonight, I have to do my hair myself, so I go for the simplest style. I braid a few strands while leaving the rest of my hair unbound down my back. A scandalous style for a debutante—but an accepted one for a more seasoned lady. And since no one shall know my identity tonight, I can be a little more risqué.

When my hair is done, I put on the mask, carefully securing it in place with pins.

And the last step—rouge.

Since I'm about to be quite scandalous, what could be more so than red lips?

Applying some red tint to my lips, I can't help but admire myself in the mirror and imagine what Amon will think when he sees me.

The black of the mask accentuates the blue of my eyes, while the red pops against my pale skin and black hair.

I'm not immediately recognizable, but if you looked closely enough, you could tell it was me by my eye color alone. But that is easily remedied. I will just not interact with anyone *but* Amon.

When I'm done, I put my slippers on and I'm out of the room, walking briskly towards the stairs to avoid detection.

The music from the orchestra resounds through the entire house, the melody lulling me closer just as a sigh escapes my lips. Excitement thrums through my veins and for some reason, I *know* this night will irrevocably change my life. Like a seed planted in fertile soil, this, too, feels like the beginning of something

Once I enter the ballroom, it's quite easy to get lost in the throng of people—but quite hard to find Amon.

My first inclination is to look for his white hair, but there are many men wearing wigs, making it hard to differentiate among them.

Grabbing a champagne flute, I let my gaze roam about the room, surprised at some of the costume choices. Some had resorted to extravagance, their costumes embodying historical or mythological. I think I spot a Cleopatra, an Aphrodite, a gladiator, and a Roman Emperor. Most people, however, had simply opted for simple masks and a change of hairstyle, not wanting to be entirely unrecognizable.

A low hum of energy travels down my back.

"Looking for someone?"

I feel him before I hear him, his body heat surrounding mine, his presence never failing to make every inch of my skin radiate with tension.

"Maybe," I reply saucily, suddenly turning.

My eyes widen as I take him in.

His hair has been dyed black, just like the mask that's hiding his perfectly sculpted features. Like me, he's dressed entirely in black, his light eyes the only contrast.

"You look spectacular as always," he takes my hand in his, laying a kiss on my gloved knuckles.

My pulse accelerates, and I find myself tongue-tied before him.

If for the past year I'd kept imagining thousands of scenarios in which we would meet again and what I would say to him if that happened, now that he is here, in flesh and bone, I do not know what to say.

What do I know about flirting, or being charming, or witty when I've rarely had the chance to interact with *anyone*—let alone men.

"You don't have to say anything witty to have my full attention, Lizzie mine," he murmurs against my hand, his warm breath penetrating the lacey glove and meeting my naked skin. "You only have to exist and you're all I see," he continues, coming closer and tugging a strand of hair behind my ear.

His proximity makes me feel light-headed—though maybe that's the champagne, too?

"Let's dance," he suddenly suggests, and without waiting for my reply, he whirls me towards the dance floor.

Seeing him against the sea of people I can admit to myself that there's nothing inconspicuous about his height and build. Even without his signature white hair I would have been able to find him—I'll *always* find him.

"And I you," he says, his eyes flickering with intensity.

"Hm?" I blink.

"Wherever you are, wherever you go..." he pauses as his gaze pins me to the spot. "*Who*ever you are. I will find you. That is my promise to you. Always."

My lips tug in a smile as a blush creeps up my cheeks.

Can he be more charming?

Following the cue of the music, he spins me in the middle of the dance floor, the physical exertion making my heart pound and my cheeks flush. Yet it's the little touches that set me more aflame than anything, the small brush of his chest against mine, the feel of his big hands swallowing mine, or the way our bodies seemingly fit together like they'd been cut from the same mold.

A giggle escapes me when the music changes to a brisk tune and he leads me into another dance, twirling me continuously. Our eyes connect, our lips moving in tandem as a smile appears on both our faces. He's laughing, too, enjoying the moment as much as I am.

Despite the intensity I've come to expect from him, there's a levity to his expression, a blithe smile that I don't think many have gotten to see before. He looks right at home—comfortable, light, carefree.

We both laugh as we throw ourselves fully into the music, simply enjoying the freedom of the night and this one moment of pure serendipity.

By the time a slower melody comes along, I'm breathing hard, yet he seems completely unaffected, swaying to the notes with innate fluidity.

He's watching me intently, and it doesn't escape me the scathing looks he sends to every other male that dares come closer.

Yet he's not the only jealous one. Not when all the women in attendance are gazing up at him like he's the eighth wonder of the world. The whispers, too, reach my ears—the fact that everyone knows it's Amon, but no one can tell who his mysterious partner is.

Amon is unbothered by all the interest he's generating in the female population, and the fact that his attention is solely on *me*—not even once swayed by a show of skin, or a too low bodice—thrills me to no end. More than anything, it gives me a confidence I've never had, making me feel beautiful—*desirable*—for the first time in my life.

"You are the most beautiful sight I've ever seen, Lizzie," he compliments me as he draws me close. "Never doubt that."

And there it is—that uncanny ability of his to guess my thoughts. If I had a superstitious bent like my mother, I would have said he wasn't entirely human. Alas, I prefer a more realist approach, rooted in evidence and facts.

The man before me might be mysterious and too alluring for his own good, but he is flesh and blood, muscle and sinew coiling right under my fingertips.

"I still haven't quite figured you out, Amon d'Artan. Are you a roué, trying to steal my virtue? Or are you after something else?" I inquire languidly, studying him in an attempt to decipher him.

"Oh, I will categorically steal your virtue. But you are correct. I *am* after something else," he pauses, a dangerous glint in his eyes.

"And what is that?"

"Your soul. Your very essence and everything that makes you, *you.* Will you give me that? Lizzie mine? Will you surrender everything that you are to me?"

I blink, suddenly taken aback by his request and the severity of his tone. No longer playful, his entire countenance changes as if everything depends on one answer.

"Will you deserve it?" I ask in a small voice, lost in the way his light blue eyes seem to turn even lighter—so much so they are almost white.

"No one will *ever* deserve it, Lizzie," he rasps. *"No one,"* he states emphatically. "But I would devote an eternity to earn the right to call it mine."

I stop in the middle of the dance floor. Time stops as everything fades away until there's only he and I. My eyes on his. His on mine.

Slipping my glove off, I bring my hand to his cheek, cupping it gently.

He seems startled by the gesture, but he doesn't move to stop me. In fact, something akin to a purr escapes him as he sighs in pleasure, his own hand reaching out and covering mine, keeping it firmly in place.

His skin burns where it touches mine—a forbidden caress.

Yet as he slowly moves my hand, leading it to his mouth as he lays a chaste kiss atop my wrist, my heart simply stops in my chest.

My lips part of their own volition, my pupils becoming so enlarged as if I'd used copious amounts of belladonna.

He doesn't move.

His lips are on my skin—on my *naked* skin. In the middle of the ballroom.

It's with a marked delay that I realize people have stopped dancing all around us, everyone gawking at us. Their whispers become louder and louder, the question of the identity of the masked girl with Amon pervasive on everyone's lips.

Yet it's only for a moment. As if compelled, everyone suddenly turns their attention to their dance partners.

"Shall we go somewhere more...private?" He asks, and I find myself unwittingly nodding.

I only know I am caught in his spell—ready to follow him everywhere.

Taking my hand in his, he steers me towards the French double doors that lead to the Duchess' gardens.

The night air surrounds us as Amon shows me a secret spot deep within the maze-like garden.

"We shouldn't be disturbed here," he starts, though his mouth curls into a smile, "or stared at."

"That was quite scandalous, wasn't it?" I chuckle, waving my ungloved hand in front of him.

He grabs it, the hold gentle, as is his touch when he swirls his thumb over my skin in circular motions.

"That's nothing compared to what I want to do to you, Lizzie mine," he whispers as his other hand comes to my face. He strokes my cheek lightly before moving further into my hair and pulling on the pins that keep the mask together.

When it falls to the ground, he takes a step closer, his own mask seemingly falling, too.

Our gazes meet again. This time, our expressions are naked, our faces bared to one another.

"But I won't. Not now. Not until you trust me wholly and irrevocably," he says in a low voice. A sad smile pulls at his lips, and an odd feeling of déjà-vu overtakes me.

"So no ravishing for me tonight?" I joke in an attempt to dispel this unusual melancholy that suddenly comes over me.

"Don't sound so disappointed, love," he drawls, pulling me closer. "You might just change my mind," he says as he leans in, his breath caressing my cheek.

"Is this your way of proving to me that you're not after my virtue?" I raise a brow.

"No, this is my way of showing you that it's not your body I want, Lizzie, though that is always an added bonus," he chuckles. "I want *all* of you. I want to slowly unpack you. Know your likes and dislikes. Explore your mind as if it's the first time."

I blink, surprised at his choice of words.

Before I can speak, though, he swoops me in his arms.

A small gasp escapes me, but when I see where he's taking me, my eyes widen just as my pulse accelerates.

We reach the end of the maze. A white blanket has been laid on the ground, and on top of it is a bottle of wine with two glasses and a selection of finger sandwiches. On both sides of the blanket are lit candles, creating a dreamy atmosphere that simply leaves me speechless.

"You... You prepared this? For me?" I ask incredulously.

"I meant what I said, Lizzie. I want to earn your trust first. And I want to show you I am no roué, though everyone undoubtedly thinks that."

Slowly, he lays me down on the blanket, taking a seat next to me.

"Why do they think that?" I frown.

"Because they only take into account what they see," his lips curl up, though it's not the smile of someone who is infatuated with his appearance—it's the smile of someone who is aware of how attractive he is but thinks it's a burden rather than a blessing. "And of course, because they don't know me. So they would rather speculate and create mythical scenarios," he laughs.

"They do that?"

He purses his lips.

"They *always* do that."

Shrugging his coat off, he throws it to the side, popping a few buttons on his shirt and releasing a sigh of pure contentment.

I swallow hard as my gaze travels from his exquisite face to his Adam's apple and the hint of skin peeking through at the top of his shirt. Even in this poor lighting I can see the contours of his muscles and the way they mold to his clothing.

He's strong. So much bigger than me.

It dawns on me then that I've placed myself into a truly terrifying situation with someone who could crush me. Yet why is it that in his presence I feel safer than I've ever felt?

"What is the truth, then?" I suddenly ask. "Who is the real Amon d'Artan?"

That pleasant smile lingers. And as he slides his elbows back, resting on them, he tips head towards the sky.

"Who is he indeed?" he muses. "He's a lonely man, Lizzie," he says in a low, sad tone as he turns to look at me. "He's a weary man who has seen and lived through too much. A man who has *done* too much. Some good, some bad. Some reversible, some irreversible," he wets his lips. "He's a man who's waited all his life for something," he pauses, intently watching me.

"For what?" I whisper.

"For someone to call his own," he states.

I fall silent, wondering if the implication is as clear as I perceived it.

But it's a second later that his hand is atop mine, threading our fingers together as he shifts on his side to have a better view of me.

"You," he says.

One word.

One word and my breathing intensifies.

One world and he claims my heart as his—irrevocably.

My cheeks heat up as I glance at him from beneath my lashes.

"But you don't know me that well, do you?"

"I know you sneak out at dawn every day at Haversham to feed your strays. I know you rescued that blasted cat and have been hiding it in your room for over a year. I know you pretend to hate certain foods so your maid could eat them instead," he pauses when he sees my shocked expression. "I may not know *everything* about you, but I know your core, Lizzie mine. And it's the most beautiful thing in existence."

"But... How..."

"I know what's important, and the rest I wish to find out."

I'm still speechless at his revelations and the fact that he knows *too* much.

"Have you been spying on me?" I inquire in a low, slightly hurt tone.

"What's paying a servant or two for details?" He shrugs, but he doesn't deny it.

"How long?" I bite my lip. "How long have you been doing this?"

"Since the day we met," he answers honestly. "I told you I didn't stay away because I wanted to. It was because I couldn't come to you sooner. But I wish to rectify that, if you'll let me," he squeezes my hand.

My mind is a whirlpool of confusion as I try to make sense of everything. Yet despite the circumstances surrounding our acquaintance, I can't help but feel like I am where I'm supposed to be.

Here.

With him.

There are a thousand reasons why I should not entertain any relation with him, yet I pick the thousand-and-first one which says I should.

"You're an odd man," I tell him. "But maybe I'm odd too, because I'm falling for you one second at a time," I admit slowly.

"Lizzie," he releases a harsh, tortured breath.

He brings his hand to my neck, softly caressing my flesh before his thumb moves to my lips, brushing lightly against them.

Once. Twice.

My lips part of their own volition, and he pushes his thumb inside —the gesture making my body grow hot and taut.

He's staring at me with such reverence, that I know I wouldn't deny him anything.

If he wishes to kiss me, I'll kiss him back.

If he wishes to do more, I'll open myself to him, letting him do anything and everything to me.

As long as he continues to look at me like that—like I'm the only one in the world for him.

Like I'm the *only* one.

Like I'm...his.

"Those are dangerous thoughts, Lizzie," he murmurs as he leans forward.

My mind blanks just as my eyes flutter closed, anticipation building in my blood.

Any moment now, his lips will be on mine.

My first kiss.

With him.

Amon.

My Amon.

Yet it never comes.

Instead, a shot rings through the stillness of the night, so loud, I fear I've become deaf for a moment. Opening my eyes, confusion swirls in my mind as I take in Amon, on my lap, blood gushing out of a wound in his chest.

My hands are soaked with red, as he gives me one pained glance before his eyes flicker shut.

Turning in horror, my eyes connect with my mother's unyielding ones.

"Die, you bloody *monster*," she spits before she shoots again.

She won't rest until he's...dead...

Chapter Nine

I jump out of bed. Tears are streaming down my cheeks as I look down at my hands, suddenly seeing the blood on them—*his* blood.

"No," I shake my head in denial. This can't be right. He can't be dead.

It doesn't matter that this was all a dream, or that I've likely imagined the entire scenario.

It certainly doesn't matter that Amon might not even be a real person.

All I can focus on is this raw feeling of being split in two—of having my heart cut out of my chest, leaving a gaping wound behind.

My tears won't stop.

I sob and sob, a howled sound of pain erupting from my throat as I bury my hands in my hands.

"Amon," I cry out. "Amon!"

You can't be dead. You can't...

The more I think of the past and of the time we spent together—the teasing, the little touches and his unique way of calling me his—the more I become inconsolable.

It might have been a dream, but I'd felt awakened to life in his presence like never before.

And it hadn't been merely lust, for I can barely conjure his features.

He'd awoken in me a deep, deep longing that even now threatens to undo me.

One moment with him, my name on his lips, his gaze on mine, and I'd been irrevocably lost.

He'd told me he was a lonely man, but I doubt anything compares to this chasm he'd opened in my heart—this abyss that's perpetually empty.

Since the first time I'd dreamed of him, I tried to rationalize everything, looking at it through a psychoanalytical perspective rather than what it truly was—a calling of the heart.

Yet now...After this... How am I supposed to move on when I physically feel as though my heart is breaking?

Stumbling out of bed, I can barely breathe for the sobs that rack my body, the pain so intense I'm about to double over in pain.

I barely get to the bathroom before I empty the contents of my stomach in the toilet. Hunched over, I heave and heave, and still, I don't think I can get myself under control. Not when my soul feels as if it's been frayed in multiple pieces, all scattered around.

I'm not...whole.

On trembling legs, I grab onto the sink as I turn on the water, cleaning my mouth and washing my face.

Yet when I look into the mirror, all I see is the redness of my cheeks, the bloodshot eyes and the tears that still trail down my cheeks—tears that don't seem to stop.

As if sensing my distress, Mr. Meow is suddenly by my side, his furry head brushing against my bare legs.

Startled, I look down to find him watching me with a curious expression.

"I woke you up, didn't I?" I murmur, leaning to grab him in my arms.

His warmth immediately seeps into my skin, and for the first time, a semblance of calm comes over me.

A few breathing exercises later and I manage to get a grip on myself. I'm not sure if it's enough to go back to sleep, though.

Carrying Mr. Meow back to the bed, I get under the sheets, placing him on the pillow and turning to face him.

"You were in the dream too," I tell him, my lips tugging up slightly. "You were named Mr. Meow then, too," I chuckle, though I barely stop myself from crying again.

He reaches out towards me with his little paw. At first, I think he wants to play. But I'm entirely shocked when he brings his paw to my cheek, swiping it lightly, almost as if catching an errant tear. Then, he just rests it against my cheek in an unmistakable gesture of comfort.

"Thank you," I whisper, patting him on the head. "I don't know what's wrong with me and why I am like this. It's just a dream, right?" I ask, feeling silly knowing he'll never answer me back. "But if it's just a dream," I take a deep breath, "why does it hurt so much?"

My voice breaks, and a high-pitched meow resounds as he comes closer, bringing his furry face to my cheek and softly rubbing it.

With Mr. Meow in my arms, I close my eyes, slowly drifting to sleep.

But it doesn't last long. Not when Mr. Meow starts hissing at me and lightly stinging me with his claws.

"Auch," I suddenly react, my lids heavy with sleep. I'm ready to reprimand him when discomfort pricks at my nose.

I start coughing, and looking at the door, I notice smoke coming from the hallway—too much smoke, which can only mean one thing.

Fire.

There's a damn fire raging in my house.

"What..."

Despite the initial shock, I'm quick to react.

Swinging my legs off the bed, I put on my shoes and quickly get my purse, fitting Mr. Meow inside. Stripping off the pillow case, I use it as a cloth and place it to my mouth to avoid smoke inhalation.

Ready to face the fire, I open the door of the bedroom, readying myself to rush downstairs. Yet as soon as I step into the hallway, my eyes widen as I realize just how far the fire had spread.

The entire lower region of the stairs is engulfed in flames, the wood crackling and feeding the fire further.

I freeze, panic overtaking me, as does the realization that there is no way out.

Damn it all, but I'm going to die here, aren't I?

Tears stab at the corners of my mouth, frustration mounting inside of me.

"Meow!"

The little sound from my purse takes me out of my dark thoughts, reminding me it's not just me who is in danger—Mr. Meow is, too.

"Don't worry. I won't let you die," I murmur, though my words belie my own increasing terror.

Going back to my bedroom, I close the door, locking it and placing the bedsheets at the bottom to avoid getting smoke contamination.

Then, my only step is to go to the window and see how I can scale the house down. And if it happens that I won't be able to...then at least Mr. Meow will.

Unlocking the window, I push it open, my mouth dropping open in shock as I note the wild flames surrounding the entire first level of the house. So much so that the entire outer wall has been compromised.

The flames are licking at the wooden structure, climbing higher and higher with seemingly every second.

Immediately, I *know* I can't possibly make it down. Not when it's a matter of minutes before the fire reaches the second floor—both inside and from the outside.

Lifting Mr. Meow out of my purse, I place him on the ledge.

"You need to go," I whisper, pointing to him the only secure ridge—one far too small and frail for me to even attempt to climb. "You need to live, Mr. Meow," I tell him, pursing my lips and doing my best to not devolve into hysterics.

He protests, pushing his head at me as if saying I need to go, too.

I shake my head.

"It won't hold," I utter the truth out loud for the first time.

The foundation is so swallowed up by flames that I'm afraid not even Mr. Meow might make it. But he has the best chance...

"Go. For me. Please," I whisper, laying a kiss against the white patch of hair atop his head before urging him out the window.

This time, he obeys me, Jumping around and managing to avoid the burning wood on his way down.

My shoulders slump in defeat. My cough is more pronounced than before, my throat is dry and sensitive the more I inhale the polluted air.

A loud crack erupts in the air, followed by a loud bang. I jump back, my eyes wide with terror as a piece of wood crashes through my bedroom door, the flames transferring from one surface to another.

Once, I'd read in the newspaper that most fire victims usually die from smoke inhalation before their bodies are charred by the flames.

Yet seeing the situation all around me, the fact that the wall connecting to the hallway is ablaze, I know I won't be one of those. Despite it becoming increasingly harder to breathe, the flames will get to me before asphyxiation does.

I pale at the thought of the agony that awaits me, and dropping my hand from my mouth, I take a big gulp of air. And another one. Anything to make this easier to bear.

Slumping to the floor in the middle of the room, I inhale and exhale, filling my lungs with the noxious smoke.

And in spite of the fact that I'm facing my end—that I'm staring death in the face—an eerie calm washes over me. My thoughts simply take me back to my dream, to the perfect moment before Amon had been killed in front of me.

In my last moments on this earth, I'm ashamed to admit that I can't think of anyone *but* him. Not my friends, the nuns, or even Caleb—real people I'm leaving behind.

No, it's just him—the product of my imagination, but the epitome of contentment.

Him, the mysterious man who'd felt like home when I've never known the true meaning of the word. Though there is no face I can conjure up, no features I can wish to see for one last time, there is pure feeling. The warmth of being someone's only reason for being. The intensity of being someone's sole focus.

Closing my eyes as my breathing becomes more ragged, I think back to the dance floor, the way he's spun me around and the blithe smile on his face. My chest constricts, and with every second, it's becoming harder and harder to breathe—to the point that I get lightheaded, my vision swimming. Still, I imagine it's from a succession of twirls and the exertion of the dance.

As the room becomes increasingly warmer, my skin prickling with the awareness that the flames are slowly making their way towards me, I imagine it's his body—his heat transferring to me.

"Lizzie mine."

My lips tip up in a smile as I hear his voice calling me—even knowing it to be nothing more than a mirage.

"I'm here," he whispers. "And I'm never leaving. Never."

"Amon," a whisper makes it past my lips, my lids heavy as I open them and see him in front of me—with his white hair, blue, blue eyes and lush lips. "My Amon..."

I barely have any strength left. Certainly not enough to differentiate between what's real and what's not. But at this point I welcome the latter, for only with it I'll be able to die with a smile on my face.

"We'll be together," I cough," soon..."

"No," he rasps, bringing me to his body just as the flames disperse around us, his presence acting as an active repellent for the fire. "You're not dying. Not again. You hear me," he speaks harshly against my hair.

His big hands cup my cheeks as he slowly draws back, his gaze searching my languid, barely present one.

"You're never leaving me again, Lizzie mine," he growls before his lips are on mine.

His body is a pillar of strength, his touch as comforting as it is invigorating.

My awareness is slowly slipping from me, and with no energy left, I slump against him.

His lips are fitted to mine—his air traveling into my battered lungs and giving me a new chance of life.

But is it among the living? Or among the stars?

MY EYES FLUTTER OPEN, uncertainty filling me to the brim as I struggle to take in my surroundings.

The ceiling is gilded, marble bas-relief adorning its entire surface.

The beauty of the room makes me wonder if this isn't perchance heaven. Especially as I move, the softness of the sheets making me purr in satisfaction.

A sense of comfort washes over me as I snuggle deeper into the clean sheets. And as I stretch, the size of the bed takes me by surprise, as does the fact that it takes me a few rolls to fully cover its width.

My lips tug in a smile as I yawn happily.

Nothing hurts. My lungs are clear, and I can breathe normally.

If this is heaven, then I am *not* complaining.

Sunlight streams through silk curtains, bathing the room in light and revealing more of its contents—and occupiers.

"You," I gasp, startled as I scurry to the edge of the bed.

Well, there goes my theory about heaven.

"You're awake," he sighs. "Good. I was worried about you for a moment," Caleb says as he comes closer, taking a seat at the edge of the bed.

"What do you mean?" I blink, confused.

"There was a fire," he purses his lips.

Immediately, the memories from before flood my mind. There *had* been a fire. And I'd been trapped, with absolutely no way out.

In fact, I remember clearly that I'd decided to embrace my death. And then...my last memory is of Amon.

Was he...there?

I frown.

But it can't be.

Not when I feel as good as new but I *know* the smoke had raked my throat, filling my lungs and making it hard to breathe. Something like that doesn't just go away.

So how come I'm here, uninjured—*feeling absolutely fine*?

"What happened? Did you..."

He shakes his head ruefully.

"I saw the fire from the hill. By the time I got to the house, you were outside, on the lawn."

"On the lawn?" My eyes widen in shock. "I don't remember that."

"You were completely out of it. Dr. Bailey was here to see you but he said you're completely fine. Not even a scratch, and your lungs are completely clear," he pauses, his eyes fixed to my forehead, and I unconsciously bring my fingers to where a wound used to be—one that is *not* there. "*Not a scratch, Darcy*," he emphasizes, something akin to hope flickering in his gaze.

"Not a scratch?" I repeat, taken aback by the revelation—though I have to admit I feel better than I ever have. My body is relaxed, energy hums in my veins and my limbs are full of strength. Most of all, my breathing is perfectly fine, which in itself is astounding.

The last thing I remember is sitting in the middle of my bedroom, hanging onto Amon's—*most likely imaginary*—body and letting him kiss me.

Of course, now thinking back, it does seem a little ludicrous that someone would be kissing me in the middle of a raging fire, which suggests I must have hallucinated the entire exchange.

But how did I get to the lawn? How the hell could I have gotten out of the house, without a scratch and without *any* smoke inhalation?

"You were so lucky, Darcy," he releases a harsh breath. "When I noticed the blazing fire from my window I thought I was looking death right in the eyes. I raced as fast as I could. That you were outside, unharmed... I can only thank your guardian angel for being there for you," he murmurs softly, taking my hand in his and bringing it to his lips for a kiss.

"I'm at the Hale house?" I blink in surprise. "Wait, this is your room?" I squeak, a blush staining my cheeks.

He shakes his head, a smirk playing at his lips.

"This is *your* room now. Mine is across the hall."

"Does your family know I'm here?"

He nods.

"They were thrilled. Both that you'll be staying with us and that you're fine after that unfortunate incident."

"But how can I stay here?" I mumble, panicking. "I can't stay here..."

"And where are you going to stay now? The house is gone. The fire destroyed everything inside."

My face falls as it dawns on me that I have nowhere else to go.

"You don't realize how welcome you are here, darlin'," he comes closer, holding my hand between his and squeezing in comfort. "This is your home for as long as you like."

"But... I wouldn't feel comfortable, Caleb," I whisper. "I barely know your family. I barely know *you*."

"Do you not?" his voice shifts, a serious tinge to it. "Do you not know me, Darcy?" he raises a brow, intensity radiating from him as he traps my hand to his side. He looks me in the eye for a moment before he suddenly tugs me forward until his face is a breath away from mine.

My pulse spikes, and a bout of fear settles low in my belly—yet it's accompanied by the ever confusing feeling of anticipation.

"I don't," I tell him honestly, meeting his gaze head on. "I've only known you for a few days, Caleb. Can you not see things from my side? That I'm uncomfortable staying in the home of the man I'm seeing," I speak softly, hoping to remove the harsh edges from his features.

"Tell me you don't feel this, darlin'," he rasps as he places my palm over his heart. "Tell me you don't feel this connection between us that's as intoxicating as it is maddening. Look me in the eye and tell me you don't feel any of this, Darcy."

I bite my lip as I regard him—with his beautiful face ravaged by these seemingly foreign emotions I have awakened in him. And he's not the only one.

"I do," I whisper. "I *do* feel something when I'm with you, Caleb. And the truth is that you terrify just as you excite me," I confess.

What I don't say is how confused I feel, finding myself drawn to Caleb—a flesh and blood man—while equally yearning for a figment of my imagination.

"But I've also repeatedly told you that I'm not used to this. I've never dated before, how could I possibly be comfortable living in the same house as you?"

"What are you worried about?" he suddenly asks. "That I'll pounce on you? Is that it, Darcy darlin'? You think I'm going to sneak into your room late at night," he pauses as he sees me swallow uncomfortably, "and do what?" he raises a brow.

"I..."

"Spy on you? Take advantage of you? Make you my woman against your will? Is that what you think of me?" he demands as he cups my jaw between his fingers, keeping me in place. "Haven't I told you already that I didn't do anything to you at the cabin? That I never touched you? What more do you want from me so that you feel comfortable?" he rasps, the accusation clear.

No matter how much I'd like to avert my gaze, I can't. Staring at him, I find myself lost in his black eyes—so dark I can see my own reflection looking back at me.

Slowly, I shake my head.

"I trust you," I say softly. "But what will your family say? What will everyone else say? They already think I'm a witch and now probably a murderer," I let a dry laugh. "Next I'll be branded a scarlet woman, too."

"Never that," his answer is immediate. "Never that, darlin'. I'll make sure no one ever speaks ill of you again. Alright?" he asks, gentling his hold over my jaw as he strokes my skin. "I don't know how many times I have to drill this into your head, Darcy, but this isn't temporary, nor is it just dating. You're mine. You were mine from the first time I saw you, and I'll be damned happy for anyone else to know it too."

My lashes flutter in surprise at his declaration.

"If I need to give you my name to make it official, we'll do that tomorrow. The very next moment if you wish so," he continues, stunning me further.

"Caleb..." I stammer. "You're getting ahead of yourself. We've just started seeing each other and now you're mentioning...marriage?"

"Darlin', do you think I'd date you with anything less but marriage in mind?" he asks, his lips curling up.

My cheeks heat up, a warmth unfurling in my belly at his words, butterflies flapping their wings all around my lower region.

Why does he have to be so attractive? And why does he have to have such a glib tongue? He says everything a woman wants to hear. I may not be experienced with men, but every word he utters assures me of his investment in the relationship and his commitment.

What sane woman would say no to that?

In fact, I'm almost beating myself up for doubting him—even for one second—and for allowing my thoughts to wander to Amon, the man who only exists in my dreams.

"Thank you," I murmur.

A huge grin splays on his face, and before I can protest, he leans in, laying a kiss on my cheek.

"Look at this as an opportunity to get to know each other better. And at the end of your two month stay, you can make an important decision."

I nod, giving him a shy smile.

Getting up, he's out the door for a few moments before he's back with a tray filled with goodies.

My eyes widen just as my stomach rumbles with hunger.

Slowly, the events of last night are coming back again.

I'd been ill. After the tragedy I'd witnessed in my dream, I'd thrown up everything I had eaten the day before.

The moment I'm reminded of that dream, however, tears prick again at my lids, as does the fact that I feel more confused than ever—how could a dream feel so real?

Yet that, too, is just one of the many odd things that have been happening around me. And with this newest incident—that I somehow escaped unscathed—I can't ignore it anymore.

Somehow, I have to get to the bottom of it all.

But where can I start?

"I brought you a little of everything," Caleb announces. He has a sweet smile on his face that transforms his entire visage, making him more youthful—more approachable.

He's so striking that I can't help my own lips from emulating his smile.

"Here you have a soup, some sandwiches, a selection of cakes, and some hot tea," he points at every little item. "So, what would you like first?"

"The soup. I'm very hungry," I blush.

"The soup it is then," he winks at me just as he props the breakfast table on top of my legs. Before I can help myself to the food, he's ahead of me, grabbing the spoon and trying the temperature of the soup.

When he's satisfied, he nods, but he doesn't give me back the spoon.

Instead, he proceeds to feed me with it, carefully wiping at my mouth when I get a little messy.

"I'm not an invalid, you know..." I mutter.

"Do you have to be for me to care for you?" he arches a brow. "Can't I enjoy pampering you?"

"You're sweet," I praise softly.

"I knew it," he chuckles.

My brows go up in question.

"There's something about you, Darcy," he gives me a wistful smile. "Something so achingly innocent that just gets me riled up every single time."

When he sees my confused expression, he continues.

"It's not bad, darlin'. You awaken this primal side of me. The one that wants to surround you in a protective cocoon and keep you safe at all cost; away from the world and any outside influences. Just for my eyes only," he drawls.

How he can be both cute and seductive at the same time, I do not know—yet he nails both.

"Are you the jealous type, Caleb?" I tease.

"Jealous?" he huffs. "That is the understatement of the century," he grumbles, eliciting a soft laugh from me.

He continues to feed me the soup, making small talk every now and then. When I'm finished with the bowl, I eye the sandwiches next—which he doesn't let me eat by myself either!

Caleb slices the sandwiches in small bits, feeding me one at a time.

Shaking my head at him, I accept the offering, my stomach finally calming down now that it's full.

"I'm happy to see you eat," he strokes my face lightly. "Now you need to rest."

Just as he rises to take away the tray, I grab his arm.

"You have a telephone here, don't you? Can I use it to call my friend and announce to the school I'm taking a longer leave?"

He doesn't reply for a moment before he nods.

"I prepared some clothes for you. Let me know when you're ready and I'll take you to the telephone."

He exits the room, letting me dress.

Browsing through the clothes he'd selected for me, I'm pleased to see how similar they are to my own style. Caleb has certainly paid attention to the way I dress, and somehow that tidbit makes him earn some bonus points for me.

When I'm done, I open the door to find him outside, waiting for me.

"You look stunning, darlin'," he rasps, his eyes hungrily roaming all over my body.

I redden from head to toe, as seems to be my default reaction when he regards me like that.

"Shall we?" he asks, offering me his arm.

As he takes me down a long corridor, I realize the house is much, much larger than I'd expected. The walls are beautifully decorated as had been my bedroom, and I can't help but admire all the work and dedication that had gone into the décor, as well as the materials.

I don't have to touch anything to see that everything must be top quality.

"We'll need to swing by the sheriff's tomorrow," Caleb suddenly says. "He wanted to question you about the fire and the murders but I told him it would happen only when you're feeling better and with me by your side," he declares, assuring me he will protect me at every step.

I nod, giving him a tight smile. I should have known that would need to happen at some point, especially with how we'd run away from the square the day before.

"Do you think..." I bite my lip, not wanting to accuse anyone. "Do you think any of the people in town who dislike me might have done this? Set the house on fire?"

His lips are flattened in a thin line.

"It could be," he agrees. "If someone tried to harm you, I promise you they will know hell, Darcy darlin'. But this is exactly why I didn't want to leave you alone—*should not* have left you alone. Fuck!"

"I know. I should have listened to you," I sigh. "But I'm not used to imposing on people. I don't know if I told you, but I grew up in an orphanage. There, the first thing you learn is to keep to yourself and not cause trouble, because then no one would want you. Not that it worked for me since no one wanted me anyway," I shrug, trying to keep the pain from my voice. "But I was ten when I arrived there. Most parents want to adopt babies."

"Darcy..." he stops, turning towards me with an inscrutable expression on his face. "Did you have anyone to love you?" he asks in a low voice.

I avert my face, since the truth *and* my ungratefulness would then show. While I did have more than a lot of my peers, I've always felt like I was missing something—craving something.

Home.

The word echoes in my head and immediately the image I've suddenly associated with that word pops up in my mind.

Him...

Amon. A figment of my imagination.

But the only person whose embrace has ever felt like...home. Like true belonging.

"I did," I reply. "I was fortunate enough to meet two nuns who took care of me. And I've had friends over the years. I wouldn't say it's the same type of love you're implying but it was good enough for me."

A pained sound escapes him.

"You're telling me no one ever told you *I love you*?"

"Of course," I wave my hand as if I'd been told many, *many* times. Yet the only one that comes to mind is when one of my pupils had said the words to me.

How sad is that...

"I don't believe you," he suddenly stops. "Tell me when and who," he taps his foot relentlessly as he raises a brow at me.

"Well, my students say it all the time. And I think my mother... But I don't remember her that well," I admit with a strained smile.

Without warning, he pulls me into his arms.

"That should have never happened, darlin'. You should have had someone tell you those words every day—a thousand times per day," he whispers poignantly as he strokes my hair. "You should have had a big, loving family..." he trails off, and I swear I hear the ghost of an *it's all you've ever wanted.*

"I'll make my own in the future," I reply with a nervous laugh, not liking having my vulnerability out in the open—my utmost desire, and perhaps deepest disappointment. "And I'll have many, *many* children to tell me that every day."

Caleb freezes. His body stills just as his breath hitches.

"You want many children?" he asks softly, the tone entirely different as the one before.

I nod.

Drawing back, he regards me for a moment, a melancholy settling over his features.

"Of course you do," he whispers, and somehow I doubt the words are meant for my ears as he amends a second later. "Of course you'll have them."

We resume walking, and he slowly urges me to tell him more about my upbringing, asking me questions that show he's genuinely invested.

He seems to be particularly interested in my reason for becoming a teacher.

"Let me guess. Because you love children?" he offers, and I chuckle.

"Part of it. But when I was younger I found my happy corner in literature and I wanted to help others find it too. Most often than not children hate reading because it's imposed on them. I wanted to make it fun for them—foster a passion in them," I explain.

All the while, his gaze on me is unwavering and arresting, making me stumble every now and then.

"You'll make a great mom, Darcy. I'm sure of it," he gives me a sad smile as he points towards a large living room.

My mouth drops open when I come face to face with the opulence of the chamber. It's almost...as if it had been taken from my dreams.

"The phone is over there. I'll leave you to it while I go sort out some business for the day," he whispers in my ear, giving me a quick kiss on the forehead before he's gone.

His sudden departure is a surprise, but as I step inside the room, I immediately forget all about it as I lose myself in the beauty of the décor and the authentic Georgian feel. Everything is decadent and absolutely breathtaking, from the garish furniture, to the combination of gilded walls with marble decorations, everything is perfect.

"And our new guest is awake," a voice comments, interrupting my thoughts.

Turning, I come face to face with Rhiannon Hale.

"Hello," I hurry to greet her.

"My niece told me you were staying with us now," she mentions, assessing me from head to toe. "Good."

Curious that she mentions Katrina instead of Caleb, but I don't have time to dwell on that since she invites me to sit with her for tea.

"I was just going to use the telephone and..."

"Nonsense. It's tea time. We shall have tea," she says right as she rings a servant.

Not a few minutes later and a tray with tea and cakes is brought to us.

Blinking, it truly does seem like I'm in a period piece for a moment —or my dreams.

"You have a wonderful home, Mrs. Hale. And I've only seen a portion of it."

"Why, thank you, Miss O'Sullivan. It's one of the few homes in the country to maintain the original Georgian décor and architecture. We've tried to limit our interference over the years, so what you see would have been part of the original design."

When she sees me look around, she adds.

"Yes, even most of the furniture. And please, call me Rhiannon."

"Then you must call me Darcy," I offer.

My eyes widen with awe as I take in the silk draped armchair and the gilded armrest, touching them reverently and briefly imagining what it would have been like to live back then.

With *him.*

Amon.

A smile pulls at my lips, and Rhiannon is quick to note it.

"You're not by any chance thinking of a beau?"

A blush stains my cheeks as I slowly nod.

"You must tell me all about it," she declares, clasping her hands together.

"It's not like that. He's just... My idea of the perfect man," I tell her, slightly embarrassed.

"Pray do tell, what is the perfect man for you?"

I pause for a moment, not knowing whether I should reveal this, but the words are out of my mouth before I can help it.

"The one who calls me his."

Rhiannon's eyes sparkle with mischief as she bursts out laughing.

"Smart man," she chuckles and I join in.

We spend some time engaging in small talk, and she tells me a little more about the architecture of the house and the period pieces.

"We Hales are a very tight knit bunch, and we always stick up for one another," she shares with a wink. "I know you're still reeling from the fire and I've heard about those awful allegations in town. All I can say is don't lose faith. Eventually, good will prevail," she adds in a wise tone.

"Is it possible then? For someone to have set fire to the house on purpose?"

She purses her lips.

"Fairydale is the place where everything is possible, Darcy. There is evil here. The type that will make grown men quake in their boots. But there is also good fighting that evil," she says cryptically.

"Why is that? Why is everyone excusing what's happening in Fairydale? I've already witnessed four unusual murders, and no one seems too concerned about them."

"I'm glad you find them odd. As you should," she nods. "But I don't have an answer for you now."

I frown.

Now?

She wobbles to her feet, reaching for her cane and turning to leave.

"You can use the telephone. I'm happy we had this chat, Darcy. I'm sure we'll have many more in the future," she shares a smile. "And when you're ready... I'll tell you everything about Fairydale."

Watching her depart the room, I repeat her words in my mind.

When you're ready.

That sounds ominous...

Shaking myself, I head to the end of the room where the creamy white telephone is laid on a table.

Trying to remember the number of the school to ask, I wheel the correct combination, waiting for the signal.

The static on the line is louder than usual, but I attribute it to the location and the fact that we're so close to the ocean.

Tapping my foot as I twirl a strand of hair while waiting, I absent-mindedly let my gaze roam around.

Suddenly, there is a loud sound.

"Hello, Saint Russell Boarding School?" I ask, hoping I hadn't dialed the wrong number.

More static, but an echo resounds in my ear. Low at first before picking up in volume, a harsh, demonic-like voice erupts from the receiver.

"Don't trust them."

Part Two

Chapter Ten

"Did you speak to the school?" Caleb asks me the following day as he brings me breakfast in bed.

I nod, a tight smile on my face as I recall the odd voice on the line.

Don't trust them.

Who? Who is it that I shouldn't trust?

At this point it can no longer be a coincidence after I'd received the same message when I'd arrived in Fairydale.

"They decided to let me go," I add with a sigh. "I can't blame them at this point since two months of absence is a long time. They will need to find another teacher when the school year starts."

I hadn't managed to reach Allison, though. The secretary had told me she was on her break and off school grounds, so I need to try again later.

"Are you upset about that?"

He comes to my side, taking a seat on the edge of the bed. Like before, he cuts my food in small pieces, feeding it to me one at a time.

"I don't know," I admit honestly. "I worked very hard to get that position. I am disappointed, but it was inevitable."

"You'll get the inheritance. And maybe you can find something around here," he suggests lightly. "We have a school. If you'd like, I can ask around and see if there's a position available."

"Really?" I blink in surprise at his offer.

Though it's very kind of him to suggest this, I can't help but feel it's his way of telling me to stay in Fairydale.

"I want you to stay here, Darcy," he confirms not a moment later. "I know it's not Boston, and it's just a small town in the middle of nowhere. But maybe..." he gives me a hopeful smile.

Lifting my hand, I palm his cheek as a smile tugs at my lips.

"I'll think about it."

It's the best I can give him right now. I've already promised I would stay for two months, but more?

Despite my connection with Caleb, there is still the fact that Fairydale scares me—with its odd deaths, witch-hunt mentality, and all the unusual occurrences that have no logical explanation.

"When you're ready, we can go to the sheriff's office so he can take your statement," he says as he takes away the tray of food.

Nodding, I wait until he's out of the door before dressing and making myself presentable.

I hadn't dreamed about *him* last night, even though I hoped I would. I *needed* to see him alive and well...

No matter how much I tried to think about him, nothing happened.

In fact, I couldn't dream at all.

Sighing as I take in my appearance, I let my gaze roam over the makeup items Caleb had bought for me.

Since everything had burned in the fire, he'd been kind enough to get me everything I need. He's been a sweetheart through this entire ordeal and I've been a...shrew, arguing with him over his goodwill and being stubborn about propriety when the reality is that I no longer have a choice.

I have no money, *nothing*. Until I get the inheritance, I am dependent on the Hales—as much as I might hate it.

But I'm not about to make myself a charity case. Every little thing he spends on me, I shall return—back to the last penny.

Uncapping one of the lipsticks, I gaze longingly at the red shade.

Why is it that every little thing brings me back to my dream—to Amon?

I release a heavy sigh as I dab some on my lips before smudging a little on my cheeks to add a bit of color to my pallor.

"I'm ready," I declare, opening the door and joining Caleb.

He gives me a sweet smile, taking my hand and leading me to his car.

It takes us a few minutes to get to the sheriff's office. By the time we pull in the parking lot, I somehow expect a mob of angry people to come after me.

Yet there's no one there.

Letting out a relieved breath, I follow Caleb as he shows me to the sheriff's office.

"Miss O'Sullivan," Sheriff Lawrence nods when he sees me. "I'm sorry to hear about your home."

I give him a tight smile.

"I was lucky to get out alive," I murmur, following Caleb's cue and taking a seat at the Sheriff's study.

"We've had men on the scene and we don't think there's any foul play involved. Are you sure you turned off your stove?"

I frown.

"Of course I did. I wouldn't have left it on," I state clearly.

"But maybe you just forgot about it..."

"Darcy says she did not leave it on and I believe her. She is always very careful," Caleb interjects, and the sheriff gives him a noncommittal grunt.

Already, I feel my temper rise. So he wouldn't believe *me*, the person who was actually there, but he would take the word of another man over mine?

"I'm certain I did not provoke the fire, Sheriff. That means someone else must have done so. I would ask you to look closer into the matter."

"As I said, Miss O'Sullivan," he repeats through gritted teeth. "We found no evidence of foul play, so we've closed the case as accidental."

"But..."

I'm about to protest when Caleb squeezes my hand under the table.

"You mentioned you wanted to interview Darcy for the murders, didn't you?" Caleb suddenly asks.

"Yes, indeed," he clears his throat. "If you could go with my secretary who will take your statement. It is just a formality. Mr. Hale has already given his statement and vouched that he spent the entire morning and the previous night with you," he says in a reproachful tone, the implication clear.

My cheeks heat up and I suddenly stand up.

"If you'll excuse me then," I murmur, knowing I am likely to explode if I stay one moment longer in his presence.

Caleb gives me a comforting smile that I try to return.

But how can I stay calm when the sheriff all but called me a hussy to my face?

He didn't even care about my words, only listening to those of Caleb—a *man*.

Balling my hands into fists, I stride to the secretary's desk, plopping myself in a chair and giving her the statement. I account for all my whereabouts and answer all the questions before I'm told I'm free to go.

"They won't do anything about the fire, will they?" I ask Caleb a while later as we exit the station. "The Sheriff doesn't care what happens to me as long as he gets his scapegoat."

Pursing his lips, he nods.

"I didn't expect that he would do much. He, like everyone else, sees you as an outsider. You would have been the perfect person to place the blame on for the murders if not for your alibi with me. Still, it's better to have everything on record so no one can argue otherwise later on."

"You're right," I sigh. "It still doesn't make it better."

"Don't worry about it, Darcy. When you're with me, nothing will touch you," he promises, his words giving me a modicum of comfort.

I nod, lost in my thoughts.

Something about the entire situation doesn't seem...right. For a murder investigation of this magnitude, I would have expected hours of interrogations, and a lot more red-tape. I've read murder mysteries, and they never let you go just like that.

Yet the Sheriff did just that, despite the fact that, as Caleb mentioned, I *am* an outsider.

Is it really that Caleb's words are so influential?

He'd only had to look at the Sheriff and the man had sung to his tune.

Maybe because they are the wealthiest in the area they are afforded more respect. Or, maybe, Caleb's history in the army adds to his credibility.

In any event, the entire visit was bizarre, and now I'm more confused than ever about what's happening in this town.

"Caleb?" I ask as we stop in front of the car. "Who do you think killed those people?"

I raise my gaze to his, watching him intently.

He merely smiles, nonchalantly shrugging his shoulders back in the most relaxed of manners.

"Someone who thought they deserved it," he answers casually. "And going by the way they all died, I'd say it was someone with a big grudge."

"But how could anyone deserve something like *that*? They weren't just killed. They were *tortured!*"

"Ah, Darcy," he smiles. "You're so innocent," he shakes his head in amusement.

I blink and he's before me—a little too close for comfort.

Slowly gazing up, it's to find him regarding me intently, a lopsided smile pulling at the corner of his mouth.

"The punishment should be equal to the sins," he murmurs. "And sometimes, the weight of the sins depends on the perspective."

"What are you trying to say?" I whisper.

"What to you was a mere moment of sadness, discomfort, or disappointment, to someone else that was a hundred fold. It all depends on the importance we attribute to things."

His words are vague enough to mean nothing, but firm enough to mean *everything.*

"Would *you* have done that?" I question him directly.

His lips merely curl up more in a wolfish grin.

"I could have done worse," he whispers.

Before I know it, he's walking back to the other side of the car.

My breathing intensifies, and as my gaze follows him, it's to note a hidden smile on his face—one of satisfaction and something more.

Something...malefic.

It also dawns on me he didn't say *would*. He said *could*.

He could have done worse.

My heart is hammering in my chest as more doubts cloud my mind.

Could Caleb have had anything to do with it?

But how?

Even if he did target Vicky for her behavior towards me, how could he have known about the man from the Ipswich station or the one from the restaurant? How could he have known who they were?

From a logical standpoint, *nothing* makes sense.

Yet if I were to allow that things are not entirely logical in Fairydale... Then what could I conclude? That Caleb has some inhumane powers and he's on a mission to kill everyone who slights me? And for what? To defend my honor when I haven't asked for it?

Or...

I bite my lip in uncertainty as I continue to watch him, more questions surfacing in my head.

The fire...

Could he have had anything to do with it too? All to drive me into *his* house, right across from his room?

But as soon as that thought surfaces I shake myself.

Don't be Catherine!

Yet it's entirely too hard *not* to find everything suspicious with what's been happening around me.

Including Caleb.

And maybe...most of *all* Caleb.

Before he can slide into the driver's seat, the sheriff's aide runs out calling for him and asking him to come inside for some new development.

"Wait for me here?"

I nod slowly, and soon he's gone.

Just as I wonder what could have happened, a man clears his throat from behind me.

Turning, I come face to face with the older gentleman I'd noticed at the funeral.

He looks to be in his late fifties, a little older than Mr. Vaughan, but more refined. He's wearing a striped navy blue suit, his hand on his hat as he removes it when he stops in front of me. His cane is in the other hand, the emerald-like stone stealing my attention.

"Miss Darcy O'Sullivan, I presume?" he asks, his accent cultured and oddly reminiscent of the period movies I'd seen with Allison when we'd get our monthly wages.

"Yes," I nod, barely wrenching my gaze from the gem. "And you are..."

"Archibald Nicholson," he gives me a warm smile as he offers to shake my hand.

"Pleased to meet you, Mr. Nicholson," I stretch my hand towards him.

A spark of awareness travels through me when his hand connects with mine, as does something akin to a long-buried memory.

"Have we met before?" I ask before I can help myself, my gaze skittering from him to the stone, seemingly unable to stop myself from looking at it longingly.

He doesn't seem surprised, merely smiling.

"You could say so," he chuckles. "I knew your parents."

"My mother, too?" My brow shoot up.

"Yes, your mother, too."

Too stunned to say anything, I merely stare at him.

To my knowledge, my mother hadn't had any living family. She'd been all alone in the world, struggling to make ends meet for the both of us. Though my memories of her are scarce, I remember her face, and the way she would tell me to never take a day for granted.

"Was she from here? From Fairydale?"

He nods.

"She was," he confirms. "But she left before you were born."

"I assume she did it because of the impending scandal?" I wince as I say the words out loud.

His lips press into a thin line.

"I can't presume what was going through your mother's head at the time. But I would assume so."

Suddenly, I'm struck by how brave she'd been.

At the height of depression, when most people were starving, she'd left the only home she'd ever known to offer me a better chance at life—one where I wouldn't be branded a bastard by everyone around.

A new sense of admiration blooms inside of me, just as new sadness envelops me that I didn't get to spend more time with her—that I don't have more memories of her.

"For that reason I wanted to approach you and offer you my apologies for how you've been treated since you arrived in our town. I know it can't erase the ugly words, but I'm sorry the Pierces didn't offer you more consideration."

"You don't need to apologize for someone else's actions," I tell him gently, though appreciating that he would try to do so.

"But I do," he sighs. "You see, Mordechai is my nephew, and the Pierces are longtime friends of the Nicholsons. By extension, they are all family. And as the patriarch, it is my duty to do so."

"Thank you," I murmur. "I wasn't aware of your connection to them. Does that mean we are related somehow, too?"

His lips widen into a thin smile.

"Does it?" he muses. "I suppose it does," he eventually amends, his eyes studying me surreptitiously.

The angle of sunlight hits the stone on his cane once more, and my gaze is drawn to it—to the point it becomes my entire focus. My skin tingles with an unnatural urge to touch it, and before I know it, I reach out for it.

Mr. Nicholson draws back, moving the cane away from my sight.

Just as the shine of the stone dies, so does this compulsion that's taken shape inside of me.

I blink in confusion.

"I'm sorry. I don't know what came over me," I murmur.

"It's quite alright," he smiles, though it doesn't reach his eyes. "In fact, I was wondering if you would do me the honor of coming for dinner at my house. I could tell you more about Fairydale and your mother should you wish so."

The offer takes me by surprise, as does the echo in my mind that whispers *no*.

My lips tremble, my polite smile wilting in the face of this unusual feeling.

"Could I bring my friend with me?" I ask, curious at knowing more about my mother, but also wary all the same.

"Your friend? Of course. Who might she be?" He inquires casually, though his gaze has an odd glint to it.

"Caleb Hale," I reply, and his expression immediately falls. It's only for a second, but it's there, nonetheless.

"Caleb Hale?" His eyes widen. "I haven't seen him in a long time," he purses his lips. "Do bring him along. I'm sure we'll have much to talk. I've heard about his feats in the war. Brave man," he mentions, but his words are empty—no hint of that supposed admiration.

"Certainly," I murmur.

"Well, it's been a pleasure meeting you Miss O'Sullivan, and I look forward to furthering our acquaintance."

I wave, but just as he takes a few steps he suddenly stops, half-turning.

"By the way. I've put in a good word for you in town. No one should trouble you again, Miss O'Sullivan. And no one should believe anymore that you had anything with those gruesome murders. Good day!"

And with that, he's gone.

I'm left staring at the space he's just vacated as I replay the entire conversation all over.

He'd been nothing but courteous, yet why is my first instinct to run away?

And it's not in the way that Caleb makes me feel—a combination of danger and seduction that borders more on animalistic attraction than actual terror. With Mr. Nicholson, the only word that comes to mind is revulsion—as if my body knows something that my mind does not.

"Agh," I exclaim in frustration as I bring my hands to my temples, rubbing them furiously in an attempt to alleviate the strain on my mind.

So many theories. So many possibilities. And in the midst of it all are my conflicting feelings.

The more I try to make sense of the things around me, the more I feel like I'm back at the start line.

Yet if there is one universal truth to everything, it's that I can't trust anyone.

Not even...Caleb. Maybe especially Caleb.

And just as I think about him, he appears before me, holding something in his hand...

My eyes widen, and I instinctively take a step back as horror fills me to the brim.

He's carrying my suitcase.

The one that had been stolen.

"The police found this in their investigations," he tells me. "They searched it and there was no money inside, I'm sorry. But your other items should be there," he explains, but I have a hard time listening.

How...fortuitous.

I bring my teeth over my lower lip, slowly biting it as I stare at the suitcase I'd thought forever lost. As I gaze up, I note Caleb's genuine smile, which slowly falls as he realizes I'm not nearly as overjoyed as he'd thought I would be.

"You're not happy?" He asks, almost confused.

"I don't know if I should be," I admit honestly, looking him in the eye and searching for the truth in his gaze.

Who are you, Caleb Hale?

And what the hell is happening in Fairydale?

BACK AT THE HALE MANOR, Caleb retreats to his office, telling me he has to take care of some business while I head to the drawing room to use the telephone again.

I'm still unsure what Caleb does for a living. I'd asked him a couple of times, and though he always avoids questions about the war and the army, he'd told me he has a private equity firm and he conducts his work remotely, mainly via post and telephone, with the rare occasions where he needs to go out of town for a meeting.

I hadn't probed more since I'm not particularly educated in how private equity firms function, but I'd still found it a little odd that he could get so much work done from home.

More than anything, I'd been shocked when he'd delivered, as asked, a notarized letter that detailed his net worth.

And it had been...something.

He owns properties all around the country, and his liquid assets are in the hundreds of millions of dollars. Right away, I'd felt a little embarrassed for being threatened for my measly one million dollar inheritance.

Still, better be safe than sorry—especially considering how fast he'd declared his interest in me.

I do share the attraction, and maybe it's because I'm neither experienced nor as daring, but I find it hard to keep up with his grandiose declarations. And though I do like him—maybe feel something more for him—I fear he's going at a much faster pace than I expected, or than I can keep up with.

Alone in the drawing room, I dial the number and wait for the connection to be made, hoping this time I will be able to reach Allison.

I'd already promised to call earlier, but with everything that had happened, I completely forgot.

"Darcy! Finally! I was worried about you," Allison's voice finally comes through, and I breathe out relieved.

"There aren't that many telephones in Fairydale," I chuckle.

"You must tell me everything! I've been thinking about you day and night."

For a moment, I truly debate telling her *everything*. But I don't want to worry her needlessly, so I give her a simplified version of Fairydale—one that doesn't include the so-called *odd* deaths.

"One million dollars?" She exclaims when I tell her about the will.

"Darcy, we never imagined that type of sum. That's... You would never have to work again with that type of money."

"You think I made the right decision to agree to the conditions?" I ask hesitantly.

"Of course! Darcy! For Goodness' sake, it's *one million dollars.* I would have thought you mad had you *not* agreed to the conditions. It's only two months. Just think about all the things you'll be able to do with that money. The books you could buy. The vacations you could take."

I smile as she proceeds to give me an example of everything I could have with that money—things we could only ever dream of before.

"We are going to take a vacation. I'm taking you with me to England," I tell her. "Do you think I'd forget about my favorite girl?"

"You better," she chuckles. "I'll even help you snag an Englishman."

"About that..." I bite my lip. "I met someone."

There's a screech at the end of the line before she comes back, the questions pouring out of her just as I knew they would.

"What? Who? Where? In Fairydale? Good Lord, Darcy, I swear to God that if you don't tell me every single detail I will take the first train there to see it for myself," she rambles on and I can't help but smile.

Her buoyancy was what I've been missing all along.

"He's from Fairydale," I tell her, giving her a brief description of Caleb and the fact that he makes me feel more alive than I've ever felt before.

"Oh my, Darcy! If you're interested in him then he must be something! How many times have I tried to convince you to go on a date and you never agreed?"

I can almost see her shaking her head at me.

"Well, they weren't him," I blush as I say the words.

"Oh, do I bet. Now I can't wait to meet him," she declares

We speak a little longer before her time on the telephone is over and we say our goodbyes, promising to catch up again soon.

After the call ends, I go back to my room, determined to go through my suitcase and see what's still inside.

Yet as I get to the corridor, I come across Caleb.

He's leaning against the wall, almost as if he knew I was coming.

"You're done with your business?" I ask as I stop by his side.

He nods, his eyes glued to me, that hunger he's always trying to subdue making its way to the surface. A shiver of awareness goes down my back, and though I try to give him a small smile, my lips are too shaky to stay in place.

He takes a step forward.

I take a step back.

There's an intensity rolling off him that scares me. There seems to be a single-minded purpose to his stride—*me*. And I'm not sure I'm ready for that.

We waltz around each other until my back meets the wall, his hands landing on either side of my head.

Leaning in, he only stops when he's less than an inch away from my face.

"What did you talk to your friend about?" he rasps, his breath caressing my lips.

"Just a little bit of this, a little bit of that," I mumble nervously. "I told her about Fairydale and that..."

"That?" He raises a brow.

"That I met someone," I swallow hard as I bring my eyes to his. They're so black his pupils blend into his irises, the effect immediate on my senses. I don't know how I could have ever mistaken their color for anything else.

"Really?" he drawls, the right corner of his mouth curling up. "And how is this person that you...met?"

"He's..." I blink, taken aback by his intensity.

His brows go up as he awaits my answer. Though his tone is playful, the atmosphere is heavy, his breathing equally so.

"Sometimes he's a bad man. Sometimes he's a gentleman," I whisper.

He smirks, and my eyes are drawn to his mouth.

"And what am I now, darlin'?"

"Now... You want to be bad," I say as I notice he's closer than before, his lips almost on mine.

"Will you let me be bad, Darcy?"

I blink, unsure how to answer the question.

Part of me wants this—*his kiss*—but the other part of me is still unsure.

"What if I want to be real bad, Darcy darlin'? Will you let me?"

"Define bad," I speak softly, looking him in the eye with a mix of desire and apprehension.

A wide smile appears on his face.

"Ah, sweetheart, if I have to define it you're not ready for it," he chuckles.

Just as I'm about to breathe out in relief at the small respite, he surprises me by leaning further in, brushing his lips across the tip of my nose.

"Let's give you a tour of the house. You've seen very little so far," he says right as he steps away from me, taking my hand in his and leading me down the corridor.

I'm flushed, my entire body burning with...something.

How can he go from seductive to casual in the span of a second?

My pulse is through the roof and I get the urge to fan myself, but I won't give him the benefit of knowing how much that one moment affected me.

Despite not being ready for what he sees as *bad,* that doesn't mean I'm not curious about it.

I'd heard some details about intimacy from Allison, but I hadn't paid much attention back then. I remember her telling me her first time was uncomfortable but that it got much better with time and practice. Now I wish I'd listened and asked more questions—just to have more knowledge on the topic and not feel so painfully naïve about it.

"Caleb," I muster the courage to ask just as we reach the landing of the stairs.

He turns to me, his head tilted to the side as he awaits me to speak.

My entire face must be flaming red at this point and after biting my lip for the tenth time, I finally blurt it out.

"Have you been with many women?"

I instantly avert my gaze, unable to believe I'd actually asked the question.

"Forget it," I say immediately, waving my hands in a stop gesture.

He regards me amused, and I feel like expiring on the spot.

Damn me and my curiosity.

"What do you think?" he inquires gently, no reproach in his voice.

I don't dare answer for fear my voice will betray me, so I just give him a nod, suggesting affirmative.

His smile widens, and bringing his mouth to my ear, he whispers.

"The answer is no."

Then he resumes walking.

He doesn't expand on that—doesn't clarify or quantify. And I've already met my embarrassment quota for the day to probe for more.

Yet the fact that he said no...a warm, fuzzy feeling develops in my lower belly.

He walks towards the main entrance of the house and I run after him, excitement thrumming through me, as well as a small sliver of anticipation.

"The Hales have tried to preserve as much of the original features of the house as they could," he explains as he points to the ladies and gents' rooms on each side.

"How many rooms are in total?"

"About sixty? I think it's around there," he says, and for a moment I think he's joking.

"You're serious?"

He nods.

"Don't worry, I won't show you all the bedrooms," he chuckles. "If we go forward, you'll see the main gallery. This houses the Creed art collection, and it has some extremely rare pieces he collected during his time," he speaks as we step into the grandiose gallery.

Larger than a museum, the gallery's walls are all adorned with various paintings—some by famous artists such as Jacques-Louis David, Rembrandt, Peter Paul Rubens, or even Botticelli, while a few are by an unknown artist signed AR. One in particular catches my eye. It's of a couple posing together, their faces painted in a colorful design as they gaze at each other lovingly.

"This is absolutely wonderful. I'm speechless, Caleb," I utter in awe as I look around.

There are also statues scattered around, placed strategically to give the impression they are real people in the room casually going about their day.

As I stop in front of one after another, I recognize the names of some artists, such as Bernini and Michelangelo. But more striking is the fact that the majority of pieces are millennia old, dating from Ancient Rome, Greece, Egypt, and even Mesopotamia. These must be truly one of a kind.

"Dear Lord. How is it possible? These must be priceless," I blurt out as I stop in front of a pair of statues of Egyptian origin—what I assume to be the depictions of a pharaoh and his consort.

"They are," he smiles, a deep melancholy reflected in his gaze.

"Shouldn't these belong in a museum? So that everyone can enjoy them?"

He's silent for a moment before he slowly shakes his head.

"They might be part of world history, but to some...they're also part of personal history," he says cryptically, stopping in front of one of the statues.

I walk towards him, gazing up at the piece that holds his undivided attention.

It looks to be Roman or Greek, though my knowledge is minimal at best. The sculpture depicts a woman holding some dainty flowers in her hand. At her feet, a sword is interwoven with serpents coiling up her leg.

"Is it Artemis?" I inquire as I inspect it.

Caleb shakes his head.

"She wasn't a Greek Goddess."

"Then who was she?"

He smiles, looking fondly at the statue before lightly shaking his head.

"You're welcome to come here whenever you want to look your fill.

There is one more gallery on the first floor, but it's been closed for years now," he resumes his tour, briefly showing me the front terraces, the drawing room and the dining room.

"And here is the library, which I'm sure you will enjoy," he tells me as he pushes the double doors open.

Like heaven opening before me, my mouth simply drops open in awe. From floor to ceiling, bookcases fill all the walls of the room, more rows piling up in the middle and leaving only one small area for reading.

"How many books are there?"

"Thousands? Tens of thousands? No one knows at this point," Caleb explains. "Another area you might want to explore more. You'll find a great deal of diversity. The Hales have updated a good portion of it," he points to some of the shelves in the middle, "but a lot are classical works. Some first editions, too," he winks at me.

He lets me wander about the room for a little, amusement pulling at his lips as he sees me gush about every little thing I see.

But how could I not? Katrina hadn't been kidding when she'd told me the house was like a museum. Most of the things I've seen so far *should* be in a museum to be admired by everyone. And these books...

"I'm going to read as many as I can," I declare immediately.

Caleb chuckles.

"You're welcome to all of them. You can even take some to your room."

The moment he gives me permission, I waste no time in picking a couple Jane Austen novels—*all first editions!*

I cradle them to my chest like the precious babies they are, barely resisting the urge to open them and inhale the scent like a creep. I don't think Caleb would find that very cute.

He watches me indulgently, letting me take my time as I peruse some of the titles. But I decide to do so more at length later instead of wasting his time now.

"We can go," I announce, hugging the books tightly.

Shaking his head in amusement, he takes me to the first floor.

"There are two wings. That one," he points to the left, "is where our bedrooms are. The one on the right is where the master's chambers are. It's been closed for a few decades now, and no one goes there."

I nod, following him to the left.

"Where does the family sleep then?"

"Second floor. *Everyone* sleeps on the second floor."

"Everyone but us?" I frown.

"I like these rooms better. They don't."

"Why?"

He shrugs.

"They think they are haunted." When he sees my eyes widen, he amends. "They aren't. I can vouch for that since I've been sleeping here for years."

"If you say so," I mutter under my breath, suddenly feeling a prickling of awareness at the surface of my skin.

Damn it, why did he have to mention ghosts?

Especially since the corridor is filled with portraits of older Hales, all looking rigid and stern.

A shiver goes down my back and I look away.

"I won't show you the second floor since it's mainly the living space for my parents and my grandmother. There are a lot of storage rooms, but other than that, nothing much to see," he explains and I nod. "But I have one more thing to show you," he says, his eyes sparkling with mischief as he goes towards the end of the corridor.

I eagerly dash after him, so excited about my surroundings that he could show me anything at this point and I'd be in awe. Especially as I hold the precious books closer, sighing in contentment as I imagine myself in my room at night, exploring the treasures hidden within the pages.

A small giggle escapes me, but I slap my hand over my mouth before Caleb can hear me.

"Here," he says as he pushes the door open.

Taking a step inside, I blink a couple of times as my eyes adjust to the bright lighting.

"It's...an art studio?"

"It is," he replies, pride reflected in his voice.

Then it dawns on me.

"It's *your* art studio."

He grins.

"Welcome to my sanctuary."

Most of the furniture in the room has been covered with white sheets, splatters of paint evident everywhere. There are canvases crowded in all corners, some finished, some in progress.

His main materials are by the window to capture the best light—a small chair facing a huge canvas with scattered paints and supplies all over the floor.

"I didn't know you painted," I say softly, my lips pulling up in a smile.

"It's not something I openly advertise," he shrugs, though I can see he's watching my reactions closely—almost anxiously.

Taking a step deeper into the room, I catch glimpses of some of his works, and the breath leaves my lungs at his talent.

"You should," I turn, telling him emphatically. "You definitely should. This is wonderful, Caleb," I praise honestly, my eyes arrested to the sight before me.

It's a simple landscape—a balcony on a cliff and the violent ocean. But each stroke has been carefully placed on the canvas to give a realistic yet terrifying effect. It's nature at its worst, merciless and unforgiving.

"Would you pose for me?"

I whip my head around, my eyes widening.

"You want to paint...me?"

He nods, his expression serious.

At once, I can tell this isn't merely a hobby for him. It's an endeavor close to his heart, and by sharing it with me, he's also sharing a part of himself.

"I'd be honored," I murmur.

He seemingly exhales in relief, almost as if everything hinged on my answer.

"As you can see, I don't paint people," he gives me a tight smile. "I haven't in... a long time," he confesses.

"Then I'm even more honored that you chose me," I blush.

He merely smiles. A different one than I'd seen from him—a warm, genuine smile that speaks of the most pure happiness.

The thought that I would have instilled that feeling in him makes my pulse race, butterflies dancing in my stomach. If before he'd drawn me to him with his raw masculinity, now it's that glimpse into his vulnerability that cements the fact that I'm falling for him.

I keep to the sidelines as Caleb moves some of the furniture around, removing the sheet off an ornate blue sofa. He pulls it towards the window and arranges it to be directly in front of his seat.

"Come," he takes my hand, leading me to the sofa and instructing me to sit down.

"I didn't realize we'd start now. Maybe you want me to put on a nice dress? Or some makeup?"

I'm wearing a white button-up sundress. It's nothing fancy and I imagine when painting someone's portrait you'd want them to be dressed in their finest clothes.

"You're perfect as you are, Darcy," he tells me when he sees my pinched brows. "I want to capture *you*, not an artificial version of you."

He's behind the canvas, a brush in his hand as his entire expression changes, a deep concentration settling over his features as he draws the initial strokes.

I nod, my nerves slowly easing. But once that concern is out of the way, a new one enters my mind. Never having modeled for anything, I suddenly feel anxious at the thought of doing this all wrong. And as I try to sit still, my hands itch to move, as do my feet and every little muscle in my body.

"You don't have to pretend to be made of stone," he suddenly chuckles.

I blink, looking at him in question.

"You're beyond rigid," he continues, and I stiffen more.

Shaking his head in amusement, he places his brush down, rising from his chair and coming towards me.

"Relax," he moves behind the sofa, his fingers on my shoulders as he softly kneads my flesh. "I want you to pose naturally. Forget about me as the artist and look at me as the man."

"What... What do you mean?" I ask softly.

He leans down, his face next to mine as he speaks.

"I want to capture your expression, darlin'. That look of wonder you always have when you gaze at me. The mix of longing, curiosity, fear...terror."

"Terror?" I wet my lips, looking away from him but feeling his nearness in my bones. His breath fans my cheek, his fingers deftly working my flesh. "What do you mean?"

"You can't lie to me, Darcy," he whispers. "Your eyes can *never* lie to me," he continues as his hands trail down, from my shoulders to my clavicle and lower.

My breath becomes labored.

"You desire me, but you're also terrified of it. Of me, of yourself, of what would happen if you give in..."

"Give in?" the question comes out breathless, my heart thundering in my chest.

His thick voice still in my ear, his hands settle on the buttons of my bodice.

I gasp when suddenly one button pops free.

I move to stop him, but his mesmerizing voice stops me—hypnotizing me into compliance.

"What if I asked you to shed all your inhibitions? Renounce all mores and morals until you're a blank canvas. Until mine is the only brush that can paint you to life..."

Another button pops free.

An intoxicating stillness claims my body, my brain foggy, my senses both sluggish and fully on alert. Anticipation builds inside me, and with his voice acting as my guide, I can only do as he says.

All other thoughts disappear from my mind until only he remains —him and his touch.

"Forget everything you know and embrace everything you don't," his decadent voice envelops me, shudders claiming my body as I let his deep rumble penetrate every inch of my skin.

I'm lost in the abyss, and he is my Vergil—the only one who can bring me to the light.

Or...drown me in the dark.

"That's it, Darcy darlin'. Give yourself to pure feeling. Abandon everything that holds you back," he speaks with a sensual confidence that demands my full compliance.

A third button pops free, his palms sliding over the swell of my almost-naked breast.

A hiss escapes him, his warm air transferring to me, his breath *my* breath.

Inhaling sharply, a sudden lightheadedness overwhelms me and a profound feeling of breathlessness—when you're on the edge of asphyxiating, but you never quite cross the threshold.

His fingers graze my left breast, his touch lingering on top of my heart as he traces the tear-shaped birthmark on my skin.

"Caleb..." a low whimper escapes me at his probing touch.

"Shhh, Darcy darlin'," he murmurs, his mouth opening over the pulse point just under my ear as he gives me a slow lick. "I am the brush," he blows hot air over the damp patch of skin. "And you are my canvas," he says right before his lips part over my skin again, this time a sharp pain spearing through my senses as my body rebels against the foreign intrusion.

I gasp, attempting to move out of his hold, but his hands hold me captive.

The pain intensifies, and even through the fog that's laid siege over my mind I can sense that he's broken the surface of my skin until he's drawn blood.

I am frozen in place as his lips move up, from my neck to my cheek, all the while smearing the blood over my pale skin.

"I am the brush," he rasps thickly. "And you are my canvas. Mine to create. Mine to breathe life into."

A low howl vibrates in the air, the sound as piercing as it is...inhuman.

Shock envelops me from head to toe as adrenaline pumps into my veins. Throwing him off me, I jump out of the seat.

"I don't think we're talking about painting anymore," I whisper, gazing at him in horror.

His entire mouth is stained with red, a trickle of blood running down his chin.

Slowly, as if barely daring to move, I bring my hand to my neck, feeling for the gash and the blood that's still pouring out of the wound.

His eyes are eerily blank as his mouth curves into a sardonic smile.

"Ah, but that look, Darcy darlin'. *That* is what I want to paint," he says as he flashes me his blood stained teeth—red against stark white.

True terror engulfs me and I dash from the studio, running straight for my room and locking the door behind me.

Panic unlike any other swells in my heart, the wound he'd inflicted on me radiating with pain.

Opening the door to the bathroom, I flick the light switch on as I bring my gaze to the mirror.

My mouth slowly parts in shock just as I bring my fingers to my neck.

The pain is there.

The feel of his mouth on my skin is there.

But there's not one mark on my neck.

Not one stain of red on my skin, though I could have sworn I felt him paint me with blood.

There's absolutely...nothing.

Chapter Eleven

"I'm going crazy," I chant to myself as I hug my knees to my chest.

Not only is my skin unblemished. My dress is all buttoned up, not one wrinkle in place.

Either I'd imagined everything, or...

"God, what the hell is happening?" I bring my hands to my temples as I squeeze my eyes shut.

For the first time, I have to entertain the idea that maybe it's not the town.

Maybe it's...me.

I'm becoming more unhinged with every passing day, seeing things that aren't there, imagining things that aren't there. What's next? Talking to imaginary friends?

But I'm already doing that to an extent, am I not? In fact, I'm doing something far worse. I'm falling in love with a figment of my imagination, conjuring up scenarios and building an entire relationship in my head.

For hours, I don't dare move an inch, the terror from before—be it imaginary or not—still fresh in my mind. It's late at night when I finally decide to get out of my room again. And it's not because I've suddenly gained more courage; it's because my stomach will not stop rumbling with hunger.

Lighting a candle, I take it with me as I slowly push my door open, looking left and right before I take a step forward.

Even if nothing happened with Caleb, I don't know if I can look him in the eye right now. Not when I'll either confirm I'm going crazy, or that he is the crazy one.

Taking a deep breath, I make my way down the corridor.

The candle in my hand is only offering *some* light—enough to illuminate a narrow path, but not much else. Not all rooms and areas of the house have electricity, and according to Caleb, some outlets are faulty so it's better to have candles on hand at all times.

On each side of me the corridor is bathed in darkness, shadows dancing with the flame of the candle, some falling over the walls, some over the paintings of the long-dead Hales.

Suddenly, I stop, my brows knit together in confusion.

Is there not one painting depicting the Creeds? Why is everything of the Hales?

Both Katrina and Caleb had spoken highly of the Creeds, and the Hale family had clearly gone to great lengths to preserve everything as it was. Then why not the paintings with the previous owners, too?

Turning with my candle, a gust of wind makes the flame flicker, its shadow falling over one of the paintings.

It's of a woman who looks to be in her thirties when the portrait had been painted. Black hair and green eyes with laugh lines at the corners, she had a youthful appearance.

Gazing at the bottom, I make out that this is Lydia Hale. According to what I remember from Katrina, Lydia was a Creed before her marriage.

I continue walking, using the light to study the other paintings as well, noticing all Hales have in common the dark hair and light eyes.

As I think more about it, I realize that everyone in the family has either green or dark blue eyes. I haven't seen any Hale with dark eyes.

Only Caleb.

Frowning, I point the candle to the last portrait, surprised to see it's of Rhiannon herself when she was younger. She was very pretty, and I have to wonder why she never married. From what I understood, she is Connor Hale's aunt—his father's older sister.

Deep in thought, I don't look where I'm walking and I trip on a small ledge. My eyes widen in shock, my first thought going to the candle and making sure I don't make any sudden movements that would extinguish the flame, or God forbid, fling the candle around and set the house on fire.

I teeter on the balls of my feet as I seek to adjust my equilibrium, the flame moving with me.

My lips tug into a triumphant smile when I manage to keep myself upright. Yet as I gaze forward, at the light emanating from the candle and reflecting in front of me, I see a shadow.

The shadow of a man.

I turn, yet there's no one.

I turn again, and again, going in a circle and covering the entire perimeter, moving my candle around as my pulse spikes, fear spreading through my veins.

"Is someone there?" I ask on a whisper.

Caleb's words about the wing being haunted echo in my mind, and I squeeze my eyes shut.

There's no such thing as ghosts.

I say that mantra a couple of times in my head, taking a step forward, and then the next. When I reach the landing of the stairs, I release a relieved breath.

"There's no such thing as ghosts," I murmur out loud, my mouth curling up in satisfaction as I look around.

Going to the stairs, I grip the balustrade tightly as I carefully make my way downstairs.

One step at a time. Just as I take one breath at a time.

Suddenly, I stop, my spine stiffening just as a whoosh of cold air passes by me.

The temperature seemingly drops out of nowhere, my breath coming out as steam right in front of me.

"Don't be Catherine," I mutter to myself, my eyes more closed than open.

At this point I'd rather fall down the stairs than open my eyes and come face to face with a ghost. If past experience is of relevance, I'm sure I will somehow heal. But seeing a ghost? Only a lobotomy could cure that—and even that might not solve my issue.

Lizzie...Run...

Despite my best efforts to *not* come face to face with the ghost, my eyes snap open the moment I hear the low whispered words.

Big mistake!

The small flame of the candle is oriented right in front of the most unfortunate looking face I've ever seen—so much so I don't know if I should run, swoon, or maybe pray for my death all at once. Especially as I get a better view of the creature—with its mangled flesh, absent eyes and only one mouth that opens wide on a loud roar.

"You're not real..." I whisper in one last attempt to convince myself I *am* crazy.

Yet as his hand shoots out towards me, claws glinting in the dim candlelight, it dawns on me that even if I'm crazy, I'd rather not have that thing touch me.

Pushing the flaming tip of the candle into his open mouth, I waste no time in giving it a kick before running away.

A loud screech penetrates the air as the creature's head burns in the darkness of the night.

With a strength I never knew I possessed, I dash down the stairs, intent on getting out of the house.

If the ghost belongs in the house, then that should solve it. But if it's a figment of my imagination... Well, then I suppose I'll see.

Running straight for the foyer, I'm barely aware of the steps following me, as well as the loud, tortured noises coming out from the creature.

Yet just as I get to the door, my hand on the knob as I try to turn it, I'm caught.

The lock turns in place without anyone touching it, and just as I try to escape towards the gents' room, the creature is in front of me. Its head is half-illuminated, and I realize it swallowed the fire from the candle.

With a loud roar, it pushes me against the wall, keeping me in place.

What... How the hell is this possible?

Even as I get a better look at the horror that is its face, I'm still of half a mind that I'm dreaming. Or going crazy. After all, how could this be real?

How can *any* of this be real?

One hand is around my throat, pushing me high above the ground just as I try to struggle, pushing against him and kicking at his gross skin-like surface. His other hand raised high, I barely manage to notice the sharp claw before it's embedded in my stomach.

I yelp in pain, but it doesn't stop, Dragging the blade-like claw against my stomach, he makes a long incision.

At the same time, another piercing scream penetrates the air. A voice I'm well familiar with.

Lizzie!

An even more powerful roar erupts in the grand hall, the echo all but making the walls of the house bend under the acoustic pressure.

The creature is off me, taking a step back and howling at the new presence.

Slumping to the ground, I can barely catch my breath as pain radiates from my belly, blood gushing out in rivulets. Yet as I look at the creature, I find it on its knees, seemingly being attacked from all directions by an invisible force.

With a loud cry, the creature disintegrates right before my eyes.

I'm so stunned, I can barely move. The pain is a continuous pulsation at the surface of my skin. As I hold my hand over my wound, I take a few fortifying breaths before I push myself to my feet.

Wobbling a little, I try to remember the way to the pantry where Caleb had said they stored medical supplies.

Without my candle, everything *should* be dark. But somehow I can see. Somehow, a low light illuminates my path and *just* my path as I force myself to continue even as I grind my teeth against the pain.

Lizzie...

The whisper is faint, but after everything I've been through, it's unmistakable.

"Amon?" I say the name out loud, half of me feeling silly for even entertaining the thought. Yet half of me... Half of me wants to weep with joy on the off chance this might be true.

If monsters exist...then my Amon has to exist, too.

"Amon, it's you, isn't it?" I ask softly.

There's no reply, just a soft caress against my cheek, something akin to the sweetest kiss.

As I reach the pantry, I search for the light switch, grinning like a fool when the room turns bright.

Immediately, I look down, almost afraid to look at the damage.

"No," I shake my head. "No, no, no."

This cannot be possible.

My hands are clean. No blood. Just as there is no blood on my gown, nor is there a cut.

Everything is as it's supposed to be.

I blink in shock, hoping that by repeatedly closing and opening my eyes the sight before me will be different. But it's not.

If...If it had been just my skin that—by some miracle—would have healed, then the gown would still be torn, wouldn't it?

It would be...

Tears of frustration prick at my lids.

"Amon?" I twirl. "Please tell me you're here. Please... Please tell me I'm not going crazy," I whisper as tears make their way down my cheeks. "What's happening? I..."

But doesn't this make me even more deranged? The fact that I'm asking a *ghost* about my mental state. The fact that I'm *hoping* there might be a ghost.

Falling to the ground, I can't contain my hopelessness anymore as a sob racks my body, tears running down my face until I can barely see anymore.

I sit on the floor and I cry.

"Who's there?" Someone asks before a man's figure fills the doorway.

Raising my gaze, I look at him through tear-streaked eyes.

"Mr. Hale?" I inquire pitifully.

"Miss Darcy? Is that you? I thought you were a damned ghost," he curses before he catches himself, apologizing.

"Ghost?" My lips tremble.

"Here, let me help you," he says as he extends his hand to me.

Glancing at it for a few seconds—far more than I should have—I eventually relent, letting him pull me to my feet.

"You might need these," he continues as he pulls on some paper towels, handing them to me.

"Thank you," I murmur, using the towels to wipe at my face.

"What happened?" He inquires gently, no doubt sensing my altered state.

"There are ghosts here, aren't there?' I swallow as I ask. The last thing I need is another person mocking me and challenging my perception of what's real and what's not.

But even as I brace myself for a dismissive laugh and a shrug, Mr. Hale doesn't do either.

He stares at me for a moment before he nods, giving me a tight smile.

"I assume Rhiannon didn't give you the rundown of the place yet, did she?"

I'm too stunned by his reaction, so I can only shake my head.

Without me saying anything, he starts speaking.

"No one knows exactly when Creed had this house built or what exactly happened here, but everyone has had an odd encounter here, one way or another. You'll get used to it," he chuckles.

"To ghosts?"

He nods, his countenance very matter-of-factly.

"If you don't annoy them they usually leave you alone. Although the first floor is a little more populated," he adds pensively.

It takes me a moment to digest his words. He didn't just admit that ghosts are real and that they are predominantly on *my* floor, did he?

"You just told me ghosts are real, and now you're telling me to be pals with them?"

He proceeds to give me a careless shrug, and my mouth drops open in shock.

"Well," he scratches the back of his head. "No one's asking you to be friends with them. Although Rhiannon is." He laughs. "My aunt has a few eccentricities, you will find."

I swallow uncomfortably.

Just one second ago I thought I was surely going insane, and now Mr. Hale is telling me the Hale matriarch has a playground for ghosts?

My jaw would be on the ground if not for recent events.

"I'm not sure what I saw was a ghost though," I say slowly.

He frowns, turning and offering me his full attention.

"What do you mean?"

"It was... Obviously, I don't know what ghosts look like," I say, "but this was more...corporeal," I explain, describing what the thing had looked like.

From mild amusement, Mr. Hale's expression turns to stone.

"You say this thing was in the house? In *this* house?"

I nod, recounting how he'd chased after me. I refrain from telling him, however, that he'd injured me, or that I'd almost immediately healed from those injuries—I may have a theory regarding that.

His lips flatten into a thin line as he appears deep in thought.

"I'll have to speak with my aunt about this," he suddenly says. "Don't worry about it, Miss Darcy. We'll make sure you're safe here."

"I don't understand... Was," I gulp down. "Was that thing real?"

He doesn't confirm, nor deny.

"Fairydale isn't a stranger to these types of situations. But... Not in this context."

"When you say types of situations, what do you mean? Everyone tells me how odd Fairydale is, but no one tells me *why*," I raise my voice, tipping my chin up so he can see I want to be taken seriously—and that I need to hear the truth.

He gives me a pitiful smile.

"I think you'll find out soon enough why Fairydale is so...odd."

Removing a candle from a place above my head, he takes out a lighter from his pants and lights it up for me.

"Take care, Miss Darcy," he gives me a nod before he turns to leave.

"What about Caleb?"

At that, he stops in his tracks.

"What *about* Caleb?" he repeats in a low, almost ominous tone.

"Is he..." I bite my lip in apprehension, almost dreading asking the question—and receiving the answer. "Is he *odd*, too?"

"My son is the most honorable man you could ever meet," he rasps, the answer more emotional than I would have expected. "He has the most pure soul. It's just that..." he releases a ragged groan, almost as if he were physically in pain. "That damned war broke something inside of him. He wasn't like this before. He wasn't..." he shakes his head. "Don't believe what people say about him, Miss Darcy. He's the finest young man out there."

I nod slowly, afraid I triggered something within him. But that doesn't stop me from voicing out my stance, and the fact that I'm not as gullible as everyone seems to think I am.

"There is something no one is telling me, Mr. Hale. Something that's being *purposefully* kept from me," I tell him in an even tone. "I don't know what it is, and I don't know if this has anything to do with your family, or the Pierces, or the Nicholsons, but I will eventually find out," I give him a tight smile. "I've spent my entire life at the bottom, and when you're down, there's only one direction you can go."

"Oh, how wrong you are Miss Darcy," he chuckles. "Maybe you've known what it's like to be at the bottom, but I doubt you've known hell."

I narrow my eyes at him.

"That is what awaits you. And everyone in Fairydale. *Hell*," he emphasizes the word, giving me a pitiful look before turning to leave.

I stare at his retreating figure, his words confusing me even more.

Yet despite that, he did give me one confirmation that I'm not *entirely* insane.

Something happened today.

"Are you here, Amon?" I ask softly, not making to move yet. Maybe because he'd spoken to me here before, but I want to linger in hopes he might grace me again with his presence.

Only a light breeze answers me back, enough to make the flame of the candle flicker.

My lips tip up.

"You're not a figment of my imagination, are you?" I probe softly.

Another gust of wind, this time extinguishing my fire before setting it ablaze again.

My smile widens.

"Thank you for saving me," I murmur. "I know it was you. At the fire. For days I thought I must have hallucinated it because my heart's been inexplicably yearning for you. But you were there. You saved me. You probably healed me, too, didn't you? Just like you did now..." I wet my lips, struggling to find the right words to convey everything I feel.

The same light breeze caresses my cheek, the contact producing the same type of reaction I'd always had in his presence—comfort, belonging...*home.*

And that's how I know it's truly him.

Emotion bursts forth in my chest, all the accumulated longing spilling forth and choking me with the magnitude of what I feel for him.

"What happened to you, Amon?" I whisper, a tear falling down my cheek. "What were we to each other?"

Lizzie...

The echo is so soft, I barely hear it.

But I know what it means.

I was his Lizzie and he was my Amon. And he's still protecting me.

"What's happening here, Amon? *Why* am I here?"

Don't trust them...

My eyes widen, understanding dawning on me.

"It was you," I murmur in awe. "You were the one warning me all this time, weren't you? Protecting me? All along..." I shake my head in disbelief.

Yet something inside of me tells me that this is right. From the beginning, Amon has been there for me, helping me, protecting me.

"Can I trust Caleb?" I suddenly ask about the matter that's been eating at me. Because if I'm not crazy... If nothing I've seen or experienced so far has been a product of my imagination, then the incidents with Caleb couldn't have been just in my mind.

But just as the words are out of my mouth, a fine mist appears before me. One second. That's how long it lasts before it dissipates, and with it, Amon's presence too.

I don't know how I'm able to feel it, but I do.

He's not here anymore.

And he never answered my question.

Getting my bearings together, I try to ignore the pounding of my heart or the echo of fear still resounding within me as I cross the ground floor of the house to get to the stairs.

Even now I feel as though there are eyes on me, strange entities ready to pounce on me the moment I have my guard down.

Now that I can no longer sense Amon's presence around, I feel like a soldier without armor.

My eyes skitter all over the place, every step I take expecting to bump into another unfortunate looking creature—as if I don't already have enough nightmare material for years to come.

Reaching the first floor, I head straight for my room, intent on putting today's incidents behind me as much as I can. And maybe, make a decision tomorrow.

I'm still unsure of the future. Should I just give up and go back home?

But what am I going back to? That's the most important question.

I no longer have a job. I don't have a place to live, and I barely have any money to my name.

Though I don't doubt the nuns would take me in, how long am I going to depend on their goodwill? They barely have resources for the orphanage as it is. The last thing they need is for me—an *adult*—to come and take food from a child's mouth.

Yet the alternative is...staying.

Just as I'm about to open the door to my room, I stop, an idea crossing my mind.

Surely, if my mind didn't play tricks on me this afternoon, the studio should be at the end of the hallway. And inside, I should find the painting Caleb started.

I hesitate for a moment, almost afraid of confirming it was not, indeed, a hallucination.

For all his faults, Caleb has managed to worm his way inside my heart, and I can't deny I *do* feel something for him. But I'm in an environment where I cannot trust anyone, least of all myself. How can I possibly trust my heart?

Especially since his behavior towards me has been, at times, questionable.

I may not be experienced with men, but that doesn't mean I lack common sense. And that's telling me that he's been repeatedly trying to cross lines, and when he hadn't gotten the desired response from me, he'd resorted to making me think I'm crazy.

But even while I consider the alternative that I am *not* hallucinating or imagining things, I can't deny the fact that, each time, there has been no tangible evidence to refute Caleb's claims.

That only leaves me with one option—checking the studio for myself.

Before I know it, my feet take me to the end of the hallway.

Holding the candle in one hand, I use the other to turn the knob, a soft gasp of surprise escaping me when I easily push the door open.

It's not locked.

If he didn't want me snooping around, or if he had something to hide, Caleb could have easily locked the door.

Stepping inside the room, I try to orient myself. The furniture is just as before, covered by white sheets, and canvases are scattered all around.

My lips tremble as they slowly spread into an optimistic smile.

If this is the same, then the rest should be too.

I go deeper into the room, stopping by the window.

Just as I suspected, the sofa I'd sat on is unveiled, and as I lower the candle towards it, I notice the color matches my memory.

It *is* the same sofa.

Turning, I spot the painting materials and the canvas sitting on its wooden support.

I swallow hard against the wave of discomfort that hits me as I move towards the canvas.

When I shine light over it, I find that it's blank.

"No..." I shake my head, biting my lip in frustration.

Thinking he might have hidden it so he could once more tell me it's all in my head, I turn my attention to the other canvases in the room. I place the candle on the little stool, dragging it in the middle of the room as I pull on the row of canvases deposited in a corner.

The first few ones depict sceneries, like the one Caleb had shown me. But as I pull one from the back, moving it towards the light, it's to find an entirely different sight.

A whimper escapes my lips as I grab the candle, holding it close to the surface of the canvas. As I stare at what I can only describe as the most lewd picture I've ever seen, drops of wax fall onto its surface. Yet I can't find it in me to care that I'm destroying the painting.

Not when the subject is so...vulgar.

A naked woman rests against the floor-to-ceiling windows, posing for the artist. Her arms are raised above her head, a dreamy expression on her face as she arches her back, the pose seductive and inviting. One leg is flexed forward, and the artist had captured her lean and shapely forms.

Swallowing hard, I drag more of the canvases from the back, lying them on the ground.

A similar sight greets me. One more lewd than the other, each painting is of the same naked woman. Like a collection of photographs, the paintings depict her in different poses and locations, but always naked.

In one, she's laying on a massive bed, the sheets half tangled around her body as she smiles at the artist. In the next, she's on her belly in the grass, smiling brazenly at the artist, while in another, she's coming out of the ocean, droplets of water coursing down her naked body.

The more I look, the more stunned I become.

But that's not the worst.

As I place the last canvas on the ground, I move the candle over it.

I gasp loudly as my brain has a hard time comprehending the image I'm seeing.

It's the same woman.

She's on her knees, looking up, her eyes big and bright as she undoubtedly gazes at the man in front of her. Her mouth is wide open as she's sucking on something...

My hand trembles, wax spilling right in the middle of the painting where the woman's mouth meets...the man's member.

I blink repeatedly, the sight entirely too shocking.

But more shocking is the expression on the woman's face.

She's enjoying it.

Peering at the man, she gives him a look of pure worship.

His hand is in her hair, almost as if he is urging her forward, his fingers lodged in her scalp yet the woman doesn't seem to be in pain.

If anything, there's a mischievous quality to her, a twinkle in her eyes as she looks up at the man.

She might worship him, but she knows she's the one in control.

Almost as if I'm in a trance, I place the candle on the floor, walking around the room and picking up all the canvases I can find and laying them down, too.

Though I stumble upon a few scenery paintings at first, I eventually come across more of the kind.

They are an erotic diary of sorts, and as I trail with my candle over each and every one of them, it's to find the woman and the man tangled in a more intimate embrace, the scenes becoming more and more shocking for my eyes.

One shows the woman on her belly at the edge of the bed, her buttocks between the man's hands as he slides his length against her.

Another has the woman on top, her arms forward as she rests them on the man's chest. One of the man's hands is on her waist, gripping it tightly, while the other kneads her breast.

But just as they all have in common the pornographic material, there is also the fact that the woman is always clearly visible, her identity out in the open, while the man is shrouded in mystery. His body is in the picture, particularly...that hard part of him. But his face is never visible.

Yet there is one feature, that the more I stare at it, makes me want to cry and rage.

The woman is...*me*.

Maybe I could have put aside the uncanny facial similarity if other features didn't match so perfectly. But it's not just my face that is perfectly depicted, my body too.

Down to the tear-shaped birthmark on my left breast.

I choke back a sob as I realize just how much I've misjudged Caleb.

I'd believed him when he'd told me he had been circumspect while changing my clothes. Instead, what had he done? He must have taken his time to study every part of my body to get all the details right.

And it's not just my birthmark. The more I study the paintings, the more I see other identifying marks. Moles no one knows I have, like the one above my belly button, or the one right above my hip bone.

These are marks no one knows about but that somehow made their way into these paintings.

Yet as soon as the question of Caleb's propriety comes up, Pandora's box suddenly opens.

How can I believe *nothing* happened?

Not only am I staring right in the face of his debauched fantasies, there's also the matter of what he might have done to me while I was passed out.

With the last developments and the unusual rate at which my injuries have been healing, would it be too preposterous to imagine he could have done something after all? That he could have...

My eyes squeeze shut just as my heart hammers in my chest, pain spreading through me like an arrow.

My head, too, is pounding with pain and confusion, and the fact that I no longer know what I *can* believe.

How the hell do I differentiate between what is real and what isn't anymore?

Yet the evidence is staring in front of me—all the pornographic scenes he'd painted of us together. It makes it hard for me to believe that he'd go to this length and not act on his desires if the opportunity arose —if I couldn't voice my objection out loud.

The more I think about it, the more sick to my stomach I feel.

When did he even have the time to paint all of these?

It's been a little more than a week since the cabin incident. How could he have had the time to paint so many of these lewd images?

The questions are endless.

But one fact remains.

Caleb Hale scares me.

Yet as much as this part of him I've uncovered terrifies me, I can't let him get away with this—with thinking he can do whatever he wants to me. Especially since I live in his home.

I don't want to contemplate what he could do at night when I'm sleeping...

A shiver goes down my back at the thought, and even with the door locked I know he could find a way to come inside.

It's his home after all.

And I'm...defenseless.

Swallowing against the wave of nausea that threatens to overtake me, I grab the worst painting—the one where he's holding me down on the bed, his hand around my throat as he pushes his member into me.

With the candle in my other hand, I stride out of the studio, determined to confront Caleb with this before he can get rid of the evidence.

My features are tense, fear filling me to the brim.

Yet I can't let this slide. I can't let him continue, because I *know* he will simply do more.

Until...

Reaching his door, I use the metal holder of the candle to bang against the door.

Waiting anxiously, I'm surprised that I can't hear anything—not even in the stillness of the night. Leaning in, I press my ear to his door.

Nothing.

No movement, nothing.

I bang again, louder this time, all the while listening for any sound.

Again, nothing.

When I bring the metal against the door the third time, the door suddenly opens.

Jumping back, my eyes widen as I come face to face with a shirtless Caleb.

He's only wearing a pair of loose pants hanging low on his hips. His hair is disheveled as if he'd just climbed out of bed—though I heard nothing of the sort.

Still, I can't help that light thump of my heart as my eyes inadvertently slip to his chest, taking in the muscle definition and the v that leads down to...

My cheeks heat up and I suddenly bring my gaze back up, only to find him watching me with amusement. Getting myself together, I remind myself why I'm here—certainly *not* to ogle him.

Muttering a low curse under my breath—*one that would make the nuns swoon*—I push the painting into his chest, almost slapping him with it.

"What's this?" I ask with all the confidence I can muster, pinning him down with my gaze to let him know I'm not playing around—and he's not going to get away with this.

"What *is* this?" he muses, his voice holding the same amusement evident in his features, and one that manages to irk me further.

"What is this, Caleb?" I repeat, demanding he look at the painting.

"A painting?" He raises his brows sheepishly, and if I could, I would probably release steam out of my nostrils with how annoying he is. And good-looking. How the hell can he be handsome *and* a pervert?

His smile widens.

"What are you asking darlin'? Be more specific," he drawls languidly, resting his arm against the frame of the door. Somehow, the pose makes his muscles bulge even more, the veins visible as they are oddly...mesmerizing.

I barely wrench my gaze off his body to look him in the eye—all the while schooling my expression so he doesn't realize that I'm getting flustered.

"I found your paintings. I know you've been..." I swallow, "that you've been..." I continue to stammer, unable to find the words—or the courage to voice them out loud.

"That I've been what?" His brow arches in question, his body angling towards me.

"I know you've been painting me naked," I burst out, my face flaming as the words are out of my mouth. "I knew there was something wrong with you after what you did today," I point at him accusingly. "After you behaved so strangely. I knew it and now I can prove it. You..." I stutter. "You're a pervert!"

A smile plays on his lips as he regards me.

He doesn't defend himself.

He doesn't seem to care that he's been caught red-handed.

His eyes are scanning me from head to toe, blatant interest in his gaze. It dawns on me that he...that he might be thinking about enacting all those lewd images.

I take a step back as I narrow my eyes at him.

Yet before I can do anything, his fingers are wrapped around my wrist, and with one pull, he has me inside his room and against the nearest wall.

The door snaps shut, the painting falls to the ground, and my fear finally skyrockets.

Remembering I still have the candle in my hand, I aim the metal handle at him, thinking I could disorient him long enough to make a run of it.

Yet it doesn't even touch him. He catches my arm mid-air, his fingers deftly dislodging the candlestick and placing it on a table nearby.

It all happens in a matter of seconds—too fast for me to react or do anything but stare at him and his damn smug expression.

"What are you going to do to me?" I ask on a whisper laced with fear. All the while, I blame my impulsiveness and the fact that I considered even for a moment that I could go against him—that I could hold him accountable when by all intents and purposes he *is* the master of the house.

Finding myself so thoroughly trapped, I have to admit to myself how silly I was in my rage.

Damn it!

I should have just packed my bags and left at first sunrise, regardless of the money involved, or the fact that I have nowhere to go.

"What do you think I'm going to do to you, Darcy darlin'?" he drawls in a smooth voice.

"I...I don't know," I whimper as he brings his face closer to mine.

His nostrils flare as he takes in my scent, a low, barely audible growl escaping him right as he nuzzles his face in the hollow of my neck.

I hold myself still, terror engulfing me, my mind swimming with the perversities I'd seen in those paintings, suddenly thinking he's going to try to bring them to life.

"You're not in any danger," he finally says, drawing back enough to look me directly in the eyes. "I'm not going to hurt you, darlin'. But I don't want you to hurt yourself either," he says as his gaze dips to where he's holding me captive.

"Really?" I snicker. "I find that hard to believe after I caught you red-handed."

"And what exactly did you catch me with?" he raises a lazy brow.

"Those...those paintings," I sputter, my pulse growing wilder with each second.

It's his damn smirk and the way he's looking at me—with a mix of want, hunger, and something else.

"What about the paintings, Darcy?"

"You know exactly what I mean!" I grit out just as I push against him.

He doesn't budge.

"Tell me what's on that painting, darlin'," he murmurs softly, his countenance changing in the blink of an eye.

"You...you know," I whisper, averting my gaze.

His thumb pressing up my chin, he brings my eyes back to his.

"I won't if you don't tell me. This is a misunderstanding, and I need to understand how to fix it."

His behavior throws me off, as does the sincerity I witness etched on his features. He doesn't act like someone who's been caught in an improper situation.

"There were paintings of me...naked," I start in a low voice, my cheeks reddening as I'm forced to recount what I'd found. "It couldn't have been anyone *but* you, Caleb. The marks on the paintings were identical with the ones on my body. And no one other than you has ever seen me naked," I swallow hard, doing my best to keep my tone even and firm, though all I want is to yell at him and ask him *why*. "You were there too, and you were doing things to me."

"What things?" he rasps, his eyes boring into mine.

"Things that shouldn't be mentioned again," I shake my head.

"What things, Darcy?" he repeats, the question more pronounced.

I must be red from head to toe from recounting him the basics, and now he wants details?

Shaking my head, I once more try to push against him.

Can't he see how embarrassed and uncomfortable I am by the entire situation?

"Tell me," he commands, his hold tightening. "Tell me what things, Darcy."

"You were doing sexual things to me," I say in a hurry, squeezing my eyes shut before I expire on the spot from discomfort.

Dear God, what has happened to me since arriving in Fairydale?

I never used to swear, and now that is a daily occurrence. And I certainly would have never imagined I would be uttering such lewd things out loud.

And what does he do?

He chuckles.

"I would ask you what things, sweetheart, but I fear you'd swoon from the naughtiness of it all."

Taking a step back, he finally lets me go.

I exhale in relief, opening my eyes to see him pick up the painting.

"Is this the naughty picture you were talking about, Darcy darlin'?" he asks in a droll tone, turning the canvas towards me.

My mouth drops open in shock.

I try to speak but no sounds will come out as I simply stare at it—at what was supposed to be on it but what is not.

"I don't understand," I murmur, stupefied.

On the canvas, the same one I'd brought with me since I can spot the wax from the candle on its surface, is a scenery painting. Not me —not *us.*

It's just a painting of a tree in bloom.

Caleb shakes his head as he lets out a soft curse.

"Come with me," he says as he grabs a candelabra from his room, lighting all the candles before taking my hand. He leads me out of his room and towards the studio.

I'm too shocked to react, my mind blanking on me even more as he opens the door and shines the candles on top of the paintings I'd laid out all over the floor.

"What do you see, Darcy?" he inquires softly, coming closer and threading his fingers through mine in an unusual gesture of comfort.

"*Nothing,*" I whisper. Because it is *nothing* like what I'd seen before.

"I told you I haven't painted a human subject in a long time. All the paintings housed here are of landscapes from around Fairydale. Nothing else."

"But... I saw..." A sob escapes me as I cannot possibly comprehend what's happening to me. "You have to believe me. I clearly saw it. I couldn't have made up all that. I couldn't..."

How could I when I had no idea some of the acts I'd seen in the paintings even existed? How could my mind have conjured something I didn't know about?

"I'm not crazy, Caleb," I shake my head, gazing up at him and showing him the terror that resides inside of me. "I'm not crazy..."

"I don't think you are," he sighs heavily. "Join me?" he asks for my permission as he points back to his room.

I nod absentmindedly and before I know it, we're back in his room.

Flicking the light switch on, he leads me to his *perfectly* made bed, setting me down.

"Are you alright?"

He brings me a glass of water, crouching in front of me and regarding me with worry in his eyes.

I slowly shake my head.

"I'm not crazy," I whisper, tears pricking at my lids. "I'm not..."

"I know," he assured me, taking my hand in his and squeezing tightly.

"First, I find out the ghosts in this house might be real, and now I'm seeing things again. I just..." my voice breaks yet I try to keep myself from crying—that's the last thing I want to do now.

"They are real," he suddenly says.

I blink away my tears, sniffling as I look at him questioningly.

"I don't think you're crazy, darlin'. This house... There *are* things in this house. Some good. Some bad. Some who like to play with people. Some who are just bored."

"What..."

"I didn't want to tell you all of this in case it scared you away. But now that you've experienced it, you should know about it."

"Your father said the same," I whisper. "He told me Rhiannon is on good terms with the ghosts."

"Is she?" he chuckles. "Of course she is," he amends, shaking his head in amusement.

"Then what happened to me..."

"One of them could have been playing a trick on you."

"But why *that*... Why show me *that?*" I ask as a shudder goes down my body. "What about this afternoon? You...you *bit* me."

Caleb gives me an intense look as he brings his hand to my face, stroking my cheek lightly before tucking a stray strand behind my ear.

"I think you already know I didn't do that," he tells me softly. "Just as you know that what happened now couldn't have been me either. In fact, I can only think of one reason why you would experience these... things," his mouth curls upwards.

"Why?"

"Don't take this the wrong way, darlin', but you're...a tad repressed."

I blink repeatedly, thinking I didn't hear him right.

"What?" I squeak.

"I don't think it's your fault. Mainly your upbringing with those nuns and your proper ways," he flashes me a smile. "But you have to admit you're a little...uptight."

"Repressed," I repeat in shock. "*Uptight?*"

"Some of the entities in this house like to play with your weaknesses, the things that you bury deep in your subconscious."

"And you think... You think I buried erotic images of the two of us in my subconscious? That I..." I keep stumbling over my words. "That I want you to bite me, and do those wicked things to me?"

He doesn't answer for a moment, merely smiling.

"I reckon you do."

"Why I...." I immediately react, scandalized as is my nature, before my shoulders sag, my eyes widening in self-reflection.

"I'm not...uptight, am I?"

"A little?" he chuckles. "What you are is awfully cute, darlin'. And I'm sure I'll get you to unwind eventually."

"But..." I bite my lip. "I'm just confused, Caleb," I confess, an echo of anguish tainting my voice. "Odd deaths. Ghosts and monsters. Now entities that prey on my subconscious?"

"Come here," he murmurs as he grabs me by my nape, enveloping me in a hug.

"Some entities are playful, but not all have good intentions," he whispers in my ear. "There are a lot of bad energies in Fairydale, Darcy. And all of them only want one thing."

"What?"

"To consume you."

Chapter Twelve

An uneventful week passes.

No ghosts. No monsters. No erotic visions—to Caleb's greatest disappointment.

After what happened that day, it's like everything suddenly stopped. I can't say I'm mad about it, but there is one thing I miss.

Amon.

Since saving me from that monster, he hasn't showed up again. No matter how much I call him at night, he never comes—nor do the dreams of the past where I am his Lizzie.

I've tried to bury my disappointment as much as possible by throwing myself into getting to know more about the town and the Hales. But, though I'm living in their house, it's very rare that I interact with them.

In all this time, I've seen Katrina a handful of times, and her parents maybe once or twice. Rhiannon has kept herself aloof, for all her desire to get to know each other better.

In spite of that, Caleb has done his best to explain to me what he knows of the *paranormal* activities in Fairydale, though his knowledge is limited. He's told me about the encounters he's had since his childhood, giving me a short introduction to the resident ghosts of the house—all previous Hales who'd decided to stay on and look over the house.

If I'm honest to myself, if I hadn't experienced all those odd interactions since I've stepped foot in Fairydale, I would have never believed that ghosts exist—or *more*.

Yet slowly, I seem to have accommodated to the idea.

That doesn't change the fact that I'm still terrified of what that means for me, and the reason for my presence in Fairydale—because I am becoming increasingly convinced that nothing so far has been coincidental.

It's just a matter of figuring out *why.*

But I've decided to take it one day at a time while enjoying my time with Caleb and our growing attachment.

Over the course of the week we've fallen into an easy courtship as we got to know each other better. Though a strong attraction between us simmers, he hasn't tried to make a move on me—despite his usual innuendoes that have me blushing.

After our discussion about the paintings and the realization that *maybe* I am a little uptight, I've decided to give it more thought and see how I could change while still remaining myself. As I'd told Caleb, it's not easy to give up on years of propriety that have been grilled into my head.

More than anything, the images I'd seen—whether real or not—had remained stuck in my brain. And though I'd been initially scandalized, now I can't help but be a little...curious. For someone with little to no knowledge about the topic, I can't deny they might have served as an... instruction manual of sorts. Before, I would have never imagined people could engage in such wicked behavior. But now...?

My cheeks heat up the moment one of the naughty images pops up in my mind.

"I trust you've had no ghostly encounters last night?" he jokes when I come down for breakfast.

"Nor did I have any naughty dreams about you if that's your next question," I add cheekily.

"Pity. I would have loved to hear the details."

"Of course you would," I roll my eyes. "I might be *uptight* but your mind is completely in the gutter."

He wiggles his eyebrows suggestively.

"What about a compromise? We could meet halfway and..."

I slap him playfully across the shoulder.

"And it's time to eat," I declare, giggling at his grumpy expression.

We're both at the kitchen table when Connor Hale suddenly comes inside.

He barely spares Caleb a glance as he greets me.

"No more monsters, I hope?" he asks as he takes something from the pantry.

"No. It's been rather quiet," I reply.

"Good. My aunt's been trying to cleanse the place. She'll speak with you soon," Connor explains, telling me that Rhiannon has a bad habit of closing herself to the world when she does one of her rituals.

My ears perk up at the term *ritual* but he doesn't explain further. He merely tells me to expect to see her soon.

I'm about to ask him more, but he's already out the door.

And he didn't even acknowledge his son.

Caleb's been sitting quietly at the table, his expression full of intensity.

"Rituals?' I turn to him. "But wouldn't that mean she's some kind of..."

"Witch," he casually states the word. "You would be correct," he forces a smile that doesn't reach his eyes.

"A witch?" I sputter.

Ghosts. Monsters. Now witches? What's next?

"Tell me more about this monster," he interrupts, his tone serious.

Though I'm still hung up on the witch term he so casually dropped into the conversation, after he hounds me for a few moments on end, I relent and tell him about my encounter with the monster. I leave out the details about Amon, not quite ready to share about our connection to the world. Instead, I tell him what I'd told his father—that he'd tried to attack me before he disappeared.

"He looked like this?" he asks as he picks up a sheet of paper, doing a quick sketch of the faceless creature that had attacked me—mangled flesh, no eyes or nose, just one huge mouth. The sketch captures its features perfectly.

I quickly nod, impressed with his talent.

"That's it. Do you know what it could have been?"

He stares at it for a moment, his gaze boring into the paper just as his fingers wrinkle the edge of the paper.

"It's not a ghost," he says carefully, turning to look at me.

I roll my eyes at him.

"I could have figured that one, too."

"What I mean is," he clears his throat. "This isn't a sentient creature. If it came after you, then it wanted something for *someone*."

"What are you trying to say? That someone *sent* it after me?" I blink in confusion.

He nods grimly.

"But wait, how do you know?"

If he has such limited knowledge, then how does he know about this unfortunate-looking monster?

"There was a legend when I was a kid. About the monster with no eyes—the *Kiaka*. He only needs a name to go after his target. He appears in the night and he will not stop until he accomplishes his mission. Unless he is destroyed, of course."

I bite my lip in apprehension as I take in the information.

"He was destroyed," I confirm.

But not before he tried to perforate my stomach.

Was that it? Was he sent to kill me? But by whom and *why?*

"That doesn't mean that more won't come. It's good Rhiannon is adding more protective wards. That thing should have never passed through her protections in the first place."

"But why would someone send that thing after me?"

"You'll learn, Darcy," he smiles sadly. "That there are many factions in Fairydale. And each wants something. Some are willing to do anything to destroy, and others will do the same to protect. It's only a matter of which camp you're on."

I blink in surprise at his words. Did he just say... Did he imply that there are people out there trying to destroy *me?* Once more, I cannot comprehend *why*.

I'm just a teacher from Boston.

Unless... Unless this has to do with my family—my mother.

And so far, only one person seems to have that information.

"What about you?" I whisper. "What about your family?"

He turns, pinning me with his gaze.

"I will *only* ever want what's best for you," he states emphatically. "I will always protect you, Darcy. From *everyone.* Sometimes maybe even myself," his lips twitch. "And my family?" he releases a dry laugh. "You're safest here. They won't harm you."

What an odd answer.

Yet the more I look at him, the more I get lost in his gaze.

Getting up from his seat at the table, he comes towards me.

"It might not seem so at times, Darcy darlin'. But everything I do is for you," he murmurs. "Already having you here, in this house..." he exhales sharply. "You're safe here—the safest you could be in this town."

"Even with the ghosts?" I crack a smile.

"Those ghosts will be your biggest protectors," he tells me in a serious voice.

"Well, enough with the morbid talk," I let out an awkward laugh, already feeling chills spreading down my spine. "Why don't we go to the library? You promised to show me those rare books," I add enthusiastically.

Shaking his head at me, he smiles.

And for the rest of the day, we spend our time in the library, reading and chatting.

Caleb may scare me at times with his intensity—or it may scare that part of me that is unused to such attention—but the more time I spend with him, the more I fall for the person he is at his core.

He's extremely smart and well-read, and his presence is simply mesmerizing.

And since he let out in passing that he has a degree in History from Harvard, I've been hounding him with all sorts of questions. There's absolutely *nothing* he doesn't have an answer to. He is like a human encyclopedia, the details so astounding it's like he's personally lived through everything.

Sometimes I wonder why even use the library when he can recite Homer by heart.

Who does that?

Despite becoming so close, though, he still changes the subject every time I ask about his time in the war. Recently I've taken the hint and I've stopped inquiring about it. Maybe his father is right and those events traumatized him. The last thing I'd want is to awaken painful memories for him.

"There are so many books in here I don't know how one person could ever read everything," I breathe out in awe as I browse some of the shelves.

"What if someone could?" he challenges.

Looking back, I spot him leaning against one of the shelves, his hands in the pockets of his trousers as he's watching me in that usual manner of his—intensely and obsessively.

Sometimes I get the feeling that he never misses one thing I do, his eyes catching everything. From my covert glances to every little sigh that escapes my lips when he shuffles closer, Caleb is able to read me like an open book—ironically.

"Only the immortal," I giggle, the topic fitting considering this house is teeming with ghosts...and other entities. "That reminds me," I turn, a mischievous grin on my face. "Can ghosts read? And do they?"

His eyes sparkle with amusement, his mouth tipping up.

"Don't laugh at me! It's a genuine question. If I were trapped for an eternity with a library like this, I would devour every single book—every word written."

"I would never laugh," he puts his hands up in a mock peace gesture.

In no time, I feel him behind me, the heat radiating from his body enveloping me and making me tense—as is usually the case when I'm in his presence.

"I think you have a wrong idea of what ghosts are," he chuckles in my ear.

I swivel to face him, narrowing my eyes at him.

"Do tell then. What *are* ghosts?"

"They are sources of energy, they are the pure intention that remains after passing—whether good or bad," he murmurs. "And though one might die with the express desire to read books for all eternity," he smiles at me, "it would lack the corporeality to do so."

"So what do ghosts do?" I bite my lip in apprehension, suddenly thinking of Amon.

"They haunt?" he chuckles.

Shaking my head, I give him a playful swat.

"Spirits remain where they do not belong for a few reasons, Darcy. Hate, resentment, or unfulfilled desire. They don't just decide not to cross over. Something is keeping them here."

His words give me pause.

If Amon is a ghost, then what keeps him here? What type of strong emotion or unfulfilled desire has impeded his peaceful passing?

A sad look crosses my face as I imagine him lonely for centuries, in search of something but never quite finding it.

Yet the question remains... Why is Amon here? Why is he in Fairydale when my dreams show me a previous life in England?

"What do you think keeps the ghosts at the Hale manor here?" I suddenly ask.

He's silent for a moment as he mulls it over.

"A common goal," he finally answers, his eyes flickering with foreign emotion. "And what most spirits have in common —vengeance."

A shiver goes down my back.

Could that be the case with Amon, too?

Could he have been killed on these grounds, remaining here to search for his vengeance?

Yet I can't imagine that, not when his presence is so soothing—so pure.

I've never once sensed malicious intent from him. Certainly not what I'd felt when the *Kiaka* had attacked me.

"Can it not be something else?" I ask in a small voice.

He raises his brows at me, and I gather the courage to ask.

"Like...love?"

"You're quite the romantic, aren't you, Darcy darlin'?"

I blush at his question, averting my eyes when his gaze seems to penetrate my every defense.

"Isn't love an unfulfilled desire, too?" I whisper.

He tips my chin up, forcing me to look into his eyes.

"Some might say it's the most unfulfilled desire of all," he murmurs, his breath fanning my lips.

When had he gotten so close?

He leans in, and instinctively, I close my eyes and pucker my lips, waiting.

Just as I think he's going to close the distance and give me my first kiss, he doesn't.

One second passes. Two. On the third, I hear his deep rumble.

"You can open your eyes, darlin'," he chuckles.

I creep my eyes open to note the amusement on his face. He's still just as close, the contours of his body fitted to mine. Yet he doesn't act on our proximity.

Instead, he lifts his arm, taking a book from behind me.

"You're a tease," I grumble under my breath.

All this time I'd been mentally preparing for *the kiss* and when I think he's about to give it to me—when I want to welcome it with open arms—he teases me like this.

"Here, I think you might like this," he says, his eyes crinkled at the corners.

Oh, the rogue! He knows exactly what he's doing.

I grab the book from his hands—*none too ladylike*—and I open it to the title page.

The Monk by M.G. Lewis.

My brows scrunch in confusion. I'm not particularly familiar with this title.

But as I read further, I note the year in which it's been printed.

1796.

"It's a first edition," I breathe out in awe.

Just how many priceless first editions can this library house?

Yet that's not the most striking thing about the book.

Right under the print year, there's a signature in bold, masculine script.

Jeremiah Creed.

"This... This belonged to the original owner of the house, did it not?" I whip my gaze up to meet Caleb's intent one.

"Indeed," he drawls.

"His name was Jeremiah? It's the first time I see his first name," I add pensively. "He and his wife died in the plague, did they not?"

"Hmm, did they," he muses. "Some say they did. Others say they were murdered."

"Murdered?" I frown. "How come?"

"You'll have to ask Rhiannon," he slowly smiles. "I'm sure she'll be a better source than me."

"Does she know everything that happens in Fairydale? Everyone seems to defer to her as the authority around here."

"She's...something," Caleb replies. "She's seen a lot in her lifetime," he says as he takes another book for himself.

"How old is she?" I ask as I follow him to the reading space.

He plops himself on the sofa, patting the seat next to him for me.

"In her late nineties," he answers.

My eyes widen.

"In her nineties?" I sputter.

Rhiannon looks to be in her fifties at best, yet she is in her nineties?

"Tell me she isn't some sort of vampire too," I mumble.

At this point would I be surprised if she were?

Caleb throws his head back and laughs.

"You should tell her that. I'm sure she would love to hear she's been compared to a vampire."

My lips twitch.

"Well, at least you didn't say vampires exist too," I add drily.

"Who said they don't exist?" he raises a brow. "They might even come and suck on your pretty neck at night," he leans in to whisper, his finger trailing down the column of my neck. "Feed on your life essence," he continues in a raspy whisper, the light touches sending a shiver down my back.

My lips part as a gasp escapes me, flashes of the previous odd encounters flooding my mind and making my pulse speed up.

"You're trying to scare me," I accuse. "*Again*," I say pointedly, giving him a look that says I don't appreciate this type of humor—certainly not after thinking I was losing my mind.

And to show him my displeasure, I open the book, making myself more comfortable on my side of the sofa and ignoring him in favor of the story.

Minutes pass, and I can tell he's getting increasingly annoyed with the lack of attention. Especially as he keeps brushing his shoulder against mine, or bumping his knee into mine.

Every time I catch him doing it, he gives me a sheepish smile.

He's almost like a lazy cat demanding attention.

"Stop that! You're distracting," I use my teacher voice on him, hoping he would feel duly reprimanded.

He doesn't.

He only gives me another smile, blatantly fluttering his lashes at me as he scoots closer.

"I won't try to scare you again," he murmurs huskily. "In fact, I'll keep you very, very safe," he declares as he clasps his hands around my shoulders. "I'll be your knight in shining armor. Would you like that, Darcy darlin'?" he speaks low in my ear, his tone a combination of needy playfulness and lethal intensity.

I still as my heart drums in my chest.

How is it that he can melt my defenses with only a few words, disarm me with the barest of touches?

"I reckon you quite enjoy it when I'm scared," I whisper as I slowly turn towards him.

"Me?" he shakes his head. "Never, darlin'."

"Oh, but you do," I continue, meeting his gaze head on. "Because then I'm at your mercy, isn't that so?"

I don't know where the words come from, but the moment I utter them aloud I know them to be true. He likes to see me on the edge, too close to the precipice. Because then he'll be the one to pull me back to safety.

Caleb doesn't deny it.

He continues to watch me closely, his eyes boring into me.

"I'd be lying if I denied it," he says in a low, even tone.

All the while, his gaze is still on mine, holding me captive.

"Your emotions are a feast in themselves. But your fear... Your fear, Darcy darlin'," he releases a deep groan. "It would keep me sated for an eternity."

"Why?" I whisper.

"Because it's so intimately linked with your desire—with everything that still holds you back," he says as he brushes the back of his hand against my cheek.

I swallow hard, unable to look away from him.

In a way, he *is* right.

About everything.

I am afraid—just as I am uptight. I am all that because something within me keeps me from fully letting go.

And I still do not know what.

"You would make quite the psychoanalyst," I note with a dry, awkward laugh.

His eyes flicker with awareness as he recognizes he touched a sore spot.

Slowly, he pulls back, letting his lips curl up into a comforting smile.

And instead of a sarcastic reply, he promptly switches the topic.

Still holding my hand in his, he opens his book—*A collection of plays by Bernard Shaw*—and starts reading one of them to me.

Soon, his voice lulls me into a state of total comfort—despite the previous uneasy conversation. It's just another facet of Caleb that fascinates me.

He can read my moods so well, he knows exactly how to react each time. He knows when to tease and when to pull back, when to challenge me and when to soothe me.

Every now and then, he pauses to recount an anecdote, telling me a humorous historical tale, or tell me the origin of a certain term used by Shaw.

I listen raptly, his intelligence more than matching his outer looks. His words are carefully chosen, his oratorical skills unmatched as he becomes the center of my attention—of my very world.

Not for the first time, I have to wonder why he's wasting his time in Fairydale when he could embark on any career he could wish for. He could become a lawyer, or a politician. He could do anything he wished, yet he stayed here. In a small town with no prospects and nothing to recommend it except some errant ghosts.

I know he has his business and he makes great money with his work, yet I can't help but wonder if he's truly fulfilled by what he does.

He's such a passionate man, a fire burning deep inside of him that he attempts to stifle at every turn. I cannot comprehend how or why he limits himself.

As he embarks on a history lesson, my interest is piqued as I draw closer to him, almost as if by being glued to his side I could absorb all his knowledge and everything that he is—awe striking and inspiring.

Damn, but he doesn't even need his looks to seduce me. He can do it by merely speaking so articulately and by transposing me to another time with his mere words.

"TELL ME MORE," I say dreamily as I place a pillow on his lap before laying my head down.

He gazes indulgently at me, his hand on my head as he softly strokes my hair.

"What do you want to know exactly?"

"Hmm," I think for a moment. "What do you know about 18th century England?"

He raises his brows at me.

"How come?"

"I've read books set during Regency. I'm interested in what happened *before*," I turn to lay on my back so I can watch him.

"Depending on what decade of the eighteen hundreds you're talking about. A lot of things have changed. The end of the century was very similar to what you know as the Regency."

He goes on to give me a quick political and societal guide to the seventeen hundreds.

I merely listen, my lips tipped up in a perpetual smile as I let his deep rumble wash through me, every vibration making me feel unnaturally alive and yearning for...something.

"Caleb?" I interrupt after what seems like an eternity.

He's on the subject of George the Third, making parallels between England and the colonies, and how people had fared under his rule.

"Huh?" he suddenly stops, tilting his head and turning those captivating eyes to me.

Rising from my—*very*—comfortable spot, I bring myself into a sitting position, sliding next to him as I cup both his cheeks with my hands. A sliver of fear blooms inside of me, but for the first time I squash it down, choosing to take matters in my own hands.

He blinks, and for the first time I note he is flustered—a fact that only makes him more endearing.

This handsome man who's been trying to seduce me at every turn is now being the one seduced. And instead of the expected resolute assertiveness, I'm met with tentative uncertainty.

His skin is soft where my fingers touch him and I caress him gently before I lean in.

My heart is thundering in my chest, but as I close the distance between us, my lips meeting his, I find that nothing else matters.

Nothing but that brief connection as I inhale the very essence he breathes.

I give him a quick kiss on the lips before I draw back, my eyes wide, my cheeks red.

To my surprise, his cheeks have a similar hue.

Unable to face him, I swing my legs off the sofa and I dash out of the library.

"See you later," I squeak.

I giggle to myself as I run up the stairs, ready to close myself in my room and replay everything in my head.

But just as I'm about to turn to our wing, I come face to face with Rhiannon.

"There you are, Darcy," she smiles at me. "My nephew told me about your misfortune, and I must offer you my deepest apologies."

I frown.

"You shouldn't encounter any more such..." she purses her lips, "creatures."

"That is reassuring," I give her a tight smile.

"Of course, you must have questions. I'd like to extend an invitation to dine with the family at the end of the week. We've all been rather absent and we've unfortunately neglected you as our guest."

"Oh, no, don't worry about it. I don't want to impose. You've already received me into your home for which I am incredibly grateful."

"It is your home, too, Darcy," she comes forward, taking my hands in hers.

For a moment, I could swear her eyes glow just as a smile slowly spreads on her lips.

"Oh, my. You are, indeed, everything I expected you to be," she tells me, giving me a warm look. "We will talk more soon, and I will give you answers to some questions you may have."

And with that, she's gone.

Heading to my room, I note how late it is and I get ready for bed, taking a shower and washing my hair.

All the while, I can't stop smiling while thinking of Caleb.

While thinking of...the kiss.

Already, my cheeks heat up as I remember the feel of his lips on mine. It had only been for a second, but it had been *glorious.*

So much so that I can't wait to repeat it.

Brushing my hair and braiding it, I put on my nightgown before I go to bed.

As I lay in bed, doing my best to fall asleep, I can't help but compare the sweet kiss I'd shared with Caleb with the one I am almost certain Amon gave me.

I shake myself. I shouldn't even try to compare. One man is dead, the other is alive.

Yet why does it hurt so much thinking of Amon dead?

I have Caleb and that should be enough. So why can't I stop my heart from yearning for Amon?

If my intuition is right, the dreams aren't just dreams—not after Amon spoke to me. They are a window to the past. One where I was his Lizzie. One where we were...in love.

But what happened? Why is he here, in Fairydale? Why is he a ghost?

The questions are endless, and I feel more conflicted than ever.

I like Caleb. I am attracted to him. And I know I'm well on my way to falling for him if I haven't already done so. But then there's Amon and the echo of feelings I had for him as Lizzie—feelings that still plague me, a gaping hole in my heart whenever I think about him.

He's the only person whose presence has ever reminded me of *home.*

"God," I groan as I twist and turn.

I'm falling for Caleb. But I'm also in love with a...ghost?

What in God's name is wrong with me?

Before, I'd never looked twice at a man, and now I'm having this infuriating conundrum.

Anywhere other than Fairydale and I'm sure I would be shipped to a mental institution. After all, who develops feelings for a ghost?

It takes me a while to fall asleep, but at some point, a loud banging noise startles me awake.

My first inclination is to get out of bed and turn on the light, already feeling myself develop goosebumps over the surface of my entire body.

Please not another ghost...

Maybe I've let myself be spoiled in the last week, but the quiet had been invaluable.

Another bang, and I jump, looking right and left.

The issue with ghosts is that you cannot just punch them and run for your life. They're not exactly...*punchable*.

The noise becomes increasingly louder, and just as I am about to go find Caleb, I hear the voice—*his* voice.

Lizzie...

It's faint, but I can hear it.

"Amon?" I ask, hating the hopeful tone of my voice.

Lizzie...

The air shimmers in front of me, and somehow I know it's him.

"Amon," I whisper softly, his name on my lips almost making me cry since I know he's...dead.

The shimmery mist moves, going towards the door.

I frown for a second until I realize he's trying to tell me something —lead me somewhere.

Before I can think anything through, I light a candle, taking it with me and following Amon's ghost—or essence, or whatever it is. At this point, the last thing I need is to argue semantics over a ghost's form. Not when the only thing that matters to me is to be able to communicate with him. I have so many questions I want to ask him—so many things I want to tell him.

Lizzie...

The voice becomes louder as I move down the corridor, taking the stairs to the ground floor before being lead to an area I hadn't to been before—but one Caleb had told me had been the servants quarters in the past.

The moment I enter it, the mist directs me to a door at the far end of the room. As I open it, shining light inside, I'm surprised to see a set of stairs that lead to an even lower level.

For a second I balk at going into such a dark place, but as the mist intensifies, I take the plunge, putting one foot in front of the other and hoping I'm not going to encounter God knows what down there.

I go down two flights of stairs before I reach another door. This one locked. I'm about to tell him that when I hear a light snapping sound before the door creaks open.

As I cross the threshold, I use the candle to see what's around me, somehow not surprised to see it's a tunnel. The ground is rocky and uneven, and I think I can hear the sound of the ocean, which suggests this is close to sea-level.

I take a few steps, but I can't feel him around me anymore.

"Amon?"

"Come to me," the voice is fully audible now, raspy, full and thick. There's almost like an echo as it fills the length of the tunnel.

"Amon, is that you?"

"Come to me, Lizzie mine," he drawls, the voice unmistakably his. I would recognize it anywhere.

Tears gather at the corners of my eyes as I hurry forward.

"It's really you," I whisper, true joy overtaking me. "It's really you, my Amon."

I don't know how far I've walked, but suddenly I hit something like a wall, the impact making me reel.

Swinging the candle in front of me, I note there's no barrier —*nothing*.

"What..."

"Come, Lizzie," Amon repeats, his voice deeply anguished.

So much so, it pulls at my soul, a melody that calls to something deep within me.

Getting up, I try to move forward again. Only to be thrust backward once more.

But I don't give up.

Moving back a few paces, I gather momentum before I run at full speed towards the invisible barrier, only to be thrown back in the air with the same force.

I hit the ground instantaneously. My head connects with a sharp rock, the pain immediate, as is the blurring of my vision and the loss of my consciousness.

But it's not before I hear a mighty roar. One that makes the entire structure around me quake.

"*Lizzie*!"

CHAPTER THIRTEEN

SEPTEMBER 1790. HAVERSHAM HOUSE, KENT

"She hasn't been herself in months, My Lady. You have to do something about it."

I vaguely hear Mary's voice outside my bedroom door.

"She'll get over it, just as she'll get over that...thing," my mother spits the words, once more making her stance regarding Amon clear.

"But she won't! It's been months, My Lady, and all she does is sit in her room and stare out the window. She doesn't eat, unless we force it down her throat. She doesn't do anything but wither away one day at a time," Mary adds, exasperated.

I feel bad for her. It's not her fault. But even the affection I hold her won't be able to move me.

"It's just puppy love. She'll get over it soon. We're leaving for London at the end of the month, whether she likes it or not," my mother declares before her steps become a thudding noise on the floor, slowly fading away.

A knock at my door and Mary slips inside, slowly coming towards me.

"My Lady," she says tentatively as she reaches my side. "You need to pull yourself together. Please," her voice breaks, and a flicker of emotion takes shape in my chest.

But I don't answer.

It's been exactly three months since I last spoke. Three months of the same recurring nightmare—of waking up and seeing the blood on my hands.

Three months of living while being dead on the inside.

At first, I'd been so inconsolable my mother had forced me into a laudanum induced slumber that had lasted almost a week.

I don't have much recollection of what happened during that time. But from the crumbs I'd gathered from Mary, I'd been in and out of it, but every time I'd regain consciousness I would go crazy with grief and I would devolve into hysterics.

That had stopped when I'd simply become numb with pain.

I'd gone from seeing my beloved bleeding out in my arms, to waking up alone and inconsolable. To make matters worse, even Mr. Meow had left me. I don't know what had happened to him, but I don't discount that my mother could have thrown him out while I was not able to defend him.

Amon is dead.

And Fiona Montford had killed him with her own two hands.

From the moment I'd heard the admission from her lips, I'd tuned her out, almost as if I stepped away from the present by closing myself somewhere deep within.

I can only recall her telling me it was for my own good—that she was saving my life. But can she not see that instead she all but damned me?

"Do you need anything?" Mary probes, laying a hand on my shoulder and trying to get me to react.

I don't. I simply continue to gaze out the window, moonlight shining over the well-groomed shrubs, the perfect outside image hiding the rot within.

With a resigned sigh, she places a tray of food on a table, telling me to help myself if I get hungry even though she knows come morning, everything will be intact.

The seconds tick before I hear the door close behind her.

I mentally acknowledge it, my body sagging as some tension leaves me.

Still, I don't move.

My limbs are stiff and numb from sitting in the same positions for hours at a time, yet, I relish the discomfort. It's the only thing I deserve for getting him killed—because if it hadn't been for me...

A sigh escapes me as I intently regard the garden that housed our first meeting, almost as if by staring at it I could undo the past—or go *back* to the past.

Back to that one first meeting.

That time when I could still hear his voice in my ear, feel his breath on my cheek or the touch of his ungloved hand against mine. The little things that made me fall for him.

The little things that are the *only* memories I have of him.

A tear makes its way down my cheek as I recall his sweet words.

Lizzie mine.

For a brief moment in time, I was his—truly his. And he was mine.

It doesn't matter what my mother says. That he was a bad man. That he was a debaucher of innocents and the epitome of evil.

He could have been that and more. But for that moment in the maze, when he'd looked at me as if I were his entire world, I know he was mine—so irrevocably mine.

If only she wouldn't have found us...

A whimper escapes me as the images of that night flood me. I can recall his smile perfectly. Yet, as soon as the shots ring out, I can barely make out blurry movements and red.

So much red.

On my hands. On my gown. Spattered all over my face.

One moment I loved him, ready to give myself to him in spite of the impropriety of it—in spite of the entire world.

The next, he was dead.

And I was dead, too.

Hours pass and the house becomes eerily quiet, everyone having gone to sleep. I stay a few moments longer before I release a weary sigh, slowly untangling my limbs as I get up from my seat by the window.

My stomach rumbles with hunger as I pass by the food Mary had left for me, yet I can't muster the appetite, nor the need for self-preservation.

Starvation is both an act of rebellion and one of pure disinterest when it comes to my wellbeing, especially as I know what will happen next.

My mother will find me a husband to keep things quiet, and I'll be locked in another form of terror. At least like this I'm still master of my own fate.

The mere thought of someone other than Amon touching me has disgust rolling deep inside of me, goosebumps of revulsion covering my entire skin.

People might think I'm ridiculous for doing this, for hanging on to something that was barely real—for what they call *puppy* love. But they can judge me all they want. *I* know what's in my heart, and what was between us. I am the one who has to live with this heartbreak, with the memory of what he made me feel both at the height of happiness, and at the lowest of the low—when his blood stained my body.

Slipping the gown over my head, I stand in front of the full-sized mirror, letting my eyes roam over my figure—or what's left of it.

My stomach has sunk in, my ribs poking through the skin. My hip bone, too, is protruding, as seemingly are all the bones in my body.

In just a few months, I've become a shell of myself.

The only question is...how long will I be able to go on like this?

For fear that I would do something stupid, my mother has ordered the servants to ransack my room for any sharp objects or anything I could use to harm myself. She'd noticed the dullness in my eyes from the moment I woke up, and she realized that with one pull of a trigger, she hadn't just killed Amon.

She'd killed me, too.

Releasing a tired breath, I drag myself to my bed, that one small movement taking all the energy out of me. My lungs are as tired as my limbs and as soon as my back hits the mattress, my eyes flutter closed.

The only light in the room is coming from the fireplace, the embers flickering with the life I wish I had—with the fire I wish still burned within me.

Yet it's that warmth that reminds me of him—of the heat of his body.

It's only in times like this that I can still hold on to him—with my eyes closed, my mind drifting to the past. Or, maybe, the potential future. The one I know I'll never have but the one I yearn for, nevertheless.

In my dreams, Amon is with me—as my friend, lover, husband and father of my children. And as I turn in bed, keeping to one half of it, I imagine it's him on the other side.

"I miss you," I whisper, the void swallowing my words and never delivering anything back.

As a tear falls down my cheek, I picture the alternative.

I see us running in the garden, smiling at one another while playing with our children.

We're...happy.

God, but we're happy.

One tear eventually becomes a hundred, until I curl inwards, hugging my legs to my chest and sobbing my heart out for the future that will never be.

Yet just as I find myself lost in my grief, a strong gust of wind blows the windows open, cold seeping into the room.

Immediately, I stand up, though it's not the easiest thing to do. It's even harder to get out of bed and trudge my way to the window to close it.

The wind blows in my face, a shiver going down my back from the cold. Wincing, I drape a red shawl over my shoulders in an attempt to warm myself.

With slow, even steps, I reach the window, my hands on the wooden frames as I struggle to close them. A storm is brewing and the wind picks up strength as I do my best to push the windows closed. Yet before I manage to seal them shut, something floats inside the room.

I don't pay attention to it until every latch is in place.

Still shivering, I pick up the piece of paper, short of breath from the mere effort of bending down.

As my fingers brush against it, I don't look at what it is, my first instinct is to dump it in the fireplace—anything to get the room warmer.

It's by chance that I gaze down at it. And two words capture my attention.

Lizzie mine.

I blink in confusion, my pulse speeding up just as a foreign feeling blossoms in my chest—hope.

It can't be, can it?

With hurried movements that my body can barely withstand, I borrow some fire from the fireplace, lighting up a candle and taking a seat at my table.

Taking a deep breath, I slowly unfold the piece of paper, my eyes quickly scanning the contents of the letter at first. Gulping down, I note the key words and phrases—all belonging to Amon—and I can't help the happiness that takes shape within me.

My fingers tremble as I bring my gaze to the beginning, reading everything with slow exactitude so I don't miss one word.

Lizzie mine,

Forgive me for not writing to you sooner. The road of recovery has been long and harrowing. For days on end I did not know whether I would be able to utter your name out loud again.

Against all odds, I prevailed.

And it is only because of you, my love.

Because of this love that burns inside my veins, this want that threatens to suffocate me.

It's because my desire for you is stronger than any weapon, or any roadblock I may encounter—in this life or the next.

Please know that I am alive and well. And I will soon come for you.
Yours Eternally,
Amon

I read the letter again. And again. I read it until I memorize each word, and still I cannot believe this to be true.

"Amon," I whisper, my chest bursting with the most pure happiness there is. "It's really you, isn't it?"

The candle burns out and I'm still staring at his words, committing to memory the curves of his letters, the hoops, and the little particularities. All so I can convince myself this is real.

Amon is alive.

He's not dead.

Dear God, he's not dead!

I stand up—albeit a little too sudden. A wave of dizziness assaults me, all the blood rushing to my head. Yet I can't find it in me to care. Not when I've been given a new purpose—to live.

What could he possibly think if he saw me like this? All skin and bone and almost expiring on the spot? Not only would he find me entirely unappealing, but he would worry.

I know he would.

Pursing my lips, I drop to my knees by the bed, searching for a little box that holds my dearest possessions. Pulling it closer, I carefully fold the letter inside so no one would find it.

Then, I bring my gaze to the tray of cold food.

My stomach rumbles again.

Yet this time—and this time only—I *know* I can keep the food down. I know that I can eat, if only to survive another day and see him again.

That day signals the start of my own recovery.

Though my appetite doesn't magically return, I do my best to eat a little more each day. The efforts are soon visible, in the new fullness of my cheeks and my figure. My hair too, slowly regains its previous luster. And with a perpetual smile on my face, things start looking up, my hope for the future growing daily.

Amon's letters continue too. Every couple of days, I find a new letter on my windowsill.

I don't know how he does it, but he never fails to surprise me with his words, promising me a future together whether my mother approves of our relationship or not.

Knowing he has plans in store for us—that at one point my dreams would become reality—I can't help the giddiness that suffuses my being.

So much so that soon everyone notices.

Including my mother.

"You're looking well, Elizabeth," she notes one morning as she sees me come down for breakfast. "You've been eating, too."

I nod dutifully.

"You were right, mother," I give her a small smile. "It *was* puppy love. I now realize that. But you can't blame me for being crushed. You saw how handsome he was," I do my best to explain, masking the distaste that assails me at those lies.

My mother's eyes widen. Placing down her fork and knife, she studies me intently.

"Do you mean that, dear?"

"Of course," I murmur. "I was courting death and for what? Because some gentleman decided to pay me attention for five seconds? I realize how naïve I've been," I sigh. "I can only blame it on my lack of experience and the fact that I was an easy prey."

My mother nods, a satisfied smile pulling at her lips as she undoubtedly thinks I've finally seen reason.

And if I am to succeed in my ruse—at least long enough for Amon to come for me—then I must convince her I am cured of my silly infatuation.

"That is good to hear, dear. You are a clever girl. I knew you'd see reason."

"I do have one question," I add as I pile my plate with food.

Her eyes sparkle with approval as she sees me eat, nodding encouragingly at me.

"You killed a man. A *nobleman.* Why is no one inquiring about that? Why is there no magistrate knocking on our door"

Her smile doesn't wane.

"I think it's high time I let you in about our family secret, Elizabeth," she says, watching me closely as I bring a piece of ham to my lips.

"Family secret?" I frown.

"Well, there are several reasons why I could go ahead with the *murder*—as you call it. At such a public event, too," she chuckles. "And that is because no one knows. No one saw, and no one heard."

"But the shot... It was so loud. Everything was so loud..."

Fiona shakes her head.

"Amon d'Artan doesn't exist, dear. He never did. There was no Marquis d'Ombre. No such title was ever created."

"You mean he was a charlatan?"

I narrow my eyes at her. It's the first time she's mentioned that. Before, the only thing she'd said about Amon had been that he was a bad man and that he was trying to take advantage of me and lead me astray.

"Oh, along those lines," she laughs. "Only much, much more dangerous. But I reckon you're finally ready to learn the truth."

"The truth?" I blink. What sort of truth could she be speaking about?

"Join me," she says as she rises from her chair,

Curious about this family secret she wishes to share with me, I grab a scone on my way out, popping it into my mouth before following her. She enters the main library, going straight for a shelf and plucking a particular volume. I don't get to see the title before a sudden noise makes me jump back.

Right before my eyes, the entire wall opens up to reveal a secret room.

"What's going on?" I whisper, my eyes widening in shock.

"Come, dear," she urges me on, taking me by the hand and inviting me inside.

The moment we're in the secret chamber, the wall moved again, closing itself behind us.

It's only then that I manage to take in the room around me.

"What..." my mouth opens and closes in wonder.

The room is almost the same size as the main library, and it seems to house another collection of books—and other items.

There are shelves upon shelves of ingredients, and odd contraptions that look strikingly similar to drawings of items I'd seen in scientific treaties.

An enormous book rests in the middle of the room, protected by a glass box. Even from where I'm standing I can tell the pages are made out of vellum, not paper.

"What is this, *mama*?"

"This is your legacy, Elizabeth," she declares, clasping her hands together as she invites me to look around the room.

"I don't understand. Did papa know about this?"

"Your father?" She frowns. "Of course not." She waves her hand in the air as if he were not in the least of importance. "Some of these items have been in my family for centuries, and the knowledge for millennia."

I take a step forward, walking around the room and studying its contents, more questions arising in my mind. There are odd looking symbols drawn on the walls, and every single book I see is in Latin, or Gaelic.

"Mother," I look up, my tone serious as I address her. "Tell me this isn't some type of witchcraft."

Though the aristocracy refuses to acknowledge such *pagan* notions, the rumors still float around. Usually among the servants who are more susceptible to superstitions. But with the past waves of witch hunting, even they are wary not to say too much.

Parliament officially passed the Witchcraft Act in 1735, thus ending the official witch hunt. That didn't stop various clerics, particularly in more remote regions, from accusing and punishing individuals. Sometimes, even a home remedy could be labeled as witchcraft, its maker branded a witch and castigated to the full extent of clerical law.

Fiona merely smiles. She doesn't deny it.

I freeze, my heart ramming in my chest as I look at the mother I've known my entire life, yet now I'm seeing someone different.

Someone with secrets.

Someone...who wasn't quite who I thought she was.

"You must realize this is madness. There's no such thing as witchcraft," I try to tell her in the nicest way possible.

Not only is my mother potentially insane, but she'd attacked my beloved based on some inane assumptions.

"You're new to all of this. I understand it might be hard for you to understand, but I'll do my best to explain everything," she smiles.

"I think I'll retire for the day," I murmur, giving her a forced smile as I take a step back, turning and assessing the mobile wall. Surely if I find the right title, it's going to move and...

"Not so fast, dear," my mother calls out.

Before I can even contemplate my exit, I feel myself being dragged backwards.

Frowning, I try to fight the pull, focusing all my strength in my legs as I place one foot forward, then another.

But it's all in vain when I get pulled once more—this time with enough strength that I fly.

I...fly.

"Whaaaat?" I squeak as I find myself floating in the air.

My eyes find my mother's knowing smirk, and somehow I know this is all her doing.

"There's no such thing as witchcraft, dear?" she asks, a smile on her face.

I blink repeatedly.

"Put me down, please," I beg, flailing my arms around as panic overtakes me.

With a wave of her hand, I'm back on the ground. My feet meet the floor and I swear I could kiss it with the amount of fear still running through my veins.

"What. Was. That?"

My features must be pale, my entire countenance mirroring the terror I feel on the inside.

"I'm dreaming," I whisper to myself. "I must be dreaming. That's it..."

"You're not dreaming, Elizabeth," my mother assures me, taking a step forward and planting herself in front of me.

She reaches for me, and instinctively I flinch away from her touch, thinking she's going to do another odd demonstration and actually hurt me.

"You're safe," she says softly, no doubt seeing the distress written all over my features. "I'm not going to hurt you."

"I don't understand..." I whimper in shock, rubbing my arms in a gesture of self-soothing. "I don't understand what's happening."

"I know," she sighs. "And I'm going to explain this to you. Come."

She takes me by my hand, leading me to the table in the center of the room that houses the vellum manuscript.

"I'll start at the beginning," she gives me a tight smile. "I'm sure you must have a preconceived notion about witchcraft—though we prefer to call ourselves the Coven of Light. The church has done a marvelous job of putting all of us in the same basket and call us devil worshippers. Yes, it is true that there are those out there who choose the dark side, and their power comes from the dark. But just as there is dark, so there is light."

She pauses, checking with me to see if I'm following.

I give her a slow nod, though my mind is still reeling with confusion and disbelief, anxiety coursing through my veins. How can I possibly believe what she's saying?

Despite the evidence staring me in the face, I have a hard time reconciling what I knew of my mother with what she's telling me—that she's some type of magical being with the ability to move objects with her mind.

I've always considered myself a rational individual, using facts to form an opinion. And though magic seems too far removed from reality, I cannot deny that my mother *is* presenting me with facts.

"There are six main families scattered around the world that fight on behalf of the light. And we are part of one of them," she says as she brings forth an old scroll with a snap of a finger.

Laying it on the table in front of me, she unfolds it with her powers. The material is yellow and worn out. As I tentatively reach with one finger, I find the material smooth and silky.

Vellum.

"This is our family—Stuart," she points to a huge genealogical tree that starts at the top of the scroll with the first Stuart, going down until

I can find my mother's name at the bottom, too. The scroll has a striking feature though—it only traces the female line.

"Only women?" I ask, tracing the ancient lineage.

She nods, a bright smile appearing on her face.

"The Stuart abilities are passed down only through the female line. Usually they are manifested through an innate talent, like my telekinesis. But we also have the ability to do rituals and spells that require different incantations, ingredients, and of course, different degrees of difficulty."

She goes on to tell me a little about the other families. For three families, the powers are passed down through females. For the other three, it's through the male line.

Most importantly, major rituals require one member from each family to perform forbidden spells.

"What do you mean by major ritual?" I frown.

"Come here," she motions me to follow her to the glass box that houses the vellum manuscript. Using her telekinesis, she removes the glass, placing it on a faraway table and giving me a direct view at the manuscript.

Up close, I can see the exquisite penmanship and the beautiful illustrations on the first page.

"This is the *Codex Stuartorum*. It dates back to the sixth century A.D. and it represents our oath to the light."

Waving her hand over the surface of the first page, she whispers, "*Revelate*," and the Latin text becomes legible in English.

My eyes widen in awe, but I don't comment on it. I'll have plenty of time to digest the information later. For now, I give the document my full attention as I read its contents.

"You swear to use your powers not for personal gain, but only for one purpose—eradicating evil entities," I quote aloud from the codex. "Demons?" I suddenly burst out.

Fiona nods grimly.

"Since we all possess these unique abilities, the elders were afraid that we would use them for nefarious purposes. As such, they came together with a solution. Each family would sign a blood oath to only do good. And to further limit abuses of power, each family's codex is incomplete," she recounts as she flips the pages of the codex, showing that many of the pages contain only a few paragraphs.

"There are spells out there that are far too powerful to belong to only one family, let alone one individual. As such, the elders broke apart fragments of the most dangerous and forbidden spells and split them among the six families."

"But what if there is an emergency? You said the families are scattered across the globe. How could you get all the fragments assembled in time?" I ask pensively.

A mischievous smile pulls at her lips.

"There is at least one teleporter per generation. It's their job to gather everyone once a year during our annual meetings," she explains.

"That's a lot to take in," I admit.

"I know," she sighs. "And it's just scratching the surface. You see, like with all aspects of life, with good comes bad. Just like there are those like us that belong to the light, there are those who belong to the dark."

"Do you mean there are similar families that belong to the dark side?"

My mother purses her lips.

"Not quite. There are those that acquire power through dark means —by selling their souls to the devil, so to speak—but they are usually solitary beings. Power is too intoxicating to share," she shakes her head in disapproval. "Our main enemies are those dark beings that encroach into our world—where they do *not* belong—and prey on those weak men hungry for power."

She gives me a short biblical explanation about the origin of demons and fallen angels and the fact that the coven of light is purported to derive its powers from divine origins.

I nod along, though I can tell she's giving me the abridged version of everything—making me wonder what she's *not* telling me.

"When earth teemed with demons and fallen, God realized he needed to protect his creations. So he bestowed gifts upon six families—gifts that would help them fight against evil and keep humanity safe," she pauses. "Or so the legend goes," she chuckles.

I narrow my eyes at her. *Or so the legend goes?*

The more I listen to her, the more I have to wonder *why now?* Why tell me now when it's clear that she should have done so years ago—if I believe that mothers should pass down their knowledge onto their daughters.

"Let me understand this. You're saying magic is real—that our family *has* magic. And now you're telling me there are angels and fallen, and demons, and evil entities?"

"That is exactly what I'm telling you, Elizabeth. And what's worse is that those evil entities live among us, wreaking havoc wherever they go. They thrive on chaos, destruction, war and suffering. And they *love* watching humanity lose itself."

"And of course, you're there to stop them," I roll my eyes at her.

She nods.

"I'm aware I haven't been the best mother to you, but know that I've always had your best intentions at heart. And all I've done has been to create a better world for my children—for *you.*"

Growing up, both my parents had been rather absent—not that it was anything out of the ordinary since nobility often let the staff raise their children. My father had lost himself in his vices, and my mother had had her commitments—which, if I'm to believe her, had included slaying demons all over the world.

"Why are you telling me this *now*?" I demand.

As I'd seen the trajectory of her story, I'd intuited how this all related to me and...Amon. Even so, I'm almost afraid to hear it from her lips.

But more than anything, I'm afraid it could be true.

It couldn't, could it?

"Because you need to know why I killed that man. You need to know *what* he was," my mother replies staunchly, setting her steely gaze on me.

"What do you mean?" I ask softly.

Flicking her wrist, she turns the codex to another page—one that has the illustration of a woman's body. My eyes go wide with disbelief as I stare from the manuscript to my mother and back to the manuscript, the question written all over my face.

"All your life, I've told you how special you were, Elizabeth, did I not?" She gives me a soft smile—one that is quite rare to see on my mother's face.

"What is this, *mama*?" I ask, almost afraid of the implications.

"My mother, your grandmother, had the gift of foresight. When I was pregnant with you, she knew you would be special—so special that the entire world would covet your gift."

"What gift?" I whisper, an ominous shiver going down my body.

"The gift of healing," my mother says, wiping a tear away.

I frown.

"Why is that so precious?"

"Because," she comes closer, bringing her hand to my chest, right on top of my birthmark. The same mark is illustrated in the codex. "Yes, there are other people that can heal injuries to a degree. But what you have," she shakes her head, pure emotion shining in her eyes. "This doesn't just heal physical wounds, Elizabeth. It heals the essence of the soul."

My brows pinch together as I try to understand what's so great about it—aside from the fact that I've never in my life healed myself, or others. How is it that I have this *gift* but I've never felt its presence?

"Though demons *can* live forever, they are not invincible. And in order to kill them, we need to destroy their essences. A demon is considered dead only once its essence is nullified," she pauses, biting her lip. "For them, your gift is like a fountain of immortality. They can drink out of it, and preserve their life forever."

"But I've never seen evidence of any such gift," I protest.

"That's because of me," she immediately answers, a sad smile tugging at her lips. "There was only one other confirmed case in history. A woman who died before she reached her majority *because* of that ability. She was a beacon for demons, and she was killed by one of them—drained of her power. I never wanted that for you, so I bound your powers at birth."

"What..."

"I thought if I did that you could lead a normal life. That you would grow to your majority, marry someone and have your own family. But I never imagined they would still find you. That *he* would find you."

"By he you mean... Amon?"

She nods grimly.

"You can't possibly think he's a demon," I shake my head, taking a step back. "No, I refuse to believe that."

"He *is* a demon, Elizabeth. I don't know what kind, and frankly, I do not care. I'm only concerned about you and the fact that you were so close to..." she chokes on a cry. "He could have killed you. He could have drained you..."

Yet as I look at her and her emotive display—one I've never seen her display towards me before—I can't help but wonder if she was concerned about me, or about the fact that Amon could become invincible because of me.

Today is the most animated I've seen my mother in...forever.

"How do you know?" I inquire, keeping my tone even though all I want is to scream to her that Amon is innocent. That he could never...

She purses her lips, her features tight and for a moment I don't think she's going to reply.

Then, the codex pages suddenly flip again.

My eyes widen, my entire being assailed by disbelief.

"That..."

"That is your Amon, dear," she says, and even through my veil of shock I can detect a hint of smugness. "A demon we've been hunting for *centuries*."

Bringing my eyes back to the codex, I peruse the drawing of a man with long, white hair and equally white eyes. The artist had done a phenomenal job, every line and every stroke matching Amon's features.

So much so that I find myself speechless.

"Every member of the Coven knows about his existence. He is one of the most powerful demons we've ever come across. And it's only because..." she pauses, her teeth raking over her bottom lip as she scrunches her brows in worry.

"Because?" I inquire, almost certain I'm not going to like her answer.

"He was the demon who killed the other girl—the one with *your* birthmark. He's the one who consumed her essence. And the moment he did that, no one could measure up to him. Even with all the six families involved, he was too powerful," she sighs.

Suddenly, things are starting to become more clear—like why Amon had survived. But there is one thing that keeps bothering me.

If Amon was so powerful, if he was so dangerous, why not cut our sojourn short at the Duchess' house? If she thought he would become so invincible if he got access to me, why did she not take me away the first chance she had?

Unless...

I swallow hard, hating that I'm doubting her, or Amon, or my own damn existence. Yet how can I not be a mass of confusion when I've just been told that my entire life has been a lie? That *nothing* is as it seems?

"You said to kill a demon you need to nullify his essence," I suddenly add. "What did you do to him? After the shooting? If he is so powerful, I doubt he would have died just from a few shots."

"You're clever," she clicks her tongue against her teeth. "You're right. The shot didn't kill him. It merely wounded him long enough so we could get our hands on him—so we could contain him until all six families were present to nullify him."

"And?"

She shrugs.

"He's dead."

But he's not. I know he's not. And *she* must know he's not.

That means my mother is lying to me.

Is it to protect me? Or is there something more?

She continues to talk, droning on about the family legacy and the fact that my sister had already been initiated into it, and she is to become the next Stuart matriarch.

Once more, I have to wonder why she hadn't told me any of this earlier—why she'd waited until I met Amon to do so. And because of that, I can't help but feel there are more things she is hiding from me.

"I really thought sealing your magic would keep you away from this life. I'm sorry, Elizabeth. But it's better that you now know. It wasn't my intention to make you suffer. I was just protecting you."

Nodding, I listen to everything more she has to say before I retire for the day.

It's close to midnight when I get to my room, closing the door behind me and managing to remove my simple gown without ringing for Mary.

At this moment, I'd rather be alone with my thoughts.

The story my mother told me is...ludicrous at best.

Yet I can't deny her ability to move things with a flick of her wrist, or the items she houses in that secret chamber of hers—including the *Codex Stuartorum*. Though a part of me may believe there is some truth to her words, I'm still skeptical about many things.

After I've removed all my clothes, I stand in front of the mirror, my attention focused on the tear-shaped mark above my breast. According to my mother, this is the core of all my problems, because it designates me as someone with the power to heal...demons.

It makes me a beacon for demons, and the reason Amon had pursued me in the first place.

But while the things I've learned cast doubt about everything that's ever happened in my life—including Amon—there are still unanswered questions.

And one still bothers me.

For all my mother's explanations about Amon being the epitome of evil who wants to leech on me to become even more powerful, some things don't fit.

That time at the Duchess' house hadn't been my first encounter with Amon. And during the first one, he could have very well done anything he wanted to me and I wouldn't have been able to stop him.

He'd been in my room. He could have easily taken advantage of me, yet he hadn't.

He hadn't even been improper.

Moreover, why had my mother not insisted we leave the house party as soon as she saw him?

Why let me be under the same roof as a dangerous demon if it weren't because...

I was bait.

Chapter Fourteen

November 1790. London, Great Britain

My first season began quite uneventfully.

Mama, my sister Olivia and I have been in London for almost a month now.

Between my introduction at court, securing vouchers at Almack's and gaining the approval of all the influential ton matriarchs, I've barely found the time to breathe.

It didn't help that my mother took it upon herself to offer me an introductory course into the ways of the coven, with my sister assisting her.

If before I would have had doubts about my mother's intentions, now they have tripled.

Olivia seems to be aware about everything regarding the coven, and when I'd asked her how she knew so much, she'd told me she's had years to study all the books and materials.

I would be lying if I didn't feel a modicum of jealousy considering I was the last to find out.

But since my last stunt, I've decided that nothing can be solved by acting out—all it does is hurt myself, and ultimately that is not the goal.

As such, I've gone along with my mother and Olivia, putting on my best behavior and becoming a veritable debutante. All in the hopes that soon Amon would contact me and I will be able to get the information directly from him.

I may have a myriad of questions, but because I am not convinced by either side. I want to hear *his* truth too. I'm not going to crucify him before offering him a fair trial.

The only unfortunate thing is that his letters have become sparser. The last one I'd received had been two weeks ago, and he'd only written one thing.

Wait for me, Lizzie mine.

The letter had been delivered at our London house, in the same manner as the others. The window would suddenly open, and the letter would float in.

That suggests he knows I am in London, and he knows where I live.

I cannot comprehend why he would not come see me since I know he could do it if he wanted to.

Then the only alternative is that he...doesn't want to.

No, that cannot be true. I am sure he is just biding his time. Maybe he has some ongoing issues that need to be addressed first. Or, maybe, he is trying to find a way to bypass my mother.

In Haversham, my mother had confessed that she'd placed magical runes all over the property to impede any unwelcome visitor from crossing our threshold.

I am not sure if she's done the same with the London house, but there are plenty of other places where he could find me.

If he wanted to...

Releasing a hopeless breath, I allow Mary to help me with my dress and style my hair.

Since the beginning of the season, I've acquired a plethora of new gowns—all in pastel colors as befitting of any respectable debutante.

From the beginning, my mother has insisted I put an effort in my appearance.

Though she hasn't directly told me so, I know she is trying to orchestrate a match for me. An eavesdropped conversation between my mother and my sister had confirmed as much.

Fiona fears Amon will not be the only one to come for me, and the best recourse for that is to marry me off and use my future husband's aura to cloak my presence. Though I'd been found before I'd heard more details about that particular process, that had been enough to put me on my guard at every event we've been to, looking around and wondering who else could be part of their society.

"You look stunning, My Lady," Mary praises as she steps back, letting me examine my hairstyle.

"Thank you," I murmur appreciatively, rising from my chair and getting ready to depart.

My mother, Olivia and her husband are already downstairs waiting for me.

"There you are, Elizabeth," my mother announces. "That pale pink suits you wonderfully. I'm so glad we picked it for you."

"It does, doesn't it?" Olivia agrees, while I merely nod, giving them a small smile.

"I hope today you won't make another silly excuse not to dance," my mother tells me when we are in the carriage and on the way to Lady Worcester's ball. "Your friend, Emma, always has her card full. You should learn something from her."

I school my features so my distaste towards dancing doesn't show. Not when the only memory I want of dancing is with Amon. Regardless of whether I try or not, I know no one will measure up to him. As such, for every ball or soiree we've been to so far I've pretended to be ill, or have a headache. I might have even broken my heel—accidentally, of course. All in an effort to avoid dancing with *anyone* other than *him*—my Amon.

"Even Emma doesn't dance all the sets," I answer with a smile.

"She's already engaged, Elizabeth," she adds pointedly, the reproach clear. If I were engaged, too, I would be given more leeway.

With how many times my mother uses Emma as an example, I would have been jealous if not for the fact that the girl is an absolute sweetheart.

We'd met when we'd both had our presentation at court, and we'd quickly become chums. She's lively, artless, and a joy to be around.

From the moment we'd found each other, we'd stuck together, always finding a topic to chat about. I've never had a close friend before, so Emma's arrival in my life had been rather fortuitous—especially at a time when I needed someone to lean on the most.

Emma is the daughter of Viscount Berkley—the title currently being held by her brother—and she'd been lucky enough to attract the attention of the Earl of Foley from the first ball she'd attended. Most importantly, though, it is a love match—something that I'm extremely happy for her.

As we reach the Worcester residence, the orchestra has already started playing and a quadrille is in full swing.

As soon as we are announced, we greet the hosts, after which Olivia and her husband are off to speak to some acquaintances, leaving me alone with my mother.

A smile pulls at my mother's lips as she regards the dance floor before she gives me a look that all but tells me I need to dance tonight, *or else.*

Sighing, I gaze around the room, spotting Emma, her mother, the Dowager Viscountess Berkley and her brother, Lord Berkley by the refreshments table.

My mother, seeing that Lady Berkley is also present, urges me to join them while she greets some of her friends on the other side of the ballroom.

"You don't look too thrilled to be here," Emma whispers in my hair as I reach her side.

I give her a pained nod.

"Mama is pestering me to dance today and I fear I'm running out of excuses," I sigh. "I've already used my entire arsenal and she knows I'm doing it on purpose."

"You poor thing," she coos in jest. "You will expire on the spot if you dance with someone, will you not?"

A giggle escapes me.

"And we wouldn't want that now, would we?"

Turning to Lady Berkley and her son, I greet both, giving them a polite smile before Emma steers me into conversation again, telling me about her latest outing with Lord Foley and how much she likes him.

I let her gush over her beau, a little jealous that she's experiencing all these wonderful moments with her beloved while mine is...missing. Or, maybe, he will never be recovered at all.

In the two weeks since Amon's last letter, I've been beside myself with worry as I've built up all sorts of scenarios in my head as to why he wouldn't write to me anymore—some more worrisome than others.

At first I'd despaired that he'd been caught and harmed by the coven, until I'd started thinking that maybe he doesn't want me anymore. That, *maybe* he'd found out that my mother had sealed my powers and as such I was no longer useful to him.

"Lady Elizabeth, you look extraordinary tonight," Lord Berkley offers me a compliment.

I give him a tight smile.

"Thank you, Lord Berkley," I incline my head.

"Terrence, you should dance with her," Emma suddenly quips.

Her brother's eyebrows shoot up in surprise.

"Emma," I hiss at her, unable to believe she'd said that.

"Your mother wants you to dance. This is your best chance to show her you're behaving without having to withstand some boor's attentions. At least you know Terry," she explains.

Her brother doesn't seem put off by the suggestion, and as I give it some thought, I nod thoughtfully, realizing it *could* help.

Seeing me consider the request, Lord Berkley turns to me.

"Would you do me the honor of the next dance, Lady Elizabeth?" He asks as he extends his hand towards me.

For a moment, I falter.

My heart thrums in my chest as I remember Amon and the

masquerade. Yet Emma is right. My mother will continue to pester me to dance and be active until she will undoubtedly force me to dance with someone of her choosing. This way, at least, it's someone I relatively know.

"I would love to," I answer, placing my gloved hand in his.

Right at that moment, the quadrille ends, the orchestra switching to a minuet.

The dance doesn't require much touching or too close proximity, and I'm grateful for that small mercy. But though I try to immerse myself in the moment, especially as I see everyone around me flushed and energized from the music, I fear I cannot do so. Not when the only thing I want to remember is Amon's light smile as he'd twirled me on the dance floor, disregarding everyone and every convention as he'd molded my body to his.

"You seem to have a lot on your mind," Lord Berkley notes.

"Forgive me," I blush as I realize I'd been caught red-handed fantasizing about someone who is most assuredly *not* my dance partner. "Just woolgathering, I suppose. I'm not very fond of dancing," I lie.

Yes, I am. I *love* dancing. But only with one man...

"I dare contradict you, My Lady. You haven't missed a step so far even though your mind is far away," he says, an eyebrow raised.

I force a smile.

"Thank you. You're an exceptionally good dancer yourself. I'm just following your lead."

He seems satisfied with my words, and as the dance continues, he attempts to draw me into conversation by telling me about his country seat in Berkley and his passion for horses.

I keep a pleasant smile on myself despite the fact that I'm neither knowledgeable in horses, nor do they interest me particularly.

"He must be a worthy horse, indeed, My Lord," I murmur after he tells me the exorbitant sum he paid for an Arabian purebred.

"I have a new mare, too. We named her Moonlight for her dark colors mixed with light. I reckon you'd like her. Maybe Emma can convince you to come visit us in Berkeley during the summer," he continues, describing his stables in great detail and telling me how much I would enjoy riding Moonlight.

For the first time, I look him straight in the eye, his words dawning on me.

Is Viscount Berkley showing an interest in me?

He gazes at me appreciatively, his eyes roving over my form and settling right...on my chest.

My eyes widen just as my cheeks redden from his blatant perusal.

I clear my throat in an attempt to steer him away from my cleavage, but he doesn't react. He only raises his eyes a moment later, meeting mine and giving me a wide grin.

Immediately, I regret having accepted his invitation to the dance. More than anything, I regret not being more attentive to the conversations around me. So busy I'd been with my own problems that I hadn't realized his words now, or in the past, could have been construed as interest.

The dance draws to an end, and just as I hurry back to Emma's side, who is now joined by my mother, Viscount Berkley proposes a turn around the room.

I am about to refuse, but my mother, sensing the situation, gives me another pointed look, leaving me with no choice but to accept his offer.

He places my arm on top of his as he continues to tell me more about his horses. I tune out most of his conversation, merely nodding along with a fake smile on my lips.

Yet just as he's returning me to my mother's side, he asks me the dreaded question.

"May I call upon you tomorrow?"

I bite my lip, ready to tell him no.

But before I can do so, my mother, who is within hearing distance, interjects on my behalf.

"Of course, Lord Berkley. She would love that."

"Oh, Elizabeth," Emma rushes to my side, her tone enthusiastic.

Though I do my best to maintain my smile, the only thing I want to do is leave everyone behind and retire to my own room.

One dance because I'd tried to get my mother off my back, and it suddenly turned into the beginning of a courtship?

The conversation flows animatedly as my mother proceeds to ask various questions of Viscount Berkley and his mother. Emma, the sweetheart that she is, tries to apologize for pushing me to dance with her brother.

"I'm sorry," she mentions when she notices that I look worse than someone waiting their turn at the gallows.

"You couldn't have known," I give her a tight smile.

"I didn't know he fancied you. But maybe you could give him a chance? I know he's my brother, but he's such a wonderful gentleman."

"I will," I tell her, the lie exclusively for the sake of our friendship.

As soon as Lord Berkley calls on me tomorrow I will make it known that I am not interested in anything more and that he should not waste his time on me.

Pleased with my reasoning, I wait for the evening to draw to an end.

And to not give my mother further reason to agree to other meetings on my behalf, I accept other invitations to dance—albeit only from married gentlemen.

Late in the night, as we make our way back home, my mother praises me for finally seeing reason.

My cheeks hurt from too much smiling, my feet from too much dancing, and my head from putting on an act for so long. Yet it seems everyone bought it—one small win.

It's only when we get back home and I excuse myself to my room that I can breathe relieved. I only let Mary undo some of my fastenings—the ones I cannot reach myself—before urging her to seek her bed.

After too much socializing, the only thing I want is to be on my own.

Once I've put on my nightgown, I let my hair loose and prepare for bed. Yet, before that, I can't help myself as I open the window, looking outside in case Amon left me something.

Disappointment fills me when I don't see anything, and as the room becomes chilly, I close the window.

Quickly checking on the fire, I finally retire to my bed.

Yet before I can draw the covers to slide inside, all the hairs on my body stand up.

My spine stiffens, my entire body freezing on the spot.

Only *someone* could trigger that type of awareness within me.

Swiveling, I come face to face with him.

Amon.

My beloved who is neither dead, nor injured, nor does he appear to be any worse for the wear.

"Did you miss me, Lizzie mine?" he murmurs, his eyes gleaming dangerously as he sets them on me.

"Amon?" I blink, taken aback by his sudden presence. "What are you doing here? What..."

I don't get to say anything else as I find myself flat against the wall, his body molded to mine, his big hand splayed over my jaw as he keeps me in place—making sure I'm looking at him directly in the eye.

"You. Danced. With. Them," he says through gritted teeth, tension radiating from him. "You let other men touch you," he rasps. "Dance with you... You're killing me, Lizzie mine."

"You weren't there," I whisper. "How could you reproach me about this when you haven't shown your face in months?"

His face contorts in pain, almost as if my words physically hurt him.

"I couldn't," he breathes, his warm air fanning my face. "I couldn't come to you. Not yet..."

"But you could write?" I raise my brows. "You could leave those damn letters on my windowsill? And for what? To give me hope where there's none?"

He shakes his head.

"You have it all wrong. Those letters were to show my commitment to you."

"Commitment?" I choke on the word. "How come I haven't seen any evidence of that?" I ask him pointedly.

"You dare question my loyalty towards you?" he raises his voice, the question seemingly getting a rise out of him. "You have no idea the things I've done for you," he hisses. "Everything I've ever done has been for you."

"For me, or for the mark I carry?" I demand suddenly.

He blinks in confusion, and with my free hand, I wrench down the neckline of my nightgown to show him my birthmark.

"I know who you are. Or, I should say, *what* you are," I tell him squarely, waiting to see his reaction.

How many times have I envisioned this confrontation? How many times did I imagine he would tell me this is all a misunderstanding. That he isn't the man in the illustration. That he isn't...a demon.

But one look at him and I know everything is true.

He is not...human.

And yet, why does that not scare me more? Why am I not more terrified of him and of everything he symbolizes?

Why is it that for me, demon or not, evil or not, he is just...Amon. *My* Amon. The owner of my heart.

"What do you think you know?" he takes a step back, giving me some space, yet he doesn't remove his touch. His hands are still on my body, one arm snaked around my waist, the other on my jaw, slowly stroking my flesh. Despite my determination to see this conversation through, my body reacts to his nearness, a raging inferno developing in my chest—quite fitting considering his ilk.

"That you're a demon?" I tilt my head to the side, studying him and his lack of reaction. "That you're after what I can do for you, not truly for myself?"

He regards me for a moment before he chuckles.

"I see your mother told you about me. What exactly did she tell you? That I'm a monster?"

I nod.

"That I'm evil personified and I need to be eradicated at all costs?"

Again, I nod.

"And of course, that I'm only after you because of this," he says as he brings his hand to my chest, on top of my gown.

Before I can answer, though, he rips the material in two, leaving me bare and gasping.

"What..."

"I'm only after you for this, am I not?" he asks again, moving closer.

Instinctively, I take a step back as I seek to cover myself.

He doesn't let me, though.

Catching my hand, he moves it aside as he lays his palm on top of my breast, covering my birthmark. His heat transfers to my body, his touch as intoxicating as it is forbidden.

"What are you doing?" I whisper, realizing I'm seeing a different side of Amon tonight.

No longer the sweet gentleman from before—*my savior*—now there's an intensity to him that scares me. Yet paradoxically, I'm not afraid.

My heart beats faster in my chest as he applies more pressure on top of my skin, and I know he can sense exactly what his nearness is doing to me.

His gaze holds me captive as he lets me witness the play of emotions on his face.

Anger. Passion. Lust.

Love?

"Is that what she told you, Lizzie mine? That I'm only after this cursed mark?"

"Yes," I whisper, unable to break eye contact.

"And what do you think? Do you agree with her?" he murmurs softly, nuzzling his cheek against mine.

"I don't know," I answer honestly. "She bound my abilities. That means the mark is inactive for now. But you could always..."

"It's irreversible, Lizzie. The binding spell your mother put on you is irreversible. Your mark will *never* be active."

I swallow uncomfortably.

My mother had never told me that. She'd implied that there was still a chance it could be useful, and that it would still attract attention.

But how could he have known? As soon as the question crosses my mind, though, I roll my eyes. Of course he would have known it. If he's such a powerful demon, he would have known it from the beginning.

"It will never be active. Yet I'm still here, aren't I?" he asks softly.

He curls his hand around my nape, bringing me closer to him until his lips hover on top of mine. All the while, his other hand is still atop of my breast, slowly caressing my skin as he brushes his thumb lightly across my nipple.

My breath catches in my throat as I stare into his eyes—into the turmoil I witness there.

"Tell me the truth, Amon. What am I to you?" I whisper, my voice almost breaking with emotion. "Are you playing with me? Is this just a game? A way to get back to the coven and my kind?"

"What if I said no?" he inquires lazily. "What if I told you that you're my entire reason for being? That you're why I wake up in the morning. Every goddamn day from the dawn of time until now. What if I told you that you belong to me in a way no woman ever belonged to a man? That I might be evil personified, but you're the only one I'll ever be good to," he murmurs huskily, his voice coated with the most potent ambrosia.

His pupils are dilated, his eyes almost black as he regards me with unfulfilled lust.

My lips part as I find it harder and harder to breathe, my chest constricting, my entire body seemingly turning against me.

"Ah, my darling girl, I know you feel it, too. You might not know why, but you will always feel this magnetic pull towards me."

I swallow hard, unable to find an adequate reply because he is right.

There are so many questions I need to ask him—so many things I still need clarified. Yet he only needs to look at me like that—like I'm the only one in the world for him—and I no longer care about anything else. Not that he is a wanted demon, nor that I am a born witch and we are on opposite sides.

I don't care about anything but this moment when he is only a man, and I am a woman.

"You *are* the only one in the world for me," he confesses thickly and my eyes widen in realization.

He's reading my mind—has been doing so from the very beginning.

"And I swear to you Lizzie mine. On my never-ending life, and on my damned soul. I swear to you that my desire for you is not conditional on the mark you bear. The only condition is you. Past, present, future. Always you," he drawls before his lips cover mine in a bruising kiss.

My hands go to his shoulders to push him off, yet instead, my fingers get tangled in his thick hair, pressing my lips tighter against his.

"Let me in, Lizzie," he rasps against my mouth. "Let me taste home again, my love," he says as he nibbles at my lips, slowly and expertly coaxing them open.

His words barely register. I'm too lost to sensation—to the feel of his mouth opening on top of mine, urging me to do the same. My lips slowly part, enough for him to swipe his tongue against the seam of my mouth, seeking entrance.

I don't question it. I don't wonder what is this madness that has taken over me as I open deeper, letting him in just as I meet his tongue with mine.

A loud moan escapes me as my back hits the wall once more. His knee is between my legs, rubbing me intimately just as he continues to stroke my naked breast, his thumb circling my nipple before pinching it.

"Fuck," he curses as he angles my head so he can taste me deeper, probe more intimately, feel me closer to his body just as I feel him to mine.

"Amon," I gasp, the word wrenched from my lips. "My Amon," I murmur incoherently as our mouths fuse to one another.

"That's it, Lizzie mine," he groans, sharp teeth pricking at my lower lip and drawing blood.

The pain is but a light pulsation compared to the pleasure of his embrace.

The kiss becomes increasingly heated. One hand continues to knead my breast while his other massages my nape, seducing me into surrendering to him.

It's a maddening dichotomy how he plunders what is freely given.

Yet just as I think I'm going to die if I don't feel his naked skin on mine, he's off me and at the other end of the room.

"I'm sorry," he breathes harshly. "I thought I could control myself," he swallows hard, his eyes glowing a deep red in the dimly lit room. "But you're not ready for me."

I'm slow to react, the fog of desire still clouding my mind.

"What if I am?" I bite my lip as I lower my torn gown to my waist in a daring gesture. His heated gaze dips to my naked breasts, pure hunger radiating from him.

"I fuck hard, sweetheart," he says darkly, his eyes never once leaving my chest. "You're not ready for me," a pause. "*Yet.*"

And with that he's gone—disappearing into thin air.

My breath catches in my throat as I stare at the spot he just vacated, and a deep flush envelops my body.

I fuck hard, sweetheart.

Why do his vulgar words only whet my appetite for...more?

LORD BERKLEY DOESN'T COME the following day, to my mother's great chagrin.

And though I'm happy about it, I can't help but think that Amon might have had something to do with it.

He hadn't been pleased to find out I'd danced with Viscount Berkley. I can't imagine how he would have reacted to us spending more time together.

Though I hadn't asked Amon any of the pending questions I have, I feel eerily calm about what happened last night.

Calm and...embarrassed.

My cheeks burn once more—*for the thousandth time today*—when I think about his kiss. The taste of him and how his mouth had fitted on top of mine.

It had been...pure wonder. So much so that I don't understand why he'd stopped when he had. He must have known he could have taken me right then and there and I wouldn't have protested. It might have been wrong of me to do so, but when I'm in his vicinity, all rational thoughts flee me until he's all I can think about.

Amon. My Amon.

I spend the rest of the day with a perpetual smile on my face waiting for night to come—for my Amon to visit me again.

Except, when midnight strikes, he is nowhere to be found.

There's only one small note.

Wait for me, Lizzie mine. I will soon have all the answers you seek.

Yours Eternally,

Amon

HOW DARE HE...

I blink as I read it again. And again. I read it until all the anger and frustration I'd held at bay simply explodes inside me. Crumpling the sheet of paper, I throw it into the fireplace.

My breathing is labored as I watch the flames envelop it. So much so that I can barely calm myself down.

How dare he?

He comes into my life when it's convenient for him to do so, and he easily leaves me when it's not.

How can he ask me to wait for him when all I've done so far has been waiting? Waiting and with nothing to show for it.

I've given him the benefit of the doubt against my own family's words.

I mourned him when I thought he was lost to me—I was ready to lose myself too.

And what does he do?

He just asks me to wait.

But how can I when it seems he's playing with my emotions? When he treats me like a mere stop instead of a destination?

"Damn you, Amon," I rage out loud, hoping his supernatural senses pick up on it so he will realize I'm not his plaything.

That night, in a moment of pure anger, I take out one of my mother's books and I draw protective runes all over my walls and on the windowsill, ensuring that if Amon wants to come in, he will not be able to.

Maybe this will teach him a lesson.

Days pass, and though my anger at him continues, it slowly loses momentum. It's especially hard to keep it going when it morphs into longing.

Why do I have to be so simplistic? Why does Amon have to inspire only l-type of emotions in me?

Longing. Lust. Love...

Even knowing he's a demon—that he's the definition of evil—my soul cannot stop yearning for him.

In an attempt to forget my situation with Amon, I dedicate more time to my friendship with Emma. We go out shopping for books together, and we spend the afternoon alternately at each other's house.

My mother is pleased about our connection, but she is still a little put off about my lack of suitors, which has been even more pronounced lately.

Though in the beginning I would receive some invitations to dance, or for a ride in Hyde Park, now there's absolutely nothing.

Before, I was the one refusing all invites. Now, they just never come.

"You must have done something," my mother snaps at me one morning. "But I can't imagine what. You have a pleasant face and figure, and I've bought you the best gowns and jewelry money could buy. By all intents and purposes you should have been declared the Incomparable of the season—a diamond of the first water. But instead of that, everyone avoids you. No gentleman would look twice at you. For God's sake, your dowry alone should have those fools running."

I shrug.

"Maybe I'm just not a great conversationalist, *mama*. I tried to talk with Lord Berkley about his horses but I fear he saw right through me. I'm sorry I can't pretend," I give her a false apology.

Her lips flatten into a disapproving line.

"Why couldn't you be more like your sister?" she huffs in a low tone.

I frown at the veiled insult.

"What is that supposed to mean? How should I be more like Olivia?"

"Never mind," Fiona waves her hand dismissively, but I'm not about to let it go.

Not when seemingly my entire life I've been somehow *less* than Olivia.

"No, please do tell me, mother. How should I be more like Olivia? Is it because she married when she was supposed to? That she was the perfect child and she never made any problems for you? Or," I pause, raising a brow, "is it because she's your successor where I lack the power to do anything but the most basic spell?"

Her eyes widen and as she opens her mouth to speak, no words come out.

"Do I come across like that?" she asks softly a moment later.

I blink in surprise at the shift.

"Yes, you do."

She purses her lips.

"It wasn't my intention," she releases a deep sigh. "I've never been as protective of Olivia as I am of you. Because I know how special you are, I need to know you are safe. And if that means finding you a husband, then I'm going to find you a husband even if it's the last thing I'll do."

"But why do you need to go to that extreme? Why would a husband help me in any way?"

"Because," she starts, looking around to make sure there's no one in our vicinity. "That mark of yours emits pulsations—*just* like a beacon. Since I bound your powers when you were born, the pulsations became so faint, most wouldn't be able to detect them. But a powerful enough demon could. So the only way for you to be safe—truly safe—is to eliminate the last traces of your mark."

"How?"

Her cheeks redden slightly.

"You'll need to marry," she starts. "And you'll need to consummate the marriage," she clears her throat. "Once you take your husband's seed, the last echoes of the pulsations should slowly ebb until they disappear."

"I see," I murmur as I direct my gaze to my food. "Why didn't you want me to marry Lord Clifford? It could have solved your issues."

"How do you know about Lord Clifford?" She frowns. "Never mind. It must be that habit of yours to listen to closed doors. Lord Clifford was a bad man, Elizabeth. I don't want you to marry just anyone. I do want you to be happy. Though we must hurry the process a little now," she gives me a tight smile.

I nod, forcing myself to return her smile.

Yet all the while, Amon's words are echoing in my mind.

It's irreversible.

Even if the mark still emitted pulsations, why would my mother go to such lengths if she knew the binding spell she'd put on me was irreversible? That I could never tap into the powers offered by that mark?

The only alternative is that she wants to keep me safe—that there is still the possibility that I could be killed if one of those hungry demons got their hands on me.

Yet why do I feel like there's more to this?

Why do I feel like neither Amon nor my mother are telling me the entire story?

Just as she gets up from the table, I remember to ask her something.

"May I spend the weekend at Emma's house? She was here last time and now she invited me over. I'd love to spend more time with her."

"Of course you may. I had tea with her mother the other day and she asked me for permission, which I've already granted. I'm sad nothing came of you and Lord Berkley, but they are wonderful people."

Thanking her, I head upstairs to prepare while Mary packs me a small bag.

Though my mother had been put off in the beginning because Lord Berkley hadn't called on us, she'd quickly gotten over it when she'd heard he'd taken ill.

By the time he'd recovered, he'd been called to his country seat and nothing more had come out of that promise.

Once more I find my thoughts drifting to Amon—as they usually do whenever I think about myself and a man in the same sentence. It's almost like he'd laid siege to my thoughts.

Or, maybe he did.

If that demon can read my mind, then who knows what else he can do?

And yet the one thing he does *not* do is honor his promise with me.

My anger at him might have dwindled over the last few weeks, but that doesn't mean he's off the hook once he shows up. In fact, I've already compiled a list of questions I need answers to—list that seemingly grows every day.

Besides being curious about him and his origins, I also want to know why he's so keen on me if not for the mark.

Despite my mother's praises, I know I am not the best looking girl out there, nor am I the best-mannered, smartest, or possessing of an even temper. If I were to describe myself, I would say I am just above average. Not quite average, but a little bit over.

My mother was right in one regard, though.

With my dowry, *everyone* should have been vying for my hand.

Yet I have absolutely no suitors—not even fortune hunters.

It's so strange that I am sure a certain demon must have had something to do with it.

Shaking my head as I try to thrust Amon out of my mind once more, I finish getting ready before boarding a carriage with my luggage and going to Emma's house in Grosvenor Square.

"I'm so happy you're here! We're going to have such a wonderful time together," Emma declares as I'm led to my room across from hers.

"Me too. Soon, when you'll be married it's going to be much harder to see each other. I'm happy my mother allowed me to come."

"I think she can see how unhappy you are," she purses her lips.

Waiting for the footman to leave, I plot myself on the bed, releasing a loud, tired sigh.

"Can she? I know she has my best interests at heart. It's just..." I trail off, not knowing how much I can share.

It is true that Emma and I have become the closest of friends—the likes I'd never had before. But how much could I share with her considering my family's secretive background. For that reason, I hadn't dared mention Amon—though she'd shrewdly intuited that I am mooning after a gentleman.

"She wants you to make a good match," Emma takes a seat next to me, taking my hands in hers.

"She wants me to make *any* match at this point. And I..." I bite my lip. "I'm in love with someone already."

"What?" She squeaks. "I cannot believe this. You must tell me everything," she says as she goes to the door, closing it and ensuring no one is around to eavesdrop.

"There isn't much to say," I shrug. "He's not someone my mother would ever approve of, so I am bound to just love him from afar."

"Does he love you back?" she asks excitedly, seemingly overlooking the fact that I told her it's a forbidden match.

"I'm not sure," I admit, my smile falling. "He's never said so though his actions suggest he might have a tendre for me."

Despite never saying it out loud, Amon had mentioned the word *love* in his letters. But considering I'm not sure about anything where he is concerned, I could never confidently say he loves me.

"Dear God, Elizabeth. Tell me you haven't done anything," she pauses, her voice dropping, "*scandalous*," she utters the word in a hushed tone.

A blush envelops my features as I think of our kiss and his heated touches. He'd made my body sing to life in a way I would have never imagined. He'd built me up to a crescendo, but he'd never quite fulfilled the promise of pleasure as he'd drawn back.

I fuck hard, sweetheart.

"You have!" Emma accuses lightly.

I wave my hands in front of me, too red and embarrassed to come up with a witty reply.

"Only a kiss," I whisper when I'm finally able to speak.

Her brows shoot up, and her cheeks flush red too.

"My God," I point at her. "You too. You and Lord Foley..."

Her reaction gives her away immediately as she looks away.

"He kissed me," she murmurs. "And a little more," she says before she throws herself on the bed, burying her head in a pillow.

"What more?" I whisper, full of curiosity.

She burrows harder into the pillow, letting out a small squeal.

When she manages to calm down, she gives me a very brief description of what had happened between her and Lord Foley.

He'd been calling on her and her mother who had been chaperoning them had been suddenly called away. By that point he'd already kissed her, but this time he did something more with his fingers.

Emma doesn't know exactly how to explain what happened, but she tells me his touch gave her great pleasure without taking her virtue.

I nod along, fascinated by what she's telling me as I do my best to imagine Amon and I in the same circumstances. Everything he'd done to me had felt pleasurable—including his slight bite.

The rest of the day passes in a flurry as we entertain ourselves talking about our beaus, while at night we sneak to her room to read passages from a novel by Ann Radcliffe that Emma had managed to secretly procure. Since reading frivolities is frowned upon, neither her parents nor my mother would ever allow us to read such a novel.

But as we delve deeper into the story, we cannot help but root for the heroine to escape her fate and succeed in her quest for love.

By the time we turn the last page of the novel, it's already late at night. Emma is snoring softly on the bed, and I know she'll want to reread the ending again when she wakes up.

Unlike her, I'm not in the least sleepy.

The candles are still burning, and measuring how much time I have left, I decide to get another book from the library.

Slowly getting out of bed, I grab a shawl that I wrap around my shoulders since the hallways are a little chilly and I make my way out of the room. Since it's Saturday night, Emma's mother is away to a ball, and with the servants already asleep, the house is eerily quiet.

Holding onto a small candle, I creep my way down the stairs to the ground floor where the library is located.

Mayhap something boring would help me fall asleep. God knows since Amon's last visit I haven't been able to sleep properly. No matter how much I tried to put him out of my mind, my traitorous heart would not give up hope.

Reaching the library, I slowly turn the knob and I push the door open.

Immediately, light floods my eyes from the inside and it takes me a few moments to get used to it.

Blinking, I bring the back of my hand to my eyes, rubbing softly before opening them and coming face to face with Lord Berkley and three of his friends.

"Elizabeth?" he calls me by my given name, making me realize the impropriety of this.

"I'm so sorry. I didn't know anyone was here. I'll leave you to it," I say as I turn to leave.

"Wait!" Viscount Berkley calls out. "You must have come here for a book. You should get one," he nods to the bookshelves behind him.

Swallowing hard, I look from him to his friends who are eyeing me suspiciously and I don't know whether it's worth the trouble.

"Thank you, but I'll just get one tomorrow. It's already too late," I murmur.

"Nonsense. Please don't let our presence dissuade you from getting a book. I would feel like a bounder if I inconvenienced you in any way," he adds, giving me a sincere smile.

I falter.

"I'll just take one book and then I'll be on my way," I nod at him, scurrying towards the back of the room.

I already know what I want since I'd perused the shelves quite thoroughly earlier in the day. Heading to the classics section, I pick Plato's Republic, hugging it to my chest as I turn to leave.

I give them a small smile as I make my way to the door.

One of Lord Berkley's friends is by the door, and he moves aside as I reach for the knob, only to realize it's not budging.

The door is locked.

I whip my head back to Lord Berkley.

"This isn't amusing, my Lord. Please open the door," I say through gritted teeth.

"Why are you in such a hurry, Elizabeth? Spend some time with us," he adds mockingly.

Too late do I notice the dangerous glint in his eyes as he looks me up and down, his lips curling up. His other friends share the same look, a couple chuckling at my expense.

"It's not proper. Please open the door," I repeat, my hand still on the knob as I try to rattle the door open.

"Is this what you want?" Lord Berkley asks as his friend throws him the key.

Lifting it in his hand, he waves it at me.

"Please open the door," I push my chin up.

"I'll give you the key in exchange for something," he continues, as if he doesn't hear my repeated pleas.

Yet I don't give him the satisfaction of asking in exchange for what. A hole develops in the pit of my stomach as I realize I stepped into danger due to my own stupidity.

The moment I saw four men, alone, at night, I should have just turned and left.

"Please open the door," I maintain my stance, looking him in the eye so he can see he won't be able to bully me.

"Give me a kiss and I will," he drawls.

One of his friends starts whistling while the others crack some lewd jokes at my expense.

"This isn't proper, my Lord," I tell him again, yet this time I can't imbue my words with the same firmness as fear starts to take shape within me.

"One kiss, Elizabeth. At least that's what I'm owed after what happened because of you."

I frown.

"I don't know what you're talking about."

It's at that moment that I realize he's only been showing me half his face. Slowly, he turns, showing me the side bathed in the shadows.

A gasp escapes me as I see the mottled red flesh on half his cheek.

What...

Emma hadn't said anything about her brother suffering such an injury. She'd just told me he'd taken ill and had decided to retire to his country seat to recuperate.

"It disgusts you, doesn't it?" he snarls, coming closer.

With every step he takes, I can see that the injury is likely the result of a hot iron being embedded in his flesh. It's a fairly recent wound, too, going by the angry red hue of the area.

"I...I'm so sorry that happened to you, my Lord, but how could it have been my fault? I did not even know you were injured," I sputter in indignation.

How dare he blame *me* for his injury?

"Not your fault?" he releases a dry laugh before his features turn to granite. "Hold her," he nods to his friend.

Before I can move, strong arms take hold of me, dragging me from the door. He removes my candle from my grasp, throwing my book and shawl to the ground as he presents me to Lord Berkley.

"Not your fault?" he repeats as he comes in front of me, his hand curled around my throat.

The other man is holding my arms captive behind my back. No

matter how much I try to struggle, I cannot move an inch.

"Guess what the person who did this to me told me?" he asks, his nostrils flaring in disgust as he peruses my face. "He told me to forget you ever existed. That this will be my mercy if I never come near you again."

My eyes widen in shock.

Only one person could have done that.

Amon...

"Let me go," I kick at the other man. "I had nothing to do with your injury, my Lord. Please let me go. This is improper," I level him with my stare.

His lips twitch.

"Hold her tighter," he orders the other man just as he reaches for the hem of my dress.

"What are you doing?" I cry out as I kick with my legs, trying to get him away from me.

Yet all it does is enrage him.

Before I know what's happening, he swipes the back of his hand across my cheek.

The unexpected pain makes me reel, momentarily stunning me to the spot.

He pulls at my nightgown, and it slowly dawns on me what he's trying to do, just as pure terror envelops me.

Enough so that I utter only one word.

"Amon," I whisper into the night, both a calling and a plea.

"What? I didn't hear you, *Lizzy*," Lord Berkley chuckles, turning his burned cheek towards me.

"But I did," another voice rings out in the library.

Air whooshes around as Amon stretches to his full height in the room, the ceiling seemingly barely able to contain him.

The man holding me stumbles back in horror just as Lord Berkley turns.

"Who the hell..." his words are cut off as his eyes widen in recognition. "You," he points at Amon. "It was *you*."

Amon doesn't even blink at Lord Berkley's incessant accusations.

Setting his eyes on me, his eyes scan me from head to toe before he gives me a brief nod.

At the same time, the man holding me is sent away flying, his back connecting with the wall behind.

"What?"

"What the hell?"

"Terry what's this?"

The others start moving around, panic and fear lacing their voices as a cacophony of sounds engulfs the library.

Amon looks completely unbothered as he takes a step towards Lord Berkley.

"What were you going to do to her?" Amon asks, raising a bored brow as he regards the viscount.

"I—I... Nothing," he gulps down, looking at his friends, his gaze pleading for help,

"Hmm, you see, I think you're lying," Amon makes a tsk sound, and as he brings one finger against the viscount's temple, tapping his skin lightly, Lord Berkley opens his mouth and starts talking.

It doesn't seem that he is in control of his words as he explains in great detail what a bitch I am and how he would have derived great pleasure from defiling me.

For the first time, a look of distaste crosses Amon's face, and with a movement of his hand, the viscount stops talking.

"What about the rest of you?" he narrows his eyes at the other men.

Before they can even blink, Amon appears behind each of them, tapping their foreheads and forcing them to admit their most depraved thoughts.

One by one, they admit they would have taken turns with me once Berkley was done, and to hide the incident, they would have killed me and made it seem like an accident or a suicide.

My lower lip trembles in distraught as I realize how close I was to my death—and to something worse.

A twitch appears in Amon's cheek as he regards the men with a murderous expression.

Yet his first target seems to be the viscount.

I'm frozen to the spot as I simply watch what's happening around me. I don't know if it's shock or morbid curiosity, but even if I wanted to, I could not move.

Amon stops in front of Lord Berkley, and lifting his hand, he snaps his fingers in front of the viscount.

Immediately, the man's head explodes.

I jump back as blood, bones and brain splatter everywhere, including on my white nightgown.

Amon doesn't flinch as blood splashes on his face, slowly dripping down.

His eye color seemingly changes, but I can't be sure it's not a play of shadows or simply my erroneous perception.

The other men scream in terror as they try to run for the exit, but as Amon turns his attention to them, they stop, as if they are no longer in control of their actions.

With measured steps, Amon walks towards them, stopping in front of the first man.

I watch with trepidation as he extends his hand. Yet, just as I think he will make the man's head explode as well, he doesn't.

Under my very gaze, Amon's hand changes shape, morphing into something sharp resembling a talon. One moment the blade glints in the dim lighting, the next it penetrates the man's chest. Everything happens in the blink of an eye.

A moment his hand is inside the man's chest cavity, the next he pulls it back, holding the man's still beating heart.

One pump. Two. Blood gushes out.

Closing his fist, the heart explodes, more blood bursting out, staining the ceiling and walls of the library, but also turning Amon's white hair red.

He looks terrifying. Like a true apparition.

Like a...demon.

I gasp just as he turns towards me, his lips pulling into a mocking smile. He gives me a knowing look, his eyes shifting from their normal light blue to blood red before they go pure black.

Flinging the man's body aside with his finger, he turns to the next one.

Two men are now left, both trembling from head to toe.

Despite not being able to move, the first one pisses himself, the entire front of his light-colored trousers now wet.

Amon shakes his head in amusement as he seemingly ponders what he should do to them.

"Lizzie mine," he murmurs, tilting his head to look at me. "They were going to rape and kill you. What punishment do you think is fit for them?

"Me?" I croak, my voice breaking as I speak—from shock or from screaming earlier, I do not know.

"Yes," he nods. "Tell me, my love. What do you think they deserve?"

"I..." I wet my lips, my limbs shaky, my heart in my throat as I take in the slaughter around me.

I'm covered in human matter from head to toe, just like the entire room is stained red.

It's a wonder I'm still on my feet—that I haven't swooned from the horror of it all.

Yet, throughout everything, my awareness was sharp. I heard everything the men said—what they would do to me and how they would kill me.

And why?

All because of a Lord's injured pride.

I have never asked Amon to act against Lord Berkley, so why should

I pay for sins that are not mine?

"As you see fit," I finally utter the words, lifting my chin up and looking Amon right in the eye.

His lips slowly curl up in pleasure as he tips his head at me.

Without any preliminaries, he turns his attention to the other two men, appearing like a flash by their side and whispering something in their ear.

Then, he simply appears by my side, threading his fingers through mine.

The man who'd pissed himself undoes the fastening of his pants while the other man falls to his knees in front of him.

Before I can see more, though, Amon whirls me around, turning me towards him and away from what is happening behind me.

"What did you make them do?" I whisper, slowly taking in his blood-streaked features and red hair. There's a savageness that clings to him—one that should disgust me.

Instead, I only find myself more drawn to him and the pure violence that radiates from him.

"Everything they meant to do to you, they will do to each other. With a small twist, of course," he smirks, his tone playful.

Blood trails down his cheek. Bringing my hand to his face, I wipe it away with my thumb.

But just as I'm about to move my hand, his fingers circle my wrist, keeping it in place.

Screams echo in the room, and from the corner of my eye I can see more blood splatter on the walls. It goes on for seconds on end before suddenly everything is quiet.

They are...dead.

"They are," Amon confirms, taking hold of my finger and bringing my thumb to his mouth.

His lips part—slowly—as his tongue peeks out to lick the residue blood.

I'm too lost in the intensity of his eyes to move or say anything. They flicker again, the color changing to a myriad of different hues.

He killed them.

He killed four people. He *slaughtered* them.

And I watched...

"How does it feel, Lizzie mine?" he asks suavely, leaning forward until his lips are a mere breath away from mine. "How does it feel to see the true face of the devil?" He blinks, and his eyes become black—wholly black.

Terrifying.

The true Amon is...absolutely terrifying.

Chapter Fifteen

Late September 1955. Fairydale, Massachusetts

"Bring me the alcohol."

"Wait! She's coming around."

My eyes slowly open as the throbbing in my temple subsides. Blinking to gain some clarity, I note four figures hovering over me.

The Hales. All but Caleb.

Rhiannon is to my right, her features wrinkled with worry. Thomasa and Connor Hale are on the left side, a step away from Katrina who's holding on to my hand.

"You're awake," she breathes out in relief.

Everyone seemingly does the same as they see me slowly regain consciousness.

Instinctively, my hand goes to my head where the throbbing had been, expecting to find an injury.

Yet there's nothing.

"What happened?" I frown, having a hard time remembering how I'd ended up here.

Rhiannon purses her lips.

"We found you in the catacombs, Darcy. You fainted there," she explains.

My brows are scrunched together as I attempt to recall how I'd ended up there, my memories slowly coming back.

Amon...

He was calling my name, was he not? I'd only followed his voice and then...

I shake my head in frustration at the huge blank in my mind.

Instead of remembering how I'd ended up in the catacombs, I recall vividly the past.

The Amon from the past.

Terrifying.

A demon. An actual, honest to God, veritable demon. Who, besides spending his time slaughtering people and spreading evil wherever he went, also spent time romancing me.

Or, rather Elizabeth.

That is a lot to wrap my mind around.

Almost two hundred years ago I was in love with a demon. So much so that I didn't even *care that he was* the personification of evil.

And then there's the matter of my former family of...witches.

I wince as my temples throb anew, pain spreading through my body.

"Are you alright, dear?" Rhiannon touches my hand, squeezing it lightly.

"Yes," I bite against the pain. "I cannot remember well what happened."

"That's fine. You don't need to strain yourself. But we will be sealing shut the door to the catacombs. It's very dangerous down there."

"Dangerous how?" I look at her, seeing the lines of worry still marring her face.

But is this because of me, or is it something else?

"There are radioactive materials there," Connor steps forward. "They used our house to deposit shipments of Uranium in the Second War. It must have been the fumes that made you pass out. It's better for everyone if we close off that tunnel for good."

Rhiannon nods.

"Here, have some tea. It should help with the pain," she mentions as she brings me a tray from the desk, placing a cup of hot tea in my hands.

"Thank you," I give them a smile. "For everything. And I'm sorry I went there without asking."

"No harm done. You're fine and that's all that matters," Rhiannon waves her hand. "Why don't you join us for dinner tonight? If you feel up to it, that is. If not, I can ask to have your dinner sent to your room."

Dinner? I frown as I look at the mantel clock on the table at the end of the room.

Three in the afternoon.

Good Lord, how long was I out?

"Dinner sounds perfect. Thank you so much," I force a smile but as my mind slowly clears, more questions appear.

"We'll leave you now if you're alright?" Thomasa asks, her eyes combing my body for any signs of distress.

"Yes, do not worry. I am quite fine," I assure them.

One by one, they slowly leave my room. Only Rhiannon lingers behind, her lips flattened into a thin line as she regards me.

"I think you and I are due for a talk, Darcy. I am in the conservatory every morning until noon. Come by tomorrow."

She doesn't wait for my reply, the door closing after her.

I wait for a few moments before I place the empty cup of tea on a nearby table. Getting out of bed, I jump to my feet, surprised there's no echo of pain.

Checking the door to my room is locked, I head to the bathroom.

Despite having my thoughts in disarray, I'm starting to gain more clarity, both about what had led me to the catacombs, and about the vision I'd had about the past.

At this point I can no longer deny that those aren't dreams—they aren't something borne out of my imagination. They are visions of a past life.

One where I was Elizabeth Montford and...hopelessly in love with a demon.

I stop in front of the bathroom mirror, and tugging on the neckline of my gown, I push it low enough to reveal my birthmark.

The same birthmark Elizabeth also had.

My lips purse in concentration as I examine it thoroughly. About two inches big, it's a dark discoloration on my skin in the shape of a teardrop.

According to Fiona Montford, this mark denotes a certain ability to heal.

Information floods my brain, as do the implications of my visions.

Am I somehow related to the Elizabeth of the past? Is this mark hereditary? Because that would make me a descendant of the Stuarts, too. In turn that would mean I have witch blood running through my veins.

Moving my gaze from my mark to the mirror, I examine my features.

Not only do I have the *same* mark as Elizabeth, but we also look like twins.

In my past life, Fiona had bound my powers so no one would take advantage of the mark. Has this happened in this life, too?

Yet the moment that question arises in my mind, I somehow doubt it.

I may not remember much about my mother, but I am certain she'd never dabbled in witchcraft, or anything pertaining to the occult. At the same time, if the Stuart abilities are only passed through the female line, then I should have inherited my powers from my mother—unless she belonged to another family?

Unfortunately, the only memories I have of growing up were of her working herself to the bone to raise me, put a roof over my head and some food in my belly. All she'd done had been to sacrifice herself for my well-being. Even when there was an alternative waiting for her in Fairydale.

That only begs one question. What was she running from?

Before I can change my mind, I open the cabinet, taking out a small blade.

There is only one way to find out if what happened in my visions has any bearing on the present.

Holding the blade between two fingers, I bring it to my forearm, cutting a straight line through my flesh. I grind my teeth in the face of the sudden pain, but I push it down as I stare at the blood pooling over the surface.

If I'm wrong, I'm going to have quite the nasty wound.

But if I'm right...

Dropping the blade in the sink, I turn on the faucet and place my arm under the warm jet of water. The blood quickly washes away from my arm, leaving behind the ghost of a stinging pain and a medium gash.

Just as I think that this was pointless and I'm going to bear the pain for a few more days, the gash starts to shrink.

Right under my eyes, it becomes smaller and smaller until it simply disappears.

My mouth hangs open in shock, and instinctively, I reach for the blade, making another gash on my upper arm.

The same thing happens. Bit by bit, the wound shrinks until it closes, almost as if the skin is mending itself at an accelerated rate.

And though there is an initial pain as the blade pushes into my skin, by the end of the process, there is both no pain and no more injury.

Cleansing the blood off myself, I turn off the faucet and brace my arms on the sink.

All those times...

It hadn't been Amon who'd been healing me. It had been me all along.

And that means...

I slowly bring my eyes to the mirror, staring at my reflection and seeing both myself *and* Elizabeth. In my mind, there's already no more doubt that we are one and the same, her feelings *my* feelings, her experiences *my* experiences.

But if Elizabeth had Fiona to bind her powers and keep her safe, I have no one.

If what Fiona had told her—*me*—about the mark is true, then it is a beacon for evil entities.

For something like that monster.

Though I've had this mark my entire life, it's only since stepping foot into Fairydale that I've gained this particular ability. And for the life of me, I cannot imagine when...or how.

Maybe the Hales can help me understand this better. I am more than certain that Rhiannon knows more than she's letting on. It's in the way she always regards me furtively, observing me for some unknown purpose.

More than anything, it makes me wonder why I've seen so little of the Hales in the time I've been here.

Caleb is always with me, yet they are rarely to be seen around.

Granted, it is a giant house. But it seems ludicrous that days at a time would pass before we'd cross each other's paths.

Almost... Almost as if they went out of their way to avoid me.

Releasing a frustrated sigh, I take a towel off the wall, drying my arms as I go back to the room.

There are too many things that are too odd for me to contemplate, just as there are too many unanswered questions. And if it weren't for these visions of the past, I would be even more in the dark.

Yet the moment I think of the past, my mind unwittingly goes to Amon and the fact that he's not a ghost.

He's a demon.

And potentially the one who wants to harm me—take advantage of my mark now that there's no spell containing it anymore.

"You startled me," I jump up as I see Caleb lounging in my bed, a book in his hand.

Peering above the pages of the book, he raises a brow at me.

"I thought I locked the door," I frown.

"It was open," he shrugs. "I knocked."

Swinging his legs off the bed, he's before me in two strides.

"You forgot this yesterday," he smirks as he places the book in my hands.

The Monk.

"Thank you," I murmur, my cheeks heating up as I recall the kiss.

"Is that all you have to say to me, darlin'? After you assaulted my lips?"

"W—what?" I sputter. "Assaulted your lips?"

"I heard about your incident in the catacombs. I wanted to see if you were alright," he goes on to say, ignoring the previous topic.

Circling me while looking me up and down, he nods quietly to himself.

"You seem fine. I'm glad."

"I *am* fine. It was just a little mishap. I didn't know the catacombs were off limits."

"Are they?" he stops, his lips pulling into a hidden smile. "Don't tell me. More ghosts?"

"No. Your father said there was radioactive residue and it could be harmful for my health."

"Hmm," he muses. "I've never heard that before."

I whip my gaze to his, surprised to see he isn't joking.

"What do you mean? He said they deposited Uranium for the Second World War in the tunnels and it's still radioactive."

I find it hard to believe Caleb wouldn't have heard about that considering it would have been around ten years ago and he would have been a teenager around that time.

"Depositing Uranium this far north? Wouldn't that have been counterproductive? It's far from Manhattan and even further away from Los Alamos," he notes quietly.

Before I can reply, though, he leans in to lay a kiss on my brow.

"I'll be away for a few days for business. My family will take care of you until I come back," he whispers against my skin. "But remember one thing, Darcy darlin'. There is no such thing as universal truth. Every story has different sides and it's up to you to assemble them together to get the final picture."

And with that he is gone.

I bring my hands to my cheeks, massaging them in an attempt to recover from the little kiss he'd given me. One small touch and I'd flushed from head to toe.

Yet even as his presence clouds my judgment, his words still ring in my ears.

There's no such thing as universal truth.

Does he mean I shouldn't wholly trust his family? But doesn't that extend to him too?

More confused than before, I go about my day as I try to make sense of all the information I have.

Pulling out a small diary, I start jotting down everything that had happened to me since arriving in Fairydale, as well as writing a chart of all the people I'd met and each specific interaction.

I already know there are seemingly two factions in this town.

The Hales are on one side, alone in their big manor but seemingly respected enough in town despite some of the rumors surrounding them.

Then there's Mr. Nicholson with the Pierces and Mr. Vaughan.

From what I've been able to glean, Mr. Nicholson is the authority in this town, and is considered the voice of reason.

As he'd promised me, he'd put in a good word with the townsfolk and suddenly any insults at my address have stopped. The police, too, had stopped inquiring into my whereabouts and I haven't been asked again to testify in the murder cases.

Drawing a diagram to map out the connections, I frown as a sudden question enters my mind.

Mr. Nicholson had said the Pierces are distant relatives of his. He'd also been the only one to admit to knowing who my mother was.

Could it be that she's related to him in some way?

Alternatively, could that mean *he* is related to the Stuarts in some way?

Caleb had already confirmed that Rhiannon is involved in witchcraft. That makes me wonder if they aren't somehow involved with the six families Fiona had talked to me about.

And if my reasoning is right...

Then why would *two* families make their home in a remote place like Fairydale?

Placing my pen down, I massage my temples.

No matter how much I think about this, it's quite clear that there are severe gaps in my knowledge that prevent me from reaching any conclusion—or, at least, any reasonable conclusion.

There's also the most important question.

How does Amon figure into all of this?

Is he a friend, or foe?

Is he after my mark, or is he trying to protect me?

Centuries ago, I loved him. And if I'm honest with myself, I still do.

I just don't know who to trust anymore.

When it's time for dinner, I put on one of my nicer dresses and head to the main dining room.

The family is already present when I arrive. Rhiannon is at the head of the table. Connor is by her right side, accompanied by his wife and Katrina. And when they notice me, Rhiannon asks me to take a seat next to her on the left side.

"Thank you for the invite," I give them a polite smile as I take a seat.

Two servants bring the first course, laying a plate in front of each of us.

"You'll have to forgive us that we only invited you now to dine with us. Somehow, it's so hard to coordinate a time when we are all available," Rhiannon starts.

"It's alright. You've already welcomed me into your home which is more than enough."

"Nonsense. I've always prided myself on being a good host. We've just had more problems than usual this time around," she says ominously as she meets her son's gaze. "But things will soon go back to normal."

"Darcy should understand. She's already met some of the resident ghosts," Connor laughs.

"You did?" Rhiannon turns to me. "Which one? Was it Lydia? I keep hoping she will appear."

"You mean Lydia Hale?"

Rhiannon nods.

"My grandmother died some fifty years ago, but I doubt she's moved on," she pauses. "I don't think any of them will until they find a resolution," she sighs.

All the while I can't help but note how nonchalant they are talking about ghosts at the dinner table. I do my best to seem just as unbothered, though the questions are piling in my mind.

"What resolution?"

"They've all been waiting for something," she smiles. "Soon, though, they will finally be able to find peace."

"Caleb told me about this house," I start, and suddenly everyone stops to look at me expectantly. "That you have wards in place to keep evil out," I amend.

"Caleb told you that?" Connor asks, frowning.

I nod.

"Is it true? That you are...a witch?" I lower my voice, almost ashamed of saying it out loud.

Rhiannon cracks a smile before she bursts out into laughter.

"Witch," she chuckles, and the others join in. "That is an antiquated term, my dear. I prefer guardian of light."

Guardian of light. Coven of light.

The terms are eerily similar, and lead me to believe that I was right in my assumption. The Hales are part of the six families.

"That means good magic, no?" I measure my words, thinking back to what Caleb had told me.

I am already at a disadvantage that I am an outsider in this town, having close to no knowledge of what truly happens here. The last thing I want to do is give away the fact that I can see my past life as Elizabeth. That is my only trump card so far.

"Of course," she exclaims. "My family has been a protector of mankind for centuries. All the women take an oath to serve the light," she gives me a short account, telling me that all women in the family are born with gifts that allow them to fight against evil.

All the information matches what Fiona had told me, making me even more certain that they are part of the six families.

"You're taking this awfully well, Darcy," Thomasa notes. "I know I reacted quite poorly when I first found out about it."

"I think I would have reacted worse had I not experienced these odd encounters myself," I admit.

Yet there's also the fact that the moment I'd obtained the information, instead of resorting to disbelief, I'd only felt a great calm settling over me as all the pieces fit in place.

I have to wonder if this isn't a result of being intimately acquainted with magic in my previous life, too, and thus being primed for accepting its existence.

Or, maybe, it's the fact that I *know* I have similar abilities and magic running through my own blood.

Nonetheless, now looking back, I cannot see the world as anything else but...full of magic.

Everyone is quiet as the meal continues, and I cannot help but ask some of my most burning questions.

"Leo Pierce's death," I look around the table, gauging their expressions. "It was magic, wasn't it?"

The tension vibrates at the table, but eventually Rhiannon responds.

"It was an evil energy unlike I've ever seen," she states emphatically. "Whatever his sins, he didn't deserve to die that way."

"What about the other murders?"

They all nod grimly.

"But why? Do you know why?"

Just at that moment, the servants descend again upon the dining room, taking away the plates and bringing the next course.

As I'm about to reiterate my question, Rhiannon suddenly changes the subject.

"I hope that despite the *odd* things you've witnessed so, you will enjoy yourself in our little town. There's a celebration coming soon for the Fairy Festival, and at the end of October I'll be holding an important event. We'll have guests from all over the world," she says enthusiastically.

From all over the world?

Immediately, my thoughts go to the other families. Could it be them?

But if that is the case then...

My eyes meet Rhiannon's and in there I note the worry, the anguish, and most of all the determination.

If all six families are reuniting in Fairydale, it can only be for one reason.

To perform one of the forbidden spells.

CALEB'S ABSENCE IS MARKED. Even though it's been just a day, I have to admit that I miss him and our discussions. I've gotten too used to having him daily with me, entertaining and challenging me with his conversation.

Without him I feel...bereft.

After a relatively fulfilling sleep, I wake up early in the morning and head to the conservatory to meet with Rhiannon, hoping that a meeting just between the two of us would bring me more answers.

As I step into the brightly lit area, I note flower beds on both sides.

Rhiannon is on her knees, digging in the corner.

Remembering she is in her late nineties, I cannot help but admire her.

"Let me help," I say as I lower myself to my knees by her side.

"Bah," she gently stops my hand. "I might be getting old but I can still do this," she chuckles. For the next few minutes I watch as she carefully plants a new rose bud in the ground.

When she's done, she asks me to join her on a bench in the back.

The conservatory is made entirely out of glass, allowing for the sunrays to infiltrate every little corner.

"You said you wanted to talk to me about something," I tell her as she pulls close a mobile table that has a teapot and two cups on it.

"Indeed," she smiles. "Let us have tea first."

She pours a cup for each of us.

"It's rose tea. I make it myself," she adds with pride as she gazes around at the varieties of roses she has in her greenhouse. I can tell this is a favorite pastime and she takes great pride in her flowers.

"It's wonderful, thank you."

We're both silent for a moment, a bird crying in the distance, the only sound around.

"This conservatory was built by Lydia's mother—my great-grandmother. I never met her, but I'm told she loved her little plants and would spend most of her time here with her husband."

I nod slowly, curious to see where she's going with this information. Instead of revealing what little I know, it's better to see what she has to offer first.

"She died during the plague when Lydia was a little girl. Despite everything, my grandmother still remembered her and would often tell me little stories about her," she smiles fondly.

I bring the cup to my lips, studying her covertly. Just like the other Hales, she has dark hair and a pale complexion with lightly colored eyes. Lines mar her forehead and cheeks, but they are not as pronounced as you would expect of a ninety-something-year-old woman. I'd been serious when I told Caleb she comes across as someone in her fifties, which in itself is a feat.

Rhiannon takes a deep breath.

"My grandmother had the gift of foresight," she turns to me. "From the time I was born she told me about one recurring vision she kept having. One that haunted her all her life."

I tilt my head, meeting her gaze.

"What was it?"

She gives me a sad smile.

"There's evil here, Darcy. So much evil, the town overflows with it. I'm sure you've already heard the rumors about the criminals in Fairydale."

I nod.

"Nothing is accidental. They're drawn to the evil here. It attracts them like a moth to a flame. We've tried to stay as vigilant as possible, but in the last few years it's been worse and worse. Murderers, rapists, arsonists. The worst of the worst. And all of them gather here."

"What evil are you talking about?"

"An entity that's been here for centuries," she answers vaguely. "Something that grows stronger every day until we won't be able to contain it anymore."

"I don't understand..." I frown.

"You will," she covers my hand with hers. "You see, my grandmother predicted that there will be one person who will help us rid the world of this evil. Someone who will be born with the sole destiny of eradicating it."

"Who?" I ask on a breathless whisper.

"The one with the mark of light," she says, waving her hand in front of me, an image appearing as if projected by a machine.

I startle, jumping in my seat.

Her other hand holds me in place.

"Don't be scared," she murmurs. "Look," she points to the image she is creating.

After the first traces of shock wear off, I realize what I'm looking at.

It's a similar drawing to the one I'd seen in *Codex Stuartorum*. It's the body of a woman with a tear-shaped mark above her left breast.

"What is so special about that mark?" I swallow hard.

Going by Rhiannon's expression as she regards me, she knows fully well I have the mark.

"No one can say for sure. The elders claimed it was of divine origins. But all agreed that it holds immense powers," she pauses, and the image shifts. "Historically, only two other people have had this mark, and both died gruesome deaths."

That gives me pause.

I know about the first one—allegedly killed by Amon.

But what about me? What about Elizabeth?

"What happened to them?"

My heart is in my throat as she explains the same I'd heard from Fiona about the first woman. But when it comes to Elizabeth...

"The second one," Rhiannon's voice trembles. "He removed her heart in an attempt to get to the core of her power. It was useless because her powers had been bound since birth, but she died a horrible death," she shakes her head.

"He?" I repeat, a ghost of a whisper as my chest constricts with visions of the past.

Of the only person who could have done that.

Rhiannon brings the back of her hand to her cheek, wiping a tear away.

"You asked about the source of the evil in Fairydale," she sighs, and with a flick of her wrist, the image changes to another illustration I'm well acquainted with.

"He seduced Elizabeth and corrupted her mind until he turned her against her own family and everything that was good. Until he..." she gulps down, the story affecting her more than I would have thought. "He killed her without remorse."

Rhiannon snaps her fingers and the illustrations come to life before me.

Amon. With his long pale hair and intense gaze. With his honeyed words and searing touches.

She's talking about *my* Amon.

"His last known name is Amon," Rhiannon starts. "The elders believe him to be an archdemon, though we've never been able to find out more. The only one who knew anything was Elizabeth but she protected him until he killed her with his bare hands."

A vision of Amon takes shape in my mind. He's standing in front of me, his hand turning into a blade and thrusting it into my chest.

I'd seen him do that before. When he'd killed that man. He'd removed his heart and crushed it in his fist.

Yet thinking about him doing that to *me?*

A shiver goes down my back.

If what Rhiannon's saying is true then...

"This Amon," I clear my throat, my voice groggy as I say his name out loud. That one word is enough to make my chest ache with longing, the love I bore him—that I still do—pushing its head to the surface and hurting me with the implications of his treachery. "What happened to him? Where is he now?"

"Everywhere," she takes a deep breath. "After he killed Elizabeth, the elders managed to contain him in Fairydale, and he's been here for centuries. But his seal is weakening. Soon... He will either go free, or we'll be able to kill him once and for all."

"How do you plan on killing him?"

The mere suggestion that anyone might harm Amon hits me like a bullet to the chest, a deep chasm opening inside my heart.

Squeezing my eyes shut against that sensation, I try to pay attention to what Rhiannon is saying.

"There is one spell. The same one they used a few centuries ago."

"But it didn't kill him back then," I interject, keeping my tone down so she doesn't detect the residual happiness.

"This time it will be amplified," she continues, giving me a knowing look.

"By the mark," I fill in the gap.

She nods.

"Yes. That is what my grandmother foresaw. The one with the mark will end everything once and for all," she pauses as she gazes intently at me. "You, Darcy."

As expected, she knows—probably knew from the beginning.

Does Caleb know, too?

"We need your help, child. We've been waiting for you for so long... For too long," she sighs.

I simply stare at her.

"You're asking me to... To risk my life..." I mumble incoherently, unable to wrap my mind around any of this.

Not only did I hear that Amon had killed me before—despite all his avowals of eternal love, but now I find out that I am the only one who can kill *him*? That they need me to perform this spell?

Even if he were the devil himself, I don't know how I could possibly do anything to harm him. How could I, when I'd seen how inconsolable I'd been in the past when I'd thought him lost to me? How could I possibly do anything to him, when killing him would be akin to killing my own heart?

"I know this might seem too sudden. I honestly did not know how to break it to you. We wanted to let you get accustomed to Fairydale on your own, so you could see the odd things that happen here. Only by experiencing it for yourself could you ever believe what I'm saying is true. Isn't that right?"

I give her a slow nod.

A small tremor goes down my body. Despite all my best efforts to control myself, it's in vain. Conflicting emotions—love, fear, disappointment—converge inside my heart, making me reel with the magnitude of my feelings.

And despite Rhiannon's explanations, I feel more lost than ever.

"You see, you are our only remaining hope. His influence is already seeping through the seal, and I can feel the evil shrouding this entire town," she laments, giving me gruesome details of the murders that have occurred in Fairydale—not only the ones I'd witnessed but also the ones from the past.

"Every year it becomes worse. But now..." she trails off, sighing loudly.

I nod.

"How do you know I have the mark?" I inquire softly.

Without taking her eyes off me, she changes the image, showing me a sketch.

"Lydia didn't just foresee your arrival. She foresaw everything about you. She knew when you would be born, how you'd look. Everything."

"Then my mother... Did you know my mother?"

A shadow falls over her face as she blinks.

"I did," she replies. "She was a great woman." There's a tightness to her voice as she continues. "She thought she was doing what was best for you by taking you away from here. But she didn't realize that she couldn't fight fate."

"What can you tell me about her?"

She shakes her head sadly.

"Everyone loved her in Fairydale. It's unfortunate that she didn't think she could share her burden with us."

Realizing I'm not likely to get more out of her, I decide to change the subject, inquiring about the monster I'd seen instead.

"Is it this?" her brows furrow with concentration as she brings to life another illustration. This time it's of a creature that looks just like the monster who'd attacked me.

"Yes," I nod. "He had huge claws and he stabbed me and..."

"Did he get your blood?" she all but shrieks.

I blink in confusion, my mouth opening and closing as I try to find my voice.

"Forgive me, but it's very important to know if he took your blood or not."

"He tried to, but he was killed before he could do it."

She releases a deep sigh.

"Good. Good," she nods to herself. "You cannot let any such creature take a drop of blood from you, Darcy. Listen to me. It's imperative that they don't get their hands on your blood."

"Why?"

"This monster. It's a *Kiaka*, a mindless lowly demon that does the bidding of its master. Since Amon cannot act for himself, he must have sent it after you. You see, your blood is the *only* thing that can give him strength."

I regard her carefully. It had been Amon himself who'd killed the monster. Why would he do it if he'd sent it in the first place?

Unless...

My pulse speeds up, my palms getting clammy as it dawns on me he's been playing with me from the beginning.

He killed the *Kiaka* purposefully *after* he'd gotten my blood. He must have done it to get me to trust him. Just as he must have been behind every little odd thing happening around me.

Remembering all the times I thought I was losing my mind, I can't help but wonder if he'd been behind that.

Could it be that he'd been trying to undermine my relationship with Caleb, too?

"Just how strong is Amon?" I utter on a whisper.

"I don't have an answer for you, child. When the elders sealed him, they gave their lives to that spell. It was a sacrifice they were willing to make, but no one realized he would be that powerful. Though he is trapped—for now—his influence lingers."

"Do you think..." I wet my lips. "Do you think he could influence my mind?"

Dear God, but what if those visions of the past I'm seeing are sent *by* Amon? What if he's trying to paint our relationship in a positive light so he can get me on his side?

She nods grimly.

My eyes widen just as my mind blanks on me.

Turning towards the beautiful roses, I stare into empty space as I realize I've reached my lowest point—where I cannot even know if my thoughts are my own, never mind my memories of the past or if my eyes deceive me.

"I can help with that," she suddenly offers.

Closing her eyes, she does a small incantation, her palms lighting up in a blinding flash before a red string appears in her hand.

"Here," she murmurs as she wraps it around my wrist. "This should be enough for now since he's still weak. But if he gains strength... There's no telling what he will be capable of," she takes a deep breath.

"You must ensure he *never* gets even one drop of your blood. If he does... I fear for the fate of this town."

I give her a tight smile, promising I will be careful.

All the while, though, I cannot reconcile what Rhiannon is telling me with what I know of Amon. Just like in my vision before, when Fiona had told me how evil he was, there's a part of me that cannot believe it—that simply cannot fathom an existence without him.

Even then. I knew he was a demon. I knew he was reviled. I knew he was a murderer.

And yet, I still loved him.

But can I trust myself?

Can I truly trust that what I'm feeling is real and not a result of his interference? He might not have the power to become corporeal and come after me himself, but as Rhiannon admitted, he *could* affect my perception of what's happening around me.

Despite knowing all that, I'm still torn...

As we finish the tea, she tells me she must retire for the day.

"You must be wondering why I've been so absent," she stops at the door of the conservatory on her way out. "I have been performing a containment ritual every day to ensure that Amon's influence does not reach this house. I will continue to do so until the moment comes that we'll finally be able to rid ourselves of him."

"What will happen to me for the final spell? You said I'm needed to enhance it. But will I...die?" I ask tentatively.

She purses her lips, her cheeks tightening in a sad smile.

"Your abilities will save you from such a fate, Darcy," she vaguely replies.

But she never gives me a straight answer.

We walk together back to the house, parting ways as we reach the first floor.

"Please consider what I told you, Darcy."

She makes to continue to the stairs when I ask one last question.

"If I don't agree. Will you do the spell anyway?"

She takes a moment to reply, nodding grimly.

"It must be done. Whether we live or die, it is our duty to cleanse the stench of evil from this town once and for all."

And with that she's gone.

I hurry to my room, all the while mulling over everything I've learned.

To say I'm shocked that she'd been so frank with me is an understatement.

From the beginning the Hales have been somehow secretive as to what goes on in Fairydale and Katrina had been quite dismissive of the rumors about the family.

Yet Rhiannon had confirmed everything.

The Hales *are* part of the six families.

And they think I can somehow help them defeat an archdemon that's been terrorizing Fairydale for centuries.

It would all be perfectly fine if not for the small fact that the archdemon in question is Amon.

My beloved. And, apparently, my killer.

There are too many contradictions, and though I can feel that Rhiannon does not have any ill intentions with me, I am still wary of trusting her.

Just how much is true and how much is fake?

How is it that I come to Fairydale to receive an inheritance from a not so dead man but instead find myself in the middle of a conflict between witches and demons?

But most importantly, how do I manage to stay alive?

Chapter Sixteen

Two days later, Caleb is still not back.

Since my talk with Rhiannon, I've been all by myself, either in my room or in the library, reading.

I've seen Katrina in passing, but she commutes to school outside of Fairydale every day so she leaves in the morning and comes back late in the afternoon.

Boredom soon pokes its head to the surface, especially as my frustration mounts at the half-truths and the incomplete information I have.

After Rhiannon had told me about Amon and the fact that the six families need *me* to kill him off for good, I've found myself going down the rabbit hole of overthinking everything.

I'd jotted down all I know in my notebook as I tried to make sense of it.

And though Rhiannon had revealed to me more than I would have thought she would, there are still glaring discrepancies.

There is the past as I know it—as I've seen it through my eyes. Then there's the version that has made it to the history books.

And while I am aware that Amon's influence could interfere with my perception of the past, I can't help but feel that my memories are real—that everything I'd seen of the past was what Elizabeth had lived through.

Otherwise, why reveal everything Fiona had told me? Why would Amon show himself to me as the blood-thirsty demon that he is instead of the sweet lover he'd been up until that point?

Yet that's not the only doubt I have regarding what I'd learned. Rhiannon had all but told me it's my fate to help kill Amon. She hadn't asked for my help, she hadn't even asked if I want to do this though it might prove fatal to me. She'd simply stated that I *would* do it—because it had been foretold.

How is that fair to me? What about what *I* want?

I sigh, blowing my hair from my eyes as I tap my pen against the wooden table. Hours of thinking, and all I have to show for it is a mounting headache and conflicting information.

Flipping the pages of the notebook, I stop at my list of questions as I circle the most important of them all—and one Rhiannon had tried her best to circumvent.

Who is my mother?

And why would she have thought she was protecting me by leaving Fairydale with me?

By my calculations, she should be a member of the six families, but which?

Wouldn't Rhiannon have told me already if she was a Hale?

The more I ruminate about that question, the more I realize there is only one person who can give me an answer. The only one who'd straightforwardly told me he knew my mother and could tell me more about her.

Archibald Nicholson.

Deciding I need to take matters into my own hands, I put on a sundress and a light blazer since the weather has turned chilly. Fiddling with the red bracelet Rhiannon had placed upon me, I have to wonder if this will help me in any way—or if it isn't a veiled threat.

Maybe I've become a little paranoid in my time in Fairydale, but everyone has their own agenda. Aside from Rhiannon's worry that some creature might get its hands on my blood and jeopardize her plans, I doubt she cares much about what happens to me.

The only one who's been there for me from the beginning has been Caleb.

He's the only person who's gone far and beyond to help me and seems to have my well-being at heart. Though I've had moments in the past where I've doubted him—due to my own mental failings—I now realize that he's only ever been frank with me. Including the fact that I shouldn't blindly trust his family.

A sudden wave of melancholy hits me when I think of him, and I wonder how long his business will keep him away. In such a short time he's become my rock. It's a little unsettling to realize that not only have I come to depend on his company, but crave it like an addict.

"You'd better come home soon, Caleb," I mutter under my breath as I comb my hair, plaiting it in a simple braid. Since he's not here, I will have to walk to town, where I will need to inquire about Mr. Nicholson's address.

Maybe it's a little rude of me to come thusly unannounced, but he had previously invited me to dinner, so I hope he won't be too bothered.

Once I'm ready, I head out, carefully making my way towards the town.

A light breeze brushes my skin as the sun hides behind the clouds.

Gazing at the sky, I hope it's not going to rain any time soon. At least not while I'm so far away from town.

Increasing my pace, I can't help but notice that the clouds are becoming darker and darker, a loud sound echoing in the sky.

Pulling my blazer tighter around my body, I try to maintain my body heat as the atmosphere changes, the temperature suddenly dropping.

"Nothing is happening, nothing is happening," I chant to myself as I pass by the Old Church and what's left of 12 Astor Place.

Until now I'd only seen it in passing from the car, but as I take in the charred wood and the barely standing structure, I cannot possibly imagine how I would have made my way out onto the lawn where Caleb had found me.

Goodness, but that was such a narrow encounter with death.

The moment that thought arises, though, I have to wonder if I can actually die. Since my injuries heal on their own, does that mean that I am invincible? Will I even grow old since my cells will just heal themselves?

Once more, I am overwhelmed with questions. I hadn't taken the time to consider the implications of my newly found abilities before, but now that the seed has been planted, I can see the countless possibilities.

Lost in my thoughts, I startle as a bolt of lightning whips across the sky, branching out in smaller lines as it takes over the entire visible horizon.

A shiver goes down my back at the sudden change in weather, especially since it had been perfectly fine when I left the house.

Even more suspicious is the fact that these sudden changes in weather have happened before—like when I'd first arrived in Fairydale.

Could it be that Amon can control the sky?

My brows pinch together in worry as the wind picks up, blowing right in my direction.

Right at that moment, lightning strikes in front of me, the bolt hitting the road and causing the ground to quake and shatter at the point of impact.

Startled, a panicked cry escapes me as I jump back. At the same time, more loud noises erupt in the sky and all around me.

My mind becomes a huge void as fear overtakes me.

Out of nowhere, a scratchy sound resounds, before something attacks me, tackling me to the ground.

I'm so stricken with fear that I fail to realize the thing is not attacking me—rather licking me.

"Mr. Meow?" my voice wobbles as I struggle to gain control over my shaking body.

I take a deep breath, and when even that doesn't help, I continue to breathe in and out while Mr. Meow languidly licks my cheek before he nuzzles his furry face against mine.

"It's just you, Mr. Meow," I finally sigh in relief when I manage to clear the fog of fear.

The storm is still brewing, and gathering myself off the ground, I cradle Mr. Meow to my chest as I walk faster and faster—barely short of a run—towards town.

Mr. Vaughan had said Astor Place was fifteen minutes away from town. Despite the rumbling thunder and the flashy lightning, I manage to get there in half the time.

I barely feel my legs when I make it to the town center. My lungs constrict in my chest, my breathing intensifying.

"We're here," I whisper to the cat in my arms.

Despite his absence, I'm happy to have come across him again. At least now I'll have someone else to keep me company while Caleb is away.

I'll have to ask first if I'm allowed to house a pet in the manor, though if they won't allow me, I'll hide Mr. Meow somehow.

Oddly enough, the moment I enter one of the shops in the town square, the clouds suddenly dissipate as if there had been no storm.

Biting my lip in consternation, I can only hope that whatever was after me is gone for good.

"Excuse me," I put on a polite smile as I enter the small shop. "I was wondering if you could tell me where Mr. Nicholson's residence is?"

The clerk looks up, surprised to see me.

Although Mr. Nicholson had assured me he'd put in a good word for me, I'm still worried that the townsfolk blame me for everything that happened.

"Oh, you're Miss Darcy, aren't you?" the older woman bursts out, her face breaking into a genuine smile.

I nod tentatively.

"It's so good to finally meet you. Archibald has told us all about you," she starts, getting up from her seat and coming towards me. "Anyone who comes as highly recommended as you is welcome here."

"Thank you," I murmur.

Unusually chatty and helpful, the woman takes out a map of Fairydale, showing me the exact route to Mr. Nicholson's house.

Before I leave, I find out just how well-respected the man is in the entire town.

"He's helped all of us at some point. Everything you see built in this town, Mr. Nicholson and his family did it," the clerk recounts, sharing that most small businesses have a personal relationship with Mr. Nicholson and his family.

"You'll be in good hands with him," she says as I head out, thanking her for everything.

Mr. Meow is getting increasingly more agitated.

"Don't worry. I'll ask Mr. Nicholson if he has something for you to eat. It can't have been easy for you these days," I coo lightly. "I'm sorry I didn't look for you more."

His paw is on my cheek, his claws sheathed as he gently strokes my skin.

I give him an indulgent smile, patting him on the white spot on his head.

Guiding myself with the map the clerk had given me, I follow a serpentine road before I reach an imposing house.

It's not as big as the Hale manor, but it speaks of the same type of grandiosity with its neoclassical façade and the entrance that simulates the Roman Pantheon.

I swallow hard as a wave of nervousness hits me. Not only because my surroundings are a little...gloomy but also because I'm coming here unannounced.

Before I can chicken out, I push my chin up, straightening my spine and marching forward. With Mr. Meow in one arm, I use the other to knock on the thick bronze door rapper.

Stepping back, I simply wait.

It's not long before someone opens the door.

It's a woman in her fifties, or sixties, and upon taking a good look at me, a bright smile stretches across her face.

"You must be Miss Darcy," she exclaims, clapping her hands together.

How is it that everyone already knows who I am in this town?

"Ah, yes," I nod awkwardly.

"Mr. Nicholson has told me all about you. He knew you'd be calling on us at some point. Do come in," she says warmly, motioning me inside.

"Let me grab your jacket, and if you'll follow me into the drawing room, I'll inform Mr. Nicholson of your arrival at once," she starts, taking my blazer and putting it on a hanger. "I do hope you're planning to stay for lunch. I'm making Mr. Nicholson's favorite stew..." she drones on, her chatty disposition making me feel better about this impromptu visit.

Leading me to the drawing room, she tells me to wait a moment as she calls on Mr. Nicholson.

Nodding, I find my attention going back to Mr. Meow, who is getting more agitated by the second, baring his teeth for no reason at one of Mr. Nicholson's portraits.

"Easy." I pull him close to my body. "We don't want to damage anything of worth around here. Until I get my inheritance I have absolutely no money," I whisper in his ear.

Once more, it dawns on me how silly I'm being. It's not as if he could understand what I'm saying. Yet his body-language tells me he does. That he's an intelligent animal and he enjoys it when I address him directly.

"Meow," he screams at me, jumping out of my arms.

Well, most times, anyway.

Just as I'm about to get up and run after him, the sound of heavy steps stops me in my tracks.

Mr. Nicholson appears in the doorway, his cane hitting the floor with a thud.

"Miss Darcy! How good to see you!" he exclaims with good humor.

My lips tip up in a smile.

"Thank you for having me. I hope I'm not inconveniencing you."

"Bah, of course no," he waves his hand. "Helena will bring us tea. Let us have a seat," he says as he steps deeper into the room.

Though I keep my eyes alert for Mr. Meow, I take a seat on the sofa opposite him, folding my legs to my right and straightening my spine.

As Mr. Nicholson takes his seat, propping his cane by the side and away from my view, Helena bursts into the room with a tea tray.

She's still chatting away, explaining that I will love the meal she's preparing and that she hasn't had a visitor to feed in a long time.

"You can retire, Helena," Mr. Nicholson adds after she's served us each a cup of tea.

"Of course, sir," she says blithely, so much so I expect her to skip out of the room, not walk.

Yet her disposition puts me more at ease, thinking that you can tell a lot about the employer by how he treats his employees. And Helena seems to adore Mr. Nicholson.

"What brings you here, Miss Darcy?"

"I was wondering if we could continue our chat from last time. You said you knew my mother and father, and I would love to hear more if possible."

He nods thoughtfully.

"Of course. I'll do my best to give you as much information as possible. What is it exactly that you want to know?"

"Who was my mother? I doubt her last name was O'Sullivan. No one so far has recognized it."

"Indeed," he drawls, taking a sip off his tea. "I suppose she tried to pass herself as a respectable widow, is that not so?"

I nod. She'd always said my father had died before I was born.

"You would be correct. Her last name was not O'Sullivan," he pauses. "It was Nicholson."

My lashes flutter in befuddlement as I stare at him thoroughly confused.

"N...Nicholson?" I repeat, swallowing hard.

He nods grimly.

"She was my daughter," he confesses with a deep sigh.

"What?" I squeak, my lips parting in shock.

"I can't say I was always a good father," he sighs. "I take full responsibility for that. But I never thought she would run away—do everything in her power to ensure she wasn't found."

"But..." I blink, slowly taking everything in.

"I may have overreacted when I heard about her relationship with Leo. He was married at that time and..." he purses his lips. "She could be very stubborn when she wanted," he shakes his head, sadness descending upon his features.

"Did you know she was pregnant when she left?"

"I suspected, but there was no way I could verify. It wasn't until much, much later that Mordechai told me he found the swan brooch for sale. That's how we found out about you."

"If you knew," I pause to choose my words carefully. After all, it's not every day you find out that you have a living grandfather—one who knew about your existence all along but did nothing. Just like Leo Pierce, Mr. Nicholson didn't think I was worthy, did he?

"If you knew, then why did you never come for me? At least visit, or send a letter," I ask, doing my best to keep my voice from breaking. "I was all alone, and I'm sure at least one letter would have made a world of difference."

He flattens his lips in a grim line as he regards me, his eyes full of sorrow.

"I'm sorry. I wanted to, but there's a reason I didn't. Just as there's a reason your mother decided to run with you."

"And that is?" I raise a brow, my tone more scathing than I would have liked.

"If you're here, then I am confident Rhiannon Hale already told you about Lydia Hale's vision."

I frown, surprised he knows about it, but wondering about the connection.

"She knew that if you grew up in Fairydale you would be indoctrinated by the Hales, forced to listen to their agenda. She knew you would no longer have a choice. And that's what she wanted for you, Darcy. She wanted you to choose."

"You know about the vision? But how..." I trail off.

Katrina had made it clear that the Hales and Nicholsons do not get along. Then how could he know...

"Everyone is aware to an extent. There's a reason they aren't well liked in town. They've laid siege to that house and continued with their outrageous *quest*," he says the last word with thorough disgust.

"By that you mean to tell me you don't agree with them? Rhiannon told me there's an evil in Fairydale that needs to be eradicated and that..."

"That you're going to do it?" he scoffs. "Plenty have tried before and have failed. What she wants is to lead to another set of deaths. It wasn't enough the first time," he grumbles under his breath.

"Forgive me for prying, but are you part of the six families?"

His eyes narrow.

"Yes," he answers curtly. "Which is how I know their quest is madness personified. No one will survive another fight with that demon. I've tried to tell her countless times that we could fortify the seal in a similar ceremony without risking everyone. Without risking *you*. But she won't have any of it."

I bite my lower lip as I regard him. There's something off about this entire situation. Something that doesn't sit right with me but I cannot pinpoint what.

All I know is that both Rhiannon and Mr. Nicholson seem to have their own versions of the story as well as different...solutions. With their added conflict, I simply don't know which one to trust.

But that doesn't mean I can't get more information.

"What's the difference between the rituals?" I inquire.

"The one Rhiannon wants to perform involves a forbidden spell that consumes life force, Darcy. The stronger the life force, the stronger the spell, which is why only the elders would be asked to perform it. And...you."

I nod grimly. I'd been right to assume that the ritual would pose a danger to my life. And if the original elders died trying to trap Amon there, then I don't know how they would manage it this time and survive to see another day.

"The ritual I suggested is a simple spell that requires a blood sacrifice," he pauses when he sees my alarmed expression, "but *not* death. A simple offering to fortify the chains that keep the demon subdued. And your blood is powerful enough to do that."

"I see," I reply slowly.

His version of events contradicts what Rhiannon told me about not letting anyone get their hands on my blood, especially Amon.

Doubts continue to accumulate in my mind, but I don't let it show.

Instead, I merely smile at him, nodding along.

"So you see, we didn't want to reach out and expose you to this. At least not until you were at an age where you could make the decision for yourself. That was our intention. But then Leo died and..." he drifts off, his eyes full of sadness.

"I'm sorry about his passing. His death was horrible. Was it the demon that caused it?" I probe carefully.

Pursing his lips, he nods.

"Just like he's caused every single *odd* death in the last two centuries. Just like he caused the plague."

"The plague?" I frown. "He caused that, too?"

My eyes narrow.

Now that is something that Rhiannon had failed to mention. Surely if she thinks he's so evil, she would have told me that he killed people en masse with the plague in order to convince me to help her. Wouldn't she?

"He did. Before the elders subdued him, he killed everyone from Fairydale to Ipswich and all the nearby villages. If they hadn't gotten in time, I fear he could have wiped out the entire East Coast. Or more..." he releases a sad sigh in an attempt to convey his feelings on the matter. Yet why does it seem so forced?

Why did I spot the slightest curl of his lip when he mentioned Amon *killed everyone*?

"Dear God, but that's horrible," I cross myself, feigning a terrified expression.

Two can play at this game.

He might be my blood relative, but I have no allegiance to him, just as I have no allegiance to *anyone* in Fairydale.

Funny, though, how everyone wants me—*expects*—me to help them.

Where were they when I was ten and wondering what would happen to me because the only person I'd had in the world suddenly left me all alone? Where were they when I spent my entire youth and teenage years trying to prove something because I felt expendable? Because I felt so grateful that the nuns had taken me in that I transformed my entire life to suit their expectations? Where the hell were they when I was working myself to the bone during the day and crying myself to sleep at night?

They were nowhere to be seen.

Not Leo Pierce. Not Mr. Nicholson. And not Rhiannon Hale.

No one had been there for me, and I don't mean in a financial capacity, since it's clear that Leo had given money to the orphanage to keep me on. But they hadn't been there for me in the way that mattered the most—human to human.

Now? They want me to risk my life for something I have absolutely no stake in.

On the contrary, a part of me—*the one that still loves Amon*—would never want to see him harmed in any way.

Does that make me a bad person? Knowing he potentially killed hundreds of people—perhaps more—and yet I know I couldn't bring myself to harm him.

If it does, then I'll acknowledge it as my fault.

Maybe... Just maybe... I am more wicked than I ever thought.

But in light of everything I've found out so far—all conflicting and potentially misleading information—I can only conclude that everyone is underestimating me.

Yes, I might be a little uptight, and maybe a little too set in my proper ways since I'd forced myself to become someone the nuns would be proud of, but I'm not stupid.

And so far, everyone seems to assume I am.

"How could anyone do such a thing," I continue in the same horrified tone. "This...demon," I drop my voice to a whisper. "Who is he? How is he capable of so much destruction? Just...how?"

He nods emphatically, simulating my terror.

"His name is Amon. He's been in conflict with the coven for centuries. Maybe more. It all started when he absorbed the power of the first..." he starts recounting the same thing Rhiannon had told me —*verbatim*.

"But is there nothing more known about him? Why would he do such a thing to poor Elizabeth?"

He shakes his head.

"He's evil, Darcy. His very essence is evil. How could you expect anything else from such a being? It's why we're here—to stop this from happening. But if we do it Rhiannon's way..." he shakes his head. "We're sacrificing good, *powerful* witches for something that might not even work."

"I understand. I agree with you. Why should we take chances when we could reinforce the seal?"

His eyes flash at my statement, his mouth curling upwards.

Interesting.

"I'm glad you are a sensible woman, Darcy. I'm sure together we can make Rhiannon and the other elders see reason."

I give him a tight smile.

"Just out of curiosity," I add pensively. "If I don't get involved at all, what will you do?"

"I will have to take drastic measures to stop Rhiannon from her folly. If I have to present my case in front of the elders, then so be it."

"Sir, sir!" Helena dashes into the room, an alarmed expression on her face. "There's something wrong with the room."

He tilts his head, awareness slowly seeping in, just as the blood seeps *out* of his face.

Whatever room Helena is speaking about must be something very important, because no sooner had she said that than Mr. Nicholson is on his feet and going up the stairs.

Walking just fine. Without his cane.

I narrow my eyes at his form—oddly athletic for someone so old.

Yet just as that thought creeps into my head, so does something else.

His cane.

Right at that moment, the sun hits the jeweled top of the staff, its brilliance flashing into the entire room.

Placing the teacup to the ground, I get to my feet, slowly advancing towards the precious stone. I no longer feel in control as I put one foot in front of the other, my eyes focused on the prize.

As if possessed, I can't stop myself from reaching out and grabbing the cane.

The stone shines even brighter, so much so it almost blinds me.

Yet despite that, there's this unnatural compulsion to touch it—to feel it against my skin.

The stone is a deep green that shines almost blue in the sunlight. And before I can help myself, I cup it with my entire palm.

All at once, my entire body starts spasming, currents of electricity going through me until I no longer feel like myself.

Until...

"YOU CAN BUY IT, YOU KNOW," he whispers in my ear, his body fitted tightly behind me.

I shake my head lightly as I gaze longingly at the gold necklace with its intricate floral design.

"I don't need more jewelry," I force myself to say.

"You can always have more jewelry," he chuckles.

"No," I say as I put the necklace down.

"*Gratias tibi agimus,*" I nod to the seller, turning around and grabbing Amon's hand as I lead him down the bustling street.

Animals are running around freely, with people stopping every now and then to watch them with unabashed amusement.

It's the fourth day of *Ludi Florae*, and the celebrations are already in full swing, the rituals taking most of the day—all in an effort to promote fertility of the land.

With this occasion, the streets are cleaner, too, despite the sewer stench that I doubt will ever go away. After all, Rome is Rome, and cleanliness has never been its strong suit.

Even so, it's been home for so long, I don't see us leaving any time soon. Not with all the connections we've made with people and the land. And certainly *not* with the wonderful climate and the beautiful Tyrrhenian sea.

The sun is shining brightly in the sky, the smell of trees in bloom intoxicating as petals of flowers are swept away by the gentle breeze.

My fingers tighten on top of Amon's, a deep sense of satisfaction blossoming in my chest. Especially as I glance up at him, a smile on my lips as I take in his breathtaking features.

So much time has passed, and it still feels like the first time.

His hair is cropped to his ears—the first time it's ever been so short. After a torturous battle, he'd finally agreed to cut his glorious mane to fit better in society, and he'd allowed me to style his hair in a modern way. Though I miss his long hair, this new style best showcases his strong jaw, sharp cheekbones and his otherworldly eyes.

That isn't to say I'm the only one noticing his striking looks.

Everywhere we go, the female gaze drifts to him, admiring him appreciatively and sometimes blatantly desiring him.

Rome isn't a prudish city. Here women take pride in their sexuality and do not shy away from making their intentions clear—as has been the case plenty of times since we've relocated to this part of the world.

Despite the fact that I cannot help but be jealous sometimes, I know my Amon. I know the type of male he is and in spite of his legendary reputation as the most savage warrior in the realm, his chief quality is his loyalty.

His unwavering devotion.

From the beginning he's been mine just like I've been his.

Wholly. Irrevocably. *Eternally*.

Catching me staring, he gives me his signature smile, a dimple appearing in his left cheek. Unable to stop, I raise myself on the tips of my toes, brushing my lips lightly against the small indentation.

"A public display, my love?" he arches a brow. "Who are you and what have you done with my wife?" he teases.

"You know what they say," I murmur softly against his skin. "When in Rome, do as the Romans do," I say as I slide my hand suggestively over his pronounced pectorals.

He's wearing an average Roman garment, just as I am. Nothing too luxurious so as to not draw unwanted attention. But even in the most ordinary garb he exudes pure strength and sensuality.

He chuckles at my words, a rich, deep sound that reverberates in my being. Immediately, though, his gaze turns serious just as it grows heated.

"Does this mean what I think it means?" he asks in a thick, husky voice.

I nod slowly, licking my lips as my eyes find his.

"Damnation," he curses, his features growing taut. "We need to get home. Now," he declares tightly, his voice full of need—one that steadily mounts in my own body.

Just as he's about to pull me into a darkened corner to avoid being seen, a cart rolls down the street, its driver nowhere to be seen.

Amon tugs me to the side, expertly avoiding the impact. But there's no one to defend the people running away from its disastrous path.

Screams erupt in the air as everyone tries to duck, or search cover, the cart wreaking havoc in its advance.

"Do something," I whisper, panic growing in my breast as I watch the ensuing mayhem.

Everyone is running for their lives, concerned only with their welfare. And there are those who cannot fend for themselves.

The...children.

There are two on the ground at the end of the street, one seemingly already injured and unable to move. An old man is by their side, moving slowly—too slowly.

Distressed, I turn to him, pleading him with my eyes.

He purses his lips, and the seconds tick.

I know he doesn't want to use his powers—has tried not to do so since the last disaster in Asia Minor.

He'd promised himself he wouldn't intervene in human lives, just like I did. After all, we'd been through enough to know that ofttimes, our interference, no matter how helpful, would only be regarded with suspicion and animosity.

Human kind is capable of great kindness. But it's also capable of the worst atrocities.

Yet at this moment, I can only see the helpless children and their imminent deaths. And as always, I can't help my traitorous heart.

"Please help them," I whisper.

He hisses in anguish, the dilemma eating at him. For despite his rough and curt manner, my Amon has a heart of gold.

With a wave of his hand, the cart comes to a halt just a few pedes away from the children.

Without waiting for his approval, I hurry forward, only one goal on my mind—to make sure the children are fine.

When the cart stops, the old man curses as he takes one of the children in his arms, leaving the injured one behind.

The boy can't be more than four or five.

My heart breaks as I see the tears on his ruddy cheeks, the dirt on his clothes and the caked blood on his legs where he'd hurt himself.

"Shh," I drop to my knees in front of him, my hands on his shoulders in an attempt to calm him. "It's fine. You're alright," I coo softly. "You're going to be alright."

I don't have to turn to feel Amon behind me, his gaze boring a hole in my back.

"Sela, don't," he grits his teeth, the command curt.

Whipping my head around, I level him with my gaze.

"I'm not one of your soldiers, General," I tell him resolutely.

Before he can act, I bring my hands over the little boy's injuries, my palms humming with energy as it transfers into his skin. Slowly, his skin starts melding, his injuries healing in seconds.

When I'm done, only caked blood remains.

"Where are your parents?" I ask gently.

He's still crying, his sobs making it hard for me to understand him. Yet as I lay my hand against his temple, I see the images, identifying his mother within moments.

"Sela," Amon calls my name, his tone firm but apologetic.

I ignore him as I simply gather the little boy in my arms, marching forward and wading my way through the crowd as I focus on his mother. It doesn't take long for me to locate her. She's pale, he features torn with worry as she looks right and left—undoubtedly searching for her boy.

"He's safe," I assure her as I stop in front of her.

Her eyes widen as she takes me in, her hands reaching out to take the child out of my arms.

"My baby," she cries out, scanning him from head to toe. "Thank you! Thank you," she bows her head to me.

I wave my hand, merely giving her a smile as I turn to leave.

Yet, it only takes a moment for my nightmare to come to fruition.

"She healed him!" She yells, and suddenly the crowd stops. "She healed my son. She healed his club foot," she declares. "A goddess among us!"

My breath hitches in alarm as images of the last incident flash through my mind, the mob of angry people, the masses of worship—the unending conflict.

"I've got you," a masculine voice murmurs against my hair. His hands around my shoulders, he lays a kiss on my brow as our surroundings change.

In just a second, we've left the busy forum only to be back to our domus.

Opening my eyes and noting my surroundings, I step away from him.

My emotions are still raw, and against all attempts to the contrary, my longing bursts through the surface, my heart aching with the hopelessness of the future.

"Sela, you promised you wouldn't. *We* promised we wouldn't," Amon says as he follows me to the peristylium.

Despite the size of our domus, we are the only ones living here.

No servants. No staff. No slaves.

We are quite possibly the only ones to live like this, in spite of our wealth. But it goes beyond the ethical implications of nexum or slavery, both of which are as distasteful to me as they are to Amon. It simply comes down to the fact that if anyone worked or lived with us, we would risk discovery.

Like today.

Like every time we decide to use our powers.

"You know what happened last time," he sighs as he comes behind me.

I swallow hard. I do know, and that is the problem—the constant predicament.

It isn't my nature to turn a blind eye, yet helping means...potentially getting crucified for it.

"I can't help it," I whisper, doing my best to keep the pain from my voice. "I see them suffering and I just can't..." I shake my head.

Columns surround the small garden of the peristylium, colorful sculptures at every corner. Since we've moved here, I've dedicated my time to growing herbs and other medicinal plants that I then donate to poorer parts of the city.

Another thing that risks our discovery.

Another thing I cannot stop myself from doing.

I march forward to the exedra at the end of the peristylium, a semi-open room that has a direct view of the gardens. The main wall had been encased with a bronze mirror that captures all the activity around.

I have my affinity for gardening, while Amon has his own—watching me.

From the corner of my eye I spot his determined stride as he comes towards me.

"Sela!"

When he sees I don't respond, he simply flashes himself in front of me, his hands resting over my shoulders as he gently stops me.

"Talk to me, Sela," he murmurs, his lovely eyes taking me in.

"You know what we promised," he continues, his voice gentle, entirely losing the edge from earlier.

I nod slowly, accepting the blame as mine.

Whenever we end up doing something like this, I'm always the instigator—always the one pushing him.

"I'm sorry," I whisper.

"It was the boy, wasn't it? That's why you did it."

I avert my gaze as I give him another nod, unable to find the strength to reply with my words for fear my voice would crack with pain.

"Ah, Sela," Amon rasps, bringing me to his body for a tight hug. "I'm so sorry, my love. So, so very sorry," he speaks harshly, and I note the same frustration—the same agony—marring his voice, too.

He's not indifferent. But how could he be?

It's not something only I have lost. We both did.

"Do you regret it?" he inquires softly, his big palms cupping the sides of my face as he draws back to look at me. "Do you regret choosing me?"

I shake my head.

"You know that isn't something I would *ever* be able to regret," I tell him honestly, though the echoes of pain are still there.

Breaking free of his embrace, I turn to the bronze mirror, gazing at my reflection and his in the back.

"Do you?" I pause, fear flickering to life inside of me.

I've always considered myself a rational female, just as I've always known he was settling by choosing me.

After all, he was Amon. The greatest warrior who ever lived—the most feared one.

Before me, he had a life of glory, his name in the history books, his reputation as awe-striking as it was terrifying.

He was Amon. A legend in itself.

And I was...Sela. Just Sela.

Poor, reclusive Sela.

"Do you regret meeting me, Amon?" I wet my lips, my eyes finding his in the mirror. "There are so many women in this world. So many who could give you more than I can..."

"No," he states categorically as he comes behind me. "How could you ever say something like that, Sela? How could you even think about it?"

A sad smile pulls at my lips.

"I see the way they watch you—*want* you," I whisper, my insecurities poking through, despite having full confidence in him.

Yet it's in times like these, when I'm reminded that I'm not whole... That I'm a healer but I cannot heal the most important part of myself. It's in moments like these that I feel like the greatest failure —like I'm not worthy to breathe the same air he breathes, let alone be his mate.

"And I would never want them back. There is only you for me. From the first moment I laid eyes on you, Sela, you've been the center of my universe. Until you, I thought life and suffering were synonymous."

His breath fans my skin as he slowly undoes the girdle at my waist before slipping the stola off my body.

The material falls to the ground, leaving me bare in front of the mirror.

His big hands are on my shoulders, slowly caressing me just as his mouth brushes against my neck.

Holding his hand to the side, he materializes an unexpected item in his palm. My eyes grow wide as he gently places the necklace I'd seen at the forum around my neck.

"Before you I only knew violence. I was born to bloodshed and destruction and I let it shape who I was—I embraced it," he kisses my skin as he fastens the necklace around my neck, the metal cold against my feverish flesh.

My breath catches in my throat, goosebumps erupting all over my skin as I react to his proximity and his molten voice, my arousal building as my body becomes primed for his.

"Before you I was chaos and ruin," he continues to speak, hypnotizing me with his voice and squashing all my doubts. "Until you showed me the alternative. Until *you* showed me there was joy to be had in the most mundane moments," he rasps, bringing his arms around my waist and holding me tightly to him.

"How could I want anyone else when I *am* only because you *are*? I exist for you just as I exist because of you," he breathes harshly against me.

His voice becomes increasingly anguished, the emotions pouring out of him as he holds me so close to his body—as if he's trying to merge us into one.

Slowly, I bring my hands on top of his, squeezing lightly just as I squeeze my eyes shut to keep the tears at bay.

We've come this far, but what about the sacrifices of the past? What about everything we've lost, or the harm we've caused because of our choice?

"I love you, Amon," I tell him with all the emotion I can muster. "I've loved you for so long, and I'll continue to love you for as long as my essence lives on."

Unclasping his hands, I bring one of his palms to my chest, covering my breast as I urge him to feel the beats of my heart and the unsubdued pulsations of my soul—every little flicker of life that is for him and him alone.

"Sela," he groans. "My darling Sela," he whispers in my ear as his other hand slides down my stomach, his fingers dipping between my legs.

"Look at us," he commands, and my eyes meet his in the mirror. "Look how mad I am for you," he says as he strokes me lightly, coating his digits in my arousal before slipping one thick finger inside of me. "Look how ravenous I am for you and you alone, Sela mina."

"Amon..." I moan loudly, arching into him and rubbing myself against the hard planes of his body.

"Sela mina, Sela mina," he chants as euphoria builds in his veins.

In my veins.

In everything that I am, only for him and with him.

As IF BURNED, I drop the staff from my grasp, taking a step back as I attempt to regulate my erratic breathing.

My pulse is through the roof, my entire body humming with foreign awareness just as liquid pools low between my legs, the arousal I'm feeling an echo of the one from the vision.

Dear God, what was that?

What the hell did I see?

Heavy steps thud down the stairs and I hurry to arrange the cane in the same position Mr. Nicholson had left it before stepping back and resuming my seat on the sofa.

Plastering a big smile on my face, I turn to him, doing my best to seem as normal as possible.

"I fear I've imposed on you for far too long," I make the excuse as I rise. "I should head back now. I'm sure people are wondering where I am."

He purses his lips, regarding me suspiciously, and for a moment I wonder if he knows I touched his cane.

"That is fine, Darcy. I am glad you visited me, and I hope you will do so again."

"Of course," I nod effusively. "Now that I know we are family, how can I not?" I offer some platitude as I inch my way towards the door.

He nods slowly, pensively.

"I also hope you will carefully consider what we've discussed today and be careful with the Hales. If you ever find yourself in danger, or in need of something, please don't hesitate to reach out to me."

"Thank you," I force a smile as I exit his home.

By chance, I spot Mr. Meow on the paved road leading to the main street and taking him in my arms, I pick up the pace.

Helena's voice echoes through the house as she makes her displeasure known at my sudden departure, but given what I'd just experienced, I can only push forward, needing to be alone in the privacy of my room.

That vision.

That damned vision.

It had been me, under yet another name. With Amon.

But that had not been the most striking thing.

I'd seen my appearance—*identical to my current one*—and I'd seen my naked flesh in the mirror.

On my body, right above my heart, there had been no birthmark.

At one point in time, I had been Sela—Amon's wife and lover.

Sela, with no mark, and no destiny of greatness.

I'd been just Sela.

And Amon still loved me.

Chapter Seventeen

"Wake up, sleeping beauty," a deep rumble penetrates my sleepy state.

Turning around in my bed, I swat a pair of hands aside as I moan my displeasure.

"Let me sleep," I grumble.

"Wake up, darlin'. There's much to be done today."

Darlin'.

Only one person calls me darlin'.

My eyes snap open as I push myself into a sitting position.

He's on the right side of my bed, a lazy smile on his face as he regards me.

Immediately, I hug the sheet to my chest, even though I'm wearing a thick cotton nightgown.

"You're back?"

"Just in time for the festival," he winks at me.

"What festival?" I frown.

"Fairy Festival. I'm sure you must have heard of it. It's the only time of the year when the town comes together and forgets about previous animosities. And even better," he pauses, a mischievous grin on his face.

My brows shoot up in question.

"It's a costume festival."

"What do you mean?"

"You'll get to dress in fancy period dresses and dance like it's the nineteenth century," he chuckles. "It will be fun. You'll see. But first we need to find you something to wear," he says as he pulls the sheet from me.

I squeak in surprise, my cheeks reddening as the sheet slips from my hands.

"Don't," I jump to grab it back.

"How did I offend your maidenly sensibilities this time, Darcy darlin'?" he drawls in amusement.

"I'm not wearing a brassiere," I admit as I avert my gaze, but not before I see his dip to my breasts.

Hugging my arms around my chest, I try to face him.

"Wait outside," I tell him, motioning to the door with a push of my chin. "I need to get dressed."

For a moment he doesn't move, simply watching me with a dangerous twinkle in his eyes.

"As you wish," he eventually says, giving me a mock bow as he exits the room.

The moment the door closes, I mutter a curse under my breath. No locked door can hold Caleb, can it?

Shaking my head, I go to my luggage as I rummage for something to wear. Since he'd said I would try on dresses, I opt for clothing I could easily wear underneath so I won't need to undress—my way of telling him he will not win in that regard.

I end up choosing a beige t-shirt and a pair of white mid-calf pants.

As I put my clothes on, I cannot stop my thoughts from straying to the day before and how my meeting with Mr. Nicholson had gone.

Yet despite the seemingly prejudiced information he'd given me, it had been the vision that had rattled me the most.

That and *how* the vision had come about.

The stone.

It must be a magical object if it was capable of showing me a previous life. One where I still had this odd healing ability, but no mark to show for it.

A life where I was still Amon's...

I swallow hard as I still in front of the mirror while rinsing my mouth. I stare at my reflection and I cannot help but remember a similar incident in the vision with Amon.

He'd...touched me.

Intimately.

And it had been...*glorious.*

Good Lord, my cheeks burn just thinking about it.

Out of everything I could analyze from that vision, that intimate moment is the one I cannot stop thinking about. The one that haunts me as does his touch—because I crave it more than anything else.

Whether I am Sela, Elizabeth, or Darcy, my feelings for him do not change.

He's in my heart, my soul, my very blood.

My fingers linger over my left breast, somehow still able to feel the heat of his palm on my skin, his lips on my neck and his fingers buried deep in...

"Get a hold of yourself, Darcy," I tell myself as I splash some water on my face.

But the truth is that I am absolutely wrecked, and the only culprit is...a demon.

Yet is Amon *just* a demon?

If what I'd seen had been real, then the Amon that had been my husband had not been evil. He's been honorable and devoted—nothing like the evil entity Rhiannon and Mr. Nicholson are making him out to be. Certainly nothing like someone who would kill me in cold blood.

He'd loved me. Of that I am sure. He'd loved me as Sela, and he'd loved me as Elizabeth too.

Once again, though the information piles up, I find myself even more confused.

Rationally, I don't think I can trust anyone. But if I look within me —my intuition is to go with Amon.

Always.

Just then, a knock at my door startles me, and I blush furiously as I remember Caleb.

The man courting me.

The man I *should* be thinking about.

Not some demon who may or may not have the power to influence my mind.

And yet another conundrum arises.

Though Amon undoubtedly has a claim on my heart due to everything that I've seen and experienced in the past, I cannot deny that I feel something for Caleb too.

He's charming, intense, and a little dangerous.

It's to a degree that my heart is just as confused as my mind.

Yes, my instinct is to trust Amon. But the same instinct wants to give Caleb a chance—live in the moment with him.

"Damn it," I curse in frustration.

Do I focus on the past with a potentially dangerous demon, banking everything on the few snippets that may or may *not* be real? Or do I focus on the present *and* the future—on Caleb?

"Darcy, are you done?'

I take one last look in the mirror before I head outside, though my heart still remains split in two.

"Where are we going?"

"While you were sleeping the morning away, I've already gone through the old clothes in the attic and have selected a few that would fit you so you can try them on," he tells me, swinging his arms around my shoulders and leading me further down the hallway.

The room he'd prepared is two doors down from his bedroom, and I appreciate that he'd been thoughtful about not making me uncomfortable by arranging everything in his own room.

"So what happens at this festival?"

"It's an occasion for everyone to be merry," he tells me with a smile. "It was first celebrated in the early eighteen hundreds to honor Mrs. Creed for her involvement in the town and with the peasant families. They used to call her the fairy," he chuckles, almost as if reminiscing about a fond memory.

"That sounds fun," I smile. "I'm curious what you picked," I say as I survey the many dresses laid out for me.

There's also a divider at the end of the room, and he gives me a sheepish smile when I look at him curiously.

"You can be quite sweet when you put your mind to it," I praise gently.

"Only for you," he whispers, coming a little closer.

Before I can anticipate what he will do, he brushes his lips lightly across my forehead.

My heart does a somersault in my chest, heat traveling up my cheeks as I feel myself growing flustered.

And there it is—my main conundrum. How can I claim to be in love with Amon yet react like this to Caleb? Alternatively, how can I say I'm falling for Caleb while holding the same torch for Amon?

Can one person even love two people? Equally?

Before, I would have said no.

Now? I no longer know...

"Why don't you start with that one," he points to a pink gown.

"Are these really from the nineteenth century?"

The quality of the silk is absolutely breathtaking.

Caleb nods.

"Most are what the Creeds left behind. No one touched them after so they should be in good shape."

"They are. These are wonderful, Caleb," I breathe out in wonder.

"Let's see how they look on you then," he directs me to the divider, telling me he will be the judge.

"Aren't you quite bossy?" I joke as I take off my shirt. "Why should *you* decide what I wear?"

"Because I'm the main audience, darlin'," he drawls in that cocky way of his. "If you're dressing up for anyone, it's me."

"You..." I take a step outside the divider, narrowing my eyes at him. "Has anyone told you how arrogant you are?"

His eyes sparkle.

"Has anyone told you how fucking sexy you are?"

My eyes widen just as my mouth forms an o, no sound coming out.

I stare at him, blinking once, twice. The third time, I squeal as I jump behind the divider again. Gazing down, I note that thankfully I still had my brassiere on, but it does nothing to alleviate my embarrassment.

"You're an asshole, Caleb!" I yell out.

His laughter echoes in the room, and it seems like my little blunder has given him plenty of material to tease me with now.

I quickly put on the dress, forgoing a corset.

"Done," I grumble as I exit, doing a pitiful twirl in front of him.

He purses his lips, tapping his finger against his chin as he considers me.

"Next," he declares, getting another dress and placing it in my arms.

I give him a deadly glare but I trudge my way back, putting on the next one.

It goes on like this for another hour. I never realized how hard it was to please Caleb. At this point we're running out of dresses and he hasn't liked any.

"What about this one?" I ask as I come out a while later.

To my surprise, I find him waiting for me with a cart full of food, tea and even dessert.

He stops the cart in the middle of the room as he straightens his spine, his eyes roving all over my figure.

I'd put on a dark blue gown that I'd thought complimented my eyes quite well.

And as he peruses me from head to toe, I rather believe he likes it too.

"You like it?" I whisper as I step closer, somehow needing to hear his confirmation.

He gives a brisk nod, his Adam's apple bobbing up and down as he regards me.

Leaving the cart behind, he takes a few steps towards me, his fingers going to my hair as he tucks a few stray strands behind my ear.

"You look magnificent, Darcy," he compliments me in a thick voice.

His eyes come to rest on my face, caressing me with his honeyed gaze.

"So very beautiful," he continues, almost as if in a trance.

"I didn't realize you found me beautiful," I blush as I push my chin down.

He'd told me he liked me and that he found me appealing. But this is the first time he called me beautiful.

He clears his throat.

"Then it is my mistake. You are the most beautiful woman I've ever seen, Darcy," he whispers as he takes my hand, bringing my knuckles to his mouth for a kiss.

I'm rooted to the spot as I stare at him, wondering what it would feel like if I just gave in—just for a taste. If I let him touch more of me just as he is touching the skin on my hand—with innate sensuality accompanied by the utmost care.

Reverence.

He might be dangerous to my virtue, but for the first time I see in his eyes that he would cherish it too—*cherish me*.

"Let's eat," he suddenly says, moving away from me.

I try not to show my disappointment as I quickly take off the dress so I won't sully it before I join him at the makeshift table.

"What did you do while I was away?" he asks casually as we start eating.

"I spoke with Rhiannon," I start, giving him a quick rundown of my discussion with Rhiannon, telling him everything but the fact that I am familiar with Amon. I also tell him about my visit to Mr. Nicholson and the fact that he'd given me some conflicting information.

He nods thoughtfully as he listens, and it's clear this is not new information for him.

"You knew, didn't you? About what's happening in Fairydale. About everything," I accuse lightly, taking in his features and his lack of reaction to even the most shocking bits.

Like the fact that Mr. Nicholson is my grandfather.

"If I knew and did not tell you, it was for a reason."

His tone is serious as he meets my gaze.

"I cannot make the decision for you, Darcy. I can only gently guide you."

"Then what do you suggest I do? One wants to do a life-threatening ritual, while the other wants some unknown blood rite. How am I to know what is right?"

"Do you have to do either?" he suddenly asks, shutting me up.

My brows pinch together as I tilt my head in confusion.

"What do you mean?"

"You don't have to do anything if you don't want, Darcy. Why should you risk anything? Why is it your duty to do anything?"

"But... Isn't this demon evil?" I probe, curious what he knows.

"He might be," he nods. "But did Lydia *name* the demon in her prophecy?"

"What..."

"To my knowledge she never said *what* evil. She only said that there will be someone who will eradicate the evil in Fairydale. What if..."

"What if there's something else?" Hope laces my voice.

"I don't trust Nicholson. All his life, he's only ever been concerned about one thing. Power. I would encourage you to be careful around him," he advises, and though he tries to come across as casual, I note the tightening of his fingers on his fork as he mentions the man by name.

"What about your grandmother? Should I trust her?"

He shakes his head, a smile pulling at his lips.

"You should trust no one but yourself, Darcy. When the time comes, you will know what to do," he assures me in a gentle tone.

"You have so much faith in me," I give a dry laugh.

"Because I know you will make the right choice," he states, his intense gaze on mine. "I trust you implicitly," he tells me, that one sentence backed by so much emotion, my own feelings seem to awaken, my eyes getting teary for no reason.

I blink away the dampness, offering him a small smile.

We continue to eat, and Caleb regales me with more tales about Fairydale and its *odd* encounters. Yet, except reinforcing his stance against Mr. Nicholson, he doesn't bring up the topic again, nor does he give me any additional information that could help me make more sense of everything.

I trust you implicitly.

Why does that feel like such a heavy burden on my shoulders? Especially when I don't know if I trust *myself*?

A few hours later we are on our way out of the house towards the beach where the celebrations are taking place—a few minutes north of the house. Caleb had described it as one of the most beautiful areas of Fairydale, where the marshes and the forest meet the sandy beach before the ocean takes over. Although I haven't had the opportunity to visit until now, I'm excited to see it. Especially since he is accompanying me—the only thing that seems to make me feel safe lately.

I'm wearing the deep blue gown while Caleb had settled for a basic ensemble that nonetheless makes him look dashing.

"Will your family be there, too?"

He nods.

"Katrina will be there for sure. I doubt my grandmother would, though. It's not really her scene."

As we get closer to the beach, music starts blasting through the air.

"A live orchestra too?" I ask in awe.

"Of course. It's a veritable nineteenth century reenactment," he chuckles. "Even better, the waltz was at the height of its popularity," he winks at me.

"I've never waltzed before," I admit as the music becomes louder, as does the crowd.

"I wouldn't have been very happy if you had," he murmurs softly, yet there's an unyielding quality to his tone.

"What?" I flutter my lashes in surprise.

Suddenly, Caleb comes to a halt as he positions himself in front of me.

"The waltz is too intimate," he states, his black eyes on mine. "It allows for the type of touch that could get a man killed."

"What do you mean?" I frown.

One hand goes to the small of my back as he pulls me to him, our fronts mashed together.

"Like this," he drawls as he caresses my back slowly. "You're only allowed to be this close to me, darlin'," he leans down to whisper in my ear. "You're only allowed to have my hands on your body like this."

"You're being absurd," I laugh, trying to diffuse the situation.

"That's not me being absurd, darlin'. It's me being at my boiling point."

I don't reply as I don't know how anyone could reply to that.

"You're being jealous for no reason, Caleb," I tell him lightly as I try to steer him towards the beach.

"I have every reason to be jealous, Darcy. *Every* reason," he states emphatically, his breath coming out in short spurts.

Drawing back, he looks me in the eye for a moment, almost as if he's trying to convey everything with his gaze—the intensity, the desire and the pure hunger rolling off him.

Giving him a slow nod, I breathe out in relief when he resumes his place by my side, taking my hand in his and leading me to the festival.

The music becomes louder, and soon we see all the townsfolk dancing and celebrating.

Everyone is dressed in period clothes, cutting a striking picture. I can easily imagine how this would have looked almost two centuries ago.

There are plenty of stands with food and beverages, as well as quite a few areas for games. The orchestra is to the side, playing different classical buoyant pieces as a few rows of men and women dance to the tunes.

"It's really the entire town, isn't it?"

There must be a few hundred people on the beach. You can barely spot a patch of empty land with how populated the area is.

"I told you it's something Fairydale takes seriously. Everyone, whether young or old, loves this festival."

"Why was Mrs. Creed so popular?" I ask as I let my eyes roam around, taking in all the fun and the good disposition of the people.

As we slowly make our way through the crowd, no one minds us. There are no strange looks, no odd whispers—nothing but merriment.

Either everyone is too focused on the festival, or Mr. Nicholson had done a marvelous job of taking the attention off me.

As it stands, no one even takes note of us.

"She helped most of the families in town, whether with money, medicine or by being there for them. She was like the big sister of the town, always ready to help."

"That was very nice of her, considering the Creeds were so rich. No one would have held it against them if they never interacted with the town."

"It's *because* they were so rich that it was unusual. They didn't differentiate in regards to skin color or amount of wealth, making everyone feel welcome."

"It makes sense she would be celebrated, then. I'm sure it must have been rare for those times."

"Come," he says as he takes me to the first stand, buying me a type of Fairydale-specific dessert—a mix of fruits and rose jam.

"There are fields of roses all around Fairydale. It's our local pride," the seller declares as he hands me a little container.

Nodding my thanks, I follow Caleb as he takes me to yet another stand, and then another, until my arms are full of Fairydale delicacies.

Amusement enters his features as he sees me juggling the many dishes, so he seats me at a small table by the side, telling me to eat.

"You're not eating?" I ask in between mouthfuls, noticing he's just watching me.

He rests his chin in his palm as he gazes at me with deep satisfaction—as if he could get his fill just by looking at me.

My cheeks color slightly, especially as his lips tip into an adoring smile.

"Have I told you how cute you are when you eat?" he suddenly says, playfully tapping my nose with his finger.

"Earlier you said beautiful," I raise a challenging brow at him.

"You're the best combination of beautiful, cute and sexy, darlin'. Never doubt that. But now..." he pauses as his smile widens, his eyes roving all over my face. "Now you're so cute, I'd like nothing more than to eat *you*."

My eyes widen slightly, and before I know it, I push a piece of fruit into his mouth.

"There's plenty of food around. Besides, I'm not that edible," I grumble, flushing in embarrassment at my abysmal flirting skills.

He releases a deep chuckle as he slowly chews on the fruit, yet his gaze tells me everything I need to know. For him, *I am* edible.

When I'm done with the food, he takes the empty containers to the trash, getting me a cup of mulled wine.

"Don't tell me you've also never had alcohol before," he inquires when he sees me regard the glass with apprehension, smelling it while considering whether I should drink or not.

"Will it get me drunk?" I ask as I look up at him.

He shakes his head in amusement.

"Go on, drink. Nothing will happen to you."

Trusting him, I take a small sip. Then another one.

There's an interesting flavor to it, and the combination of sweet and sour is potent on my senses. Before I know it, the cup is empty and I give him a doe-eyed look as I ask for a refill.

Ever the gentleman, Caleb indulges me, getting me another one. But when I'm done with that one, he tells me it's time to dance.

Right at that moment, the Blue Danube starts playing.

Though the sand is a little inconvenient to dance on, I forget all about it as Caleb sweeps me into the crowd of other dancers, losing ourselves among them.

I may not be particularly familiar with the waltz, but with his lead, I don't think I need to know anything—just how to let myself go and enjoy the moment.

He holds me close to his body—*too* close. One hand hugs mine as he raises our arms in the air while his other languidly touches my back, settling right above my hip. One dip and it could slip in dangerous territory.

But seeing the wicked gleam in his eyes, I *know* he's aware of it—he's in fact tempting fate as he caresses me softly, his fingers brushing over the light material of the dress, his touch searing even through the clothes. He moves his hand slowly, following the same rhythm of the waltz.

As he pushes me back, his hand dips, as he pulls me towards him, it goes up.

"You're incorrigible," I tell him, channeling my teacher's tone. Yet my lips are in a perpetual smile as he spins me onto the sand-filled beach, my cheeks flushed, my heart pounding relentlessly.

The light breeze of the afternoon brushes against my skin, the cool wind doing nothing to ease the heat building in my body—from the wine or his proximity, I don't know.

He has an equally carefree smile on his face, and though his eyes maintain the same intensity as before—as if he *would* eat me if he could—his features are lighter than they've ever been. So much so that I can't help the feeling of déjà-vu that takes shape in my breast—an eternity converging into one moment.

This moment.

The music becomes a faraway sound, drowning in the distance as my focus dims until he turns into my sole focus. Everything to my right or left is a blur.

The sounds of the crowd are all but drowned out as I get lost in his eyes.

He twirls me around, every time fitting me tighter to his body—to the point that I feel every hard edge of him. His muscles bulge beneath his clothing, but there is another part of him that makes me blush to the roots of my hair.

He notices it too, as he brings his mouth to my ear, nibbling at my flesh.

"My shy little maiden," he coos gently. "This is what you do to me, Darcy," he drawls as he holds me to him, his hardness fitted against my belly. "You make the blood in my veins boil with a need to possess you. To be the only man to ever touch your skin—to *sear* myself on your flesh."

A shiver envelops me, his hot breath caressing my earlobe, his heated words making me tremble in his arms.

"Will you be mine, Darcy darlin'?"

He draws back to study my reaction, and as I find myself staring at him, I cannot deny this maddening connection between us—this attraction that borders on the animalistic.

When I'm with him, all sense leaves me until I'm a mere pool of sensations, his touch creating small waves that ripple through the entire surface.

Words fail me as I can only look at him, my lips parted, my pulse drumming in my ears.

There's music in the background, and as the waltz comes to an end, the orchestra switches to a more lively tune. Yet even as Caleb leads me into a brisker dance, increasing the tempo and swirling me all around, I cannot find it in me to answer him.

Not because I do not have an answer—my reaction to him is the prime indication that I do. But because I feel so lost, yet so found. So foreign in my own flesh, yet so at home in his arms.

It's an alarming dichotomy, and one that scares me with its implications. It makes me believe that I'm more... That I'm not just orphaned little Darcy, the lonely English teacher who's never tried to do anything daring in her life. No, when I'm with him like this—when my spirit soars up high—I feel special.

I feel...capable of anything.

"You are," Caleb states as he comes closer in the rhythm of the dance, his breath caressing my lips. "Mine," he continues. "Mine. Mine. Mine, Darcy," he chants, his eyes a cloudy gathering of lust, desire and something more...

Something I should be intimately acquainted with, yet is ever so elusive.

Just as I'm about to look deeper into myself to give him an answer, a loud cry erupts in the air.

"Duck," Caleb yells, pushing me to the ground just at the same time another howl resounds. The music stops, replaced by human screams as everyone starts running and panicking.

"What..."

The word is barely out of my mouth when I see four winged creatures descend onto the beach.

"What's happening?" I ask in alarm.

Caleb gathers me to his chest, doing his best to shield me from the ongoing chaos.

"Gargoyles," he mutters. "Fuck."

"G-gargoyles? You mean..."

"Yes, those," he nods to one of the winged creatures stepping onto the beach, one clawed hand reaching out and grabbing one of the men in its path.

Just as I think it's going to throw him away, the gargoyle wraps its big hand around the body, bringing it to his mouth and popping the head off, slowly chewing on it as it lets its gaze roam around the beach.

"We need to leave. Now," Caleb says as he helps me to my feet.

Before I can ask him what's going on, he grabs the hem of my dress, tearing it in one go.

"We can't have anything slow us down."

Grabbing my hand, he tugs me after him, hurrying to the path that leads back to the main road—and to the house.

I'm still staring at the big creature munching on the human head, my eyes bulging in my head at the sight, disbelief filling me to the brim.

Thank God for Caleb and his quick acting because I'm barely starting to recover from my shock.

"Fuck," he suddenly stops, and I note that the other gargoyles have surrounded the beach, each slowly inching their way towards us while feasting on the crowd of people in their way.

"They're killing everyone," I whisper in horror. "We have to do something, Caleb. We can't just..." my voice trembles as I see more blood.

More decapitated bodies fall to the ground as the gargoyles blaze through the crowd.

"They're here for me, aren't they?" I ask, tugging on his sleeve. "They must be..."

"Even if they are, they will never get to you. Trust me?" he turns, confidence and determination radiating from him.

I give him a nod.

"Yes, they must be here for you. For your blood," he winces. "The only way to save the humans is to lead them away from the beach and allow everyone time to run..."

He quicky comes with a plan, but my attention is stolen by a small cry of help.

Turning, I note with horror the destruction the gargoyles have already wrecked in their path—the dead bodies, the crushed stalls and blood-stained sand.

But my eyes focus on something else.

A child.

He's maybe a few feet away from us, dragging himself in the sand all the while crying for his parents. People run past him, some tripping on him in their hurry to leave the danger zone. He yelps in pain as he tries to fend for himself, but he can barely move.

Everyone ignores him while they seek their own safety, and I can't help the sudden squeeze in my chest.

"Caleb," I point towards the little boy, gazing up at him and pleading with him with my eyes.

"Darcy," he groans, but he acquiesces, shielding me while I dash to the little one.

As I reach his side, my mouth parts in horror as I note the state he is in and why he's crawling instead of walking. His tibia is fractured, a part of the bone sticking out through his flesh.

"Mommy," he cries out, his cheeks red with tears.

All at once, I'm thrust back in the past and in that one vision. Sela had been able to heal injuries with a touch. Would I be able to do that, too?

I can heal myself, but can I do it for other people as well?

Although I'm not sure what I'm supposed to do, I let instinct take over as I drop to my knees before the little boy, speaking softly to him in an attempt to calm him.

"Be quick. We need to move," Caleb speaks harshly, yet his expression doesn't match his tone as he regards me with hidden longing.

My heart beats loudly in my chest as I try to focus on my breathing.

Placing my hands over the little boy's injury, I remember how Sela had channeled energy to her palms, letting it hum to the surface before pushing it in the boy's skin.

I try to do the same.

Focusing on my palms and on the energy inside of me, I summon it forth.

It takes a few attempts before I feel a flicker of something come to life, a pulsation at the surface of my skin.

"It's ok," I smile at the little boy, distracting him as I place my hand over the broken bone.

Gritting my teeth, I push all the energy towards him, imagining his bone retracting, his skin and flesh mending.

It doesn't happen at first.

But within a few tries, I can feel the transfer of energy take place. Leaving my body, it morphs into a healing mist that envelops the injured leg.

In a few seconds, no injury remains.

"Run," I tell him. "Run and find your mother."

He blinks in confusion, unable to understand what's happening. But eventually he does as told.

He runs away.

"Did you see that?" I jump to my feet. Immediately, though, a wave of dizziness hits me and I would have hit the ground if not for the strong arms that catch me. My head swims, my entire vision about to leave me just as my body becomes limp in his arms. If it hadn't been for him, I would have never been able to keep myself upright—I'm struggling as it is to keep conscious.

But...how? When I heal myself I'm fine. Sela, too, hadn't even felt the effects of healing that boy. For her it had been second nature. So why am I suddenly so weak?

"Fucking hell," Caleb curses. "I'm proud of you, love, but you can't do that. Not now. Not when you don't have your strength back," he chastises lightly before swooping me in his arms.

I don't question him, leaning into him and releasing a deep sigh as I wrap my arms around his neck, breathing his scent in.

Weak... I feel so weak...

The crowd is still running amok around us, and until now they've done a good job of masking our presence. Soon, though, one of the gargoyles spots us, its red eyes flashing across the beach as does the pure determination reflected there—its singular purpose.

"To the forest," Caleb says, holding me closer as he starts into a full on run. There are some people around who'd tried to hide in the marshes, and in an attempt to draw the creatures away, Caleb takes a different path than the rest.

The gargoyle follows, with the other three close on its trail.

"It's working," I tell him, struggling to keep my focus as my body is still languid from healing the boy. "They're coming after us and leaving the people alone."

"Gargoyles, just like the Kiaka, are creatures that have a master—someone who gives them orders. It's clear that whoever is behind this told them to target you," he purses his lips. "I thought the bracelet Rhiannon gave you would have helped."

"Why do you think they chose this celebration? Out in the open like this?"

"Because you barely go out, Darcy. And, it seems, Rhiannon's wards have become stronger so nothing can penetrate the house. The only option is to catch you outside of the manor."

"But the people..."

"Do you think they care about the people? Not when the prize is right in front of them," he adds tersely, hugging me closer to his chest as he makes his way out of the marsh and into the forest, losing ourselves between the tall trees.

As we take cover behind a fallen log, Caleb gently lays me down.

"We won't be able to defeat all of them like this. I'm going to ask you to do something, darlin'. I'm sorry about this, but it's the only thing that might help."

"What is it?"

"This," he says as he rips another bit of material from my dress. "I need your blood on it to lure them away until I can find a weapon to fight them."

"But..." I bite my lip, not liking the idea of being parted from him—of knowing he might be in danger. "Do you know how to fight a gargoyle?"

He gives a brisk nod.

"They have impenetrable skin save for one spot under their right wing. But I need to get close enough to stab them there," he purses his lips. "There are four of them. I need to know you're safe and away from them so I can focus on this. You get me?"

He seeks my gaze with his and I can see the worry reflected there.

"Ok. We'll do it your way. Just... Please take care. I don't want you to get hurt," I take his hand in mine, squeezing tightly and bringing it to my lips for a good luck kiss.

He's watching me intently, almost as if he's memorizing my features.

"I would do anything to keep you safe, Darcy. *Anything*," he emphasizes.

Leaning forward, he brushes his lips across my forehead.

"Soon you'll be mine. No more delays and no more excuses. I'm claiming every inch of you," he rasps against my skin.

Yet before I can reply, he's off me. Taking his jacket off, he removes a switchblade from a pocket, and unsheathing the knife, he gives me a questioning look.

Extending my hand towards him, I point to my palm.

Gingerly taking my hand in his, he brings it to his mouth for a kiss before he lays the blade against my flesh.

"I'm sorry," he whispers.

The pain is brief. Blood pools to the surface, and he wastes no time in smearing the red liquid all over the piece of fabric.

Moments trickle by and slowly, my wound starts closing. Yet it doesn't happen as fast as before. The healing process is sluggish, and I anxiously wait for my wound to seal.

Eventually it does, and only a few errant drops of blood remain on my skin.

Bringing it to his lips, Caleb licks my hand clean before he gets to his feet.

"Stay out of sight. If anything happens, run and find another hiding place. I'll find you, don't worry about me."

With that, he's gone.

More noises erupt in the air—howls from the gargoyles and screams from the people.

Though we'd drawn them away, I don't doubt the others have to deal with the casualties and the destruction the gargoyles had wreaked around.

Fear mounts inside of me as I think of Caleb alone out there facing these terrifying creatures. Though I don't doubt his physical prowess since I know he spent almost a decade in the army, these aren't enemy troops he has to fight against. These are supernatural creatures with who knows what abilities.

Bringing my hands together, I say a quick prayer for Caleb, hoping he will be victorious and he will find me—as he promised.

At the same time, I can't help but think about *who* would send the gargoyles after me.

I'm sure everyone will be quick to say it's Amon. Yet why do I not believe that?

The sound of leaves rustling puts me on my guard just as it dawns on me that there are four.

Four against one.

Dear God, but how can Caleb survive against four creatures by himself?

The more I think of him overpowered and hurt, the more I blame myself and my uselessness. Not only am I in the middle of this conflict I want no part in, but I have absolutely no clue how to defend myself.

So what if I have these abilities? These healing powers? They are useless in open combat.

Some time passes as I continue to despair over Caleb, huddled against the fallen log and shielding myself from view.

A sudden thud gets my attention, and mustering enough courage, I move slightly out of my hiding place to gaze in the clearing ahead.

Nothing.

Thinking it might be a ground dweller and nothing else, I take a deep breath as I return to my spot. Yet the moment I turn, I come face to face with one of those ugly creatures.

A few feet from me, he's staring at me with those red eyes, his nostrils flaring as it studies me.

The gargoyle's skin is a muddy brown with an ashy tone. The wings themselves remind me of bat wings but one hundred times bigger.

And when he releases a loud howl, I realize that not only am I in trouble, he likely announced my location to his buddies.

Swallowing hard, I get to my feet, finding a piece of harder wood on the ground and using it as a sword-stick of sorts. Even in this life-and death situation I can't help but laugh at the absurdity of it.

I'm facing a creature with impenetrable skin and I'm waving a...twig?

It doesn't matter, though, I'll give my all to this fight. I'm not about to back down just because I'm ill equipped or not equipped at all for such a situation.

"Bring it on, bad guy," I push my chin up, wielding the twig as I step over the log and back away.

The gargoyle is still in front of me, its eyes narrowing dangerously just as he takes a step forward.

His wings flap once and he's in front of me.

Jesus, but he must be over ten feet tall.

I blink, my eyes widening as I realize I stand no chance.

Especially as one of his enormous hands reaches for me, his fingers wrapping around me even as I try to step out of his path.

Good Lord! Is he going to eat my head next?

Squeezing my eyes shut, I pray for a brief death.

Do you feel if someone rips your head off your body? I suppose you don't get enough of a warning to do so, considering how fast he chewed that other man's head off.

The scenarios are piling up in my mind at an alarming speed, and I barely realize that nothing happens. Not only is my head still attached to my body, but the gargoyle hasn't moved an inch.

Slowly opening one eye, I realize why he hasn't moved.

My entire body has an odd glow to it, and the gargoyle is tilting his head right and left as he's studying me, probably as confused as I am with its origin.

Yet just as I'm about to start struggling in his hold—or do something with my twig—the gargoyle's body explodes.

That's it.

One moment I'm being held by this giant creature who's probably wondering what I taste like, the next I'm falling to the ground covered in all types of gargoyle matter—his blood is gray!

My face scrunches up in disgust, especially as the stench hits me.

Not only did the whole giant gargoyle blow up, but so did his gut, which happened to be digesting all those human bits.

Bile rises up my throat, my stomach in knots as I drag myself away from the slaughter.

Of course, I'm very relieved to find myself still in possession of my head, and other limbs, but I still can't *wrap* my head around what happened—pun intended.

It wasn't me. That, I know for sure.

Whenever I'm using my abilities I can feel the energy surging around, almost like it's a separate entity. This time, I'd felt nothing until I'd seen the odd glow surrounding my body before the gargoyle had detonated in front of me.

Still, not one to overly question my good luck, I take a few clean breaths as I force myself to my feet—a little wobbly from the surge of adrenaline and fear that still resides in my limbs.

When the thoughts of danger subside, I can only think of Caleb.

Is he fine? Is he...

I don't even want to entertain the thought that something might have happened to him.

Knowing I cannot remain here with the gargoyle remains—who knows if they have a super developed sense of smell—I start in the direction Caleb had taken off.

At the same time, I know I'm also running the risk of discovery by virtue of my stained clothes alone.

Not a while later and I hear the sound of water—as well as remembering that Mr. Vaughan had told me about a river with a waterfall around Fairydale.

Thinking I could go and quickly rinse the gargoyle goo off my body, I follow the sound of water.

Luckily, it doesn't take me long to find the river.

Despite being the beginning of October, the surrounding area is still somewhat green. The water is crisp and clear and exactly what I need.

Walking alongside the river bank, it takes me about five minutes to reach the waterfall.

Just like Mr. Vaughan had said, the view is breathtaking.

The waterfall is some fifteen feet, and the river currents don't seem to be overly strong.

Satisfied with my assessment of the area and the fact that I could take a chance and clean myself, I waste no time in tugging the dress off my body, holding my breath every time I smell some gargoyle on me.

When I reach my underthings, I decide against taking them off. I guess I am a little daring, but not *that* adventurous.

Dipping my toes first, I wince at the first bite of the cold water.

We're already in autumn, and the temperature in the river must have dropped a lot.

Still, it's either that, or monster bodily fluids that might attract other monsters.

All things considered, I think I'm going to take my chances.

Steeling myself against the cold, I proceed to dive head first into the river. Surprisingly, it's not very deep, and when I'm standing in the middle of it, the water only reaches the top of my breasts.

Smiling as my body acclimates to the coldness, I duck under water a few more times as I scrub my scalp. Blood, guts and probably bone got tangled in my hair, and it's not exactly easy to get it out.

When I feel thoroughly clean and ready to go, I emerge to the surface and I start wading towards the shore.

Except...

"I told you I'd find you, darlin'," Caleb smirks at me as he's leaning against a tree.

I gasp at his sudden appearance, but I forget all about my shame as I study him carefully for any sign of injury.

Even better, he helps my perusal as he takes off his shirt and pants until he remains only in his underwear.

My cheeks heat despite the coldness of the water, yet I can't look away.

It's my first time seeing a man in such a state of deshabille, and I have to admit, I am not disappointed.

Just like my first impression of him, Caleb Hale is a mountain of a man. His body is only muscle, his abs hard and defined, his thighs equally as powerful. Every inch of him is pure brawn, and I don't think I've ever seen a more mouth-watering sight.

"What happened?" I ask as he dives into the water, slowly coming towards me. "What about the gargoyles? Are they..."

"They're dead," he confirms and I release a relieved breath.

"Thank God," I exclaim. "And you? Are you hurt anywhere?"

He shakes his head, that arresting smile still playing at his lips.

"I killed three, and a fourth I found already dead. You left the clearing," he raises a brow.

"I couldn't stay and wait for more to appear," I grumble. "And I was covered in gargoyle bodily fluids, not exactly the best perfume on the market."

He chuckles as he reaches my side. He brings his hands on my shoulders as he stabilizes me next to him.

"What happened to it?"

I give him a short summary, finding him as perplexed as I was at how easily the creature had exploded.

Pursing his lips, he seems deep in thought.

"But," I nibble at my bottom lip. "I wonder if they weren't here to kill me?" I ask, a theory going through my mind.

"You would be right. Whoever wants to use your blood would not risk that. They would kidnap you to have it all readily available. The gargoyles were your escorts, so to speak," he laughs.

"I'm conflicted, Caleb. Why now? Why not when I went alone to Mr. Nicholson's house?"

"Why indeed," he muses, though his expression tells me the exact reason.

"Is it him?" I ask on a whisper. "Is it him who wants me? But why if we're related? I just can't make sense of this."

"Don't trust anyone, Darcy," he states resolutely as he cups my cheeks with his big palms. "Everyone is looking out for their own interests. You must do so as well."

"What about you?" I draw back, searching his face. "Are you looking for your interests as well?"

Yet there's the unspoken question.

What are your interests?

So far I've inferred that both Rhiannon and Mr. Nicholson have a stake in Amon's imprisonment and though I don't know what their personal goal is, I am sure it has something to do with that ritual they want me to help with.

Yet Caleb?

He's secretive and mysterious. So far, I haven't been able to pinpoint what his goal is.

"Of course," he readily admits. "And I only have one interest," he continues as if reading my mind.

I tilt my head as I wait for his answer.

"You," he declares.

"Me?" I echo, confused.

"You've asked me about war before, sweetheart," he sighs. "It's true that I've seen many wars. I've fought too many battles to count. At some point in my life, all I knew was devastation. I did as I was told because I never knew otherwise. I never knew how to live my life without bloodshed. But then I met you and..." he smiles. "You're just a ray of sunshine, aren't you? Making everyone fall in love with you everywhere you go."

"F-fall in love?" I falter, afraid I didn't understand him right.

"Yes, Darcy darlin'. That is exactly what I mean. I've fallen in love with you. Fast. Hard. So fucking deep. Like I never thought I would fall for someone," he confesses, his voice thick with emotion.

My lids flutter as I regard him, committing his features to memory as he looks in this moment—all hard edges and killer aura. Yet there's the gentlest smile on his lips, and the most intoxicating love in his gaze, and I know he speaks the truth.

Slowly, as if he's handling a precious jewel, he brings me closer to his body.

All the while, his gaze is on me to gauge my reactions, showing me that he can be a true gentleman mindful of my sensibilities.

"I want you to be mine, darlin'. I want to taste and worship every inch of you, drive you so fucking mad with passion, you will never think of anyone else but me. Only ever me. That's what I *need* sweetheart," he growls, almost as if frustrated with himself. "I want to keep you to myself, tuck you away from the world and protect you from all the dangers out there, all the perversities and all the fucked up shit that goes in this fucked up world. I only want that for you," he breathes harshly. "I only want you to be mine, Darcy darlin'. Now, tomorrow and to the end of time."

"Caleb..."

I don't get to speak as he fits his lips to mine in what can only be considered an assault to the senses.

The previous kiss I'd given him is quickly forgotten as I realize I'd been playing a child's game. Then, I'd brushed my lips against his in what I considered to be a *kiss*.

Now, he proves me wrong.

He channels all the aggression, all the emotion bottled up within him in this kiss, his lips on mine, his mouth devouring mine until I lose myself.

Until just like he said, I become his and only his.

But just as it starts, it's over.

He draws back, breathing hard and studying me closely for my reaction.

He's testing the ground.

But how dare he give me a taste of paradise only to take it away?

Wounding my arms around his neck, I raise myself on the tips of my toes—easily done in the water—and I press myself against him.

The length of my body meets his just as I reclaim my kiss.

"Fucking hell, Darcy," he curses against my mouth before he kisses me like I never thought a kiss could be.

His tongue dives into my mouth, meeting mine and inviting it to a tantalizing dance that has me squirming against him. Heat builds up in my body—so much so, the water must be boiling by now.

Dragging his open mouth on top of mine, he gives me a languid lick. Then another. Almost as if he's tasting and savoring me.

A deep groan erupts from his throat as he brings his big hands to my bottom, cupping my ass and inviting me to open my legs so he can step between them, so he can bring his hardness in contact with my center and...

"Caleb," I moan into his mouth. "What..."

"Tell me you're mine. Tell me you're mine, love," he chants, nibbling at my lips between earth-shattering kisses. "Tell me!" he suddenly demands.

"I'm yours," I agree. "Yours," I repeat as I emulate his movements, threading my hands through his thick hair and biting at his lips.

"That's it," he speaks softly, encouragingly. "Just like that, darlin'. Suck my tongue in your mouth," he commands, and I can only obey. "Fuck, you're so hot," he rasps, alternating between kissing me deeply and licking my face as if he wouldn't want to leave any inch of me untasted.

Just like he promised.

"I never knew kissing could be so..." I trail off, simply at a loss of words.

My breathing is harsh, my heart hammering in my chest and my soul...my soul is singing in my body, asking to be let out for a true mating dance with this man.

Heat builds inside of me, so much so it's close to bursting to the surface.

All the passion. All the longing. All the...want.

All that I've repressed before is now emerging—is now coming to the surface for this man, and this man alone.

"You make me hot, Caleb," I admit, slowly biting on my lip as I bring my naked gaze to his. "You make me want to shed all my inhibitions and everything that holds me back. But I..."

"Marry me," he suddenly says.

My eyes grow wide as I still in his arms.

"W-what?" I stammer.

Did I hear him right? Did he just ask me to...marry him?

"Marry me, Darcy," he repeats, and I can sense the sincerity that laces his voice, as does the emotion and the true desire behind his words.

He...wants this.

"What? How? I..."

"It's not only this maddening attraction that's simmering between us. It's also the fact that you bring me more peace than I've ever known," he tells me with a soft smile. "I respect your principles and I would never try to pressure you into doing anything you didn't want or weren't ready for. But I also want to make my commitment clear to you. I *want* you—and everything that you are."

"T-that's a lot to take in. I've never been proposed to before," I let out a nervous laugh.

"Well, you better not, or I would have to comb down this world and get rid of every man who thought he could have a shot with you."

I giggle at the absurdity, but why do I have the impression he's not kidding.

"Marriage is a big thing," I continue.

"Exactly. It's a lifelong commitment—and beyond. So marry me, Darcy. Be mine—forever."

The sun is setting, the sky turning into an orange hue as the light becomes sparser and spares. Still it's enough to illuminate his handsome features and his black, black eyes that hold my heart captive.

In spite of everything that has happened—in spite of my dreams and visions, and admittedly strange encounters with Amon—I cannot deny that Caleb owns my heart.

Slowly yet steadily, I've been falling for him from day one.

A pang of guilt reverberates in my chest as I think of Amon, but he's nothing more than an echo of the past—if that's even real.

There are too many doubts to even begin assembling a concrete picture.

He's...a demon—a captive demon believed to terrorize the entire town.

Caleb is a man. A flesh and blood man that's present before me, telling me he is in *love* with me.

"Ok," I whisper, deciding to push my thoughts about Amon aside—shove them into a little box and seal it shut.

Caleb is the present. He is my *now*. And he is the one who's been on my side—fighting for me and with me from day one.

"I'll marry you."

Chapter Eighteen

I wake up at dawn.

The house is dead quiet, which gives me hope that no one else is mad enough to be up at this unconscionable hour.

Yet despite the strain on my body from yesterday's events, I could not sleep.

Not with so many erratic thoughts and never-ending dilemmas.

My stomach is still humming with pleasure from Caleb's proposal, the taste of his kiss lingering on my lips and making me look forward to seeing him again today.

But this time it's not *him* who is the cause of my confusion—he's the only thing I am sure of. Rather, it's everything that's happening around me and the fact that my blood seems to be so precious for no specific reason. It's the fact that I've recently discovered I have powers, but now I realize they come with severe limitations.

More than anything, it's in the fact that someone is directly targeting me. Whether it's Amon, Mr. Nicholson, someone in the Hale family, or someone I do not yet know, I can't help but suspect everyone.

Light filters through the wide windows of the hallway, illuminating the staircase and every corner of the house. Thankful that I won't need to use a candle, I slowly make my way downstairs.

Aside from the Hales, few people work in the staff kitchens on the lowest level—between the ground floor and the catacombs. As far as I'd understood it, they do not reside in the house, rather they are townsfolk who'd agreed to work for a wage.

I hadn't interacted much with them—whether because our paths never really crossed, or they purposefully avoided me, I do not know.

But the one time I'd seen them, they'd advised me against visiting that area of the house due to its infestation with rodents.

One of the older women had told me they've been having a hard time controlling the rodent population down there, and they've resorted to all types of traps and poisons to ensure they didn't spread further to other parts of the house.

Though it had barely been a passing mention, as I became increasingly frustrated with my situation and the fact that I do not understand my abilities, nor do I know my limitations. As such, the idea had come to me as I'd woken up.

Determination brims inside of me as I stride over to the lower quarters. Luckily, though the staff hasn't arrived yet, the doors aren't closed.

Remembering the areas I'd heard were most infested, I check those first—the cupboards, and the small crevices.

To my great surprise, I find plenty of rats squirreled away in a corner—some dead, some half-alive.

Grabbing a box and a pair of gloves, I pluck them by the tail and I drop them in the box, one at a time. There are about three that still move a little, which leads me to believe they've likely ingested poison and are well on their way to the grave. There's a fourth dead one, and I add it too, thinking Mr. Meow might like some food.

For a wild cat, I haven't really seen him chase mice, or birds, as is the way of cats. He accepts what I feed him, but he doesn't have the inclination to procure his own.

It's a wonder how he's made it on his own until now.

Still, he's not a domesticated cat and I have no doubt he misses his prey and raw meat, so I'm sure he will appreciate my little gift.

Box in tow, I head back to my room.

Mr. Meow is on my pillow, stretching languidly and grooming himself—he always makes himself at home in my bed.

I think I'm the only human he likes, though, because whenever someone else comes along he either runs away or bares his teeth at them—not very nice cat behavior, which I've reprimanded him for.

"I have a surprise for you, Mr. Meow," I declare as I close the door behind me, locking it just in case. The last thing I need is for someone to come across my little experiment and think me mad.

Mr. Meow jumps up, his ears perking as he hears my voice. Coming towards me, he regards the box in my hand curiously.

I beckon him to the bathroom where I place the box on the floor.

Still wearing my gloves, I take the dead rat out by its tail, waving it in front of Mr. Meow.

"I got you raw meat," I tell him, dropping to my knees and placing it in front of him. "I'm sorry I've only fed you human food until now, but this is your special treat."

The rat isn't particularly big, but it should fill Mr. Meow, nonetheless.

Yet as I regard my dear friend expectantly with a wide smile on my face, I realize he doesn't seem particularly thrilled. At least not as I expected him to be.

He's flinching away, and if he had a human nose, I'm pretty sure it would be scrunched up in disgust.

"Don't tell me you don't like it..." My face falls.

Yet when he sees my disappointment, he immediately reacts.

If at first he'd seemed put off by the dead rat in front of him, now he leans forward, smelling the meat before bringing his sharp claws to scrap at the hide, digging into the rat and bringing his snout into its cavity.

"That's my sweet boy," I coo at him, patting him on the head.

Seeing him munch with gusto, I decide to switch my attention to my own little experiment.

Settling on the floor next to Mr. Meow, I pluck one semi-alive rat from the box, placing it in front of me and regarding him carefully.

Do I need to remove my gloves, I wonder?

Not entirely thrilled about the prospect of touching a rat, I slowly take my gloves off, depositing them to the side.

The rat has a few spasms as he undoubtedly struggles between life and death.

"What fails for me is more food for you, Mr. Meow," I tell him with a wink.

"Meow."

I'm not sure if that's a *yes, please*, or a *no, thank you.* But seeing that he's enjoying the rat, I'll take it as the former.

"Now let's see," I murmur as I bring my hands over the rat, focusing my energy into my palms.

Like before, I need to *feel* the energy at the surface of my skin, almost like a sleek film covering my palms.

A slow hum accompanies it, and my skin starts pulsating. At the same time, the rat becomes increasingly more active, moving around until he suddenly jumps up—newly revitalized.

"It worked, Mr. Meow. It worked," I exclaim in wonder.

Yet just as I try to move, the same lightheadedness as before descends over me, to the point that I feel my eyes roll back in my head. I fall back on my ass, stretching my arms back just in time so I don't fall flat on my back.

At the same time, the rat becomes straight up rambunctious, wasting no time in running around.

"Mr. Meow," I call out, my eyes growing wide.

It was fine when the rat wasn't moving, but now, seeing it slither his way around my bathroom, heading straight for me, has my skin erupt in goosebumps—an unwelcome add-on to my mounting headache.

Mr. Meow, though, proves to me that he is a veritable wild cat by jumping on top of the rat and catching it with his claw, effectively stopping his movements.

"Maybe I shouldn't have brought so many," I sigh.

One or two would have sufficed seeing that I can barely heal one before I get dizzy.

Turning my gaze to the box, I note that the other two have already stopped moving—likely a sign that they've died.

"Damn it," I curse softly.

Yet there's still something else to be done.

A little more difficult than I would have liked, I slowly manage to get to my feet. Washing my hands with soap and water, I take a blade from the cabinet and aim it at my open palm. Since I don't know how fast I will be healing now, I can't afford to nick any important veins.

"This is the moment, Mr. Meow. Let's see if my theory is correct."

Making a shallow cut, I watch as blood slowly seeps to the surface.

Mr. Meow surprises me by climbing on the cabinet and pushing his little snout against me.

"What?" I turn to him.

He takes advantage of my momentary lack of attention to dive straight for my hand, lapping at the blood until the wound is clear.

And not healing.

Or, if it is, it's very slow.

Quickly glancing at my wristwatch, I note the time as I wait for it to close.

Usually, it takes a second for it to do so. Now? After five minutes and there is still a tiny scar,

It's only at the seven minute mark that the wound disappears completely.

"What do you think, Mr. Meow?" I ask pensively as I stare at my hand.

"It seems that by healing someone else, my energy goes down to such an extent that not only do I get physically weak, but my own wounds no longer heal at the same rate," I start, voicing out my observations. "On the other hand, if I focus only on healing my own wounds, they heal within seconds. I think we can surmise that I have a limited supply of this...energy or ability or whatever it is. It seems to be a replenishable resource, since once I rest I do feel better, and my wounds heal faster again. But overall there seems to be a limit to how much I can do. And that means..."

I swallow hard at the implications.

How foolish of me to think myself invincible when I'd first found out about these strange abilities. It was my own hubris and folly that could have led me down a dangerous path had I not realized my own limitations.

"This means I can die. Without enough energy, my body will *not* heal, and I can die," I whisper in horror.

"If I participate in the rituals Rhiannon or Mr. Nicholson want me to, there is a very good chance I *will* die."

And there is one more variable I have not considered.

What is the basis of my energy?

Is it my blood? It could be since everyone seems to want it.

But if that is so, then if I lose too much blood, I will be in danger.

"Mr. Meow... Is it just me or..." I pause, focusing on my now non-existent wound. "I might die either way."

Mr. Nicholson wants to use my blood for some alternative ritual, while Rhiannon wants to use *me* to channel the spell. By her own admission, she would happily *die* to rid the town of evil.

No matter *how* I look at this, there is only one potential outcome—my demise.

To perform *any* spell would mean my end.

Then what about Amon?

It is my understanding that if the spell they mean to cast doesn't succeed, he will walk free.

Amon... Free...

I gulp down against the wave of emotion that hits me as I think of him.

Rhiannon, nor Mr. Nicholson, had given me any details about his state of imprisonment—where or how. They'd simply stated he was somewhere in Fairydale and his influence extends to the borders of the city.

Yet as soon as I think about Amon walking free, I can't help but wonder what I would do then. Maybe I could meet him and...

"God, I'm such a fool..." I mutter to myself.

I am a confused fool that agreed to marry one man while still wavering about the other—*while still very much having feelings for him.*

I've never personally met Amon in *this* life.

But we've been together in at least two lifetimes before—one where I did not have the mark, and one when I did.

If he weren't trapped, would I be with him now, too?

Would he have found me and seduced me as he did in the past?

Some things simply don't add up—from Rhiannon or Fiona's sides.

If my mark was so important, then why would Amon have been with me when I didn't have it? Hundreds of years—if not thousands—before I ever had that mark.

The more I dwell on this dilemma, the more I get to only one primary question.

What does this mark *truly* mean?

I think Rhiannon and I are due for another talk—one where she no longer *lies* to me.

"Let's clean this mess up, Mr. Meow," I sigh as I bring myself to the present and place the dead rats back in the box before I go trash it.

As soon as the hour becomes more reasonable, I steel myself and head to Rhiannon's lodgings.

Luckily I bump into Katrina on her way to school and she shows me where Rhiannon's room is.

"Just be careful. She doesn't really like when people invade her sanctuary," she gives me a warning before she leaves.

Invade? That sounds ominous, doesn't it?

Steeling myself, I walk towards the end of the wing where Rhiannon's rooms are, knocking on the door.

Surprisingly, it slowly opens by itself and I'm beckoned inside.

"Rhiannon?" I ask as I step inside.

The entire room is like a jungle, overgrown plants everywhere.

I slither my way through the tall branches and leaves, wondering why she would need to have them in her room when she had the entire conservatory at her disposal.

There's a small arch a few steps in front of me, and passing through it, I find myself in a seemingly entirely different location.

"Rhiannon? It's Darcy," I call out, looking right and left.

Whereas the other room was full of plants, this one is full of books. And not just *any* books. As I peruse some of the volumes, I note I've seen them again once before.

In Fiona's library.

But how would they have ended up with Rhiannon?

"In the back," Rhiannon's voice sounds out.

I put the matter out of my mind as I go to the back as instructed.

Yet another arch delimitates this room from the next.

Frowning, I let my gaze roam around, finding Rhiannon tending to a boiling pot.

All around, there are jars with ingredients and vials of potions, making me believe this is a laboratory of sorts.

"What a surprising visit, Darcy. What brings you here," she smiles at me as she rises from her seat. Pushing her glasses up her nose, she regards me intently.

"I wanted to talk to you more about my birthmark," I jump straight to the topic. "I wish to know everything there is about it."

Her brows go up.

"And what brought about this...curiosity?"

"I'm curious about this ability you say I have."

She nods to herself.

"Well, since we are here we can look at the original source material," she says as she leads me to an empty table.

Before I can wonder what she means, she waves her hand, whispering a phrase in Latin, and the bottom of the table opens up to reveal a huge vellum manuscript—*a codex.*

As it reaches the surface, its pages flip until it settles on the illustration of the woman with the mark. Just like before, the drawing is accompanied by a few rows of text.

"This is the main information we have, but there's also the account of the elder who encountered it."

"When did that happen?"

"Sometime in the sixth century A.D.," she sighs.

My eyes widen as I remember Fiona mentioning the *Codex Stuartorum* was from the sixth century, too. Could there be any connection?

"It was the year 536 A.D. somewhere near Ravenna. It's not a coincidence they call it the '*worst year to be alive*' and it's all because of that demon," Rhiannon spits the words in distaste.

Using her abilities, she projects the account from that elder on the wall. "The scroll with the original account is kept in the archives at the Vatican, as are all the important documents that have not been incorporated in the *codices.*"

I can make out the script, but I'm not the best at Latin so I rely on Rhiannon to translate it.

The elder describes noticing an unusual male in Ravenna in the summer of 536. The male seemed to have particular abilities and he didn't belong to any of the covens. That raised the alarm for this elder and he proceeded to follow him.

The male was often in the company of a woman, and the elder immediately thought she might be in danger from him.

He triggered the alarm with his superiors, thinking it might be a demon preying on a poor and unassuming woman, but his request to intervene was denied.

The elder didn't give up and he continued to follow the male around until he heard a ruckus in the lodgings the male was sharing with the woman. He immediately burst through, hoping to save her.

But it was too late because by that point, the demon had already fed off her life's energy.

He had not been strong enough to defeat the demon, and the creature had fled off with the body of the woman.

The elder had noticed the mark above her left breast and he'd thought it odd, so he'd remembered to sketch it in case it proved of importance later on.

"The saga didn't end there," Rhiannon purses her lips as she brings forth another page. "Back then, our codices weren't split. There was a single one that belonged to the Supreme Authority. The demon stole the original codex."

"What?" my eyes widen.

"We don't know what he meant to do with it, or if he used any of the forbidden spells. But when the Supreme Authority delegated a team to go after him—a member of each of the current six families—they were easily defeated. Amon incinerated the codex. Luckily, the elder who'd rang the alarm on him was one of the experts on the codex during that time and he was able to recreate most of it from memory. For the first time, the Supreme Authority decided that having all precious information in one place was too dangerous, so the most powerful spells were split."

"What about Amon?"

"He disappeared for a long time. But not before wreaking havoc on Earth. Many thought the apocalypse was upon them," she says as she pulls up multiple other accounts from the time.

Some recount that the sky had darkened, similar to an eclipse, others say that a cloud of darkness had descended upon them. Historically, however, soon after, a devastating plague had started in the Byzantine Empire. One that the coven attributed to Amon.

"There isn't a lot of information about the mark, but the elder who discovered everything theorized that the energy from that woman must have been enormous for we had never encountered such a powerful entity before. Amon was, and is, the most powerful demon the coven has ever fought."

"If there isn't a lot of information about the mark, then how did you come to the conclusion that the owner of it has such powerful healing abilities?"

Rhiannon gives me a sad smile.

"The elder had some theories. And they were confirmed with Elizabeth Montford. When she was born, her mother was declared dead. It was a difficult birth and she bled out. Everyone who was at the scene witnessed the pure cloud of energy that formed around them. One moment the priest was ready to give her the last rites, the next she was perfectly fine—no injuries. Even her scars from the pregnancy had been healed. It was then that they recognized the mark and made the connection."

"And then you bound her powers," I note, narrowing my eyes.

"No one could take a chance. We've seen healing abilities before but *never* to that extent. Fiona was *dead*. There are people who can heal small injuries, but there has never been anyone to raise someone from the dead."

"I didn't realize the mark was that powerful," I whisper, though the rat comes to mind.

I can't say for sure, but it had been more dead than alive. Could it be that...

"The elders gathered together and they voted to bind her powers. The spell was one of the forbidden ones, and as such irreversible. They hoped that by doing that they could avoid the same situation."

I give a dry laugh.

"That is what I don't understand. Was it for Elizabeth's good, or was it to avoid anyone else getting their hands on her abilities?"

"Both," Rhiannon replies firmly, and I can tell she believes it implicitly.

If there's one thing I'm getting out of this meeting, it's that Rhiannon has blindly put her faith into the coven and their version of events. Regardless of the questions that arise regarding their policies and manner of action, she truly believes the coven can do no wrong.

"Alright," I nod, going along with her explanation. "Then tell me something. Why did my abilities only develop *after* I came to Fairydale?"

"I cannot give you a proper answer, Darcy. I'm telling you what I know as well, but I agree that there are gaps in our knowledge when it comes to your birthmark."

"Then how could you ask me to risk my life in your ritual if you don't even know what it will do to me? I might be able to heal, but it's not an exhaustive supply. Once it's gone..." I trail off, letting the words sink in.

"And the alternative? Amon walks free. Is that what you want? For him to terrorize more people? Kill more? Didn't you hear what I said until now? Fairydale wasn't his first time triggering a plague, or unleashing total destruction. It wasn't his first time abusing and killing an innocent woman—one who was foolish enough to fall for his demonic charms," she grits her teeth at me, her words full of frustration.

Isn't all this circumstantial evidence at best? To say that he caused the Justinian plague... I want to laugh at the absurdity of it all.

The Amon I know is a good and honorable man. He might have his vicious side, but I've only ever seen him act when provoked. He would *never* do something to an innocent.

I do not know how I am certain of this, but it's a feeling deep in my gut.

Amon d'Artan would *never* act unprovoked. Would he?

"How can you even be sure it was him?" I counter.

If they want me to believe all this nonsense—if they want me to help their cause in *any* way then I will need proof—*tangible proof*.

A snarl pulls at her lips and before I know it, the entire room is engulfed in darkness.

What...

I don't get to voice my concern as the black walls suddenly become animated.

I'm sitting in the middle while all around me images are being projected onto the wall. I know this is all Rhiannon's power, yet that doesn't make me feel any less uneasy about it.

"Watch!" Rhiannon's voice booms. "Watch what he did to Fairydale and dare to tell me we can't be sure it was him!"

"W-what's this?" I ask tentatively, a shiver of doom going down my back.

"This is the collective memory of that day—of every little organism that witnessed the wickedness of Amon," Rhiannon explains. "But I should warn you, Darcy. It gets bad. Real, real bad," she whispers in a sad tone.

Her warning has me on my guard as I expect to see a version of Amon like the one I'd seen before—the bloody killer who'd slaughtered four men with one snap of a wrist.

Yet it's an entirely different sight that appears before me.

My eyes widen as I realize the surroundings are familiar.

It's the Old Church as I'd seen it that night. Everything is exactly the same as in my vision. But how... If it's sealed, then how could I have known how it looks like.

Unless...

I swallow hard. Maybe it's just a dormant memory from my life as Elizabeth.

The organ is playing just as it had that night. Even the melody is the same—Bach's Toccata.

The image focuses on the person playing.

Elizabeth.

God, but if before I'd seen Elizabeth through the foggy memory of my dreams, aware of her appearance only as it had been reflected back to me through the looking glass, now I can see her clearly.

I can see *myself* clearly.

It's eerie gazing upon someone who is identical to me. So much so that we could pass for twins.

Yet another question arises. How in God's name had Elizabeth ended up in the Old Church of Fairydale? How would she have gotten here from England?

I purse my lips, keeping my focus on the images before me.

Elizabeth is focused on playing the organ, seemingly lost in the music when someone steps inside the church.

Amon.

With a loud bang, her fingers still on the keys, her head slowly turning as she gazes upon him with disdain.

"Lizzie," an anguished cry is wrenched from his throat as he addresses her. "Look at me, Lizzie mine."

If before I would have been unsure of the veracity of this film, now I am more than certain.

Only Amon—the *real* Amon would have called me like that.

"Please talk to me," he pleads with her as he walks down the aisle of the church towards the organ.

She resumes playing, ignoring him.

Even when he stops by her side, she keeps playing away, purposefully snubbing him.

"Please talk to me," he whispers, his hands coming down on hers.

"Why? So you can tell me more lies?"

She slowly turns, her expression stony.

"So you can deceive me again?"

"I never lied to you," he rasps, grabbing her into a tight embrace.

Her body is languid as she lets herself be pulled into his arms. Her expression is blank—as if she's reached the end of her tether.

"Please, Lizzie mine. Don't do this. Don't do this to us," Amon whispers.

"Excuse me, but what am I supposed to see here?" I suddenly inquire of Rhiannon. "This is clearly just a lovers' quarrel. I don't understand why we would look into something so intimate."

Something that *she* has no right to see.

It feels like a defilement to witness such an intimate moment without permission. And this is coming from the reincarnation of the person starring in the vision.

"Just watch, dear. You will get all your answers soon," Rhiannon tells me just as the angle of the image changes.

If before we'd been looking in from the entrance of the church, now the view is from the altar.

"My sister," Elizabeth starts, stepping away from Amon. "I thought she had an accident with her husband. That they were injured and..."

her voice breaks. "It was all a lie," she accuses, suddenly looking at him with a combination of disgust and contempt.

"It's what happened. You know..."

"No," she cuts him off. "They didn't have an accident. *You* killed them," she points her finger at him just as a tear falls down her cheek.

"Lizzie, how could you say that?" Amon tries to placate her, taking a step forward.

She flinches, jumping back.

"You killed them just so they wouldn't interfere with you? You knew they were coming to warn me ,so you decided to take matters into your own hands..." she trails off, overwhelmed by emotion.

My head whips towards Rhiannon, questions written all over my face. But she merely nods at me, telling me to watch the ensuing scene.

"Just tell me the truth, Amon. For one goddamn time, tell me the truth!"

He's staring at her, a forlorn look on his face before he releases a resigned sigh.

"Yes," he whispers, the word barely audible.

"How could you? How the hell could you?" Elizabeth cries out as she launches herself at him, beating her arms against his chest. "Who's next? The children? Me?"

"You have it all wrong. I did this for you. So you would be happy," Amon tries to explain himself.

Elizabeth keeps shaking her head, her cheeks red with tears, her expression one of inconsolable pain.

"No. You did it for *you*. Never once did you think of me," she suddenly says, her voice cold—too cold. "I can't do this anymore, Amon. I'm done."

Stepping back, she gives him one last look before she walks away.

Yet she doesn't get to take one step before Amon flashes himself in front of her.

"What do you mean you're done?" he snarls, his hands on her shoulders as he shakes her. "You're mine, Lizzie. You're mine and only mine. Do you think I'll ever let you go?"

"That's right," she releases a dry laugh. "I'm yours because that's the only thing you care about. That I'm yours and no one else's," she scoffs at him, pushing him off her. "You're wrong if you think you can own me, if you think you can dictate my life in *any* way," she tells him resolutely before she continues on her way out.

"Lizzie!" Amon's voice thunders in the church, the intensity of his roar making the walls quake and tremble. "What do you think you're doing?" he asks, and suddenly, his voice changes.

No longer the human-like voice from before, now it's a full on demonic one, a perverted quality to it that makes my skin erupt in goosebumps.

God, but I don't think I've ever heard something so...vile.

There's no other way to put it. His cadence carries a negative energy with it that makes me want to scrape all layers of skin off my body to get rid of its stain.

"Go to hell, Amon," Elizabeth snaps at him. "But that would be just an exotic destination for you, wouldn't it?" she snickers as she walks away.

Yet just like before, she doesn't get to go too far.

In just a second, Amon has his hands around her throat as he pushes her against the wall.

His eyes flash a mix of red and black—like I'd seen him do before—as he bares his teeth at her.

"You think you can just leave me?" he snarls in the same demonic voice. "You think you can just walk away and what? Find someone else? Let another puny male human put his hands on you?" he demands roughly.

Elizabeth's eyes widen, her features bathed in fear.

It's the first time I see that emotion flash on her face.

"Let me go," she wheezes out.

Amon doesn't listen. Instead, his hand pulls at the material of her dress, tearing the entire bodice.

"Amon what..."

"Tell me again," he demands. "Tell me again how you're going to leave me, Lizzie."

"What are you doing?" she asks, her voice laced with anxiety.

He doesn't answer as he continues to pull at her clothes, ripping her gown to pieces until she's standing naked before him.

Suddenly, I have an inkling of what's about to happen, and I do *not* want to witness anything like that.

"Turn this off," I snap at Rhiannon. "I don't want to watch this, turn it off," I repeat.

But she doesn't reply. It's so dark around save for the projection of the images, that even as I turn three-sixty, I can't find her.

"Rhiannon!" I yell.

And it's exactly at that point that it happens.

One moment he has her against the wall, the next he lays her flat against the ground, his hands on his breeches as he unfastens his falls.

It feels like I'm swallowing glass as I'm watching what comes next.

She's struggling in his hold, crying out for mercy and for him to stop, yet he doesn't.

He holds her to the floor, his hand still on her neck as he parts her legs, settling between them before...

I turn away, squeezing my eyes shut just as her first cry of pain resounds in the air.

More screams follow in a quick succession, as well as his own grunts of pleasure as he ruts her like a beast.

Despite her continuous cries of anguish and physical pain, despite her pleas for him to stop, he doesn't.

He keeps raping her, forcing himself onto her like it was his right to do so.

My eyes are still closed, the accompanying sounds the only indications of what's happening. Even so, I feel my stomach churning, nausea overtaking me just as a soul-searing pain consumes me at witnessing something like that.

Amon... My Amon... How could he do something like that?

But he's not my Amon after all, is he? Because if this is true... Then I never knew him. I only knew the pleasant face he wanted to show to me —to the world.

The true him is this beast. This merciless creature that takes and takes as if it was his God given right to own every piece of her—of me.

And that's the worst.

Because Elizabeth isn't *just* one of his victims.

It's me.

I just watched myself get raped by a beast, and I don't think I will ever be able to erase those images from my mind, nor the sounds.

Everything is ingrained deep in my memory and will likely haunt me for an eternity.

"She lived through it. You must watch," Rhiannon finally speaks. "Look, Darcy. Now!"

Opening my eyes, I peer tentatively to see Amon lift his arm, his hand turning into something resembling a lance before he brings it over her heart, stabbing her with it.

One second.

That was all it took for him to kill her.

And as he steps away from her, I see the entire devastation. Her thighs are bloody and covered in semen, her eyes wide and unblinking.

She's unmoving.

Dead.

He...killed her.

He really did kill her.

Yet the destruction is not done. As he steps towards the nave of the church, he falls to his knees, a wild cry escaping him. A blast of power emanates from him in circular waves.

At the same time, the walls to the right and left of my field of view change, showing me different sights.

The village.

Everyone is dying.

People are spilling their guts, blood pouring out of every orifice.

They are dying *just* like Leo Pierce died.

Is that... Is that the plague?

"Look what he did. Not only in Fairydale, but to all the villages nearby."

More images appear of people dying everywhere, and in the worst of manners.

Amon bellows in the church, and it's at that moment that six people arrive, a portal opening right next to Elizabeth's body.

The first to come out is Fiona. The rest, I do not know, but I can guess who they are—the other families.

What ensues next is a bloody battle between them. Six against one, and they're barely hanging on.

The fight goes on, until Amon is shackled with iron bonds, while the other witches are wasting away to the sides.

And suddenly, I realize just how they'd died. How they'd given up their lives to seal Amon.

They'd formed a barrier and closed themselves off in the church with him, tying their own life-forces together as a net to keep him away from the world.

They had killed themselves—sacrificed themselves to the spell so Amon would not walk free.

As the images slowly disappear, the room comes back to its previous state.

"So you see now," Rhiannon comes by my side, laying one hand on my shoulder.

My lashes are stained with tears, my soul shattering in my chest. I try to contain my erratic breathing, but the only thing I seem to be capable of is to keep myself from choking as I painstakingly inhale and exhale.

Amon. He...

"He killed Elizabeth and everyone in Fairydale. He *tortured* them before they died. We call it a plague now, but it was malice of the highest order. And to stop him, the elders gave their lives to the seal. All so they could keep Amon from walking free—from killing more."

Her words barely register in my mind. Not when I'm still shaken by what I've seen. By the fact that...

"You must have already noticed that you're the spitting image of Elizabeth. We believe you to be her incarnation in this life. That means that you, more than anyone, should not want him to walk free. He raped *you*. Killed *you*. As he did everyone in the village. And you know what's worse? He killed even those children—the ones he stole from your sister. The ones you raised as your own babies. How could that not convince you of the evil he is capable of?"

"You're not any less evil for showing that to me," I croak, barely keeping myself together.

"What?" She frowns. "It is the truth and it shows you how bad this Amon is. It's something you *need* to know."

A dry laugh escapes me.

"You don't even realize, do you?" I tilt my head. "Do you care about anything other than this stupid quest?"

"W-what?" she sputters. "Stupid quest? How dare you! You saw how many people died. You saw what he did. And you dare..."

"In case you didn't realize," I pause, my throat clogging with emotion. "You just made me watch myself get raped in another life. Yes, Amon may have been awful for being the initial perpetrator. But what you did..." I shake my head.

Her gaze is full of indignation, ready to defend herself and her priceless mission.

What about me then?

What about the fact that I may never in my life forget what I saw?

But then it dawns on me. Why would that matter if I might not even live long enough?

My mouth twists into a sardonic smile. She doesn't understand it. She thinks herself so self-righteous standing there, on the side of the coven and telling me what a bad guy Amon is, that she doesn't see herself.

Without saying another thing, I simply leave.

I fear that if I stay on, I won't be responsible for my actions.

The only thought residing in my mind as I dash down the stairs is that I need to be alone—close myself to the world so I can let the tears fall freely.

I barely look where I'm going as I hurry to my room, closing myself in the bathroom.

Mr. Meow sees my anxious state, and tries to claw his way at the door. But I don't let him in.

I can't even face him at this point.

With shaky hands, I snap open the buttons on my dress, letting it fall to the ground as I stand naked in front of the mirror.

My gaze moves over my face—*Elizabeth's, Sela's*—before going lower, to my birthmark and to my body.

Good Lord, but what I'd seen...

A sob racks my body as the images continue to assault me—the sight of Amon with his hand around my throat, holding me immobile while he had his way with me. His bruising hold, and the way he'd snapped at me replay in my mind, his voice echoing and making me physically flinch.

Bringing my hands to my ears, I try to push it out of my mind, yet I cannot.

It's there, taunting me, mocking me and my foolish feelings.

I stumble out of my clothes, stepping into the tub and turning on the shower, letting the water wash over me and drown out the sound of my sobs and tears—the cries that no one cares to hear.

Because hadn't Rhiannon said just that? It doesn't matter what happened to me before, it only matters what I'll do about it now.

She only needs me to act against Amon—as a weapon, not a human. She cares nothing about me or my feelings, only what I can provide for her and her coven.

And Amon...

Good God but Amon, *my* Amon. How could he do something like that?

My wails become louder as something inside me shatters, the mere thought that he could act against me in violence—in such a vile manner —proving my undoing.

I'd been told time and time again what type of person he was—that he was evil personified—but I still kept the belief that he was good to me.

Just like he'd promised.

Maybe he was bad to the world, but to me he was good.

It's so hypocritical of me to admit it, but as long as he was mine—as long as he did everything for me and never against me—I would have been fine with it.

I would have accepted anything and everything.

Because he was mine.

And that was my ultimate fault.

Thinking that someone could change who they are at their core— that I would be the exception to the rule.

Over and over again I'd been told about his deeds against Fairydale and the world. By Fiona. By Rhiannon. By Mr. Nicholson. Everyone had agreed that he was a powerful demon who only cared about himself and wreaking destruction to the world—that he relished spreading evil wherever he went.

I'd been told this, and still, in my heart, I chose to keep a glimmer of hope. That it was all fake. That it was a misunderstanding.

Because otherwise my heart couldn't have been so damn full of him. My soul couldn't have belonged so entirely to him.

If he'd been that evil—that type of scourge—it wasn't possible that I would have ever fallen in love with him.

And yet I had.

That is what hurts the most.

I'd fallen for him, time and time again.

As Sela, he'd been my whole world and I considered myself unworthy of him. I'd sensed that the moment I'd gazed upon him. I'd loved him deeply—*too* deeply one might say.

As Elizabeth, I'd slowly fallen for him. Second after second in his presence and he had me wrapped around his finger—he'd made me his thrall.

And as Darcy... As Darcy, I remember every other life, and I remember all the feelings. For that and that alone I know that a piece of myself belongs to him—irrevocably.

But now?

Now I have to come face to face with my own failings, and the fact that I'm in love with a monster—that I gave away a piece of myself to that monster.

The tears continue to fall just as the water courses down my skin, its warmth enveloping me in a big blanket of comfort.

"Why?" I croak between sobs.

Why did I have to come to Fairydale? Why did I have to return to this miserable place that is the root of all my misfortune?

Though I am lost to my sorrows, I can't ignore the fact that the water is becoming increasingly colored—at first a pinkish hue before becoming redder under my gaze.

I suddenly stand up, confused, terrified, and heartbroken.

For a moment, I can't possibly figure out where the color is coming from, but as a trickle of blood makes its way down my thigh, I finally realize the source.

My period.

Damn it all to hell, but why did it have to come right at this moment?

Right when I look at the droplets of blood, I'm reminded of the images Rhiannon had showed me—of the fact that Amon had forced himself between my legs, hurting me until my entire body was bloody and battered.

Something snaps within me at that moment, and grabbing a small block of soap, I move it all over my skin, lathering myself in it in an attempt to cleanse myself and get rid of his soiling touch.

I wash myself everywhere—every inch of my skin. Yet when my hand reaches between my legs, I hesitate.

A cry is wrenched from my throat as I fall to my knees into the bath, the impact bruising my flesh. Yet I can't bring myself to care. Not about any injury I might sustain, or the pain I will feel.

After all, pain is what I'm looking after.

I want to hurt—anything to dim the guilt and heart wrenching sadness I'm feeling. And so I bring my nails to my skin, scrubbing myself clean. What the soap didn't cleanse, my sharp nails will. Dragging them down my arms, I see the red trails left behind, the irritation of the skin and at times, the deep lacerations. Blood trickles to the surface just to be drowned out as my skin melds together.

So I do it again.

And again.

I scrub myself until I feel like my skin is about to fall off, and still it's not enough.

Will it ever be enough?

Yet no matter how much I clean my body, I can barely bring myself to touch that spot at the junction of my thighs.

After moments of deliberating—of hesitating and of sobbing out loud in an attempt to soothe my own battered heart—I finally slip the soap between my legs, slowly cleaning myself.

More red accompanies the bubbles of soap, the clear of the white stained by my period blood.

"Damn you," I cry out, dropping the soap from my hands just as I fall into the tub.

Bringing my hands to my face, I hunch over as I weep loudly, consumed by pain and consuming every little bit of tears I have left.

The crying, the washing, the wailing.

It's my catharsis.

It's my mourning of things that never happened to me, but happened to me all the same.

More than anything, it's the last time I'll let Amon influence me in any way.

Too many times I've given him the benefit of doubt when I shouldn't have.

Even now, I know I would have made excuses for him—that it was all a mistake, that it couldn't possibly be him—if his words had not been so irrevocably his own.

Who else would have known he called me *Lizzie mine*?

Who else would have been able to contrive his manner so perfectly?

It *was* Amon—my lover and my heartbreak.

But from now on, he will only be my regret and disappointment.

My...enemy.

I don't know how much longer I spend in the bathroom. I seem to have an endless supply of tears where he is concerned, and no matter how much I try to stop myself, they will simply not stop.

I cry.

I cry and cry and cry until my heart breaks and my soul fractures.

I cry until I'm ready to relegate him to the past.

When the water grows too cold for me to be able to sit in it, I finally get out of the bath.

Getting a towel and wiping myself, I wrap it around myself before I exit the bathroom.

As I open the door, though, I come face to face with the last person I want to see.

Caleb.

His face is ravaged by pain, his features scrunched up in worry.

"W-what are you doing here?" I whisper.

But as I take a step forward, I trip on the door frame.

My arms flail out, and before I know it, I'm on the floor on my ass, my towel unwrapped all around me.

My knees are spread, my elbows back as I'd tried to keep my balance.

And I'm...completely naked.

Caleb mutters a curse under his breath as he picks me up from the floor, placing me gently on the bed.

"I..." I gulp down as I try to say something, but no words come to mind.

I can only stare at him. So strong. So reliable. So damn handsome.

More tears form at the corners of my eyes, before I release a loud sniffle, breaking once more into sobs.

"Shh," he cradles me to his chest. "What happened?" he murmurs in my hair, drawing back just enough to study my face.

"I-I..." I bite my lips as the tears stream down my cheeks. "I'm sad," I eventually say.

It sounds stupid to my ears, it should sound the same to his. But he doesn't seem concerned as he looks at me with worry and far too much love than I deserve.

Certainly not after I spent the last hour crying about another man.

"Why?" he asks softly.

I shake my head, unable to give him an answer.

"Ah, darlin'," he coos gently, tucking my wet hair behind my ears as he leans forward to catch a tear with his tongue. "I'm here now," he whispers. "I'm here and I'll take care of you," he says as he licks my cheek from my chin to my eye. He does the same to the other one, capturing my still falling tears, eating my sorrows away.

"All these tears," he rasps. "They're mine now, aren't they?" he asks in a smokey tone.

I can't help but nod as I lose myself in his gaze and the intensity of his presence—everything that makes me forget the past.

He's so big in my small room, taking far too much space and for a moment I feel slightly alarmed. Yet it's not for long. Certainly not with how careful and gentle he is with me.

So much so that I forget that I'm completely naked with him. I forget everything but the touch of his hand on my back, slowly stroking me—comforting me in a way I didn't know I needed.

My knees are to my chest as I huddle into a small ball. He fits his body against mine, his arms drawing me into his embrace. His mouth is still on my face, licking at my tears, swallowing every bit of my heartache and turning it into something different.

Something...

"Caleb," I whisper, cupping his cheeks with my hands as I search his face. "Kiss me."

"You never have to ask, darlin'," he says before his mouth is on mine, his lips clashing with mine as he forces me to open to him, let him in and share everything that I am with him.

I cling to him, my arms wound tight around his neck as I rock myself back and forth against him—seeking to absorb every bit of his heat.

From the moment his lips touch mine, the kiss is wild and *out-of-control*, mirroring my emotions and this *out-of-control* need for him—for his touch and for his unique brand of comfort. I want to feel his arms around me, his big hands on my body. I want to feel him everywhere—just so I can erase the violation from before.

Just so I can be whole again.

"My darling girl," he rasps against my lips as he continues to lay kisses all over my tear-stained cheeks and my red-rimmed eyes. He holds me reverently to him as he places his lips on one eyelid, lingering for a moment before moving to the other.

In his embrace, I feel so safe—like I never have to wonder about tomorrow again. Like all the worries in my life have suddenly disappeared.

When he's done kissing every little inch of my skin he moves lower, his mouth trailing down my neck right as he scrapes his teeth lightly against my skin.

I'm so lost to this sea of sensation—to this maelstrom of pleasure—that I no longer care how far this goes.

I'm simply his for the taking.

His mouth opens over my pulse point, sucking my skin in at the same time as his hands cup my breasts, his thumbs brushing softly over my erect nipples.

A gasp escapes me, my spine arching as I urge him to continue what he's doing.

"Please," I moan softly, feeling him absolutely everywhere.

His mouth continues its descent down my neck, alternating between kissing and sucking and biting every now and then. I can feel him lay his claim on me, his red kisses embedded in my skin and leaving a mark for all to see that I'm his and only his.

Because, regardless of what happened in the past, in this life I'm his. *Only his.*

"Fuck, love, you're killing me," he speaks harshly, his breath on my skin.

His lips move downwards, and before I know it, he has one nipple in his mouth, sucking on it before biting every so lightly.

"Ah," I arch my back encouragingly. Desire pools low in my belly, and I find myself growing wetter and wetter between my legs. In no time, I've lost all my inhibitions as I seek to have his mouth on me—time and time again.

"More, please," I mumble incoherently, my hands in his hair as I urge him on.

He alternates between licking and sucking on my nipples, his hot mouth proving to be my undoing as I feel a storm build inside of me. I lose myself in his touch—in everything he does to me and every little bit of pleasure he racks from my body.

"I'm all yours, darlin'," he tells me huskily. "Just like you're all mine, aren't you?"

I nod effusively—anything to get him to touch me more, kiss me in more places and give me the blessing that is his mouth.

"All yours," I agree, hugging him closer.

"That's all I want to hear," he murmurs softly. "That I'm the only one to touch you."

I gasp softly as I push my chest towards him.

He chuckles when he sees my enthusiasm, and giving me one long lick between the valley of my breasts, he moves lower. His mouth opens over my stomach, and he lays sloppy kisses everywhere, licking me thoroughly.

Dipping one hand between my legs, he finds me completely drenched as he parts my folds with two fingers.

He touches me lower and lower until...

My eyes widen as I remember I'd just gotten my period, and I'm likely drenched from the blood.

"Wait," I squeak, pushing at his shoulders.

He pauses, his black eyes pinning me to the spot as he gazes at me assertively. His mouth tips up in a wicked smile and before I can tell him that he can't touch me there—that it's messy and he'll get dirty—he brings the same red-stained finger to his lips, sucking it clean.

My eyes flash wide open.

"You're mine, darlin'. In any way, shape or form. That means this is mine, too."

Biting my lip in apprehension, I can only nod, unable to form a coherent reply.

Do people do this?

I'm not knowledgeable enough to know if it's the norm, but if he says he's fine with it then...

My train of thought is interrupted as he pulls me to him, his hands on my butt as he spreads me open to accommodate the breadth of his shoulders.

"What..."

His lips settles over my sex, and he gives me an open-mouth kiss *there*.

To say I'm scandalized by the naughtiness of it all would be an understatement. But I can't muster any maidenly concerns as he brings the rough pad of his finger over my bundle of nerves, caressing it softly until I'm bucking in his arms.

"You're so wet, darlin'," he blows hot air over my damp folds, the effect immediate on my senses. He brings his tongue to my opening, breaching me and flicking it in-and-out while his thumb massages that sensitive bud. "So wet for me," he drawls as he drinks my very essence.

The entire action is infinitely decadent as he touches me in places *I*'ve barely touched myself before, kissing me and tasting me so intimately. But more than anything, I can see how much he enjoys it, my pleasure automatically converting into *his* pleasure.

"Delicious," he praises, speaking against my core and making me buck against him with every vibration of his mouth. "You're so fucking sweet, Darcy darlin'," he continues, pausing to inhale my scent into his nostrils.

My core clenches with every little touch of his lips, every feathery brush of his tongue, every wet slide of his mouth against me. But it's nothing compared with the guttural sounds he makes, the noises of pure male satisfaction that fill my ears as he simply devours me.

He savors with gusto the combination of blood and arousal, lapping at my sex as if it's the best meal he's ever had.

"You're my sweetest miracle," he groans as he gives me a long lick. "My innocent little temptation," he continues as he flicks his tongue in and out of my entrance.

Everything he does to me is designed to titillate and push me to the edge in a slow and torturous dance—but one that has me enjoy the journey more than the final event.

He's too good at this, reading my body like an open book and taking note of every little cue and non-spoken signal—almost as if he knew my body better than I know it myself.

"My lovely enchantress and my fucking seductress, aren't you, darlin'?" he coos gently.

"Yes," I whisper. "I'll be anything you want me to be," I tell him in a moment of pure madness as a new Darcy emerges from somewhere deep within me.

"Good," he purrs against me, nuzzling his face between my legs in a way that is both ticklish and pleasurable and I can't help but release a half-giggle that echoes into a moan.

Though initially I might have been embarrassed to have him so intimately between my legs, I soon lose all inhibitions as I give in to pure sensation and *him*—letting him be my guide and master of my body.

"This is all mine, isn't it Darcy? Tell me," he rasps as he raises his head to look at me. "Promise me," he repeats.

My lids are half closed, but even so I can make out the blood clinging to his lips and trickling down his chin.

And yet, the sight doesn't disgust me. If anything, it makes me deliciously tense, knots appearing in my lower belly as more wetness gushes out of me. There's something incredibly primal and sexy about the way he's tasting every bit of my essence—my arousal and my life's blood.

"It's all for you," I moan, wiggling my hips to get him to continue his ministrations.

Still watching me, he continues to work my bud with his thumb, alternating between caressing it softly and rubbing it vigorously, so much so that every muscle in my body strains and weeps for relief.

My breathing intensifies, and I know I'm simply at his mercy.

"Have you orgasmed before, love?" he suddenly asks as he nuzzles his stubble against my inner thigh, scraping my skin lightly before kissing it softly. "Have you made yourself come before?"

I shake my head, and a devilish grin appears on his face.

"Good girl. All your firsts are mine, Darcy. Now and forever, you understand me?"

I swallow against the wave of pleasure that hits me as I move my chin up and down in a tentative nod. Yet as soon as he shifts the tempo of his fingers, my head falls back, my mouth open as I release moan after moan, chanting his name as the sweetest and most torturous melody.

The pleasure keeps on building inside of me and as he brings his mouth once more to my sex, licking me thoroughly before wrapping his lips around my bud and sucking hard on it.

His hand moves lower, a finger probing at my entrance.

Soon, he establishes a rhythm as he licks me while thrusting his finger in and out of me.

My mind blanks on me just as every muscle in my body suddenly tenses.

"Caleb," I gasp as the orgasm overtakes me, taking me to the highest high, before unfortunately making me crash back to earth.

"I'm here," he whispers as he continues to lick me—almost as if he's devouring me. "I'm all here, Darcy, and I'm never letting you go."

The flat of his tongue covers my entire sex as he gathers all of my wetness into his mouth, imbibing everything that I am.

"One more," he whispers. "Give me one more."

I'm about to tell him I can't possibly do that, but he adds another finger to my opening, slowly stretching me. Moving both fingers in and out of me, I find myself screaming my pleasure out loud.

My hands are tightly wrapped in his hair as I keep him between my legs, my eyes fluttering closed as I gyrate my hips around, seeking more of his touch.

And he gives it to me.

God but he gives it to me.

"Fuck me, darlin', you're so hot. So fucking hot. Come for me," he demands harshly as he increases the rhythm of his thrusts. "Come on my tongue, Darcy. Give me everything sweetheart. I want to taste your blood, your pleasure, everything that makes you, *you*."

I'm no longer in control of my limbs as I thrash my head from side to side, my fingers tightening in his scalp as I feel another wave wash over me.

"That's it, sweetheart. Give me everything. Every. Fucking. Thing," he orders, and I do.

Oh, but I do.

So much so that my toes curl as I push the heels of my feet into the mattress. My back arches off the bed and my thighs squeeze him, keeping him rooted to the spot.

Pleasure pulsates in every atom of my body—in every single cell.

And it's all because of him.

All because of this magnificent, selfless man before me.

My body becomes languid and relaxed as my eyes close, my consciousness drifting from me. Yet as drowsiness slowly seeps in, I have the vague impression that for the longest time he's still lapping at me, drinking me in as if what hides between my legs is the most potent ambrosia.

Only when he's truly sated does he move up, gathering me in his arms and letting me use him as my pillow.

That night, despite all the heartache and disappointment, I sleep better than I have in my entire life. And I know there's only one reason for it.

Him.

Sometimes, doors close just so others could open—journeys end just so new ones could begin.

Caleb Hale is my next destination.

Chapter Nineteen

January 1791. London, Great Britain

"What did you find out? When are we leaving for the country?" I inquire as Mary comes inside. I'd asked her to inquire among the other servants, sure one of them would have heard when my mother planned to leave for Haversham.

Mary shakes her head slowly.

"Your mother has no intention of leaving for the country any time soon, My Lady," she tells me with a sigh.

"But..."

My shoulders slump in defeat as I plop myself back in my chair. My eyes are blank and unmoving as I simply stare at the empty wall.

"Maybe you could talk to her..." she offers kindly.

"No. Thank you, Mary. That would be all," I give her a small nod.

She takes my meaning well as she soon retires, closing the door behind her and leaving me alone.

All alone with my misery.

In the two months since Amon's attack at the Berkley house, everything had devolved into chaos. Thankfully, he'd saved Emma and the rest of the innocent people in the house. But that hadn't been much of a consolation for the Berkley family, who is still mourning the death of their only son.

Emma, too buried in grief, slowly stopped talking to me. Not that I blame her after everything that happened. She doesn't know the extent of what occurred that night, or what the real cause of the fire was. She thinks that I'd somehow been awaken by the smoke and carried her out.

Initially, I'd tried to be by her side and help her through her pain, but it hadn't worked. Not only had I felt like an impostor by her side, comforting her about her brother while knowing that I, too, had a hand in murdering him. But I'd seen her need to be alone and deal with everything by herself so I hadn't pried further.

When she's ready to talk to me again, I will be here, waiting. But I fear the guilt that assails me every time I look upon her will never go away.

The papers had called the fire an unfortunate incident, and the entire ton is mourning the death of the young Viscount Berkley. Yet it seems very few people knew how wicked he was behind his easy-going façade.

Certainly, I would have never thought he could be so depraved as to wish me harm for something entirely not my fault.

Something Amon had done out of his inane jealousy.

I'd only had one moment with him before he'd disappeared and I'd made my stance clear towards him—that I don't approve of his actions and his *solutions*.

After that, Amon hadn't lingered. I'd barely finished telling him off for the disaster he'd created when he'd vanished into thin air—as he always does.

And he hasn't returned since.

Now I'm regretting my words.

At the time, I'd been too volatile. I'd just seen him slaughter four people with his inhumane powers and with no remorse at all. To say I'd been slightly shocked would be an understatement. As such my words may have been more biting than I would have liked.

Despite everything, I would have hoped he would show up again and hear me out.

And...he hasn't.

I sigh as I rest my elbow on my table, disappointment filling me as I realize my mother will not allow us to return to the country until summer time—unlikely even then.

She is absolutely bent on finding me a match, and even though she'd seen my reaction to the fire and the slow decay of my friendship with Emma, she'd continued with her absurd quest to see me married.

That has manifested itself in several ways, not in the least the fact that she's forcing me to attend every ball and gathering, introducing me to various bachelors in hopes something would work.

Of course nothing will work.

I do not want to wed, not now, nor ever.

Amon might be a blood-thirsty demon and a monster, as my

mother doesn't shy away from calling him. But he is still the only one who claims my heart.

He is mine, just like I am his.

Now, and for the days to come.

I am certain, in fact, that if I were to wed anyone, Amon would ensure that man never made it to the wedding day. If before I'd thought that his jealousy was out of bounds, what he'd done to Viscount Berkley had cemented it.

Amon would take offense for any little thing, I'm sure—which is why I haven't danced with anyone despite attending all these events. I might get the urge to irk him just like that, but I would never risk an innocent man's life to do it.

The perks of falling for a demon.

Tired of feeling sorry for myself, I take a blank piece of paper, dip my quill into the inkwell and pen the first words.

Dearest Amon,

I pause, pursing my lips as I realize I have no idea what I want to tell him.

Sorry for reacting adversely to murder? That sounds mildly deranged.

Thank you for saving me.

There, that's better. He had, after all, saved me.

Yet as I try to continue, I cannot for the life of me find the words to tell him to come back—to return to me. Deep within me, I am sure he hasn't abandoned me. I don't know how, but I simply do. I'm more concerned about him thinking I hate him when I don't—that I feel disgusted by him after I'd seen him act like that.

Though I'd been quite scathing with my remarks, I hadn't *really* meant any.

Yes, I am aware his nature is more bizarre than I am accustomed with. But that is solely by virtue of his otherworldly abilities.

I dare say, the men he'd killed had been more monstrous than he can ever be.

He might be a demon. But he is *my* demon.

The tip of my quill touches the paper as words of affection suffuse my being. Instead of thinking too much about it, I just let my heart dictate the letter.

Dearest Amon,

Thank you for saving me.

I'm sorry for my ungrateful behavior and biting

words. I was beside myself with worry and terror and I fear I might have come on too strong towards you.

I do not begrudge you what you've done. I can only be happy that you appeared when you did and protected me.

It's been two months and I haven't heard from you.

I miss you.

Maybe it's wrong of me to feel so, but I cannot stop my heart from yearning for you.

You've shown me your true face—the destruction you are capable of—and I want to let you know that I am not scared.

Not anymore.

I want you as you are.

Just Amon.

My...Amon.

Eternally Yours,

Lizzie

ONCE I'M satisfied with the letter, I fold it carefully, dabbing a little bit of scented water over it.

Rising up, I head to the window, opening it and arranging for a little nook on the ledge where I can deposit the letter. I may not be entirely sure how he does it, but there's no doubt in my mind that he will receive it—mayhap even grace me with his company soon.

A silly smile appears on my face as I bring the letter to my lips, giving it a quick kiss before leaving it in that spot.

Yet as I'm about to close the window, my brows scrunch up in confusion as I spot a foreign carriage stop in front of our townhouse. It doesn't have any recognizable emblem or coat of arms though it looks to be new and expensive.

But at this hour?

A quick glance at the mantle clock tells me it's entirely improper to receive visitors at one o'clock at night.

Sliding close to the edge of the wall so I won't be seen, I sneak a peek at the people who get out of the carriage. Two tall gentlemen whose looks, strength and countenance remind me of Amon.

I blink in confusion when I note they are swiftly received within the house.

A little odd.

I don't trust my mother where Amon is concerned, and I know she would do whatever she could to kill him—neutralize him as she'd so objectively put it.

Curiosity gets the best of me as I quickly pull a shawl over my shoulders and slide the door to my room open. Just in time to hear my mother greet the gentlemen and tell them to adjoin in my late father's study.

With years of experience sneaking around and eavesdropping on my family, I do my best to quiet my steps as I go down the stairs.

It's already late and save for my mother's ladies' maid, everyone has retired for the day.

Careful to avoid the creaking of the floors, I successfully get to the landing of the stairs before I tiptoe to the back of the house where the study is.

Yet as I get in front of the door, I realize my mother had closed it shut. No matter how much I try to fit my ear to the wood, I can't make any sounds.

Even more odd, isn't it?

Why would two strange men visit my mother in the middle of the night if it wasn't some type of coven business?

Not one to be deterred by a closed door, I put on a pair of slippers and I go outside the house through the servant's entrance.

Rounding the house until I reach the study's window, I smile to myself as I note it's half-open. And if I climb just a little higher, I can listen to everything.

It's unfortunate I cannot see, but with my situation precarious as it is, I'm not going to risk it. Especially as one of the men speaks first, my eyes widening as I realize my hunch had been right—this *is* about Amon.

"The Holy See has received your request, Lady Montford, and we are here to provide you with guidance."

"I didn't think they were going to send *you*," my mother clasps her hands together. "It's so good you have come. As I've outlined in my previous letter, I am sure this is about the same demon that Elder Ambrosius spoke about in his account. Considering the lives lost more than a thousand years ago, I would say this deserves immediate attention."

A thousand years ago?

Amon is that old? My eyebrows crease with the new information. I'd never asked him his age—maybe I should have.

"You would be correct, My Lady. The Supreme Authority delegated us to assist you with our knowledge about this...demon," the other man notes, yet his tone suggests skepticism. "Our job as demonologists is to study these entities and make notes on them."

"I am happy the Supreme Authority decided to take my claims seriously," Fiona says. "Why don't we just go to the topic. How do you *kill* this Amon? I've already tried everything the elders wrote in the codex, and none of the usual spells worked on him. Not even the hallowed barrel powder we used when we shot him. I've consulted with other members of the coven and they were equally as mystified."

One of the men clears his throat.

"Amon is not a regular demon, My Lady. It wasn't coincidental that the Elder Ambrosius named him an archdemon. His powers are far above those of regular evil entities, and you will not be able to defeat him with one codex alone."

I frown. He must be referring to the forbidden spells then, since those are the only ones for which you need *all* the codices assembled together.

"What can you tell me about him?" Fiona's voice wobbles as she asks the question.

"There are accounts of him going some two thousand years before," one man starts. "Ancient scrolls talk of an Amon who influenced kings and emperors, leading from the shadows. In fact, we have reason to believe he could have been the inspiration behind the Ancient Egyptian god Amon."

"Dear Lord," my mother gasps.

I would, too, if I could afford to make any noise.

Ancient Egyptian God Amon? But that would make him... Not just one thousand years old but *thousands.*

Cold seeps through my clothes. My shawl is not enough for the temperature outside. Despite forcing myself to stay still and listen, I can't help my own body rebelling against me as shivers overtake me.

Taking a deep breath, I do my best to be quiet as I fit myself better to the outer wall.

"No wonder I wasn't able to harm him. If he's capable of such things... I don't want to imagine what he could do if he ever got his hands on my daughter."

"We are here to ensure that doesn't happen, Lady Montfort. And we haven't come empty-handed."

There is some noise coming from inside the room, but I'm afraid I will be seen if I try to peek inside the room.

"This is..." my mother trails off in awe—the best thing to pique my curiosity even more.

"This is a sword forged by a holy metal called rhodium. It is an extremely rare metal, and I urge you to be exceedingly careful with how you wield it," one man explains.

That's all it takes for my curiosity to shoot up. Placing my hands on the window ledge, I slowly raise myself up—enough to glimpse the form of the two men and my mother as they gather together around the sword.

I can only make out a powerful gleam before I have to duck again. The cold has affected my fingers, and my grip is tenuous at best. If I try to hang on to the ledge, I might slip and fall, attracting attention to myself—which is the *last* thing I want.

My teeth start chattering uncontrollably. I slap my hand over my mouth in an attempt to control it and focus on the conversation.

"You're saying this can kill him?" my mother asks.

"Not much can injure Amon, let alone kill him. But this, accompanied by the spells of the Elders, should work."

"Do not worry. Some of the other families have been made aware of this, and I will work to convince the rest too. He won't escape again," Fiona declares.

"We have all the faith in you, Lady Montford."

"I've managed to find a husband for my daughter, too. Just as your letter mentioned. But are you sure that will deter him from going after her? I..."

What?

She found me a husband?

My pulse speeds up as shock and fear accumulate in my heart.

When did this happen and why was I not informed?

But then it dawns on me that my mother wouldn't have told me until the last moment—all so she could ensure the wedding would go smoothly and I will not put up a protest.

After all, despite my feigned disavowal of Amon, she is aware I am not interested in finding myself married off to some stranger—though it's all my mother has ever wanted.

Now...

Despite my shivering, my lips flatten into a thin line of determination, for I know I will do whatever I can to prevent such a marriage from taking place.

"We are absolutely sure. Once your daughter is mated to another man, Amon will no longer have a claim over her," the man assures her,

So this is where my mother's odd idea that marriage is the only way to hide the pulsations from my birthmark had come from. These two men have been the ones to put it into her head that the only way to subdue the pulsations of the mark is to *mate* me to someone else.

They continue to outline a plan, and as I'd guessed before, it involved using *me* as bait for when my mother has secured the cooperation of all the other families.

With the rhodium sword and the ancient spells, they still only *hope* to neutralize Amon, which tells me just how powerful he is.

Yet it seems that my mother isn't the only one who wants Amon caught. These gentlemen and the Supreme Authority seem to be hunting for him too.

God, Amon, what did you get yourself into?

My limbs are frozen from the cold outside. It's to the point that I'm barely in control of my movements anymore.

As I try to step away from the window to get back to the house, I barely take a few steps before I get a cramp in my lower leg.

Limping for a couple of steps, I don't manage to regain my balance as I fall face down onto the even colder ground.

A pained cry is wrenched from my lips despite my best attempts to stay quiet.

"What was that?" one of the men suddenly asks.

"What? I didn't hear anything," my mother says.

"Check the window," the other suggests.

I punch my calf as I try to drag myself back up. But even so, I am more than certain that I will be caught. Never in a million years will I be able to make it back to the house undetected. And if these people also have magical powers, then...

Fear grows in my breast just as the pain in my leg continues to echo in my body.

The seconds tick by as the men come closer to the window.

Before I know it, though, strong arms pull me to an equally strong embrace.

I blink in confusion.

One moment I'm behind my house, struggling to move my frozen limbs, the next I'm in a luxurious chamber, the fire sparking to life as heat engulfs the entire room.

The sudden change in scenery would be enough to scare anyone, but I'm not afraid.

His touch sears my chilled skin, his smokey scent invading my nostrils.

I know exactly who this is.

Just as I know he always comes in my hour of need.

"Amon," I whisper as he carries me to the big upholstered bed. "You came for me."

He doesn't reply as he sets me on the edge of the bed. A thick blanket appears on my shoulders, and I pull it tighter around me as I lose myself in its warmth.

Amon takes a step back, regarding me closely.

He's wearing a loose silk shirt half unbuttoned at the neck and a pair of black trousers. His white hair flows down his back, the sheen making it look silver in the firelight.

Slowly raising my gaze, I take in his features—that otherworldly beauty that makes my heart clench. His jaw is strong and masculine, his cheekbones sharp and defined, a mix of beauty and danger that never fails to take my breath away. And then there are his eyes. Those pale, almost white eyes that spark with life whenever he gazes at me.

Like now.

He peruses me from head to toe, his jaw twitching when he sees my deplorable state.

"You're hurt," he states curtly.

The frost had taken away the sensation from my limbs, so I can't localize the pain, nor do I feel anything but a dull ache radiating from every part of my body.

It's only when he drops to his knees in front of me, laying his hands on my knees that I spot the ugly bruises forming from my fall.

"It's nothing," I give him a tight smile. "I don't even feel it."

"But *I* see it," he counters, raising his unyielding gaze to mine. "You can't get hurt, Lizzie mine. Not under my watch."

"Well, technically I didn't fall *under* your watch," I raise a brow at him.

After all, he's been missing for two months.

"I'm never *not* watching you," he enunciates slowly, the meaning clear.

"What..."

"I may not be with you at all times, Lizzie. But I'm always watching. I'm always there for you."

"Then why?" I frown. "Why would you *not* come for me?" I ask dejectedly.

How many times had I yearned for him, wanted to see him only to be ignored for months at a time.

"It's complicated," he sighs.

"Uncomplicate it for me, please. Help me understand this," I urge softly as I place my hands on his shoulders, stopping his movements.

"You're always giving me vague answers and explanations and expect me to accept everything without questioning you. It doesn't work like that, Amon," I tell him gently as I cup his cheek with my hand, swirling my thumb across his marble-like skin. "I know your nature and I haven't shied away from you. I know you're capable of extreme destruction, yet I haven't run away. I'm still here. So whatever it is you're keeping from me, you can tell me. It won't change how I feel about you. But I do need to know where we stand."

He's staring at me with a frightening intensity. Slowly, he takes my hand in his, bringing my palm to his lips for a searing kiss.

"You want the truth?"

I nod.

"I was petrified," he admits in a thick voice. "After you told me what a brute I was, I was terrified to face you again. I merely wanted to give you time to come to terms with everything."

Emotion laces his every word as he opens up to me, revealing his weakness.

This man—this *strong, strong* man—was terrified of what I would think of him.

I don't know why, but that one admission has the power to make my heart stop in my chest before expanding like never before—all for him. With feelings for him.

Without taking his eyes off me, he materializes some sort of tincture that he applies softly to my injured flesh. After he's done, he bandages each wound carefully, as if he has plenty of experience with such things.

"I'm here," I whisper. "I'm not going anywhere, Amon. If you want me, you have me," I confess, knowing just how much power I'm giving him with those few words. Yet as I utter them out loud, I know them to be true—my entire being knows them to be true.

From the moment I'd met him I felt a strange connection to him—one that befuddled me and messed with my senses. He hypnotized me with his presence before he seduced me with his words. He awoke my body with his decadent sensuality just as he made my heart sing with every little gesture—every proof of his devotion.

Mayhap this is madness—pure, unadulterated madness.

Yet somehow I know he is in it with me. He feels it just as much as I do.

"From the beginning, I've been trying to find a way for us to be together, Lizzie mine," he sighs as he leans to lay a kiss on one knee, then the other. "And I'm closer than ever to accomplishing it."

"How?" I ask the question as I wet my lips.

"I shall tell you more about this over dinner," he flashes me a smile. "There is much we need to talk about. But first, are you warm enough? Do you need anything?"

I shake my head, watching him curiously.

There's a frightening dichotomy to him—to the tender and sweet Amon that I know and the blood-thirsty monster I'd last seen. It's as though there are two different entities residing in the same body. As that thought arises, I whip my gaze to his.

He shakes his head slowly, amusement playing at his lips.

"No, Lizzie. I am not possessed. All of this is me. The killer," he whispers as he leans into me, brushing his lips across my cheek before he reaches my ear, nibbling at my skin. "The lover. This is all me, love. You can't have one without the other."

"I want *you*," I tell him with all the emotion I can muster. "All that you are, Amon."

His lips tip up into a satisfied smile, and before I know it, we're in a different room.

"What... What is this?" I ask in awe as I look around, taking in the racks upon racks of gowns and luxurious furs. At the end of the room, there is a full wall full of jewelry cases, diamonds upon diamonds, pearls, and other precious stones. Everything must be worth a fortune.

Yet as I'm admiring everything, I can't stop the ugly jealousy that takes root within me.

Whose room is this? Whose clothes are these?

"This is all yours, love," Amon murmurs, not for the first time sensing my switch in mood. "I bought them for you."

"You...did?" I blink, surprised.

"Choose something beautiful for tonight. I'm keeping you all to myself until dawn," he tells me as he takes a step back, letting me move around the room.

"But...how?" I mumble to myself, still stunned by the contents of the room and the fact that he'd gotten it all for me.

"I have more surprises," he chuckles. "The night is young, love. Let's take advantage of it."

Nodding effusively, I turn my attention to the wardrobe, browsing the selection of clothes he'd chosen for me. My lips tip up as I imagine Amon in all his imposing glory, shopping for women's clothes, remarking on color and style in search for the perfect gown.

There must be at least a hundred gowns in this room, for all types of occasion.

Locating the evening section, I go by color since it's obvious that all are exquisite and high quality.

"Amon?" I tilt my head to peek at him.

He's sitting in the middle of the room, his hands behind his back, his legs apart, his stance powerful and warrior-like. When he hears me call his name, he whips his head in my direction.

"What's your favorite color?"

"Mine?" He asks in a perplexed tone, pointing to his chest.

I nod, a hidden smile on my lips.

"Red. Why?"

"Red it is then," I declare as my hands settle on a deep red gown.

We have an entire night together—*I* have an entire night to entice him to touch me. After all, how many times have I thought about this in the last months? Especially after that kiss that left me entirely unfulfilled and longing for more.

"I'm guessing you won't give me privacy to change, will you?" I raise a brow at him as I present him with my choice for the night.

"You'll need a ladies' maid, Lizzie. And I'm nothing if not accommodating. You'll see that these hands can do a great deal of things," he says as he brings his hands down my shoulders, the tips of his fingers lightly tapping my flesh.

A gasp escapes me as air whooshes around me, tenderly caressing my skin in all the right places—in all the *hidden* places.

"You rogue," I accuse playfully when I look down at my suddenly naked body. "You don't need your hands for anything."

Despite not having been naked before someone of the male sex before, I don't feel shy. If anything, all maidenly concerns are thrown out the window once I see the way he looks at me, raw hunger emanating off him.

He circles me in a predatory manner, his nostrils flaring as he takes in my body.

Goosebumps cover my entire skin, whether from the light breeze or from his probing gaze, I don't know.

"Ah, Lizzie mine, you'll see *just* how I use my hands on you," he chuckles as he stops behind me. His breath is on my nape, his presence absolutely intoxicating me until I become lightheaded—almost as if I'd consumed copious amounts of alcohol.

"So, what are you waiting for?" I ask as I lean into him, undulating my body against his.

His lips part, his breathing intensifying. Yet just as I think he's going to finally touch me—he merely steps back. With swift movements, he helps me put my dress on, fastening it at the back. Every now and then his fingers brush against my bare skin, eliciting a soft gasp from me as I imagine he's changed his mind.

But as I find myself fully dressed, I belatedly realize it was all part of his plan.

Though initially I'd thought to entice him with my naked body and the desire I witnessed in his eyes, in the end I'd been the one seduced, my skin flushed, my heart hammering in my chest every time I feel him get closer to me.

I swivel to face him, narrowing my eyes at him.

"Seduction isn't merely the consummation of the act," he tells me with a knowing smirk. "Seduction is in the anticipation, Lizzie mine. It's in wondering whether every little touch will amount to more," he pauses as he caresses my face with the back of his hand. "Seduction is the intention without the certainty. It's all in the element of surprise."

My breath hitches as I find myself lost in his eyes.

So much so that he surprises me once more as he disappears only to appear behind me.

Cold metal touches my skin as he fastens a necklace around my neck.

"Beautiful jewelry for a beautiful lady," he murmurs in my ear, laying a soft kiss on my shoulder blade.

I'm entirely too dazed by everything to be able to react in any manner, except awe.

There's something about Amon that goes beyond his strange abilities. Maybe it's the way he holds himself, as if he's the guardian of some ancient knowledge. Maybe it's in the play of emotions on his face that I sometimes witness—the pain and the loneliness that ravage his features before he remembers to put on his carefree mask.

The truth is that no matter how deeply I feel for him, there's so much I don't know. So much I *wish* to know. But I won't until he thinks I am ready to do so.

He is the one dictating the pace of our relationship.

Yet in spite of all the control he has over the situation and over me, there's this certainty that every little move he makes, he does so only after he's carefully deliberated it—only after he's read me thoroughly.

"Shall we?"

"I have one question, Amon. Answer it truthfully, and I'll go wherever you want me to," I suddenly turn to him.

His eyes turn molten as he regards me intently, waiting.

"Did you kill that girl? The one with the birthmark like mine? Did you do what my mother and the coven are accusing you of?"

He blinks. Slowly.

"What do you think, Lizzie?" he murmurs, his question loaded. "Do you think I did it?"

"No," I whisper. "I don't know *how*, but I know you wouldn't. Just like I believe you are not with me for my mark," I say as I bring his hand over my heart, the heat from his palm transferring to my naked skin and making me shiver in response.

"Trust your intuition. Always," he gives me a tight smile. "I might not always be able to tell you everything, but know that everything I do is with your best interests at heart," he pauses briefly. "To answer your question directly, no. I did not kill her, nor am I after that mark—*your* mark. In fact, the coven doesn't have the least idea what it means, and how it came to exist..." he trails off.

"And you do?"

He nods, his gaze searing.

"Thank you for telling me," I smile as I lay a kiss on his knuckles.

"Even if the entire world hates me—even if they all revile me—as long as I have your love and your regard, nothing else matters. I can be the enemy of people, Lizzie. But if I am your lover, it's more than enough for me. I told you before," he purrs huskily, "I may be bad to everyone else. But to you, *just* to you, I'll be good."

I don't get to reply as double doors open before us. Tucking my arm in the crook of his elbow, Amon takes me through a small ambulatory before we reach the hallway. It seems that this time he's decided against teleportation.

The entire corridor is brimming with light. There are candles everywhere, and I can tell he's spared no expense with this.

As we walk further and further, I'm floored by the sheer size of the location. Especially as we reach the staircase, the top of it overlooking the foyer and what looks to be the entrance to the dining room.

A crystal chandelier hangs from the ceiling, so high I don't know how anyone would have reached there to replace the candles. Yet this is Amon we're talking about. Of course he would be able to replace them —mayhap even with a snap of a finger.

"What is this, Amon? It's absolutely stunning!" I exclaim as we slowly go down the stairs.

"Do you like it?" He smiles, pleased with my praise.

"Like it? I adore it!"

I've been to plenty of balls and soirees in some of the most beautiful locations in England, yet I can't recall ever seeing something so splendid.

My opinions are reinforced as we enter the dining room.

Entirely bathed in candlelight, it makes for a stark contrast with the darkness of the night.

The room is fully adorned with Ancient Greek motifs, while the gilded furniture boasts a Louis fourteenth style.

"It must have cost you a fortune," I whisper as I note the artwork on display—all pieces by reputed artists.

"It better," he chuckles. "I made it for you."

I stop, my fingers digging in his arm.

My eyes open and close in confusion.

"For...me?" I ask in a small voice, afraid I haven't understood him properly.

"I built this entire place for you, love," he confirms. "I made it just as I knew you'd like it."

"But how... When..." I mumble, at a loss of words.

Everything about this location speaks of quality and the best materials money can buy—nothing hurried. How could Amon have built something like this so fast when it can take years to build something so flawless.

"I've been waiting for you for a long time," he gives me a sad smile. "When all you have is time, you devote it to perfection," he replies, a note of melancholy lacing his words.

He leads me around the big dining table, pulling a chair for me. When I see him moving to the other side, I grab his sleeve, stopping him.

His brows go up in question as he looks at me. I slowly shake my head as I bite my lip.

"Stay," I whisper.

I don't want to have him across from me—so, so far away. We're together at leisure for the first time in forever and all I want is to have him close, feel his body heat and let his deep rumble reverberate through my being.

"As you wish," he gives me a nod as he takes a seat next to me, but not before I spot a small smile pulling at his lips.

It pleases him too.

Though the table is set, the food isn't here yet. Just as I'm about to wonder if he'd hired servants, the food appears out of nowhere.

Well, there goes my answer. It seems we are to be truly alone for the night.

"How does this work? This conjuring things out of nowhere?" I ask as I watch him portion a piece of steak before placing it on my plate.

"They're not out of nowhere," he chuckles. "I'm not *that* powerful. I merely call to me things which I am familiar with—things I have interacted with before."

"So, for example. If I asked you for a pie. Would you be able to get it here?"

He shakes his head.

"I can only call forth specific things I have touched and know the location of."

I nod thoughtfully. That makes sense.

"What else can you do?" I inquire eagerly.

After the reveal of his true nature, we'd never gotten around to talking about it or what it means for him.

"How did you turn your hand into a sharp blade to kill that man? What about the mental suggestion? Oh, and reading minds," I keep firing one question after another at him.

I'd had plenty of time to think of all the things I wanted to know about him—all the curious aspects of his arcane nature.

He chuckles at my enthusiasm.

"You're adorable," he suddenly compliments.

I don't know if it's the excitement of the moment or his honeyed tongue, but I feel myself blush from head to toe. He notes it, too, because his gaze suddenly darkens as he trails his eyes from my face to the generous décolletage of the dress and the swell of my breasts where my flush had extended to.

Suddenly, he clears his throat as he wrenches his gaze away from that area.

"My powers are mostly combat-based, though I've learned to give them other uses. The teleportation you speak of? It's my enhanced speed in a fight."

My eyes widen as I take in all the information. Combat?

"You were a soldier?"

He nods.

"I am a war machine, love. I was built with the express purpose to kill and slaughter," he says as he lifts his right hand. Under my very gaze, I see it morph into a sharp blade.

"My mental abilities, too, are an extension of that," he smiles bitterly. "For interrogation purposes," he clarifies. "That isn't to say that I was born this powerful. I trained for centuries to get to the level I am now."

Though his tone is moderately objective, I can tell this is an area of his life that he doesn't like talking about. Now that I know at least something, I decide to not probe further.

"Can you read my mind all the time?" I wet my lips, awaiting his answer with apprehension. Can he see everything I feel for him and the way my mind is inundated by thoughts of him? That since the moment we've met he's been my very own elusive obsession?

"Not all the time," he answers ruefully. "I can do it if I concentrate enough, but some thoughts are louder than others. Just like how people have better mental defenses than others," he explains. "In your case, I can read your loudest thoughts, but not all of them."

"Thank God," I whisper, exhaling in relief.

He throws his head back and laughs.

"Ah, my dear Lizzie, what is it that you hide in that pretty head of yours and you don't want me finding out?"

His lips are tipped up in amusement, his countenance relaxed unlike I've ever seen him.

Before, he would always be tense, almost rigid. And though I'd been drawn to that magnetism he exudes when he channels his warrior self, I can't help but feel my pulse pick up at the handsome picture he makes like this.

Blithe. Carefree. Absolutely breathtaking.

He looks like...home.

"You might find out if you're a good boy," I wink at him playfully.

He bursts out laughing.

"Damn, if I wouldn't spend an eternity just like this. You. Me," he pauses as he catches my eye. "*Us*. Forever. How does that sound, Lizzie mine?" he murmurs thickly.

"You might have to convince me," I counter cheekily. "But is it true that you're immortal?"

He chuckles.

"You could say so. But that doesn't mean I am impervious. I can get mortally injured, but I have a very, *very* long lifespan."

The image of the gleaming sword flashes in my eyes.

"Rhodium," I whisper.

His eyes widen with alarm.

"There were two men visiting my mother. They gave her a sword to kill you with and they mentioned it was forged from rhodium—the only thing that can harm you."

He takes a deep breath, exhaling slowly.

"I know who you are talking about. Yes. It is correct that rhodium can kill me," he explains, telling me that the only thing that can kill him is a blow with a pure rhodium weapon to his heart. Anything other than that would injure him, but not enough to finish him off.

The mere fact that he's telling me in detail how he could be killed means that he trusts me implicitly—a fact which warms my insides.

"Aren't you scared then?" I ask, biting my lip.

He releases a dry laugh.

"Those two have been working against me for a long time. They didn't succeed last time, it's unlikely they will this time."

I narrow my eyes at him.

"What about the wedding advice? They instructed my mother to marry me off because," I pause, blushing as I say the next words, "if I take my husband's seed you will stop looking for me—or, rather, my mark?"

The moment he hears my words, the temperature drops in the room, his eyes shifting color. From the light blue from before, they turn a deep red before settling on the blackest black.

"Nothing would stop me from coming to you, Lizzie. But that would definitely piss me off. And when I'm pissed," he flashes his teeth in a predatory smile. "Few people survive."

"So it's not true?"

He shakes his head.

"They assume that if you were touched by another I would renounce my claim on you, which is erroneous from three points of view," he says matter-of-factly as he raises three fingers.

"One, you're mine. No buts, no conditions or prerequisites. You're simply mine."

His words make me warm and fuzzy so I nod along.

"Two, no man would ever get close enough to you to do so."

I roll my eyes at that, since I haven't forgotten his little stunt with Viscount Berkley. Did he really have to scar the man for dancing with me?

"And three," he smirks arrogantly. "You would never let another man touch you."

My brows shoot up.

"That's rather presumptuous of you," I challenge.

"I'd rather call it confidence," he chuckles. "But it's a fact, isn't it Lizzie mine? Have you ever felt *anything* at all for another man?"

I don't reply, merely averting my gaze. He is right in that regard. I've never felt even a glimmer of something for another man. But I'm not about to inflate his already enormous ego.

"Then you should know that according to my mother, she's already found me a husband," I add flippantly, watching him from the corner of my eye.

He doesn't react. He doesn't rage as I would have expected him to.

"So she has," he merely answers, lounging in his seat.

Still his eyes are on me, his mouth curled at the corners, and that tells me everything I need to know.

"You had something to do with it," I accuse. "I know you did. What did you do? Kill the poor man? Ship him off to the colonies?"

His smile widens.

"I'll let you in on a little secret," he leans in to whisper. "We *are* in the colonies."

"What?" I squeak.

Before he can stop me, I pull my chair back, getting up from the table and going straight to the exit.

Pulling the door open, I'm met by a completely foreign sight.

We're on a hill, and before me stretches what looks to be a village.

"This will be our home, Lizzie," he whispers in my ear. "Away from everyone who is against us. Away from the entire world."

"You... Where are we?" I swallow hard against the panic that threatens to overtake me.

"Northern Massachusetts. Your new home."

"But... How? I don't understand," I say as I turn to face him.

Taking my arm, he closes the door before he leads me back to the dinner table.

Seating me down, he places more food on my plate, urging me to eat as he starts recounting his plan.

"I know you love your family. Despite their best efforts to hunt me down and break us apart, I will not hurt them. As long as they love you and *never* harm you, I swear to you that I will never lay a finger on them, Lizzie."

The sincerity in his voice is unmistakable, as is the fact that I believe him—I *fully* believe he would never hurt them.

"You've been wondering why I've been so absent. The truth is that I've been planning a way for us to be together without having to fight against your family or the coven. Just a way we could be together, only the two of us."

"But," I purse my lips. "You're...immortal," I whisper the obvious. How would this work when I would grow old and die while he would just...

"Don't," he growls. "Don't even think of that. I told you I would take care of everything and I mean it, Lizzie. You will *never* die on me again," he tells me resolutely.

"Walk me through this, Amon. From the beginning."

"I knew about your mother's quest to find you a husband and instead of fighting it, I decided to play her at her own game. You will, indeed, wed someone," he pauses. "*Me.*"

My eyes widen.

"What?"

"Your family and everyone will, of course, think that you are married to someone of your mother's choice. But it shan't be so," he proceeds to explain that he will use an irrelevant man and gain control of his mind throughout the courtship period and until the wedding takes place.

"After the vows have been said, to me of course," he gives me a sheepish smile, "we will relocate to the colonies to start a new life."

"And my mother won't catch on?" I ask skeptically.

"She won't be able to tell," he chuckles. "Despite what your mother and that coven of hers seem to think, I'm not averse to holy water, nor holy ground, nor any of those silly runes she's placed all over her house to keep me out. So you see, she has a very poor understanding of who —*what* I am."

"If you're sure this will work then..."

"I am certain it will work," he assures me gently.

"Then what about the other part? The immortal problem."

He chuckles.

"There is one item I am searching for, Lizzie mine. And if I'm correct, that should stop you from growing old, or..." he drifts off as his eyes rove over my body. "Be so fragile."

"Fragile? What do you mean?"

He scowls.

"With the way Fiona bound your abilities, you cannot heal at all. That means I could hurt you if I'm not careful," he swallows hard, and I spot the vulnerability in his eyes—the fact that he is terrified of hurting me. "And I could never forgive myself if I hurt you in any way."

Suddenly, it dawns to me why he's been treating me with kid gloves —why he'd always kept his distance.

He's afraid of hurting me.

God, but his features are torn up with such immense anguish, that my heart squeezes in my chest. He can't bring himself to touch me because he thinks he might harm me in any way...

Getting out of my seat, I slip between him and the dinner table. He's watching me closely, his gaze heated, his eyes hooded as he awaits my next movement. Pushing his empty plates out of my way, I hoist myself up the table, placing my legs on either side of him—so close; too tantalizingly close.

His hands automatically come to rest on my bare ankles, his touch so delicious, I cannot help but yearn for more. Yet first I must have my answers.

I bring my hands to his face, cupping his cheeks and slowly stroking his skin with my thumbs. Not for the first time, I find myself getting lost in his gaze and the hypnotizing combination of his physical presence and searing touch. I take in his broad shoulders, his prominent collarbones and the muscles that seem to hide under his shirt. I look at him like the exciting, desirable and oh, so arousing man that he is, and I only have one question.

"Is that why you won't bed me? Because you're afraid to hurt me?" I ask softly.

His jaw clenches as he gives me a brisk, pained nod.

"I can't trust myself with that yet, love," he releases a weary sigh. "I want to touch you more than I've wanted anything in my life but... I can't risk it. I can't risk that I'll become lost to sensation and everything you make me feel. You already saw that one kiss got me so worked up I drew blood from your lovely lips," he pauses as he gently caresses the column of my neck.

I swallow audibly as his palm closes over my throat, the hold light, yet menacing. In spite of that, all I want is for him to squeeze tighter—touch me everywhere. God, but I want everything he can give me—pain, pleasure, *love.* I'll take him as he is.

Violent. Brutal. *Suave.*

I'll take the killer and the lover. If only he'd give it to me...

"Fuck, when you look at me like that it's fucking impossible to resist you," he curses, his features tensing. "But it's been so long since I've been with someone that I don't know how I would react. How...frenzied I would become."

My eyes widen.

"How long?" I ask before I can help myself.

His eyes flash at me.

"More than a thousand years."

I gawk at him, though his answer makes my insides flutter in an unexpected way.

"A thousand years," I repeat in awe. "And now you're mine."

He shakes his head, a sad smile on his lips.

"I've always been yours, love. *Always,"* he states emphatically.

"Then touch me. Do something. Anything," I inhale sharply. "Please, Amon. I *burn* for you," I plead just as I take hold of his hand, lowering it from my neck to my breasts, urging him to touch me—anything to quench this incessant thirst I have for him.

"Lizzie," he releases a deep, guttural sound, his features contorted in pain as he visibly fights himself and his own desires. I can see the conflict in his gaze, the way he's looking at me as if he'd die if he didn't touch me in the next second but at the same time is entirely too afraid to take the plunge.

"We don't have to do everything. Just...something. I know there's more to lovemaking than copulation."

His eyes flash at me.

"And how would you know that?" he grinds his teeth, a murderous aura surrounding him.

"Emma," I whisper. "She told me that her fiancé touched her." I take hold of his other hand, moving it under my dress, up my leg until it reaches my inner thigh. "Here."

"Lizzie," he growls.

Before I know it, he's out of his seat, the chair flying back across the room from his residual strength, and I finally realize his reticence.

He is...absolutely super human.

A demon.

God, he is magnificent.

He doesn't allow me any time to change my mind as he has my dress bunched around my hips, his hands parting my legs for him. I'm not wearing my drawers—or anything that could impede his access.

"Fuck, Lizzie. Fuck. Fuck. Fuck," he curses to himself, his eyes turning to molten lava as he lowers his gaze to my core.

I'm almost ashamed of the unusual wetness that gushes out of me and I barely fight the urge to squeeze my legs shut. It's only his appraisal and the look of pure wonder that he's sporting that has me equally frozen to the spot.

"One touch," he says, as if trying to convince himself. "Just one touch. One taste," he breathes harshly.

"One touch," I nod enthusiastically, curious about what he's going to do to me—dying to feel his big hands on my body.

That thought alone makes my core clench, more wetness accumulating between my legs.

"Sorry," I whisper, making to shield myself from his view.

"Sorry? Why the hell would you be sorry? Fuck, your sweet little cunt is the most beautiful sight I've ever seen. So plump and rosy. So fucking mine," he says right as he dips one finger between my folds, gathering all the moisture and swirling it around.

I'm so sensitive there that I can't help but arch my back, moaning at the barest touch.

God, but I am wanton.

So. Damn. Wanton.

And I can't find it in me to care.

Nothing else matters but this moment.

Him.

My Amon.

He teases me with soft touches and when he brushes his thumb against a particularly sensitive spot, I all but jump off the table.

"Amon," I gasp. "What..."

"So responsive," he murmurs softly, his eyes almost black. "Gods, Lizzie, you're so beautiful. So fucking sensual."

Raking my teeth over my bottom lip, I peer at him from beneath my lashes as he continues to touch me there, caressing me softly as he watches every play of emotion on my face.

"So wet for me," he rasps as he brings one finger to my entrance, pushing it inside. "Fuck. You're going to be the death of me, Lizzie mine."

"Big words for an immortal," I giggle, but I barely manage to get the words out as he pushes another thick finger inside of me, stretching me.

There's a slight burning sensation, but it's all drowned out by the richness of feeling and the buzzing thrill.

His thumb is circling my sensitive spot while he thrusts his fingers in and out of me.

"Amon," I breathe out. "What are you doing to me?"

"I'm giving you what you asked for, love. I'm touching you, petting you," he says just as he increases the speed, applying more pressure to my bundle of nerves.

Just as I feel something mount inside of me, he stops.

"Amon," I call out, confused and unfulfilled.

"Shh, my darling girl," he coos, and I feel his hot breath against my wetness. "Let me take care of you."

A shiver goes down my back.

He can't possibly mean to...

But he does.

God, he does.

My back hits the table as he throws my legs over his broad shoulders, his tongue making contact with my core. He gives me a long lick, covering that entire sensitive area with the flat of his tongue.

"Such a bad girl, Lizzie mine. Taunting me with this naughty little cunt," he speaks against me, languidly licking me until I'm a thrashing mess in his hold, gasping, moaning, whining.

Anything to get him to continue this sweet torment.

"This naughty little cunt that begs to be claimed, isn't that right? It needs to be marked and owned."

"Yes," I moan out loud. "Please."

His fingers are back at my entrance, stretching me anew as he pumps them in and out while his lips are wrapped around my bundle of nerves, sucking and nibbling and driving me absolutely insane. Every little touch, every little brush of his tongue against me has me tense up, anticipation building inside of me as I know this time I'll find that elusive peak.

"So deliciously wet and sweet for me," he murmurs. "So mine. Only ever mine."

"Yours," I chant incoherently. "I'm your Lizzie. Just like you're my Amon. My everything," I cry out as my muscles strain with this kiss of pleasure.

Something pulsates inside of me, the pressure mounting higher and higher, until it reaches that ineffable pinnacle. I fall apart, seemingly breaking into a million pieces as I chant his name, again and again—the tone alternating between a loving caress and a worshiped whisper.

"*My* Amon," I barely find my breath as I raise myself on my elbows to look at him.

He's holding himself still, tension radiating from him. His muscles are taut, the veins on his arms even more prominent than before.

Hunger still gnaws at me as I let my gaze roam over him. Especially as my eyes move from his solid chest that moves with every labored breath lower—to the hardness that dents the material of his trousers.

I may not know much about this love making business, but I'm quite certain that is for me—meant to go inside me.

Slowly biting my lip as I hold his gaze, I slide myself to the edge of the table, my hands trailing over his hard chest as I feel his muscles coil under my touch.

"You're so strong," I murmur appreciatively.

He's so big compared to me. He could crush me in one second, and I know that's what he is afraid of. Yet *because* he could, I trust him even more not to. Because I can see in his gaze what I mean to him—all the love, tenderness and possession.

Despite everything, I trust him implicitly—with my heart *and* my body.

I move my hands lower, and his eyes flash dangerously as he senses the direction.

"Lizzie," he gives me a rumbling warning.

My hands hover over his hardness, slowly tracing the outline of it.

And it's...quite massive.

Certainly more than I would have thought.

"Lizzie, I..." he groans as he covers my hands with his, stopping my advance.

"I want to see," I whisper as I search his gaze. "Show me, Amon. Show me everything."

"Fuck, Lizzie. You're really killing me here."

"This is because of me, isn't it?" I murmur softly as I cup him through his trousers.

"Of course," he groans at my touch. "Only for you, my love. Only for you," he says harshly, his nostrils flared as he exhales sharply.

"Are you... Are you in pain?" I ask worriedly as I lighten my hold.

He shakes his head.

"Show me," I coax again.

He bites back a curse as he takes a step back.

Just as I think he's going to deny me, I see his hands go to the fastening of his trousers.

"You want to touch me, sweetness? You want to put your hands on my cock?"

My eyes widen briefly as I continue to nibble at my lip, anticipation and desire mingling inside of me.

"Is that what it's called?" I ask curiously.

He grunts.

"Cock," I repeat, tasting the word on my lips and finding that I don't mind it. Not at all. "Let me touch you, Amon. Let me touch your cock," I say eagerly.

"Fuck me, Lizzie mine," he groans out loud. "Say that one more time and you won't need to touch me at all."

My brows scrunch in confusion, but it's all quickly forgotten as he places my hands on his hardness. Full of curiosity, I reach inside his trousers. Warm flesh greets me, so hot and silky I can't help the gasp that escapes me.

Slowly, I take him out, my eyes widening when I see the entire extent of him. God, but how is that supposed to fit inside of me? It must be the size of my forearm, the thickness even more daunting as I can barely fit both hands around him. Angry veins run along the entire length, the thick head at the end leaking some clear liquid the more I handle it.

Yet that's not even the most alarming feature. There's a thick silver ring at the end of it, intertwined through his flesh in what I can only imagine had been a painful experience.

"What is this?' I tentatively touch the ring as I bring my eyes to his.

His hand is on my cheek as he caresses me softly, looking at me almost reverently.

"That is a symbol of my commitment to *one* woman for eternity. In my culture, mated males get it after they find the woman they want to be with forever."

My breath hitches at his explanation.

"Me?" I whisper, barely daring to ask out loud.

"Only you," he confirms, his tone firm and unyielding.

Pure joy bursts inside of me, my chest contracting with the power of my feelings for him.

"This is for me," I repeat numbly, bringing my eyes back to his cock —his jeweled cock.

All for me.

That he would risk pain to do something like this to prove his commitment is beyond what I would have ever expected. And that makes me want to please him all the more—give him the same pleasure he's given me.

"Show me how to touch you."

He gives me a curt nod just as he shows me how to stroke him, moving my hands up and down his shaft while giving special attention to the thick head at the end.

"Spit in your palm, love," he commands, and I do.

I spit both my palms before I bring them back to his length, lathering the wetness all over the soft yet steely surface of his skin. I massage his flesh slowly, doing my best to cover his entire shaft before I reach the head. I carefully flick my thumb over it, taking some of his arousal and playing with it. Yet I'm startled to see that the metal ring moves, too.

A low hiss escapes him, but I don't think it's one of pain. Not with how his eyes change color again, the light blue becoming darker and darker until it's fully black—the color of his desire.

I add more moisture as I touch him, tentatively at first before gaining more speed as I watch for his cues—the way his lips part, his breath coming in short spurts when I massage the head of his cock. My eyes on his face, I see all the sensations echo in his features—the tension, the relief, the *desire*.

"Damn it all to hell, Lizzie," he releases a tortured cry as I start working him faster and faster. "Just like that. Fuck, but your hands on my cock... I didn't dare... I didn't think you..." he mumbles incoherently.

His hands rest on either side of me on the table as he leans into me and my touch, his warm breath fanning my face as I continue to stroke him, delighting in every little sound that escapes his lips.

Yet it's when a loud snap erupts in the air that he wrenches himself from me.

He's breathing had, his eyes wild as he focuses on the spot next to me—the fissure that appeared in the wood.

Dear God, he nearly broke the table!

"I can't..." he shakes his head, a look of pure disappointment flashing across his face.

"No, no. Please don't," I whisper, hating to see him so far away—so forlorn. "Please, Amon. Let me..."

"I can't risk it," he releases an anguish sigh. "Damn it, Lizzie. Damn it," he curses in frustration.

"There must be a way. Please. I need you, Amon. I *need* you," I'm close to begging him. And if I have to do it, I will—anything for him to come back to me.

He must read my mind because a defeated look descends upon his features.

"How can I deny you anything, Lizzie mine?" he murmurs as he slowly comes closer.

I watch him with trepidation and the precariousness of the moment. I want him too much to think coherently. I only know that I can't stand another moment with him so far from me, without his hands on my flesh, or mine on his.

I've never known greater torment than this unleashed passion that's revealed itself within me—all for him. There's such depth of feeling, of want and desire that I feel like I will physically wither away if I don't act on it.

He's a few inches away—miles still. But as he closes his eyes, he materializes a gleaming metal around him. The chains swirl all around his torso until his arms are fully trapped.

"You'll have to help me take them off later," he chuckles a moment later.

"What..."

"Rhodium chains. They will ensure I don't accidentally hurt you," he gives me a sad smile, explaining how to take them off at the end.

I can tell how much it's costing him to do this. He's so used to being in control, yet for me, he's willing to give it up.

To make me happy.

To please *me.*

"I love you, Amon," the words flow out of my mouth. "I love you and everything that you are," I confess.

His eyes widen, disbelief crossing his features before an eerie calm settles over him—an unusual certainty that shifts the currents of the air surrounding us with its strength.

"I love you so damn much, Lizzie. You have no idea just how much," he rasps just as he steps between my open legs. "I'm yours, sweetness. Yours to do as you please."

Wetting my lips, I give him a nod.

"Kiss me," I whisper as my hands reach for his cock, resuming my previous ministrations.

Though he is still slightly hesitant, he leans in, softly touching his lips to mine.

Once. Twice. On the third time a groan escapes him as he gives himself fully to the kiss, plundering my mouth with his tongue and laying small, claiming bites all around my lips.

I increase the rhythm of my strokes, his cock twitching in my hold as he nears his climax. My own core grows wetter and wetter from his proximity, my muscles tensing with desire and a need to be possessed by him—to be fully his.

"I need you, Amon," I murmur against his lips. "I want to feel you."

He draws back just enough to gaze at me. I topple all my mental defenses as I beckon him to look inside of my mind and see everything he makes me feel—the absolute inferno that burns in my veins because of him.

From the first moment I'd seen him, he'd opened something within me.

I may not have known what it meant at the time, but I do now.

An all-encompassing need to belong to him—to be one with him.

"I need you inside of me," I whisper, blinking in fear as I may have pushed too far.

His control is already tenuous as it is, the chains only doing so much to keep him from taking over. And though I know he's doing all this for my benefit, I can't help but yearn for more—regardless of the consequences.

"Just a little. Enough so I can feel you for a second," I continue when I see the mix of pain and arousal on his face. He wants this as much as I do—maybe more.

Yet beyond the desire there is the need to protect me even if that means denying himself.

"Please..."

Breathing hard, he takes a moment to look at me. His eyes are wholly black, and they seem to bore into me with the power of their perusal.

"Just a little..." he repeats on a ragged breath, almost as if he's trying to convince himself of it. "Just the tip, Lizzie mine," he rasps as a dangerous gleam enters his eyes. "I'll tell you what to do and you do it for me," he murmurs seductively.

I nod effusively. Leaning in, I lick his lips as I search for access to his mouth, all the while scooting to the very edge of the table and wrapping my legs around him.

"That's it. Now take my cock and bring it to that sweet wonder that hides between your legs."

I maneuver his cock right at my core, a gasp escaping me as I feel the cold metal of his ring slide between my folds.

"Fuck yes, Lizzie mine! That's it. Rub me against that rosy cunt of yours and lather me in that sweet honey," he growls against my lips.

I can only comply, the sounds of pure male pleasure echoing in my ears the more I rub him against me.

"Push my cockring against your little nub," he commands, and I acquiesce, moving the metal-covered head against that sensitive spot. A low moan escapes me. "Just like that sweet thing, just like that," he groans, his pelvis tilting in small but punctured thrusts. The combination of hard metal and silky skin is maddening against me, the friction delicious as he drives forward before drawing back.

In no time, I'm tensing all over, my eyes rolling in the back of my head as my muscles tighten with the power of my release. So much so that I lodge my nails into his arms, holding onto him as the climax cascades through me.

"So beautiful," Amon whispers. "So fucking beautiful. And mine. My love. My lover. My other half," he speaks huskily in my hair.

"Now slide me to your entrance," he continues. "Let me feel your tight little cunt squeeze the life out of me, Lizzie."

As if hypnotized by his voice, I can only comply, sneaking one hand between our bodies to grasp his cock and move it lower to my entrance.

I instinctively know it's going to hurt—it can't be otherwise with his monstrous size. Yet I want that pain more than anything for it will make this real—*his possession.*

Nudging the head of his cock against me, I slowly push it in. The ring makes it inside me first, the texture of the metal making me release a small gasp. Just that small jewelry and it's already a tight fit. Not one to be deterred, I wrap my hand as best as I can around his shaft and I push him into me at the same time as I cant my hips, the double action helping him breach me successfully.

A loud pop erupts in the air at the same time as a searing pain radiates from my entrance.

"Fuck, Lizzie. Fucking hell," he rasps loudly, the chains rattling around him as his entire body vibrates with pure strength. For one second, I think he's going to break free of them and have his way with me. But despite all my hopes, they seem to hold.

"My God, Amon," I whisper in awe as I rotate my hips to find a more comfortable position.

He's mine. Just as I am his.

Good Lord, he's inside me.

Well, maybe just half an inch, but the stretch is unmistakable as is the burn.

"You're so big," I breathe out. "So..."

"Are you ok?" he asks suddenly, his voice tinged with worry.

"It hurts a little but I'm fine. I feel...*glorious!*"

He chuckles against me, a deep rumble that makes my insides tingle.

"I never dared to imagine this would happen," he whispers softly. "Not this soon. Not when I'm still a danger to you."

As he speaks, I realize that he feels the same all-encompassing awe I do—the same endless love that pulsates between us.

The head of his cock throbs inside me, the ring bumping against my inner walls with every little move and making me jerk in pure pleasure.

Though only barely, we are united—and that in itself makes my entire being soar with unadulterated pleasure. If this feels like this... Then I can't imagine what having him wholly inside me would be like.

"No, don't," he grits his teeth when I continue to undulate my hips in an attempt to draw more of him inside me—despite the renewed pain. "I'm losing control, my love. The chains... I don't know how long they will hold me."

I whip my gaze to his.

"But...rhodium..."

He smirks at me.

"It might slow me down, but it's temporary. It's why a puny sword will never fell me," he tells me confidently.

"My big and strong protector," I coo at him, nuzzling my face in the crook of his neck.

"But that doesn't mean I'm not marking you today, Lizzie mine. I want you dripping with my cum, smelling of me, feeling me everywhere," he drawls smoothly.

"Yes. Yes, please," I agree wholeheartedly.

"Put those hands on me," he rasps. "Put those soft hands of yours on me and stroke me like before," he commands me.

I use both hands to cup him, keeping his head inside me as I follow his instructions and move them up and down his shaft.

Soft groans escape him as the chains rattle more and more.

"Fuck," he moans, dropping his forehead to my shoulder. "Just like that, my darling girl."

His sounds grow increasingly louder. His musky scent invades my nostrils as I feel him like never before.

And his cock. God, but it feels like his cock is swelling in size with each pump—each stroke of my hands.

"I'm coming," he roars, and before I realize it, he lodges his teeth deeply in my shoulder just as the hot liquid of his seed fills me to the brim.

My mouth opens on a soundless moan as pain and pleasure mingle together.

He sucks on my wound, animalistic sounds escaping him as he laps at my blood.

Reaching around, I find the small mechanism of the chains, quickly unscrewing it. They fall to the ground with a thud, leaving him completely free. But just as I think he's going to continue—claim me fully—he draws back.

Blood trickles down his chin, his eyes swirling red and black as he regards me with an odd expression on his face.

"I'm sorry," he hangs his head low, fastening his pants back on.

"No," I shake my head. "I'm not. Please, Amon. You didn't hurt me," I whisper, holding my hand out to him and urging him to come near.

He's like a savage beast as he takes his first step. Yet as he approaches, his nostrils suddenly flare, his eyes pinned to my shoulder before moving lower. Slowly, he tentatively moves in front of me, bringing his lips to my wound and licking it clean.

I smile at him and the tenderness I note in his eyes—just as I see the guilt.

"I liked it," I confess. "I like the pain and the feel of your mouth on me."

His nose wrinkles some more, and it's as though he doesn't even hear me as he pushes me back on the table, pinning my dress above my hips as he regards me with a crazed look on his face.

"Amon?" I call his name, but he doesn't reply.

He trails his nose down my body until he reaches between my legs.

"I made you bleed," he suddenly says. "Again."

"No, you..."

I don't get to speak, though, as his tongue connects with my slit, licking me clean.

He laps at me for what feels like an eternity, and as two more orgasms rack my body, I find myself too spent to protest when he finally gathers me in his arms, flashing us back to the bedroom.

"This should have never happened, Lizzie mine. I was too impatient," he murmurs in my ear as he gently places me on the bed.

"No," I hold him to me. "This *should* have happened. I don't regret anything, Amon. I'm yours. And you are mine. Don't tell me you regret that?" I ask, a tinge of hurt in my voice.

He shakes his head vigorously.

"Never," he states resolutely. "But you're hurt. *I* hurt you..."

"I wanted you to do it, and I loved every moment of it. Just like I love you."

"Lizzie," an anguished cry makes it past his lips as he hugs my waist, laying his head over my heart and holding me tight. "I'll make this right. Soon, I'll make this right," he promises.

And I know he will.

THE FOLLOWING day I wake up in my own bed with Amon nowhere to be seen. As promised, we only had one night together—but many more to come.

As Mary comes to tend to me, I ask her to run me a hot bath before starting the day. I am still sore between my legs despite the fact that I took so little of him inside of me. But seeing how he'd fretted about me afterwards, my guess is that he broke my maidenhead, which is why it had been both painful and a little bloody.

Yet how could he expect anything less with his frightening size? I wonder if human males are similar in that regard, yet somehow I doubt it. Everything about Amon is in the superlative. I don't think anyone in the world could measure up to him. But again, I may be a little biased on the subject.

For the next hour, I lounge into the hot bath, enjoying the many fragranced oils Mary adds to my water.

Yet as she helps me dress, she informs me that my mother wants to see me in her office.

That in itself would sound ominous, considering what I'd overheard yesterday.

But I trust Amon implicitly.

So when my mother gives me the dreaded words, *"I found you a husband," t*he only thing I feel is anticipation for the future.

For my mother's sake, though, and to maintain our cover, I pretend to be entirely surprised.

"His name is Jeremiah Creed. He's an American industrialist. He may not have a title, but he wishes to relocate to his home with you. I've had him checked, and his credentials are sound, as is his fortune and his morals. He is everything I would have wished for you."

"And I don't get a say?" I mumble drily.

"Of course not," she gives me a tight smile. "I know best for you, dear. He will call on you in," she pauses as she glances at the mantle clock, "one hour. Please do make an effort. This is your only chance to escape that...demon," she grits her teeth, unable to even say his name out loud.

I mumble something before I make my exit, going to my room and waiting for the so-called meeting.

No matter how much my mother may love me, and I do believe she does, she is also entirely too invested in her coven.

Unfortunately for me, not only am I the second-born, but I also have my powers bound, which means that aside from the curious mark on my chest, I won't serve for much in her world. As such, as long as she thinks I am safe on the other side of the ocean, I know she will not bother with me again.

Mary helps me prepare to receive Mr. Creed, and all the while I cannot help but be curious about what Amon had in mind.

Just who would he send to play the role of this Mr. Creed?

When the hour comes, I go to the drawing room to meet my intended.

"Elizabeth, come," my mother exclaims. "Just in time. This is Mr. Creed."

"A pleasure to meet you, My Lady," he drawls, the bass reverberating through my entire being.

My lips tip up in a polite smile.

"A pleasure to make your acquaintance, Mr. Creed."

Our gazes meet, holding, arresting.

Oh, the rogue!

I don't know how he managed such a ruse, but he looks like another person.

Dark hair, dark eyes, everything about him is different.

Everything but the essence, and the voice that I would recognize anywhere.

"Why don't you sit there with Mr. Creed and talk."

My mother is quick to steer us to the sofa, telling us to take our time getting to know each other while she moves to the other end of the room to give us some privacy.

I maintain my pleasant smile as I gaze at him, studying him. Despite looking so different, he isn't in any way less striking. In fact, my attraction to him goes beyond looks. It's something at a more primal level.

It's his mere presence, his *essence* that intoxicates me.

"You're crafty, I'll give you that," I murmur in a low voice.

"And you're not too sore, I hope?"

I shake my head lightly.

"How can no one tell? How did you even do this?"

"I can change my eye color at will," he says just as he does a brief demonstration. "My natural color is light, but my mood often influences the shifts."

"And the rest?"

"I can slightly alter my physical appearance so I won't be recognized. But the rest is here," he taps his forehead.

"You're using your mind tricks, aren't you?"

A quick nod.

"I won't be able to stay long because of that. Though I changed my appearance a great deal, it's the mind glamor that gives the impression I'm a completely different person. I didn't want to risk anything with your mother in case she might find some familiarity."

"You can do it with more people at once?" I ask in wonder.

"Not for long though. It depletes a lot of my strength to control that many people. It's even worse because your mother has strong mental barriers, so it's almost double the effort to trick her."

"I see," I purse my lips. "I appreciate what you're doing for me," I whisper, wishing I could reach out to touch him.

"I'd do anything. This is but a small price to pay for knowing you will be mine. That we will be together, away from this place."

My lips pull in a loving smile.

"You're quite the charmer, Mr. Creed," I speak out loud, feigning a giggle as I draw back.

My mother peeks over at us, nodding approvingly.

Amon takes my cue and engages in a monotone conversation to suit the circumstances.

Unfortunately, soon it's time for him to leave.

The visits continue for a month, after which Mr. Creed makes his formal proposal, and I, ever the dutiful daughter, accept.

The bans are soon read and the following month we are both wedded and ready to depart for the colonies.

"I can't believe this is happening," my mother cries after the wedding, giving me a tight hug. "You know I love you and I want what's best for you. You know that, don't you?"

I nod.

"I know. And I will be happy. I happen to like Mr. Creed and I am sure we will be happy together."

She sniffles at my statement.

"You know, if your courtship hadn't worked out, I would have never forced you to marry him."

"You wouldn't have?" My brows shoot up in surprise.

She shakes her head.

"I wanted you married, but I would have never forced you to accept someone you abhorred. I know how my marriage with your father went, and I'd never want that for you."

"Thank you for telling me," I say as I kiss her cheeks. "We may see each other again in the future."

"Anytime you need something, I'm one missive away."

We hug some more and I help her wipe her tears before we say our goodbyes. Next I say farewell to my sister and my brother and I am finally ready to leave.

"Please take care of my daughter," my mother tells Mr. Creed, giving him a warm hug.

Ah, but if she only knew she was hugging the exact demon she'd sworn to eradicate.

To keep up appearances, we embark on the vessel headed for the colonies, but as soon as the ship takes off, Amon gives me his signature smile and taking me in his arms, he transports us directly to the manor he'd built for me.

"Welcome home, my bride," he drawls as he presents me with the entire grandiosity of the place.

Up on the hill, it's far enough from the village to give us all the privacy we need.

"I now have a surprise for you," he tells me as he leads me to our suite.

The bedroom is just as I remember it, but as Amon shows me around, I realize there's more I didn't get to see last time.

Two double doors lead to a small balcony, and Amon invites me to step inside.

"What..." I trail off as I see the wonder around me.

The balcony protrudes from the building, and looking down I note that the hill turns into a rocky cliff before it meets the ocean. Up here as we are, it feels as though we're right above the shore—over the water.

"I knew you would love this," he says tenderly as he fits his front to my back, cupping my midriff and hugging me close to him.

"It's such a wonderful view."

"Doesn't it remind you of something?" he inquires softly, laying his chin on my shoulder.

I don't reply immediately as I stare at the picturesque scenery, something about it tugging at my heartstrings.

"I-I don't know," I whisper. "There is a certain melancholy, despite the beauty of it, but I do not know why."

I feel him smile against me.

"I have something for you."

He draws back, but before I can protest his absence, he places something around my neck.

"What..." I bring my hand up to touch the necklace, feeling the smooth stone.

A current of electricity goes through my body, jerking me back.

"Amon... What..."

"It's time you learned the truth, my love. It's time you learned how it all started."

"What started?" I frown, suddenly overwhelmed by a mountain of sensation.

"Us."

A simple word, but a complicated history.

Chapter Twenty

October 1955. Fairydale, Massachusetts

Sweat clings to my skin as I open my eyes, wildly looking around. The unfortunate realization that it was all a dream crashes on me, while my frustration mounts that it couldn't last a while longer.

What was Amon talking about?

I remember most of the details of the dream before he showed me the balcony, yet I can't recall anything of what he told me after and something tells me it was very important.

My hands go to my neck, feeling for the missing necklace. I hadn't gotten a good look at it, but for some reason I feel its absence to my very soul.

The moment it had touched my skin, I'd felt more complete than ever before.

I sigh as I rub my eyes in an attempt to chase sleep and disappointment away. My limbs are sluggish as I get out of bed, and I'm barely able to stand on two feet. Yet as I glance at my wristwatch, I note it's three o'clock at night.

I'm alone in my room, with Caleb nowhere to be seen. If before I would have been upset at his absence, now I don't know anymore.

Certainly not with this last dream and what I'd learned about Amon.

He...

I swallow hard, certainty washing over me the more I think about the past.

Amon would have *never* hurt me.

I am absolutely sure of it. More than I've ever been about anything in my life. So much so that I can't conceive of ever believing Rhiannon's lies.

He loved me—he *loves* me.

And I love him.

How vile do you have to be to lie to someone about something as severe as rape? To show them what would look as their own abuse and murder? How evil do you have to be to do that just to push your own agenda?

Ironic how everyone blames Amon for being so evil but at every turn I'm getting more and more convinced everyone else *but* him is evil.

Amon would never do anything unprovoked, and I remain staunch in that opinion.

I may have wavered for a moment, and I deeply regret that. But at least that showed me that Rhiannon isn't as saintly as she makes herself to be—perhaps none of the Hales are.

Crashing on the edge of the bed, I blink back tears as I recall all those perfect moments and the utmost care he had for me. He chained himself with a harmful metal to please me, even knowing he would be at my mercy while doing so.

Goodness, but he was absolutely wrecked when he saw he'd made me bleed just a little.

That Amon would *never* do anything to hurt me, physically or emotionally.

For God's sake, the man plotted an entire elaborate scheme to marry me just so our relationship wouldn't cause a bloody conflict—so he wouldn't hurt my family. He'd built me a castle a continent away, dedicating every little architectural quirk to me.

Someone like that would never, *never* do anything against me.

And that complicates everything in my life. With me. With Caleb. With what Rhiannon and Mr. Nicholson mean to do to harm Amon.

Conflicting thoughts arise in my head until I can no longer make sense of my own mind. I no longer know what to do, or whom to trust.

I only know that I am in love with a demon. And I must do whatever I can to ensure that he walks free.

Swiftly getting dressed, I open the door to my bedroom, glancing around the hallway. Relieved I don't see any sign of movement, I take a candle with me to the other wing on the first floor—the forbidden Creed matrimonial suite.

Creeping my way towards that area, I can't help but think back to the past and how everything had originally looked like. Though the Hales have undoubtedly maintained the authentic feel of the house, there are some things that have changed. Yet as soon as that thought crosses my mind, I come to a halt just in front of the big double doors.

Katrina had told me Lydia Hale was the daughter of the original owners—the Creeds.

Dear God, but does that mean that...the Hales are my descendants?

If Lydia was my daughter in a past life, then that would make me Caleb's great-great-grandmother.

What sick twist of fate is this?

I shake my head at the absurdity of it all. Surely there must be another explanation. Seeing how nothing is as it seems with this family, I won't despair just yet.

Steeling myself, I muster the courage to probe the door.

To my surprise, it easily gives way.

Not so locked...

Pushing my way inside, I come to a narrow corridor. As I wave my candle around, I note the various paintings on the wall.

The first three are of people I do not recognize—one girl and two older boys. But it's when I reach the end of the corridor that I stop in my tracks, my eyes slowly widening with disbelief.

If I would have had any doubt about the veracity of my dreams, then this would have erased all doubts.

It's a painting of five people—a family.

Elizabeth and Amon are in the back, looking lovingly at the artist painting the portrait. His arm is across her shoulders as he holds her close to him—scandalous for the period, no doubt. Her head is on his chest, a look of pure happiness on her face.

"God, but we're identical," I can't help but whisper as I let my eyes roam over her features. The same blue eyes, dark hair and pale complexion.

Taking a step closer, I move the candle higher to study Amon's features, which are just as beautiful as I remembered. Strong jaw and cheekbones, a lush mouth and mesmerizing eyes. Then there's the unmistakable strength of his body, his height and breadth of shoulders impressive and breathtaking.

"Amon," I whisper, hovering my fingers over the surface of the painting in the ghost of a touch. "My Amon..."

Lizzie...

I startle back, my eyes wide, my breathing punctured as I look around me.

"Amon... Are you here?"

My smile dies down when I don't get any reply.

It must have been my erratic mind, for I wish for nothing else than to meet him again—tell him I still love him. Against all odds, he still has my heart.

Returning my attention to the painting, I see the same three people from before in front of Amon and Elizabeth.

The girl looks about eight or ten years old, while the other boys are older, in their late teens.

Who are they?

Elizabeth had wed Jeremiah Creed in seventeen ninety-one. This painting looks to have been commissioned in eighteen-five—the year of the plague.

Could they have had three children in that period? *Those* children?

More questions arise in my mind, but hopefully I will be able to find some answers.

Taking a few more steps, I spot another portrait of Elizabeth and Amon.

There are none with them individually. Just the two of them together, always holding each other, always gazing at one another with love.

Melancholy settles deep in my soul as I glance at them—at us. I know at once that this is what I've been looking for my entire life—that restlessness that's always lurked beneath my skin, making me dissatisfied with every moment, even the joyful ones.

It was because of him.

I was missing a crucial part of myself.

Him.

Forcing myself to move on, I come to a small ambulatory before I walk into a big closet—the same one from my dreams.

My breath catches in my throat as I recognize some of the gowns—particularly the red one I'd worn that night for him. Reaching for it, I trail my hands over the worn silk, the material damaged by the passage of time.

More memories appear in my mind—the first time it has happened during daytime. Yet as I brush my fingers along the fine fabric, I can envision all the occasions I'd worn it on. And every time it had been to please Amon.

We'd made love countless times while I was wearing this gown, every time the passion between us burning brighter.

"Amon," I sniffle a cry as tears stream down my cheeks. "I miss you. I *need* you," I whisper.

But there's no reply.

Turning, I come face to face with the wall of jewelry, where there are even more pieces than in my dream. Picking up a small, red box, I barely open it and I'm thrust into the past.

"You got me another pair of earrings? Amon, I already have more than enough," I'd admonished him softly, gazing at him with tenderness.

"You love jewelry, Lizzie mine. And I love gifting it to you. Do you begrudge me this small pleasure?"

"Of course not. Never. Thank you," I'd leaned into him, giving him a kiss and allowing him to put the earrings on.

Back to the present, I can't help but audibly sob at the beautiful ear pieces. Without even thinking whether I should or not, I pluck them from their box, putting them on—the only way I can feel closer to Amon at a time such as this.

Yet as I search through the various boxes of jewelry, I can't find the necklace he'd given me after our wedding anywhere.

Odd.

That is the one piece I wish I could get my hands on, not only because of its symbolism to our relationship, but also because I'd felt *something* when it had touched my skin. A strong current of electricity had entered my body, the necklace acting like some sort of armor around my skin.

Somehow I force myself to move forward even though my heart yearns for that one piece.

Maybe I'll find it in another place...

As I open another set of double doors, I come to a small living area that leads into the main bedroom.

The matrimonial bedroom seems to take up the space of the entire wing. But it's not just the sheer size of it that is striking, but also the design.

Though everything is dusty since no one has been in here in decades, if not more, everything is as we'd left it.

I don't know how I am so sure of it, but as I take in the design, the furniture and the items lying around, I get a strong sense of déjà-vu.

Everything is a combination of red and gold. The walls, the furniture, even the bed.

Drawn to the bed, I reach down to touch the red covers, images dancing in my brain—of us together, wrapped in each other as we made love. I see flashes of our temporary happiness, when it had been just us.

Amon and Lizzie. Husband and wife. *Lovers.*

My throat feels ragged as I cannot stop myself from crying at what I've seemingly lost.

"Who did this to us, Amon?" I murmur between sobs. "Who destroyed our happiness?"

Most of all, who killed me?

If Amon didn't do it, then who did?

Wandering around the room, I touch every little thing as I get more snippets of the past—yet it's nothing concrete. I see bursts of happiness, but I don't see a coherent or linear narrative. And now, that is what I need the most to make sense of things.

Next to the bed, there's a brown, wooden chest that I slowly open, coughing when the dust flies into my face. Rubbing my eyes with the material of my blouse, I peer inside.

"No..." I whisper as I reach down inside. "It can't be..."

Yet it is.

There are tens, if not hundreds of letters in the trunk. All in a decidedly masculine writing.

The letters I'd received from Amon.

They are all here.

Settling on the floor, I place the candle next to me in a secure location before I unfold a couple of them, reading their contents.

If before I'd been sobbing, now I can't help but wail as I read those precious words.

Eternally Yours,
Amon

The letters are just as I'd seen them in my dreams, once more confirming the veracity of my visions. But it's the intense feeling at seeing them up close, of having them in my own hands, that proves to be my undoing.

"Amon, Amon," I chant his name between uncontrollable sobs.

The letters attest to his love, and patience. To his care for me.

Each word is like manna for a woman on the brink of hopelessness, each word bringing me closer to him and steering me towards the truth.

I don't know how much time I spend lost through the letters. But I can't stop myself from unfolding every one of them, poring over his beautiful script as I imagine him sitting at a desk, penning them slowly and carefully.

In my mind, I see my beautiful Amon as he brought his quill to the paper, staining the sheet with ink just like he'd stained my very essence with his presence.

He imprinted on me just as he imprinted these words on paper.

Irrevocably.

Eternally.

Light streams through the curtains, particles of dust dancing in the air. Dawn is here, and I'm nowhere near ready to leave this place. Not when it still holds a piece of him.

Yet as I look up towards the source of light, I suddenly remember the balcony.

Carefully placing the letters back in the chest and closing it, I blow the candle out and leave it on the floor. Getting up, I slowly make my way to the other end of the room, pulling on the curtains and peering outside.

A medium-sized balcony appears before me, sparsely furnished with only two chairs, a small table and many, many blue flowers that are somehow still alive.

My eyes widen at the wonder of it.

Wiping a finger down the table, I note the thick layer of dust that coats not only this surface, but every single one on this balcony. There is absolutely no trace of anyone having been here to tend to the flowers in the recent past.

Yet in spite of that, they look perfectly healthy.

My brows scrunch in curiosity as I go down to my knees to take a closer look at them.

I've always had a fascination with flowers and plants. Unfortunately, save for the books I'd manage to find at the orphanage or at Saint Russell, my education has been sorely lacking.

Even so, it's impossible not to recognize this one—anyone would be able to.

Forget-me-not.

Given their pristine condition—not one flower is wilted—someone must have taken religious care of them.

And I can only think of one person.

Amon.

Somehow, he'd kept these flowers alive. Even trapped, he focused his strength into them.

"I didn't forget you," I whisper as a tear rolls down my cheek. "I could never forget you. Even when I couldn't remember, I knew I was missing something—a central part of myself. How could I forget you when you're part of me?" I confess softly, plucking one small flower and placing it in my hair.

A little wobbly, I slowly get up and turn towards the big windows at the end of the balcony, the memory from before appearing again in my mind.

Placing my hands on the windowsill, I lean forwards to watch the breathtaking scenery, made even more so by the slow ascent of the sun into the sky, its orange-like beams bathing me in the purest light.

Closing my eyes, I inhale the clean air as I lose myself in the moment —in this place that bears the dearest memory of our wedding.

An eerie calm unlike I've never experienced before settles over me, reaching deep inside of me and touching my soul. Feather-like touches caress my cheeks just as the warmth of the young sunrays cascades over me.

I remain like that, hanging onto the windowsill while freeing my mind and letting it roam—all in an effort to draw more visions of the past.

I want—*need*—to see more of Amon. Of our past together. Of that past happiness.

So I open myself up like never before, somehow knowing I will be safe on the other side.

Tipping my head up, I lean forwards onto the railing. The sound of the ocean becomes increasingly louder, the water hitting against the rocky shore before retreating—a perpetual movement.

Seagulls squawk in the distance, the combinations of early-morning noises washing over me.

Yet just as I find myself firmly planted in the present, I'm suddenly thrust forward in another time.

The view is a similar one. A balcony on the edge of a rocky cliff overlooking the ocean. But I can tell immediately that this is an entirely different place.

Turning, I note the change in furniture and the fact that this balcony is far smaller, only accommodating two people with almost no wiggle room. Taking a step forward into the adjacent room, I'm surprised to see how sparsely furnished it is.

A bed lies in the middle of the room, and a chest of drawers next to it. At the end of the room, there is one table and one chair, suggesting this is only occupied by one person.

My feet take me inside, but I don't stop in the room. Opening the door, I follow a small corridor before I go down a spiral staircase. Everything is small and secluded, the living quarters away from everyone else.

As I reach the bottom of the stairs, I look right and left, realizing there are two rooms to the left and glass doors to the right.

Full of curiosity, I march to the right, opening the glass doors and stepping into pure sunlight.

I instinctively squint my eyes and I bring a shielding hand to my forehead. My eyes get teary from the direct contact with the light, but as they slowly accommodate to it, I manage to take in my surroundings.

It's...an indoor garden.

A glorious garden.

It's the size of an entire yard, the only difference being that it is walled on every side, the light coming through a glass ceiling at the top.

There are rows upon rows of flowers and plants, many of them medicinal.

Yet my eyes take me to the top right corner where I spot the beautiful blue hue of the flowers—*forget-me-nots.*

I squat down in front of them, bringing my hand and touching their silky texture.

The questions continue to assail my mind. Though I am seeing a foreign sight—one which I am sure belongs to my memories—I cannot for the life of me remember what this all meant.

Where am I? What is this place? And why is it so solitary?

Taking out a handkerchief, I pat down each flower, the action foreign.

That is when I realize that despite maintaining my own awareness, it is not I who is performing this task—who is moving about the garden. I am merely a spectator in this body, watching things that have already occurred in the past.

I carefully tend each flower, making sure they are all clean, healthy, and well-watered.

Yet as I lose myself in this menial task, a sudden creaking sound startles me.

Jumping to my feet, I bring my hand to my breast, my heart beating wildly in my chest. I cannot say for sure if I am afraid, or curious.

"Show yourself," I call out, my voice booming in the enclosed space.

Yet again, I'm struck by the accent and the words, immediately aware the tongue is not English but instinctively knowing its meaning.

Slow, thudding steps resound in my ears. Turning towards the entrance I'd come from, my eyes widen as I see an imposing form walking towards me.

"You've been taking care of them," he tips his head towards the flowers, his eyes glinting with pleasure at seeing me again.

"A gift should always be treasured," I reply with a huff, though there is no mistaking the warmth that spreads to my insides at the sight of him.

"What are you doing here, Amon?" I ask softly, my pulse picking up speed just as he picks up his pace—until he's standing right in front of me.

He's dressed in formal clothes, black silk and leather mixed in a lethal combination. All tied together with bones—what little must have been left of his greatest adversaries.

He looks absolutely dashing, and I cannot seem to tear my eyes from him.

There's a quiet pride shining in the tilt of his chin, a deadly aura surrounding him as he walks with such casual leisure, as if he could end the entire world if he wished to.

"I'm here for you, lovely Sela," he murmurs softly.

Before I can reply, though, I'm wrenched back into the present, crouching in pain from the unexpected push. My breath becomes labored just as my heart slowly breaks as I reach out for Amon only to find nothing before me.

"Amon," I whisper, my voice tinged with anguish as more tears leak from my eyes.

I do not know when that flash was from, just as I do not know where we were.

The only thing I do know is that my feelings for him never changed.

Then, just like now, I placed in him all my girlish dreams and childhood fantasies. I saw him for what he was—a war machine—but I also knew a side of him the world did not.

Amon d'Artan was not just a killer.

He was the most tender lover—*my* lover.

Feeling more alone and forlorn than ever, I drop to the ground, hugging my knees to my chest as I rock myself lightly, all the while thinking of him and of this situation that's threatening to make me go insane.

What do I do now? How can I help him when I don't have all the information, let alone knowledge of who *I* am?

As the hour grows late, I realize I need to head back to my room to avoid being discovered. The last thing I want is for Rhiannon to know I suspect her and her motives.

Yet I cannot ease the turmoil that resides within me.

If Amon cannot tell me anything, it means I need to find everything out for myself. And I fear the only way to do so is to dream more—see more of the past and understand the hidden truths.

If I am able to find out who killed me, I may be able to find a solution to this.

With my mind made-up, I climb back in bed, closing my eyes and forcing myself to sleep.

"Do I have to carry you out of bed?" an amused voice whispers in my ear hours later, when despite my best efforts, sleep has proven elusive.

"What are you doing here?"

My eyes snap open as I come face to face with Caleb hovering over me.

A lopsided smile pulls at his lips as he regards me, and my heart skips a beat. Yet at the same time, a big chasm opens inside of me as I find myself caught in yet another conundrum.

I *love* Amon. I love him unlike I ever thought myself capable of loving someone. At the same time, I have to admit to myself that I'm in love with Caleb, too. Against all odds, he's ingratiated himself in my heart with his unwavering support.

There is also the fact that I accepted Caleb's proposal, not Amon's.

Why does it feel, then, that I'm betraying *Amon* when I am with Caleb?

Frustration gnaws at me the more I ruminate about this. Yet one thing is absolutely certain. I cannot marry Caleb, nor can I continue a relationship with him. Not with everything I know now. I just need to find the right moment to let him know that, too.

"Let's go. I have a special treat for you today," he winks at me just as he yanks the sheets from my body.

All at once, the scene from the night before replays in my mind and my cheeks heat up in embarrassment. Well, at least this time I'm wearing clothes.

"You know, women need their beauty sleep," I grumble as I get out of bed and put on a pair of shoes.

"If you were more beautiful, Darcy darlin', you'd give me a heart attack," he says smoothly.

"You're such a charmer," I shake my head at him, though his words make my insides melt.

He doesn't allow me any respite as he takes my hand, leading me out of my room and towards the exit of the house.

Despite my previous decision, my body reacts to his nearness, a tingling that starts at the surface of my skin which then extends everywhere, until my mind is filled entirely with thoughts of him.

Is it possible for someone to be attracted to two people the same? Can the same be said about love? Because no matter how much I mull over this issue, or how much I compare Caleb and Amon, a side of me wants them both.

Is it possible to *love* them both?

The moment that thought arises, I chastise myself. How could I be so fickle?

"Here," Caleb suddenly says, startling me from my thoughts.

"What's this?" I blink in confusion.

"What do you think, silly? It's a picnic," he tells me just as he swoops me in his arms, laying me on the spread blanket. "I prepared all your favorite foods and drinks. Since I don't have any business pending today, I wanted to spend the day with my fiancé," he declares as he leans in to give me a kiss on my cheek.

I'm speechless as I'm trying to catch up with everything.

Everything is laid out before me perfectly, from food, to wine, to a couple of books and board games to read and play, he's been entirely too thoughtful.

And I, ever the ungrateful, get hung-up on one word.

Fiancé.

"Here," Caleb says as he places two plates of food in front of me, both boasting a selection of cheeses, ham, and vegetables.

"I also got your favorite bread," he continues as he removes a French baguette from his bag. Taking a knife, he proceeds to cut it into little pieces for me.

"You're too sweet," I smile at him.

"Not enough," he answers gruffly. "My purpose is to make sure every moment of your day is sweet—regardless of the circumstances."

I raise a brow at him, but I don't get to reply as he holds a morsel of food to my lips. He'd stacked cheese and a slice of salami on a piece of bread, topping it off with some red pepper.

Opening my mouth, I let him feed it to me.

"You need to take care of your health, darlin'. You've been slacking off with eating, haven't you?"

My cheeks redden from his observation.

With so much stress, I might have forgotten to eat a time or two.

"I eat when I'm hungry," I mumble.

"Which is when you remember, and it's not good for you. You've already lost weight."

My eyes widen.

"It's not polite to comment on a lady's weight," I reproach lightly, trying not to let his comment get to my head.

Looking down at my body, I have to wonder if what he says is true. I haven't paid much attention to how my clothes have fit me since I've had other things on my head. Yet now that he mentioned it, I can't help but wonder if he finds that unappealing.

Then I realize that from the beginning he's been plying me with food at every turn, urging me to try this, try that. Was it all some covert mission to get me to fill up in places?

He draws back, blinking in confusion, and it dawns on him that he misspoke.

A flush mars his cheeks as he finds himself speechless for a moment.

"It wasn't my intention to offend you," he murmurs, his hand seeking mine and squeezing tight. "I don't care about your weight, Darcy. I care about *you*. And that means watching out for you to be healthy, to eat at the right times and make sure you're taking care of yourself. I know you have a tendency to forget about that when your mind is preoccupied with something."

His tone is laced with so much sincerity as he urges me to meet his gaze.

In such a short time, he's observed me quite thoroughly, hasn't he?

Always looking out for me, always there to help me if I'm in trouble. Why does that thought alone make my heart beat faster in my chest, my stomach clenching with that familiar sensation?

I shouldn't feel like this, yet I do.

"I apologize. I truly didn't mean it like that, trust me," he reiterates.

"Alright," I nod.

"I mean it," he continues, seemingly making it his mission to convince me.

Sliding closer on the blanket, he tugs me to him, his hand trailing down my back as he places my head on his shoulder.

"Do you know why I fell in love with you?" he asks softly in my hair.

I shake my head.

"Your heart," he tells me, and I can feel him smile against me. "You have the purest soul, darlin'. I've never met someone more kind hearted than you. I mean, who would save a damn cat from a fire instead of saving herself?" he chuckles.

I freeze.

How...how does he know about that? I haven't told him about it. In fact, he's never even met Mr. Meow. So how would he know about that incident unless he was there?

Unless...

Goosebumps cover the entirety of my skin as an ominous feeling envelops me.

Dear God, but could he have something to do with the fire?

He continues speaking, singing me praises yet I can't listen anymore as doubts cloud my mind.

Could he have done that to force me to move to the Hale manor?

He'd certainly been insistent about it before.

"So trust me that it's not your appearance that holds my heart, Darcy. Though I must say you're the most beautiful woman I've ever seen," he chuckles, and I force a smile on my lips.

"Thank you," I murmur.

I don't get to say more as a loud crash resounds in the air.

Caleb stiffens.

"We're still on Hale land, we should be protected by Rhiannon's wards," he frowns.

"We should see what's wrong," I offer, and before he can refuse me, I'm already out of his arms and to my feet, hurrying towards the noise—anything to avoid the deep discomfort that settled in my stomach at his words.

God, but I really hope it's just my paranoia coming to the surface and Caleb had nothing to do with the fire.

But what if he did?

"Darcy! Wait!" Caleb calls after me. "Don't..."

He doesn't get to finish his sentence as I stop in my tracks, shock overtaking me at the sight I'm seeing.

"Darcy," he breathes hard as he catches up with me, taking my hand.

But then he looks ahead, too, and notices the same thing.

Rhiannon is at the big gate of the estate, and she's opposite Mr. Nicholson.

Both are glaring at each other while screaming, and before I know it, a laser beam erupts from Mr. Nicholson's cane, which is directed at Rhiannon.

"You damn old man," she curses before a shield envelops her.

Like a mirror, it serves to refract the laser beam. Yet it's unfortunate that the direction is...us

"Down," Caleb yells just as he pushes me to the ground.

Even so, the trajectory of the laser is downwards, and as he emits a low, pained groan, I know he got hit.

"Oh God, Oh God," I start panicking, my hands all over his body. "Are you alright? Are you..."

"I..." his features tense and strain as he squeezes his eyes shut, holding himself over me, his palms on each side of my face as he supports himself on his arms.

"You're hurt. God, Caleb..."

"Don't," he grits out. "It's just...temporary," he grinds his teeth as he breathes in and out, doing his best to control himself.

Yet as he opens his eyes, I'm struck by the change of color in his irises as they swirl a deep red.

Surely not... Surely it's just a play of shadows...

"Darcy!" Rhiannon calls my name, followed by Mr. Nicholson as they both reach my side.

Caleb is quick to regain control as he rights himself back up before helping me to my feet.

"Are you hurt?" she asks, her voice full of worry.

"You're not hurt, are you?" Mr. Nicholson addresses the same question.

"No," I give them a tight smile. "I'm fine."

"This is all your fault," she snaps at Mr. Nicholson, her hands gaining an odd yellow hue before she blasts him into a tree.

I jump a step up, my eyes wide in shock.

"You fucking shrew!" Mr. Nicholson yells.

Red stains his white shirt as he rights himself up, a gash forming where his forehead meets his hairline. Yet despite the visible injuries, he is fine.

He grips his cane tighter, his entire palm cupping the top of the handle as he rights himself back up. And just like they appeared, his injuries heal under my very gaze.

I shoot a concerned look at Caleb, but he slowly shakes his head at me. His lips are pursed, his entire countenance stiff.

"You should know by now that you can't hurt me, Rhiannon," he snides.

"Oh, you might heal, but I'll just keep blasting you. Let's see if you can heal forever," she smirks at him as her palms color with magic again, energy humming all around.

"I just came to see Darcy, not an old and bitter crone like you," he spits out at her, his eyes full of malice.

"And you'll have to get past me to see her," Rhiannon challenges, placing herself in front of me and channeling the same shield she'd used before.

"Bring it on," he spits out in distaste, and lifting his cane to his chest, he closes his eyes.

"Darcy, go inside the house," Rhiannon yells at me.

The sky blackens, bolts of lightning marring the previously clear expanse.

I'm rooted to the spot as I just stare at Mr. Nicholson and the energy that swirls around him.

His eyes snap open, his irises swirling a combination of white and blue as he blasts that lightning towards Rhiannon.

It's at that moment that Caleb takes my hand in his, tugging me towards the house.

"But..."

"You don't want to be anywhere near them now," he says tightly.

Reaching the house, he pulls me inside, closing the door.

Yet I can't help my curiosity as I go back to the window, watching Rhiannon and Mr. Nicholson fighting from a distance. They seem to be equally matched, with the only difference that Mr. Nicholson can heal while Rhiannon cannot.

"I didn't know Mr. Nicholson had powers too," I mention absent-mindedly as he continues to wield the lightning in his favor.

Caleb grunts, taking his position by my side as he wraps a possessive arm around my shoulders, pulling me into him.

"But how is it possible?" I suddenly frown. "If he is my grandfather and powers are passed down the female line, how is it possible he has them, too?"

"What do you think?"

"Then my grandmother *must* have had powers, too."

Caleb smiles in my hair.

"Or, maybe, she was the only one who did," he muses quietly.

My brows pinch together in concentration as I try to make sense of what he's saying—or, rather, what he *isn't* saying.

I continue to watch the ongoing fight, grimacing when Mr. Nicholson is once more thrown to the side by a powerful blast. Yet this time, the impact is so great, his cane slips from his hand, falling onto the grass a few feet over.

He struggles to his feet, teetering from side to side.

Even from a distance I can see he has a nasty wound at his temple, but unlike before, now it's not healing immediately, bleeding profusely onto his cheek.

He moves slowly, his sights set on his cane as he tries to evade more blasts coming from Rhiannon.

But what is most striking is that not only has the sky suddenly cleared of all the clouds, but Mr. Nicholson is unable to channel any of the previous lightning bolts for his use.

"The cane," I whisper, realization dawning on me. "The cane is the source of his power."

Caleb nods.

"Look now," he urges, just as Mr. Nicholson gets his hand on his cane.

In no time, the wounds are healing on his body, his strength seemingly reinvigorated.

"Is the cane a magical artifact? What is it, that it can confer so much power to its master?"

"Is it," Caleb hums, his eyes steely as he regards Mr. Nicholson.

Tipping my head up, I blink in surprise as I see the naked hatred and anger radiating from Caleb—all directed towards Mr. Nicholson. There's so much negative emotion coming from him that it swirls in the air, a bitter taste erupting on my tongue.

Somehow, I know this is personal. From the beginning Caleb has been against him, though he'd never outrightly told me why. He'd given me hints he disapproves of him, but never with such an astounding vehemence.

As such, I can only infer one thing.

"What did he do?" I whisper in horror, seeing Caleb as I'd never seen him before. "What did he do to you?"

"He bit the hand that fed him," he pauses, his jaw tense. "And stole what I held most dear in life."

IT'S late afternoon when I find myself face to face with Rhiannon in the drawing room. The conflict between her and Mr. Nicholson had ended at a standstill and the man had reluctantly left the premises when the other Hales had appeared to back Rhiannon up.

In the meanwhile, Caleb had excused himself to attend to some business and it seems I am to meet with his grandmother alone.

I swallow hard as I plaster a smile on my face.

"I'm sorry about the incident outside," Rhiannon purses her lips. "I'd have never imagined Archibald would seek you out here. Although, given your rare appearances in town, he must have found himself at the end of his tether."

"Katrina told me there is a historic conflict between the Hales and the Nicholsons. But that seemed personal," I note.

Her features darken at my words, and she lifts a glass of water to her lips, taking a big gulp.

"It is personal just as much as it is generational. I'm an old woman, Darcy. I've been around for a while. Archibald? He's been around for even longer. Always waiting. Always looking out for a weakness."

"Longer?"

Although Rhiannon looks great for being in her late nineties, I got the impression Mr. Nicholson was younger than her.

"I gather you spoke with him before?" she probes carefully.

"Once. He mentioned he knew my mother and I wanted to ask him some questions."

She releases a dry laugh.

"Did he now?" she shakes her head. "He knew your mother as well as anyone in town, I assume."

"What do you mean?" I frown, unable to understand what she's hinting at.

"Let me guess, child. He told you he was your grandfather, didn't he? That you were blood relatives and he asked you to help based on that."

I frown.

"Was he lying?"

Her right cheek twitches as her mouth screws up in a sneer.

"No," she chuckles. "He wasn't lying alright. But I don't think he mentioned *who* Lizette's mother was, did he?"

I slowly shake my head.

Rhiannon rises from her chair, walking to a drawer and opening it. From it, she withdraws a small photo album, handing it to me.

"These photos were taken in the twenties," she says, urging me to look through them.

With some apprehension, I open the album to the first picture, my eyes widening in the process.

"This is..."

"Lizette and Connor when they were younger."

"But that would mean?"

"They're cousins," she purses her lips. "First cousins."

I flip the page, finding another picture with my mother and Rhiannon. Both looked far younger, and the resemblance is astounding.

"Lizette was your daughter," I whisper, lifting my gaze to her in horror. "Which makes you my grandmother."

And that makes me related to Caleb...

She gives a bitter nod.

"I admit I kept some things from you. But it wasn't for lack of want to tell you, but rather because it's a difficult subject in the family," she swallows hard. "Like I said before, Lydia Hale foresaw your birth and the fact that you would be the one to eradicate the evil in Fairydale. But she foresaw something else, too," her lips tighten as she exhales deeply. "Your blood is like a fountain of power, Darcy. It is why that monster and the gargoyles came after you. It is why we need you for the ritual just as much as Archibald needs you for his own nefarious purposes."

I nod along. I'd heard similar information from Fiona, but I'd never realized that my blood would be valuable for rituals, too. I'd assumed it worked for demons only.

"Archibald knew everything about Lydia's visions, and he knew exactly when you were going to be born and to whom. So he made sure to tie himself to you in a way that you could be useful to him."

"He made sure to tie himself to me? What do you mean?"

She swallows hard.

"Lizette's conception was not consensual," she admits in a low voice. "And I have every reason to believe neither was yours."

My mouth opens and closes as I try to find my words. But ultimately I am speechless.

"You mean Mr. Nicholson raped you so you could conceive my mother, and then had Mr. Pierce do the same with her?"

She nods, pain reflected in her eyes as she averts her gaze, looking out the window as her hands tremble in her lap.

From the moment I've met her, Rhiannon has been poised and calm, so to see her this rattled is entirely unusual. Despite my reticence against her, and the previous erroneous information she shared, I can't help but believe she is telling the truth with this.

"He wanted to ensure he had a link to you so he could convince you to join his cause."

"Then why didn't he come to me earlier? Why wait until I arrived to Fairydale?"

Her lips flatten in a sardonic smile.

"He cannot leave Fairydale," she confesses. "When Lizette realized she was pregnant, she knew what would happen were she to stay in Fairydale. She didn't want you to step into this life. She didn't want us, or Archibald, to influence you so she felt that the best way to offer you a normal life was to leave. When she did, knowing that Archibald would likely follow, I asked my coven to help me perform a spell to trap him."

"But he still found me. Through Mr. Vaughan."

"Yes. That rat," she sneers.

"I assume there is no inheritance either?" I ask drily.

Rhiannon chuckles.

"Oh that was quite the interesting plot he devised to get you here. Including attempting to fake Leo's death," she shakes her head, her eyes crinkling with amusement. "But to answer your question, yes. The inheritance should still stand if you abide by the conditions. It is still a legal document, and Leo wasn't a poor man."

My brows go up in surprise. Somehow I would have expected the entire thing to be one big farce. But if I get the money...

Get it together, Darcy! There's still the matter of your survival and freeing Amon. Besides, with Amon's powers, what is one million dollars? In fact, who even needs money?

"But why would he use that to get me here?" I ask pensively. "Why now?"

"Archibald's time is running low. He needs your help or he will continue to decline," Rhiannon explains.

"What do you mean by my help?"

"Oh, so he didn't tell you?" she chuckles. "I would have thought he must have found a way already to hint to you his plans."

"He only told me he does not believe in the ritual you mean to perform to kill Amon. He believes you're risking the lives of precious witches when it is not a certain thing."

She regards me for a moment, unblinking. Then, she throws her head back, laughing.

"He said that? Oh, Lord, that fucker," she holds to her stomach as she continues to laugh.

I stare at her, not sharing the amusement since I do not understand *why* it is so funny in the first place.

After she seemingly calms herself, she wipes the tears at the corners of her eyes.

"He doesn't care about anything other than himself. Certainly, he doesn't care about our coven or the people who stand to lose their lives."

"Then what is his purpose? Why is he doing all this?"

"Because he's dying."

"Dying?" I repeat, frowning.

"When he first appeared in Fairydale, everyone knew there was something evil about him—something dark. We realized too late that he was dabbling in dark magic—stealing people's life essences and using them for his own."

"I don't understand."

"Archibald arrived in Fairydale in the eighteen hundreds, not too long after my grandmother relocated with her husband here."

"But that would make him..."

"Over a hundred years? Yes. I am not sure how old is he. Lydia knew about him, and she always told us to be careful, but she never shared more," she sighs. "From the beginning, he'd been dabbling in a forbidden magic meant to increase his lifespan and give him those abilities you saw."

"What about healing? How does he heal like that?"

She shakes her head.

"I am not entirely sure, but it must be a consequence of the forbidden magic. But even that isn't enough. I may not be very knowledgeable about it, but from what I've gathered, it corrodes at the soul until there's nothing left. Turn to the end," she nods to the album in my hands.

I do as she says, flipping to the last page.

My brows furrow as I try to make sense of what I'm seeing.

"That picture was taken a few years before you were born, at the Fairy Festival. Most of the town was present. In the far end corner, you can see Archibald."

"But... He looks to be in his twenties here."

Rhiannon nods.

"That's how he looked for as long as I can remember. He never aged. Not until..." she pauses, her eyes meeting mine. "Not until you were born. I don't know what happened—*how* it happened, but he started aging rapidly. It's to the point that he now looks like a grandfather where just ten years ago you would have still thought him in his thirties. He's degenerating faster and faster, and I am absolutely convinced he contrived to get you here to use *you*."

"You mean my blood," I whisper, realizing why I'd been attacked so many times.

She nods.

"Unfortunately, with Archibald's greed, it's not just your blood he wants to maintain his strength. He wants more."

"More? Where..." My eyes widen in comprehension. "Amon."

"He doesn't want to put the demon away. He wants to take his powers. And for that, too, he needs *you*."

"But how?"

"The prophecy was two-fold, Darcy. It said you could eradicate the evil that resides in Fairydale. But it also said you could unleash it," she admits sadly. "We want your help to end Amon's influence over this town. Archibald wants your help to free him into the world so he can take his powers. Yes, we might be risking our lives with a forbidden ritual, but the alternative is much, much worse."

And with those words, Rhiannon leaves me alone to mull over the issue. Not before I'd noticed the confident gleam in her eyes. She thinks she's won me over with her arguments and that there is absolutely no way I would help Mr. Nicholson.

Little does she know, though, that I can't find it in me to care about their conflicts or anything other than Amon and how to free him.

But first, I think I need to have a very serious chat with Caleb.

I need to know if he was aware of any of this—of our familial connection, or the foul history between Archibald and Rhiannon.

More than anything, though, I need to ask him about his eyes.

For the first time since I've arrived in Fairydale, I do not think I am mad anymore, nor do I think my mind is playing tricks on me—or that it ever did.

Later that evening, I take dinner in my room as I add more details in my notebook, circling in the new connections.

If Rhiannon is my maternal grandmother, then it makes sense that my abilities had been passed down to me via the maternal line.

The only question I still have is regarding Lydia Hale and Elizabeth. How were they related? Was she truly Elizabeth's—*my*—daughter?

No matter how you look at it, though, the connections are slightly baffling.

Though it does make sense that I would be born in the same family as before, there are still some details that are throwing me off.

How is it that I was reborn looking the same, having the same abilities, and clearly the same soul? This isn't just a matter of my soul reincarnating into another body in the future. Rather, I'm back in the *same* body, with the *same* abilities, and with my memories seemingly intact but locked.

I may not be an expert in witchcraft, or genetics, or even reincarnation, but something is odd about the entire situation.

And then there's Sela.

Who is *she?*

Bringing my fingers to my temples, I rub them gently as I try to clear my mind.

It certainly doesn't help that I've developed a romantic connection with Caleb, who, technically, is my...second cousin?

Clearly, I'm not an expert in genealogy either.

But we are definitely too related for this to be comfortable in any way, which will need to be addressed as soon as he wraps up his work—though I have plenty of pending doubts about him.

As I type down my questions, there's one last one that niggles at my mind.

Why had Rhiannon waited so long to tell me we are related?

Isn't that something usually said at the first meeting? She certainly hadn't seemed overly affectionate or maternal towards me, which, granted, could be attributed to her hate of Archibald and the fact that my mother's conception had been via rape. At the same time, I find it entirely odd that she hadn't reached out directly. Not when I'd first arrived in Fairydale, and barely after.

She'd slowly tried to inch her way towards me while keeping her background and our connection a secret.

Why?

Was she afraid I would find out about my connection with Elizabeth and Amon? That it might skew my perspective? It could certainly be the case since from the beginning she'd tried to paint Elizabeth as the weak-willed victim of Amon's charms—someone he'd completely destroyed in his search for power. And considering I know she lied about everything regarding Elizabeth's death, it makes me wonder what else she might be hiding, or what other information she might be misrepresenting for me.

The same goes for Mr. Nicholson, too. Though I have a feeling that Rhiannon might be telling some truth about him, I can't write him off completely.

As it stands, both Rhiannon and Mr. Nicholson want to convince me to join their sides, and that brings me back to the beginning.

I end up spending more hours than I should have, poring over all the information I have in order to come to a conclusion. Yet all I manage to do is run in circles, making unreliable inferences and setting myself up for failure if I consider them the basis of my judgment.

"Damn it," I grit out as I put my pen down.

I can already feel a headache mounting on top of my period cramps.

To relax, I opt for a long steamy bath. When I'm done, I change into some comfortable clothes and I look for Mr. Meow.

He's been missing all day, and I wonder if he went in search for more rats.

"Mr. Meow," I call out in a small voice, careful not to wake people up.

Holding on to my candle, I look all over the first floor for him, puzzled that he would disappear like this. Then again, he does seem to drift in and out of the house. Maybe he's just too wild, and doesn't like to live in enclosed spaces.

As I continue my search for him, though, I can't help but think back to Caleb's mention of Mr. Meow and the fire. How could he have known about that incident when I had been the only one in the house —save for Mr. Meow (but he's a cat!).

There is also the small—or not so much—matter of his eyes.

This wasn't the first time I'd seen them change color, and though he'd managed to convince me before that it had been all in my head, I can't help but question that.

I already know I am not mad, nor am I the type to entertain fanciful notions as I've been led to believe.

Which can only mean one thing.

Caleb might not be who he says he is.

And there could be just one explanation for it...

I whip my head around as a loud sound penetrates through the stillness of the night. The melody is so familiar it tugs at my heartstrings.

It's the Old Church organ, and the sound from the music has somehow reverberated across such a great distance. Except I know that would never happen unless someone else was involved.

Amon.

Is this his way of calling me to him?

Yet even as questions pile in my head, I ignore them. My body has a mind of its own as I put on shoes, and shrug a coat over my long dress.

Without thinking twice about the distance I have to walk, or the fact that it's close to the middle of the night and it might be dangerous to go out, I head for the exit.

There's pure instinct at this point—the fact that I know my beloved is calling for me and I can only respond in return.

After all, wasn't this already in my plan? Find a way inside the Old Church so I can find Amon—so I can finally see him after all this time.

If he's calling for me, then maybe he can help me find a way in.

Out in the cold of the night, I wrap the coat better around my body, hurrying my pace as a shiver of fear goes down my back. My limbs are frozen, yet it's not the chilly wind that caused it, but a feeling of doom that somehow makes my skin prickle with discomfort.

In spite of that, though, I don't stop as I reach the estate gate, nor do I turn back. I simply push on, going down the hill.

The church soon appears in sight and I can all but weep of happiness.

I'm coming. Wait for me. I'm coming.

The music of the organ continues to blast through the night, the sound clear and crisp as if the instrument were next to me.

Five more minutes of walking, and I will be right there.

My walk is brisk, my mind solely on Amon. Yet I still keep my eyes on my surroundings, that ominous sensation continuing to assail me.

Two bright lights appear at the end of the road and my eyes widen as I spot a car coming my way.

Pulling the hood from my coat over my head, I move to the side of the road, hiding by a tree and waiting for it to pass.

If it's on this road, coming this way, then there is only one destination.

The Hale manor.

And who could be visiting at this hour?

For a moment I wonder if it's Caleb, but that theory is immediately disproved as I note the different car brand.

There are two men in the front. The inside of the car is faintly illuminated, and as it passes by me at a moderate speed, it's enough for me to get a clue as to the identity of the newcomers.

My eyes widen just as my jaw drops open as I realize I'd seen them before.

Both of them—though briefly.

They had been the two men visiting Fiona on behalf of the Supreme Authority. The ones that had given her the sword with which to defeat Amon.

But that...

That had been almost two hundred years ago. They should be dead and buried, regardless of their affiliation with the coven or the Supreme Authority.

Unless...

Dear God, why is this getting more and more complicated?

Because if those men are the same men who'd visited Fiona in seventeen ninety-one, then they are not regular people.

One thing is for sure: they are enemies.

When they've passed the Hale gates, I feel confident enough to resume my journey. The music continues to blare through the night, and somehow I am sure I am the only one able to hear it. Otherwise, the men would have stopped to check the source of the noise.

"Amon?" I ask on a whisper as I stop in front of the Old Church—just as imposing as I'd last seen it. If before I'd been a little frightened by its appearance, now a deep melancholy overtakes me as I take it in.

"You're here, aren't you?" I continue in a soft voice. "You've been here all along."

The wind picks up from all directions, and before I know it, the door to the church opens before me.

Shock flares in my breast, yet I don't question it.

I simply put one foot in front of the other, stepping inside the Old Church, ready to meet my beloved.

"I'm here," I tell him, emotion bursting in my chest. "I'm finally here, my love."

Then everything goes black.

Chapter Twenty-One

December 1795. Fairydale, Massachusetts

The snow has blanketed the entire courtyard, the horizon all white. I release a satisfied sigh as I huddle deeper into my blanket, cupping the hot cocoa in my palms.

"I have the cards," Amon declares as he enters the room.

"And I have your cup," I wink at him as I move from the window, taking a seat at the table by the fireplace and pushing his cup in front of him.

His brows go up in curiosity. Taking the cup from me, he brings it to his nose, inhaling deeply before taking his first sip.

"I still can't believe you've never had hot cocoa before."

"My palate is decidedly common," he chuckles. "But of course I will drink it if you've made it for me."

"So?" I look at him expectantly. "How is it?"

"Sweet," he pauses, his lips curling up in a smile. "Somehow it tastes like you," he drawls.

The rogue!

"You're such a charmer," I wave my hand at him, though a blush climbs up my cheeks.

His eyes sparkle at me as he takes another sip—this time bigger.

But as he puts the cup down, I can't help the giggle that escapes me.

"What?" He asks, a suddenly serious expression on his face.

Somehow that makes it worse, the brown stains from the cocoa resembling mustaches on his pale skin. And as he purses his lips, they move, too.

"What is it?" He repeats, thoroughly confused.

I barely manage to subdue my laugh as I stand up, still smiling as I head over to his side. Seeing me come to him, he pushes the table further away to allow me to sit on his lap, which I promptly do, wounding my arms around his neck.

"What are you finding amusement in, wife?" he demands in a low, gravelly tone that makes my insides tingle.

Giving him a mischievous look, I lean forward, licking the cocoa stains.

He keeps himself still as he lets me clean him thoroughly with my tongue.

Leaning back, I glance at his face, not surprised to find his eyes swirling red and black—as they do when his emotions are out of control.

A small gasp escapes me as I move against him. His hardness is poking in my backside, the heat emanating from him threatening to be my undoing.

Just as I see him about to pounce on me, I jump out of his lap, heading back to my seat as I take the deck of cards and start shuffling them.

His eyes are boring into me, the atmosphere tense, the air growing hotter.

"Let's play," I say, a little breathless.

Licking my lips, I taste the sweetness of the cocoa and that flavor that is specifically his.

"Here," I push his cards towards him when I note he isn't speaking, merely watching me intently. I take hold of my own, and I do my best to focus on the game.

Four years of being his wife—of being his in any way possible—and every time we're together still feels like the first time.

I'd never had great expectations about what marriage would entail. Especially considering the abysmal model my parents had set. But then I'd never imagined myself married to him—my Amon. I'd certainly never believed anyone could be as loving, attentive, or sweet as him.

Slowly, he takes his cards off the table, sparing them a brief glance before his eyes find mine again, the irises completely black.

As I try to focus on my own hand, I hear one whispered word.

"Run."

My eyes widen as I whip my gaze to him, finding him on the verge of snapping.

Pushing my chair back, I let my blanket drop as I start running, heading for the gallery and losing myself among the many sculptures.

Amon doesn't strain himself as he merely puts one foot in front of the other, trailing after me slowly. His lips are drawn into a predatory smile, his teeth gleaming dangerously.

My pulse picks up as I feel his energy swirl around us.

With his powers, he could easily find me in a second. But that's not what our game is about. It's all about the thrill and the slow build of the anticipation that now simmers in my veins.

My Amon is a born warrior, a predator that lives for the thrill of the chase.

Looking back, I note him walking slowly towards me, his hands slowly going to his shirt as he pops open the buttons.

I emulate his movements, my fingers pulling at the simple laces that hold my gown together. Just as he yanks his shirt off, I let my own dress pool to the floor, remaining in nothing but a cotton shift.

Next, his hands are on his trousers, and my breath catches in my throat, my belly tightening with desire.

I'm past the gallery when I look back to see him discard his pants on the cold tiled floor, standing before me entirely naked and aroused.

Slipping the straps of my shift off my shoulders I let it fall to the ground just as I step inside the conservatory.

There is a narrow path between beds of plants and flowers and I turn around, walking backwards as I zone in on him.

The scent from the flowers wafts towards me, the atmosphere intoxicating despite being the beginning of winter. But my husband would never neglect them. Knowing how much joy they bring me, he ensures that they are perfectly healthy all year round in spite of the ever changing climate.

The rule is simple.

Here, in our conservatory, no plant dies—ever.

As I reach the end of the path, he appears in the doorway, leaning against the wooden frame and giving me a languid smile as he lets his eyes roam all over my body, his gaze stopping on my breasts, the mark that mars my flesh and the necklace that completes me.

To give him a better show, I take a seat on the bench at the far end of the conservatory, my hands on my knees as I slowly part my legs for him.

A growl echoes in the enclosed space, the sound vibrating through me.

My lips pull in a smile as I let my eyes wander up and down his body, too. He is so deliciously masculine, I don't think I could ever get tired of the sight before me—not even for an eternity.

His tall form and well defined muscles make my mouth water. I study his wide shoulders and those strong arms that can snuff the life out of me, but can also give it back with one simple embrace. Going lower, his abdominals are as defined as that of a Greek God statue—even more so. They are equally as hard to the touch, but warm where the statues are cold.

He is all flesh and fire, masculine ferocity and predatory energy that gets my pulse to spike with desire laced by an ever present current of fear. Yet it's never that he will hurt me. It's that he will not reach for me—that he will not take me.

I lick my lips suggestively as my eyes go lower, to the hardness straining against his stomach, the size as daunting as the thick metal ring attached to the head.

"Lizzie," he rasps harshly.

Moisture accumulates at the junction of my thighs as I crook one finger, beckoning him closer.

He wastes no time in coming to me, and despite the strain of his muscles and the want that drips from his gaze, he is in no hurry. He takes his time as he slowly approaches me, all the while eating me up with his eyes.

"Where are you taking me for Christmas this year?" I murmur softly as he kneels in front of me.

His eyes close, his nostrils flaring as he brings his face to my body, inhaling my scent.

"A surprise," he says heavily, the tension mounting with every little movement as I wonder where he'll attack first.

"You won't tell me?" I ask in an innocent voice. "Not even if I..." I trail off as I bring my lips to his neck, parting them over his flesh and sucking it in before biting it gently. I repeat the action as I move down his chest. "Tell me..." I coax.

Every year, he surprises me with a destination for the Christmas celebrations since he knows how much I enjoy the holidays. Last year he'd taken me to Prussia and we'd attended a wonderful Christmas celebration, enjoying the buoyant market and local traditions.

"You little minx. You're trying to seduce it out of me, aren't you?" he chuckles, bringing his mouth to my ear and nibbling at my lobe. "It's called a secret for a reason, Lizzie mine. You won't get a word out of me."

"You know I do love a challenge," I tell him, my eyes sparkling with mischief.

He shakes his head in amusement, but catching him off guard, I push him down.

His back meets the floor, his eyes wide with curiosity as he sees me climb on top of him.

"I bet you I can change your mind," I say as I trace a finger down his rock hard muscles.

"And I want to see you try," he growls, almost in pain as I shift over his erection, placing the head of his cock between my wet folds, his ring brushing against my sensitive bud at the right spot. Moving up and down, I watch his features darken, his breathing intensifying.

I rest my palms on his hard pectorals as I increase the rhythm, feeling myself get closer and closer to that pinnacle.

My lips part as low moans escape me.

"That's it, Lizzie mine. Fuck, I love it when you take your pleasure from me," he groans, his hands cupping the sides of my hips, squeezing my flesh as he urges me on.

"Amon," I moan out loud as I shatter into a million pieces.

I barely come down from my high and I find myself on my back, his hand around my throat as he positions his cock at my entrance.

"Mrs. Creed!" A distant noise penetrates my euphoria-filled mind. Vaguely, I hear knocking and screaming.

But I don't have to say anything as Amon is already on his feet, materializing clothes for himself and for me. Dressing quickly, he leads me to the main entrance, his hand on the small of my back as he lays a kiss on my forehead.

"We'll resume this later," he whispers in my hair as he opens the door.

Mr. and Mrs. Dunn, a couple from the village, are waiting anxiously for us. Mrs. Dunn is holding her newborn baby close to her chest, her face red from the cold.

"Oh, Mrs. Creed," she bursts out when she sees me, tears appearing at the corners of her eyes. Her infant is crying uncontrollably in her arms, no matter how much she's trying to sway or pacify him.

"Come in," I tell them immediately, urging them inside by the fireplace. "Get warm first."

Amon is quietly standing behind me, letting me do the talking as usual.

I don't know if he has a hard time interacting with people who are not me, but he prefers to keep to the shadows, watching, observing.

Though he is the man of the manor, he relegates all the domestic power to me, telling me I can run the house as I see fit. That power also extends to the village and our interactions with the people living around us.

I know Amon prefers solitude, and for us to be separated from the world—all alone in our little bubble. But for me, he'd promised to make an effort. Especially as he knows I cannot sit by and watch people suffer when we have the ability to do something for it. Whether it is money, or medicine, or food, we're always willing to help.

After all, I'd told him long ago that I do not care for riches, or for what he is able to provide for me. I only care about him—*us*. The fact that we are together against all odds.

We could be paupers for all I care. Maybe we'd have to work a little harder, but the satisfaction at being together would be the same. The winters would be just as warm with the heat of his body alone.

"What is the matter?" I ask as I hurry to Mrs. Dunn's side.

"It's Little Johnny. He won't stop crying. He's been like this for the past two days and we haven't been able to calm him. He won't even nurse," she cries just as the baby continues to wail in her arms.

"I'm so sorry," I murmur. "May I?" I motion to the bundle in her arms.

She gives a brisk nod as she carefully places the baby in my arms.

His little face is a splotchy red from crying, his skin dry and dehydrated.

"Mayhap you could help him with a potion or something," Mrs. Dunn suggests coyly. "You helped Mrs. Saunders' baby a few months back and she's been telling everyone that you're a miracle healer," she fires rapidly at us, her husband nodding alongside her.

"I only work with what I know, Mrs. Dunn. I am familiar with medicinal plants, but I am no physician."

"Mr. Daniels already saw Little Johnny and he said he couldn't do anything," she sighs, dabbing the tears from her eyes. "You're our last chance, Mrs. Creed. If only he could eat something..."

"I'll see what I can do," I murmur, looking down into the sweet face of the infant crying in my arms.

My heart squeezes in my chest at the sight, and despite my best efforts, I can't help but find myself overwhelmed by emotion as I hold him tightly, swaying with him in an attempt to calm him.

"Come with me to the kitchen, will you?" I give her a tight smile as I lead her to the back of the house.

For all my knowledge of healing herbs, I must admit to not being an expert on children. After all, I have none of my own.

A hole opens in my very soul as that thought crosses my mind, an emptiness assailing me.

Amon is immediately there, his hand on my back as he gently massages my skin, his touch revitalizing. But even his presence fails to fill me with the usual joy as I am faced with my very failure.

"Shh, Little Johnny," I whisper, trying to think what could ail him.

It seems his fit of crying is so intense, he isn't able to get proper rest or nutrition. And when he wears himself out he only sleeps for a few hours before he's back to crying uncontrollably again.

"Can you do something?" Mrs. Dunn is watching me with a hopeful expression, the black circles under her eyes obvious. Both her and her husband have probably been unable to sleep due to Little Johnny's crying, and worry that this could be a symptom of something worse.

"I have a calming tincture. We could put a few drops on his tongue, maybe it will help?" I offer uncertainly.

Though I have treated plenty of people in the past, I am still wary about children since I have neither the experience nor knowledge. They are so small, gentle and frail that I always second guess myself when handling them. Yet despite that, I push forward, wanting to do my best so they can recover and be healthy.

Laying a kiss to his brow, I pass him to Mrs. Dunn while I grab my tincture.

"If you could hold his mouth open," I instruct her.

It takes us a few tries as Little Johnny becomes increasingly more agitated, but we manage to get some drops on his tongue, which he swallows.

"It's valerian-based, so it should help him calm down a little. But the effect is not immediate," I purse my lips.

"Thank you," Mrs. Dunn tells me sincerely. "Thank you so much, Mrs. Creed."

"Thank me if it works," I tell her tightly, inviting both her and her husband to our drawing room.

Since we don't generally hire staff during the winter, Amon takes over as he feeds the fire and prepares some hot tea for our guests.

"You're a wonder," I lean in to whisper as I see him carefully add the tea to the boiling water. What other man of his station would do this?

None.

But he is not intimidated by any type of work, lowly or otherwise. For him, a chore is a chore just like a person is a person. Despite passing himself off as a nobleman for a long time, he confessed that he has no affection for their station.

Setting a few teacups on a tray, I bring them to the drawing room.

Yet as we enter the room, I'm shocked to find it entirely quiet.

Mrs. Dunn sends me a shocked glance before looking down at her son who is currently nursing peacefully from her breast.

"You're a miracle, Mrs. Creed," she whispers, her throat clogged. "He... He's nursing. He hasn't nursed in so long," she sniffles a sob. "Thank you. Thank you," she bows her head.

They don't end up staying, deciding to go back home. But not before both give me their thanks again.

"It's true what they say about you, Mrs. Creed," Mr. Dunn stops in the doorway. "You're the village's fairy godmother," he tips his hat at me before they are both gone.

When the door closes, however, I slowly make my way to the drawing room, taking a seat by the fireplace. Amon, too, does the same, sitting opposite me.

"It was you, wasn't it?" I inquire softly.

"I don't know what you mean," he flashes me a smile.

"I know it was you," I smile. "That tincture could not have acted so fast, and I was already uncertain whether it would work or not."

"Does it matter? The baby is nursing, and should be fine from now on."

"You probed his mind, didn't you?" I continue, curious what he'd done.

He grunts.

"I merely infused his mind with tranquility," he confirms a moment later.

Releasing a weary sigh, I stand up, coming to his side and laying my head on his chest.

"Ah, Amon. We'll never be so blessed to have a child, will we?" I inquire softly, though I know the truth deep in my heart.

"Lizzie," he says my name in an anguished tone. "You know... I told you..."

"I know," I whisper, my spirits plummeting. "I know, and yet I still hope. How foolish is that of me?"

"It's not," he declares staunchly, wrapping his arms around me.

"I know it's impossible, but why do I still feel this deep disappointment in my heart whenever I see a babe? Rationally, I can accept it. But emotionally..." I trail off as my voice breaks.

"Goddamn it, Lizzie. This is all my fault," he rasps against me just as sobs rack my body. Slowly at first, before everything I'd held inside crashes down on me.

"No, Lizzie mine. Please, love, don't cry. You're breaking my heart," Amon murmurs.

"I..." hiccup, "can't..." hiccup, "stop..."

"Damn it," Amon curses as he brings his lips to my face, kissing my forehead, my eyes, before licking my tears with his tongue. "One day, Lizzie. One day we will have a child," he promises raggedly, even as he knows the words to be useless. But though they are for my benefit only, I find myself agreeing—even if it might be the height of delusion.

"We will, won't we?" I sniffle. "A piece of both of us," I continue, letting myself dream, just as the tears continue to pour down my cheeks.

My dear husband listens and soothes me, validating my hopes and dreams and promising me a better future.

Yet it all makes me feel even worse.

I have everything a person could ever want, yet I'm still dissatisfied.

What does that say about me?

It's why I always try to push these thoughts down and not dwell on my unhappiness, rather embrace what makes me happy.

Yet it's not easy when all around me people are having children. When all the women gather together to speak *about* their children. When in this world, the sole purpose of a woman is to bear children.

When I look at myself through that prism, I only see failure. Inadequacy.

And of course, there are those questions.

When are you having children?

You've been married quite some time already, when will the children come?

More often than not, the question is tinged with the unspoken—are you *ever* having children? And if the answer to that question is no, regardless of want, ability, or chance, then there must be something wrong with you.

Carefully picking me up in his arms, Amon flashes us back to our bedroom, placing me on the bed while he tends to the bathroom, fetching hot water and filling the tub with it.

When he is done, he undresses me slowly, lowering me into the bathtub before stepping back and removing his own clothes to join me.

My eyes are red from crying, my throat hurting with every little sound I make.

"Don't speak," Amon whispers softly as he caresses my cheek. "I'll take care of you, my sweet girl," he gives me a gentle smile. "I know what's missing from your life—from both our lives—but I'll do my best to fill that gap for you. I'll always do my best to make you the happiest you can be."

My lips tremble as I attempt a smile for his benefit.

"I am. You're the only thing in my life that brings me joy, Amon. Now and ever. You know that, don't you?" I push down my sadness so I can be present in the moment.

More than anything, I shouldn't be selfish about this—not when it's something that affects both of us. It's not only me that cannot have children, but him, too. We're both in the same situation and though he doesn't always voice his sadness I know it to be just as great as mine.

Oh, God, but what a wonderful father Amon would make.

He would be absolutely magnificent. I am sure of it.

He brings the soap to my skin, slowly lathering it on my skin.

I let out a small purr as I give myself over to the sensation of his hands on my body, his presence the only balm to my battered heart.

Amon can sense the turmoil in my heart and as is his nature, he tries to overcompensate by making me happy in whatever way he can. God, but I know he would give me the moon in the sky if I asked for it. Yet for all his powers, we're both useless in the face of fickle fate.

"I love you," I tell him later as he lays me in bed, hugging me close to him.

"I love you too, Lizzie mine. Always."

Though we don't speak of the issue again, it remains looming in the horizon, my mood slowly going downhill the more I dwell on it.

Our first year of marriage had been absolutely perfect. I'd been so lost in the happiness of the present that I hadn't spared a moment's thought to the fact that I was not getting pregnant. After all, that was something taken for granted with a married couple. And with the frequency of our bedroom activities, I'd thought it a given that it should happen at some point.

Until I started questioning *why* it wasn't happening.

He was spilling his seed inside of me every coupling, yet nothing seemed to take root.

It was when the second year mark was approaching that I finally mustered the courage to ask him if there was something wrong with me.

Though he'd told me all about our past, he hadn't mentioned one detail.

The fact that I could never have children.

As I'd heard the explanation, I understood the ramifications of the decision, and that I'd given that up to be with him. And so because I *had* him, I didn't dare think too much on it, on the off chance regret would surge forward.

If someone mentioned children, I would push the thought down.

If someone asked me questions about children, I put on a smile and changed the topic.

Even in my own head, I did my best to thrust that topic aside.

Yet because I'd stifled my own desires for so long, once they reached the surface, they couldn't be contained anymore.

Amon, my sweet husband, does his best to cheer me up. He senses that I'm drifting farther and farther away—from him, from us, from everything—so he doubles his efforts to help me overcome this rough patch.

Except things get exponentially worse when I receive a letter from my mother the day before Christmas.

"What's wrong?" Amon's eyes widen as he comes across me, tear-eyed and inconsolable.

"My sister and her husband are dead," I whisper bleakly, still unable to fully internalize information. "Of course, due to the timing of the letter, they've already been dead for weeks."

"I'm so sorry," he immediately comes to my side, taking me in his arms.

"The children, Amon. What will they do? My mother says she will take them in, but she doesn't seem quite certain of it," I add on a trembling voice.

"How old are they?"

"The boys are ten and twelve. The youngest is only a few months old."

He's silent for a few moments before he offers his suggestion—one that makes my heart swell with hope in my chest.

"What if we took them in?"

I draw back, blinking in surprise.

"You're... You're serious? You wouldn't mind that?"

He shakes his head.

"It would be nice to have some young ones around the house, wouldn't it?" he smiles. "I'm sure we could manage the logistics. I'd probably have to change my hairstyle," he chuckles, referring to the fact that everyone knows Jeremiah Creed to be dark-haired.

"Tell me you're not joking about this," I breathe out in awe.

"I would never," he tells me vehemently. "In fact, why don't we go back to England on Monday? We can say we were already en-route to visit and we didn't get the letter and you can convince your mother to give us custody of the children."

"Amon," I pause, my voice crackling from too much emotion. "You're so good to me. Thank you. Thank you," I tell him profusely as I palm his cheeks, laying a hard kiss on his lips. "I love you. So, so much. Thank you," I repeat.

Though I am undoubtedly sad to hear of my sister's passing—in a carriage accident no less—I can't help but think this might be our only chance in life to be parents.

I'd met the boys when they were younger, but it's been four years. I do hope they are agreeable to live with us.

As promised, Amon transports us to London on the following Monday. We don't immediately go visit my mother as we need to procure lodgings first and Amon needs to change his look.

When we visit the following day, my mother is thrilled to see us, but she is clearly deeply upset about Olivia's passing. And I can't blame her. She's always been her favorite, and she was going to carry on the family legacy within the coven.

With my bound abilities, I can't even count as second best.

We give our condolences, after which I ask my mother for a private meeting.

"Oh, Elizabeth, it's so good you're here," she sighs. "I've been going crazy with grief by myself. Your brother is away at Cambridge and I've been beside myself with worry for the children. I'm already in my fifties as it is. I can't raise another brood—a baby no less!"

I nod, giving her my sympathies, and nodding along to everything she says. Somehow, I know I won't even have to suggest the custody issue since she is well on her way to do so.

"You and Jeremiah don't have any children," she bits her lip, her eyes teary. "Wouldn't you be better off taking care of them than me?" she finally asks on a tentative note. "Can't you ask your husband about it?"

I pretend to mull it over for a minute.

"My husband would be fine with it, mother. We'd love to have the children around if they didn't mind moving across the ocean..." I trail off.

That is my only doubt regarding this entire situation. The boys are old enough to know what they are leaving behind and I would never dream about splitting the siblings up if they do not agree to come together.

"They will," she's quick to assure me, and I realize she truly does not want to worry about them. "The only condition I have," she pauses, her cheeks red. "When Lydia comes of age, you'll have her visit me? She needs to learn about her heritage and the legacy she's carrying on her shoulders."

"Of course," I give her a tight smile.

"The boys already know more or less," she continues, and my eyebrows go up in surprise.

Well, it seems I was the only one who did not know anything.

"They do?"

"Olivia wanted them to know from early on," she releases a loud sniffle. "Mind you, it's never a prerequisite for men to be told in our family, but we prefer to do it so they can be aware of what's happening around and, at times, offer protection. Olivia knew she would have a daughter at some point and she wanted them to be ready and know that their mission is to protect her."

"That's a very good idea," I nod. "Do you know what gifts Lydia might have?"

"Goodness, no. It's too early. She's only three months old, Elizabeth. But the moment she exhibits her first gifts you must write to me, alright?"

"Of course."

We spend a little more time talking and delineating everything she wants me to know, and in an act of unprecedented kindness, she offers some books from her collection.

"To guide Lydia," she nods.

Knowing how keen my mother is on her coven business, and especially on having someone to carry the name further, it seems entirely too odd that she would let me raise Lydia an ocean away.

Yet as I dwell on that a little more, my questions are answered over dinner, when Fiona introduces a certain General Powell, who happens to be a friend of hers.

Of course, the manner in which they behave is clearly *more* than friendly, and I soon understand why she wouldn't have time for children.

That isn't to say I'm begrudging her for it. After surviving my father, she deserves to be happy in any way she can. If this General can do that, then I will be supporting her decision.

But even as the issue with my mother is solved, there is still the matter of the children.

"I'm not taking them with us if they don't agree, Amon," I tell him the night before we are to meet them. "What if the boys don't like us? What if they don't want to move to America? There are so many things at stake..."

"What is there not to like about you, love? You're the warmest person I know. They will love you just as I do and I am sure they will eventually get used to the move. Certainly, they must still be in shock after the death of their parents, so we can only go at their pace."

"You're right," I nod, placing my head on his chest. "I feel so bad, you know," I breathe out, feeling a sliver of discomfort.

"Why?" he asks, his chest rumbling with deep vibrations.

"My sister just died and all my thoughts are on the children. I feel a little...selfish," I admit.

"Lizzie..."

"It's true. I've barely had time to mourn her before we set out with this plan. Not to say that I'm not happy about it, but I feel guilty getting this small happiness while my sister and her husband are gone. The children lost *their* parents..." I trail off, not knowing how to put into words what I'm feeling.

There's a mix of sadness, guilt and joy all mingled together and I don't know on which to focus.

Do I succumb to grief? Or do I try to forget and focus on the positives—making sure the children are well?

The questions seems to be harder to answer the next day when Amon and I meet them.

My mother isn't present, but she'd left instructions to the wet nurse to present Lydia to me. The boys are still at Haversham, but she'd sent word out for them to be returned to London as soon as possible.

"You do know our entire life is going to change from now on," I whisper to Amon as we anxiously wait to meet Lydia.

"For the better," he winks at me, giving me an assuring hand squeeze.

"My Lady," a girl curtsies as she comes into the room carrying the babe.

"I'm Mrs. Creed now," I wave my hand.

Curiosity eats at me as I bite my lip, waiting for her to come closer.

"This is baby Lydia," she says as she hands her to me.

Amon is behind me, his body heat enveloping me as he shows his silent support.

Carefully, I take her into my arms, my heart immediately bursting with love as I look into her sweet face.

She has a tuft of dark hair on top of her head, her eyes a deep blue. As she takes me in, her eyes grow wide, just as her mouth spreads into a big grin. She's the prettiest baby I've ever seen and God...now she's mine.

"Hello, Lydia," I coo softly, and she releases a giggle as she takes my hand in hers, her small palm curling around my finger.

"Look," I tell Amon, my lashes wet with tears of happiness.

"I think she likes you," he whispers, his eyes equally as entranced as he looks down at her. "She looks like you, Lizzie."

"She does, doesn't she?" I murmur, still shocked by the intimacy of the moment and the pure emotion that bursts forth in my chest.

"Is it crazy that I already love her?" I ask stupefied by my own reaction to the baby.

"Never," he shakes his head.

I cradle her to my chest for what feels like forever before I turn to my husband.

"Here, you can hold her, too," I wipe my eyes and nose as I hold her out for him.

He looks slightly alarmed as his gaze swings between me and the babe.

"Hold her like this," I show him how to hold her head, and he gives me a brisk nod.

Though still a little uncertain, Amon picks Lydia up with so much care, you wouldn't think he's a powerful warrior with extraordinary abilities. And when he holds her closer to his chest, cradling her little head and gazing down at her, I know I've fallen in love with him again.

Tears spring in my eyes anew as I realize this is what I've been wanting all along.

A family.

This family.

"She's our daughter now," Amon whispers in awe.

"She is. And she will be very, very loved," I add, dabbing at my tears.

We spend more time with her as she laughs at every little gesture we make before her wet nurse tells us she must take her nap.

Reluctantly, we part with her for the rest of the afternoon so she can get her sleep.

Unfortunately, due to the fact that we'll be traveling with the children, too, we will have to go back to America via ship, which will not be the most pleasant process, especially for a baby.

With Lydia sleeping, Amon and I decide to head out and do some shopping for the voyage and ensure we have everything we need. I am particularly excited about getting some fabrics for baby Lydia to make her little outfits.

"You can buy those, too, you know," Amon mentions when we get to a fabric shop.

"What's the joy in that? I've always wanted to make baby clothes from scratch. I just..."

Never had the chance, or hope before.

He purses his lips, giving me a tight smile.

We go from shop to shop to get everything I had in mind. Amon trails behind me, putting up with all my whims in a way that I start feeling sorry for him.

"You didn't need to accompany me, you know," I add when I see him blank out at the milliner.

"And leave you alone?" he narrows his eyes at me. "Never."

Shaking my head at him, I proceed to pick a few hats for everyone in the family. As we get to pay, I notice the clerk is a little sluggish, his gaze drifting from the hats to me and back to the hats.

For a moment I wonder if he thinks I cannot afford them since I'm not wearing the most fashionable clothes at the moment.

Yet a low, ominous sound from behind me takes me completely by surprise.

"Did you just growl?" I ask on a whisper.

"He was looking at you too much," he shrugs, his tone biting.

The clerk, seeing Amon put his arm over my shoulder in a way that is entirely improper, blushes profusely before packing all the other hats with renewed swiftness.

Realizing the clerk somehow triggered him, I simply take his arm as we head out with our purchases, deciding to call it a day. After all, I cannot wait to get back to baby Lydia.

We spend the rest of the day with her, watching the wet nurse and learning everything I can from her despite the fact that she will have to join us—Lydia still needs to nurse.

Yet it's the following day that has me on pins and needles when we're told the boys have arrived from Haversham.

Though I'd met them before, I want to introduce them to Amon as well, and make sure they are comfortable with the arrangement.

At noon, we're called to the drawing room. Their governess is with them, instructing them to be polite.

"Hello," I add tentatively.

"Say hello, boys, and introduce yourselves," the governess chides.

"Hello, I am Abraham," the elder of the boys says, a small smile on his lips.

The other, though, doesn't seem inclined to say anything.

Abraham elbows him in the side.

"I am Abel," he mutters under his breath.

I give them both a wide smile. From the first, I can tell that Abel will be the hardest to get across. But I decide to make it my mission to get both boys to accept us.

"I am your aunt, Elizabeth, and this is my husband," I motion towards Amon. "We're so sorry about Olivia and Jonathan's passing," I add, pursing my lips. "We were wondering if you'd like to come live with us."

Both of them are silent, only looking at us.

Wetting my lips, I feel my anxiety climbing as I try to find the right words for them.

"What your aunt is trying to say is that I have a castle in America and we'd very much like you to join us. There's a lot of space to fill," Amon winks at them.

Abraham chuckles, but Abel maintains the same aloof expression.

"Will Lydia come, too?" Abraham asks.

"Of course," I nod. "She's just a baby and she needs a mother. I was hoping I could fill that role for her," I explain carefully. "That doesn't mean that I'm trying to replace your parents in any way. But if you'd let us, we'd love to welcome you into the family."

"If Lydia's coming, I'm coming too," Abraham declares, looking at Abel for his opinion.

"I'm coming," he grumbles under his breath, seemingly unconvinced.

We spend some time with them describing our life in America and what they can expect by moving in with us.

Amon does most of the talking and by the end of the day, he has both Abraham and Abel eating from his hand, despite the fact that the younger one still seems a little reticent.

Yet as our preparations come to an end, it's time to head back home.

No one is looking forward to close to a month of travel aboard a ship. But as we book a full suite on a passenger ship, I'm grateful for the close quarters as we can become more acquainted with the children.

During the day, I'm mostly busy with Lydia while Amon plays games with the boys, teaching them different card games and amazing them with his infinite knowledge.

As I watch him with them, I can't help but smile and feel myself fulfilled for the first time in a long time.

It takes us a little under a month to get to Boston, after which we take the train to Ipswich and hire a hackney to take us home.

The kids are becoming increasingly excited as they see the surroundings, especially when we get to the manor. Both Abraham and Abel are sporting awed expressions as we get out of the carriage.

"So, what do you think of our little castle?" Amon asks them as we walk towards the entrance.

"It's...not little," Abel answers, and we all laugh.

Despite a slightly rocky beginning as we are all accommodating to living together, things go much, much better than I'd ever expected.

The most marked difference is the next year during Christmas, when Lydia has already taken her first steps and spoken her first word.

Mama.

To quantify the joy I felt at hearing that would be blasphemous.

For one moment in time, I'd felt happier than I've ever been.

We haven't made any demands of the boys, though, and we are pleased to have them call us aunt and uncle.

"Are you happy, Lizzie?" Amon asks me late that Christmas night. Draped around him after a bout of fervent lovemaking, I nuzzle my face in the crook of his neck as I wrap my arms and legs around him, keeping him to myself.

"I've never been happier," I confess, kissing his skin. "And it's all because of you and everything you've done for me. You are the best father I could have ever hoped for and," I pause to drag in a deep breath. These damn tears just won't stop falling. "Watching you with the boys and with Lydia warms my heart like nothing else," I whisper.

"Ah, Lizzie mine," he rasps, cupping my face in his big hands and pulling me back so I can watch the raw emotion on his face. "Your happiness is *my* happiness. But this past year," he swallows hard. "I never knew one could be this happy."

My lips pull up in a smile as I gaze at him.

"As long as we're together, we'll always be like this," I murmur.

"Always," he whispers, bringing his lips to mine in a searing kiss.

Chapter Twenty-Two

Late September 1805. Fairydale, Massachusetts

"The children are out for the day," Amon says as he closes the door with his foot, mischief crackling in his eyes.

"Are they?" I breathe out in anticipation, slowly dragging myself out of bed.

I'm wearing a loose cotton nightgown and as I push the strings off my shoulder, it slowly falls to the ground.

His eyes meet mine with intense longing before his gaze travels down my body.

"I promised you a birthday gift, my husband, did I not?" I ask as I take a step towards him, sinuously moving my body to distract his attention.

His throat bobs up and down as he gives me a nod of assent, yet he can't seem to take his eyes off me.

"And what..." he clears his throat. "What did you have in mind?"

"Another episode for your collection," I whisper when I'm in front of him.

Giving him a knowing smile, I move to the right as I remove his painting supplies from the drawer I'd stashed them in.

Amon's eyes widen in surprise.

With time, I've learned to shield my mind so I can surprise him every now and then. And watching his expression, I know it's worth all the effort.

"You..." he swallows hard. "You'll let me paint you again?"

"Yes," I answer as I move back to the bed, lifting myself up while still watching him intently. "But this time, I'm in control."

"Fuck, Lizzie mine," he groans. "You're killing me," he says in a pained tone.

Beckoning him closer, I watch as he takes a pencil and a blank canvas before he moves toward me.

Shuffling in bed, I rise to my knees, moving to the edge of the bed as I slide my hands down his robe, getting a hold of the tie that holds the material together and pulling on it.

He doesn't take his eyes off me as he helps me take it off him until he's left only in a pair of silky pants, his erection unmistakable as it strains against the material.

"Show me," he rasps. "Show me what's in that lovely head of yours."

A sneaky smile pulls at the corners of my mouth as I let my hands roam over his hard chest.

"What do you think I have in mind?" I ask on a seductive drawl.

As I bring my cheek against the front of his pants, nuzzling my flesh against that part of him and inhaling his musky scent, so male and so breathtaking, I already feel myself on the edge. But this is all for him—only for him.

I've been anticipating this moment for far too long. Ever since I'd seen the rapt expression on his face as he'd painted me while he was deep inside me, I knew I wanted to prepare a special treat for his birthday—the one day where he is the only one on the receiving end.

Opening my mouth on top of the material, I suck lightly on the head of his cock before I trace his outline with my tongue.

A hiss escapes him, his eyes snapping closed. Moving the pencil in his other hand, he threads his fingers through my hair, massaging my scalp as he urges me on.

"Today is my day to worship you," I whisper, looking up at him and letting him see all the naked desire in my eyes—the fact that I'm dying to touch and please him.

"Lizzie," he rasps, biting back a curse as he opens his mouth on a labored breath. "You know you don't..."

"Shh," I whisper, hooking my fingers on the band of his pants and pulling down. "Anything that gives you pleasure gives *me* pleasure," I murmur lovingly.

His cock springs free, the length slapping against his stomach just as he releases a harsh groan. I lick my lips as desire pools low in my belly, arousal dripping from me as I take him in.

He's so beautiful. So male. And all mine.

I've never failed to be astounded that this man is all mine. Mine to touch, kiss, and hold dear. He's *only* mine and will only ever be mine.

His muscles strain just as his cock twitches, moisture accumulating at the tip. His ring gleams in the dim lighting, the evidence of his eternal commitment never failing to get me all hot and bothered, goosebumps erupting all over the surfaces of my skin as my core tingles with awareness.

I waste no time in putting my hands on him, touching him, trailing my fingers lightly all over his shaft, and marveling all over again at the velvety feel of his skin and the warmth emanating from him.

Repeating the action from before, I bring my cheek against his erection, brushing my flesh against his in the barest touch as I continue to inhale his musky scent.

A small tremor goes through him, his breathing intensifying as I nuzzle my cheek against his length.

"Ah, Lizzie. My beautiful Lizzie," the words slip from his mouth as he continues to pet my head, twirling his fingers through my hair and encouraging me to continue what I'm doing.

"I love the feel of you, Amon," I whisper as I bring my lips to his skin, trailing reverent kisses all over the surface. "The sight. The smell. Everything."

He groans when I reach the tip, swiping the moisture with my tongue.

"Fuck, Lizzie," he hisses as I lightly lap at him, slow and precise movements that I know will get the most out of him. "Your lips on my cock and I'm done," he says harshly. "Your pretty mouth swallowing my cock and I'm fucking done."

"Not yet," I reply cheekily, winking at him.

Bringing my hand to the base of his shaft, I palm his balls with the other one, kneading softly while I lavish attention to the tip with my mouth, wetting it thoroughly and getting him mindless with frustration.

When he's almost wild with want, I give him a long lick from base to tip before I wrap my lips around the head, his ring clanking against my teeth as I suck him in.

"Fuuuck," he curses out.

"Like this," I say as I move back an inch, lathering his cock in my saliva. "Paint me like this. At your mercy with your cock in my mouth. Paint me like this, Amon," I tell him fervently, knowing this will give him the most pleasure.

"Lizzie," he calls my name in a stained voice. "Is that what you want? To paint you choking on my cock? With it so far down your throat that tears will fall down your pretty cheeks?"

I nod, my eyes on his as I get lost in the intensity of his words.

"Lass, you do know how to turn a man's fantasies to life," he continues, his eyes the deepest shade of black as he regards me. "And when I'm done, I'll fuck you in a room surrounded by all these paintings so you can see yourself taken in all ways as I lay claim to your sweet body again and again. What do you say, Lizzie mine?" he drawls dangerously, the corners of his mouth quirking up as he looks at me with the same predatory hunger I'd seen on his face from the beginning.

Will this ever abate, I wonder? This volcanic desire I feel inside of me—that *he* feels?

Years pass, and I find myself wanting him more and more, never less.

"Yes," I breathe out. "Yes, Amon, yes!"

Anything for him.

Being with him for so long, I've found that no act is wrong, no desire forbidden. I'm always willing to push my limits for him just as I push his. In our bedroom, it's only us. Only ever us and the love we have for one another that translates into an insatiable desire that burns stronger every single time.

"My darling girl. Show me how deep you take me," he rasps as he brings his cock to my lips again, pushing it in my mouth.

I open wide as I take him in, letting him thrust into me until his ring hits the back of my throat. Gagging, I look up just as my lashes dampen with unshed tears, my gaze on his just as his pencil hits the blank canvas, his strokes quick and masterful.

"Gods, you take me so good," he praises. "Your mouth was made for my cock just like my cock was made for you, darling girl. Made to claim every fucking inch of your body."

His hips tilt, rocking into me as he feeds me as much of his length as he can fit into my mouth. Still, I don't make a sound even when he is too deep. I let him use me as he wants—as I know he *needs.*

Lips parted, his eyes are half-lidded as he breathes harshly, fucking my mouth while laying down the contours of my form on the canvas.

"That's it, Lizzie," he rasps, and once the first sketch is finalized, he materializes the canvas and the pencil out of his hands and on the table opposite the bed. Suddenly, his hands are on my face, cupping gently as he pulls out all the way, wetness dripping all over his length as he lets the ring cling to my lips.

"You're so beautiful, love," he murmurs as he strokes my hair. "So fucking beautiful and all mine," he says before he pushes his cock inside my mouth again, the thrust shallow.

I extend my tongue, licking the underside every time he pushes it in my mouth.

My eyes are on his face as I admire every slight change in expression, every twitch in his jaw and the grind of his teeth—everything that tells me how much I affect him.

"Good girl," he rumbles. "My very special girl."

"More," I whisper as I lick him fervently. "Use me, Amon. Fill me up and use me for your pleasure."

"When you say things like that, Lizzie mine," he moans as he squeezes his eyes shut. "You inflame me," he confesses. "You fucking make me lose all reason until there's only you. My good, good girl who is only bad for me, isn't that right?"

"Yes," I admit unabashedly. "I'm only bad for you. I'll only ever be bad for you," I moan as I wrap my hands tightly around him, sucking the head into my mouth before allowing him to fuck me as he wants—wildly and out of control.

His hands go down to my throat, circling my neck in a light hold as he starts thrusting. Slow at first, he gains more and more speed, grunting as the head of his cock reaches the tight space at the back of my throat.

I hum lightly around his cock, the vibrations giving him additional pleasure.

"That's my bad girl," his breath catches in his throat as he throws his head back. "Fucking hell, Lizzie mine. You own me. You fucking own me. Body and soul and everything else that I am," he mumbles, almost incoherently.

Moving my hands to his ass, I let him fully take control as he chases his pleasure.

God, how I love it when he uses me like this, when I'm the only thing that can make him feel good—a medium through which he can reach his peak. And as I lose myself in his features, I forget all about gagging or choking or the tears that fall unbidden down my red cheeks. There's only him before me.

Amon.

My lover, my protector and my master.

For him I would do anything. For his happiness, I'm capable of anything.

One hand remains tightened around my neck while the other goes up, tangling in my hair and pulling my head back.

His eyes collide with mine as blackness stains the white of his eyes until everything is black. Dark currents surround us as he watches me, a mix of lust, want, and unyielding tension that tells me just who is in control.

I may have fooled myself into thinking I was the one leading this, but that role belongs entirely to him.

"Just like that. Suck on it like the bad girl you are, Lizzie—*my* bad girl."

Just as I think he's going to come, he suddenly pulls out of my mouth.

I inhale sharply through my mouth, dragging a harsh breath into my lungs just as he pushes my hands aside.

My eyes widen, yet it's not in shock but pure anticipation as I cannot wait to see what he's going to do next.

His left hand curves alongside my neck, palming my nape as he holds me tightly to him. His other hand grips the base of his cock, bringing the length against my face as he smears all the wetness on my skin.

"How bad will you be today, Lizzie mine?" he asks me in a hypnotic voice. "Tell me, where should I come?"

His arresting gaze has me pinned to the spot and I find myself at a loss of words, simply staring into his beautiful features ravaged by the most extreme lust.

He slaps his shaft lightly across my cheek and my lips. His mouth has an arrogant tilt as he taunts me with the promise of his release.

"Should I come down your throat?" he drawls, pushing an inch of his cock between my lips. He only lets me give him a couple licks before he moves. "Should I come on your beautiful face?" he continues, dragging the tip across my face. "Or," he pauses as he licks his lips. "Should I come on your lovely tits?"

I gasp at his question, but before I know it, his fingers tighten over my nape and he looms dangerously close to my face.

He licks my lips, giving me a maddening kiss before he pulls back—too, too fast.

"Cup your tits, Lizzie. Hold them for me and play with your nipples," he suddenly commands.

Though the thick fog of awareness makes it hard for me to think straight, I slowly bring my hands to my breasts, squeezing them before I pinch my nipples.

His features darken.

"Fucking hell," he curses, his eyes glued to my chest as he strokes his cock in slow, languorous movements.

Arching my back as I thrust my breasts forward, he takes advantage of the position to slip the head of his cock between the valley of my breasts.

My breath hitches as I feel him there, and bringing my breasts together, I create a tight and hot environment for him as he starts thrusting.

"That's it, my bad Lizzie," he rasps.

"Amon," I moan as I touch myself while he takes his pleasure from my body. "Come on me. Everywhere," I breathe out. "Cover me in your seed."

"Ahhh, Lizzie mine. You want to feel me everywhere, don't you? You want to smell of me everywhere you go so no one can ever doubt who you belong to," he pauses on a groan as he increases the rhythm of his thrusts.

I keep my breasts together for him, and when he releases his hold on my neck, I dip my chin down, licking him every time he surges forward.

A string of curses are wrenched out of his mouth as my teeth catch his ring, holding it in my mouth for a moment before opening my lips over the tip of his cock and sucking.

"You're so fucking hot," he moans harshly, his features tight as his climax builds. "I just need to look at you and those fucking pouty lips of yours and I'm about to burst, Lizzie. You drive me so fucking insane with want," he rasps. "You're my fucking madness, the fever in my blood, a never fucking ending psychosis that leaves me breathless, helpless and so fucking weak with want for you."

His words arouse me to no end and when he rips himself from me with a biting curse, I present myself to him.

"I'm your canvas," I whisper, my fingers on my nipples. "Paint me, Amon. Paint me," I moan as I meet his crazed gaze with my dazed one.

He furiously works his cock, his grip tight as his muscles tense with his impending release.

Ready to receive everything that he is, I drag myself closer to the edge of the bed just in time for the first spurts of cum to hit my face before going lower to my neck and chest.

He comes so hard in never-ending jets of cum as he marks me all over. His grunts become louder as he paints my entire front in his seed, turning me into his very own canvas, his creation.

"Just like that, Lizzie mine. Take my cum. Take everything that I am," he grinds out as he finishes.

"Yes," I reply in a breathless voice.

There are still a few drops hanging on to the tip, so I lean forward to catch them with my tongue, sucking him in and cleaning every inch of his cock.

He's barely in control of himself, his breathing harsh, his eyes still full of lust.

Giving him a come hither look, I lean back, falling on my elbows. Still holding his gaze, I bring one finger to where he'd come on my face, swirling the semi-white liquid all around my flesh before dipping my fully coated finger in my mouth.

I do the same with the remaining seed on my neck, but when I reach my breasts he suddenly stops me.

Gathering his cum with his own thicker, bigger fingers, he brings them to my mouth, pushing every last drop inside my mouth.

But just as I think I have his trajectory figured out, he surprises me by flinging my legs over his shoulders and burying his head between my legs.

His tongue connects with my bundle of nerves and I barely keep myself from jumping out. I'm already overstimulated that even one touch can set me off.

"You're so fucking wet," he growls against my center. "All for me," he hums as he catches my bud between his teeth.

"Yes. Oh, Amon," I writhe under him.

"All from sucking my cock. Because you're a bad, bad girl who gets off on being face-fucked by her mate," he rasps, blowing hot air against my wet slit.

"Yes. Yes. Yes," I mumble incoherently.

I only need two flicks of his tongue and I'm already coming, squeezing him tightly between my legs as my hands find their way to his hair, gripping tight as I scream his name.

The orgasm is so powerful, I barely catch my breath as I fall against the crisp sheets, too worn out to do anything.

"Lizzie mine, Lizzie mine," he whispers against my inner thigh before he continues to lap at me.

"I-I can't..." I wheeze out. But he isn't deterred. He's determined to wring everything out of me until I'm a quivering mess—until I can't even utter another word.

My eyes snap shut and before I know it, sleep claims me.

I don't know how much later I wake up, but when I open my eyes, I find myself completely cleaned up—the sweetheart must have given me a bath while I was out. Amon is sitting on the chair opposite to the bed.

He's still naked. Dipping his brush into his color palette, he brings it to the canvas in elegant, smooth strokes.

"You're awake?" He raises a brow, an arrogant smirk playing at his lips.

"How many times did you make me come?" I yawn languidly as I get out of bed, pulling a robe over my body.

"You passed out on the fourth," he chuckles. "I think you need more practice, Mrs. Creed," he winks at me.

"I rather like Mrs. d'Artan better," I quip as I make my way to his side.

"What's in a name, love," he murmurs lovingly as he lays a kiss to the top of my head. "You would be mine under any other name. Just like I would be yours."

My lips tip up in a smile, but as I take in his painting, I can't help but gasp.

"That is..." I trail off, suddenly at a loss of words. "You made me so beautiful," I whisper.

"You *are* beautiful. But with my cock in your mouth..." he whistles suggestively.

I chuckle, swatting him playfully as I continue to study his work.

He'd painted us perfectly as I lay naked before him, my lips wrapped around his cock and my eyes on him—always on him.

"You're so talented," I praise sincerely.

He merely grunts.

For a fearsome general such as he, his passion for painting had not been something he'd been able to indulge at will. Not until he'd gotten here.

Not until us.

I feel sad that this world will never know his talent, but he insists on making me the subject of all his paintings, and given the intimate nature of the poses, neither he, nor I would ever want these made public.

They are for our eyes only. For our enjoyment.

Later in the afternoon, the children come back from their little ocean adventure and we set about preparing for the celebration that will take place the following day when our tiny village will finally be upgraded to the designation of town with a new name.

Fairydale.

The town council had come together to vote on it, and to my dismay, everyone had wanted to name it Fairydale for Amon and I and the help we've lent to the people of the area.

It won't just be a celebration of the town, but it will also be a personal one for us.

We finally belong somewhere!

Unfortunately, the future will be challenging. It's been almost fifteen years since we've moved here, and considering that neither Amon, nor I, have grown any older, people are bound to start asking questions at some point.

When we decided to have a family and raise our children here, we had to consider the implications, and so we came to the agreement that once Lydia is settled at her home, we would take some years and travel around the globe before returning with new identities.

Amon has already taken his *aging* role seriously, and has slowly renounced his darker hair in favor of white, his natural hair color.

The following morning, we all wake up early in preparation for the town fair.

Giving Amon a quick kiss on the lips, I leave him to deal with the boys while I go help Lydia dress.

To my great surprise, instead of finding her still abed and hard to get her out of bed, she's already up and spry.

"Mommy, mommy," she squeals when she sees me, jumping straight in my arms.

"You're rather cheerful this morning, aren't you?" I chuckle as I kiss both her cheeks.

"It's the fair. Of course I'm happy. I can't wait to see the sign, and I want to eat some yummy food."

"You're saying it as if we don't give you any yummy food."

"Well," she pauses, deep in thought. "It's not that. It's just that food on special occasions tastes better than the same food on normal days."

"You're so witty, aren't you?" I pat her head affectionately as I open her closet, asking her what she'd like to wear.

"Lydia?" I repeat when I see she doesn't reply.

She's deadly still next to me, and immediately, my worry mounts.

Going to my knees, I take her cheeks in my palms, looking her all over.

"Didi, baby, what's wrong?"

Her eyes are out of focus even as she looks at me.

"He will wait for you. At the Old Church, he will wait for you. He will always wait for you."

What? What Old Church? There is only one church in the village, down the hill from our home.

As soon as the words are out of her mouth, she recovers, blinking as she takes me in.

Immediately I realize that she likely had a vision, though she's never reacted like this before.

Since she started speaking, she would always blurt out things that never happened or that were not real and we didn't know what to make of them. That was until they did come to pass and we realized it was her gift that was manifesting through visions of the future.

"Lydia, baby, who will wait for me?" I ask softly.

"Papa," she answer, a sad smile on her face. "He will wait for you to defeat the bad people and save him."

"Me?" I smile. "I'll save him?"

She nods.

"But I'm not there," she suddenly says, and her face falls.

"Didi..." I trail off, pulling her into my arms. "Don't say that. We'll always be together, you know that," I tell her gently.

"We won't," she replies. "But it's fine, mommy. You have a more important mission to fulfill," she adds ambiguously.

Just as I'm about to question her some more, she jumps out of my arms, going to her closet and rummaging for a dress to wear.

I try to plaster on a smile, though her words worry me.

My Didi has never been a normal child. The visions she has affect the way she interacts with the world, often giving her a far more mature and jaded outlook than she should have for her years.

When my mother heard about her gift she was beside herself with happiness. She even visited once a few years back, but since she has remarried she's been more preoccupied with her marital life than with the coven. For the first time, I think she's truly in love and has found someone who cherishes her just as much.

"This one," she takes out a pretty yellow gown.

I smile appreciatively at her choice.

"Let's put it on, then."

I help her into her gown, after which I spend some time doing her hair, plaiting it in a simple braid. Since she'd seen me wear mine like that, she'd demanded I do hers too in the same manner.

"Look how pretty you are," I gush when she's done.

"I love it," she declares, putting on her shoes and telling me she's ready to go.

Shaking my head at her amusement, I take her hand as we head downstairs.

Amon is deep in conversation with Abraham while Abel is a few paces away.

I purse my lips at the sight, not liking that Abel is always keeping himself separate from the family.

While Lydia considers us her parents, Abraham and Abel remember their real parents, we would have never asked them to forget them and accept us instead. Yet whereas Abraham had embraced our family, and as of a few years back had started calling Amon father and me mother, Abel had not.

Though he has his good moments, he is always distant, preferring to spend his time in town, or going to Ipswich rather than be with his family.

Lately, though, his visits home have become even rarer.

Maybe he has a girl he's seeing in Ipswich?

He is already twenty, so it wouldn't be out of the question for him to court someone. But he hadn't told me anything when I probed a few weeks back.

And if he is semi-engaging with me, with Amon he's even worse.

Luckily, Amon has the patience of a saint because every attempt to get closer to Abel has blown in his face. Even so, he never quit. He always tried to find a way to include him in activities and converse with him.

"Are you ready, boys?" I call out as we near the landing of the stairs.

"Abraham," Lydia exclaims as she runs towards her older brother.

He takes her in his arms, laying a kiss on her temple.

"You're so pretty today, Didi," he murmurs.

"You think so? I like this dress so much."

"You're the prettiest princess," Amon leans in to give her a kiss, too.

Abel snickers from the side, and I fear he's going to ruin today as usual. Amon gives him a reproachful look and he huffs at him before walking ahead of us.

Unfortunately, it's not only his relationship with us that is strained. He's not particularly close to his siblings, either, though he is at least more courteous.

I know he loves Lydia in his own way, but he isn't very demonstrative, preferring to keep to himself. Abraham, on the other hand, couldn't be more different.

He's the sweetest boy and he's made me and Amon extremely proud by graduating from Harvard with a degree in classics and apprenticing for a lawyer in Boston. He's already set to start his own practice in the future. Despite having a title waiting for him in England, he's decided to make America his home for good.

Amon, in particular, has been extremely happy with Abraham's choice, and as a subject they both enjoy, they've dedicated evenings to debates and animated discussions.

"You look wonderful, mama," Abraham says as he gives me a kiss on the cheek.

"Thank you, dear," I smile. "You look dashing, too. You're going to see Annie, aren't you?" I wink at him.

He reddens, giving us a brief nod.

"You need to make the courage and propose," Amon says. "She needs to know you're serious about her."

"As a matter of fact," Abraham pushes his chin up. "I'm going to visit her parents on Monday."

My eyes widen in surprise just as Amon claps him on the back, congratulating him.

"You've grown so much," I blink my tears away, unable to believe my baby is already at a marriageable age. "I'm so, so proud of you."

"Thank you, mama," he smiles.

"Shall we?" Amon motions to the door.

Abel is already far ahead of us, almost as if he didn't want to associate himself with us.

"I'm surprised he came," Abraham nods towards his brother.

"Honestly, me too," I sigh, wondering where we went wrong with him. "Didn't he rent some lodgings in Ipswich? You know more about him than us," I add on a sad note.

"Barely. Other than the few times he randomly decides to come home, I have no idea what he's up to. He didn't even show up for Didi's birthday," he presses his lips in a flat line that shows his disapproval.

Abraham is very protective of Lydia—has been from the moment she was born—whereas Abel as always had a more independent streak, preferring to do everything on his own, Abraham had been content to rely on us, both for company and for advice whenever he needed it.

In a way, I am almost glad that Abel isn't as close to Lydia, though that makes me feel like such a bad mother. Yet I wouldn't want him to influence her with his negativity.

He's made his distaste towards us quite clear. I wouldn't like him to poison Lydia's mind, too. The last thing I'd ever want is for my daughter to believe his propaganda and alienate herself from us as a result.

"He's a loner. We shouldn't try to impose on him too much," I add weakly. "He's also a grown man now and can make his own choices."

Amon is watching Abel closely, his expression tinged by sadness. "At least he comes home every now and then," he finally says.

"My love," I whisper, taking his hand and squeezing hard.

He sees Abel's behavior as his own failure, and though Abel often behaves in an impetuous manner, Amon always finds excuses for him and tries to not punish him too much.

"You're too soft on him, papa. He needs to understand that he won't get anywhere with that type of behavior. More than anything, he needs to know that family is family. We have to stick together."

"You're so right," I nod.

Lydia jumps out of Abraham's arms as she finds her way between me and Amon, taking our hands and firmly plastering herself in the middle.

We all laugh at her antics, and the noise prompts Abel to look back.

At the same time, my eyes connect with his and I note a flash of yearning on his face—one that makes my heart hurt.

At that moment, I resolve that I shall have a conversation with him. Maybe there is still time to solve our differences before he leaves and gets married as well.

It takes us some twenty minutes to reach the newly minted town square, but we opt to walk the distance as we talk and banter, getting in the mood for the upcoming festivities.

As soon as we reach the area, the music resounds in the air from the people who'd decided to take their instruments out and help with the atmosphere.

Amon had also donated a piano for the pastor's son who had learned to play, and he is leading the local orchestra.

There are stalls of food and other services, almost as if this were a veritable international festival.

We stop by a few of them as we buy Lydia some dessert before the elected mayor clears the space to give his little speech. He does us great honor by including our names in his acknowledgements and declares the town hereby named Fairydale.

As soon as the announcement is over, the music starts anew, as does the dancing.

Couples hurry in the middle of the square, getting together and moving to the music.

"Let's dance," Lydia tugs on our hands.

Giving Amon a look, I wink at him and push him forward as he takes his daughter for a dance.

He's so tall and she's so small that the size discrepancy is absolutely hilarious.

"Dance with me, mama?" Abraham comes to my side, taking my hand in his.

"Of course," I immediately agree as we join Amon and Lydia on the dance floor.

They are both laughing and after some time Amon takes her in his arms, dancing with her like that.

My lips pull up in a content smile as I hug my son to my chest.

"Are you really fine with me proposing to Annie? I know she's not of our station and..."

"Nonsense, dear," I cut him off. "You should know that I, more than anyone, have no care for stations or conventions. Do you love her?"

He gives me a confident nod.

"Does she love you?"

Another equally certain nod.

"Then you know what to do. I only want you to be happy, dear. If that is with Annie, then so be it," I give him a smile.

"Thank you. I wasn't sure whether you and papa were going to agree to the match."

"Your father wants you to be happy as much as I do, and he's known about your feelings for a while now. He was just wondering when you were going to give us the big news."

"I'm hoping for a quick wedding so I can take Annie with me to Boston in the spring," he tells me, explaining his plans for the future and the fact that he'd done his best to make contacts in the city to help him with his future law cabinet.

"That sounds fabulous. I'm so proud of you and how you've thought this all out," I praise him gently, my heart swelling in my chest.

God, my son is about to get married and move to his own home. I can't believe how the years have passed.

"If you need any help, you know you can count on us, right? Not just money. Anything at all," I assure him.

His lips spread into a big smile.

"I know, mama. I know. I love you," he tells me as he gives me a tight hug.

I can barely contain my tears.

"I love you, too, son. All of you are my joy."

We dance as we make more small talk, steering away from the serious topics and giving into merriment. By chance, though, I spot Abel at the other side of the square, deep in conversation with someone.

"Do you know who Abel is talking to?" I ask Abraham.

He turns to look in Abel's direction and he frowns.

"Isn't that the mayor's son?"

"Is he? I didn't recognize him," I say vaguely.

I hadn't realized Abel had any connections here, but I'm happy if he made friends.

The first dance ends, and Abraham ends up swooping Didi in his arms for the next one while I wink at Amon, beckoning him to my side.

Just as he reaches me, though, Abel is also here.

"Would you do me the honor of a dance?" he asks.

Amon purses his lips but gives me an encouraging nod. He's probably thinking, just as I am, that this is the first time Abel has reached out like this and we shouldn't refuse him.

Amon takes a step back, watching us like a hawk as I let Abel lead me back to the dance.

"We were all surprised you came today," I speak first in an attempt to break the ice.

His features are tense, his body stiff. As he looks down at me, his mouth curls at the corners in a barely disguised sneer.

"I came," he shrugs.

"Abel..." I take a deep breath. "I know we haven't always been on good terms, but you know you will always have a place with us. I told that to your brother too. It doesn't matter if you move out or start your own family. We'll always be here."

"And my spineless brother probably agreed, didn't he? Because he's such a pussy he can't think for himself without the help of father dearest."

"Abel!" My eyes widen, scandalized at his words. "How can you speak like that about your brother?"

"Because it's the truth. I don't blame Lydia since she's young, but you two managed to turn my own brother against me."

"You... You're accusing us of turning Abraham against you? How in

God's name did you get that notion? We've never done such a thing. On the contrary, we've always tried to be there for you..."

"Cut the crap, *mommy*," he snarls, his expression darkening. "You think I don't know everything? That I don't know your *secret?*"

"What... What are you talking about?" my voice trembles as I ask.

His eyes scan my face, his upper lip twitching.

"I've lived with you for ten years and in all this time you haven't gained one line on your face. As a matter of fact, your husband hasn't either, despite his white hair. He's what, forty something, yet doesn't look a day over twenty-five?"

"I don't know what you're talking about," I whisper.

"Of course you don't. Grandma told us all about the family legacy, but she didn't tell me that you have some age-defying abilities. Or, do you?"

"I think this is enough for today," Amon cuts in, taking Abel's hand off me.

He's a head taller than the boy, and as he gives him a scathing look, Abel has no recourse than back off.

"You're shaking," Amon says as he draws me into his arms.

"He... He..." The shock is too great and for a few moments, I cannot find my words. When I've calmed down a little, I tell Amon all about our conversation.

"Do you think that's why he resents us?"

Amon shakes his head.

"I'll have a talk with him."

"Don't be too harsh," I wet my lips as I look into his eyes. "He's still our son."

"I know, Lizzie, I know," he sighs. "I love him, too, but that doesn't mean we have to accept his behavior. Especially since it might be harmful for his siblings."

"You're right," I nod.

Resting my head on his chest, I let him sway me to the music as I turn my attention to where Abraham and Didi are dancing. She's giggling at something Abraham said, grinning to her ears.

I wrap my arms around Amon's waist as I hold tight, needing his body heat and the support of his presence.

"Don't be sad, Lizzie mine. I'll find a way to fix this," he murmurs in my hair.

As always, if Amon says he will fix it, I know he will. After all, he'd *never* disappointed me in the past.

The celebration lasts another few hours and Amon is invited to the make-shift stage to give a small speech, which he dedicates to me, making me blush from head to toe.

Yet as everything comes to an end, we all start walking home for dinner.

Luckily, I'd asked Esther, our cook, to have the food ready for a later hour.

When we arrive home, I just ask her to bring it to the dining room, which she obliges right away.

"I missed having these events as a family," I say as I look around the table. Everyone is present, even Abel, who'd surprised us once more by coming home with us and sitting down for dinner.

"May I have more potatoes?" Didi bats her lashes at me.

"Who did you learn that from?" I chuckle as I add more potatoes to her plate.

"You," she says pointedly. "You always do this when papa is around and he does whatever you say, isn't that true?" She looks at Amon to confirm her words.

My eyes widen as I turn to him too.

His lips are curled up as he barely keeps his amusement in check.

"She is right, you know," he shrugs. "You only need to give me one of those looks and I'm your servant."

A little embarrassed, and quite scandalized, I move my gaze between the two of them.

"You two are conspiring together against me, aren't you?"

"Who? Us?" Amon puts his hands up, just as Didi does the same.

Letting out a small laugh, I shake my head at their antics.

"How about this then," I suddenly straighten my back. "May I have another glass of wine, darling?" I ask as I lean into him and bat my lashes.

"See, this is exactly how it's done," he says in a serious voice as he fills my glass to the brim.

We all laugh—all but Abel, that is, who is watching us with unrestrained disdain.

I try to ignore it for the rest of the dinner, though it doesn't help the heavy feeling I have in my heart.

"Let's retire to the drawing room. We can play some card games, what do you all say?" I clasp my hands together as I address them after dinner.

Everyone but Abel agrees. Seeing him go out, Amon follows to have a talk with him.

"Come, let's start without them," I tell Didi as the three of us make our way to the drawing room.

Just as Lydia takes a seat next to me, though, she grabs my hand, holding it in a deadly grip.

"Don't give it to him," she whispers. "Don't give it to him, please."

"What..."

Turning towards me, she gives me the saddest smile I've ever seen as she launches herself at me, hugging me tightly.

"It's not your fault, mama. Please don't blame yourself. I will be fine. Even if it hurts, I will be fine."

"Didi, what are you talking about?" I ask, suddenly worried. "What hurts? What happened? What did you see?"

She shakes her head slowly.

"I love you, Abraham. You're the best brother ever," she suddenly tells him, taking him by surprise.

"I am?" He looks taken aback before he amends. "I love you, too, moppet."

"Why don't you play with him for a little bit while I find your father," I tell her gently as I try to hide the storm that's building inside of me.

To say that her words scare me, would be an understatement. I am certain she saw something bad and she won't share it with me.

Rising up, I give both of them a small smile as I head towards Amon's study.

I don't reach it, though, as I'm stopped by an echoed voice down the hall—Abel's voice.

"I want to see you tell Elizabeth the truth then. Tell her," he taunts. "Tell her how you killed my parents, because I *know* it was you," he accuses.

My hand flies to my mouth in shock.

"You don't understand, Abel," Amon tries to intervene, but Abel doesn't let him speak as he continues.

"You forget one small detail, *papa*. I was there that night. I saw the accident and everything that happened. I saw *you*."

"You couldn't have seen anything, Abel..."

The voices drown out as a loud thud signals the door closing.

Fearing I'll be found eavesdropping I turn away, yet I'm barely able to process what I'd heard.

It's preposterous. Ludicrous even.

Where would Abel have gotten the idea that Amon was behind Olivia and Jonathan's deaths?

He couldn't have.

Could he?

THREE DAYS later and I haven't been able to move on from what I'd heard.

It's not that I don't trust my husband—or so I tell myself. It's that I know he *would* be capable of that. To please me, I know he would do it.

On top of that, I am exhausted from putting up my mental defenses so he doesn't see what bothers me. At least not until I get a better grip on my emotions.

That day, early in the morning, I decide to leave the house for a moment and be on my own with my thoughts. But since there is nowhere else I can go, I make a visit to the church.

Surprisingly enough, it is empty.

As I allow myself inside, my eyes drift to the organ at the end of the aisles, and before I know it, my feet take me in that direction.

Sitting down, I tentatively place my fingers on the keys, the rich sound reverberating in the entire church.

There's a melancholic quality to it in the way the bass fills my entire being, yet I'm at a point where not even music can help the turmoil in my heart.

Could Amon have done something like that? Otherwise why would Abel accuse him of it?

It is true that he'd been the only one to survive the carriage accident that claimed the lives of my sister and her husband, but he'd never once intimated that it was something else.

That Amon could have been guilty of it.

Yet I still can't believe he would do it.

He'd promised me he would *never* hurt my family. And my Amon would never go back on his promise. Of that I am absolutely sure.

Yes, I nod to myself as I continue playing.

It's senseless to accuse Amon of that since there is no way he would do it.

Abel must have been mistaken.

At the same time, why would he accuse Amon now? Is this a new strategy of creating a rift in the family?

A tired sigh escapes me, all the regret piling up.

Dear God, but where did we go wrong with him?

Why would he hate us so much when we've only wanted to offer him love and a family?

What could we have possibly done that he hates us so much?

Tears trickle down my cheeks as I remember him growing up and becoming more and more distant until even the polite words he'd say to appease us had turned into veiled insults. Every time he would say something like that he would break my heart a little more each time.

Yet now? To go as far as to accuse Amon of such a heinous crime?

It's clear I have to do something about it. I'd never want that type of rumors to reach Didi's ears, or put any semblance of doubt into Abraham.

I'm lost in my own thoughts and I barely recognize there's another presence in the church.

Turning to the entrance, I see my husband tentatively walk inside.

"Lizzie?" he asks softly.

My fingers falter on the keys.

"Why are you crying? What's happening?" he comes forward, his voice anguished as he regards me.

I shake my head lightly.

But as I regard him, doubts assail me once more.

"Amon," I wet my lips. "I have one question, and please answer truthfully."

He blinks in surprise.

Dear Lord, but I feel guilty just thinking about this, but uttering it out loud? Somehow that wills it into existence—both the doubts and the allegations.

"I heard you arguing with Abel a few days ago," I start, fully turning to him and fidgeting with my fingers in my lap.

His eyes flare with alarm.

"What did you hear?" he speaks slowly, methodically.

As I look at him, though, I can recognize the signs of distress. God, I know this man better than I know myself.

"Why was Abel saying that you killed Olivia and Jonathan? Where would he even get that idea?"

He's still looking me in the eye, not answering. Just...watching me.

"Lizzie..." he whispers, and something inside his voice scares me. Something about this entire encounter scares me more than anything.

"Amon," I gasp. "Tell me the truth, please."

"Lizzie mine, you know I would do anything for you," he says as he stops in front of me.

Dropping to his knees, he takes my hands in his, bringing them to his lips and laying kisses all over.

"I would do *anything* for you," he repeats, the emphasis unmistakable.

"You promised you would never lie to me," I tell him as more tears accumulate in the corners of my eyes.

He gives me a pained nod.

"You also promised you would never hurt my family," I continue, and his features darken.

"Please tell me the truth," I whisper. "Did you have anything to do with Olivia and Jonathan's deaths?" I ask, dreading saying the words out loud.

Yet the pain on his face is unmistakable.

He squeezes my hands, bringing them to his heart.

"Trust me that I had no other alternative," he speaks slowly, yet I cannot hear anything more than the confirmation of what I would have thought inconceivable.

"You killed them..." I repeat, averting my gaze.

"Lizzie, please..."

I swallow hard as a thick lump forms in my throat. Pain radiates from my chest, my mind blanking on me as I'm sure this isn't happening.

It cannot be happening.

My husband, my beloved husband, would never do something to hurt me.

"Please leave," I croak, wanting to be alone before I break into a thousand pieces.

"I can't do that, you know it. I can never leave your side."

"Please... I... I need time. I need you far away from me, Amon. Please, just this time," I mumble incoherently, the pain slowly unfurling and becoming far too much than I can handle.

"Let me explain what happened," he protests but I shake my head.

"Not now. I can't... I can't even look at you, Amon," I tell him as a sob breaks through. "I need space. Time. Please..."

"Promise me we'll talk. That you'll let me explain. *Please*!"

I nod absentmindedly.

"Go," I whisper.

He backs away a few steps but falters as he freezes on the spot, his eyes on me, his expression more anguished than I've ever seen it.

For a few moments he just stares at me before he gives me a pained nod, disappearing from my sight.

Unable to hold the tears at bay anymore, I bury my face in my hands as I let everything out.

My marriage, the only thing I'd thought most secure, is now no longer so secure.

He'd promised me. He'd...

Sobs rack my body as I fall down the chair and onto the floor, gathering my knees to my chest as I continue to cry out in an attempt to exorcize all this disappointment and pain that flickers in my chest.

The worst thing?

It's been ten years and he'd never once thought to tell me. Never once did he think I deserved to know. And if I hadn't overheard that conversation, he likely would have never told me.

Good Lord.

My own husband killed my sister and her husband. He killed our children's parents.

How could he...

The more I think about it, the more I break out in tears, my heart unable to find any mercy from the onslaught of emotions that are slowly destroying me.

Is this why Abel has hated us from the beginning? Because he'd witnessed Amon at the scene?

Somehow that pains me even more.

No child should see his parents murdered, and by the man who was to become his new guardian.

God, but how must he have felt all these years living with us?

How could he have borne it?

For the first time, I understand why he'd always be so distant. Why he would prefer to go far away rather than be with his family.

He didn't want to be in the same room as his parents' murderer.

"How could you do this, Amon," I whisper softly, my heart breaking bit by bit. "How could you hurt me so badly?"

A sudden noise startles me from my thoughts. Whipping my head up, I note the door to the church opens again, and I quickly dab at my eyes.

Getting up from the floor, I wobble a few steps before I realize who it is that entered the church.

Abel and Abraham.

"We were looking for you, mama," Abraham comes forward. "What's wrong?" he immediately asks when he sees my red face and tear-streaked eyes.

I slowly shake my head.

"What happened?" he asks as he takes me in his arms, hugging me tightly to his chest.

"It's nothing," I whisper. "Just a minor disagreement between me and your father."

"It doesn't look little to me," he frowns as he draws back.

I do my best to not let my heartbreak show, forcing on a smile and patting his shoulder affectionately.

"Don't worry. We'll work it out between ourselves."

As I raise my gaze, my eyes connect with Abel's behind Abraham.

He's looking at me intently, almost as if he was privy to every secret I ever held.

"How are you Abel?" I ask, feeling like a goddamn impostor as I do.

"I wanted to come check on you with Abraham," he says glibly.

I frown, assessing him thoughtfully.

There's a sinister air about him, his mouth curled in a derisive smile, his eyes glinting with hidden intention.

"I am quite fine, thank you," I nod as I let Abraham hold me, rejoicing at the little comfort I find in his arms.

Yet my true comfort is far away—not only the cure to my heart but also the poison that dances in my veins.

In all these years, we never fought. We never had a disagreement. We lived in such perfect harmony, that I became one with him just as he became one with me.

To have that ripped apart? To realize I've been living a lie? To exist as a sole entity instead of a united one?

It's not just the news that Amon had something to do with Olivia and Jonathan's deaths that guts me. It's the fact that for ten years he's been lying to me, making everything we lived together a *lie.*

And to my great shame, the disappointment at his deception trumps the pain of losing my sister. I am a horrible human being, am I not? That alone makes me too ashamed to look my sons in the face.

"You found out, didn't you?" he taunts as he sees the emotions play on my face.

"I don't know what you mean," I reply weakly, my hands trembling with fear.

The last thing I want is to discuss this problem here, and with Abraham present, too.

"We should tell good ol' Abraham, too," he offers, a malicious smile pulling at his lips.

"Maybe we should talk. Just the two of us. Will you let us for a moment, Abraham?" I ask softly of my eldest son.

He looks in confusion between the two of us, nodding reluctantly.

I breathe out in relief that he doesn't question my decision, yet I'm still wary about discussing this with Abel.

"No," Abel declares. "He needs to hear this too."

"What's happening?" Abraham's brows are pinched together as he addresses me.

"I..." I stammer, suddenly at a loss of words. "You should go," I urge softly—anything to have him away from this confrontation.

"Our parents' accident wasn't quite an accident, was it?" Abel smirks.

"What? What are you talking about?"

"Your brother and I need to have a conversation. It's better if you go," I repeat, true terror taking shape within my breast.

As Abraham starts to move, Abel jumps in front of him, his eyes crazed.

"Tell him, Elizabeth! Tell him who killed them."

I shake my head at him.

"Please don't..."

He throws back his head and laughs at my fearful expression.

"What are you saying, Abel? You know it was an accident," Abraham argues.

"It wasn't!" he spits out. "It was all her husband, who isn't even a bloody human," he accuses, his eyes flaring with disgust as he looks at me.

"Abel..."

"What is he talking about, mama?"

"Jeremiah Creed doesn't exist, brother. He never did," he continues, seemingly taking great pleasure in revealing everything to Abraham.

I freeze at his words.

How... How would he know?

"Her husband's real name is Amon and he is a demon. A fucking demon who killed our parents and disguised it as an accident. A demon who's been killing people for centuries!"

"Abel, please..." I mumble in an attempt to stop him.

"Tell us. Tell us it isn't true," he adds smugly as he places a hand on Abraham's shoulder.

Abraham looks at me for confirmation and I cannot find myself to say anything. Yet it's exactly that which serves for confirmation.

"Did my mother tell you?" I ask softly.

"Grandmother? No," he laughs. "Although she should know by now, too. The entire coven should know where that bloody demon is."

No... Amon... Is he safe? Is he...

"You have it all wrong, Abel. Please let us explain it. Amon isn't..."

"Isn't what? A murderer? A demon? A fucking evil entity that killed our parents just because he could? You're insane if you think I'll listen to anything you say, Elizabeth," he tells me pointedly.

"Mama, what the hell is happening?" Abraham's gaze flies between the two of us in confusion.

"Yes, *mama*. Tell your precious son everything. Tell him you've been protecting a demon; that you forced them to call their true parents' murderer *father!*"

"Where in God's name did you hear that from? Who told you, because everything you think you know is *wrong,*" I burst out, sick of hearing Amon be called a demon when he is anything but.

"Kress and Finn told me," he replies smugly. "They told me everything."

What?

"They also told me the secret to *your* ageless appearance," he continues.

"What are you talking about?" I frown.

He nods to my neck—to the necklace I'm wearing.

"You have it all wrong, Abel. If you'll just let me explain," I take a deep breath as I try to keep my head straight.

But after everything that has happened, I find myself slipping one second at a time.

"I don't want any explanation," he yells. "I don't want anything! You already killed my parents. Do you think anything can bring them back? That you can just give me back the years I lost with them? No! It doesn't work like that."

I shrink back from his tone, a sliver of fear going down my back.

Abraham comes to my side, and despite the obvious confusion on his face, he grabs my hand, squeezing tightly.

"You're mad, Abel," his brother tells him. "I can't believe I didn't see this earlier. All this time you've drifted further and further and I didn't even notice..."

"I'm mad?" he laughs. "Oh, how wrong you are brother," he shakes his head.

Removing a knife from his coat, he waves it around, a sick smile on his face.

"If I'm so mad, then your *mama* should bleed if I do this, no?" he says and before I can realize what he means to do, the knife is embedded in my shoulder.

I bunch over in pain, but gritting my teeth, I grasp the handle, pulling it out of my flesh.

As it drops to the floor with a thud, my skin starts mending together.

Abraham looks at me with shock in his eyes.

"But... But..." he stammers.

Abel has a smug expression as he comes closer.

"She should have no abilities, no? That is what grandma said. Yet she does."

"But how?" Abraham asks dazedly.

"From the demon, of course," he chuckles. "Because she's a demon's whore, that's what she is. A fucking Satan worshipper."

"What do you want, Abel?" I ask through gritted teeth. Though the wound is closing up, the physical pain is still there—just like the one in my heart where it feels like I've been stabbed over and over again.

"Simple. An eye for an eye," he smiles. "And a little extra something."

Before I know what's happening, Abel has Abraham in a choke-hold, dragging him backwards and restraining him in his arms. Silver gleams in the light as he places a blade at his brother's throat.

My eyes widen in alarm.

"What are you doing..." I whisper in shock. "He's your brother."

"He's a waste of space. Like you," he scoffs.

"Please don't do that. Please! Let Abraham go. Your grievance is with me not with him," I beg.

"Let me go," Abraham struggles in his arms, yet somehow he's no match for Abel.

How?

When had Abel become so strong? How had he even found out all of these things? How, when some of them were only known to me and Amon?

God, but I shouldn't have sent Amon away.

He would have been able to deal with this. And in a last attempt to salvage what's left of our family, I whisper his name, knowing he will come to me.

"Amon. Come."

With the call in the wild, I know it's a matter of seconds before he will appear. Until then, I need to deal with Abel myself.

"Let Abraham go," I speak slowly as I take a step forward, keeping my eyes on him.

"I might. For a price," he suddenly says.

"A price? Anything," I readily agree.

My eyes meet Abraham's and I witness the pain and confusion that resides in there. My Abraham has always been a gentle spirit, and to be put in this position by his own brother must be utterly heartbreaking.

As long as I can hold him off until Amon comes, I'll do anything.

"Your necklace. I want your necklace," he demands with a sneer. "I know it has to be given of your own free will, so don't try to trick me. Gift the necklace to me and I will let him live."

My eyes widen at his outrageous request. How could he have known about the necklace?

"He's your brother, Abel," I exclaim, unable to believe he would kill his own blood.

"I have no family, Elizabeth. You took it from me. Now I have *nothing!"*

His blade touches Abraham's neck, a drop of blood spilling. Already it's a drop too much as I feel myself panic.

Amon, Amon, where are you? Please come!

The seconds trickle by and my husband is nowhere to be seen while Abraham is still in danger. And I know Abel means it. There's a deranged look in his eyes, a self-righteous conviction that he's using to justify his actions.

Somehow, I am *sure* he would harm his brother to get what he wants.

"Fine. I'll give it to you. But you promise to let him go?"

"A fair exchange, as I said."

I don't have time to think what the implications are for giving away my necklace—the source of all my powers. Yet at this moment, Abraham is more important than that. He's the only one that matters.

Bringing my hands to my neck, I unclasp the necklace, taking it off.

Immediately, dizziness assails me at being separated from such an integral part of myself, and my soul weeps at being fragmented again.

"Here," I extend my hand. "It is freely given. Now please let Abraham go."

"A deal is a deal," he nods to himself, giving Abraham a strong push just as he wrenches the necklace from my hand.

I quickly make to go to Abraham's side, but just as I take one step, a strangled cry echoes in the church.

"No," I shake my head as blood spills onto the ground.

On his knees, Abraham is still looking at me as blood gushes from the cut at his neck. The blade is stained with his blood as Abel waves it back and forth, looking entirely too pleased with himself.

"No, no, no!" I scream, fear unlike any other erupting inside of me.

Panicking, I throw myself over to him, my hands over his wound in an attempt to stop the blood.

Where are you, Amon? Our son is dying! He's...

"Ma..." Abraham tries to speak, the word obvious, yet one that never reaches my ears before he slumps against me.

His breath is gone. His pulse is gone.

He is...dead.

A savage wail escapes my lips as I hold on to him, wishing with all my might I could save him—that I could return his breath and life essence.

But I can't.

My powers are gone.

My abilities are bound.

I am absolutely useless as I stare into my son's lifeless face, his eyes still open, his lips parted on a word that will never come out—one I will never hear again.

In all my life I've never felt as helpless as in that moment. What good does it do to have all the power in the world but be powerless still?

"Abraham, please don't," I whisper, my voice becoming erratic as I will him back to life. "Please, my baby. Don't die on me. Please," I plead continuously, yet there is no one to hear my prayer.

No God. No Gods. No deities. There is nothing but this aching emptiness that forms inside my heart.

Even if Amon came now, he wouldn't be able to do anything. Even he doesn't have that much power.

Abraham is dead. He is...dead.

"What have you done, Abel?" I ask in an anguished whisper. "What... How..."

I'd never thought my heart could take this much hurt, but as I cradle my dead child to my chest, I feel like howling in pain.

"How could you..."

Tears cloud my vision as I hug him closer.

He can't be dead.

No, my son can't be dead.

I chant it in my head, thinking that maybe I will be able to will it into reality.

"I'm merely righting your wrongs, *mama*," he laughs as he looks at his brother on the ground. Placing the necklace to his own neck, he takes a deep breath before setting his eyes on me once more.

"I'm paving the way for a new future. One where the coven recognizes *me* and my new powers. One where they *bow* to me," he continues, and I get a glimpse into his plan.

I shake my head in dismay, not recognizing who he is anymore.

"Who the hell are you, Abel?" I whisper.

"Oh, I'm glad you asked, Elizabeth," he gives me a wide smile. Coming closer, he leans into me until his words are dead whispers in my ears.

"I'm the last thing you'll ever see."

Just as he draws back, I take a labored breath into my lungs.

My gaze goes lower to where a knife is protruding from my chest. Compared to the last hit, this is a ghost of a pain—ironically.

Yet unlike the other wound, this one doesn't heal.

This one doesn't close up as it keeps bleeding and bleeding, slowly taking with it my life's essence. I don't even know if I realize it at that moment, or if I can coherently categorize my thoughts.

I only know that I'm falling to the ground with Abraham by my side. My limbs are languid and unable to move just as my consciousness slowly slips for me.

The last thing I see is Abel, proudly cradling the necklace in his palm, his evil smile burned on my retina forever.

But the last thing I hear...

It's a roar that soars through the sky, echoing through every building, every space.

A battle cry unlike any other and one that tells me *he* knows. And he is coming for me.

He's coming for me.

He's coming for *us.*

If only I can hold on until then...

Part Three

Chapter Twenty-Three

October 1955. Fairydale, Massachusetts

Groaning, I shift to my side as pain radiates from my breastbone. Bringing my hand to my chest, I expect to see it covered in blood. Instead, it comes back empty.

I frown, then blink before my eyes widen in surprise.

Bringing myself to a sitting position, I take in my surroundings. The sun is barely up in the sky, which suggests it's fairly early in the morning.

I'm in...a field.

I quickly get to my feet just as panic threatens to overtake me, but as I turn around, I note a familiar building.

The Old Church.

I slept in a field behind the Old Church.

Plucking some twigs from my hair and dusting my clothes, I scrunch my brows in concentration as I try to remember what had happened.

I followed the sound of music that led me to the Old Church, and then...

Slowly, all the events from before come to me.

I'd seen my death.

I'd witnessed my death as Elizabeth.

A pang erupts in my heart as I recall everything that had happened —and *how* it had happened. And by God, it couldn't have been more different than what Rhiannon showed me.

Amon did not kill me. He would have *never* killed me.

Instead, I was killed by Abel. My own child.

I *died* together with Abraham.

Tears fall unbidden down my cheeks as I go over every little moment, reliving every bit of pain, of disappointment and of heartbreak.

For moments on end I can't seem to get a hang of my feelings, and no matter how much I try to rein in my emotions, they are too powerful —too out of control.

It feels like an eternity before I can breathe properly without sobbing my heart out. And as I slowly calm myself, my mind becomes sharper, the realizations trickling in.

The necklace.

Amon had given me the necklace to confer me an equal lifespan to his that would make me stronger. Previously, when he'd told me he was searching for an object that could help me, he'd been speaking about the necklace.

Though some details are still fuzzy, the origin of the necklace still unclear, I know it's something extremely important to me.

And I know exactly where it is now.

Mr. Nicholson.

If I hadn't seen those pictures of Mr. Nicholson in his twenties, maybe I wouldn't have believed it. But now I am absolutely certain.

Mr. Nicholson *is* Abel. And the gemstone on his cane is my necklace.

His powers and his healing were dependent on the cane when he'd fought Rhiannon, and now I know why.

Because they are not his. They were *never* his.

Oh my God....

My hand flies to my mouth as realization sinks in.

Mr. Nicholson—*Abel*—had killed me almost two hundred years ago in order to steal my power. And if I remember correctly, he admitted to alerting the coven to Amon's presence, which had undoubtedly led to his imprisonment.

The only question is...how had he known about it?

The why, I can wager a guess for. He'd been angry at us since a young age for the death of his family, and that had only festered as he'd grown older until he'd decided to take the revenge into his own hands. Yet it's more than that, isn't it? He'd wanted recognition from the coven and abilities that he could only get through stealing.

What might have started as revenge turned into a foolish quest for power. One he is still pursuing to this day.

I cannot recall too much about the necklace, but given Abel's rapid decay, I think he's used up all the power inside of it and now he needs more. And the only way to get more is through Amon.

Even as I understand his thirst for power, I still cannot comprehend how he could hurt his own brother. How could he kill him in cold blood?

Maybe in a twisted way I can understand why he would go for me, or Amon, because we were guilty in his mind. But Abraham? He'd never done anything wrong in his life.

My heart hurts every time I think of my fallen son and the way he'd died—with his throat slit from behind.

Damn you Abel! Damn you and your cowardice!

Despite my renewed sorrow at Abraham's death, there is a modicum of peace at knowing my Lydia had fully lived her life. She'd somehow escaped unscathed and she'd lived a happy life.

Don't give it to him.

Lydia had known.

She'd had a vision about it, and I'm quite certain she'd seen Abraham's death, too.

Why hadn't she warned us? Why hadn't she said anything?

More theories are going through my mind the more I think of the past, yet one thing question will not leave me be.

How could Abel have known about the necklace, or about Amon's identity? For him to accuse Amon of being a demon means he must have had a source from the coven.

But who?

As I stop in front of the church, I try once more to open the door, cursing out loud when it doesn't budge. It seems the only way I can access the church would be...through the catacombs.

Yet I'll have time to think about that later. With the hour growing late, I trudge my way back to the Hale manor, all the while ruminating over the new information I'd received.

Kress and Fin. Abel had mentioned those names. Could it be...

A gasp escapes me as I think back to the two men who'd advised Fiona in the past, and who had now made a sudden appearance in Fairydale.

Could it be that they are the Kress and Finn Abel was talking about?

Certainly, they seem to be present everywhere and have a vested interest in Amon.

I increase my pace as I remember it's still dangerous for me to be outside. At least now I know who is sending these creatures after me.

Abel.

Ironic how he'd branded Amon a demon, but he's not above using those evil creatures for his own gain.

What I'm still a little unsure of is how my blood figures into all this. Is it really a source of power, since as I'd experimented before, my abilities are quite finite? Or is there something more that I am not aware of?

How could it be useful to both Abel and Rhiannon, yet for completely different purposes?

Reaching the Hale gate, I make my way to the main entrance of the house, getting inside.

Yet before I can stealthily sneak to my room, Rhiannon calls out my name.

"Darcy, do join us in the drawing room."

Curious, I head for the drawing room.

"Hello," I greet everyone, not surprised to see the two men from before present.

"These are my special guests. They are here from the Holy See and will oversee the ritual at the end of the month," Rhiannon explains.

I put on a smile as I take a seat opposite them.

"I am Kress d'Pio and this is Finn d'Reig," he introduces himself and his friend.

"Darcy O'Sullivan," I nod.

Both of them have impressive physiques—taller than any men I've ever seen except Amon. Kress is dark haired and dark eyed with an olive complexion. Finn has equally dark hair, but his eyes are a hazel shade, his skin lighter.

Their poise and demeanor remind me of Amon. But it's the format of their last name that makes me more suspicious. How are they related to him?

Yet the more I watch them, the more I realize there is something about them... Something that makes me wary and anxious at the same time.

"They are here to help us with all the logistical aspects of the ritual. They are specialists in demonology and know about Amon best."

"I see. Is there anything I can help with?" I ask politely.

Right as the words are out of my mouth, I get struck with the most potent headache.

Gritting my teeth, I try to not show the physical symptoms as I push against it with all my strength. Yet as I meet Kress' gaze, I note his eyes narrowing at me, his mouth slanting down.

Finn is also regarding me with an odd expression.

It's a second later that it dawns on me what could be happening.

This headache isn't a regular one, is it? Especially as it feels as though there is a relentless pressure against my skull—almost as if someone was trying to probe into my thoughts.

The realization is startling, and as more information aligns in my brain, I am inclined to make the educated guess that these men have similar abilities to Amon.

And if that is the case, then they are definitely trying to read my mind.

A little too annoyed at the prospect, I focus all my strength into building a solid mental barrier as Elizabeth had done in the past. But going one step forward, I visualize my mind as a wall they are trying to break, hitting against it without stop.

Focusing my attention on the outside forces, I build an offensive as I mold the wall into a weapon, pushing them out of any corner of my mind.

Everything happens at once.

The moment I attack, Kress and Finn physically recoil, giving each other a secretive nod before they resume their positions as if nothing happened.

"We will have a meeting at the end of the week," Kress says. "The other members of the coven will be present too and we will detail the terms for the attack."

"Attack?" I frown.

"Amon is a very dangerous demon, Miss O'Sullivan. As Miss Hale must have told you, his seal is weakening," he purses his lips. "Amon was locked in the Old Church on the thirty-first of October eighteen-five. In just about ten days, it will be exactly one hundred and fifty years since then and it will be the perfect time to perform the ultimate ritual to kill him."

Ten days?

Rhiannon had mentioned there would be guests coming at the end of the month, but I hadn't realized they were planning on completing the ritual so soon.

"While he is still weak, we must focus all our energies into neutralizing him. If not, it will be increasingly difficult to do so."

"Why?" I suddenly ask. "Why couldn't you kill him the first time?"

Kress and Finn share a look.

"As I mentioned, Amon is no ordinary demon, Miss O'Sullivan. Even with the entire coven circle present we could not defeat him."

Dear God, what happened after I died?

My heart squeezes in my chest at thinking what my Amon might have endured. Yes, I might have been upset with him momentarily, but even as I lay dying, he was my last thought—my last hope.

And he had come for me. Of that I am certain. It's how they'd trapped him in that blasted church.

But just thinking of him hurt makes me physically ache.

I swallow hard, closing my eyes for a second as I banish that thought. It's not the moment to lose myself in my grief. I need to be strong to navigate the circumstances at hand. And the best way I can do that is if I have as much information as possible.

Rhiannon had been very vague about the ritual except to specify that they would need my blood to fuel the spell.

Yet I am still uncertain what happened the first time. How had that one failed?

"I understand that," I fake a smile. "What I do not understand is *how*. Can you walk me through the events of that day?"

"I don't see why that is necessary," Finn adds, narrowing his eyes at me.

"You require my participation, is that not so?" I raise a brow.

"We do," Kress takes over as he lightly touches Finn.

"Then I would like to have all the details. I would like to know what I am risking and what the chances of success are for such a risk. Hasn't Rhiannon told you that I have not yet fully agreed to participate?"

They turn to Rhiannon for confirmation. She gives them a bitter nod.

Kress exhales in annoyance.

"We received information that Amon was sighted in Fairydale and we made a plan of attack. Unfortunately, by the time we arrived, Amon had already killed Elizabeth Montford when we caught up with him," Kress pauses, and following a hand cue, Finn continues.

"We engaged Amon in a fight to keep him distracted until the Elders arrived. When they did, they tried a nullification spell, which was unsuccessful. After that, they decided something was better than nothing and settled on another powerful containment spell."

My lip twitches in amusement as they don't seem to realize their slip. They just confirmed it had been them who'd fought Amon in the past.

"The reason why they died, Darcy, is that they attempted multiple forbidden spells one after another. Their energy was depleted, but they used all of it in one last effort to seal Amon," Rhiannon interjects.

I nod thoughtfully.

"You're saying there isn't much risk as long as everything goes according to plan."

Rhiannon nods.

"But what if you can't neutralize him now, either?"

"We can. With your power, we will be able to. Just like Lydia foresaw."

I feel a pang in my chest at the thought of my daughter.

"Let's say that it is so," I nod, turning to the two men. "Why could you not kill him?" I ask pointedly. "With rhodium."

Their eyes widen for a brief second before they compose themselves.

"And how do you know about rhodium?"

"Oh, Rhiannon must have mentioned it when she was telling me about Fiona and Elizabeth, is that not so?" I plaster a smile on my face.

She frowns, but she doesn't disprove my claims, seemingly thinking she might have told me something of that nature.

"You are correct that rhodium is a metal that is poisonous to this... demon," Finn admits, his voice strained. "But it is not that simple. The only way for him to die is to pierce his heart with a pure rhodium weapon."

"So why could you not do that?"

My question seems to have struck a sore spot as both stiffen, their fists clenching. Yet just as before, in a matter of seconds they have themselves back under control.

"Amon is a skilled fighter. He is a master sword fighter and undefeated in hand-to-hand combat. To pierce his heart, one would need to get close enough to him, and that was impossible."

I narrow my eyes at his answer. Odd that he would focus only on Amon's skills on the battlefield when he is supposed to be a vicious demon with countless abilities.

"What about while the elders attempted the spell? Surely that amount of energy could have held him immobile," I counter.

"Anyone interfering with the spell would have suffered the same repercussions as he. Trust me, Miss O'Sullivan, there was no way to kill him back then," he assures me though it clearly pains him to make that statement.

"And what makes you think there will be a different outcome this time? How would you even go about this neutralizing spell if rhodium is the only way to kill him?"

My questions seem to enrage them further, which to me signifies that there are severe gaps in their plan, and that they are not at all certain anything will work.

"Because," Kress grits his teeth. "He will be far too weak this time to pose the same challenge as before. And he *will* be neutralized with rhodium. In a slightly different manner," he clicks his tongue against his teeth, his eyes like two razors as he cuts me with his gaze.

And with that, I know I will not get any more information from them.

I nod with a smile.

"We will discuss this more in depth when the coven members arrive here, Darcy. Don't worry, you will find out everything when the time is right. Though this is dangerous for everyone involved, I do believe that we will succeed this time," Rhiannon adds. "And no more people will die."

"Thank you for the information," I incline my head to the two men. "I was just wondering if you could tell me more about why my blood is so important, and how Mr. Nicholson figures in all of this. Since you're from the Holy See, you must have all the information."

My cheeks hurt from smiling so much, but it's imperative they believe I'm going along with their plan. Especially since they must be put out that they cannot access my thoughts—another reason why I think they must be related to Amon in some way.

"I trust Rhiannon has already told you about the story in the codices? The ability has been dormant in your family for millennia, but it only pokes its head to the surface every few hundred years or more. Unfortunately, Elizabeth was the exception to the rule since her mother bound her powers and the coven could not use the properties of her blood in the ritual. But they have been thoroughly documented before," he says confidently.

I nod. Nothing new there.

"And Mr. Nicholson?"

"He is someone who will be dealt with by the Elders when the time is right. He has gone against our standards and has procured forbidden spells for himself which he has been using for decades. Rest assured that he will be punished accordingly," Finn adds.

"Thank you for clarifying everything," I murmur, letting my gaze roam about the room and observing every little movement.

Isn't it odd that Abel has been in Fairydale for more than a century, seemingly using forbidden spells, and no one has intervened? Even as he threatens the coven's mission, he's been left alone.

Why?

Could it be that he has someone on the inside? He'd certainly known plenty about Amon before.

"The gentlemen must be tired already. Why don't we let them retire," Rhiannon suddenly says. "They will be lodging with us for the duration. Their rooms are on the second floor."

I barely stifle a sigh of relief at hearing they will not be anywhere near me.

The last thing I need is to have these highly suspicious men in my proximity. Especially since it seems I must be on my guard at all times since they might be able to read my mind.

Just as they are about to leave, though, someone appears in the doorway.

"Your cook let us in, Miss Hale," Sheriff Lawrence says as he knocks on the wooden frame of the door. There is another deputy behind him and they are both sporting severe expressions.

"Sheriff. What a surprise," Rhiannon exclaims. "Is everything alright?"

"Where is your nephew, Miss Hale?"

"Oh, he is upstairs. His wife too," she says before she frowns. "I'll tell Frida to call them," Rhiannon says as she heads to the kitchen to ask Frida to call the entire family down.

"Would you like anything, sheriff? A coffee? Tea? You know my rose tea is the best around here."

"I'm sorry, Miss Hale. But we're here on police business."

Rhiannon swallows hard, nodding.

From the police officers' expressions, it's clear they aren't bringing any good news with them.

In just a few minutes, Connor Hale and his wife come down the stairs, joining us in the drawing room. Katrina is at school so she cannot be present.

"If you will sit," the sheriff tells Mr. and Mrs. Hale.

Their features are gaunt as they absentmindedly nod and I have a feeling they suspect what the sheriff is about to tell them.

"There is really no way to tell you this, Connor. I'm really sorry to come here bearing such bad news but..." he takes a deep breath. "We found your son."

He found...Caleb? I frown at the wording, but the others don't seem to share my confusion.

Thomasa gasps, her hand flying to her mouth as tears fall down her cheeks.

Connor's hands are clenched tightly into fists as he takes her in his arms.

"What do you mean? Be more clear, Lawrence," he demands.

Rhiannon shakes her head, her eyes teary as well.

What the hell is happening?

"He's dead," the Sheriff states.

Loud gasps permeate the air.

"We found him in the marshes a few weeks back, but he'd already been out there for at least a couple of months. He was completely unrecognizable so we had to ask a coroner from Ipswich to come help us identify the body. We used everything at our disposal to make a correct identification..." he continues to speak, but I can no longer hear.

All I'm focused on is the fact that he said they'd found Caleb dead. A few weeks back in the marshes? He'd been dead for months?

How?

He was with me yesterday. Right in front of them.

I open my mouth to argue, yet no words come out. Because just as I question everything, the answers come naturally as if I'd known from the beginning. Every little doubt I've had in the last few weeks is suddenly resolved until a quiet certainty washes over me.

There was never any Caleb. There was never anyone else but him.

Only ever him.

Every little point suddenly aligns as the story gains a new perspective.

The odd eye color shift. The odd disappearances.

Everything that didn't make sense about Caleb suddenly does.

The paintings. His subtle warnings. The way he seemed to know me better than I knew myself. But more than anything, there's the obvious: the way he made me feel.

The way only one man could ever make me feel.

Just as I'd asked myself before how could I be in love with both men, it dawns on me that my confusion was not because I loved two men, but that I loved one man under two different identities.

What had he said before? That I would never let another man who is not him touch me.

And he is right.

Only one man can evoke those deep feelings inside of me. Only one man can make me feel alive with one touch.

Only him.

Amon.

My Amon.

The man who's been by my side from the beginning.

I may not know why he felt the need to assume someone else's identity to do that, but I will question him the moment I get the chance.

"How... How did he die?" Connor asks, his voice breaking.

"There were lesion marks around his neck. We believe he may have killed himself," the sheriff purses his lips. "I'm sorry about this, Connor."

"Can we see him?"

"You can but I do not advise it. He does not look like the young man you knew."

"It's that war. That goddamn war. He's never been the same since he came back. Always on his own. Always in his own head," Thomasa cries out. "We should have been more vigilant. We should have helped him somehow," she wails.

"Shh," Connor hugs her, doing his best to comfort her.

Seeing the grief and pain on their faces, I cannot help but empathize with their situation despite never knowing the real Caleb.

But as they continue to discuss personal matters, I realize it is not my place to be privy to them. Giving everyone a tight nod of acknowledgement, I move stealthily towards the exit before dashing up to my room and closing the door behind me.

My breathing is out of control, exhaustion clawing at my mind as I try to make sense of this infuriating realization. And I just...don't know how to feel.

I am not thrilled about the deception, that is for sure. At the same time, I cannot help but feel for Amon and his circumstances, the fact that he's been waiting for me for so long and he felt the need to take another identity to approach me.

Why?

Even as I ask the question in my mind, I have a few theories, the most salient one being that he was afraid.

Without my memories of the past, I would have been susceptible to the things said to me and around me—all which painted Amon in a bad light. And he would have been right to fear that. If I hadn't seen the truth of the past, I would have likely fallen prey to Rhiannon's machinations, or God forbid, that of Abel.

As I mull over our entire acquaintance, I have to wonder how come no one ever saw him. Clearly, Rhiannon's wards do not work against him in the house. But for no one to have seen him, how is that possible?

Unless...he'd used his mind controlling abilities. But how?

I'd been with *Caleb* around town, and I'd interacted with people, yet no one ever noticed? What about his appearance? The Caleb I know doesn't look like Amon. Though...

I frown as I try to mentally change his coloring and some of his features.

Whereas Amon has white hair and light blue eyes, Caleb had black hair and black eyes—though Amon had admitted he could change his eye color at will.

Yet as I superimpose their images on top of one another, I have to admit that the bone structure is similar, their physiques identical and their mannerisms the same.

He looks...just like Amon disguised as Jeremiah Creed had.

And I feel absolutely ridiculous for not making that connection earlier. The only excuse I have for myself is the fact that I'd only recently remembered about Amon as Jeremiah and his ruse. Add to that the fact that sometimes my dreams can be a little...foggy, and I don't think it's too far-fetched that I couldn't recognize him.

More than anything, in my mind, Amon had been trapped in the Old Church this whole time.

God, I'm such an idiot. Embarrassment colors my cheeks the more I remember things that were dead giveaway that he was my Amon—but only retrospectively. At the time, I'd only seen what I wanted to see. I'd been so drunk on the happiness of the moment and the attention Caleb was lavishing over me, that I would have never questioned his identity. Not when, despite the little odd behaviors every now and then, everything else seemed to check out.

Though I am still a little upset about his deception, especially as it dawns on me that those times he'd made me question my sanity due to his uncontrollable outbursts, I can put everything in perspective and see the big picture—the fact that he'd been by my side from the beginning.

He'd protected me in his own odd ways, and he'd always been there for me from the shadows. Even when I did not know who he was and I could not remember our past relationship, he still risked everything for me.

The incident from the cabin comes to mind, the way he'd been unusually ill, his eyes flashing different colors. Now that I'm aware it hadn't been my erroneous perception I can surmise a guess that he might be ill.

All this time, he's been protecting me at the cost of his own wellbeing. God knows what state he might be in, and that thought alone is enough to make me break out in a sweat.

Everyone had agreed the seal is weakening and his influence is growing, but no one had realized there is a cost for it.

Good Lord, the blast yesterday!

He'd taken that hit for me, hurting himself in the process even while he knew I would have healed. Maybe it would have been initially painful, but I am certain I would have healed.

But he... Since then, he's been absent, and I can't help but think of the worst.

If I close my eyes, all I can see is his tense jaw and the pain clinging to his features as he'd braced himself over me after that hit.

Already weakened and he'd still sacrificed himself for me despite my healing abilities. He'd known that, too, but he'd done it, nonetheless.

"Ah, Amon," I whisper as tears coat my lashes. "I love you," I whisper into the empty air. "Under any other name, and I would still love you."

I don't know if he can hear me, or what is the limit of his abilities, but this overwhelming emotion bursting out of my being cannot be quieted down anymore.

"I love you. Oh, how I love you," I repeat, wanting to scream the words so everyone would know. But more than anything I need *him* to know that there is no other for me.

Only him,

But first, I need to find a way to the catacombs. And to reach him, I will need something to nullify the barrier placed in the tunnels.

A weary sigh escapes me as I try to think of my next steps. Undoubtedly, I will require a spell to clear the way for me to advance to the Old Church. I do not, for one moment, believe there is radioactive material down there.

The only danger is Amon.

But not for me.

Only for those who'd done nothing else but hurt him. Time and time again.

My fists clench together in anger.

Abel. Kress and Finn. Rhiannon. The coven.

Everyone has sought to hurt him and take advantage of him at every turn.

And this is not merely something that started a couple of centuries ago. This has been ongoing from the very beginning, with the first sighting of Amon and the mystery of the first woman with the birthmark.

They've had a silly vendetta against him for far too long, and the thought that anyone would harm my beloved tears at my insides.

The pain is sharp and continuous as anger mounts inside of me.

Do I still have a lot of unanswered questions? Yes. But what I may not know, I *feel*.

Everyone who's ever had a hand in hurting my beloved will pay. They need to suffer just as much as he has, wither in the same timeless torment that he has.

A sob escapes me as a ghost of dread slithers against my skin.

He's been alone for almost two centuries, unwaveringly waiting for me. And for twenty-four years I lived in blissful ignorance while his loneliness increased one day at a time.

Letting myself be led by pure instinct, I open the door, stepping into the hallway and heading towards the Creed suites. The small hallway is now eerily familiar, and as I turn to look at the portraits hanging on the wall, my heart bleeds in my chest at the sight of my precious children.

"My precious Lydia and my sweet Abraham," I whisper as I stop in front of the family portrait. Even now, I can see his lifeless face and the blood pouring out of his open wound.

One moment he'd been alright, the next he'd been dead, slumping in my arms as he'd given his last breath.

The only relief is at knowing that at least Lydia escaped the carnage.

I linger for a moment as I take in the happiness on all our faces—the time we'd still been a family.

God, but I don't want to imagine what Amon must have felt like when he'd come to the church to find both Abraham and me dead. That amount of pain would have been harrowing and I choke back a sob as I imagine his reaction.

Shaking myself, I continue to the master bedroom. There is one more room I hadn't entered. One I hadn't known existed until the last dream, but one that he had mentioned before.

The Creed private gallery.

It's a hidden door right by the wardrobe, and as I place my hands against the wall, feeling for a slight protrusion, I push gently until the door pops open.

More dust assails me as I take a step inside.

Given the nature of Amon's paintings, he'd always insisted on an enhanced security mechanism. So I'm certain it's been exactly one hundred and fifty years since anyone has been in here.

"I'm the only one who can see you like this, my love," he'd told me.

And so he'd built a secret chamber that was to be our love nest.

The moment I'm inside, I can see that everything is as it's been left. But more than anything, my eyes widen at the fact that while the ground is covered with thick layers of dust, there is none on the paintings. Just like the flower from the balcony, they'd been cleaned and well-kept.

"Amon..." his name slips past my lips as his regard never fails to astound me.

Even while suffering alone in his cell, he devoted what little of his powers he still had to this—to make me happy. To preserve our happiness in these little moments despite it slipping from us in the real world.

Ah, but how I love this man.

From floor to ceiling, the entire room is covered in canvases—all of them depicting us.

I have to admit there was one instance when my mind had played tricks on me—though it had been of Amon's making. That had been when I'd seen the erotic paintings in the studio.

Now, seeing them in their original location, I know it had been Amon who'd placed the ideas in my mind—*potentially to remind me of the past*? Regardless of his reason, he hadn't included the most scandalous of paintings, where not only *I* am the main subject, but he, too.

The entire room is one debauched scene after another as my husband had painted us together in every erotically charged moment and in every position.

There is one small window that allows for minimal sunlight inside the room, and as I close the door behind me, I let the memories wash over me.

"Soon, my love," I murmur lovingly as I stop in front of a painting.

Though not as sexual as the others, this one shows us in our natural habitat.

We are both naked, but that is the extent of salaciousness.

I'm on my back on the bed while he's lying on top of me, hugging my midriff while his head rests atop my breasts. We're languidly wrapped around each other, limbs intertwined, gazes locked together.

He's looking up at me with absolute love and devotion while I smile affectionately at him, threading my hands through his long hair and cradling him close to me.

The scene is so warm, so intimate, that a pang of longing hits me right in the chest.

Bringing my finger to the canvas, I trace his features, and for a moment, I wish for nothing more than to curl in bed and sleep—dream of that wonderful past in which we'd been so happy, so in love, so...full.

Yet there's also the sickening realization that it would have never last. Despite all those happy times I yearn for, *this* is the present—the consequence of all those past actions. And as such, I need to steel myself to the future instead of losing myself to the past.

Now, more than ever, I need to find a way back to him.

"Give me a sign, Amon. Tell me what to do..."

The truth is that I'm lost.

With everything happening around me and despite my continuous struggle to understand everything and keep afloat, I am absolutely lost.

There is only one purpose that keeps me adrift—Amon.

But while I have the goal, I do not have the steps to accomplish it.

No matter how much I call out his name, he doesn't answer—likely cannot. And that makes me worry even more, leaving me in a state of near-frenzy as a mix of anger and frustration explodes in me.

He needs me. Amon needs me and my stupid brain won't work to find a solution.

Exiting the secret room, I make sure it's fully closed before I turn to the bedroom, letting my gaze linger a little as I absorb the residual memories of the past.

I need a spell to break the barrier from the tunnels.

But would I be able to perform *any* spell?

Pursing my lips, I plop myself on a chair as I bring my hands to my temples, rubbing them gently as I mentally backtrack.

First, I need to find a way to get my hands on that spell. Unfortunately, I am sure it's part of the codex, or belongs in some spell book, all of which are located in Rhiannon's quarters.

Maybe I *could* sneak inside while she is away, and if I'm lucky enough I could find something.

But...

"Damn it," I mutter out loud.

Even if I did find something, it would be in Latin—as are all the texts related to the coven.

Just my luck.

Couldn't I have studied Latin instead of English? I doubt there would be too many positions to fill, but at least I wouldn't find myself in such a predicament at the moment.

Unless...

A bulb lights up in my brain—ironic considering this wing of the house does not have any electricity—and my eyes widen with excitement.

The library! I am more than certain I will find some Latin dictionaries there and they should help me find the spell. To make my job easier and smoother, I will make a list of potential words—all synonyms of barrier—and flag them for easy reach.

As I calm down, the ideas start coming to me. And what better moment if not now when the family is undoubtedly grieving the real Caleb Hale?

Doing my best to keep quiet, I sneak to the servants' staircase, which leads straight to the kitchen. The library is right around the corner and I successfully manage to avoid any detection as I slip inside, closing the door behind me.

Amon—since I can no longer think of him as Caleb—had showed me all the book categories as they'd been arranged on shelves, and I remember quite well that he'd pointed out the selection of dictionaries as being in the far back of the library.

Heading there, I start browsing, noting quite a variety of German, French and Ancient Greek dictionaries, but only one of Latin.

Relief courses through me that there is at least one, and I pluck it from the shelf, noting the thick layer of dust.

Damn, but it seems no one has been interested in Latin in a long time.

Just as I am about to turn with the tome, the door slides open.

My spine stiffens with fear.

"We should leave them for now. Maybe find somewhere else to sleep the night," one of them suggests and I recognize the voice—Finn.

Kress grunts.

"We need to stay out of it as much as we can until the others come. We can't afford any questions at this point. Not when everything's already set in motion."

"We still need to see Nicholson. That old fool is going to ruin all our plans," Finn curses.

Aha! So I was right about their acquaintance. But even that doesn't help my increasing anxiety at being in the same room with them. Especially since it becomes clear I'm listening to something that I'm not supposed to, and my pulse quickens at the thought of being discovered.

Stepping further back into the shadows, I bump into one of the shelves.

Oh, God...

Yet to my surprise, no sound erupts in the air.

There's only a light breeze that brushes against my cheek and the quietest whisper that I'm still unsure whether it's real or not.

Shhh.

I keep myself still as I let the mist envelop me in a protective cocoon, somehow instinctively aware that it's *him.*

"Fuck," Kress curses as he comes deeper into the library, taking a seat on the couch on the other side of the room. Finn follows him. From my angle, I can see them but I doubt they are able to see me too. Not when Finn looks directly at me without any reaction.

Thank you.

I whisper the words in my mind, convinced he will be able to hear me.

Yet he doesn't reply.

I don't let that disappointment overtake me as I focus on what Kress and Finn are talking about.

"So, what did you think?" Finn asks.

Kress flattens his lips in a thin line.

"I'm not sure. She was asking too many questions."

"You think she knows something?"

"I couldn't probe her mind. Could you?"

He shakes his head.

"I tried but there was a strong push," Finn answers, clearly put off by that.

"Damn," he curses, suddenly standing up. "She can't know, Finn. She *can't* remember."

"You really think she's Sela?" Finn rises, too, his features hard.

"You saw her too. She's identical. Just like Elizabeth."

"But how could it be? Even among the General ranks, no one has that ability—to die and come back all over again," Finn counters.

"You forget this is Sela we're talking about, Finn. She's the exception to the rule."

"No. She doesn't have her powers anymore. It *can't* be of her own doing," he argues.

"You think it could be that damned spell Amon performed? The one that went missing with the original codex?"

Kress nods.

"It's the only explanation. But that doesn't solve our problem. We've known about that damn prophecy for two centuries but we never realized the chit would be Sela's reincarnation. That changes everything," Kress grits his teeth.

"But the prophecy said she would be the one to end him. Do you think maybe it's true? You know that even weak Amon will pose a challenge, regardless of the coven's presence."

"Don't I know it," Kress says drily. "The prophecy also said she would unleash that evil, and both events are equally possible," he pauses. "But maybe we can make some use of this. Amon and Sela were mated, were they not? You know that a male's greatest weakness is his female."

"But how? There's never been a documented incident of a female going against her mate," he sighs. "At least not among our kind since the mating requires free will."

Our kind?

"Yes, but look at it this way, Finn," Kress turns towards him. "Even if they are still technically mated, Darcy does not remember what happened as Sela, or that she mated Amon. That is vital to our plans. We can't risk her having knowledge of the past. More than anything, she can't know that Amon isn't a demon."

My eyes widen in surprise at his words, yet there's a familiarity to that sentence—a knowledge deeply buried inside of me.

"You're right. We should probably talk to Rhiannon about it and have her check for her memories. If Hale thinks she is Elizabeth she will also be alarmed of the potential switch in loyalties."

Kress grunts, but his features are still unyielding.

"Fuck it! This complicates our plans too much when we don't have the time. The search party could be here any time in the next decade."

"I still can't believe they haven't let it go. They are using precious resources on a traitor," Finn spits out.

"A traitor with enough underground support that could wipe out the entire empire. They know what they are doing, Finn. I might not like it, but it makes sense they require evidence that Amon is dead. Otherwise, we will always be under threat. I don't like it any more than you do, but I would do the same."

"Even after all this time?"

Kress gives him a sad smile.

"You haven't known Amon as long as I have. But you've seen what he is capable of. He didn't become the youngest General in history for no reason, Finn. His reputation wasn't unearned, which is why we need to finish him off while he is weak. If he regains his strength, we won't be safe. The empire won't be safe. Fuck, the world as we know it will not be safe."

Finn shakes his head as he paces around.

"How did he even become so strong? I know back home he was a legend, but what we saw him do in that Church was beyond anything I've ever seen," Finn adds, his voice tinged with awe.

"I don't know," Kress takes a deep breath. "It might be a spell from the original codex. We already know the spells in this world are compatible with us. That could have given him more power than he already had."

"He can kill with his mind, Kress," Finn accused. "If we didn't have that shield protecting us, our brains would have become mush just like everyone else in town. He made everyone's insides melt. That's some fucked up shit," he exclaims.

"I had no idea he would be capable of that, either. For fuck's sake, you saw that even the Elders had trouble restraining him," Kress shakes his head. "In Arkgor, he was famous for his combat abilities, but no one ever mentioned that type of matter manipulation. It's something only the Reva in the North Woods were capable of, but their kind is nearly extinct. Unless...you think Elora might have known? She said she had one last trick up her sleeve to get Amon ostracized by the people."

"Maybe," Finn shrugs. "At this point I just want to finally be rid of him. I'll be able to sleep well at night again, without thinking we would be found out and..." he swallows hard. "You saw what they did to his supporters when he was accused. If we don't kill him, we are next, Kress."

"I know," he answers somberly. "I, more than anyone, know what's at stake."

"We need to deal with Darcy and make sure she has no knowledge of who or what Amon is. This entire operation hinges on the belief that Amon is an evil demon out to destroy humanity. If they find out that isn't true..." he trails off.

"Don't worry about it," he waves his hand. "Humanity's greatest folly is its unerring condemnation of that which it does not understand. That hive mentality will not perish anytime soon. We'll merely take advantage of their ignorance again."

"That doesn't mean..."

"Shh. Someone is coming," Kress stops Finn.

A few moments later, Rhiannon opens the door to the library, stepping inside.

"I'm so sorry about this, gentlemen," she says, her tone sad. "It seems it's not a good day for our family. But if you'll allow me to show you to your rooms," she gives them a smile.

"Thank you for your hospitality," Kress inclines his head. "And allow us to pay our condolences. It can't be easy to lose one so young."

Rhiannon shakes her head, her eyes glossy.

"He's been missing for a while now, but we always thought he would come back. He used to do this before. Leave for a couple of months and then return," she sighs, barely able to hold back her tears. "The funeral will be in a few days. You will have to excuse me if I'm not as present as I would have liked. We will discuss and plan for everything afterwards."

"Do not worry on our account. We are already more than grateful that you've received us in your home. Take as much time as you'd like."

"Thank you," Rhiannon murmurs.

They make small talk for a while longer before they all leave the library, closing the door behind them.

The moment the room is empty, I feel the air curl around me as it frees me. And before I can say anything, that warm presence is gone.

I'm frozen to the spot as I mentally go over everything I heard, my confusion mounting again.

Dear Lord, but this is more complicated than I could have ever thought. And if Amon is not a demon, *what is he*?

Somehow, the statement rings true in my mind, but my memory of the past is incomplete. I cannot remember anything about *what* or *who* Amon is.

Although I do know he used to be a General, and that he'd dedicated all his life to the army before, I do not know when and where. It seems to me that the only one who would have had the full version of the past was Sela. And though I have memories of my life as Elizabeth, Sela is a complete mystery.

I'd had that one vision in Ancient Rome and nothing more.

Moreover, what spell from the original codex was Kress talking about?

"Agh," I huff out loud. There are too many narrative threads for me to make sense of, and without all the information I feel like I'm running in circles.

The only way to understand everything is to go straight to the source.

Amon.

Anticipation courses through my blood as every little part of my body throbs with longing.

Opening the book, I look for the translation of the barrier.

With the family busy with the funeral, I might manage to find the time to infiltrate Rhiannon's quarters.

Flipping the pages in search of the letter b, I'm surprised to see something fly out of the book, landing on the floor.

The paper is worn, the edges yellowish.

Bending to pick it up, I note the beautiful penmanship as well as the name and date scribbled in the corner.

Lydia Creed, May 1835.

As my eyes scan the document, I realize it's a spell.

A spell to nullify the barrier.

My God!

I cannot believe what I'm seeing, or the fact that Lydia had written this more than a hundred years ago. She must have known I would need it in the future.

"My Didi," I whisper, my lashes coated with tears.

Is she here, I wonder?

Rhiannon had said there are ghosts, but is Lydia here, too?

God, but what I wouldn't give to talk to her again. Tell her I'm sorry about everything that happened...

A sob escapes my lips and I wipe the tears off my face with the sleeve.

"Thank you, Didi," I tell her, hoping she will somehow be able to hear me.

Folding the piece of paper and slipping it into my blouse, I place the book back in its place and go back to my room.

Once nightfall comes, I prepare myself to proceed.

My heart threatens to burst in my chest thinking I might see Amon soon, yet I don't want to put my hopes up in case it doesn't work.

I'm already dying to touch him again, to hear his voice and feel his skin against mine. If I don't succeed, the disappointment would prove too much.

Dressed in my best gown, I put on some make-up and arrange my hair in loose curls around my shoulders.

My cheeks are already red with shame at being so vain while my beloved is suffering. But I don't want him to see me ragged or unkempt. Somehow, his opinion of me matters too much.

Smoothing my hands over the dress, I hide the spell inside my brassiere as I compile a small basket of items for him, too. I don't know what state I might find him in, so I need to be prepared for every eventuality.

I pack a few towels, medicine and even some food as well as a few weapons that might be helpful later on.

Maybe I'm silly about it since I don't know what someone as powerful as Amon might need. But just thinking about him not having basic items makes my blood boil and my heart hurt.

If it weren't for the weight, and the fact that I'm not that physically strong, I would have taken with me an entire infirmary.

With everything ready, I take a deep breath and open my door, stepping into the hallway. I do my best to be quiet as I move about the house. The last thing I need is for Kress or Finn to catch me and interrogate me on my whereabouts so late at night.

Taking the servants' staircase, I head to the kitchen where the entrance to the catacombs is.

As expected, the Hales had somehow locked the door.

Sighing, I bring my candle next to the lock, examining it closely and noting it's not something I'm likely to unlock on my own. Instead, I'll have to find some way to break it—but without drawing any attention to myself.

Removing a screwdriver from my basket, I jam the pointy tip inside the lock.

It might not open it, but it should definitely *break* it.

I struggle for minutes on end to push it inside when, suddenly, I hear a small click and the door opens on its own.

Blinking in surprise, I withdraw the screwdriver and dump it in the basket.

"Thank you," I whisper in a low voice as I take a step inside, closing the door behind me and going down the stairs.

The candles allow for some light, but the entire area is pitch dark.

I swallow hard against a wave of discomfort that hits me, just as a small shiver of fear goes down my back.

It would be fair to say that after a while in Fairydale I've developed a certain distaste of dark places that might be rife with the supernatural.

But even as that thought crosses my mind I force myself to focus.

This is for him—all for him.

I walk for a couple of minutes before I come across the invisible barrier from before.

Taking out the piece of paper from my brassiere, I bring the light over it as I clear my throat and start reading.

The words are all in Latin, and although I can't be sure my pronunciation is on point, I hope it will still work.

I channel all my hope in the words I'm saying—all the love and longing in my heart.

When I'm done, I find myself completely out of breath.

Peering up, I expect to see something happening, yet the tunnel is just as before—dark and foreboding.

My heart hammering in my chest, I take a tentative step forward.

Then another.

My lips tremble as they tip up in an optimistic smile the more I walk, the path clear for me.

From hesitant steps, I slowly pick up speed until I'm running for my life.

Adrenaline dances in my veins as my feet take me closer and closer to him. My skin tingles with every moment, my body humming with something utterly indescribable.

A blinding light suddenly appears before me.

Blinking, I slowly accommodate to the light as I take in the new surroundings. The tunnel funnels into a wide space that looks like a chamber. The walls are a light color, the area clean and tidy—clearly indicative of someone living here. A bed rests against the northern wall, some books piled on top of the blankets. There are various items around, all well-kept and unusually clean considering the circumstances.

And there...right before me, it's him.

Chapter Twenty-Four

"Amon," I whisper through misted eyes.

He's standing before me, eyes wide, features gaunt and filled with pain.

For a second, I simply take him in, drink in the sight of him and bask in the sheer magnetism of his presence. A few feet apart and I still feel it—the way the air crackles around us, the atmosphere heavier than it's ever been.

My heart hammers in my chest.

Thud. Thud. Thud.

The sound would be deafening if not for the loudness of my thoughts—the way my entire being is screaming with happiness.

He is just as handsome as I remembered, with his chiseled features, full mouth and mesmerizing eyes. He's wearing a black fitted shirt and a pair of loose pants that only serve to emphasize the muscular build of his upper body.

His white hair flows down his back unrestrained—a contrast to his dark clothes.

But it's his eyes that have me riveted to the spot as they shift color under my very gaze.

Blue. Red. Black. Then Red again.

The colors of his eyes are the evidence of his volcanic emotions—as out of control as mine. He gazes upon me as if I'm a mere mirage, something he's conjured up in his mind.

His eyes slowly move over my form, blinking as he swallows hard, a torrent of longing written on his face.

My breath hitches as our gazes connect, an invisible tether irrevocably tying us together.

In that moment I know.

I simply know that this is what I'd been searching for my entire life. His absence is the reason for that restlessness that simmered in my blood for so long. And his presence...

His presence makes my essence sing.

Without him, I was lost. With him, I am found again.

Instinct takes over as I move. The basket drops to the ground as I fling myself forward.

One step.

Two.

On the third I am in his arms, his heat penetrating my skin and telling me this is real. That I am not imagining it, just as he isn't imagining it.

"Amon, my Amon," I whisper as I hold tightly onto him, almost wishing I could become one with him so he could never be apart from me. So this moment would survive in all eternity. Just the two of us like this.

Together. Touching. Feeling.

Being as we were always meant to be—two, never one.

"You're here," he whispers, his voice bleeding hope and anguish. "You're here," he repeats as he draws back.

Tentatively, his hands reach for my cheeks, cradling my face between his big palms.

He swirls his thumbs over my skin—slow languorous movements that make me want to purr out loud and present myself to him in an ancient mating ceremony.

"Darcy," he groans. My name on his lips is quite possibly the greatest joy I've ever known.

"I'm here. I've come for you," I tell him fervently. "I would always come for you. I'm just sorry it took me so long," I say as tears fall down my cheeks.

Before I know it, his lips are on my skin, his tongue catching my tears before he kisses my eyes. Every touch is slow, tentative, as if he's still convincing himself this is real.

"I would have waited an eternity for you," he murmurs. "Knowing you would come for me is the only thing that kept me sane."

I hug him harder, wrapping my arms around his midriff and burying my face in his chest.

A low hum vibrates in his chest and he winces as I tighten my hold.

Immediately, my eyes widen as I step back, assessing him with questioning eyes.

His hand goes to his ribs as his cheek twitches in pain.

"You're hurt," I state plainly. Before he can deny it, I grab the hem of his shirt and slide it up his torso, the ugly sight making me gasp.

His entire upper body is purple, gashes running from his pectorals all the way to his belly.

"It's not that bad," he gives me a tight smile.

"This is not bad?" I demand, horrified. "Amon, you're hurt all over. It's from that blast isn't it?"

He shakes his head.

"It's really not bad. It will heal," he nods, his eyes big and round as he looks at me as if he'd like nothing better for me to drop the issue.

Just as I open my mouth to speak, though, he grips his midriff as a coughing fit assails him, blood splattering all over his hands and trickling down his chin.

Panic erupts in my chest.

"That is not bad?" I ask numbly.

"I'm...fine," he says between coughs and more blood.

I shake my head at him.

"You're not fine. You need to sit," I tell him, taking his hand and leading him to the bed.

He doesn't protest, merely staring at me. Either he's too weak from his injuries, or he's simply abiding to my wishes to please me. That thought alone makes me lean in to kiss his brow before panic takes hold of me anew and I pull at his shirt.

"Tell me the truth, please," I murmur as I slide the shirt off his body, only to discover more wounds, some deep and bleeding while others faded and in the process of healing.

His face is the only area on his body that isn't injured.

God, but I didn't imagine he'd be so hurt, and to this degree. This isn't *just* from the blast, is it?

It can't possibly be.

Recovering my basket, I place it by his side as I remove some of the items I'd brought.

"Why are you like this, Amon?" I ask, hurting just looking at the state he is in.

His lips flatten in discomfort just as his hands come atop of mine, stopping my fretting.

"It's the price I pay for leaving this place," he tells me in a soft voice.

"Wh-what?"

"This," he nods to the area around, "is a prison with a mind of its own. And just like any other prison, it punishes its inmates when they try to escape."

"You mean..." I wet my lips, my forehead creasing with worry.

He nods.

"I can go out for limited periods of time, but that always comes with a price."

"This?" I can only stare at him flabbergasted. "You... Please explain."

His hands tighten over my own.

"It took me decades to gather the strength to fight against it. Eventually I managed to get out, but it's only for a limited time and within the town radius. But the prison always fights back."

"Tell me more specifically. What is the exact price," I demand softly.

"I'm not sure what their policy is," he gives a dry laugh, "but one day out usually equals about a thousand lashings."

I gulp down against a wave of nausea that threatens to overtake me. "A thousand lashings? But who..."

"The spell that trapped me is not static. Just like action and reaction, it responds to any disturbance."

My eyes widen.

"Then what about my being here? Please don't tell me that's going to get you punished again."

He smiles.

"No. You're not the first one to come down here. There is no side effect of you being here," he assures me quietly, but all I can think of is the fact that I'm not the first one here with him.

"Who was it?" I bite out, jealousy unlike I've ever experienced fueling my words.

He chuckles, and bringing his hand to my cheek he caresses me lightly. "Lydia," he answers.

"L-Lydia?"

He nods.

"She used to come visit me often until she passed. She is the one who put the barrier spell in the tunnel so no one else could come here—no one but you."

"Oh, Amon," I take his hand, bringing it to my mouth for a kiss. "I'm so happy she was there for you."

His features turn sad, his eyes glossy with unshed tears.

"It was the most unusual thing, Darcy, to watch my child grow old and die. I suppose I should have known it was going to happen eventually, but I never realized how hard it would be."

"She was happy, was she not?"

He nods, his lips tipping up in a slight smile.

"She came to ask me for permission before she married Hale. She was so happy and in love that I could only encourage her to follow her heart. But because I was here, she decided to move back with her family," he relates fondly. "She was devastated when you died..." he trails off as his voice breaks.

"She knew," I tell him. "She saw what would happen, both with me and with Abraham. I'm sure of it. She tried to tell me," I choke on a sob. "She tried to tell me not to give Abel the necklace."

"Shh, please don't cry," he murmurs as he cups my cheeks, resting his forehead on top of mine. "It breaks my heart when you cry, my darling girl."

I wipe at my eyes as I take a water bottle from my basket, wetting a towel and bringing it to his chest.

He releases a hiss when the cold material touches his wounds.

"I need to patch you up," I say as I sniffle—anything to take my mind off the past. At least for now.

It's still too sudden, too raw.

It might have happened in the last century, but for me it's like it happened yesterday.

"How is your healing?" I bite my lip as I focus on cleaning him carefully.

Some of the injuries are nasty looking and potentially infected. To realize that he's been getting these to come be with me is absolutely devastating. Especially since I now understand why he's been absent for the last few days.

He's been here suffering. Alone.

All for me.

"Slow," he answers. "The prison inhibits some of my abilities, but even if I were operating at full capacity, the recurrent injuries take a toll on how much I can function and move around."

"And you got hit with that blast, too."

"Compared to the prison lashings, that was like a light caress," he laughs.

"Amon..." I look up at him, my features torn with worry, sadness and absolute frustration at being unable to help him in any way.

"Don't worry about me, Darcy darlin'. I'm used to the pain. Flesh wounds come and go. They are nothing new to me. Just having you here, with your gentle hands on me is like a balm to my soul. For this alone I would endure much, much worse."

"But these are *because* of me," I sigh. "Because you went out to see me. If I'd known..."

He shakes his head.

"I would have never wanted you to know," he declares.

"You silly man," I sob as I clean his torso. "If you hurt I hurt more, don't you know that?"

Slowly, I bring my misty eyes to his, watching the play of emotions on his face.

He's clenching his jaw in an attempt to stifle his feelings, but I know.

"I'm sorry," he whispers. "I never wanted to worry you."

"From now on, you're not coming out. I'll come to you every day, but you're not risking more for me, ok?"

"Darcy..." he groans.

"Ok?" I repeat, a steely determination in my voice.

"Unless you're in danger. Then I'll come," he counters.

"Amon..."

"Darcy..."

We're at a standstill as we stare at each other, neither willing to make a concession on this.

"Fine. Only if I'm in *grave* danger."

"You have a deal," he chuckles, though the action makes his injuries hurt.

"That reminds me. All those times when I felt a change in the air, it was you, was it not?"

He nods.

"When all you have is time..."

"You devote it to perfection," I fill in his words.

His brows go up in surprise before he throws his head and laughs.

"Ah, my love, how I've missed you," he tells me sweetly. "You are correct. Since I've been trapped here for so long, I've learned a trick or two. In this world, it's called astral projection. Lydia was the one who taught me how to do it. Since I already have enhanced mental abilities, she used to bring me books on the topic. You could say I've learned a lot in the last one hundred and fifty years."

I look at him in awe.

"What else can you do?" I whisper, remembering what Kress and Finn had mentioned. "Something like...matter manipulation?"

He nods.

"It's something that no one else, apart from you, knew about me," he confesses.

"You were the one who killed the gargoyles, weren't you? Just like you were the one to kill those people..."

His lips flatten as he gives me a tentative nod.

"It's ok." My hand stops on his chest, the combination of blood and water coursing down his skin. "I won't judge you, nor will I blame you. I understand."

"I could never let anyone who threatened you live. *Never*."

"Is that what happened with my sister?" I ask before I can help myself.

His features harden.

"Yes," he confirms. "Your sister and her husband were working with Kress and Finn. Somehow, your sister found out about our relationship and she was about to tell everyone."

I purse my lips as I think of the past.

"One of her gifts was mirror divination."

"I couldn't let her tell anyone, love. I'm sorry," he apologizes.

"I understand," I give him a tender smile. "You know, in the past, I was disappointed you'd never told me about it. That you hid something like that from me for ten long years. If you'd told to me about it... I wouldn't have been that upset, I think," I admit.

It might make me a bad person to be so inconsiderate of my own relatives, but for me, he comes first. Always.

"Darcy," he whispers, his eyes full of emotion.

"That day... I was waiting for you. I kept waiting for you," a sob escapes me. "Even as my life was fading away, I was waiting for you because I knew you would always come. And you did come. You came for me."

"Fuck. Fuck. Fuck," he curses, and before I know it, he pulls me towards him, burying his face in the crook of my neck and hugging me to him.

My hand falls away and I let him hold me. The blood from his wounds soaks the front of my dress, but for one moment, I can't seem to find it in me to stop him.

Not when it's clear he needs this just as much as I do—maybe more.

"I came too late," he croaks, his voice gravelly from the intensity of his feelings. "I'm so sorry. So very sorry, my love. I failed you."

I shake my head.

"You didn't. I'm here. You're here. And I'll get you out of this damned prison if it's the last thing I do. You have my promise on that, Amon. They won't win."

"I won't fail you a third time," he whispers in my hair, dragging his mouth across my cheek before he reaches my lips.

He hesitates for a moment, his forehead on mine as he looks into my eyes for confirmation. And I give it to him—*this* is something I would never deny him.

Slowly, he lays a soft kiss to my lips, a tentative brush of his mouth on top of mine.

I sigh as I tip my face up, giving myself to him.

"My beautiful mate," he rasps against me, nibbling at my lips and laying small bites all over the surface of my skin before he gives me our first proper kiss.

His mouth opens on top of mine, his tongue brushing against the seam of my lips as he demands entrance.

I'm powerless against him as I gasp and moan, my hands grasping at his shoulders in an attempt to ground myself. Yet it's useless when pleasure unlike I've ever known bursts inside of me as he continues kissing me.

I taste a mix of blood and that male flavor that is specifically his and I feel myself slipping, my body humming with unreleased tension.

There's nothing more potent than knowing I am with the only man who completes me in the entire world—the one who claims my heart, my soul, my goddamn essence and everything that I am.

His lips on top of mine are like homecoming. Like an euphoric potion that gets me drunk on life and the happiness of living—of being in this moment.

Present. Taking. Yielding.

We kiss for what seems like an eternity, and although we are both breathing hard and gasping for air, we'd rather gasp for each other and with each other. My lungs, just like every cell in my body, is full of him, his breath my breath, his essence my essence.

He could consume me and I wouldn't care because for once, for the first time in this life as Darcy O'Sullivan, I am happy.

I am home.

"Easy," he whispers as he wrenches himself from me.

His eyes are fully black as he barely contains himself. Yet the tension in his jaw is unmistakable, as is the fact that he is in pain.

"I'm so sorry," I apologize as I scramble off his lap—*how did I even get there?*

Getting to my knees on the floor before him, I pick up the discarded towel and I set about cleaning his wounds again. Yet he doesn't let me continue, suddenly stopping me.

His body radiates with unleashed energy—something I can feel in the way the air around us crackles with danger.

"What..." I blink in surprise as I see him climb off the bed and lower himself to the floor to be on the same level as me.

"I never want to see you kneel before me," he murmurs softly as he rests his back against the cold wall. "You will never kneel before *anyone*, Darcy. If anything, the world will kneel in front of you," he states, his voice completely serious.

"If you move around like that I won't ever finish this," I grumble, though my cheeks heat up from his pronouncement.

I bring the towel to each wound, horrified to see just how much blood pours out, some of his wounds already swollen and infected.

"How long does it take for these to go away?"

He shrugs.

Frowning, I look up at him to clarify.

"I haven't been injury-free in a long time. I suppose," he pauses as he thinks, "maybe a few weeks or so?"

"Even if they are infected?"

He grunts.

"I have to open them back up if they are infected."

I wince at his comment, already imagining him cutting open his own flesh to drain the pus so he can heal properly.

"I don't have your healing abilities," he chuckles. "I never did. Even at my full capacity it would take me quite some time to heal."

I nod, though it doesn't help the squeeze of my heart as I conjure up images of him alone and in pain. God, but those simply gut me.

"Would it work if I gave you some of my blood?" I ask softly.

His eyes turn red before he can stop himself, hunger etched on his features.

"Yes," he replies.

"Then why did you not say so from the beginning?"

"I would never ask you to do that for me..."

"If I want to? God, how can you even think otherwise. Here, take some," I extend my arm towards him.

He's staring intently at me, not making to move or accept my offer.

"Amon, you need to heal and be at full strength for the next few weeks. If this helps, then please," I tell him gently, caressing his cheek as I bring my hand to his mouth.

"If you're sure..." he murmurs, and before I know it, his hand is on my nape as he brings me to him, his nose nuzzling against my throat before he opens his lips over my skin.

I part my legs as he pulls me on his lap, my dress bunching around my hips, my center resting on top of his erection. God, but he is hard and pulsating with strength. The slight material between us is an inconvenience that we could do without, though I don't dare voice that thought out loud—not when it is imperative he heal first.

His lips on my skin, at first he simply laps at the area, licking it thoroughly before I feel the sharpness of his teeth against my flesh. But he doesn't bite immediately.

He grazes the surface, the effect immediate as goosebumps erupt all over my body. The entire gesture is so erotically charged I find myself getting increasingly aroused by it.

The heat and wetness of his mouth, the sharpness of his teeth—all make me want to combust in his embrace.

I arch my back into him, gasping just as he pierces the skin, deep enough that I can feel the blood flooding to the surface.

My lips part on a silent moan as the combination of pain and pleasure bursts through me, my entire body growing feverish and out of control. I squirm against him, seeking to feel him closer, harder, *deeper*.

I want him like I never thought I'd want anything in my life, and if he decided to take me on the spot, I would not protest. I would let him thoroughly have his way with me, hard and fast as he wants—as we *both* need. Already, I can picture him pulling his cock out and impaling me in one swift thrust, ripping through my virginity and claiming me as his —always his.

My imagination continues to fill the gaps as his hands cup my ass, kneading my flesh as he brings me closer to his hardness, moving me on top of him in circular motions that have me weep for relief.

At the same time, he drinks greedily, sucking in my skin as his tongue gently soothes the puncture wounds. There's pain, but there's also pleasure in pain—a special brand that only he is capable of giving me.

My breathing intensifies. I'm panting harshly as I rub myself against him in an attempt to alleviate the growing discomfort between my legs. My core pulses with a need for release—one that I know only he can give me.

Keeping one hand on my ass, he moves the other up my body, caressing me softly before pulling at my dress. The buttons pop and as he tugs on my brassiere, it gives way, my breasts spilling out in the open.

He brushes his fingers against my nipples, alternating between soft caresses and harsh pinches of pain that startle me as they excite me.

"Bite me," he groans, lifting his mouth just enough to speak that one command before he's back at lapping at my blood.

Euphoria fogs my brain, my mind slipping from me as I can only obey him. Bringing my mouth against his neck, I brush my lips against his warm skin, inhaling his clean yet musky scent. My tongue peeks out to lick his flesh, a hum of appreciation escaping me at his taste.

I don't know how I'm going to bite him. My teeth aren't as sharp as his to penetrate the skin. But at this point, I'm too gone to consider that. I simply open my mouth wider, lodging my teeth in his skin and biting.

Hard.

So hard that I draw blood.

The sweet metallic taste hits me immediately, as well as something else—something that leaves me breathless and wanting. My head swims as I become intoxicated by the flavor of him. I suck his flesh in, my lips making love to his neck just as his do to mine.

The more I taste him and feel myself tasted in return, the greedier I become for more of him.

Sneaking my hand between our bodies, I undo the buttons of his pants, reaching inside and wrapping my hand around his hot flesh, stroking him.

He's so big and thick—just as I remember. I squeeze my inner muscles in response, the thought of having him inside and stretching me making me mad with desire. Especially as my thumb brushes against the ringed head, feeling that thick metal that symbolizes his loyalty to me.

I'm growing hotter and hotter just touching him, feeling the moisture at the tip of his cock and imagining him filling me with his hot seed.

A ravaged cry escapes him as his hand skims the surface of my underwear, pulling it to the side so he can touch me freely. His fingers dip between my folds, finding me absolutely drenched for him. My breath catches in my throat at the sensation—at finally having his hands on me.

Everything is hot and growing hotter—the air around us, the blood in my mouth, in *his* mouth; his silky hardness that throbs in my hand, my damp core that purrs against *his* hand. Just feeling him like this and all sensations are suddenly amplified, his presence my only requisite for pleasure.

God, but my dreams had never prepared me for the reality that is Amon, the sheer physicality of him or the unspeakable pleasure he's capable of racking from my body—with just one touch.

I squeeze his erection just as he slowly circles my bud, making me whimper as I get drunk on his blood and the taste of him. When he has me on the brink of insanity, he pushes two thick digits inside of me, stretching me and leaving a pleasurable burn behind.

That's him. My Amon. The only one who can hurt me and love me at the same time—whose bite of pain is as heavenly as his lick of pleasure.

Soon, he establishes a rhythm as he pumps his fingers in and out of my tight channel, my climax building and building until I come—harder than ever before.

"Yes, please," I cry out against his skin as I continue to suck on his blood.

My vocal confirmation sets him off, and before I know it, he has me on my back, my legs spread as he drives his thick cock inside me in one smooth thrust.

My eyes widen at the sudden rip of pain, but just as it comes, it's gone, replaced by a maddening fullness as he pushes his way inside me until he's buried to the hilt.

God, but I feel him everywhere.

"Amon," I thrash on the ground, wrapping my legs around him and holding on to him.

He leans back, blood clinging to his lips and staining his teeth, his eyes equally red as he regards me with a crazed expression on his face. One filled with lust, love, and an insane animalistic attraction that makes my own heart pound, that restlessness in my blood moving in tune with his.

"Darcy," he rasps as his fingers dig in the soft skin above my hip bone, holding me in a bruising grip.

"Mine," he declares on a ragged voice. "My love. My lover. My fucking mate," he says as he withdraws all the way before slamming back inside me.

Pain mingles with pleasure as his cockring hits a deep spot within me.

He repeats the motion, gripping my ass and pulling me towards him until my pelvis meets his. He is so thoroughly inside of me I swear to God, I feel him in my belly. I release a startled breath as he circles his hips, his cock moving inside of me until no place is left untouched.

He's on his knees while I'm on my back, held immobile by his deathly grip and the way he surges back and forth, every savage thrust making me reel.

Yet from my position I can see him entirely healed. His wounds, previously ugly and jagged, have now closed, and only the stain of red remains.

"I love you, Amon," I confess, the sound torn from my lips.

"Dreamed of this too long," he grunts. "Too fucking long. Love you too much to go slow..."

"So take me. I'm yours. All yours. Don't hold back, please," I whisper, tears appearing at the corners of my eyes at the onslaught of sensations that rack my body.

I am absolutely at his mercy, yet I wouldn't have it any other way.

Yet no sooner are the words out of my mouth than I find myself on the bed, on my knees, with Amon mounting me from behind. He nudges his cock against my entrance but he doesn't push it inside. Sliding it against my folds, he lathers it in my wetness as the ring bumps against my sensitive bud, rubbing and stimulating it until I'm screaming his name as I come.

Taking advantage of my climax, he grips my hips as he thrusts all the way inside me, this position making me feel him deeper than before, and almost impossibly larger.

"Gods, Darcy, how well you take me. Your tight little cunt's strangling the hell out of my cock, lass. Fuck," he growls, his voice reverberating in the entire room, the walls seemingly shaking from the echo.

"More, please," I breathe out.

"That's it, love. Only I get to fill you." *Thrust.* "Only I get to fuck you." *Thrust.* "Only I get to pleasure you." *Thrust.* "Only I get to touch you. For all fucking eternity."

"Only you, Amon," I moan. "Only ever you."

His fingers dig in my flesh as he thrusts in and out of my body, every time a little harder and faster—every time filling me deeper.

Suddenly, his fingers move to my neck as he pulls me against him, my back meeting his front as he continues to push into me. His teeth nibble at my skin in the exact spot he'd bitten me before.

"You're so wet, lass. All wet for me," he murmurs in my ear, his voice more sedated even as he plunders my body with the same ferocity as before.

His teeth lodge in my skin as he bites just like before, more blood reaching the surface before he licks it all. The sting of pain overstimulates my body until I'm clamping on his cock with the power of my orgasm.

"That's it," he groans. "So fucking tight. You're gripping me like a fucking vise. Come," he bites my skin. "Come again."

Tremors rack my body as I start trembling uncontrollably with the power of the next climax.

"It's too much," I gasp. "Too..."

"I'm right here with you," he breathes harshly. "I've got you," he says as he holds me tighter to his body, one hand still on my neck while his other arm snakes around my front, gluing me to him as he pistons in and out of me.

The sound of flesh slapping against flesh echoes in the room, as do my frenzied moans and the fact that I'm no longer in control of my body.

He is.

Climax after climax, he takes advantage of my tightening muscles to fuck me harder, pushing himself deeper inside me, with so much strength that I feel like I'm being ripped apart—yet the ghost of pain that accompanies his brutal fucking only serves to enhance the pleasure, making me wetter. I'm becoming increasingly more aroused where I did not think it would ever be possible.

"Just like that, lass. Take me. Take everything I fucking am. Everything that is yours and yours alone," he groans.

His cock twitches inside of me, seemingly swelling in size as he fills my insides with his hot seed. He comes in long, never-ending spurts, and I feel his release everywhere.

Slumping against me, he holds me in his arms as we both struggle to find our breaths.

He nuzzles his face in my neck, giving me long, unhurried licks as he cleans the blood off my skin.

I purr softly against him, feeling utterly content and at peace.

My entire body is lethargic, and I can hardly move my limbs.

Amon doesn't seem to share my languid state as he turns me around, laying me on the bed and pulling my legs apart to examine me.

"What are you doing?" I whisper in a barely audible voice. My throat hurts from too much screaming.

"Watching you," he says, his tone tinged with wonder. "Watching my little treasure," he continues as he brushes a finger against my battered sex, sliding it through my folds and gathering the combination of our releases, only to push it back inside of me.

"I didn't hurt you too much, did I?" he asks as he circles my entrance, massaging all of the cum that drips out of me back inside. He swirls his fingers masterfully, eliciting small moans of approval from me.

I shake my head.

"It was absolutely perfect," I sigh dreamily.

"Are you sure?" he murmurs worriedly. "It was your first time in this body and I..." he swallows. "I have no control when it comes to you."

"You gave me more pleasure than I could ever imagine, Amon," I smile at him.

"Good, good," he nods, more to himself.

Tugging on his long hair, I pull him towards me.

"Kiss me," I whisper.

And he does. For moments on end, he does.

It's a while later that he brings a wet towel between my legs, cleaning me carefully.

Once the frenzy from before passes, I tug on my dress and underwear, putting myself together as I blush at my wanton behavior. He certainly has the *how to get me mad with lust* recipe down to a t.

We hadn't even taken our clothes off before he'd fucked me harder than I thought someone *could* get fucked. And as I feel tender all over—but slowly mending—I understand why he'd been so wary about taking me before, when I hadn't possessed my healing abilities. He definitely bruised and made me sore, but it was all in the most delicious type of way.

Though I'd thought about how our first time would be many times in the past, I have to say that this is beyond anything I could have imagined.

It was raw and animalistic, rooted in the most primal feeling there is.

And I have absolutely no regrets.

It seems that most of my prudishness has gone away with his wicked influence.

I smile to myself just as he comes next to me, pulling me in his arms and kissing my brow.

"You know," he smiles sheepishly. "Everyone got it so, so wrong."

I raise my brows in question.

"Your blood. Yes, it is precious, but only for me."

"What do you mean?"

"That damned coven and everyone else seems to think your blood has some magical properties. What had Fiona said, that it's the fountain of immortality?" he chuckles. "It's not. To any other person, it would be useless."

"I still don't..."

"You're my mate, Darcy. *Mine*. Your essence feeds me and only me, just like mine feeds you," he explains.

"That's why you didn't mind that I was on my period," I mumble embarrassed under my breath.

He chuckles.

"Guilty," he says as he puts his hands up. "I *loved* tasting you on your period. And I hope you might let me do that again," he drawls, but there's a hidden gleam in his eyes—something that looks like...*hope*.

Mortification colors my cheeks as I avert my gaze. Yet it's not before a *maybe* slips past my lips. After all, for him I'd do anything, wouldn't I?

"Wait," I whip my head around, realizing something. "But why would they think my blood is so special then?"

"Because the coven operates on a mountain of misinformation. Most of it perpetuated by Kress, Finn and the Holy See," he shrugs. "But also because our dear daughter had a hand in helping it spread in a way that would help us."

"What do you mean?"

"Lydia's power was not to make clear-cut predictions. She saw *versions* of the future. Potential events that could happen. She saw everything like a map where a chain of events would lead to an outcome, but if even one event were to change, the entire outcome would be different too."

He takes the towel and cleans the residue of blood from his torso before materializing another shirt that he shrugs on his body.

"She had many visions regarding us and what would happen when you were born again, but in all of them we...failed."

"Failed?"

"We died," he states, his features grave.

I stare at him open-mouthed.

"Only in one version would we succeed, and for that to happen we had to endure some hardships along the way. She did her best to ensure that version of the future would be the only one."

"Then the prophecy that I can eradicate evil or unleash it..."

"It was two-fold to confuse both the coven and Abel. I think you already know what he means to do..." he trails off, disappointment marring his features.

"He wants to use me to release you so he can then take your powers. Just as the coven wants to use me to kill you," I add carefully.

"Indeed," he sighs. "And the only way for us to win is for you to get your necklace back from Abel, and then get access to the forbidden spells of the coven—in that order."

"I see," I bite my lip as I regard him thoughtfully. "So everything needs to be played according to a script."

"Yes."

"Is that why... Is that why you pretended to be Caleb, too?" I inquire softly, though the curiosity is killing me. I've been wanting to ask him that from the beginning, but with his injuries it didn't seem like a good time.

His lips curl up in a devastating smile—certainly one that makes my insides tingle, butterflies having an all-out celebration in my stomach.

"You're right. Lydia advised me against meeting you as myself until the time was right—until you fully remembered your past as Elizabeth. And the truth is... I couldn't stay away," he admits with a sigh. "Are you mad at me?" he suddenly asks, panic flaring in his eyes.

"I am confused. Maybe it might not seem so, but you played with my feelings," I admit as I fidget with my hands in my lap. "During the day you made me fall for you as Caleb and at night I'd see the past and I would love you as Amon. At one point I was wondering how I could possibly love and desire two men equally. To an extent I think I did know, deep down, that I couldn't possibly fall for two. But in my mind I was just...confused."

He nods thoughtfully, his mouth set in a grim line.

"I'm sorry about deceiving you. You have every right to be upset about that, love. But..." he takes a deep breath. "After Rhiannon showed you that false memory from o-five, you gave in to me for the first time as Caleb. If you want to know the truth, it's that I was afraid," he confesses as he tucks my hair behind my ear. "Without your memories, I was afraid they would all poison your mind against me and take advantage of you. But most of all...I was jealous. Mad, mad with jealousy."

"What?" I blink in surprise.

"When you first came to Fairydale, I was a fucking mess thinking you might have had someone else. You spent so much time away from here—away from *me*. And with no recollection of what we were to each other you could have..." he trails off on a pained groan. "I was consumed by jealousy," he states vehemently.

The little moments come to mind, especially the time at the cabin where he'd been scary in his jealousy.

"You scared me at the cabin," I murmur.

"I scared myself. I was so mindless just thinking about you with another man, that I almost ruined everything," he groans.

"But why Caleb? Did you know he was dead?"

"Yes. It was why it proved to be the perfect opening for me. I would be there for you while using my mind control to ensure no one else but you saw me. That way, I could gently steer you in the right direction but without too much interference. The goal was to make you remember on your own, and reach your own conclusions."

"Is that why you never told me too much?"

He nods.

"You have no idea how painful it was to see you so oblivious of our past and everything around. I wanted to tell you everything *every single day*. But Lydia had foreseen a version of the future in which I told you the truth from the beginning, and the coven ultimately convinced you it was all a lie."

"I understand," I tell him softly. And I do—especially as I see how conflicted he is about the entire situation. "But I hope you now know you have no reason to be jealous of *anyone*," I smile warmly at him.

"No reason?" he scoffs. "Darlin', I was fucking jealous of myself," he suddenly says.

My eyes widen in confusion.

"Every time you called me *Caleb* instead of my name, I was dying inside. Especially when I made you come. That was, quite honestly, the biggest blow."

A snort escapes me, followed by a giggle before I can't help myself but laugh. He is so serious about this, so full of indignation that I feel bad for finding it amusing. But how can I not?

"So let me get this right. You were jealous of yourself?"

He grumbles something under his breath, looking away as he realizes how this all sounds, too.

"Ah, my beloved Amon," I whisper as I come closer, nestling against his chest and nuzzling my face against it. "You're so cute."

"I'm not cute," he huffs, though his arms are locked tightly around me.

"Yes, you are," I tell him pointedly. "And you are also the only man I've ever wanted. In this life, or the one before. Yes, I was away from you for a long time, with no memory of you or of our love. But I *never* looked at another man. Of that you have my vow."

Leaning back just enough so he can look into my eyes, I topple all my mental barriers as I give him unfettered access to my mind, showing him my entire life before him.

"Darcy..." he whispers in awe as he sees everything that happened in my life before Fairydale. Most importantly, he can see my naked feelings and the fact that even as I was falling for Caleb, my heart was irrevocably his.

"See? There is no reason to be jealous," I murmur lovingly.

"My darling girl," he whispers as he brings his lips to my face, peppering kisses all over my skin. Tugging me to his chest, he rocks softly with me—almost as if he didn't dare let me go for fear this is all a dream. His warmth penetrates my skin as he imprints himself on me, his presence making me feel complete for the first time in my life.

"I've never looked at another female in my entire existence," he answers my silent question. "Only you, my love. Before, or after. Only ever you."

I would have never doubted that, but hearing his verbal confirmation brings an ineffable peace to my soul—as if I've been teetering on the edge of the precipice until now but I've finally found my balance.

Holding me in his arms, he explains everything from the beginning —how he'd used Caleb's identity to get closer to me but also protect me from the people in town. His telepathic abilities had helped him sow different thoughts into people's minds to create a reality where it seemed that his Caleb was part of the town's fabric. And since I can't not question him about Grace and her supposed crush on him, he confirms that her crush had been on the real Caleb, not on him and that he'd never met her. He'd merely borrowed some of the real Caleb's life history to have a more solid background while still being himself.

I nod, happy he's giving me a detailed account of everything. I may be still smarting about his small deception, but I can't help the way my heart warms at his efforts to be by my side.

"Can you tell me what happened in eighteen-five? How did the plague come about?"

I remember my own side of the story, but I still do not know his.

"Kress and Finn ambushed me at the outskirts of the town. They were no match for me, but they slowed me down. When I tried to get to the church, most of the residents went against me. I realized after that

Abel had made a deal with the mayor's son to raise the town against us —they even sent some people to raid our house. Luckily, Lydia knew about it and she hid," he smiles against my skin. "But when I arrived at the church and saw you and Abraham..." his voice breaks just as his arms tighten around me. "I was out of control, love. I didn't even realize what was happening. I only knew I wanted everyone to hurt as much as I did. And if the coven hadn't come at that time, I fear..." he swallows hard. "I fear no one would have been safe. Guilty or innocent. I would have killed everyone. Just like before..." he trails off and I instinctively know he means when Sela died—events which I still do not remember.

I bring my hand on top of his, swirling my finger over his skin in a comforting gesture.

"It's ok," I whisper. I'd already intuited he would have been devastated by that sight. "I don't blame you. If I were capable of it, I would have done the same," I admit, even as it pains me. After all, I'd once thought Amon was lost to me, and I lost myself too.

"It was a coordinated attack they'd been planning for years, Darcy. And because I trusted Abel, I was never aware," he whispers, telling me how much he regrets never probing his mind.

"Don't beat yourself for it. He was our son. It's normal to *not* suspect him."

"I should have paid more attention to him. I would have realized that all he wanted was power. Just like Ambrosius, just like everyone else we ever met. All they ever want is power," he says in a ragged voice.

"Ambrosius?"

The name sounds vaguely familiar.

"You might know your life as Elizabeth," he murmurs against my cheek. "But you still need to remember your life as Sela."

"You won't tell me?"

He shakes his head.

"You need to remember everything on your own, love. Compared to your past life, your life as Sela stretches across thousands of years. I could never summarize something of that magnitude and do it justice."

"Thousands of years?" I echo in awe.

"Soon you'll know the entire truth. And then you'll be able to act accordingly."

"You said I need to get the necklace first. That will give me back my memories, no?"

He nods.

"That necklace holds all the secrets. Not only to your memories, but also to your true powers."

According to Amon, the necklace only recognizes me as its master and as such I do not need to ask for permission to use its powers.

Anyone can take it, but to use it, the necklace needs to be freely given, just as Abel had asked me for verbal consent when he'd demanded it in the church.

"I touched the stone once, and I had a flash of us in Ancient Rome. It was brief, but I didn't have the birthmark there."

Amon stiffens against me.

"You didn't," he confirms.

"You're not going to tell me why, are you?"

I draw back to look at him.

He purses his lips, a sad smile on his lips as he shakes his head.

"The only thing I can tell you is that I am not a demon, nor are you one. They called me as such because it was the only thing they could use to instill fear in people. Regular people knew the biblical tales and they feared the devil and his army of demons. When the Holy See became aware of our existence, the entire Church was terrified of the ramifications. At first, they tried to use us, but when it didn't suit them anymore, we became the foe. Kress and Finn helped in large part, playing on people's beliefs in order to turn them against us. At the end of the day, we were the *other*—something they couldn't understand nor make sense of."

"Kress and Finn. They are the same as us, aren't they?"

Amon nods.

"It's my fault. They were always after me since I am a liability to everyone if I'm not dead. They've been following us for centuries."

"Why?" I whisper.

He merely smiles, and I realize I'm not likely to get anything out of him.

"When you see the past, you will know everything. I never had any secrets from you. You know my entire history, who I am, *what* I am, and why we've been on the run for so long, love."

Biting my lip, I regard him for the longest time before I tip my head in a hesitant nod.

I am curious about everything, but if Amon says I need to remember by myself, then I will trust him.

More than anything, I trust Lydia and the fact that she's looking out for us—even from the grave. She'd certainly arranged for everything to play out according to her vision.

"Although, while we're at it, I might as well confess something else," he murmurs softly, and I could swear I note a blush on his cheeks.

"What?"

"Mr. Meow," he clears his throat.

My eyes widen in fear.

"What happened to Mr. Meow? Is he ok? I haven't seen him around in so long," I burst out, panicking.

Dear Lord, but I hope nothing happened to him.

"No, nothing happened to him."

"Where is he then? You know where he is, don't you?"

"You could...say so?" he scratches the back of his head in discomfort.

"Amon... What is it?"

He's really scaring me at this point.

"Well, you're looking at him," he winces as he says it, averting his gaze.

My mouth opens and closes as I stare at him.

"Can you repeat that? You're a cat?"

"Darcy darlin'," he laughs at my scandalized expression. "No, I am not a cat. But I have, at times, inserted my consciousness into one."

"I don't..." I trail off as it dawns on me.

He was Mr. Meow. That's why the cat was so damn smart, because it was actually Amon.

"I took you in my bath," I accuse, pointing a finger at him. "I slept with you!"

"You also gave me dead rats to eat," he mumbles dryly. "Which, by the way, are not at all tasty."

"But you ate them anyway," I raise a brow as I cross my arms over my chest.

"Of course I did," he says in indignation. "It was that or you'd be sad."

I blink.

"And I didn't want you to be sad," he grumbles.

"Amon..."

My gaze softens as I look at him.

"I needed to be by your side somehow. Even when I was down here and couldn't get out. I needed a way to be with you," he adds vehemently, as if he's trying to explain himself for fear I would be upset.

"Amon, I'm not mad. Maybe surprised, I guess. But how could I ever be mad that you'd go through so much trouble to be with me? If anything, I'm extremely flattered," I admit.

"You're sure you're not mad?" He repeats, his eyes wide and wary.

I give him a brisk nod.

His arms shoot out as he brings me to his chest, his lips on my temple as he gives me one loud smooch after another.

"Is there anything else you want to tell me?" I chuckle.

"No, I promise."

"Good, now maybe we can go over our plan of action? We have ten days until the coven will perform the spell. That means I need to get the necklace back as soon as possible."

He grunts, suddenly serious.

"You need to be careful with Abel. Though he has access to your powers, it's limited. You're the only one who can fully master the necklace. For anyone else it would be one percent of its actual power."

"Rhiannon said he's weakening. Since my birth..."

"Yes. It's exactly as you think. The jewel recognizes you as its rightful owner, and since you came back into the world, it stopped working as well for Abel. That isn't to say he hasn't learned a trick or two. He can summon those odious creatures and they can help him in a fight. The only bright side is that it requires him days to do a summoning ritual, which means we need to plan for a quick intervention."

"He never goes anywhere without his cane," I mention. "Aside from that one instance when I was visiting," I frown. "There was a disturbance upstairs and he left it unattended."

"Upstairs you say?" He inquires, deep in thought.

"Why? What are you thinking of?"

"I was with you at his house last time if you remember," he adds and I nod.

Mr. Meow had suddenly joined me on the way. Now, I see it as his way of taking care of me.

"I was looking through his house while you two talked. And when he was called upstairs, I went with him."

"And?"

"I couldn't go inside. There's a room on the second floor, at the very end of the hallway, that has a strong barrier spell around it. In Mr. Meow's body, it was too much for me."

"What do you think he's hiding there?"

"Something important enough for him to leave his cane unattended."

I nod slowly.

"You think if I manage to get there I might stand a chance against him?"

"I don't know," he takes a deep breath. "Honestly, I'm afraid of what he's capable of either way. Even if I go out, I won't be at full capacity to help too much," he sighs dejectedly.

"You're not coming," I suddenly tell him.

"Of course I'm coming."

"Amon, you said only if I'm in danger."

"And this constitutes the worst danger, Darcy. I'm coming and there's absolutely no room for discussion."

"But... You... You'll be hurt for it, you silly beast!" I cry out in frustration. "I won't have you hurt on my account. I'll figure something out to tackle Abel."

"No," he shakes his head, crossing his arms and telling me it's final. "He's my son, too. I need to be there for it."

Well, when he puts it like that...

"But you'll get hurt," I make another feeble attempt at countering his arguments.

"And you'll give me more of your blood, won't you?" he murmurs softly. "And more of your sweet pussy," he continues as he licks my cheek.

"You're not playing fair," I stammer, the heat of his body making me forget my thoughts.

"Say yes," he continues as he takes my lower lip between his teeth, nibbling softly at it. "Say yes, darlin'."

"Fine," I sigh. "Now kiss me properly."

"Much obliged," he chuckles.

Then his lips are on mine.

Properly this time.

And as I melt in his arms, I truly hope this is the right decision.

Because when he hurts, I hurt more.

Chapter Twenty-Five

The following day, I wait until nightfall when everyone is asleep before I attempt to go down to the catacombs. I'd spent the entire day preparing some nice food for him since I doubt he's had anything stellar in a long time—dead rats notwithstanding.

I wince as I think of him eating those to please me. My sweet beast.

As I come to Amon's quarters, I find him already waiting for me.

He's shirtless, only wearing a pair of loose pants that hang low on his hips, all his muscular splendor in the open for me to admire.

His hair is wet and droplets of water cling to his skin.

The moment he sees me, he pulls me to him for a deep kiss that makes me dazed.

"You took a shower," I whisper. "Where?"

He points to a corner at the end of the room, separated by a divider. That's when I realize that he's installed an entire bathroom down here.

"I have to say, your tastes in interior design are not bad."

He chuckles.

"I had to make do. Since I spend all my time down here, I figured I would make it as comfortable as I could."

"Let's eat," I say as I take his hand, leading him to the table.

Placing the basket I'd brought with me on it, I start unpacking it, removing some food, water, and wine.

Since I knew I would be seeing him again, I wanted to prepare something special for him so I made him a few dishes.

"You cooked?" he inquires softly as he pokes his head in my basket, his eyes filled with excitement as he examines everything I brought.

"Of course. From now on, I'll bring you food every day."

He licks his lips as he gazes longingly at the stew I made.

"Did I tell you how much I love you?" he murmurs, though he isn't looking at me.

I release a soft giggle as I place a plate in front of him, filling it with a little of everything.

And as he digs in, I can't help the way my heart warms as I see him eat with so much gusto.

"I haven't had food cooked by you in so long," he moans softly. "I almost forgot it's an experience in itself."

Taking a seat opposite him, I rest my elbows on the table as I watch him, *that* sight being an experience in itself.

Maybe yesterday I was a little too lost in his presence that I didn't get to appreciate him fully, but as I stare at him, I can't believe this man is mine.

He is so handsome and kind, and despite having a slightly chaotic bent that might be construed as evil by some, he is just my big, bad protector—the man who always put me above everything, including his own welfare.

For that alone he has my ultimate loyalty too, because he deserves nothing less than someone who would also put him first. Someone who would never doubt him, even when the worst evidence is presented.

And that is what I've realized about myself since I've arrived in Fairydale.

I might have had a slight lapse in judgment when Rhiannon had showed me that false memory, but from the beginning I'd known that he was never capable of something like that.

Even his evil deeds—as others perceive them—are nothing more than his reaction to the world that seeks to harm him, or me.

My Amon will never intentionally hurt someone unless they ask for it. It is true that when it happens, he is capable of mass destruction. But I would never begrudge him that.

Never.

I know he's worried I'll see him differently if I see him in his destructive mode. But how could I, when I know his core?

"What are you thinking about?" he asks, raising his gaze to meet mine.

"Can't you read my mind?" I challenge.

He shakes his head, his lips tipped up.

"I want to hear it from your lips."

"I was thinking that you might very well have the ability to destroy the entire world," I whisper, gauging his reaction to it.

He grunts, his lips flattening.

"I might. If something were to happen to you again..." he trails off.

"I don't know how I would react, Darcy. It would be easy to tell you I would never do it again. But after what happened in o-five, I fear I don't even know myself anymore. I've never felt despair like that before and I struck out—*violently.*"

I reach across the table to place my hand over his, squeezing his fingers gently.

"I know," I whisper.

"People can think the worst of me. They may think I'm Satan personified, the epitome of evil or destroyer of worlds, but as long as you love me and see *me*, I don't care."

"I don't care either," I give him a sad smile. "All my life, for one reason or another, I tried to live up to people's expectations. Be proper because it was expected of me and my position, and be *good* because of my upbringing. If not, people would immediately associate the stigma of being an orphan, with me being bad. So I tried to beat it. I pushed down all other wants and desires and I pursued what I was supposed to," I take a deep breath, remembering all those moments in the dark when I would yearn for more—when I would see myself as being more.

With time, I'd managed to stifle those feelings until only a light restlessness remained. One that could be ignored as I went about my life—ignorant and complacent about everything else that happened around me.

"But I'm done being that person. I'm done letting others dictate how I should feel or behave, or who I should love. So I don't care about what outsiders think of you—of us. I only care about our relationship and the fact that you are so good to me unlike anyone's ever been."

"My darling girl," he smiles. "I'm proud of you."

"Thank you. I'm rather proud of myself," I add bashfully. "It's not easy to beat those voices inside my head that hold me down, but slowly, I find that I'm able to do it. Remembering my life as Elizabeth has helped me enormously. Because even then..." my lips tremble as they pull into a smile. "I went against everyone for you. Just like I would now."

"You've done it before," he comments before he can help himself.

My eyes widen and I realize he's talking about Sela.

"I never asked you. How do you feel calling me by different names? Isn't it...odd?"

He shakes his head.

"For me you're still you, and any name of yours I would infuse with just as much love," he answers matter-of-factly.

"You're such a charmer."

"It's the truth," he shrugs.

"There is this famous psychoanalyst Carl Jung and in his view, the persona is made up of experiences and social and cultural context. In that instance, without any experience of the past, wouldn't you say I am an entirely different person? Doesn't memory *create* a person?"

He thinks on it for a moment.

"You're right to an extent. Yes, memory does constitute the basis of a person, and their experiences shape who they are. But I also believe in intention and reaction. In that integral part of your essence that would react the same to a situation regardless of whether you were Sela, Elizabeth or Darcy."

I nod slowly, thinking back to myself and Elizabeth and agreeing with his assessment. Though the time had been different, I hadn't felt any less myself, regardless of the different upbringing and socioeconomic status.

"But you also said social context," he smiles. "And in this case *I* am your social context. You might find it a bold claim, but you are you because of me, just as I am me because of you. We're so tightly interlinked, Darcy, that sometimes we're not two individuals—just one. It's been like this from the very beginning. From the first moment we met, made even more so by our mating. It doesn't matter what world we're in, or how far we are from each other. We *are* relative to one another."

I pick up a piece of bread, chewing slowly on it.

"Do you remember what I told you the first time we met in seventeen-ninety?"

"What?"

"My madness recognizes yours; just like my essence recognizes yours. As individuals, we're semi-whole. Only together do we feel finally fulfilled. I know you've felt it before."

Biting my lip, I give him a sharp nod.

"Memory or no memory, it's your presence alone that completes me. Never doubt that."

"I know what you mean. I saw you and my entire being wept with an unknown relief. Never have I experienced something like that, Amon."

Taking my hands into his, he lays a kiss on each knuckle, all the while maintaining eye contact.

"I don't want you to ever doubt that I love you for *you*, not for the name you bear—never that."

"You too," I whisper as a blush mars my cheeks. "You have no idea how confused I was with Caleb because how could I feel the same way about two different people? Maybe I was a little slow, or maybe I didn't want to admit what was in front of me. But even then, I *felt* it."

"Let's not mention that name again," he grumbles. "I think I'm traumatized from hearing you say it too many times."

"Amon!" I giggle. "Didn't you just say it's the essence that matters, not the name?"

He pouts as he turns away, and he reminds me so much of Mr. Meow I just want to take him in my arms and kiss his white hair—though it might prove more difficult with Amon considering he's at least twice my size.

"I'm a jealous man, darling," he admits with a weary sigh. "You'll have to get used to this small flaw of mine, but I become quite rabid if anyone dares to sniff around you."

"Small flaw, huh?" I raise a brow in a playful manner.

"I promise to refrain myself from killing them *just* for looking," he puts a hand up. "It's the most I can do. If they put a finger on you, then all bets are off," he smiles, quite pleased with himself.

"What about me then? Do I get the same courtesy?"

"What do you mean?" he frowns.

"Well, you're a handsome man. What if a woman touches you? Can I kill her too?" I ask innocently, curious to see how he'd react.

He stands up abruptly, the chair flying a distance away from him.

"W-what? Another woman touching me?" he asks incredulously. "Another woman that is not you?" he repeats, almost as if he cannot believe I would even suggest such a thing.

"Yes. Can I kill her if she does that?"

"No. I'll kill her myself first," he declares fervently. "Any person who upsets you, whether by intention or implication, *regardless* of sex, will die by my hand," he pushes his chin up, placing his arms over his chest in a confident stance.

I stifle a laugh.

"So let me get this straight. You're allowed to get jealous and consequently off people, but I'm not, because you will kill them before I can even get jealous."

"That is absolutely right," he nods. "It's my job to protect you, and that means your mental state too."

I stare at him a little flabbergasted, yet I can't help the way my lips pull up into a smile.

How is he so adorable?

"Fine, fine. You win," I tell him. "Now bring the chair back and finish your meal. It's probably cold already."

"Ok," he murmurs, grabbing his chair and sitting back at the table as if nothing happened—as if he didn't just give me an impassioned speech.

And just like that, he's back to eating, slowly savoring the food while staring at me.

Well, adorable might be an understatement.

We spend moments on end in companionable silence as we eat while our eyes feast on each other. When he's finished, he helps me put the dirty dishes aside before placing a stack of books on the table.

"So, what do you want to start with?" he asks as he opens each of them to the title page.

I look at the books with a mix of horror and apprehension.

"Are you sure we should do this?"

"We convened to go to Abel's house in a few days. That gives us only a little time to prepare. And since you're technically a Stuart descendant, you can use these spells."

"But I've never done a spell before," I whisper as I look at the tomes before me—all in Latin.

"Sure you have. You took down the barrier. That was you performing a spell."

"But..."

"I'll help you," he smiles as he takes my hand, giving it a quick squeeze. "Lydia explained to me enough to guide you, and she even picked the spells she knew you would need. Besides, I happen to be fluent in Latin."

"I'll have to memorize them, though, no?" I ask as I bite my lip.

"Well, yes. But first we need to make sure you do them right."

"But Amon," I burst out. "I was never good at memorization. Even at school, I could never get it right," I sigh. "I have this thing where if the letters of the words are similar enough, I'll mess them up. Surely that will be a problem with a spell that needs exact wording. I might even make it worse."

"You won't," he shakes his head, giving me a roguish smile. "I'm here to ensure you will do just fine. Besides, you only need to learn some defensive spells. I'll take care of the offensive."

I pout as I look at him, hoping he would change his mind, but he seems quite staunch in his conviction.

Taking a seat at the table, I drag a deep breath in my lungs.

"Fine, let's do this."

"We need a specific plan of attack to ensure we are successful. More than anything, we need to make sure we are not found out by Kress and Finn."

I nod.

"I guess it will help that Abel's power is dwindling. But..."

He tilts his head, waiting for me to speak.

"Will we have to kill him?" I ask on a whisper.

Why is it that killing him leaves such a bad taste in my mouth? This is the man who killed *me* and his brother. Yet at the same time, he was still our son. How could I ever justify raising a hand to my child?

"We must do what we must do, darlin'. There is no other way around this, unfortunately. Abel made his bed when he decided power was more important than his family. I can understand why he would hate me, since I am guilty of killing his parents. But you? Or Abraham? Or Rhiannon and your mother?" Amon pauses, and in his features I note the same deep pain that stabs at my heart.

Abraham should have *never* died. The fact that he did, in my own arms... That I felt life go out of him... The sight of that still haunts me. And I doubt it will ever stop.

But Amon is right, the Abel we knew is gone. He's not only committed the murder of his kin, but he'd raped and perpetuated violence, all in an attempt to get his hands on *more* power.

"In his mind, we are both just as guilty. But to go against his own brother... To commit those atrocities..."

"Power corrupts," Amon purses his lips. "But it's not power itself that poisons the brain. It's the euphoria of chasing after it—of always getting more and more. It's an addiction, Darcy. And unfortunately, too many people have fallen prey to it."

"You mean that Ambrosius, don't you?"

He nods, his features tight with sadness.

"We've been around for too long not to experience the worst of humanity. Have we seen the best, too? Yes. But more often than not, we're shown that the bad outweighs the good—at least where it matters."

"I don't understand," I frown.

"I know you don't," he smiles sadly. "And I promised myself I wouldn't say too much. But we've seen empires come and go, we've seen men in power and *what* they do with that power. And unfortunately, nine times out of ten, they choose to abuse it."

"So you're saying he cannot be saved," I sigh.

"It's too late, love. Believe me, it pains me just as much as it does you. But we cannot let that obstruct our view. We need to get you that jewel back. I really hope nothing happened to it while it was in his possession..." he trails off.

"Alright," I say, imbuing my voice with determination.

I pick up one of the books at random since all of them have Latin titles.

"This one is all about barriers and shields. I know you can heal, but your power isn't fully formed. You saw what happens if you overtax yourself."

I nod.

"I stop healing if I use up my energy."

"That means we need to make sure you get minimally injured—

ideally not at all. You might be able to handle superficial wounds. But anything more than that..." he shakes his head.

"How is it that my blood works for you, then?" I suddenly ask.

He smiles.

"Because it's not only your ability to heal that gives me strength. It's the fact that you're my second half. We're bound together, Darcy. We complement each other."

"Does that mean your blood would help me too?"

"Theoretically, it would give you some of my energy, but it wouldn't heal you," he grimaces, about to say something else before he shakes his head and continues. "You're the super healer in the family, and when you're at full strength, you can heal more than just yourself."

"I saw in that vision. I was healing a little boy."

"At full capacity, your power is boundless, love. It's why everyone is after it."

I study him for a moment and the way he regards me with such love —such confidence. Just knowing he trusts me with this makes me want to give my best.

"Then let's do this," I declare.

I turn the page to the spell he'd marked. He reads it out loud while I follow with my finger, trying to remember the right pronunciation.

"This one should give you a temporary armor."

"How temporary are we talking about?"

His lips flatten in a pitiful smile.

"One and done. It's why we need a combination of spells."

I grumble something under my breath, but eventually I say the words out loud like he'd done.

"Nothing happened," I frown.

"Well, let's see," he lifts his hand, and under my very gaze, it morphs into a sharp blade.

I'd almost forgotten he was capable of that.

He brings it to me, stabbing—or more, like poking—me with it.

Instead of penetrating my flesh, though, it seems to be stopped by some invisible barrier.

"Oh, God. It worked," I exclaim as my eyes widen in surprise.

"It did," he chuckles. "But remember that this one can only be used once every ninety minutes. You might want to save it for hard impacts."

I nod as I throw my eyes over the words again. They aren't too hard to memorize—just a couple of lines.

"Ok, what's next?" I meet his gaze, suddenly feeling excitement simmer in my blood.

Maybe this spell business isn't as hard as I'd thought. Certainly, the reward at getting it right is quite intoxicating.

We go over a few more protective spells, and I recognize one of them as being what Rhiannon had used in her fight with Abel. That one is slightly more complicated, though, and the moment I'm done reciting it, I start feeling lightheaded and we need to put a temporary halt to our practice.

"Here," Amon seats me on the bed and gives me a glass of water.

"Thank you," I murmur.

"You're doing great, darlin'. I know this is a lot, but honestly, most of it is for my peace of mind. I need to know you can defend yourself when the time comes."

"I understand."

For the rest of the week, we spend every possible moment together as we practice the spells Lydia had left for me.

Amon proves to be quite the teacher with his unlimited amount of patience and amazing insight. If I hadn't been completely in love with him already, I would have fallen for him simply for his pristine work ethic and sweet personality.

Though I don't know much about the past, I remember that he was a general in the army. And I can clearly see how that reflects in his manners. He speaks with a certain assuredness that makes me want to hang on to his every word and obey every command. But more than anything, I can see his vast experience in how he approaches this one mission.

He's already made one main plan and countless spare ones as he tried to account for everything that might go wrong.

"Are you sure you're ready for this, love?" he murmurs in my hair as he holds me in his arms the night before we're set to put our plan in motion.

"Yes. And we need to succeed. The coven is coming to the manor soon. We need to get this done before they arrive."

"You're right. Depending on how experienced the members are, they might be able to feel the disturbance if we do it with them in Fairydale."

"We can do this," I whisper, hoping to cheer myself on.

"Remember that if you happen to forget words from the spells, call my name and I will feed them to you in your mind."

"It will all be fine," I whisper as I nuzzle into him.

We go to sleep wrapped in each other, and as I'm getting used to sleeping with him, I don't know how I ever managed to do it by myself in the past.

Amon was right that there's something about our connection that goes beyond just being a couple. When I'm with him, I feel unusually whole. Every little part of me vibrates with every little part of him, each so thoroughly complementary we're like two pieces of a puzzle matched to perfection.

He'd implied the reason for this hides in my memories as Sela, and I cannot wait to find out about our past—how everything started.

I can tell that Amon has a hard time not telling me about our past and sometimes he has to censor himself to not give away too much. At the same time, it's clear that most of our fondest memories are in *that* past. And that is all the motivation I need to see this to the end.

I need to know who I am—who I was.

The following day, we both wake up and slowly dress while going over our plan once more. When we're ready to head out, Amon flashes us in front of the church.

"Are you ok?" my eyes widen when I see his eyes flash between light blue and a deep red.

He strains a smile.

"I'll be fine in a moment. It's always bad in the beginning. The prison seeks to hold me inside, and though I am here, I can feel tendrils of pure energy that try to drag me back down. It takes a bit of concentration to fight it."

He takes a seat on a boulder as he takes a deep breath—in and out as he tries to stabilize himself.

"This is what happened at the cabin, wasn't it? You were having problems fighting the prison's hold."

He gives a brisk nod.

"I'll be fine soon. Please don't worry."

Once his eyes stop flashing, he gets up and takes off his already blood-stained shirt, discarding it.

My hand flies to my mouth when I see the wounds appearing on his back and torso. Almost like someone had clawed his skin out.

"Amon," I whisper, tears accumulating at the corners of my eyes. I don't even think as I bring my wrist to his mouth, encouraging him to drink.

He shakes his head.

"I don't want to weaken you now," he gives me a sad smile as he cleans the best he can of the blood flowing down his skin before taking out a new black shirt.

Seeing him in so much pain shakes me to my core. My actions are entirely instinctive as I bite hard on my tongue—enough to draw blood. Raising myself on the tips of my toes, I cup his cheeks, bringing him in for a kiss. As I open my mouth, I urge him to suck my tongue.

"You shouldn't have done that," he rasps as he wrenches himself from me. His breathing is ragged as he stares at me, his tongue tracing the remnants of blood on his upper lip.

Maybe it was a few drops, but some of his injuries are already healing.

"There will be more, Darcy. You can't heal all of them now. We can worry about this later, ok?" he watches me closely, waiting for me to agree.

"Ok," I sigh.

Putting on his clean shirt, he makes himself presentable so there is no trace of blood, or of injury. He changes his hair and eye color to black once more, taking the appearance he'd used when he passed himself as Caleb.

When he's finally done, we start hand in hand towards Abel's house.

It takes us a few minutes to reach it, and as we give each other a look of encouragement, I knock on the door.

As before, the same elderly lady opens it.

"Helena, right?" I give her a small smile. "Is Mr. Nicholson home?"

She looks us both up and down before she beams at us.

"Of course. Why don't you come into the drawing room while I tell him you're here. I hope this time you're staying for lunch."

"I'm so sorry about last time. I wasn't feeling very well. But this time I promise we'll stay and taste your cooking."

"And this is..." she moves her gaze from me to Amon.

"Oh, this is my husband."

"You're married," she gasps. "But I thought you were a Miss."

I purse my lips as I try to look convincing.

"Truth to be told, I've never revealed this before since my husband and I were not on good terms when I came to Fairydale. But he ended up chasing after me and here we are," I sigh. "But now that he's here, I wanted him to meet Mr. Nicholson since he is my only living relation."

"Oh, dear! Of course! He will be so pleased to hear about this. Let me get him for you. Come," she adds effusively, showing us to the drawing room before going upstairs to call on Abel.

We both take a seat, our hands still linked together.

My heart is beating fast in anticipation and a touch of fear since I do not know how all of this will unfold.

According to the plan Amon had concocted, we are to engage Abel in conversation at first, lull him into a sense of security while dropping enough hints to unsettle him.

"Darcy, how nice to see you!" Mr. Nicholson suddenly appears in the doorway, slowly walking inside the room. He's using his cane for support, and as before, my eyes are drawn to the jewel resting atop it.

"Mr. Nicholson," I greet him. "This is my husband, Anthony."

"Pleased to meet you, sir," Amon extends his hand.

"Husband?" He watches him with narrowed eyes. "What a surprise," he adds drily, and I can tell he doesn't seem to like the fact that I'm married.

"Have we met before?" he suddenly asks as he takes Amon's hand.

"Hmm, have we?" he murmurs softly.

"I came to speak to you about a most urgent matter," I intervene.

Abel grunts, still watching Amon warily, studying him as if he can tell there's something wrong.

"What is it?" He barely wrenches his eyes from Anthony to look at me.

We all take a seat. Amon and I on the couch, while Abel sits on the armchair opposite us, resting his cane against the outside of the chair—just as we'd anticipated.

"The coven will be here shortly, and they will proceed with the ritual. Two emissaries from the Holy See have already arrived at the Hale manor and they've taken over the preparations. The coven members are set to arrive soon to discuss the plan for the spell," I take a deep breath. "I haven't been able to dissuade Rhiannon."

"I see. I was afraid it would come to this," he sighs dramatically.

"What can we do? I tried to approach Rhiannon with it and she told me the most awful lies about you," I start, putting on my best act.

He shakes his head, and I know he's already anticipated that Rhiannon would tell me everything. And despite her track record with lies, I am quite certain she wasn't lying about this.

"Of course she would," he agrees. "You saw how she treated me just for attempting to talk with you. It's actually a wonder that you've managed to come here today," he says as his eyes stray to Amon. There's a twitch in his cheek as he studies him carefully, almost as if trying to place him somewhere.

"She is busy with the people from the Holy See."

"I am happy you understand that it's all lies. Rhiannon and I had a fully consensual relationship some fifty years ago. When she became pregnant she decided to lie about the abuse because she didn't want to be seen as a single mother. The times were very different, you see. Now you might be able to survive the stigma, but back then the entire town shunned her. It was only her name and some decades of hiding that allowed her to show her face again."

"I knew there must be some explanation for it," I nod emphatically. "How could she say that you instructed Leo Pierce to rape my mother to get her pregnant? All because you seemingly knew of some prophecy that stated when and to whom I would be born," I give a dry laugh.

"Right," he clenches his teeth. "Of course it is not true."

He brings his gaze to Amon again.

"How come you've brought your husband with you?"

"You see, we had a huge row just before I left for Fairydale and I swore I'd never see him again," I explain, giving him a fake history of myself and *Anthony*.

He nods along to my story, but it's clear he has doubts.

"So you see, we've come to ask for help. I don't know how to proceed, Mr. Nicholson. You're the only one that can guide me," I tell him, proud of myself for not wincing at such a blatant lie and even more suffocating pandering. God, I might have to bleach my mouth after this.

"But how could I help if they are so set on performing the ritual? I am a mere old man against an entire coven of witches."

"Well, you see..." I bite my lip in uncertainty as I look to my husband then back at Abel. "I had a dream."

"A dream?" his interest is suddenly piqued.

I bite my lip as I do my best to appear uncertain.

"My ancestor, Elizabeth Creed, appeared in my dream."

He blinks repeatedly, unable to mask his shock.

From what Amon had told me, no one is aware of the fact that I *am* Elizabeth. Not even Abel who knew Elizabeth. They all put it down to an eerie similarity both in appearance and purpose.

"You dreamed about Elizabeth Creed?" he swallows hard.

I nod.

"It scared me so bad. Good thing my darling Anthony came to find me on time otherwise, I thought I would go crazy."

"Why," he wets his lips, leaning forward. "What happened in that dream?"

"A frightening thing, Mr. Nicholson. She said the ritual will fail and Amon will be released and he will avenge her death. That he will unleash death over Fairydale again."

"Avenge her death?" he repeats, seemingly only caring about that aspect.

"Right? Didn't she die so long ago? How could he avenge her death when her killer must be already dead?"

"Indeed... Did she say anything else?"

I shake my head.

"She didn't mention the identity of her killer?" he continues to probe.

"No, she didn't tell me who it was. But she showed me the entire scene. It happened in the Old Church, did it not?"

His eyes flicker with surprise.

"What else did she show you?"

"The killer was a young man, I think. I've never seen him before. He demanded her necklace after which he killed someone else at the scene.

Another man," I bring my fingers to my lips, nibbling on them. "While she was grieving for him, he stabbed her. God, I've never seen anything more horrific," I recount as tears stream down my cheeks.

Abel's face is white as he struggles to open his mouth to say something.

"You seem distraught, Darcy," he mentions, his lips trembling slightly.

"I suppose the scene affected me too much. Would you mind telling me where the restroom is so I can refresh myself?"

"Certainly," he gives me a clipped answer, his jaw ground tight.

He directs me to the end of the hallway and I give him a sad smile as I exit the drawing room.

I don't go to the restroom, though. Instead, I enter the kitchen where I find Helena toiling away at what would be our lunch.

"Helena," I call out. "Mr. Nicholson asked me to tell you that he needs something urgently from town. Would you mind going there to buy it?"

"He did?" She blinks.

"Yes," I purse my lips. "We need a selection of red, white and purple candles, some marine salts..." I give her an entire list of inane purchases that she needs to get.

She regards me skeptically in the beginning until I assure her it's for a secret ritual.

Remembering she'd been the one overseeing the secret room on the second floor, I assume she is familiar with Abel's witchy pastime.

The moment I mention that, she finally relents.

"He's trusting you to choose the best items, Helena. Please don't disappoint us."

"Of course not. Mr. Nicholson knows to expect only the best from me," she says as she puts a coat and a hat on. Grabbing her purse, she is already out the door.

This way, Helena won't be harmed in our upcoming altercation.

I tarry a few more moments before I return to the drawing room.

"Your husband was telling me how you two met. Quite interesting that you did not tell anyone you were married. Mr. Vaughan certainly didn't find any documents relating to your civil state."

"Why would he?" I raise a brow.

"Because he looked into your situation, of course. There's quite a bit of money at play, and anyone could pretend to be Leo's long lost daughter, isn't that right?" he strains a smile.

"Of course. He had to do his due diligence."

I resume my seat, and Amon takes my hand, his heat seeping into mine as he lets me know he is there for me. Although I am leading this conversation, he was the one who suggested we take this route—play up on any potential guilt Abel might have.

"But tell me more about that dream. What else did you see? What did the young man look like? Did you tell Rhiannon about it?" His barrage of questions takes us by surprise.

Yet one question stands out among the others.

Did you tell Rhiannon?

Why would he care if I told Rhiannon about it?

"I was going to, but she's been awfully busy with the guests. Why? Do you think it means anything?'

"No, of course not. Everyone is aware that Amon killed Elizabeth and their children. It was quite horrible. He raped and killed her. I am certain the man you saw in your dream must have been Amon," he nods, almost as if to himself.

"Really?" I frown.

How would he know about the erroneous version of the *collective* memory which shows Amon as the killer?

"I did not see it as such," I counter. "No one raped Elizabeth. She was stabbed to death."

"I am sure you must be mistaken, Darcy."

"But how would you know?"

"Why, everyone knows. It's in the coven archives."

I narrow my eyes at him at the same time as Amon squeezes my hand—sign to not let my emotions get the best of me.

But the question remains—how does he know about the archive version if he is not part of the coven?

"I am told Amon had long white hair. The man I saw did not. He had short dark hair."

"Did he," he murmurs in discomfort. "I'm sure it was just a bad dream, Darcy. You shouldn't bother Rhiannon with something like that," he tells me quite emphatically.

My God! Could it be that he was the one to interfere with the images from the archive? Otherwise why would he be so scared of anyone finding out *my* version?

"But there's more," I mention, barely stifling a smile as I see him fidget in his seat.

"More?" he whispers, his eyes widening.

"Elizabeth called him her son."

He stares at me, seemingly struck speechless.

"I think it's time for you to go, Darcy," he suddenly says, jumping to his feet and reaching for his cane. "I forgot I have an appointment later in the day and Helena must be..."

I give Amon a look and he nods. The doors to the drawing room immediately close.

"I'm afraid Helena has left on an errand," I tell him.

"What is happening here?" he asks in a thundering voice.

"Odd that you don't remember me, *Abel*," I smile sweetly. "I'm told I look quite the same," I say as I push my hair off my face and strike a pose—anything to infuriate the damned man.

"W-what..." Abel stammers, his eyes like two saucers.

And just like that, Amon changes his appearance to look back like himself.

"You... It can't be," he whispers. "You should be locked away. Not here. Not..."

"Not interfering with your plans?" Amon chuckles. "I bet you'd love that."

A snarl appears on Abel's face as he fully turns towards us. Energy swirls around him, but as he channels it towards us, I quickly say the words to the spell I'd learned, erecting a shield around us. The blast dispels around, too weak to penetrate our defense.

Abel tries to summon another blast, but this time, he's unsuccessful in hitting us.

"I think you might need a power source for that. Something like this?" Amon asks playfully as he raises the gem.

While Abel had been captivated by my story, Amon had focused his abilities on getting the gem, successfully dislodging it from the cane. We hadn't known it would be so easy, but since this worked, then the first part of the plan has been successfully completed.

Amon carefully pockets the gem, keeping it safe until we're able to fashion it into a necklace again, while I regard Abel's pitiful form.

"How... I don't understand... You can't be Elizabeth..."

"But it seems I am. How does it feel, Abel? To stare into my eyes once more?"

"No... " he shakes his head. "You can't do this!" he yells, bringing his palms together to gather more energy.

Amon rolls his eyes and with a snap of his fingers he has him across the wall, arms and legs apart.

"You won't want to see this, Darcy," he whispers, but I shake my head.

"I have to."

Stepping forward, I stop in front of him.

"Why did you kill Abraham? I understand that you hated me and Amon, but your brother? *Why*?"

He gives a maniacal laugh.

"Because he was convenient," he scoffs. "He'd always been a pussy, at least he died like a fucking man," he spits out.

"You think you deserve any praise for the way you killed him? For the way you slit his throat from behind like a coward?"

Amon places his arm around me, grounding me even as my emotions threaten to get the best of me.

"You know nothing, you stupid cow," he yells at me. "You know fucking nothing!"

"Don't," I whisper to Amon as I feel him tense. "Let me talk to him."

Turning to Abel, I look him in the eye.

"Then tell me why you did it. I know you worked with Kress and Finn from the beginning. But why?"

"Why do you think?" he snarls. "I spent my entire childhood being told I wasn't good enough on account of my sex only. Abraham was the heir to my father's fortune and Lydia was the heir to my mother's coven. Where did that leave me? Nowhere!"

"But you never wanted money, did you?"

He would have had plenty of opportunity to become a very wealthy man, and by all accounts, he is the richest one in Fairydale. Yet from the beginning he'd stayed here.

He gives a dry laugh.

"Money," he snorts. "I have plenty of money."

Of course he would. After all, Abraham's money all went to him after he died, did it not? Not even the money he owns is his by right.

"But you don't have power. You never did."

"It's all because of that stupid coven and their rules! I can perform spells! I can do everything a woman can!"

"But you do not have the energy source to do so," I fill in the blanks.

He is able to do spells, potentially on account of his blood relation to the Stuart family. But only the female line is blessed with innate abilities.

"That's what Kress and Finn offered you," Amon, who'd been silent until now, finally speaks. "They bought you with the necklace, promising you it would give you everything you ever wanted."

"My cooperation in their plan was a small price to pay for immortality, wouldn't you say?" he asks sarcastically. "Who in their right minds would not jump at that?"

He tries to move as he mutters a few words in Latin under his breath, but Amon is quick to shut him off, clamping his mouth shut.

He struggles, making muffled noises and thrashing as much as he can before Amon restrains him even more, shaking his head at his pitiful efforts.

"Except that for the last twenty-four years the necklace hasn't been working too well, has it," I add.

He frowns.

"You didn't know, did you? The necklace isn't just a source of power," Amon interjects. "It's part of her, and it will always recognize her as the master. It's why it might have given you *some* power, but never to its full capacity."

More muffled sounds, and Amon removes the mouth clamp for a moment.

"Kress and Finn will fucking end you! You think you're so high and mighty now, but wait until they get their hands on you, you fucking filthy demon," he curses. "They will send you back to hell where you belong..."

Amon stops him from talking again.

Turning to him, I give him a confident look.

"I'll do it."

"Darcy, are you sure? You don't have to..."

"I *need* to. If not, I'll probably be haunted my entire life by that scene and the way he killed us," I shake my head. "It's my duty. For Abraham."

He looks unconvinced for a moment before he nods.

"For Abraham," he repeats, taking a step back.

Turning my attention to Abel who is throwing daggers at me with his eyes, I bring my fingers together, remembering one other spell I'd learned.

This might not have given me the answers I wanted to hear. He'd made no excuses for his behavior and in his mind, he doesn't see himself as guilty—he'd simply acted in his best interests.

I look at him and I try to imagine the ten year old he'd been when we first picked him up from London. I remember the youth he'd been before all the corruption—before the fratricide and the abomination he'd become.

Yet no matter how hard I try, everything is tainted by his actions.

I can no longer see him as my son, Abel. Only Archibald Nicholson, an old, pitiful man who'd sold his entire family in his quest for power. A man whose chief qualities have been his greed and treachery.

"There is nothing more disappointing for a mother than seeing her son turn out the way you did. But you never did consider me your mother, did you? Not even your aunt. You always saw us as the enemy and you let your hate poison your heart until you turned against your own brother," I speak, my voice unwavering. "I no longer recognize you as any relation of mine, Abel, or Archibald Nicholson. You are *nothing* and you will perish as nothing but an afterthought in the history books."

His cheek twitches as he stares malevolently at me. If he'd been able to, I don't doubt he would have spit in my face and cursed me some more—after all, that's all he can do being as helpless as he is.

Neither Amon nor I imagined he would rely almost entirely on the jewel for his powers, or that he would remain so thoroughly vulnerable without it.

Alas, my husband is right. He made his bed; he will now rest in it.

Forever.

"Incendia," I whisper as I channel my attention towards him, watching his entire body catch on fire.

I'd picked the spell randomly while reading through the ones Lydia had marked for me, thinking if the time came, this would be the most appropriate way for Abel to go. He'd blamed Amon for being a hellish creature when he'd been the worst evil all along. It's only fitting that he should be the one to burn in hell.

Black flames swirling around him and consuming him until nothing is left of his flesh.

My eyes widen as I realize this is the exact way Leo Pierce had died after he'd had an attack.

But...how?

"Amon...did you kill Leo Pierce?"

He looks pensive for a moment.

"I tried, but someone else beat me to it. I thought it was Rhiannon."

"I don't think it was," I whisper. "He died just like this, with the same spell."

"You think..."

"Someone else killed him. Someone who would have known this specific spell."

Before I can speak further, a loud noise erupts in the house, followed by another.

Like a howling sound, it's absolutely terrifying in its intensity.

My hands go to my ears just as Amon takes me in his arms, ready to flash us out of the house.

"No," I whisper. "The second floor. I'm sure it's coming from there."

"It could be a trap. Who knows what type of creature Abel could have summoned and is now going berserk without a master?"

"No," I shake my head.

I don't know why I'm so convinced, but I do not believe the source of the noise means us harm.

The sound reverberates again in the house, this time sounding more like a wail than a howl.

"It's a signal of distress, Amon, not one of attack," I whisper, wrenching myself from his arms as I hurry to the staircase.

Amon is right on my tracks as I chase the source of the sound.

It's not on the first floor, though. It's on the second.

"That's the room," he says as he comes behind me. "The one I couldn't go into."

"There's someone inside," I whisper. "I'm sure there's someone inside."

We walk towards the room, yet as I reach out with my hand, I come across the same barrier Amon had mentioned.

"Let me try again," Amon suggests. He creates a ball of energy in his hands that he launches at the barrier.

Yet just as it reaches it, there's a light ripple before the blast is thrown back at us.

Amon is quick enough to remove me from its trajectory, but that means the barrier will not budge no matter how much power we throw at it.

The sound continues to come from the room, now more potent than ever.

"Wait," I suddenly say as I grab onto Amon's arm. "What about the spell Lydia left me to disarm your barrier? Would it work?"

His brows furrow together before he gives me a nod. Holding out his hand, he materializes the piece of paper I'd found in the Latin dictionary.

Taking it from his hands, I say the words out loud just as I'd said them before. When I'm done, I give Amon a look as we both step towards the door. This time, Amon tells me to stay back while he tries the door.

"It worked," I whisper in awe as he successfully turns the knob.

Opening the door, we both enter the room.

"What..." I blink in shock as I take in the sparse furnishings.

There is only one chair placed with its back towards us and orientated towards the window but not close enough to it so it would be visible from the outside of the house.

But the most unusual thing is that there is a person there. Someone sitting in that chair and rocking slightly with it.

As we go deeper inside, Amon places himself in front of me, assuming a protective stance.

"Hello?" I call out as we tentatively walk around the chair.

The closer we get, however, the more I can make out the features of the person sitting on it. She seems to be female, her hair the whitest white, her face serene and almost wrinkle-free despite her seemingly advanced age.

"Ma'am, are you alright?" I ask slowly, worried she might be having some sort of crisis with the way she'd been screaming.

But why? Why would Abel lock her here? Is she a former lover or something of that nature? Her age certainly seems to match.

"Darcy, wait," Amon rasps as he stops in front of the woman, putting his arm in front of me.

"What is it?" I frown.

Slowly, she raises her head to look at us, her eyes a deep shade of blue, tears coating her lashes. She has a slender frame, looking even smaller due to her low weight.

God, but would Abel have held her prisoner here?

"She..." Amon trails off, his face one of disbelief.

"You're finally here," the woman croaks, her voice harsh and seemingly overused.

"What is it? Who is it?" I ask him since he looks as if he knows something.

"But it's not possible. How can this be..." he whispers, staring at her as if he'd seen a ghost.

"Amon? You're scaring me..."

"You don't...remember me...mommy?" the woman sets her eyes on me, her lips pulling up in a gentle smile.

I freeze, my heart hammering in my chest.

"It can't be..." I trail off in absolute shock. "Lydia?" I choke out her name, unable to help the tears from pouring down my cheeks as she gives a small nod.

"Oh my God, no," I mumble as I reach out to hug her and hold her in my arms. "You're Lydia, my God," I sway lightly with her, barely in control of my feelings.

Strong arms surround me as Amon wraps us both in his embrace, holding tight.

"I can't believe this is happening," he whispers on a ragged voice, and as I turn my head to look at him, I note he's crying too.

We stay like that for moments on end, unable to speak, only hug each other.

God, this is Lydia? How can it be?

Yet even as the questions pile in my head, my heart knows it to be right.

There's an ineffable warmth at hugging her, at holding her once more in my arms and I feel as if I'm transported again in the past when she was just a little girl—when the world was still a beautiful place and we'd still been a family.

Eventually, though, we separate, the lack of touch creating a crack in my soul.

"What happened? How come you're here?" I ask.

Amon is doing his best to control himself, wiping at his tears and breathing hard.

"Abel," she answers, and it dawns on me that she has difficulty speaking. "He wouldn't...let me...die."

"How?"

She takes a deep breath.

"Spell...necklace," she manages to get out, slowly explaining that Abel had used the necklace for a necromancy spell that had put Lydia in a limbo as she was about to die—stuck in a perpetual state of dying but never actually doing so.

"Oh my God," I gasp as the enormity of it registers.

She's been like this for years. For *decades.*

"I should have fucking tortured that little shit," Amon bursts out—unusually so for him. "He should have suffered more. Fuck!"

"But why? Why would he do that?"

"He...needed...predictions," she swallows. "He...wanted... the...future."

"He wanted you to help him get Amon's powers too, didn't he?"

She gives me a nod.

"It wasn't enough to kill his brother. He had to enslave his sister and torture her like this... My God, but how is this possible," I cry out, unable to comprehend how someone could be so evil.

"I didn't...give...him," she coughs. "I...helped...you."

Slowly, her mouth tips up in a satisfied smile, and it dawns on me that she's been doing this from the beginning—helping us by leaving little clues.

"You knew," Amon whispers. "You knew this would happen to you and you never told me a thing. Damn it, Didi, you *knew!*"

She shakes her head lightly.

"I...had...to. For...the...future...to...become...the future."

"What do you mean?" I frown.

"For...you...to...live," she nods, her smile brightening. "I...helped...as I...could."

"Lydia..." I trail off, unable to believe she would sacrifice herself for us.

"Don't...trust...them," she says, managing to wink at me.

My eyes widen in surprise.

"It was you. My God. Leo Pierce, too. It was you," I whisper.

She nods.

"All...I...could."

"Thank you," I tell her from the bottom of my heart. "I would have never agreed for you to sacrifice yourself for this, but thank you, Didi."

A tear falls down her cheek and I catch it with my thumb, brushing it off her skin.

"I love you. We both love you so much," I whisper as I fight my own tears.

"I...know. I...love...you...too."

She looks at me and Amon with the most beautiful smile. Even through a curtain of tears, her smile is still brighter than the sun.

"Now...I...want...to..." she pauses, swallowing hard. "Die."

"What?" I jump up.

Amon's arms are around me, keeping me from falling.

"She's been in limbo, love. All this time, she's been on the verge of death but she's never been allowed to. It would give her peace."

"Didi," I murmur as I regard her and the weariness on her features.

Yet how can I deny her something like that?

Even as my heart breaks for this short reunion, I know that her time has gone—that she needs to find her peace.

At the same time, I look at her and I'm unable to believe that I found her again only to lose her...again.

"Please," she whispers, a broken word that has the power to unravel me.

"How? Tell us how," I get to my knees in front of her, holding her hands in my own. "Tell us how."

"Daddy," she looks at Amon. "You...do...it."

Amon gives her a pained nod.

"You...will...do it," she says as she regards both of us. "You...will... return...to...Arkgor."

I frown as I don't understand what she means, but I don't interrupt her.

"You...will....reign."

"I don't understand," I tell her, but she just smiles.

"You...will."

She gives me a feeble squeeze before she asks Amon again for death.

"Darlin', you should go out."

"I'm not leaving her," I shake my head at him. "I'll stay with you," I assure Lydia.

After everything she's done, the least I can do is this.

Her lips move as she whispers a barely audible thank you.

Taking one of her hands, Amon brings it to his lips before moving it to his forehead and staying like that for a moment.

"I couldn't have done this without you, Didi," he murmurs. "You turned into such a wonderful woman and I couldn't have been more proud of calling you my daughter. I love you," he whispers before he moves his other hand to her heart, resting it over her chest.

She still has the most beautiful smile on her face as she looks at us.

I monitor her chest as it rises and falls. It does so for a few more times before it stills completely, her head dipping down.

Swiping my palm over her features, I close her eyes as I say a silent farewell, thanking her once more for everything she'd done and apologizing for not being a better mother.

And that's when I also know what to do next—what she would have wanted.

"Incendia." I murmur.

Her entire body is swallowed up by black flames until only the ashes remain. But this way, no one will be able to disturb her from her peace.

One second. That's how long I can hold everything in before a loud cry escapes me, the sob wrenched from deep within me as I fall to the floor.

"Darcy, darlin'," Amon's arms come around me, his presence the only thing that keeps me from falling apart—and barely.

I cry unlike I'd ever cried—for everyone we'd loved and lost.

"Shh, please," he rasps in my ear, holding me tight and trying to comfort me even as his own heart is breaking.

"Take me home, please," I beg him, my nails lodged in his skin as I hold onto him.

In no time, though, we are back to the catacombs.

My cries are out of control, tears coursing down my cheeks, my heart continuously breaking in my chest. But as I step away from him, I look into his eyes and see the same sadness mirrored there, mixed with physical pain and soul-searing agony.

"Amon. My beloved Amon," I reach for his shirt, tearing it from his body to reveal the absolute horrifying sight that is his flesh—now wholly mangled by deep lacerations.

Blood flows down his chest, so much so that his entire torso is painted red.

My fingers are on his trousers as I undo the buttons and push them down his legs, shocked to see even more damage.

There is not one inch of skin untouched.

My panicked gaze flies to his, but he just shakes his head.

"No," he whispers. "I won't ask you for anything, love. Not now. Not when our hearts are mourning."

He turns to head to the shower to wash the blood away, but I reach for his arm, stopping him.

"I'm offering," I take a deep breath as hiccups rack my body. "Please," I whisper as I slowly unbutton my dress, letting it fall to the ground.

"Make love to me, Amon. Please love me and help me forget. Help me..." My voice breaks as more cries erupt from my throat, the pain of it making me double over in pain.

"My darling girl," he breathes out, and before I know it, his naked chest is against mine as he lays me on the bed. Our bodies are fitted to perfection as we stare into each other's eyes—both equally heart-broken, both grieving Lydia's loss.

Parting my legs, I wrap them around his waist as I reach between our bodies, grabbing his length and positioning it at my entrance.

He's still staring into my eyes, a sadness unlike any other reflected in those beautiful, beautiful light eyes as they shift between red and black. He knows how precarious this moment is and is holding himself still so I can be in control.

"Please," I whisper as I push his ringed head inside of me, his thickness immediately stretching me.

"My love," he releases a ragged breath as he pushes himself into me, his arms holding me tight as he brings his mouth to mine for a kiss that tastes like death—like tears, sorrow and heartache. We kiss and kiss as he thrusts into me with slow precision, making love to me just like I'd asked him, yet even as we touch and reach for each other, the emptiness in our souls remains.

Pushing his head to the side, I encourage him to take what he needs from me just as I bite into his skin, tasting the blood as it reaches the surface.

So does he.

The bite of pain makes me spasm around him as I feel his blood everywhere.

In my mouth, on my body, even between my legs.

At this moment, it's only us and the essence of life despite the fact that death hangs over us.

"I love you. I love you so much," I tell him as he increases his pace. "Please never leave me, Amon. I would never survive it."

"Never, darlin'. Where you go, I go. If you exist so do I," he confesses thickly before he kisses me anew. "And if you're not, nor am I."

I lightly rake my nails down his back, feeling his wounds closing.

He holds me in his tight embrace as he slowly pushes inside of me before retreating, doing so all over again until we both climax at the same time—our minds, just as our hearts, pulsing as one.

It feels like an eternity later that I've calmed enough to stop crying.

Amon takes me in his arms, leading me to the shower and cleaning me thoroughly before sliding a big shirt over my head and putting me back to bed.

I'm so spent, I can barely move.

Tinkering with something to the side for a while, he comes back to me holding a necklace—*the* necklace.

He'd placed the jeweled stone back to its original design.

"Lydia would have wanted you to wear this, darlin'," he whispers as he kneels on the bed beside me, placing the string around my neck.

"Thank you," I strain a smile as I skim my lips across his cheek.

As I lower the neckline of the shirt to sneak the necklace inside, the jewel meets my skin, causing a heat unlike any other to erupt within me.

My eyes widen in alarm, and I open my mouth to ask Amon what's wrong, yet no sound comes out. There's just a scorching pain as the stone melts within me, searing itself on my skin and becoming a part of me.

That's when I see it.

I see everything.

Chapter Twenty-Six

Eons ago. Vissirian Empire, Arkgor

"You're so pretty," I murmur lovingly as I gently wipe the leaf of the pale pink flower.

It still does not have a name, though it's been close to a season since I've created it through a mixture of two other flowers.

It's been a hard endeavor, but as it has grown increasingly larger, I'm close to declaring it a success. Even better, it's just in time for my birthday tomorrow, when my mother will finally visit me again. I'll be able to show it to her and hopefully earn her praise.

Hopefully.

A sigh escapes me at the thought.

My mother is not one to give out praises that easily, just as she is not usually impressed with anything.

She knows of my love for flowers and she'd equipped my home with a large conservatory to grow any flower or plant I'd like. But in many ways, that is only to excuse her absence and the fact that most often than not she forgets she has a daughter.

I continue to wipe every little leaf carefully before I step back, admiring my years' worth of work.

Alas, it's not like I have many options.

I've been trapped within these walls my entire life. I have absolutely no idea how life on the outside world is, except that it is dangerous.

The first time I asked my mother what was outside my front door, or whether there was something else beyond the ocean, she'd told me there was—a bad, bad world that would only hurt and exploit me.

At that time, I wasn't very knowledgeable, nor did I understand much of what she was telling me, so I repeated the question a few years after.

"Why can I not go out, mother? Saima does so all the time," I'd asked, confused why Saima, my maid and cook at the time, was able to step out into the world while it remained completely forbidden to me.

It was at that point that, on one of her rare visits, my mother had gifted me a set of history books about Arkgor, telling me to study them and pose the question to her again when I was done.

Hungry for anything that would tell me the secrets of the outside world, I'd devoured the books, reading them again and again until I memorized everything by heart.

The stories all revolved around the Vissirian Empire and how it had gained supremacy over the entire continent, subjugating smaller, less powerful kingdoms, while declaring war on the stronger ones.

It was then that I understood what my mother had meant by the fact that the outside world was bad. It was filled with war, famine and disease. It was a world in which the Vissirian Empire waged war continuously, killing everyone who stood in its way.

And since the empire had first appeared on the map, fifteen thousand years ago, there had been not one day without war, with casualties that kept on piling.

So on my mother's next visit, I'd posed the question to her once more.

"Here," she'd said, pointing to the map of Arkgor. "Hundreds of years ago, this used to be the Kingdom of Milena."

The area she'd showed me was right at the border of the Vissirian Empire, and it was the latest kingdom it had incorporated after a lengthy war. It was also the area we found ourselves in.

"With the Empire growing in size, its population became more diverse, too."

She'd explained that there were many types of peoples, with different abilities and appearances—some humanoid, some non-humanoid. To me, who'd only ever seen a handful of people in my entire life, everything had seemed so interesting.

"Yet everyone on Arkgor has something in common. Despite the fact that some may be stronger, faster, or more powerful than others, everyone has one fatal weakness."

The books had detailed all about the varied species on Arkgor, most of which boasted a slew of abilities, with some of them able to live tens of thousands of years. Despite that, though, there was one thing that was able to kill any life form on Arkgor—*rhodium,* otherwise known as Vissirian silver.

To the weaker, even a scratch could prove life-threatening, for the metal had some properties that did not allow the body to heal itself, the wound ultimately festering and leading to death. To the strongest, though they were able to withstand shallow cuts of rhodium better, they were still threatened by it—one strike to the heart and that person would be dead.

The metal was widespread in the northern part of Arkgor, the region which coincided with the first settlement of the Vissirians.

According to legends, the first Vissirians had seen the devastating effects of the silver and had weaponized it. Because their region was so abundant in it, they managed to turn it into an advantage by equipping every soldier with it and building a never before seen army.

That turned to be the prime advantage of the Vissirians.

Though they could be felled by the silver as well, they had the upper hand in battle against foreign soldiers who were not properly equipped with such deadly weapons.

While all the other parts of the world scrambled to find their own supplies of rhodium, the Vissirian Empire grew exponentially, investing everything in its military and arming it with the perfect weapons to subjugate the rest of the world.

It was only when a coalition of the Western Kingdoms had managed to find a deposit of rhodium deep in their mountains, that everything had changed. And though the states remained at war, there has been a long standstill.

With the rhodium scales evened out, everything else became a matter of individual prowess rather than any hidden advantage.

Unfortunately, the effects were far-reaching.

Because the world has been at war for so long, only a few cities are livable, with clean water and food. The rest are all wastelands, ravaged by the military and scavengers.

But that hasn't been the only effect.

Previously long-lived species have seen a decrease in their lifespans as a direct result from the famine and disease that followed the war.

Though initially everyone's weakness had been rhodium, the conflict had caused some species to develop other vulnerabilities—one of which was childlessness: the decreased ability to carry gestations to term or birth viable offspring.

The books had also detailed never-before seen plagues that attacked *some* species, and there was the implication that they'd been created by the Vissirians as an alternative to rhodium.

"The Vissirian Empire is always looking for a way to regain its dominance. Since rhodium became widespread in the entirety of Arkgor, they've lost their bargaining chip. And that's where you come in."

"Me?"

"You have a never before seen ability of withstanding any rhodium injury, or any type of plague," she'd said just as she'd removed a small rhodium blade, cutting my skin with it before cutting hers, too.

While mine had healed immediately, hers had not.

"If my assessment is correct, your ability would be priceless for the Vissirians, and they would use it in the most horrific ways. Not to mention what they would do to you..."

My mother had detailed the atrocious ways in which the Vissirian Empire would use my ability to lay siege to other nations and effectively conquer the entire Arkgor. With my healing powers, nothing would stop them.

"They are absolutely despicable, Sela. The Emperor is a vile man whose god is power and only mistress is greed, and his General is the worst scourge to ever be born in this world."

The Shadow General, so called for his ability to move faster than shadows, is purported to be the most dangerous man alive. A rare warrior breed, no one knows exactly what his ancestry is, or why he is as powerful as he is—allegedly more than the Emperor himself.

He'd been the one to lead the Empire's armies into Milena, conquering the Kingdom and executing its ruling monarchs before the entire population while giving them a choice—submit and live, or rebel and die.

The same night, the General alone had slaughtered more than a thousand people who'd dared stand up against Vissiria.

"Though our Kingdom is long gone, we haven't forgotten what the Vissirians did to us. We'll never forget," she'd added vehemently, telling me that they would ultimately regain what was originally theirs, but that was imperative on me being hidden.

"You'll be our hope when the time is right. Until then, you need to stay safe and the Vissirians must *never* find out about your power."

"I understand," I'd told her,

Since then, I stopped asking her about the outside world and I have become used to my own little haven. After all, I am safe here. I have food and drink, and there is no one who could experiment on me.

When I'm done with one row of flowers, I move to the other, cleaning them thoroughly.

There aren't many things to do here besides tending to my garden, and spending moments on end gazing out at the ocean from my balcony.

I have a small library that's ever expanding with the books Meli brings me weekly—after my mother has approved them, of course.

It was only by chance that I found out that Meli has to run everything by her first, and I cannot understand why. I already know most there is to know about Arkgor and what goes on in the outside world. As I'd told her, I have no intention of going outside if it means putting myself in danger. Yet she still continues to monitor the contents of my books.

So far, I've noticed that she's restricted me access to anything that might have romantic content—I'd received none of the ballads I'd asked for. Yet I'd still managed to read summaries of them in other works.

My guess is that my mother believes that such fanciful notions might make me sad, since I am unlikely to ever experience them.

She is right to an extent, since who would *not* want to live an epic love story?

Yet I also know the reality of what is implied in the history books.

The outside world is so horrible, there is absolutely no place for romance.

When everything is rotten to the core; when the only relationship model is of master and vassal, what is there to emulate?

Marriages are conducted for business purposes only, either to conjoin two strong lines for the powers their future offspring would have, or for political reasons to make alliances.

Despite the fact that my mother had told me she thinks I would be useful for the Milena cause in the future, I hope she did not mean that I would have to marry someone.

The mere thought of it makes my skin crawl.

I'd rather stay in my tiny home forever than let that happen.

"Miss, Miss," Meli's voice reaches my ears.

Turning, I see her dash into my conservatory.

"Your mother is here!"

"Now?" I blink in surprise. "But tomorrow is my birthday, not today," I frown.

Had I gotten the day wrong? I'll be the first one to admit that I'm not the best at tracking time. When you're losing yourself in the same thing on a daily basis, the days tend to blur into one another. I don't discount that I might be mistaken about the date.

I'm about to be eighteen, and if I've become so bad about keeping track of time so young, then I don't know what will happen when I'll be a couple hundred years old.

Will I become insane?

Despite being used to my lot in life and trying to make the best of my situation, I'm more than aware that it's not ideal. Though most days I enjoy my time with my plants, there are those when I feel like throwing myself off my balcony and into the ocean—I probably would have done that if not for the rocky cliffs that would destroy me on the way down.

"She wants to see you. In the office," Meli relates.

Nodding, I follow her out of the garden and into the house.

Aside from the ground floor that houses the kitchen and a study, there is only one room upstairs where I sleep.

"Mother?" I incline my head in greeting.

Immediately, I take in her fancy gown, green with specks of gold, the bodice being sown onto geiki bones—a rare and expensive creature. This type of couture is only available to the rich—or at least that's what I'd read in books.

I bite my lip as I cannot help but compare the difference in our clothes.

Looking down, I stare for a moment at what used to be a dark blue gown but has now faded around the hem and in some areas I'd dropped fertilizer on. I don't own too many clothes since my mother has always said I'd never need them, anyway. But the few that I have are all in dire condition and need replacing.

I should probably ask her for some new clothes as a birthday present.

But there's also something else I want more than anything. And though I might have to endure another year of tattered gowns, I'd rather have *that*.

"Come, Sela. I must speak with you at once."

I nod, worried at her tone.

Reaching for the chair across from her, I take a seat and assume my stance—back straight, hands politely on my thighs and gaze forward.

I might be isolated from society, but I am not a savage—or I don't believe I am.

Truth to be told, I'd learned everything from those damned books in an effort to impress my mother and maybe...maybe have her visit me more often.

"Has something happened, mother?" I ask in an even voice.

My mother strains a smile.

We share the same features, black hair and dark blue eyes set against a pale complexion. We could potentially pass for twins if not for two differences. My lips are plumper than hers and she has a birthmark in the shape of a clover on her upper left cheek—*Lady Luck* as I'd heard Meli call her.

"There's been a disturbance in the Empire. I'm going to station more guards around the house. If you hear something, or if anyone comes inside, you know the protocol. You hide in the East chamber."

"What disturbance?"

She purses her lips.

"The emperor was assassinated. There's a rebel group that's been sighted all over the capital and around the borders of the empire. It's better to be vigilant."

"But isn't that a good thing if he's dead? It's what you've been waiting for all along!" I burst out in happiness for her.

Ever since I was young she'd told me how much she hated the Emperor and the Empire. Yet as I look at her, my smile slowly falls.

She doesn't look happy. If anything, she looks weary, dark circles forming under her eyes, her features slightly gaunt where they were full before.

"It would have been a joyous event, indeed. But with the rebels at large, it only makes this situation more dangerous."

"But... What about the Milena resistance? Maybe it could ally itself with the rebels and..."

"Since when do you know what's best in politics, Sela?" she gives me a grave look. "A new emperor has already been crowned and the entire Empire will be searched for traitors, after which they will all be executed as an offering to Vessar," she says, mentioning the ancient Vissirian god —coincidentally, a god of war.

"I don't understand..."

"Of course you don't. These are topics for grown-ups. In any event, I want you to be careful if you hear anything out of the ordinary. I will not be able to come again for quite some time until matters are stabilized in the capital."

I frown.

Why would she be reliant on the matters in the capital? She doesn't even live there.

I don't understand anything.

She should be more happy that the Emperor was killed.

"How is the new Emperor?"

Her lip twitches in disgust and something akin to guilt flashes across her face.

"He will bring the Empire into a new era," she vaguely answers before standing up and heading to the door.

"It's my birthday," I call out, surprised she hasn't mentioned it at all.

"That's right," she says after a moment of deliberation, as if it had completely escaped her mind. "Happy Birthday."

"And my present?" I smile sweetly.

She opens her mouth to speak before closing it.

"I'm sorry. I couldn't find it."

"But I gave you the clipping last year," I say dejectedly, the implication clear.

She'd had time to find it.

Every year on my birthday, she gives me a gift while asking me what I'd like for the following year.

Prepared with my most wanted wish, I'd given her a page from one of my books that detailed the existence of a purple plant in the Northern part of the Empire. It might be quite far away, but during the year she could have had someone get it, could she not?

I'd been wanting it from the moment I'd spotted it in the book, knowing it would complement my other flowers perfectly. But more than anything, it would help me attempt a new hybrid.

"Maybe next year," she tells me in a dead voice as she heads to the door. "Remember what I told you. If you hear anything, you hide."

I nod, straining a smile as I wave her goodbye.

And as the door closes, I realize I won't get any birthday celebration.

This was it.

I stare for a moment at the door, for one moment truly wishing I could wrench it open and run out into the world—live like I'd never lived before. Yet just as the thought comes, a wave of fear goes down my back.

Besides my books, what do I know about the outside world? What do I know of conversing with people or avoiding danger?

Truth to be told, even if I had the chance to leave, I would be too scared to do so.

"I left you the food in the kitchen, Miss. There's plenty for the entire week since your mother has tightened security," Meli's words startle me from my thoughts.

"You're leaving, too?" I turn to her, doing my best to hide the hurt from my voice.

She nods.

"I've washed all your clothes and cleaned your bedroom. I'll see you in a week, Miss."

And just like that she's out of the door too, and once more I'm left feeling lonelier than ever before.

Trudging my way back to my garden, I try to think of ways to amuse myself so this awful feeling can go away.

"We're alone again," I murmur as I squat next to my roses. "What do you think I should do for the rest of the afternoon?"

I nod as if the flower spoke to me.

"Yes, I could re-read the book on Lyrian botany."

A sudden noise at the end of the garden startles me and I jump to my feet.

"Who's there?" I demand, remembering what my mother had told me.

But...if the noise is coming from the end of the garden, and the trap door to the underground room *is* at the end of the garden, then what should I do?

Is this all in my head, I wonder?

Maybe my mother's tale had scared me a little more than I admitted to myself.

Just to convince myself that I'm being silly, I walk towards the end of the path, all the while scanning my surroundings.

Nothing seems out of the ordinary... Maybe it is all in my mind.

When I don't spot anyone at the end of the garden, I sigh to myself just as my pulse seemingly settles down.

Yet it's too soon. In just one second I feel a cold metal against my throat.

"Don't move," the deepest voice I've ever heard whispers in my ear, the warm air from his mouth sending shivers down my spine.

Terror engulfs me at once.

"W-who are you?" I ask, barely keeping my voice from trembling.

"Why was Lady Luck visiting you?" he demands in a thick voice, the blade digging into my skin.

The sun hits the metal, its shine revealing it's rhodium.

"I don't know what you're talking about," I murmur.

All at once, he pulls me closer, fitting my body to his hard, big one as he slices the blade across my neck. His other hand comes to rest across my waist, keeping me still against him.

"You have one more try, lady. Why was Lady Luck visiting you?"

Seeing as the blade continues to advance into my skin, I debate whether I should tell him or not. Yet the most important thing is that he cannot know I can heal from rhodium—that it does not harm me as it does everyone else.

Maybe cooperating for now is the only way to keep him from finding out.

"She's my mother."

"Lies," he grits. "Lady Luck has no children."

"I'm telling the truth," I breathe out, trying to push down the panic that's threatening to overtake me.

This won't end well. I just know it.

Tears appear at the corners of my eyes as my entire body starts shaking.

"Who is your father then?" he asks again.

"I don't know. She never told me. Please... I'm telling the truth."

His teeth clank together and I know he doesn't approve of my answer.

By chance, I look down and see blood soaking his sleeve, drops falling to the ground.

"You're injured," I quickly add. "I can help you if you let me go."

"Prove to me that Lady Luck is your mother," he says, ignoring my previous words.

"I don't know how," I whisper. "She comes to visit me a few times every year but never stays longer than a few hours. You could look at me? We look alike," I offer, wincing at my own words.

Suddenly, he releases me.

Before he can turn me around to look at me, I bring my sleeve to my neck, wiping the blood away. The wound is already healed, so I can only hope his precision with a sword isn't too great that he'll know something is wrong...

I barely put my hand down when I find myself face to face with him.

Slowly, I look up, my eyes widening in even more terror as I look upon him.

He's...absolutely gigantic.

He must be twice my size. His arm alone looks like it could squeeze the life out of me and I doubt I would heal from *that*.

As I examine him, I come to a stop when I note his eyes—the lightest shade of blue I've ever seen. His hair is white, tied together to his back in a warrior-type of fashion I'd seen drawn in my books. His body is fully garbed in black leather, the combination with his light features making him look awe-striking indeed.

He would be breathtakingly beautiful, if not for the scowl that mars his features and the annoyed twitch in his jaw.

His gaze sweeps over me, studying me from head to toe in a manner that makes me want to run and hide. But seeing what I'm dealing with, I know he would not hesitate to do something to me if I defied him in any way.

I keep my spine straight for his perusal despite the fear that's settled in my stomach. Yet I can't find it in me to let him see how much he affects me.

"You say you're her daughter," he repeats.

His thumb touches my chin as he tips my head up to regard him.

"Look at me properly, female. Not like a scared mouse," his voice booms, making every cell in my body vibrate with...something.

I squeeze my eyes shut for a moment to push against a sudden wave of nausea.

Breathing harshly through my nose, I feel his fingers on my skin as he grasps my chin tightly.

"Now," he commands, and something in his tone makes me obey.

My eyes snap open, my gaze meeting his.

His eyes flare with interest as he takes a step closer to me, bringing his face to mine and...sniffing me?

He inhales deeply, moving his nose around my hair and neck before stopping right in front of my face. His nose is almost touching mine as he watches me intently.

"What is your name, female?" he asks in a honeyed voice, entirely different than the one before.

"Please don't hurt me," I whisper, afraid of what his interest in me might be.

I'd read enough about the violence happening in the world to know what could happen to a helpless woman. Yet I'd never thought it would visit me here, in my very own home.

"Your name," he repeats.

"S-Sela," I answer, swallowing hard.

"Sela," he nods to himself. "And you are Lady Luck's daughter. I can see the similarity," he muses, more to himself. "Yet I can also see the differences."

I nod slowly.

"M-my mother has a clover on her right cheek. And her lips are thinner," I recite the differences like a fool, not realizing my last statement brought his attention to my mouth.

His own twitch in response, the corners curling into a sardonic smile.

"Wrong," he clicks his tongue against his teeth. "There's one more difference."

"What?" I blink in surprise.

"Your eyes. They are warm where hers are cold," he states matter-of-factly.

The words stun me, but more than anything, I'm still reeling from the fact that there is a stranger threatening me in my own home—one who seems to be well acquainted with my mother.

All at once, a spark of outrage erupts within me as I imagine what type of relationship my mother would entertain with this...brute.

Surely they aren't...

"I would never lay a finger on that viper of your mother," he snarls, the mere allusion making him angry.

Just as I open my mouth to reply, I close it as I realize I hadn't spoken that accusation out loud. The only way he could have known it is if he...read my mind.

"You cur!" I push him off. "You could have read my mind all along to see I am telling the truth. Why torment me so?"

A smile plays at his lips as he regards me, almost as if one would look upon a jester at court.

"You're an interesting little thing," he drawls.

"And you're an unmannered brute," I point my finger at him, seemingly having lost all my fear from before.

But so be it. If he's going to have his wicked way with me it's going to happen eventually and I will still be powerless to stop it.

Isn't that the truth?

That I know absolutely nothing about defending myself—against anything.

"You said you could treat injuries," he changes the subject as he folds his sleeve to reveal a very nasty gash on his forearm.

I shake my head, my expression mutinous.

"I don't treat vile people such as yourself. Please see yourself out," I demand as I point to the exit.

He doesn't move. He simply regards me with the same lazy smirk as before, his eyes skimming outrageously over my body.

"And stop looking at me like that," I mumble.

"Like what?" His brows go up in question.

"You...You know what," I huff.

"Ah, lovely Sela, you're a fiery lass, are you not?"

"W-what?"

My eyes widen as my mind hones in on one word.

Lovely.

He called me lovely.

Instinctively my hand goes to my face as I feel heat climb up my cheeks.

No one's ever called me lovely before.

Yet just as I realize the direction of my thoughts I shake myself. I can't fall prey to him just because he's spouting flowery words to me.

"I've decided to let you tend to my wounds," he says as he plants himself on the bench at the end of the garden, his hands unfastening his vest as he lays it on the ground.

"You've decided? I repeat incredulously.

He continues with his chemise, slowly unbuttoning his blood-soaked shirt.

"What are you doing?" I ask in horror as I see the direction he's taking.

"What does it look like I'm doing?" he raises a brow as he gives me a lopsided smile. "I'm getting ready for you."

"I said I won't tend to you."

"No, you said you would tend to me if I let you go. I'm accepting your bargain."

I narrow my eyes at him.

From his previous murderous mood, this one is too...laid-back and jovial. Almost as if he is having fun at my expense.

I do not know who he is, but I know he is not welcome in my garden. And I tell him so.

"You already let me go. Now please leave," I say with all the confidence I can muster, folding my arms over my chest.

He tilts his head to the side, shaking it slowly and releasing a tsk sound.

Before I know it, he's behind me again, his big—entirely *too* big—hands splayed over my waist.

"Are we back to the negotiating table, lass?" he whispers in my hair.

"Let me go," I breathe out.

My pulse accelerates in what I think is extreme fear. But it makes no sense the way my body quickly yields to his in a way I've never experienced before—nor read about.

It's almost as if, despite knowing he represents danger, my body's decided the opposite.

Quite alarming, if I'm honest.

Especially as a sigh escapes my lips and I lean into him.

I. Lean. Into. Him.

What type of madness is this?

"Let me go, you brute," I repeat, attempting to push him off me.

But he doesn't budge—after all, how could someone *my* size take on someone *his* size?

"Treat my wounds and I will let you go. You have my promise, lovely Sela," he murmurs softly. "I can see you have various healing plants in here. You're a healer, are you not?"

I gulp down as I fear discovery—if he hasn't already looked into my mind and found out everything.

"Fine," I reply.

Just like before, he disappears from behind me and appears once more on the bench.

I've read about the diverse species on Arkgor and I've gone through their abilities, yet I can't seem to place his.

He looks...humanoid. Like me. At the same time, though, there's something that makes him so much more. Something I couldn't even begin to imagine.

He leisurely unbuttons the rest of his shirt before discarding it on the floor.

It's at that moment that I freeze in shock.

Not because his physique is just as impressive as his size, or as mesmerizing as the beauty of his features.

But because there's a sharp arrow protruding from his chest, right below his heart.

A rhodium arrowhead.

"You're not dead," I whisper.

How?

"Decidedly not," he chuckles. "Though my guess is that not for long," his eyes then flash a dangerous red, sending a shiver down my body—yet I'm not sure if it's still one of fear.

I give him a brisk nod as I come closer, my eyes moving all over his chest.

"I'll need to clean it and add some *zveka*," I murmur as I take note of all the injuries on his body. There are a few deep lacerations that are oozing blood, but they are almost drowned out by the myriad of scars marring his skin.

Just how many times has he been hurt?

"Are you going to do something or stare at me all day?" he drawls.

My cheeks heat up as my eyes meet his before I avert my gaze.

Grabbing a towel from the basket I always have on hand, I take it to the small well on the far right of the garden. I wet it thoroughly, and I pour some water into a small container. Bringing them to his side, I place them on the bench next to him before I go to my *zveka* row. A plant from the far East, it's reputed to be one of the few plants that can combat the anti-healing properties of the rhodium, acting as a cleanser and flushing everything out of the wound.

Because of its use, it's also exceedingly rare, having been used to near-extinction.

Bringing everything back to his side, I take a mortar and pestle and I make it into a paste.

I can feel his gaze burning into me as he studies every move I make, his shrewd eyes taking everything in—doubtlessly also reading my mind to make sure I don't do anything to harm him.

There's something savage about him, an intensity that makes me react with both fear and curiosity.

Dropping the mortar to the ground, I bring the wet towel to his injuries, cleansing them of blood and other debris before applying a thick layer of paste.

He never makes a sound. Not when I cleaned his wounds, nor when I push the paste into his open flesh. He's just...silent.

Somehow, that's even more frightening.

When I'm done with his more minor wounds, I focus on the arrow.

Biting my lip, I debate how to go about it. It looks to be so close to his heart that I'm afraid that by tipping it even a little to the right it could kill him.

Maybe I should...

As I bring my hand to grasp the arrow, he suddenly stops me.

Looking up, I find his grave gaze on me.

"Try to kill me and I'll blow your brains out with one thought, lass," he tells me in a gravelly voice, his glare as icy as the light color of his eyes.

I nod slowly. That seems quite far-fetched, but why do I believe it?

It must be his eyes.

His eerily light eyes.

They absolutely frighten me.

Gripping the end of the arrow, I try to remove it, but it's lodged right between his ribs and I don't have the necessary strength for it.

"Can you do it?" I whisper. "If you pull it at this angle," I pause as I take his big hand and wrap it around the metal, angling it upwards, "it shouldn't touch your heart."

He grunts, his eyes still on me.

And just like that, he continues to watch me as he wrenches the arrow out of his chest successfully.

Blood gushes out of his wound, flowing freely down his chest.

Immediately, I grab the towel, holding it on top of it.

"Are you not in...pain?" I ask tentatively as I see no change in his expression—not even a hint of pain.

"Pain and I are intimately acquainted," he grunts, though he doesn't expand on that.

Infuriating male.

When the bleeding slows down, I repeat the process, stuffing the paste inside his circular wound until not one drop of blood can come out.

"Done," I murmur as I get to my feet.

Yet before I can take a step back, I find myself firmly on his lap as he cradles my hip, his hand close—*too* close—to my bottom.

My eyes widen at his scandalous behavior.

"You brute," I whimper as I push at his shoulders. "You'll open your wounds again."

"Shh," he says and places a finger to my lips, all the while staring at me as if he can't quite decipher me despite obviously having the ability to read my mind.

Unless...

He can't do it all the time.

Once more, he leans into me, inhaling deeply.

"You're not mated," he states.

"H-how could you know?"

The corner of his lip tips up.

"Any male of sound mind would have put his mark on you if you were," he says, his hand cupping my cheek and tipping my face up towards him. "You smell fresh, Sela. Like an unplucked daisy."

"You should p-put me down," I whisper when I see how close he is to me.

"In a moment," he murmurs as he leans forward, brushing his cheek against mine.

The heat from his skin transfers to mine, making me still as unnatural thoughts erupt in my mind—things I should have no business imagining.

Yet his pull is too strong—so much so, in fact, that I can't help but lean forward, inhaling his scent too and marveling at the sweet musk that emanates from his skin.

The combination of blood and sweat should repulse me, but if anything, it makes my loins heat up as something bubbles inside of me.

I release a soft sigh as I bury my nose in his hair, breathing him in deeply as he does the same with me. I don't know what type of madness this is, what kind of wicked mind sorcery, but my body has a will of its own as it can only yield to his.

His face is nestled between my shoulder and my neck as he releases an unnatural growl just as his lips skim the surface of my skin, his teeth scraping lightly over my flesh.

The slight pain is enough to make me regain my composure as I jump out of his arms.

"You need to leave," I tell him pointedly.

His eyes flash a deep red at me, his nostrils flaring as animalistic energy rolls off him. Especially as he gets to his feet and takes a step towards me.

Yet before he can reach for me, his ears perk up, his features twisting into a scowl.

"I'll be back, Sela."

I blink and he is gone, as is any evidence he'd been here.

Not a few moments later, the door to the house burst open as my mother, together with some soldiers, come into my garden.

"Where is he?" My mother demands as she wildly looks around the place.

"What do you mean?" I frown.

"The rebel must be here! Search the place!"

The soldiers quickly run all around my house, searching every nook.

"What is this, mother?" I demand sharply.

"That blood. Whose is it?" she hisses accusingly.

"It's mine," I boldly lie. "I cut myself while tending to the garden. It's nothing new," I roll my eyes.

She won't be able to demand to see my injuries just as she won't want to let any soldier get too close to me in case they start asking questions.

Giving me a pointed look, she steps back. But not before she leaves me with a warning.

"Be very careful if you ever lie to me, Sela. Or you will not like the consequences."

Her words startle me, as does the malicious expression on her face—something I'd never seen before.

"I won't," I tell her—a lie in itself.

Huffing at me, she turns and commands everyone to follow her out.

Soon, I'm all alone and wondering how I got myself into this. Because no matter how much I look at it, something deep inside of me tells me my life as I know it is about to change.

And it all starts with a frightening warrior with a beautiful face—the one who becomes a recurrent theme in my dreams.

———

THE HOUSE IS EERILY quiet at night, and as I twist and turn in my bed, I realize sleep is unlikely to come—especially after I'd woken up from the most scandalous dream I've ever had.

It's that brute.

It's all because of him and his terrifying eyes.

But you liked them.

I huff to myself as I get out of bed, wrapping a shawl around my shoulders and stepping out onto the balcony.

The light breeze of the night brushes against my skin. I release a deep sigh as I tip my head up, inhaling the clean air.

The turbulent waters crash against the rocky cliffs, the sound comforting to my ears as I lean over the railing, looking over the ever familiar background.

Who was he?

Not for the first time since he'd left, I can't help but wonder about his identity.

According to my mother, he is a rebel.

Remembering how he'd looked, I can definitely see it in him.

He'd been so big and strong, his body frighteningly massive. Yet he hadn't hurt me. Aside from the initial prick of his blade, he hadn't done anything to me.

Maybe I'm looking too much into this. After all, it had been a first for me to come into contact with such a male specimen. One that not only scared me but also...

A blush goes up my cheeks as I realize the direction of my thoughts.

But that's exactly why he'd intruded in my dreams. Because despite the initial fear, I'd also felt...*want*. Or at least that's what I think it had been.

His touch alone had made my skin erupt in goosebumps, my pulse shooting through the roof.

When he'd looked into my eyes, I'd felt every little part of my body heat up, a strange tingling developing in my lower belly.

Retrospectively, maybe everything I'd felt had been because he is the first male I've ever seen up close—*too* close.

All my life, I've only been around my mother, her friends, and the various servants she'd hired. Is it any wonder that I'd been so struck by his impressive presence?

Yet somehow I doubt any other male would compare with him. At least in the books I'd read, they'd never appeared as large, or as...hypnotizing.

I slap my cheeks twice as I chastise myself. No matter how I think of him, I end up at the same conclusion—he intrigued me. Maybe a touch too much.

Giving up on sleep even though there are a couple of hours left until dawn, I head downstairs to the kitchen to check what Meli left for me.

I'm pleased to find an assortment of cooked meals as well as cold cuts which she'd thoroughly bathed in salt to hold for the entire week.

Despite providing for me as best as she can, my mother would never allow anyone to *live* with me. The more time someone spent with me, the more likely it would be for them to discover my abilities. And as she'd repeatedly told me, that was simply out of the question.

There had been an incident when I was younger with one of my maids. She'd seen me heal after cutting myself on some glass. The next day, she'd been gone.

I don't know what happened to her, but I hope my mother didn't do anything unseemly to her.

Taking advantage that some of the dishes are still fresh, I pour myself a bowl of stew.

As soon as I taste it, though, I wince, realizing it's missing seasoning.

Not one to despair, I take a pair of scissors and head to my garden since I have an entire section dedicated to spices and edible plants.

Yet the moment I step into the moonlit area, I'm struck by something at the end of the garden—something sitting on the bench that brutish man had previously occupied.

Frowning, I slowly step towards it, afraid it could be something dangerous.

The poorly lit area obstructs my view at first, and though I can make out the outline, I don't realize what it is until I stop in front of the bench.

My hand flies to my mouth in surprise, my heart beating loud in my chest.

There, placed haphazardly in a makeshift bowl, are the flowers I'd been desiring as my birthday gift—the purple blooms I'd only seen in the pages of a book.

I swallow hard as I take the bowl in my hand, surveying its state.

Immediately, I can tell that this had been done by someone unfamiliar with gardening, the entire situation messy. At the same time, the root of the plant has been perfectly preserved so I can move it into my garden.

At once, I know it's not my mother who's done this. She hadn't even remembered what I'd wanted for my birthday. And she certainly wouldn't have been able to journey to the other end of the Empire to get it for me.

Only someone with the ability to cover great distances in moments' time would have been able to do this.

Someone like...

"You like my present, Sela?" his smooth voice hits me right in the chest, causing my heart to stop for a second before resuming beating.

Thump. Thump. Thump.

As if being reset, it assumes a different rhythm that coincidentally matches his breaths.

"You," I state accusingly, turning and coming face to face with *him.* The same male from before—the one who'd been haunting my thoughts ever since he'd disappeared from my sight.

"What are you doing here?" I narrow my eyes at him as I try to decipher his intentions.

"I told you I'd be back."

He's wearing different clothes from before, a pair of beige linen pants and a loose white shirt. Even though his garb is ordinary, it does nothing to decrease from his formidable appeal. It certainly doesn't make an effort to hide his massive chest or his muscular thighs.

Despite the loose fit of the clothes, his muscles strain against the fabric. If he'd wanted to pass for a simple peasant, he most definitely failed.

No peasant would look that...decadent.

Yet there's another feature that makes me still in my tracks.

His white hair, previously tied tightly at his nape, now flows down his shoulders, its sheen absolutely magnificent.

"Why would you be back?" I stammer.

He'd seemed acquainted with my mother, though his opinion of her had struck me as abysmal.

Is that why he's here? To use me to get to my mother? Exact some type of revenge on her? But why? Surely if he's a rebel then he should recognize they are on the same side against the empire.

"Perish that thought, lovely Sela. I'm only here for you," he murmurs as he steps closer.

Instinctively, I take a step back until my legs meet the bench. I teeter for a moment before I fall.

Yet it's not as gauche as I would have imagined. Not when my bottom meets a soft yet hard surface, strong arms wrapping around me and taking the little potted flower out of my hands.

"You'll hurt yourself," he whispers in my ear.

Just like before, I find myself speechless not only in the face of his impressive abilities, but also his equally devastating presence.

I drag a ragged breath into my lungs as his heat engulfs me, seeping through my clothes.

"I haven't given you leave to touch me," I muster a feeble protest.

"You haven't vocalized it. But your eyes do not lie," he speaks in my ear. "I'm not the only one feeling this madness, am I, lovely Sela?" he murmurs softly.

Damn it, but why does he have to be so appealing? Even operating under the impression that he is some kind of ruffian, a rebel who is sought by the authorities, I still cannot steel myself against him.

Is this normal, I wonder?

Am I just so starved for interaction that I lose my head to the first male I meet? Would I react the same to another?

A growl escapes him, the sound so potent it travels through my veins as shivers overtake me—yet I'm not afraid. At least, it's not the type of fear one would have for one's life. It's something utterly different...

"It's not normal. Of that I can assure you," he rasps against me, once more, reading my mind.

"Stop reading my thoughts," I hiss at him.

"It's not my fault you broadcast them so loudly, lass," he chuckles. "But maybe this will answer your question," he says as he brings his lips down my neck again, inhaling me deeply while trailing his open mouth down my flesh.

A wave of awareness hits me at once, places I'd never given much thought to flaring to life and throbbing. And it's all because this stranger is...licking me.

"Remove all thoughts of other males from your mind," he states savagely. "You will not react to another the same, Sela. Of that you have my vow."

My lips tremble as I attempt to form a reply. His touch is everywhere, lulling me into a sense of security unlike I've ever known.

It's not just interaction I'm starved for. It's touch, too.

And when he buries his face in my neck, I can only arch against him, purring happily at the way his touch feels.

When was the last time someone had given me a hug?

I can't remember.

Maybe it is madness that I am yielding with nary a protest, but starvation gnaws at me as I cover his hands with my own, throwing my head back and allowing him more freedom of movement.

I wiggle in his lap, feeling the hilt of his sword poking me in my back but trying not to mind it too much.

He lays small, sweet kisses all over the column of my neck.

"You smell so good. So fucking delectable I'd like nothing more than eat you."

Somehow that one sentence is enough to put a damper on my shameless behavior. Especially as I'd read about some species that...well, eat others.

Jumping out of his arms, I take a few steps back, biting my lip and regarding him with apprehension.

His eyes flicker between red and black. Now, *that* is something I've never read about. Do they change at will, or does something influence them?

He rises from the bench, a smirk pulling at his lips.

It's at the same time that I notice that the front of his pants have become tented.

Is that... Is that what was poking me in the backside?

My wide eyes meet his as I continue to walk backwards.

"My eyes change according to my mood," he answers casually.

"What does red or black mean, then?"

He smiles lazily, almost like a cat.

"Black is when I'm at my tipping point. Red is halfway there," he explains.

"Where?" I frown.

"Ah, Sela, you're such an innocent, are you not?"

"Well, will you tell me or will you not?" I snap as I cross my arms over my chest, tapping my foot at him.

Odd that I'm feeling so daring with this man when he has the power to snap me in two. My healing abilities aside, I have no doubt he would do what nothing seems to have ever worked—destroy me.

"War," he says and as I blink, he appears right before me. "It's the bloodlust in me that claws its way to the surface."

"You want to...hurt me?" I ask as I gulp down a sliver of fear.

"No," he shakes his head, his lips drawn up in an amused smile. "I'm finding there's a second reason for it."

I flutter my lashes in confusion.

Leaning towards me, he brushes his lips across my earlobe before speaking.

"*Lust.*"

"Lust?" I repeat, dumbfounded.

"I'm a war machine, Sela. I was forged with the explicit purpose of bathing in my enemies' blood. Slaughtering, marauding, *killing*. If my eyes turn black, make no mistake, I don't lose myself to the bloodlust," he drawls seductively. "I *give* myself to it."

"Is that what this is about?" I ask as I bring my hand to my neck, trailing my fingers over the surface he'd scraped the other day. "You want my...blood?"

He smiles.

"And if I did?"

"You can't have it," I answer sharply, narrowing my eyes at him.

What is he?

"I am ruin, Sela. I will be *your* ruin," he states seriously. "If only I could stay away..."

"You...should?" I murmur weakly, thoroughly lost in his eyes.

The last of the red has faded away until only the clear blue remains—the most beautiful blue.

"If you continue to look at me like that, I won't be able to stop myself, lovely Sela. You're far too tempting for a man who's never denied himself anything in his life."

"I..." I lick my lips, still staring at him. "I have food. I'm not sure how much better than blood that is, but you can join me to eat." I don't know what prompts me to utter that foolish invitation.

His eyes crinkle at the corners as his mouth spreads into a breathtaking smile.

"As you wish," he inclines his head.

Taking my hand, he leads me to the kitchen, taking out a chair for me and seating me at the table. My gaze follows him silently as he moves around the kitchen as if he's been here a million times before.

He doesn't ask me any questions, or demand anything of me.

He simply heats up the food before pouring me a fresh serving and pouring himself another one.

I keep watching him, barely even breathing for fear I'm going to disturb this scenery in front of me, that I'm going to blink and everything will turn out to be just a dream—just a figment of my imagination.

Yet I doubt I could ever conjure up a male as striking as him, one who is equally ill-mannered as he is sweet. I doubt I am capable of such mental acrobatics.

So I just watch, letting that tingle of awareness spread all over my body.

My heart thuds in my ear, my pulse seemingly going berserk.

And as he surprises me by cutting some thyme and basil over my stew before doing the same for his own, I can no longer deny what is happening.

I am smitten.

Unfortunately, it had to be with an outlaw.

The books certainly did not lie when they mentioned that you cannot command the heart.

"You read my mind about the flower, did you not?"

He nods.

"How did you get it so fast? It's endemic to the other end of the Empire. On horseback that would take at least a month."

"I can move fast," he smiles.

"What are you?" I finally make the courage to ask.

He falters for a moment.

"It's better you don't know."

I frown.

"Why?"

He doesn't answer me, merely watching me with naked hunger in his gaze despite having a sizable portion of food in front of him.

"You could at least give me your name," I mumble.

"Amon."

"Amon?" I'd seen that name before in the history books. But I imagine it must be an immensely popular one since it's associated with one of the most infamous figures in the Vissirian Empire's history.

"I love hearing my name on your lips," he murmurs.

His hand reaches for my face as he brushes his thumb under my lip, swiping a stain of food off my skin and bringing it back to his own mouth. He sucks on his thumb with gusto, all the while his eyes never leaving mine.

I blush, but I don't look away. Is it a dare, or an invitation? A promise for the future or a tease?

Despite the unusual feelings he instills in me, there is something utterly comfortable about being in his presence.

A deep desire unfolds inside of me to climb back on his lap and let him put his massive arms around me, surrounding me with a protective cocoon and never letting me go.

Foolish, isn't it? I've only met him twice and yet his arms feel like the home I've never had despite living very self-sufficiently.

"Then I should tell you, Amon, that I am not versed in the politics of our world. I may have the theoretical basis down, but there are many things I do not know. If I ask, it is because I am genuinely curious," I tell him seriously.

A brow goes up as he looks at me expectantly, almost as if I surprised him with my words.

"I've read all the canonical literature on the species of our world, and I have *some* knowledge about that, but I must confess I've never met anyone in person aside from my mother, a few of her acquaintances and the staff that changes with the season."

He purses his lips as he takes a moment to ponder his next words.

"Do you know what a Reva is?"

I frown and shake my head. The name is awfully familiar but as I try to remember, I cannot do so.

"They were a people in the North of the Empire, many, many eons ago. They were few to begin with, but their numbers dwindled over the years since the Empire hunted them down to near extinction."

"Why?"

"Because their abilities were...unique."

"How unique?"

"There are species on Arkgor that can wield the elements, but only the Reva of the North could wield matter."

"Matter? Can you be more specific?"

He smiles. Holding out his hand, he materializes the flower pot from before and places it down on the table.

My eyes widen in shock.

I'd never read about anyone able to do something like...that.

"This is but one of the consequences of this ability. The most deadly one is wielding the matter of being. Quite simply put, I can make someone's insides explode. And to the Vissirian Empire that is something as dangerous as Vissirian Silver. Maybe more, because rhodium does not have a mind of its own."

"So you're a...Reva?"

"Part. But I've never identified myself as such, just as I don't use those abilities so I won't draw unnecessary attention to myself."

"You're telling me it's dangerous for people to know you're part Reva."

"That is correct."

"Then why are you telling it to me if it's so dangerous? Aren't you afraid I'm going to tell someone?"

He shakes his head, his mouth curled up in a perpetual smile.

"But how would you know? I could very well be a spy planted here in the middle of nowhere to ply tales out of weary travelers," I shrug.

"You've a very active imagination, lass," he laughs. "But I am not worried you will tell on me."

"Why?" I narrow my eyes. "I could be dangerous," I throw the idea out there. "Mayhap not a spy since clearly I would have failed at holding my own," I pause as I tap my jaw with my finger. "But what if I was stationed here to *seduce* this information out of you?"

"You're trying very hard to convince me you're not to be trusted, lovely Sela," he chuckles. "But say you *were* instructed to catch me here and seduce me. You'd be doing a rather poor job of it."

My cheeks flame at his insult.

"W-what do you mean?"

"You thought a *sword* was poking you in the backside, lass. Need I say more?" he asks, amused.

"But there was a sword..." I reply lamely, embarrassment coloring me red from head to toe.

"Sure there was," he laughs. "I only told you in an attempt to show you I am in earnest about my intentions, my darling Sela. I hope that by knowing this one weakness of mine you will feel more at...ease with me."

That...That somehow makes me feel warm inside. Damn it! Why does he have to be sweet at the perfect moments? Now, not only do I feel flattered by his attention, but I'm also thrilled to be the only one knowing that secret of his.

"Is that why people were looking for you? Because of your ability?"

He shakes his head, suddenly sobering up.

"No. You would be the only one to know I am part Reva now," he adds, stunning me with that piece of information. "They were looking for me for another reason altogether."

"Why?"

"It hasn't escaped my notice that you lied for me," he suddenly says. "You're not as indifferent to me as you try to seem, are you?" he drawls seductively as he reaches across the table to cover my hand with his own.

Damn it, but who was I kidding?

He'd be more equipped to seduce *me* than I could ever be to seduce him. Especially as heat pools low in my belly, the sensation utterly disconcerting as I rub my thighs together to alleviate the pulsation in my loins.

His nostrils flare as he looks at me, and his eyes shift to red again.

"Stop moving," he rasps, squeezing my hand.

"W-what?"

"If you want me to be civilized, you need to stop moving, lass," he pauses as he releases a pained groan. "I can smell your arousal."

I blink, thinking I haven't heard him right.

"You...what?"

"The more you move, the more potent it is for me. Stop. Moving."

All at once, I freeze.

For a few moments, he gulps down deep breaths, almost as if he is suffocating.

"I was right, wasn't I? You *are* a brute. There's nothing *civilized* about you, Amon," I accuse, staring mutinously at him.

"Ah, my lovely Sela, how right you are about that. Yet for you, I'm trying to be," he murmurs as he tries to contain the red in his eyes from becoming the darkest black.

"You're one of those rebels on the run, are you not? My mother told me they are accused for the assassination of the Emperor."

He simply shrugs.

"You're not denying it."

"It is true. And you are correct on another point. *Accused.* That doesn't mean guilty."

"So you're saying you're not guilty?"

"Exactly. Though I don't doubt the entire world wishes I were," he sighs.

For the first time, I note the signs of weariness on his face. If until now he'd seem entirely jovial and charming, bent on teasing me at every turn, now he looks almost...disappointed.

"How do you know my mother, then? You called her Lady Luck. How did you know that's her nickname?"

"The question is how well do *you* know your mother, Sela?" he fires back.

"I know she is a good woman," I push my chin up.

"A good woman who keeps her daughter hidden from the world?" he snorts.

"She has very good reasons to do so. I don't begrudge her. Just because you don't know her, it doesn't mean you're allowed to make judgements about her character."

Yes, I am aware how my situation might seem from the outside. But my mother is doing it for my protection.

"But that's the issue. I do know her. Far better than you do."

My lip twitches in displeasure.

"I thought you said you'd never touched her," I grit out, surprised at myself for the wave of jealousy that hits me, my entire body tensing up for his answer.

"And I haven't," he rolls his eyes. "But I know her from court."

"Court?" I frown.

"Sela, Sela. You truly have no idea who your mother is."

"I don't understand what you mean. What court?"

"She is—*was*—the Emperor's mistress."

I blink repeatedly as I don't think I heard him right.

"What did you say?" I whisper.

"You heard me right. She was the former Emperor's favorite mistress, and currently an advisor for the new Emperor. Isn't that quite the coincidence?"

"I don't..."

I swallow hard, feeling as if I'm munching on sharp glass.

He's implying that my mother was involved in the assassination, is he not? Because otherwise why would a new Emperor bestow such an important function on his predecessor's mistress.

Whenever the Vissirian Empire had changed Emperors, it was always a bloody process. There has *never*—not once—in the history of the empire been a peaceful succession. Of that much I am aware. The court is a battlefield in itself, war reigning supreme even at the most elevated title in the Empire.

And whenever there was a new leader, he would execute the retinue of the former one.

"You're not suggesting that my mother is a...traitor..." I barely get the words out before realization dawns on me.

From an early age she'd told me she wanted to see Milena back to its former glory, and that one day it would happen. I just never gave much credence to her words because of the current situation and the fact that the Empire had been more stable than ever.

Yet as I slowly ruminate over this piece of information, I wonder if she could have done that. If she could have bedded the enemy just to infiltrate the court and his confidence...

"You need to leave," I suddenly get up.

No! My mother may be many things, but she is an honorable woman.

After all, I've grown up with tales of Milena's bravery and honor in battle. There is no way that someone who would have preached those values would have resorted to such...tricks.

"Sela..."

"Please leave," I repeat, though my voice cracks.

If I don't believe it to be true, why is my voice breaking? Why do I feel like I'm suffocating?

"Lass, let me..."

"Leave, Amon. You are no longer welcomed here," I tell him with all the strength I can muster.

His eyes darken just as his lips harden into a flat line.

"You are overwrought. I apologize for making you so. I will take my leave now," he inclines his head. "But make no mistake, Sela. I am coming back for you."

My brows crease in confusion. Even believing my mother would be a traitor, and the Emperor's harlot to boot, he still would come back?

"Why?"

"Because I claimed you as mine."

Chapter Twenty-Seven

Carefully wiping the leaves of the flower, I pause to marvel at its beauty.

The illustrations in my books had not done it justice. Though the scent is extremely light, the color is absolutely stunning and complements the rest of the row perfectly.

Not for the first time in the days that have passed since Amon had brought it to me, I wonder if he's going to come again.

He'd said he would, but we'd parted on rather sour terms.

Yet in the time since, I've given his words more thought, and have decided that he...could be right.

At the end of the day, despite our mother-daughter relationship—which is more by virtue of our biological relation than anything—I do not know her.

The few days we meet yearly have not allowed me to know more than the surface level she wants to present to the world.

As such, I cannot defend her based on her character when I do not know it.

Immersed in my activity, I barely realize there's someone else in the garden with me.

Turning, I spot him immediately—there's not one hint of shock at seeing him again, though there is plenty of longing.

For all this time, he's been haunting my dreams and every waking moment.

And as I gaze into his eyes again, my pulse quickly picks up.

Come to me...

"You've been taking care of them," he murmurs, watching me intently.

"A gift should always be treasured," I reply.

My body immediately reacts at his nearness. There is something impossibly irresistible about him, yet I could not say what. I only know that when he is near, I seem to give in to my baser instincts, craving touch so ardently for the first time in my life.

"What are you doing here, Amon?" I inquire softly, my eyes taking him in.

He's dressed in formal clothes, black silk and leather mixed in a lethal combination. All tied together with bones—what little must have been left of his greatest adversaries.

He looks absolutely dashing, and I cannot seem to tear my eyes from him. There's a quiet pride shining in the tilt of his chin, a deadly aura surrounding him as he walks with such casual leisure, as if he could end the entire world if he wished to.

"I'm here for you, lovely Sela," he murmurs softly.

I give him a light nod as I invite him to take a seat on the bench.

"I'm afraid I can only offer you water."

"I don't require anything from you but your company," he smiles, taking my hand in his.

The effect is instantaneous as my skin tingles from where it touches his.

The corners of my mouth tip up as I cannot help the giddiness that mounts inside of me.

"You like it when I touch you, do you not, Sela mina?"

My lashes flutter at his question and a blush colors my cheeks.

Slowly, I tip my head in a tentative nod.

I also like it when he calls me *his*.

"I like it too. Immensely," he whispers as he brings my hand to his mouth, skimming his lips over my knuckles and kissing each in turn.

"Why are you so interested in me, Amon? Tell me the truth, please. Are you trying to use me as some political pawn because of my mother?" I ask him as I bring my gaze to his.

Though I'd pondered many things during his absence, I couldn't help but develop doubts that this could be too good to be true.

Why would someone like him suddenly develop an interest for someone like me? I'm neither worldly nor an incomparable beauty that would make him lose his mind.

What could have prompted him to say those words...that he claims me as his?

"You're wrong," he says quietly. "To me you're the most beautiful woman in the entire Arkgor—in the entire universe. And believe me, I've lived long enough and traveled far enough to know it."

Biting my lip, I avert my gaze.

"Don't," he immediately says. "Don't take those beautiful eyes off me. Let me see you," he murmurs as he grasps my chin between his fingers, making me face him.

My lips tremble as I force myself to return his regard.

"I've waited for a long time for someone like you, Sela."

"Someone like me?" I echo.

"Someone who completes me," he replies. "You might not understand now. But you will. Soon," he promises, and for some reason, I believe him.

"How... How long are we talking about?"

"Are you fishing for my age?" he chuckles.

I nod.

He doesn't look older than his late twenties, but as I've read, appearances can be deceiving with many species. There had been no information about the Reva, however.

"It's been four hundred thirty nine years since I was born."

I blink in surprise.

"That's...a lot older than me," I whisper.

He purses his lips.

"In many ways, I'm just as young as you," he smiles.

"What do you mean?"

"Sometimes, they say you must experience the worst before you can experience the best. I think I got that with you. If I hadn't lived through the worst before, I would have never found this place...you."

"But that's the thing, Amon. I haven't experienced *anything* besides these walls. My only knowledge comes from books. I do not know how to behave in society, nor do I know how to interact with people."

"Shh," he places a finger over my lips. "We all have our roles, Sela. I, too, haven't experienced plenty of those things."

When I frown, he continues.

"I joined the army when I was eleven."

My eyes widen in shock. Isn't that too young?

"It is," his lips flatten in a tight nod. "My parents were very poor, and they knew they couldn't afford to feed me. This was right around the time of the Uridic plague, when food was more scarce than ever. My parents were regular peasants. Though they each had the right ancestry, they had never manifested any abilities. But I did," he sighs. "From the youngest age, I showed great promise. At first, I simply helped around the house, but when it became clear that starvation was upon us, they decided to sell me to the Special Unit of the Emperor's army."

"Special Unit?"

"It's for the most gifted people. There are many species on Arkgor, that is correct. But not everyone is born with abilities, just as not everyone measures the same on the power scale. The Special Unit was created for those people that showed most promise."

"I didn't know that was a thing."

"It's not too widely known. As you can guess, the military relies on the strongest people. In many ways, the Special Unit was a training ground to make sure we could all reach our full potentials. Yet there was one difference..." he trails off as he squeezes my hand.

"What was it?" I ask, riveted by his storytelling.

"Due to how aristocratic and upper-level marriages work, most often than not, the most gifted people are within those ranks. That put me firmly at the bottom."

"You were the poorest," I whisper.

He gives me a tight nod.

"But that only made me work harder than the rest. Whoever got into the top five at the end of every month got to take home a few coins and grain. So much grain it could feed my family for an entire year," he speaks wistfully.

"So you did it," I smile, expecting nothing less from him.

"Not immediately," he takes a deep breath. "I was young and untutored. My parents had no idea how the Reva powers had been passed down to me after so many generations, but they'd always told me not to show them off because that could lead to death. So I had to rely on my other abilities. My speed, and mental control among others. But more than anything, I had to train my body. I needed to learn how to fight with an arsenal of weapons since we would be tested on each. Many of my peers had already wielded those, and had been trained since young with some of the most famous masters from all over Arkgor. Compared to them, I'd never touched anything but a scythe during harvests."

"So, what did you do?"

"I trained. I trained and trained until the skin on my hands peeled off from overuse—until I could barely stand on two legs. It took me a year and a half until I finally scored into the top five percent. But..." he trails off, swallowing uncomfortably.

I scoot closer to him, my thigh meeting his as I wait for him to continue.

"After I finally got the reward, I had one free day on which I could see my family. Since we lived quite far away from the capital where I was doing my training, I used my powers to get back home. I... They were dead when I arrived there. They'd been dead for at least a couple of months, either from the plague or from starvation. I was almost thirteen when that happened—by all accounts almost a man. But I still bawled like a baby," he shares on a ragged breath.

"Amon," I whisper, the hurt in his voice echoing in my heart.

"My mother's parting words to me had been to become the strongest. To climb my way to the top so that nothing could hurt me—no disease or starvation. So that's what I did. I took her advice to heart and since then I haven't stopped. I trained more. Every waking hour of every day. I trained until I honed every single skill required of me, excelling in all categories. And so I climbed the ranks. A mere peasant's son climbed the ranks right to the top. So you see, Sela, I've never known anything *but* war."

He turns fully to me as he gives me a sad smile.

"I dedicated myself so fully to war, my name became synonymous to war."

My eyes slowly widen as realization dawns on me.

"Amon. You're Amon d'Artan. The Shadow General," I whisper.

There are entire sections dedicated to him in the history books, all speaking of his abilities and leadership.

He is the man who captured the Kingdom of Milena for the Vissirian Empire. He is the one that annexed tens of other territories since he became the General of the entire Vissirian Empire army.

"I am," he confirms, sadness descending on his features as he watches me warily.

And that's when I realize why...

He's waiting for me to be repulsed by him.

I don't know his reputation in the outside world, but the books sing him homage.

He has a fearsome reputation, that is true. But for Vissirians, he is also a celebrated hero.

"Have you ever killed a child?"

He shakes his head vehemently.

"Have you ever killed or harmed an innocent?"

"I may not have killed an innocent with my own hands, but plenty have died during the wars I've helmed. And for that, their blood stains my fingers as if I'd killed them myself," he admits, regret dripping from his voice.

"Then why do it? Why do it at all?"

"Because," he gives a dry laugh. "Until very recently I didn't live. I was only a tool of violence, nothing else—alive but not living."

"What happened?" I ask when I see his features darkening. "It has something to do with the assassination, does it not?"

"You're correct," he nods quietly. "My closest friends betrayed me. I'd never thought them capable of such a thing, but they allied themselves with certain members of the aristocracy to replace the old Emperor with someone new. But for that to happen, they needed someone to take the blame for the death of the old Emperor. And they found me," he laughs. "Even after all this time, I was still peasant shit to them. It didn't matter that I was their superior—that I had the seals of the army and could move it freely to my will. It never mattered to them."

"That's why my mother brought the soldiers after you. She..." I bite my lip. "She's involved, is she not?"

He grunts.

"Does that make you hate me?" I ask tentatively, remembering the state I'd found him in.

He'd been hurt, and badly. Just a little higher, and that arrow could have ended his life.

"Darlin', I just told you all the terrible things I've done in my life, and you think I'm going to hate *you*?" He shakes his head, a smile probing at his lips.

Snaking his arm around my shoulders, he pulls me into him.

"I do not begrudge you your parentage, Sela. It would be the height of hypocrisy for me to do so."

"I'm sorry all this happened to you, Amon," I murmur, hurting for him and everything he's been through. "My heart breaks for you."

Gods, but just imagining the child he'd been—the child he *never* got the chance to be—and my chest contracts with pain.

"Please, don't. It made me who I am. And the male I am now can protect you."

"What...?" I whisper, raising my gaze to look at him..

"From the first moment I saw you, I knew you were mine, Sela. My female. The only one made just for me."

"How?"

"It's part of my Reva heritage. They were one of the few species who mated for life. According to what I know about them, they recognize who their mate would be upon meeting. It would converge in all the senses—smell, touch, taste, sight, sound. Everything about you made my heart pound and my blood boil with a need to have you. One I've *never* had before."

"Never?" I repeat in awe.

"Never," he confirms. "You'll be my first female, Sela mina. Just like I'll be your first male. The *only* one."

My breath becomes labored as I stare into his mesmerizing eyes, his words slowly sinking in.

"No one?" I ask again, unable to believe this beautiful male wouldn't have taken another female before.

"No one," he states firmly.

The color of his eyes starts shifting again and I remember what he'd told me—that it changes because of lust.

"My lovely Sela," he murmurs as he skims his lips across my forehead. Slowly, he moves to my cheeks, not leaving even one part of my face untouched.

He breathes me in deeply, almost as if he's memorizing my scent.

And I do the same.

It's not only him that experiences this maddening compulsion. I, too, felt it from the first. The need to bury myself in his arms, bathe myself in his scent and have his big hands all around my body.

Initially, I'd thought it a bout of madness—an effect of years of solitary existence. But what if it's not? What if it's just...him?

He trails his tongue over my flesh before he reaches my mouth, swiping it over the seams of my lips and demanding entrance.

I open, tentatively at first, before I become more emboldened as his mouth consumes mine, our lips fusing to one another, our tongues mating with a ferocity that leaves me breathless and absolutely dripping with want.

"Gods, Sela... You take my breath away," he murmurs reverently against my lips.

"I'll give you mine," I whisper, blowing gently against his lips.

His hands move to my ribcage as he encourages me to sit astride him, our bodies fitted together as we give ourselves to the kiss.

I sigh into him, letting him in deeper—wanting anything he can give me.

His taste coats my tongue, his flavor infiltrating my senses and making me drunk on pure sensation. There's only his kiss and the stroke of his tongue against mine, every little spar of our mouths sparking something deep within me.

He's hard where I'm soft, strong where I am weak—simply a perfect fit.

"I'll make it right," he breaks off the kiss, leaning back and watching me with hooded eyes. His pupils are close to black now, and for the first time there is no trace of fear as I take in his beauty. "I have a plan to clear my name. But until then, I can't risk your safety, Sela."

"What do you mean?" I ask in confusion as the fog of lust still clings to my mind.

"The Emperor might be the most powerful man in the realm, but he is nothing without his army. Yes, there are a lot of soldiers whose loyalties are with the Empire first and foremost. But the majority of them would follow me," he says as he twirls a strand of hair around his finger. "It was me who fought side by side with them, who trained alongside them. It was me they put their faith in when we went to war, not the Emperor."

"You want to organize an uprising," I whisper.

He nods.

"It's why they are after me. They aren't as afraid I'm going to tell the truth about what happened as they are about me raising an army against them, which they know *will* happen."

"How much time are we talking about?"

"A few weeks to organize everything. Maybe more," he sighs. "I need to reach out to every legion and see who will follow me. And at the end, we will plan for synchronized attacks on the capital. The goal isn't to get to the new Emperor. I could have done that on my own. It's to get the support of the people."

"You're telling me so much... Aren't you afraid I might say something to my mother?"

He shakes his head.

"I *know* you wouldn't betray me. How? I cannot say. But the conviction is deep in my heart, Sela."

"I wouldn't," I assure him. "I don't have any loyalties to the Empire."

He grunts, his mouth set in a lopsided smile as he watches me.

"I didn't know *how* to approach you," he chuckles. "I was so overwhelmed by what you made me feel that I didn't know how to convince you to give me a chance. Especially as I got to know your circumstances. Your thoughts can be pretty loud sometimes."

I roll my eyes at him.

"I thought that if I shared my secrets with you, you would see I am in earnest. That I'm not trying to take advantage of you in any way."

"You went about it the right way," I wink at him. "The flower helped."

"You've been taking care of it daily, haven't you?" he murmurs.

"How do you know?" My eyes widen in surprise.

It's embarrassing how much care I've been giving to that flower—to the extent that I've neglected everything else *but* her.

"That you've been cleaning its leaves twice a day? Or that you would sit down in front of it and stare at it for hours at a time? Or maybe..." he pauses, his smile widening as he sees my scandalized expression. "That you've been talking to it the entire time."

"You... You spied on me?"

He shrugs.

"Guilty. I waited for you to come to terms with what we talked about before I came back. But that didn't mean I could stay away. I find that even a moment is too long when I'm not by your side."

"Is that normal?"

"I don't know, and frankly I don't care. You're mine, Sela. And that means I must always be there for you."

"I like that," I blush as the corners of my mouth tremble in their upwards movement. "I like being yours," I say as I lay my head on his chest.

For someone who's never belonged anywhere, hearing him call me his makes my entire being hum with pleasure.

"And you are mine, too," I state.

"Always," he whispers in my hair.

We stay like that, wrapped around each other as the sun ascends into the sky and then begins its descent. All the while, I cannot find it in me to tear myself away from him.

My head on his chest, right over his heart, I listen to the rhythm of his beats, finding that they match mine perfectly.

It's the oddest thing to find ourselves so in sync.

His chest rumbles with every word spoken, his voice deep and husky as he recounts more of his time in the army, telling me about battles, about his comrades, but most of all, sharing the profound pain he'd suffered when his lieutenants and close friends had tried to kill him in his sleep.

Due to the nature of his work, Amon doesn't sleep on a daily basis, only going into a deep regenerative slumber at the end of the month.

When he is in that slumber, he is ignorant of what goes on in the world, and can hardly be roused until he completes his entire cycle, which makes this his greatest weakness.

For that reason, he'd had a special chamber built in the Army's garrison to which only he and his right hand man would have access to —in case of an emergency.

But he'd never counted on waking up with a rhodium sword sticking out of his chest and Kress, his right hand man, attempting to kill him.

My heart aches as I hear the disappointment in his voice, especially knowing Kress had been with him for the last hundred years.

"He was the first person I called a friend," he says on a weary sigh.

"How are your wounds now? Did the *zveka* help?"

"It did," he smiles. "They are healing well thanks to your gentle touch, Sela mina. In no time I will be as good as new. Just in time for my plans."

"And after? What's your plan after?"

"I'll marry you," he simply states. "The moment I stop being a fugitive and I vanquish all my enemies, I'm marrying you."

A blush suffuses my cheeks as I flutter my lashes at him.

"Shouldn't you ask the bride-to-be first?" I mumble.

He throws his head back and laughs.

"I would, if it were something negotiable. But it's not. You'll be my wife, my mate and the mother of our children," he drawls seductively before leaning down to whisper in my ear. "You'll never get rid of me. *Never.*"

Maybe the vehemence in his voice should scare me, yet I'm too gone to care.

If this is madness, then I fully embrace it.

"If you are mad, Sela mina, then I am madder. You're like the most potent poison that's infiltrated my blood, one that is as deadly as it is sweet for I can see in you both my beginning and my end. Gods, but you consume me, lovely lass," he groans. "You've become my most recurrent thought, which is as enthralling as it is infuriating," he breathes harshly, his eyes flashing the darkest black.

"We can both be mad," I whisper. "Together."

"Together," he repeats before he kisses me again.

It's late at night when he takes me in his arms, tucking me in my bed and kissing me goodbye before leaving to deal with his work.

I barely manage to sleep as I worry about his safety. With everyone on his tracks, I fear he might get cornered and caught.

He might be the greatest General who ever lived, but he is still just one person facing tens of thousands—if not millions.

But he cannot be parted from me just as I cannot be far from him, so he promises that he will spend time with me daily.

A week passes in which we spend every waking day together, and to my greatest surprise, Amon doesn't spare any details about his ongoing military actions.

In fact, he even asks *me* for advice on some of his ideas. And that is... entirely inconceivable.

Though I haven't lived in the outside world to witness a proper relationship between a man and a woman, the text I'd read had had quite a misogynistic bent to them.

There were rarely any women depicted in positions of power. If there were, they certainly must have been from their shadows since their names had never made it to the history books.

But it's more than that.

I'm surprised he prizes my opinion when my own mother had not thought it important in the least.

Our last visit is proof of that, when she'd chided me for merely mentioning politics. Yet that isn't the first time it happened.

Though we'd discussed the history of the Empire at large, it had always been from the prism of understanding why it's mandatory for me to stay hidden. There had never been a debate between the two of us, only information relayed with the express purpose of being internalized without any questions.

Yet the more time I spend with Amon, the more I realize just how narrow my view has been. And one of the main reasons for it is the fact that the books that my mother has been supplying me with have been written from very biased perspectives.

"These aren't canonical," he'd said when I had presented him with my treasured library.

He'd gone through them one by one and had told me that some of them had never even been in circulation in the Empire.

"No one would approve this, Sela," he'd mentioned while looking at a book on military history. "And it's not because it doesn't coincide with the views of the Empire. It's true that history is written by the victor, but in this case it's a matter of changing the facts. I was there during this battle," he'd pointed to one of the key battles in the conquest of Milena. "And this never happened. There was no convoy sent to execute women and children. The Empire might be vicious but my army would *never* do something like this. I would never approve it," he tells me vehemently.

"But... Then all my books..." I'd been absolutely devastated to find out the books that I'd learned by heart, those tales that had been my driving force for so long had been...false.

I am still reeling from that information, and the urge to burn all the books is almost too intense—but that would only alarm my mother that something is wrong.

Instead, Amon had taken to filling the gaps in my knowledge and telling me the truth about key events in the Vissirian Empire history and that of Arkgor by and large.

Yet aside from his tales—and he is quite the storyteller—he would always invite me to debate on different topics that have to do with military strategy or court politics.

To have my voice heard for the first time is quite...something.

It's rather unfortunate that I've gotten used to being silenced all the time—to the point where I would have never believed someone would value my opinions.

But Amon keeps showing me the opposite. He keeps challenging my views of the world and of my reality and shows me that there is another way of living.

On the other hand, I can tell that I'm also teaching him new things.

His life has always been on the move. From one war to another, he's never had a day to just relax and unwind.

While he debated politics with me, I taught him the basics of gardening—specifically, I showed him how to prepare the *zveka* plant in case he ever finds himself in need of one.

Of course, I couldn't let him go out without making him plenty of *zveka* poultice to have on hand.

He travels from one side of the Empire to the other on a daily basis, encountering so many different dangers along the way. Just thinking about what could happen to him, and my heart stops in my chest.

But despite his extremely busy schedule, he somehow always finds the time to bring me a gift—every single day.

Usually, he brings me flowers he'd spotted on his journeys—at least that's what *he* says. I somehow doubt that he would know to bring me *exactly* the flowers from my botanical texts. Especially the ones that I've marked as being interested in.

He's sly, but he's not *that* sly.

But it's not just flowers that he brings me. He'd figured out early on that I have a sweet tooth despite not being given too much by my mother and the staff she hired.

I'd never quite understood why sweets were out of the question since it's not like I can get ill, or develop cavities when my body is practically an unnatural fortress—nothing can damage it.

My Amon had taken it upon himself to bring me delicacies from all over the world, getting me to try something new every day.

"Let's see. What did you bring me today?" I ask as I feel him step into my garden.

He smirks at me but his hands are behind his back as he holds something.

"What do you think?"

"Another flower? Healing plant?" I bat my lashes at him.

Gods, but as the days pass, my love and regard for him increase exponentially.

All my childhood, I'd been told he was a bad man who'd subjugated Milena when the truth is as far from different as possible.

"Something different," he smiles sheepishly as he motions me to the bench.

I skip around the paved path and sit down on the bench like a dutiful child though I'm dying of excitement and curiosity.

Stopping in front of me, he raises a shameless brow as he baits me for a moment, showing me empty hands.

My face falls and I pout at him.

"I know you brought me something," I playfully point a finger at him. "Please stop teasing me and show me," I say as I flutter my lashes at him some more.

"One kiss and I will show you," he murmurs, beckoning me closer.

Not one to miss a chance, I jump up, twining my arms around his neck and giving him a kiss.

As soon as I turn to the bench, however, my eyes widen as I take in the exquisite gowns laid down in succession.

"Amon..."

"That's what you wanted to ask for your birthday, isn't it?" he speaks softly in my ear as I continue to gawk at them.

"They are absolutely stunning. *You* are the best male I could have ever hoped to fall in love with," I declare effusively.

His arm tightens around my waist.

"Sela... You..." he stammers.

Amon *never* stammers.

Turning to him, I note his slightly tinted cheeks and the way he blinks repeatedly as he stares at me.

It's with a marked delay that I realize it's because of my words, because I...

"You..." he scratches the back of his head as he looks anywhere but my eyes. "You're in love with me?"

I don't think I've ever seen Amon flustered before, and what a sight.

"I am," I confirm.

A whoosh of air escapes him before he draws me to him.

"I love you, too, Sela mina," he whispers in my hair, his arms tightly wrapped around my body.

He holds me like that for what feels like an eternity before he finally releases me, urging me to try the dresses on.

I do a quick show for him as I try each dress on.

They are much more glamorous than the dress that my mother had been wearing.

I don't know where Amon got these from, but he has great taste.

"I'll treasure them," I tell him as I twirl around.

Yet when I look at him, his jaw is clenched, red seeping into his eyes.

"Amon?" I ask carefully.

"Just a moment," he breathes out as he storms out of the garden.

I blink in confusion as I look at his retreating figure, thinking what could have affected him so.

Yet the answer is quite clear as moments pass and he still doesn't return.

It was me.

I affected him—maybe too much.

He'd had similar episodes in the past where he'd withdrawn when his eyes had started rapidly shifting color, and he'd told me it was because he was desiring me too much.

"I'm dying of want for you, Sela. But I'm not going to dishonor you.

I'm already a lucky bastard that you allow me to put my hands on you and taste your mouth. But I can't ask for more until you're wed to me. More than anything, I can't risk getting you pregnant when the situation is so precarious. I would never be so cruel as to steal your future from you," he'd told me then.

At first, I hadn't been able to comprehend why he was denying himself when it was causing him great pain. But as I'd learned more about the outside world, I'd realized that he was only protecting me. Not only from the stigma of having a child without a father, but also because it would be *his* child—the child of a traitor.

He can't risk that until his name is cleared in front of the entire Empire.

Yet it's exactly that gesture that makes me absolutely convinced of his intentions towards me and the fact that he *is*, without a doubt, the best male I could have ever had the luck to fall for.

We'd spent a lot of time talking about how our future would look like and I'd told him in no uncertain terms that I would like a household full of children. The more the better. It doesn't matter how many we are blessed with. After my lonely childhood and the isolation in which I'd lived, I want nothing better than to have a big family. And I know he would be a great father.

And because of that... Because I already see him as the father of my children, I need to be honest with him, too.

"I have something I need to tell you," I say suddenly when he reemerges from the house.

He frowns.

"What is it, love? Is something wrong?"

Walking to his side, I reach out and unsheathe his rhodium sword, the blade gleaming in the sunlight.

For all its poisonous effects on the residents of Arkgor, it is the prettiest thing to behold.

"Sela, what are you doing?" his voice holds a grave note to it.

"Don't stop me, Amon. I need to show you something."

"What..."

Before he can finish his sentence I bring the blade down my arm, slicing a long line on the inside of my forearm.

"What have you done, Sela..." he whispers in shock.

"Watch," I tell him as I extend my arm towards him.

Immediately, the skin starts melding until in no time the wound disappears completely.

"What... It can't be. What..." he mumbles as his eyes flitter from my healed wound to my face.

"You've told me your secrets, now I'll tell you mine. The reason my mother kept me isolated from the world."

"Because your power changes everything," he whispers, still shaken by what he'd seen.

I give him a brisk nod.

"What's the extent of it?"

"Rhodium can't kill me. At all. Not even a stab in the heart."

"But how would you know unless..."

"My mother tried it on me when I was six. I went through a lot of trials to determine the nature of my ability."

"Gods, Sela. But that means... She could have fucking killed you. A child!" he bursts out, his eyes crazed with worry. "That damned woman," he shakes his head. "I'm sorry, but if I ever cross paths with her, she will not survive the end of my sword," he declares solemnly.

I nod slowly, not contradicting him.

If there's anything my time with Amon has shown me, it's the fact that I've been lied to my entire life. My mother has manipulated me for her own purposes, and when she'd spoken of the final goal—the ultimate test of my abilities—who knows what trap she had in mind.

She's *never* had my interests at heart despite swearing on it.

"I can also survive being cut into pieces," I admit reluctantly.

"*Vessar*, my fucking gods," he jumps up as he places his hand over his face, his breathing harsh and barely subdued.

"Continue," he nods at me, though his muscles are straining under his clothes, his eyes red when it's decidedly *not* because of lust.

"If you cut a limb, the severed one will dissolve and I will regenerate," I explain.

"Do you feel pain?"

"Of course I do."

"Then you realize what you're telling me? That your mother's been torturing you? Fucking experimenting on you?"

"I know," I answer quietly.

"What else? Tell me everything, Sela. Every. Fucking. Thing. And while you're at it, tell me who else was involved. Who watched? Who knew? Who was there?" he fires question after question, his eyes now turning black.

Though I know he's on the verge of losing control, I tell him everything they'd done to me when I was younger. How they'd hurt me in all the ways imaginable to see if I could heal. I also give him the names of the people I remember from that period aside from my mother. It had been five or six people who'd called themselves scientists of sorts.

"They what?" he whispers in disbelief. "They burned you alive to see if you could heal?" his voice cracks as his eyes turn glossy—black for his raging wrath, but glossy for the tears he's shedding for me.

I haven't thought about those days in a long time, and despite trying to keep my emotions under control, I cannot help my own tears from falling as I recall the pain I'd been through.

"They drowned you... How long?"

"At most a day. Though it went progressively longer after they realized I could be submerged under water, die, and then come back as my lungs would regenerate. In all honesty, I don't think there's anything in this world that can kill me. Likely not even your power to blast me from the inside," I wrinkle my nose in distaste. That would hurt. A lot.

"Don't even speak about that," he shakes his head.

"There's more," I whisper.

"Fucking Vessar. I can't imagine what else there can be and I've doled out torture for centuries! I hope you realize just how bad this is, Sela. It's not just a test, it's *torture*."

"I know," I nod grimly. "I think I coped with it by not thinking about it."

"I can't believe you would still be sane after all of that, Sela. I've seen countless wars and disasters. I've seen people die in the worst conditions. But for someone to withstand that type of torture repeatedly?" he scrubs his face with his palms, wiping his tears away.

Suddenly, I find myself in his arms.

"I'll kill them. Every. Single. One. I'll make them rue the day they decided to experiment on a fucking child."

"It's in the past," I whisper.

"No, it's not. For me, this is the present, and it's a fact that those bastards will *all* suffer."

I nod absentmindedly, somehow not feeling any pity for the fate those people will suffer at Amon's hands. I suffered, too. I cried in pain, and never did they stop. They just continued.

But there is still more he needs to see. I don't want to hide any facet of myself from him.

Stepping away from him, I take a deep breath as I channel my power.

He watches me closely, not understanding what he's seeing until tendrils of electricity sneak up my arms and legs, creating a field of pure energy all around me.

Amon blinks in shock.

"Sela...you..."

"They called me a source of pure energy," I tell him. "They didn't know if this was the core of my power and what gave me my healing abilities, or if it was the other way around. They only knew that I was a source of unlimited energy."

"What did they do?" he asks in a defeated tone.

My lips tremble.

"They wanted to siphon the power from me, to feed themselves or their weapon. They tried, but they couldn't succeed."

"My brave, brave girl. I've got you, Sela mina," Amon swallows hard as he kisses my forehead. "I won't ever let anyone abuse you again. In *any* way."

"I trust you," I reply, realizing just how true those words are.

"And I trust you. Unequivocally. So much so that I would like to go through my slumber here if you don't mind that."

"You... You would trust me with something like that?" I whisper in awe.

"I *am* trusting you with my life," he confirms.

"When is it?"

"At the end of the week. I'll come after your maid has left."

He recounts that usually it takes him a couple of days to recharge, sometimes less, sometimes more depending on his energy levels—which at this point are fairly low due to his extensive travel.

It's the following day, however, that Amon instructs me to put on my favorite gown from the ones he'd gifted me.

"We're going out today."

"Out?" I repeat, a little scared of that.

How many years has it been since I've been out of the house?

Gods, I've become so used to this solitary existence that even the thought of putting one foot outside of the house absolutely terrifies me.

"I've got you, love," he assures me with a wink.

Knowing I can trust Amon but also the fact that I need to do this at some point—challenge myself even further—I do as he says and I dress nicely.

In the beginning, I think he's going to take me to an establishment somewhere in a more remote part of the city.

But as he takes me in his arms, murmuring how pretty I look, the entire scenery shifts around us.

One second I'm inside my house, the next we're in another location altogether.

"What's this?"

Yet as I look up at him, I nearly jump out of my skin at his changed looks.

His hair is dark, his eyes equally so, yet it's not in the way the color spreads to the entire area when he is in the throes of bloodlust or *lust.*

"You can manipulate your appearance?"

He nods.

"To a certain degree. But at least this way I won't draw attention to myself. There aren't too many white-haired, blue-eyed men around," he adds drily.

"Where are we?"

I look around, noting the brightly lit corridor and the many people jostling around us—all wearing the finest clothes I've ever seen.

"It's a..." he smiles. "House party."

"House party?" I frown.

"I investigated some of the names you gave me. Even if you didn't remember much, it was enough to track at least three of them. All attending this party tonight."

"What did you find about them?"

"Hans is somewhat of a scientist in these areas. He has some very lofty ideas about giving ordinary people abilities."

"How?" I frown. It's a known thing that it's entirely by virtue of your birth and your ancestry.

"That is the question, is it not?" he narrows his eyes. "At first he claimed he could unlock abilities for those with the right pedigree, but now he claims to be able to *give* abilities to someone who has neither. Bollocks, if you ask me, and entirely too suspicious."

"What about the rest?"

"One is his wife, Andrea. She is purported as an occultist."

"Occultist? What is that?"

"In her case, she claims to be an expert in the science of the soul. There are quite a few faiths around the Capital that claim the same thing. Charlatans, the lot of them."

I nod along.

"And then there is the third, and quite possibly the most dangerous. Aristol. I couldn't find much about him except that he dabbles in the dark arts."

"Sorcery?" My eyes widen.

I'd read that it was banned in the entire Empire for fear that it would be misused, which Amon had confirmed to be correct.

The issue with sorcery is that it's unpredictable. You only require a powerful source of energy which you can wield to suit your needs.

"Yes," Amon's lips flatten into a thin line.

"I could see why they would all be involved. Sorcery could be the answer to Hans' problem, could it not?"

"It could. If they found a way to give someone an energy source first."

His eyes bore into me, the implication clear.

"They would have used me, wouldn't they? If they could figure out how, that is."

Amon nods.

"Fuck, but I'm going to have so much fun breaking their bones today," he mutters under his breath.

"Can I do something, too? I don't want you to do all the work," I pat him lightly.

"Sela, love. If you want to help, you can. But you are in no way obliged to do so, alright? I can handle it just fine."

"We'll see."

Walking arm in arm, we reach an enormous ballroom where everyone is busy dancing the night away.

My pulse accelerates at seeing so many people at once, a sheen of sweat covering my skin as I force myself to bear it.

"I'm here," Amon whispers, his touch the only soothing thing.

One hand on the small of my back, he uses the other to rub circles on my inner wrist as he leads me to the back of the ballroom.

"That's Hans," he points out to an elderly male being accompanied by a relatively younger female. "And that is his wife Andrea."

"Where are they going?"

"I don't know. But we're following," he winks at me.

Making our way through the crowd, he swirls me effortlessly on the dance floor in an attempt to blend in as we follow the two.

"You're a good dancer," I note, jealousy gnawing at me as I think of other women he would have spun on a dance floor in the past.

"It's my first time dancing, Sela," he chuckles. "I've been to celebrations, that is true. But I've only stayed on the sidelines for a polite period of time after which I took my leave. I'm not the type to care for frivolities such as this."

"So you *don't* like dancing?"

"I like dancing with *you*," he says pointedly, eliciting a smile from me.

"Right answer," I chuckle.

"I knew it was a tricky question," he laughs, his eyes crinkling at the corners. "But I quite like you being possessive of your male like this."

"Really?" I raise a brow. "Does it inflate that already gargantuan ego you have?"

"Ah, Sela mina," he opens his mouth in a wide smile, his tongue swiping over his white, sharp teeth. "It inflates something for sure. Something like...my sword?"

I blink twice before my cheeks turn red as I realize I've been caught in a trap of my own making.

"Well," I clear my throat. "I am very glad your sword reacts to me," I say, barely able to look him in the eye.

"Are you?" he raises a brow.

"It should *only* react to me, of course."

"Of course," he repeats, his amusement seemingly increasing by the moment. "And you'll take good care of it, won't you?" he drawls wickedly.

My lips tip up in a teasing smile.

"*Of course.* I'll polish it quite thoroughly. First I'll use my hands. Then my tongue and..." I trail off when I note the usual change in the color of his eyes.

"I win," I lean in to whisper in his ear, quite satisfied with myself.

"Fucking Vessar, Sela. You want me to spill my seed right here on this dance floor? Before I get to torture those bastards? That's just mean, lass."

"We should probably get on with the plan then, they're rounding the corner."

"Trust you to be the voice of reason when my baser instincts take over," he groans.

Taking my hand once more, we follow swiftly after the couple, stopping only when they enter a strange room.

When the door closes behind them, Amon fits his ear to the wood.

"They are alone," Amon whispers. "And getting quite busy from what I can hear."

"Maybe we should go in before..." I trail off since I'm sure he gets my meaning.

"Naturally. I wouldn't want your pretty eyes to be damaged by such a sight," he winks at me.

Taking my hand, he pushes the door open as we step inside.

Andrea and Hans are kissing against a bookshelf, both suddenly breaking apart when they realize they aren't alone anymore.

"What's this?" Hans demands sharply. "Who are you and what are you doing here?"

Amon uses his power to close the door and lock it.

"What?" Hans frowns.

Andrea is trying to put her dress back together as her gaze flies sharply from Amon to me.

Yet one thing is clear. Neither recognize me.

They don't, Amon speaks into my mind.

"I'm sorry for the rather impromptu visit," Amon starts in a feigned diplomatic tone. "I was told only you would be able to answer a question of mine—one that cannot wait any longer."

Hans tilts his head in obvious interest.

"Speak," he commands.

Amon's lips twitch in amusement since it's ironic for someone to give *him* a command.

"I've heard about your study into sources of energy. I've acquired one of my own and I'd like to use it to fuel my own abilities."

"What type of energy source are we talking about?" Hans takes a step forward, his eyes glinting with curiosity.

"This," Amon says as he gently pulls me forward.

"The girl? How so?"

"It's quite unprecedented, but she can withstand a rhodium blade and heal from it in a matter of seconds."

Both Hans and Andrea freeze on the spot, their eyes widening in shock.

"You say she can heal from rhodium?"

Amon nods.

"Why don't you give them a demonstration?" he coos softly.

Trusting that he knows exactly what he's doing, I take his sword, cutting myself lightly on the finger and showing them how the cut mends.

I'll make it up to you, my love, Amon whispers in my mind.

I stifle the urge to smile at his caring tone, instead focusing on the moment at hand.

"You see, unprecedented, I tell you."

Hans brings a finger to his chin, tapping it lightly as he regards me closely.

"I've seen one person exhibiting this ability before. Unfortunately, we were not able to siphon the energy out of her," he says, confirming what we already knew. "However, my associates have developed a new protocol that we will start testing very soon. You are more than welcome to join. These...*creatures* are exceedingly rare and we must amass all the data we can on them."

"Creatures indeed," Amon repeats, a twitch in his jaw.

Hans doesn't seem to note that as he continues to speak.

"Everything we'd tried in the past has failed, but we'd approached it from the wrong angle. We tried to siphon *just* the energy."

"So what is this new protocol, if I may ask?"

Amon is barely holding himself together as he grits each word out.

"Transplants," Hans smiles. "You see, we wouldn't try to take just the energy since it seems to be rooted in its owner. We would try to gather the energy through body parts."

My eyes widen.

That is absolutely sick.

Hans doesn't shy away from going into detail with what he plans to do—take out my organs and place them in another body in hopes my energy would transfer as well.

"That is an innovative idea for sure," Amon notes. "But what about the other *creature?* In all my life I've only encountered her, and trust me, I've lived long enough."

Hans chuckles.

"They are rare, are they not? The one I know of is being contained at an isolated facility as we speak," he says, undoubtedly referring to me. "Her guardian still needs some coaxing in regards to the new plans since she has some silly notions about using the creature for her own goals. But science will prevail."

He seems very pleased with himself as he invites Amon for something to drink in order to discuss further plans.

"Alas, I will have to decline," Amon gives them a predator smile before they are both thrust backward and nailed to the wall.

"W-what?"

"Hans..." Andrea opens her mouth to scream, but Amon somehow makes it so she cannot talk.

"Thank you for enlightening me on your future plans. And here I was of a mind to punish you only for past transgressions," he makes a tsk sound as he uses his power to draw two chairs back and situate them in the middle of the room.

As if we're in front of a theatrical spectacle, Amon invites me to take a seat next to him as we continue to look at the two people currently stuck to the wall.

"May I introduce you Sela? Although, I'm sure you must recognize the name."

The only reaction from the two is the flare of their eyes as panic overtakes them.

"You might also recognize me," he smiles wolfishly as he changes his appearance to his original one.

Oh, yes, they must recognize him alright, because a wet spot appears on Hans' trousers, piss trailing down his leg and dripping to the floor.

Amon laughs as he leans into me.

"They were so brave a moment ago, were they not?"

"So brave," I shake my head dramatically.

"What do you think, my love? What do they deserve?"

I think on it for a second, not really knowing what to say.

"You do whatever you want to Hans. I'll take Andrea," I eventually say.

Seems only fair that I get a chance at this.

Though it's been so long and I barely remember some of the events —more due to my effort to forget than due to my young age—I can still recall the pain.

Maybe their faces have been erased from my memory, but what I felt as a result of their experience will never fade.

"Whatever I want?' Amon's eyes sparkle like a child receiving his most desired gift.

I nod.

"We can start with an apology. What do you have to say for yourself, Hans?" Amon asks as he removes his hold on Hans' mouth.

"I-I-I'm s-s-sorry," he whimpers, close to tears.

Amon releases a loud sigh.

"That sounds rather fake to me, Hans. Let's see if you can do better."

Amon raises his hand, and with one finger he moves Hans' left arm so it's stretched outwards. Before I can even think what he means to do, there's a loud explosion as his entire arm blows up before his flesh and bone liquify to the ground.

"What do you say now?"

Amon allows him to speak again but this time he releases a shrilling cry.

"Now, that's not fun," Amon chuckles.

He does the same thing with his other arm, until Hans is completely arm-less.

"Quite fitting, wouldn't you say, love? He wanted to chop you to pieces, now he gets the same treatment."

I nod.

"I think you're right. Good should be repaid with good just like evil should be repaid in kind."

He leans in to kiss my temple.

"Agreed. See how compatible we are?"

I roll my eyes at his playful tone as I turn my gaze to the two people.

Hans is slowly bleeding out while Andrea has also peed herself and is now silently sobbing while begging us with her eyes to let her live.

"Let's add another level, shall we?" Amon narrows his eyes at Hans.

He doesn't even move as Hans' legs explode next, both being cut right at his upper thigh as his flesh liquifies onto the floor.

Yet against all odds, the man is still conscious, probably ruing the day he was born—just as Amon had intended. His face is red since Amon will not allow him to cry in pain, and the entire situation feels eerily familiar.

After all, hadn't they afforded me the same treatment once upon a time?

They'd never cared about my pain as long as the experiments yielded *data.*

"Why don't we show Hans that there's one more type of suffering? That of watching your beloved one in pain?" Amon murmurs in my ear.

Giving him a brisk nod, I focus my energy to the surface, tendrils of electricity forming on top of my skin and slithering onto the floor. As if having a mind of their own, the tendrils snake up the wall until they reach Andrea's side.

Hans is watching the entire display with wide eyes as the tendrils touch Andrea's skin, the electricity so potent it burns every inch of her skin. And as they continue to climb up her body until they reach her head, nothing recognizable remains in their wake.

Tears stream down Hans' cheeks as he looks at his wife turned into a mass of burned flesh. And with a flick of a finger from Amon, what is left of her liquifies to the floor.

In the end, nothing remains.

"This is my message to everyone who was ever involved in Sela's torture, Hans," Amon smiles. "And they need to see just what type of pain awaits them."

Raising his palm, Amon slowly squeezes it. At the same time, Hans' body is squeezed down, his bones breaking and contracting, his flesh almost dissolving until only a ball of mangled matter remains—but it's one that still holds some sort of resemblance to Hans.

Getting up, Amon narrows his eyes at the wall, and lifting a finger, he controls the liquified matter from the floor, slapping it onto the wall in the shape of words.

Welcome to Krovj. Hell. The dimension where Vessar was supposed to have banished the souls of his defeated enemies to be tortured for an eternity.

"Shall we?" Amon turns towards me, his intense gaze washing over my form.

I take his hand, laying a gentle kiss to his knuckles.

"You could never scare me, Amon," I answer his unspoken question.

"Your appetite has grown, miss," Meli jokes as she shows me the assortment of food she'd brought for me. "I brought the extra stuff you requested, too."

I look around the kitchen, nodding in satisfaction when I see the cuts of meat and the ready-cooked stews.

Since Amon is with me throughout the day, he eats here too. He sometimes brings food, too, but I like to be prepared in any case and have something to offer him.

After all, he is more than twice my size and as such needs more nourishment.

"Thank you, Meli. This is wonderful."

"I cleaned your room and dusted the library. This should be it for this week," she gives me a tentative smile as she takes off her apron. "Do you have any requests for next week?"

"Just the regular. Thank you."

Nodding, she finally takes her leave. And now I can breathe more relieved as I call out for Amon to come back.

"That smells divine!" he exclaims as he appears in the kitchen.

"You're hungry?"

"When am I not?" he mumbles.

With the energy he expends every day, it's not a wonder that he requires plenty of food.

"I hope you eat when you're away, too," I say as I pick up two bowls, filling them with stew and placing them on the table. On a separate tray, I cut pieces of meat and arrange them in a row.

"Here, come," I beckon him.

Giving me a breathtaking smile, he takes a seat next to me.

"I do. Unless I forget, but then I get reminded when I become ravenous," he chuckles.

"You've had a lot on your mind lately."

He grunts.

It's been four days since the incident with Hans and Andrea, and though that went well, Amon has had trouble locating Aristol again. We'd looked for him after we'd finished with the other two, but Amon thinks he might have realized we were trailing him and disappeared.

Yet that's not everything that's been weighing on his mind.

In his attempt to unite the people who are loyal to him and rouse his own army, he'd come across a few roadblocks. Some of the lieutenants he'd been counting on had turned their backs on him. In the best case, they'd declared that they didn't want to get involved since they had their own families to think about. In the worst, the ones he'd visited had rang the alarm on him and he'd once more had to escape being followed by trackers—a special branch of the army designated with tracking down individuals of interest.

Their abilities are so specialized that Amon had to make some stops around the world in order to lose them.

"Are you hurt?" I ask softly as I see him eat with such an appetite.

Though his abilities are extraordinary, he's never risked revealing his Reva side before—and I doubt he would start now when he needs people's approval, not their hate. In that regard, we are quite similar as we are both outsiders—what many would call *creatures.*

But even knowing he is a flawless sword master and a born warrior, I cannot help but worry about him since he purposefully holds himself back so no one will find out about his heritage.

"Not more than usual," he shrugs. "I should be fine after my slumber."

"You need to let me patch you up first," I tell him sternly. "After you eat, go take a bath and I will meet you in the bedroom to examine your wounds. Then and only then you can sleep."

He grunts.

I can tell he's tired, his face paler than usual. He is also rather quiet when he is usually talkative, always teasing me about this or that.

We eat in silence before Amon goes upstairs to bathe while I pick up some plants as well as my pestle and mortar and a few clean rags to use as bandages.

When I enter the room a while later, I find him sitting on the edge of the bed, wearing only a pair of loose pants.

His naked torso is covered in cuts and bruises, some of them still oozing blood.

"You said it wasn't bad," I chide softly as I come by his side, assessing the state of him.

"It doesn't hurt," he shrugs.

"It might not hurt you, but it hurts for me to see," I murmur.

His eyes widen and for a moment, he doesn't speak, merely watching me as I apply a mix of paste to the deeper wounds and some balm to his bruises.

"I did not realize. I apologize," he says quietly. "I will attempt not to get hurt from now on."

"You..." I draw back as my lashes flutter in confusion. "It's that easy? If I tell you not to get hurt anymore you won't?"

"I'll do my best," he inclines his head.

A smile pulls at my lips.

"What am I going to do with you, Amon?" I whisper lovingly, my hands still working on his wounds.

"Love me?" he offers lightly.

"That I already do," I chuckle. "And now you're all done, too. Get into bed."

"Will you stay with me for a while? Until I fall asleep?"

His question makes me still. Why does this one question convey such an aching vulnerability? My heart clenches in my chest at his words, and I give him a small nod.

Taking me in his arms, he fits his big body on the bed (taking most of the space) and places me on top of him.

"Your wounds," I burst out, but he doesn't budge.

Just as he assumes a comfortable position, his eyes close and soon his breathing evens out as he is deep asleep.

That was...fast.

Gods, he must have been so tired. He's really been running himself ragged these past few weeks trying to take care of everything.

I can't help but feel a little guilty that I've added to his load.

During the day, he spends all his time with me, going out into the world and dealing with his issues at night. Rinse and repeat.

Has he taken a break since everything imploded? Has he even had another slumber before this one?

The answer, unfortunately, is no.

He couldn't have when he's been by my side *daily*, and he's already confessed that once he's in that deep state it takes him a couple of days of *uninterrupted* sleep to recover.

I nap for a couple of hours with him as well, but I later go back to my garden to wet and clean my plants for the day.

When I'm done later in the evening, I quickly wash myself and get back into bed with him.

The following day, I do the same, thinking he would awaken in the evening.

Yet he doesn't.

Once more, when I go to bed at night, he's still deep asleep, as he is when I awaken.

Goodness, but I can't imagine how he must have stayed on his feet if he was *that* tired.

Without the blessing that is his company, I get bored easily by mid-afternoon.

I have no idea how I'd gone about my day before he appeared in my life, because now everything seems...tedious.

I sit in front of my purple flower, admiring it once more. It still doesn't have a name—a *proper* name. In my botany book it had been referred to by its geographic location since it is endemic to one area in particular.

It's sometime later that a loud noise startles me. Jumping to my feet, my lips spread into a big smile as I dash down the pathway, thinking Amon must have awoken.

Yet as I reach the landing of the stairs, my smile dies down as I come face to face with my mother, her expression thunderous.

"Where is he?" she bites out, striding towards me.

Instinctively, I shrink back, but not before her palm connects with my cheek.

"What are you talking about?"

"The male you're hiding in here. Where is he?" she asks as she comes into my garden, her eyes scanning every corner.

"I'm not hiding anyone," I reply.

"Lies," she grits out as she comes to face me again.

Yet this time when she tries to strike me, I channel my power to the surface, my entire skin becoming electrified, which seems to make her pause.

"Aristol saw you, you stupid girl. He saw you at his party on the arm of a male."

"I don't know what you're talking about," I continue.

She's unrelenting as she barges into the study, then the kitchen, inspecting everything around.

"I know you're hiding him somewhere. Who is he?"

"I have no idea what you're talking about mother."

"So it's just a coincidence that Aristol sees someone who looks exactly like you and then two of my friends die in the most horrific ways?" she yells at me, a vein throbbing at her temple.

"I... I don't know what you're talking about. I swear," I lie, demurely shrinking back.

Yet it's when she decides to go upstairs, to my bedroom, that panic gets the best of me.

Amon trusted me with this! He trusted me with his life, and with his most vulnerable state. I can't fail him.

I don't even know what my mother is capable of. She might know about my abilities, but I know nothing of hers.

"Mother, just stop for a moment and explain to me clearly what this male thinks he saw. It's preposterous that you would assume it was me when I haven't exited this house in more than a decade," I call out as I follow her up the stairs.

Panic surges in my chest as I hurry and plant myself in front of her so that she won't be able to open the door to the bedroom.

"I thought it odd when Meli requested additional food, but then it all makes sense if you're fostering some vagrant. What did he tell you, Sela? What idiocies did he fill your brain with that you would allow him to do something like that?"

"I-I don't know what you mean, mother."

"No one else would have targeted Hans and Andrea like that," she hisses. "Who else would have known about them?"

"I don't know, their other victims?" I add drily. "I can't be the only one they experimented on."

"Experiment? That's my confirmation," she shakes her head in disgust. "Only someone else could have introduced that word in your vocabulary. And I demand to know who he is."

"No one. I keep telling you. There's absolutely no one. I don't know what you heard from that friend of yours, but I never left this house. I'm terrified to take one step in the outside world and you think I would go to some party? *How*?"

Her nostrils flare, and before I know it, she pushes me aside as she barges inside the bedroom.

"Mother, stop..."

My mouth drops in shock as I note the empty room, just as a feeling of tranquility overtakes me.

He's gone. Amon is awake and gone.

"See? There's no one here."

She releases a string of curses before she marches back downstairs. But as she's about to leave, she levels me a harsh stare.

"This isn't over. I know it was you. And I know you're working with someone, you ungrateful little bitch. After all I've done for you, and this is how you pay me back? By betraying me? By going after my friends?"

"But I haven't done anything," I complain.

"I don't have proof yet, but rest assured I will get it. And when I find out who the male you're hiding is, you will pay for this transgression, Sela."

Just as she opens the door, I spot at least twenty soldiers in front of the house.

"What..."

"They will keep watch, both inside *and* outside the house. You chose the wrong moment to rebel, Sela. And by Vessar, I'm going to enjoy killing that male of yours."

As she gives the soldiers orders, five of them enter the house, one in each room.

"Mother, this is preposterous! You're letting a *male* in my bedroom. To stand there at all times?"

"I don't trust you," she shakes her head. "Too bad you're still useful to me."

Her words confuse me, but I don't get to dwell on them as I return to find my home entirely occupied with strangers.

The front door closes and I know my mother has already left, leaving me to deal with these strangers.

No sooner had the guards assumed their positions that they drop dead. One by one, they melt in a puddle of grime on the floor.

"Tell me I can kill her," he demands as he appears, anger radiating from every pore in his body. "Tell me I can fucking slaughter her for putting her hand on you."

He reaches out to touch me, carefully stroking the cheek my mother had slapped.

"It's not too bad."

"She wanted you to live with five males. FIVE, Sela," he grits out. "And if you knew what was on their mind..." he exhales deeply as he leans down to place his forehead on top of mine.

"She didn't care that she was leaving you here to be raped, for those men only had one thing on their mind."

A shudder goes down my body at his words.

"Thank you for keeping me safe," I murmur, hugging him close.

"Let me kill her."

"I..." And just like that, I hesitate.

She's the only mother I've ever known. How could I possibly condemn her to death?

"We need to leave," I whisper instead. "I can't stay here anymore under her scrutiny. Not like this. Not when I could endanger you too."

"But your home...your garden," he draws back to search my features. "You would abandon your beloved garden?"

"It's no longer my home," I confess. "Flowers and plants can be replanted. A house can be rebuilt. But the feeling of home can never be restored. This," I motion to the house, "ceased to be my home the moment you appeared in my life."

Our gazes find each other, grasping—arresting.

He stares at me as his breathing intensifies, his nostrils flaring.

"Damn it, Sela. You're making me lose what little control I still have," he rasps.

I'm about to ask him why, but the moment I open my mouth, his lips claim mine as he kisses me so hungrily, my heart feels like it's about to burst in my chest.

His hands cup my head as he angles my head to the side so he can kiss me deeper until my head swims with euphoria, my body humming with approval for every little touch of his skin on mine.

Taking hold of his hands, I move them lower to my breasts, encouraging him to touch me further. He always pulls the breaks when our kisses get too heavy, but in this instance it's not enough.

"Amon," I whimper against his mouth.

His sharp teeth nibble at my lips, drawing drops of blood which he laps at, sucking my tongue into his mouth. A growl escapes him as he fits me to his body, so tightly I can feel his hardness protruding against my stomach.

Yet just as I think he's going to take it further than ever before, he wrenches himself from me. His eyes are wholly black as he tilts his head, his ears pricking at some inaudible sound.

"Soldiers," he suddenly speaks, his lip twitching in distaste. "They're close. *Very* close, Sela. They must have used a cloaking spell."

"Cloaking spell?"

"Sorcery," he spits as if it was the most disgusting thing. "We've encountered those in battles before. It means there must be a sorcerer nearby too."

"Aristol?"

Amon nods.

"It must be him," he grits out. "Don't worry. I'm going to end this once and for all, Sela mina," he promises before he disappears.

My eyes widening, I run towards the exit, opening the door and stepping outside on my own for the first time in too long.

My entire body trembles as my eyes accommodate to the change in scenery in front of me.

Yet as soon as I take everything in, my mouth opens in shock.

There are tens, maybe hundreds of soldiers stationed in front of the house.

All at once I realize that my mother's visit had only been a bait as she'd tried to draw Amon out.

"Amon, don't," I shake my head at him when I spot him facing off all those soldiers. "Don't use your powers, please."

The last thing he needs is for the world to find out he is part Reva. Then all his efforts would have been in vain. Everyone would fear him by virtue of his heritage alone.

He half-turns.

Dressed in a pair of black linen trousers and a loose top that's tied with a belt around his waist, he removes his sword, the movement slow as the metal shines in the sunlight.

Despite seeing Amon use his abilities before, this is the first time I'm seeing him fight with his sword.

He gives me a sharp nod.

Only as long as you are not in danger, Sela, he speaks in my mind.

A battle cry resounds through the air and the soldiers march forward, charging at Amon.

And this is what it has come to. One standing against hundreds.

Gods, but the sight sickens me to my stomach, and I know I can't let Amon fight this on his own.

Tensing my muscles, I let all the energy course through me as I call it to the surface. Once it's simmering on my skin, I let it seep in the ground, controlling the tendrils of electricity as I send them to the soldiers, burning them alive the moment they touch them.

I walk towards them as I send everything I have in me towards the envoy.

A blast of fire comes my way, but due to my misplaced focus, I see it too late to avoid it.

It catches the side of my head, the heat so powerful, it blasts off half my face.

I blink against the scorching pain as I turn slowly towards the assailant. My face is slowly mending together, the tissue repairing under everyone's sight.

I've been trying to protect Amon's secret and I've revealed mine. Yet I can't seem to care. *He* matters. He is the hope of the Empire. As long as his reputation suffers no damage, I'm willing to be his shield.

Turning my attention to my attacker, I send him a blast of electricity that fries his entire body.

"Sela," Amon roars when he sees my mending flesh. "Don't do it, lass. Don't get involved."

He just felled ten, if not more warriors just to be able to tell me those words. And even as his attention is on me, his sword is slashing through enemy skin, deftly avoiding the armor and going for the weak points.

"I'll protect you, Amon," I tell him.

What good does it do to be invincible and not use it?

With that thought solidified in my head, I proceed forwards, using my energy to fight off one line of soldiers while Amon cuts through lines of people.

Yet it's still not enough as more and more soldiers appear.

How could my mother have gotten access to this many forces?

Another moment of inattention and a sword slices through my arm. The pain makes me hiss as I see my arm drop to the ground only to turn into smoke, disappearing into thin air as my flesh starts to regenerate.

Everyone is staring at me as if I were, indeed, a creature.

But before I can unleash my electric snakes at them, Amon teleports to my side.

Blood drips from his face, staining his hair and every inch of his skin. His eyes are wholly black just as more darkness seems to seep from his eyes into his skin.

"Amon... What's happening?" I whisper when I see him.

"You're hurt," he rasps, his voice deeper than before, the bass making the hairs on my body stand up.

He lifts my still regenerating hand as he stares at it, his cheek twitching in displeasure.

"You're hurt," he growls, the sound louder.

The soldiers advance towards us, but with one look, Amon has them stop in their tracks, an invisible barrier seemingly holding them in place.

"Amon..."

"You. Hurt. Her," he screams, the sound of his roar turning into a physical blast that as soon as it reaches the first row of soldiers, transforms them into little else but goo on the ground.

It's almost as if he's not himself anymore.

"Don't..." I whisper, but he doesn't listen.

He's already charging at the soldiers, his feet barely reaching the ground as if he's stepping on air.

Yet that's not the most alarming feature. It's the fact that the black from his eyes is seeping into his skin, his body almost doubling in size as his hands turn to claws. And...

I blink, thinking I'm certainly not seeing this right. But...there's a tail? That's a tail, isn't it?

"You. Hurt. Her," he yells once more.

If before most of the males had been regular soldiers, the ones arriving now seem to have special abilities, too, as blast after blast is thrown at Amon.

Immediately, I become scared that he could get hurt by this.

But it seems that with his changed appearance there are new abilities coming to light. Like the fact that his darkened skin seems to serve as some sort of armor. The black linen gets blasted and burned off his body, but his chest doesn't get injured at all. But it's not like me, where I get hurt and then I heal. No, his skin seems like a thick shield that can block any attack so far.

Like this he's...unstoppable.

I know it, just as the soldiers are realizing it, too.

More people come towards him, but even if they land a hit on him, it doesn't affect him at all. At this point, Amon is a mindless war machine, bent on destroying *everyone.*

My lips part in a combination of horror and awe as he uses his bare hands to smash people to pieces. Given his change in size, his fists are now the size of a soldier's head—*helmed* head. He can easily grasp it and squeeze, causing it to pop.

Soon, I can see his strategy, *and* his weakness. He can't use his mental abilities while using his physical ones at the same time, and that means that while he's slaughtering one row with his hands, he reduces the next to mush with his matter manipulation, then goes back to using his hands.

I wonder if there's an interval at which he can use his ability, and that's why he alternates like this.

But even as I study his movements, I can't help but admire the way he is absolutely magnificent in fight. Despite his monstrous change—maybe *because* of it—blood has never looked better on someone.

His skin-armor is so strong that I doubt even my energy could penetrate it.

The sight of him alone is enough to inspire terror in everyone, some of the soldiers fainting before Amon even gets to them.

As I admire the fight, I note a couple trying to tackle me from the side and I decide to do something else.

Instead of letting the electricity tendrils seep into the ground, I use them as lassos. Holding my hands out, I will the energy to materialize before me, one in each hand.

They have a yellow-bluish tint, and as I grasp them, I feel a slight tingling sensation in my palms.

Turning my eyes on my adversaries, I use each lasso concomitantly as I throw them towards the soldiers, watching with satisfaction when they coil around their necks, suffocating them at first before sending the first high voltage of electricity and frying them.

Amon must be halfway through the soldiers who'd arrived here. At this point, in no time he'll run through all of them.

I smile at my big protector. He would stop an entire army from getting to me.

As I step forward to go to him, I feel fingers coil around my arm, thrusting me backwards.

I'm about to call up my tendrils of electricity again when I note it's my mother, a scowl deeply embedded in her features.

"Call off your pet," she sneers.

"He's not my pet," I push her hand away. "He's my mate," I declare proudly.

Her expression changes immediately. From a disapproving one, it slowly morphs into a terrified one.

"What have you done?" She whispers in horror. "You don't know what you've done, Sela."

Her eyes travel down my body, almost as if she's searching for something.

"Have you bedded him?" she asks suddenly.

"What..."

"Have you or have you not bedded him?" she hisses at me.

"It's none of your business. And I'm done hiding away from the world."

Her lip curls in distaste as she scoffs at me.

"It's a world that will chew you up and spit you out damaged beyond belief, Sela. I did you a service hiding you all this time. Giving you the best money could buy. And this is how you repay me? By mating with a...creature?"

"He's not a creature," I tell her.

Despite the erroneous literature I'd been digesting my entire life, Amon told me it's true that non-humanoid creatures are not welcomed in society. Nothing that doesn't fit the norm is. You have powers? Perfect. You don't look a certain way, then you don't matter.

"Whatever he is. Call him off or you're going to regret it. Both of you."

I look at her in disgust and I cannot believe *this* is my mother.

"How could you treat me so? I'm your daughter. Your blood. Don't I matter in the least? Doesn't my happiness matter?"

"It doesn't when there's a greater purpose at play," she says as she grabs me again.

This time, however, her touch hurts.

Looking down, I note her hand glowing just as her lips are moving in a low chant.

"What are you doing? Stop this," I try to push her off me, summoning my energy, but I find that I cannot do it.

"Selaaaa!" Amon's cry resounds through the clearing now littered with tens if not hundreds of corpses. He can feel my alarm and my silent struggle, and as he appears before us, my mother smiles.

It's then that I know she means to do something. She...

I can't even form my next thought before her other hand is on my chest. But it doesn't stop there. No, it penetrates my skin until I feel her fingers clench around my heart.

My eyes widen in disbelief.

"Surrender, General, and she will live," my mother adds smugly.

I can only see Amon from the corner of my eye. His new shape is absolutely breathtaking in its savageness. But as he sees the danger, he starts to morph back, his tail and claws already fading and leaving way to weakness.

I shake my head in horror, afraid they could hurt *him*.

"I can heal. Don't do it, Amon," I call out confidently, wrapping my fingers around my mother's wrist and tugging at her hand.

"Can you?" She raises a brow. "You think you have no weakness do you?" She smiles arrogantly.

"I can do it, Amon. I know I can do it," I tell him.

But he's not listening.

He's staring at her hand in my chest, the way she's holding on to my heart.

"If I squeeze too tightly, her heart is going to explode in her chest. Even if you think she can heal, will you take a chance on it?"

"Amon, no."

"Sela," he releases a ragged breath as his dark form is completely gone, leaving behind the Amon that I know. He has a crazed look of fear on his face as his eyes go from my mother's hand to my chest, almost as if he doesn't know what to do.

"I can't risk it," he shakes his head.

Some soldiers move from behind, approaching slowly and waiting for my mother's command.

"No, Amon, please don't," I whisper, realizing what my mother plans to do.

This had been her goal from the beginning, hadn't it?

It wasn't to scare me, or threaten me. It was to catch Amon somehow.

Except... How had she known? How had she known the male from the party was him?

"I can't risk you, Sela," he says. "I can't risk that she's right."

"Surrender, d'Artan and I will remove my hand."

His eyes flash red at her as he releases an animalistic snarl.

My mother flinches, and I note that despite her air of confidence she's afraid of him.

"Let her go," he growls, his eyes growing black again.

"On your knees," she commands him.

He gives me a look full of longing as he mouths a *sorry*.

The soldiers come forward holding rhodium chains in gloved hands.

They plan on...

My breath hitches as panic hits me. Full-blown, horrifying panic that clogs my airways as I take him in and the intention reflected in his gaze.

I can see the love, but I can also see the sacrifice.

Slowly, his knees buckle before they hit the ground, yet his proud demeanor doesn't change.

Head high, back straight, he looks my mother dead in the eye as he says.

"You may chain me this time. But next time you will meet the end of my sword. Or," he smirks. "You will join your soldiers on the ground."

"Shut him up," my mother commands.

I'm helpless as I watch the soldiers put the rhodium chains around his body, as well as a gag in his mouth. The chains must have been bespelled because the moment they meet his skin they shrink until his movements are fully restricted.

Wait for me, Sela. Nothing will stop me from coming for you. Just as nothing will save them from my wrath.

The moment Amon is restrained, my mother withdraws her hand from my chest.

I draw a deep breath in as my heart beats harshly in my chest. Yet as I move towards Amon, a needle pokes at my skin as my mother injects something into my veins.

"Amon," I whisper as I wobble towards him.

But I don't reach him.

I just...fall.

Chapter Twenty-Eight

My limbs are sluggish as I drag myself on the ground. My mouth is dry and parched, and as I open my eyes, I find myself in a foreign location.

The events from before slowly come back to me and my eyes widen as I remember how I'd last seen Amon: on his knees, sacrificing himself for my sake.

Just as horror sinks in at the thought of my Amon in danger, so does my determination soar.

He'd surrendered for me. On the off chance that my mother was telling the truth and my heart *is* my weakness.

He gave up *everything* for me at that moment. Because it's not just his life he's forfeited, but that of those loyal to him and any hope for justice.

According to what we'd spoken, Amon was certain they wouldn't kill him immediately if they captured him. They would torture him to get a confession out of him before publicly executing him. All of it is a well-crafted plan to ensure that any ongoing loyalties to him within the Empire would be squashed.

Amon had been rather modest when he'd told me that he has followers in all corners of the Empire, and not all in the military. Seeing the effort my mother and whoever else she's working with are putting into this, it's clear they consider him a threat.

I'm coming for you.

Even if it takes the impossible, I'm not going to let anything and anyone stand in my way.

My pulse accelerates as strength flows through my limbs as I force myself to my feet.

Taking in my surroundings, I note it's something similar to a cell, but the location is not familiar.

Where had my mother taken me?

The cell is dark and the only door that leads outside of it has a small grilled window. There is no other source of light inside.

Making my way to it, I grasp onto the metal bars as I raise myself on the tips of my toes so I can look outside.

"Is anyone there?" I call out, my echo traveling far through the hallway.

This tells me the location is quite big, and as such, might be guarded by a fair number of guests.

Flexing my palms, I try to summon my energy to the surface, afraid that my mother would have messed with it somehow. After all, she'd definitely pulled some tricks I was not aware of when she'd gone for my heart and injected me with that magical sedative.

I am certain it was magical because they'd experimented with normal ones on me in the past and my body would break down the compounds extremely fast so they ultimately never achieved their intended effect.

Within seconds, I feel the usual tingling, my entire body becoming surrounded by the familiar tendrils of electricity.

Maybe it's sheer determination that's causing this, but my power pulsates to life like never before.

Placing my hands on the door, I push some of the energy into the metal. At first, my purpose is to melt away the closing mechanism and open the door. As soon as I touch it, however, something completely different happens.

The door is thrust backwards almost like a projectile, hitting the back of the hallway and freeing the way for me to move.

I don't linger.

Already I hear people moving around and yelling orders as they undoubtedly heard the crash and are coming to check it out.

Running towards the end of the hallway, I come to a narrow staircase that is quickly filling with guards as they march towards me.

Closing my eyes, I focus on the same energy to create a blast that I throw towards the first five soldiers I see in front of me.

"Ops," I mutter under my breath as they turn rather crispy in front of me.

"Stop her!"

More voices echo in the building as I climb up the stairs just as more males charge towards me.

As I advance, I hone in on my concentration, keeping the same level of electricity at the surface of my skin. The moment anyone tries to touch me, whether with a hand, foot or weapon, they get burned.

Remembering the way Amon's skin had turned into an armor, I try the same.

No one stands a chance as I make my way to the exit.

Even when soldiers with powers are sent after me, it's quite easy to block their attacks. More surprisingly, I find that I can manipulate energy no matter the source—whether it's mine or theirs. And as one of the soldiers sends a blast towards me, I open my palm, absorbing it.

Instead of using my electricity as a shield that reflects back the blast, I use it to consume it instead, adding some of my own energy as I redirect it stronger than before.

With no defenses to speak of, they stand no chance.

"Wh-what are you?" A male asks me as he watches in horror his burned arm, my tendrils sneaking up on him and burning an inch at a time.

"Death," I whisper when his heart stops.

And I will be death for as long as I must to get back my beloved.

I shield my eyes from the sun as I finally find the way out.

Odd how even my anxiety about going out into the world has dimmed to a mere afterthought. Despite the ever constant fear of what I will encounter out there, it's something I need to do—I need to push my own limits.

For him. For me. For us.

Looking around, I note I'm somewhere at the edge of a forest.

I still don't know where my Amon could be, but my intuition tells me they would have taken him to the palace to interrogate him and have him admit to assassinating the former Emperor. That means I must go to the capital.

But how do I get there?

Looking down at myself, I cringe at the state I'm in. My dress, though not one of my prized gifts from Amon, had still been in fairly good condition before the fight. Now it's ripped and torn at the bottom, one sleeve is missing and there is mud and blood caked all over it.

As I rake my hands through my hair, I note there's more mud and blood there, too.

Good thing there isn't a mirror in front of me or I would probably have a heart attack.

Taking a deep breath, I start in the direction of the forest.

My knowledge from books and Amon's stories are the only things that can help me find my way at this point. And one thing I remember is that sturdy roads were built all around the Empire some thousand years ago. All of them had been designed to provide easy access to the capital.

If I come across a road and follow it, maybe I'll be lucky enough to come across some travelers who could take me with them.

Since I don't know where I am on the map, I have no idea how far I am from the capital.

The Vissirian Empire is absolutely enormous. So much so that I have no idea how it's endured as it has until now without breaking apart due to revolts or civil war. There are plenty of factions inside that aren't exactly fans of how the Empire has been operating in the last centuries. Specifically, there's a lot of bad blood with the recently annexed territories that still maintain their national identity, no matter how much the Empire had tried to force its language and traditions upon them.

There is only one recognized official language: Vissirian. But the more you travel, the more language and dialects you will find—one of the reasons why there is so much unrest in the Empire.

When you have so many group identities, which sometimes go beyond the national in the case of some species, it's hard to find common ground and establish a strong Vissirian identity.

As Amon had told me, one of the most polarizing issues in the Empire is the fact that non-humanoid species are mostly enslaved and robbed of any benefits that basic citizens have.

They would be the first ones to oppose the empire, but because one of the earlier Emperors had already foreseen this issue, he'd passed laws that ensured they would be spread out all over the vast territory of the Empire based on their species so they wouldn't come together and rebel. He'd taken advantage of inter-species enmities and had created a new map for the empire where every people was placed strategically to avoid coalitions.

So while the army is leading perpetual wars outside of the Empire, it also polices what happens inside since a civil war could start at the drop of a hat.

And *that* is why the Empire is so terrified of Amon.

Because he has the potential to *unite* all those factions under a common goal. With his name and prestige, he would be the only one who could entreat different species to involve themselves in a potential war. But more than that, he has the power to sway the citizens, too.

"Wait for me," I whisper.

I don't know what state I will find him in, but I am praying with all I have that I won't be too late.

I've never been a believer, or practiced any religion, mostly because my mother prohibited me from doing so. And like the good girl that I was, I always obeyed her.

Now, looking back, I realize it had been manipulation on her part, just as she'd done with the false books she'd given me to read.

If I'd believed in anything other than *her*, then I would had reason to hope for another future that didn't have anything to do with her. I would have probably been curious about the outside world and I might have rebelled earlier—all things which she tried to avoid.

For that reason I'd never had books that covered the topic of religion in the Vissirian Empire, though it had been, at times, briefly mentioned in other writings.

It had been Amon who'd opened my eyes as he'd told me about the practices in the capital.

"The other areas of the Empire are more different, and just like languages, you will find plenty of religions, gods and pantheons throughout the Empire. But the only recognized one is the Vissirian pantheon, led by Vessar, the god of war. There are plenty of other major and minor deities in the Vissirian pantheon, but the cult of Vessar has been the most popular for thousands of years for no other reason that it gives credence to the Empire's mission to conquer the entire known world."

Oh, Amon. How I miss you!

Just thinking about him being hurt and in pain makes me want to raze the entire damned Empire to the ground.

Even being separated for this short amount of time and already I don't feel whole.

After walking what feels like an eternity, I reach a road.

My face lights up, and I'm about to do a celebration dance when I see a carriage coming up. Not knowing *which* is the direction for the capital, I just dash towards it, waving my arms up like a crazy person in hopes they will see me.

Lucky for me, it stops.

"Are you lost, miss?" The door to the carriage opens, and I note the features of a male a little older than me. I suppose it's hard to know someone's age when they could be equally thirty or thirty hundred years old.

"Could you point to me the way to the capital?"

"*You're* going to the capital?" his brows go up as his eyes rove over my dirty clothes, his lip twitching in disgust. It's soon masked though as he gives me a pleasant smile.

"We're going in that direction. I can take you with me. There is one spare spot in the carriage."

As I move closer, I see there are two other male inside.

The thought of being in such close quarters with three strange males is not a comfortable one, so I simply ask.

"Could you tell me how long it will take me on foot?"

"On foot," one of them exclaims in dismay. "One or two days, I reckon. No one should make that distance on foot."

"But..."

"It's only a few hours with the carriage if you will join us," the male from the beginning interjects.

"I don't know..." I bite my lip in apprehension.

But as I think of Amon and his suffering, I know that I must put my sensibilities aside and approach this from a practical angle. I need to get to him as fast as possible.

My mind made up, I look up at him and I give him a determined nod.

"Wonderful! Hop in, miss," he says as he opens the door wider for me to step inside.

I do my best to not touch any of the occupants as I plop myself on the empty seat.

The carriage starts moving again and I take a moment to observe the males. They are dressed in quality garb, and the carriage itself looks to be constructed with expensive materials.

"So what is your business in the capital?" the first male asks me.

I force a smile.

"I'm supposed to meet with my husband," I lie.

He frowns, his eyes once again on my tattered dress.

"Looking like that?" another man bursts out, but it's clear he's voicing out what everyone else is thinking.

"I had a little accident on the way," I release a small laugh.

"Well, I hope you're fine now."

"Of course," I reply, happy when they stop questioning me and go about their own discussions.

The first hour passes quite uneventfully, and when I inquire how much longer, I'm told we're around halfway there.

Yet as night falls and the carriage veers off the road, my suspicions start to mount.

So much so that I'm already with my guard up when I feel a sharp metal against my neck.

The blade glints in the moonlight, its sheen confirming it is a rhodium one.

"Take off your dress, girl, and I won't have to hurt you," one of them says, and the others laugh, shuffling around to remove their own clothes.

"You commented on my torn dress and now you want it?" I ask ironically.

"You know what I mean," he barks.

"No, I don't think I know," I say as I move closer, letting the blade dig into my neck.

"Foolish wench. You're going to fucking die," he rebukes me, though he doesn't take the knife away from my throat.

"Isn't that what your plan is?" I inquire languidly as I build a shield around myself. "After all, I doubt you'd let me live after you had your way with me."

"But you have to be alive first," he laughs, and the others join in.

"I'd rather take my chances with death," I mumble under my breath.

Lifting one finger up I turn to them, letting the blade swipe over my skin some more, drawing blood.

"What do you think you're doing?"

"This?" I ask innocently as I bring my finger to the blade, electricity pouring into the metal which conducts it straight to the man's body.

His cries of pain echo in the carriage before he slumps against his seat, his body charred.

The smell of burned flesh permeates the air, and the other two seem to realize that they will not be having any fun times. Scrambling to exit the carriage, one of them trips and falls to the ground while the other runs straight into the woods.

I take my time to get out, pushing the smelly corpse onto the ground before creating two lassos with my hands, using both to bring the runaways back.

"It's not very nice of you to accost a lady," I tsk at them. "You really should be thankful my husband isn't anywhere near, or he wouldn't have been twice as merciful," I smile.

They blabber some more, but I'm not inclined to hear silly excuses when their intentions were clear.

"Why couldn't you prove my mother wrong that the world *isn't* a dangerous place?" I sigh as I imbue the lassos with electricity.

The driver of the carriage looks in shock as he places his hands up, dropping to his knees and begging me to spare him.

"I still need to get to the capital. You can take me there."

My voice doesn't leave room for discussion and he nods fervently, thanking me for saving his life.

Before I get in the carriage again, though, I take out the luggage the men had brought with them. Using my palm as a source of light (it seems I'm finding more and more uses for my abilities), I sift through the clothes in hopes I can find something I can use.

Clearly, with my current appearance I'm only going to attract the wrong kind of attention, which is the last thing I need.

The only thing that seems to be remotely useful is a pair of loose pants, a shirt and a jacket. Sighing, I decide it's better than nothing. Luckily, I also find a pouch full of coins, which should serve me well—especially since I need to get some food and water.

I might be indestructible—at least to a certain degree—but I still need sustenance.

Taking the clothes with me inside the carriage, I instruct the driver to get going while I change. And for the next hour and a half, I make myself comfortable as I wait to get to the capital.

"Here we are, miss," the driver tells me as the carriage comes to a halt.

"You were their hired driver, were you not?"

He nods.

"Then you're welcome to keep the carriage. I'll be off," I incline my head before turning to look at the capital.

Amon had made it sound like it's the center of decadence. But from where I'm standing it looks a little...decrepit.

There are street lamps in the distance, and I make my way towards them.

I walk for a few minutes in absolute silence before the atmosphere begins to be more buoyant. Shops appear on each side of the road, merchants still selling their items at this late hour of the night.

People are bustling up and down the street, some peddling their trade, others shipping from stall to stall.

I'm guessing this is a more mercantile area—still not in the center of the capital.

Walking around, I note the people around, some humanoid, some not.

In fact, with how busy the street is, I can't believe I'm not in the least afraid of walking around since I've never been among so many people on my own.

Yet after the previous events, I find that there's little to be scared of when I can take care of myself. After all, people might look frightening, but when it comes to a direct confrontation, I am the *more* frightening one.

That isn't to say I can go around flaunting my powers. Considering how distinctive they are, it's the one thing I need to refrain from doing if I don't want to draw attention to myself.

Walking deeper into the city, I come to a halt when I can make out the shape of the Emperor's palace in the distance.

Though the darkness of the night affects the visibility, the palace's windows blare with light, illuminating the sheer size of it and making me blink in surprise at the opulence I'm seeing.

Soon.

First, I need to gather some information. If they captured the great Shadow General, rumors are bound to swirl around—if only to emphasize the status of the new Emperor. I just need to find the right hub and listen.

Feeling the weight of the coins in my pocket, I swallow hard as my stomach rumbles with hunger. Maybe I can do that while eating too.

As I throw my gaze around, I spot a place that's overflowing with clients.

Straightening my spine, I confidently walk inside and seat myself at a table as I see others doing.

"What can I bring ya?" A girl wearing a colorful apron asks.

"Uhm," I bite my lip as I look around. "What do you recommend?"

"We have the specialty pie that's the most popular. That and the ale," she chuckles as she nods to some patrons chugging ale from an enormous mug.

"I'll have that then. Thank you."

"I'll be right back," she winks at me.

Fidgeting with my hands as I look right and left, I surreptitiously push my table forward so I can hear what the people at the other tables are talking.

"Here you go. One pie and an ale," the girl lays them on the table.

"How much is it?"

"One runa," she smiles.

I might add the fact that I'm not familiar with physical money as another thing that I'm not proficient in.

Looking through my pouch, I take out one of the smaller coins, thinking this could be it.

The girl's eyes widen.

"That's a vessa. No, no," she shakes her head as she leans in to look at my pouch. Fishing one bigger coin, she shows me the side of it which has a woman wearing a headpiece—the goddess of the household. Next to it, the letters R U N A are carved at the bottom.

"Ah, thank you," I tell her honestly, and because she was so helpful and without ill intention, I take out another runa and I hand it to her.

"I can't take that..."

"Please," I push the coin towards her. "Thank you for everything."

"If you're sure," she teeters on her feet before eventually taking the coin and leaving.

I hadn't exactly looked at the money when I'd found it, but now I find myself curious to see what the rest of the coins look like.

The vessa has an engraving of Vessar, the god of war. There are mostly vessas in the pouch, with a few runas and another one called treva for Trevio, the god of metals.

Since Vessar is the head of the pantheon, I assume the vessa has the highest value.

Putting my money aside, I take a fork and I dive into the hot pie. The smell is already intoxicating and as I take the first mouthful, I can't help but be surprised at how good it is.

I force myself to eat slowly, washing it with sips of ale. Yet the mere fact that I'm eating alone, without Amon, takes away from my enjoyment of the meal.

How can I eat with such gusto when I don't even know if he's been fed? If he was afforded even one sip of water?

Though I finish my meal, it's hard to hold the tears at bay. It's only when I hear some murmurs, followed by the words Shadow General, that I shake myself, my ears perking up as I strain to hear better.

"They're lying. The Shadow General wouldn't be captured so easily."

"Everyone I spoke to heard the same, and a few said they witnessed it, too."

"They did?"

"There was a procession at dawn on the main road when they took him to the palace. They had him all chained up. Everyone swears it was him. How many people do you know with his signature white hair?"

"But... The General's never been defeated in battle. How could anyone..."

"Who knows what tricks they used to catch him. I'm telling you, this is all that new Emperor's plan. He knows we don't like him."

"But this will make people not like him even more," someone protests.

"Yes, but it will also make people fear him. Everyone knows how strong the General is. For him to be defeated..." he trails off, the implication clear.

So Amon is indeed in the palace.

"I heard they plan to execute him regardless of whether he confesses or not."

"Of course they will. Even if he doesn't confess, it will send a message to anyone who thinks to stand up to the Emperor."

As the discussion turns more political, I realize that my window is much smaller than I believed.

If they plan to execute him anyway, then it could happen at any point.

My heart speeds up as fear overtakes me.

Somehow, I need to act.

Getting up from my table, I move to the back as I spot the nice girl who'd served me.

"I'm new around here and I had a question," I tell her as I catch up with her for a moment.

"Yes? What can I help with?"

"Do you happen to know how one could get into the palace? I've always wanted to visit..."

Her frown cuts my words as I hurry to ask what's wrong.

"No one visits the palace. It's forbidden. You need a special invitation to even be allowed through the gates."

"And who would have one of those invitations?"

"Only soldiers and officials. Sometimes the aristocracy. But I wouldn't recommend it. There have been people who've tried and they've been killed for it."

"I see... Thank you for the advice."

"Have a good night," she offers as I wave her goodbye.

Mulling over her words, I decide that the best course of action is to head to the gates and observe who gets in and who gets out.

Ideally, I don't want to use my powers and draw attention to myself in case they have another army ready to send after me. I might be strong, but I don't know *how* strong I am. Certainly, I doubt I could take on an entire army as Amon had.

Though it is night, the road is becoming increasingly more illuminated as I head towards the area where the palace is located. And though I am a little spooked by the sheer fact that I am walking by myself, alone, at night, I am more comfortable than I ever thought I would be on my own—in the outside world.

Yet with everything happening, I've barely had time to think about the implications—the fact that I interacted with strangers, or that I went to an establishment and ordered food for myself. They are all milestones for me and I suppose when I will have time later to mull over everything that happened, I will be able to analyze everything more thoroughly.

Right now, the most important thing is to get to Amon—no matter what.

It takes me more than an hour to get to the palace gates, and this was only following a straight road. The capital is a big place, indeed.

As I come across the big gates, I spot two big torches lit on either side, accompanied by two surveillance towers. In fact, everywhere I look, there are soldiers.

The sound of hooves resounds in the air, and I hurry to the side, hiding in a bush as I watch a carriage draw up to the gates. The driver shows a permit to one of the guards after which the gates slowly open up for him to come inside.

Without even thinking, I act.

Summoning the same lasso I'd used before, I pray what I have in mind will work.

Feeling the energy materialized, I throw it at the back of the carriage, willing it to hook on a lower railing but without sending any electricity through the lasso. Instead, I use it as it's been intended, as a rope.

Considering this is *my* energy, I should be able to manipulate it at will.

I force myself to focus as I pull on the lasso, imagining it shrinking in size as it pulls me forward at an insane speed.

I almost yelp out loud as I find myself flying in the air, the other end pulling me towards the carriage as the rope continues to shrink.

My eyes widen when I realize I'm going to collide with the back of the carriage, so I use my other hand to create another lasso, this time to stabilize me when I get to the carriage.

Releasing a worried sigh, I find myself right between the carriage wheels as I secure myself to the metal railings. And it seems the entire process is finished right on time as no one noticed and the carriage speeds past the gate and towards the palace courtyard.

Noting a slope to the side, I grit my teeth as I release my hold on the carriage, falling to the ground and rolling down the slope. I stay there for a moment as I try to assess what's happening around me and what the position of the guards is.

Well, getting into the palace certainly wasn't as hard as I thought it would be.

Eventually, I get up, surreptitiously making my way around the courtyard and towards an open door that leads to the palace.

As soon as I get inside, though, I note that it's the kitchen—a grandiose kitchen by the sight of it, with tens of tens of staff members.

"You," someone points at me. "You're the new girl, aren't you?" she wrinkled her nose at me.

"Y-yes," I force a smile.

"Stop dallying and go change. You can't go around in those awful clothes," she says in disgust.

Luckily she shows me where the staff uniforms are and I quickly change into one. Maybe this will afford me more anonymity as I make my way around the palace.

Going back to the kitchen, I pretend to work for a while as I try to find someone who can give me an idea about the palace's layout.

On one side, some girls are rolling dough, so I join, too, since that's not too hard—especially for someone like me with no experience to speak of.

"I heard the Shadow General is being held here," I start, thinking a bit of gossip won't hurt anyone.

They frown as they look at me, giving each other an odd look and ignoring me.

"Wouldn't you want to see the Shadow General?" I attempt again, but it's to no avail.

"There's a no speaking policy, new girl," the same woman from before comes from behind, looming over me.

"Oh, sorry. I didn't realize," I give her a look of regret. "I was just curious about the General since he's such a famous figure."

"We don't see, we don't hear. And we certainly don't talk," she tells me none too nicely. "Come, I have another task for you."

"Wha..."

I don't get to protest before she pulls me aside, putting a tray full of food into my hands.

"The feast is short staffed. You go into the hall, you don't talk. You don't make eye contact. You keep yourself in the background, understood?"

"Uhm, yes..."

"Good, now go," she gives me a light push.

I don't even know where to go, but as I see an army of other servers head to the hallway, I quickly get in line to follow thinking I could sneak off at some point.

The line becomes so ordered, almost as if it was an army drill. And as they enter a big illuminated ballroom, I find that I cannot move out of formation without drawing too much attention.

Swallowing hard at the discomfort that prickles my skin, I watch what everyone else is doing and proceed to do the same, moving silently around and laying the food from my plate on the table.

Curiosity gnaws at me, though, and from the corner of my eyes, I try to see what's happening at the table.

The entire scene is what I would have imagined a feast for kings to be. And it's quite fitting considering at the top of the table is the Emperor—at least going by the incredibly garish crown he has seated on his head.

But that's not the only alarming thing I see.

As I scan the rows of people, my eyes come to a stop on my mother.

She's not too far from the Emperor, seated between two males around Amon's age. They are both wearing formal army clothing. Going by the intimate body language between the two, I have to wonder what their relationship is.

My mother brings a goblet of wine to her lips as she chuckles at something one of the males says before her gaze meets mine.

Her eyes flare with shock when she recognizes me.

But I'm even more surprised since this was the last thing I needed.

Luckily, the army of servants is returning to the kitchens, so I take my spot in the line. When it comes to entering the kitchen area again, I remove myself from the line.

My pulse is racing.

She shouldn't have seen me. Not yet.

Fear pools in my stomach that she's going to sound the alarm and I will lose any chance I have to save Amon.

My breathing intensifies as panic continues to grow within my breast. But I cannot let it stop me. I came here with one purpose only, and I'm going to get Amon back—whatever it takes.

If I have to confront my mother while doing it, then so be it.

I may have been reluctant in the past, but after the tricks she pulled with Amon, risking me like that, I'm clear where her priorities lay.

More than anything, I'm certain she's never cared about me for more than the value I can bring her. The future she'd been telling me about from the beginning had been one where she groomed me to her liking, a mere puppet who didn't asked questions and just followed her lead.

Unfortunately for her, I stumbled across Amon, who opened my eyes to a life outside the walls of my house.

Turning to head to the other side of the palace, I take another hallway so I can lose my trace.

Yet just as I step onto the new corridor, I still in my tracks as I hear my name called out.

"Sela!"

My mother's voice echoes down the hall, and I clench my fists in fear that she will alert more people.

"Good to see you, too, mother," I mumble drily.

"I should have known that jail wouldn't hold you," she observes as she comes closer, a hint of respect in her tone.

"Then why did you put me in one?"

"I hoped it would delay you. The execution is at dawn."

I gulp down the wave of uneasiness as I fully turn to face her.

"Well, here I am. And I'm not leaving without him."

"You would risk everything for him?" She raises a brow at me.

I nod.

"That and more."

"He's played with your mind, Sela. Why can't you see that? How long have you known him? A few weeks at most."

"So? In a few weeks with him I found more about the world than in all my previous eighteen years. Of course you wouldn't understand. All you've ever wanted was to keep me ignorant. You think I don't know about the books? About every lie you told me?" I grit out. "I was so brainwashed, I even justified those experiments you did on me when I was a child. Why? Because I thought it was your manner of looking out for me. But when have you? When?"

"You don't understand," she shakes her head. "All this. Everything I've been doing from the beginning has been for the future—for the good of the Empire and everything that will follow."

"Really? And how's that? By killing the Emperor and framing an *innocent* man for it? By executing him in front of the entire capital?"

"Innocent?" she sputters. "Amon d'Artan is the furthest thing from an innocent man, Sela. You think you know him?" she laughs. "Shadow General is an apt term for he's been the shadow of this Empire for too long, Sela. He's killed and slaughtered *nations, towns and villages.* How is that innocent? You saw what he did to the army," she spits out, and I can see that there's some personal bad blood there. "He destroyed Milena, and you're telling me he's an innocent man?"

"He did what he had to do?" I raise my chin confidently.

"You didn't see him at the time. So mighty on his horse and covered from head to toe in Milean blood. I saw him, and I'll never forget the sight. Amon d'Artan is a scourge for this Empire. Let's not forget about the fact that he's been hiding his Reva heritage all this time. Do you know what the punishment is for hiding non-humanoid ancestry within the army ranks?"

"Non-humanoid...?"

"Ah, I see you don't know everything. The Reva were the monsters of nightmares. Their abilities were as terrifying as their appearances. When they were wiped out, everyone rejoiced. And tomorrow, everyone who's ever looked up to the famed General will find out just what type of monster he is."

"You're vile," I tell her, disgust rolling in my stomach as I look at her.

We're so close together in resemblance yet miles apart in our personalities.

"Maybe I am," she shrugs. "But you will not succeed today. I'm sorry, Sela. But one day maybe you will see reason."

Just as she finishes talking, she starts chanting something in a muffled voice. Like before, her hands start glowing.

My eyes widen at the sight, and I immediately channel my energy forward, sending a blast her way and stopping her from mouthing her words.

Remembering Amon's lessons about sorcery, I realize it hadn't been Aristol who'd cloaked the soldiers. It had been her.

She is the one dabbling in sorcery.

The blast sends her to the ground. Her breath comes in short spurts as she tries to put herself together and start chanting again.

Her eyes narrow at me, and before I know it, the earth opens up, tree-like branches extending from below and coming towards me.

"What are you doing?" I breathe out.

"You're not the only one with abilities in this family," she smirks as she straightens herself, her hands moving in time with the branches.

"That's sorcery," I accuse.

"Maybe," she shrugs. "But it only gives me an edge. Hasn't your lover told you already? To do sorcery, you need a big source of energy to draw from," she brags before she sends the branches towards me.

Summoning my lassos, I hurl them to the ceiling, coiling one around a chandelier and pulling myself up while using the other one to reach for the branches, sending zaps of energy deep in the ground so I can sever the roots.

Pushing myself more than usual, I focus as much energy as I can towards the hole in the ground.

"Don't tell me this is your plan when you know you can't hurt me?"

"I can't?" she smiles. "You think you know yourself, Sela, but I know *everything* about you. Including your future."

"Future? What do you mean?" I frown.

She shrugs, and at the same time another blast catches me by surprise from the back, sending me reeling to the ground. I slide on the floor before I'm knocked against a wall, the power of the blow so strong, I know I've broken something—or more.

I breathe through my nose against the pain as I feel my ribs perforate my skin and poking to the surface. Lifting my shirt I see the bones sticking out, blood pouring out from the wounds.

Gritting my teeth, I push them back into my body, my skin melding afterwards.

"Is that all you have?" I provoke her as I spit blood onto the ground. "You know that if you hurt me I'm just going to heal. All over again."

Before I can blink, my mother is in front of me, her lips twitching in distaste.

"I could kill you easily if I wanted to," she tells me matter-of-factly. "You're not as invincible as you think you are, Sela."

"Thank you for letting me know. Unfortunately, I can't let you do that. By the way, thank you for telling me that your sorcery is energy-based. You see, you're not the only one with new tricks up her sleeve," I smile at her as I put my hand on her shoulder.

As I'd done with the blasts before, this time I focus on absorbing the energy *from* her.

Her eyes widen as she tries to shove my hand away, especially as a pained cry erupts from her mouth.

"Stop," she whispers, pushing against me.

I'm staunch in my position.

She claws at me, scratching me with her nails and hitting me with her mini blasts whose size decreases the more I hold my hand on her flesh.

"I'm sorry, mother. I truly am."

She starts trembling as she falls to her knees, her breathing harsh, her skin turning a pale shade. She gasps for air but it's becoming harder and harder to breathe.

"You...will...regret...this," she grits out.

Before I know it, her arm reaches out and she buries her hand in my stomach just like she'd done with my heart on the battlefield.

My mouth opens in shock, my eyes widening as I feel her fingers moving under my skin, almost as if they were signing something over my organs.

"You...might...kill me...today," she coughs. "But...I...will...kill... your...future," she says, just before she removes her hand, blood dripping down her arm as she holds something clenched between her fingers.

"What..." I jump back, an aching emptiness overtaking me.

"No children...no prophecy...no future..." she continues, giving me a crooked smile as she says two barely audible words and the organ in her hand catches fire.

That's when I realize something. Whatever she took from me...it's not healing.

It's not...

"I win," she laughs.

"No, you don't," I shake my head as I send the most powerful blast of electricity her way, watching as her entire body burns and turns to ashes.

Just like what she stole from me...

I barely register the noise of feet thumping and heading in my direction.

Still dazed, I quickly move out of the way, finding a different path so I won't be discovered. Yet I can't stop thinking about what she meant and what she took from me.

Opening a random door, I get inside and lock it behind me. I can't make out anything in the darkness, but it seems to be unoccupied so I take some time to gather myself.

No children...

My hand goes to my lower belly where the emptiness still persists. Did she... Did she take part of my womb?

The implications are too much for me to ponder right now. Not when I still have to get to Amon and not when, if that is true, it will wreck me for my entire life.

More noise erupts from outside, and I keep myself still as soldiers run around the corridors in search for whoever had done the damage to the hall. Luckily, my mother's remains had melted away and they won't ring the alarm about her murder yet. I doubt that wouldn't be an important issue seeing how close she was to the Emperor.

My pulse continues to race as I barely come to terms with the fact that I killed my own mother—with my own hands...

A few breathing exercises and I have myself under enough control to move forward. I'll have plenty of time to dwell on my actions later—when Amon is safe.

Opening the door, I glance around, quickly closing it when I see two soldiers walking down the hallway.

"It's a kitchen girl, so she'll be wearing the uniform. But be careful. If what happened in the hall is any indication, she's not someone to underestimate."

The voice of one of the males registers, as well as the fact that they think I was the suspicious one. That means that I won't be able to move around freely dressed liked this.

Pursing my lips, I open the door, choosing a narrow pathway as I listen for any other loud noises. If previously I've hidden from the soldiers, now I need to find some who can lead me to where Amon is being held.

I wander around for a few moments before I see my chance, using my lasso to drag one of the soldiers to me.

The entire ordeal lasts surprisingly little time as he tells me what I need to know immediately. But as my eyes rove over his uniform, I realize that I might need something else from him.

Careful not to burn his clothes when I turn him to a crisp, I shrug the uniform on, putting on his helmet and hoping I won't be recognized this way.

I may not fill the uniform as well as a male, but in the darkened hallways I shouldn't be spotted.

According to the soldier, Amon is being held in the dungeon, which can only be accessed from the army garrison in the west wing, so that's where I am headed.

All the while, I can't help but keep Amon in my thoughts and hope I won't find him near death. With how my mother had been speaking about him, I don't doubt that everyone who carried him any grudge or hated him simply for his position, might have tried to make him suffer.

The fact that the execution had been scheduled for *tomorrow* at dawn tells me just how afraid they are that they won't be able to contain him, or his supporters.

I reach the army garrison, and I'm lucky to see that it's mostly empty. Everyone is so busy doing their own thing that they don't notice me going down to where the prisoners are being held.

There is a tunnel that leads down a narrow path before I note some light coming from torches on the walls.

As I slowly walk inside, I see rows and rows of cells, each of them full.

Taking one of the torches, I swipe the light at every cell in my search for him. But the sights I see are absolutely horrifying. There is not one person that is still whole. Some have had limbs amputated and left to rot, barely clinging to life. But others have already perished, some freshly dead, others well on their way to putrefaction.

I bring my sleeve to my nose and mouth as I try to ignore the smell of death and waste that lingers in the atmosphere.

Yet there is one commonality I see in most prisoners. The majority are non-humanoid.

The Empire really has a vendetta against those that do not fit into its designated mold.

I walk for minutes on end and the cells seem to be endless. There's so much pain and death here that my heart cannot help but be moved by the sadness that permeates the air.

The more I walk, though, the more confused I get when I cannot find Amon anywhere.

Where is he?

I'm getting increasingly afraid that something might have happened to him as I can't spot him in any cell.

But it's only when I get to the end of the tunnel that I realize why he was *not* in a cell.

As the row of cages ends, there is a wide area at the end that holds a myriad of torture devices. All the instruments are dirty and bloody, with a few people wasting away while strapped to them.

And one of them is...my Amon.

His white hair is the first thing I see, and knowing it must be him, I rush forward, holding the torch closer so I can ascertain his state.

"Amon?" I whisper.

He groans in pain, slowly lifting his head towards me. And that's when I realize what his torture had been.

I gasp, my hand flying to my mouth in shock as I take in his condition, tears streaming down my cheeks at the pain he must have suffered.

Both his eyes have been removed, the eye sockets empty as blood pours down his face.

But that's not the worst.

His entire chest cavity had been opened, his ribs cut to expose his inner organs, and his guts had been pulled out, currently hanging on the ground.

"Sela..." his voice is barely audible as he moves his face, using his other senses where his sight cannot help him. "Is this an illusion," he whispers brokenly. "Is this how you're going to torture me next, Elora?" he grits out, and it dawns on me that he's addressing my mother.

Gods, but was it her who doled out this torture? If that is so, then I cannot find it in me to regret ending her life. Not when...

I bite back a sob as I force myself to be strong for him.

"It's me. It's really me, Amon. I've come for you and I'm getting you out of here."

He takes a moment to reply, probably still trying to ascertain if I'm telling the truth.

"Sela? Sela mina? Why are you here?" he eventually answers. "Go. You need to go and save yourself. I..." he trails off, choking on the anguish that's seemingly holding him in a tight grip.

"No. Never. I'm here for you and I'm not leaving without you."

"Look at me," he states harshly. "I'm... halfway to the grave."

"No, I refuse to believe that," I tell him staunchly. Anything but that.

I will not let him die, no matter the cost.

Going closer to his side, I study the mechanism of the chains that hold him together. They are made of pure rhodium and even while restraining him, they keep hurting him by rubbing against his skin with no hope for relief.

Pushing down the hurt I feel at seeing him like this, I look around for the keys to unlock his chains. Luckily, they aren't too hard to find. It's harder to get him down considering the damage to his organs.

"You need to leave me here, Sela," he groans in pain as I help him onto the floor.

How he is not dead with all this damage is beyond me, but I can only be thankful to whatever force kept him alive.

I stifle my tears as I focus on him.

"Not leaving you," I tell him, softly brushing his hair as I lay a kiss on his skin.

"Sela... Please don't endanger yourself for me," he rasps.

I ignore his continuous pleas for me to leave, and I focus instead on his open rib cage. Trying to fight against the wave of nausea that comes over me, I pick his intestines off the floor and place them back in his rib cage, arranging them to the best of my ability without causing him more distress.

"I'm going to save you, Amon. I'll do it even if it's the *last* thing I do," I murmur lovingly.

Maybe this isn't the time for more experimentation with my abilities, but the situation makes for exceptions.

Focusing my energy to the tips of my palms, I feel them tingle and heat up with vibrations. If it had worked to absorb energy, then it should work to give it, too. And maybe, if I concentrate enough, I can channel that energy into healing.

My hands become two beacons of light as they charge up with energy. Bringing them to his head, I close my eyes as I will every little bit of strength I have left into him, picturing in my mind how his eyes are regenerating and how his ribcage is slowly closing, every open wound healing until he's perfectly fine again.

I feel the energy transferring from me to him, and suddenly, his entire body lights up.

My eyes flare open as I take in the blinding show before me.

As I'd intended, every little wound starts to mend. His eyes are completely regenerated, and his ribcage is closing, the ribs fusing together before the skin heals completely, leaving no scar behind.

When it's done, I feel slightly light-headed, but I quickly compose myself when I see him drag himself in a sitting position, his features full of disbelief.

"Sela, you..."

"It worked!" I don't give him time to say anything else as I jump on him, hugging him to my chest and peppering his face with kisses.

Tears of joy coat my lashes and I let them flow freely for he is fine—my Amon is fine.

"You're healed. Oh, Amon," I whimper as I hold him so tightly, I wish I could sear myself on him so we're never parted again.

"It worked," he repeats numbly. "Sela mina, Sela mina," he chants in a deep voice as he wraps his arms around me, giving me the gift that is his embrace.

We may not have time to waste, but this moment is too precious.

"I love you," I whisper fervently. "I love you, you silly beast. I still can't believe you'd sacrifice yourself for me like this."

"I would have done so much more for you, my love. Ah, my darling Sela but you have no idea how much I love you," he pauses as he catches his break, his powerful emotions flashing on his face."I didn't think you would ever come for me," he confesses. "I thought you saw my true form and I... I would have never dared believe you would risk everything to come here."

"And that's your first mistake," I chide as I draw back, giving him a pointed look. "I would always come for you Amon. We're in this together."

"I accept it as my fault," he nods thoughtfully. "I will not doubt you again," he says as he lays a kiss on my forehead. "Now we have to get out of here. I already hear soldiers coming towards us."

We both get to our feet as Amon regards his now healed chest with awe.

"You're incredible," he praises quietly as he feels his strength come back.

"Now, let me give a little parting gift to my friends coming for us," he says as he closes his eyes. The next time he opens them, they are fully black as a flicker of white swirls through them. Screams echo through the palace walls and I already know that Amon must have killed the first wave of soldiers coming after us. Yet it's not enough as he uses his abilities to open every cell in the prison.

"You are all free to go," he yells to them.

I look at him in awe, that he would still do something like this when our time is running short. But then Amon has never been the type to shy away from a confrontation if it gave him the desired result.

"You did good," I tell him as he pulls me in his arms.

In the blink of an eye, we are not in the palace anymore.

"Where are we?" I open my eyes to see we're somewhere in a cave. Yet it doesn't seem like a regular one.

"This is one of my outposts. No one knows about this one so we should be fine for a while."

I take a step further into the cave as Amon manifests a lit torch in his hand, going to the torches on the walls and lighting them too until the entire cave becomes illuminated.

"Wow," I whisper in awe as I take in what he'd done with the place.

There's a bed to the side, a chest of treasures and a hearth in the back. Yet that's not the only thing that gets my attention.

"Is that the sound of water?"

He smiles.

"There's a hot spring. Come," he takes my hand, showing me to a separate area. There's a pond in the middle, steam coming out of it.

"A hot spring?"

"It's why I chose this location. It was perfect to have some time to myself when I was in the area. And it's on the edge of the Empire so they shouldn't find us too fast."

"But you think they're going to find us?"

He gives me a pained nod.

"They have deep ties with dark sorcery. It's not only Aristol, but also your mother and the new Emperor. They are all practicing, and with the right spell, they can find us—*will* find us eventually.

"But..." I bite my lip. "Where does that leave us? We can't run forever, can we?"

He has a grim expression on his face.

"Let's get cleaned up first and I'll tell you the options I've thought of. How does that sound?" he murmurs lovingly.

I nod absentmindedly.

Amon has just survived the most painful day, and he is still covered in blood and grime. Of course he'd like to take a bath. And if I'm honest, even for me it sounds a little too attractive.

I start removing the heavy armor, shedding it to the ground until I'm left in a long button-up linen shirt. At the same time, Amon takes off his tattered clothes until he's completely naked.

My eyes widen just as my fingers still on the buttons.

It's my first time seeing him in such a state of undress and he is... absolutely glorious.

I blink as I take him in. He is one solid block of muscle. There is not one inch of fat on his body, his muscles hard and clearly defined as if they'd been carved in stone.

Yet there's one thing that claims my attention as I survey him from head to toe.

My gaze zeroes in on his hips, shamelessly dipping lower to the length that sways between his legs as he moves.

I suddenly bring my hands to my cheeks, feeling my skin heat up.

Is that... I think it must be...

It's the oddest thing I've ever seen, and though I have a vague idea about how the bedding business works, I'd never expected it to be quite so...big. And then there's some type of jewelry adorning the end, which makes me even more confused.

"Come, lass," he chuckles as he stops in front of me, his fingers deftly undoing the buttons of my shirt before letting it drop to the side.

"It's the first time we're completely naked with each other," I whisper, averting my gaze.

Though I'd been in my shift in front of him and he'd been shirtless before, this is a true first for us.

"Indeed," he drawls, his eyes dipping to my breasts, his gaze caressing my entire body as he studies me. A hum of appreciation escapes his lips. "And I like what I see. Do you?"

"Uhm...Yes," I whisper, my cheeks turning even redder. "I'm just a little confused about..."

"This?" he asks as he takes his member in hand, his thumb swiping over the head before settling on the ring.

I nod as I slowly bring my gaze down, curiosity getting the better of me. But now it's even stranger, for it seems to have doubled in size from before, appearing frighteningly large.

As I look up at him in alarm, I find him watching me with amused fascination.

"I told you the Reva mated for life," he murmurs as he pushes my hair out of my face to lay a kiss on my shoulder blades. "This ring is proof of that. Only one female is ever allowed to see it. The one I'll take as my mate."

"No one's ever seen it before?" I ask on a whisper.

"Only you."

That one statement makes me melt like nothing else, my inhibitions disappearing as he takes me into his big arms and carries me to the pond.

Slowly, he submerges the both of us in the water. It's so warm and comfortable that I can't help the sigh that escapes me.

"Oh, Amon. This is exactly what we needed."

"Relax, my beautiful Sela. I'll take care of you," he speaks against my ear as he proceeds to wash my hair, his movements slow and careful, as if he's enjoying the mere act of it.

After he's done washing my hair, I return the favor as I do the same with his own.

When we're clean, we simply sit in the warm water and relax.

"I was afraid I'd never see you again," he confesses, his words breaking my heart.

"Me too. How is it possible that after so little time you've become such an irrevocable part of me?"

"We belong to each other, Sela," he smiles. "And I promise you that I will protect you better from now on. Still, to know that you risked your life to save me... My brave mate. I'm immensely proud of you."

"Thank you. You were my driving force all along. For you..." I smile. "For you I can be strong."

"You don't need me for that, Sela. You're the strongest female I know, and not only by virtue of your abilities. But because of here," he says as he skims his fingers down my collarbone before setting his palm over my heart.

"I killed my mother," I confess as I relate what had happened with my mother, including the odd thing she'd done right before her death.

"What prophecy could she have been talking about?"

He purses his lips as his arm tightens over my waist.

"She visited me while I was being tortured. She was very angry that I *soiled* you because she had everything planned out for your future."

"What is it?" I draw back to look at him.

"She wanted to gift you to the Emperor."

My eyes flare with shock.

"Apparently, she was under the impression that there was a prophecy about your first born, that it will have so much power, it will conquer the entire Arkgor. She planned to use you as a bargaining chip to gain a position at court and power over the Emperor."

"But surely that can't be true," I gasp.

"I don't know the veracity of it. She believed it to be true. But she could have also made it all up to appeal to the Emperor and trick him into not only letting her live but also promoting her as court adviser."

"She did something to me, Amon. I'm not certain what, but she took something from me when she reached inside of me."

His features darken.

"We'll find out what. I promise you," he says as he takes my hands and brings them to his mouth for a kiss.

"But where does this leave us? We can't run forever, can we?"

"They executed most of my supporters in a position of power. There might still be a chance I could gather up a resistance. But I don't want to risk it."

"What do you have in mind?"

"We can either go to one of the kingdoms that's on bad terms with the Empire, although with my identity, they wouldn't receive us with open arms."

I nod. "Or?"

"We can leave Arkgor."

"What? Leave Arkgor? What are you talking about?" I frown.

"Not many people know this aside from the high officials in the Empire, but there are portals that lead to other worlds. They are very sparse and scattered across Arkgor, but I was sent on a scouting mission a century back. The portals do, indeed, lead to different worlds, but they are highly volatile. The former Emperor started a unit to document them and the worlds they lead to, but it was discontinued for lack of funding since the Emperor wanted to focus on domestic wars first."

"What are they like? Those worlds?"

"Some are very much like ours. The inhabitants look similar too. In some, they have abilities as we do, while in others they don't. There are also wastelands, where only foul creatures live."

"And you think we could go to one of these worlds and they would lose track of us?"

He nods.

"It's the best option I can think of. I know it's a lot to ask since we would be taking a chance on a totally unknown world. But..."

"Let's do it. My home is with you, Amon. As long as you are with me, I don't care where we are."

How could he even ask that of me? He is the one who has the most to lose. If we stay here and fight, he could achieve greatness and maybe even take on the leadership of the Vissirian Empire. But if we leave, he is forfeiting all his history, all his military accomplishments and his legendary status.

Most of all, he's letting everyone think he is, indeed, a traitor.

He gives me a brilliant smile.

"I'm the same. As long as we're together, nothing else matters. I don't care if they write me off as the villain in their history books," he says as he reads my mind. "I might be a traitor to them, but I'll be a husband to you."

"You have a way with words, Amon d'Artan," I wink at him playfully as my heart speeds at his proclamations. "I don't care about glory either, or prophecies, or power. I only want to be a wife to you," I tell him gently.

His hand reaches out to cup my cheek and I purr softly into him.

"We'll do it. We'll find one of these portals and leave Arkgor for good," I state determinately.

"But first," he says, a mischievous twinkle in his eyes. "Before we leave, I want to wed you properly with our Vissirian traditions and the Reva way."

"How are you going to do that?"

"Let me worry about that, alright?" he leans in to lay a kiss on my nose before taking me out of the hot springs and leading me to the living quarters.

Laying me on the bed, he rummages through his coffers for some cloth to wipe the moisture off my skin. He dries me first, before doing the same with himself.

When he's done, he dons on a simple white tunic.

"I'll be right back," he says just as he disappears from my sight.

I don't even see him get back as more and more items start to litter the empty cave.

It all starts with a beautifully wooden carved altar, a table and two stools, a mix of paints and candles and a set of wedding garments. Lastly, he places fresh food on the table as well as a wedding cake. When he's done, he's back for good.

"That was fast," I note.

He colors slightly.

"I may or may not have already bought the items before," he admits.

"So you've given this a lot of thought, haven't you?"

He nods.

"I bought them as soon as I met you," he smiles, satisfied with himself.

I shake my head at him, though his regard never fails to amaze me.

"Since you don't have a maid to help you, will you let me do it?"

"Of course. You probably know the traditions better than I do."

"I've been to a few weddings in my lifetime," he chuckles.

First is the dress, an exquisite white gown with gold thread interwoven in stunning patterns. He helps me into it, buttoning it at the back before seating me at the table.

He dresses himself in the matching two piece suit featuring a pair of white linen pants of the highest quality and a white top interwoven with the same gold designs.

"Each wedding set has different patterns embroidered into them. There are never two identical ones so that each couple may prosper independently of the world."

"I like that," I smile. "A marriage is only between two individuals, and it should be unique to them."

"Now for the next step," he declares.

He draws the other chair for himself as he picks up the paints he'd brought.

"What are those for?"

"Women are traditionally painted in the style of Yula, the goddess of marriage, while men are painted in the style of Yul, her consort."

He spreads red paint all over my face before adding some black to my eyes and white to my lips. He does a similar design to himself but the colors are inverted, his entire face black, his eyes white and his lips red.

"You look funny," I giggle. "But handsome. My handsome husband," I murmur as I send him an airy kiss.

"You look funny too," he chuckles as he taps my nose with a little bit of white paint. "Now a little more so."

Startled by his touch, I move back and his finger ends up dragging a white line all across my cheek. Not one to back down, I smear white paint on his nose too, continuing on his cheek in an identical pattern.

"Now we match," I say in an amused tone.

"A pattern of our own, isn't it?" He smiles as he picks up a small mirror, holding his arm back so we can both fit the frame.

"Perfect," I whisper.

We sit like that for a moment, simply watching our reflection and the way we fit together.

"One day, I'm going to commission a painting of us like this," he says quietly.

"Why commission it when you could do it yourself? You're quite the artist," I tell him.

He pauses for a moment.

"You think so? You think I could do it?" he asks in a soft voice laced by longing.

It's moments like these that I fall deeper for Amon. When, despite knowing the massive strength that lies inside of him, he shows me his vulnerabilities, trusting me to protect them as he does mine.

"I know you could. I would only ever trust *you* to paint my likeness."

He nods to himself, though there's a quiet determination that shines in his features.

When we're done with the preparation, it's finally time for the ceremony.

Taking a couple pillows off the bed, Amon positions them in front of the altar for us to kneel over them.

"Ready?" He takes my hand, helping me to sit down and fold the dress under my legs.

I give him a nod.

The altar depicts the union of Yula and Yul and the scene of their wedding when they'd said eternal vows to each other.

Amon takes his place by my side as he hands me a candle and keeps one for himself.

We twine our hands while holding the candle in the free hand.

"Goddess Yula, I present to you my chosen wife, Sela," Amon speaks first. "She is the female who's stolen my heart, my head and everything that I am. She is mine just as I am hers," he murmurs as he looks at me with such love, I feel the emotion overflowing in my own chest. "Please bless our union for an eternity to come. Please bless me with the ability to protect her at all times. For as long as she exists, I shall exist, too."

He places the candle on the altar.

My turn comes and I give him a shy smile.

"Goddess Yula, I present to you my chosen husband, Amon," I repeat after him. "He is the male who utterly and irrevocably stole my heart. He saved me from my lonely tower and showed me the joys of life and of love. More than anything, he taught me how to be strong. How to get stronger every day. And it's only because of him and *for* him," I whisper, the words meant for the goddess, yet my gaze is all meant for him.

"Please bless our union for an eternity to come. Please bless me with the ability to make him as happy as he makes me," I squeeze his hand. "Our lives will be forevermore intertwined. As long as he is, I shall be too."

I place my candle on the altar, too, and I follow his cue as we both rise.

Still holding hands, we make a bow before the altar before we turn and we bow towards each other.

"We're married," I breathe out in wonder.

Amon's eyes crinkle at the corners as he watches me with rapt fascination, his love so very evident in every little facial expression and every small gesture.

Taking a chair out for me, he sits me at the table before seating himself next to me.

We have a small wedding feast as we talk about anything and everything. It doesn't matter that this isn't a grand wedding, or that there are no guests. That we are together is all that's important.

"Were you scared of my Reva form?" he asks quietly as he cuts a piece of steak for me.

I shake my head.

"Why would I? It's part of you. A part that was willing to slaughter an entire army for me."

His lips tip up.

"It was my first time fully turning," he admits. "I'm still uncertain how it all came about, but it was also the first time I didn't hold back."

"How do you know so much about the Reva if they are nearly extinct?"

A melancholic smile pulls at his lips.

"I met one once. A few hundred years ago, I went on an expedition with the army. My entire regimen had been killed and I was lost in the woods. By chance, I stumbled across one of them and we engaged in a fight. When he saw my eyes shifting color, he realized I was part Reva, and he invited me to his home and he taught me a lot of the things I know about them," he remembers fondly. "Because I'm not full-blooded, my Reva form isn't permanent. But that male told me that once I activate it, it will become an impulse to do it again. More and more every time until I gain complete control over it," he relates, telling me what else the Reva he'd met had taught him.

"I tried to go back a few years later, but his home had been destroyed. Because of their monstrous forms, the Reva were never welcomed in society, so I assume some villagers had found out about him and tried to drive him out. Or worse," his face scrunches up in horror.

"That's horrible," I whisper.

"It's the way of this world," he shrugs. "It's why I'm not keen on pursuing this silly vendetta against the Empire. Even if I do get to the top, they will never accept me. Your mother was right in one respect.

They might venerate Amon, the military legend, but they will always shun Amon, the Reva."

"Maybe things will change."

"Will they?" he gives me a sad smile. "In the time I've been alive, if anything, people have only gotten more intolerant of those that do not look like them. There are so many factions in this Empire, just as there are so many peoples who hate each other to the bone. I must confess that I won't be sad to leave this world."

"Hearing your stories makes me very happy I grew up in isolation. I can't imagine living in constant fear that people would find out what I am and...hate me, too. I am fully aware that despite the fact that I look humanoid, my abilities would make people regard me with skepticism. Just like those experiments when I was younger, there will always be those who will want to get to the bottom of my ability, or who will want to replicate it."

Amon nods.

"I feel like I've only told you about the ugly parts of Arkgor," he chuckles. "There are the good parts too, the warm people, the traditions and the history, and of course, the absolutely breathtaking nature. It can be a haven for some. Just..."

"Not for us."

"We'll find our place, Sela. It might not be this world, or the next. But we will eventually find our happy place."

I reach across the table and squeeze his hand.

"Alright, enough morose talk. It's cake time," I say as I pull the beautiful cake he'd bought closer.

Amon uses his knife to cut it into a few pieces, placing one on my plate and one on his.

As soon as the flavor bursts on my tongue, my entire face erupts in a bright smile.

"This is wonderful, Amon. My favorite flavor, too!"

He shakes his head in amusement but continues to feed me. And to be a little cheeky, I feed him too, bringing mouthfuls of sweet cake to his lips.

We take our time eating, but when we're done, Amon is the first to get up, excitement sparkling in his eyes.

"Now that I've sweetened you up, it's time for the consummation, dear wife," he winks at me.

I giggle at his eagerness.

Rising from my chair, he wastes no time in snapping my buttons open before the dress pools at my feet and I'm completely naked before him.

He swoops me in his arms as he carries me to the bed, laying me down on the clean sheets. Leaning in, he grabs my nape as his mouth opens on top of mine, his kiss as potent as it is maddening. The paint on our faces smears and mixes together, creating brand new colors and patterns.

Drawing back, he takes his top off, throwing it to the ground before hooping his fingers through the band of his pants and removing those too.

My eyes widen when I realize that part of him is even bigger than before. Just how big is it going to grow?

As I drag myself backwards on the bed, Amon's knee presses into the mattress as he comes forward, his body blanketing mine as he captures my lips again.

"Don't be scared," he whispers against my lips when he feels me tense.

"It's not that. It's just..."

How do I tell him that I want him more than anything but I don't know what to expect? That I'm both curious and scared at the same time but it's all overpowered by this desire I have for him—to be one with him.

"You don't have to tell me anything. I know," he assures me. "And I'm just as scared."

"You?" I raise my brows at him.

"I don't want to mess this up, and I want to make it good for you, too," he confesses.

I lick my lips as I take in the intense expression on his face. His eyes are wholly black to complement the paint on his face. Gods, but I want nothing more than to please him, too. It seems hard to believe that this is his first time as well and he is as nervous as I am.

"Tell me what to do," I whisper.

"Just... touch me. Anywhere, everywhere. There's no wrong way to go about this, Sela. I'm yours."

"I'm yours, too," I smile as I cup his cheek, leaning in to lay a kiss on his lips.

My hands go down his body as I touch him, becoming familiar with every scar and indentation on his torso.

At the same time, Amon dips his head and brushes his lips over my pulse point, laying open-mouthed kisses all over my neck as he moves down my body.

His teeth tug at one nipple before he swirls his tongue around the bud.

"Do you like this?" he asks as he looks up, his eyes finding mine, curiosity, desire and love all mingling together in his gaze.

I nod fervently as I urge him to continue, slowly losing all my inhibitions as desire takes over. My worries disappear as I focus on pure sensation and the feel of him.

He gives the same consideration to my other breast before he continues his journey down my body. Cupping my ass, he places my legs over his shoulders as he nuzzles his face against that place between my legs that weeps for relief.

"You have no idea how long I've dreamed about this, Sela. Your scent," he pauses as he inhales deeply. "It's been haunting me, lass."

The first swipe of his tongue surprises me, my eyes flaring open in shock as pleasure courses through my veins.

"You like that, don't you?" he chuckles against me.

"Yes... More, please," I whimper as he kisses me there just as he kisses my mouth, seducing at first as he licks me thoroughly before resorting to full-on plundering as his tongue delves inside of me, lapping at me as if I were a delicious dessert.

"You are. You're so fucking sweet, Sela mina. So wet, so mine," he purrs, gently blowing air over my wetness and making me shiver.

"Amon...what..."

"Come for me, Sela. Give me your pleasure," he rasps before he wraps his lips around my bundle of nerves, making me thrash and moan. My fingers lodged in his thick locks as I urge him to continue.

I don't know what's happening to me, but there's a delicious tension building inside of me, my muscles tensing the more he pays attention to that particular spot.

Gods, but his mouth on me, down there... I'd never thought something so scandalous could feel so good.

"Amon," I moan. "I..." My spine arches, my toes curling into the mattress just as my words are cut off. A wave of pure pleasure crashes through me, followed by light pulsations as I feel myself creeping to the edge again.

"Give me more, love. I need you wet and ready for me," he says. "Let me please you, lass."

"It's... It's too much, Amon. I..."

"Let your male please you, Sela," he growls before resuming the same ministrations from before. Wave after wave, I lose count of how many times I jump over the edge just as I lose track of the time he's been spending between my legs.

"You're so fucking beautiful, Sela," he whispers, licking me languidly. "So fucking sweet."

"I need you, Amon. Please..." I whimper, opening my arms and beckoning him to come to me—fill this aching emptiness I feel inside.

He relents and climbs up my body, once more kissing every inch of my skin before kissing my mouth and making me taste myself on him.

"You're going to let me eat this sweet little cunt every day from now on, Sela," he speaks against my mouth. "Multiple times a day. Every time I want to eat, you open your legs for me. Alright, wife?" he rasps seductively.

My entire body is entirely too languid to argue with him so I just nod. I would agree with anything right now as long as he gave me more of himself.

"Good girl," he purrs.

Before I know what's happening, he has our positions reversed. He's sitting on the bed with me on top of him, that hard part of him brushing against my thigh.

"Touch me," he asks in a gruff voice, his eyes hooded yet still watching me with resolute alertness.

Giving him a shy smile, I cup his cheeks first, leaning in to give him a sweet kiss before I move lower, doing to him what he'd done to me.

I kiss every inch of his chest, swirling my tongue around his nipples and sucking each in my mouth. His reactions are so fascinating that I'm soon becoming addicted to touching him, curious how he will react next and how much pleasure I can give him.

Continuing my descent down his body, I bring my hands to his chest, raking my nails over his skin before soothing the light sting with my tongue.

"Such a good girl," he purrs, his chest vibrating with the sound. His deep rumble echoes in the cave as he praises my every little action.

My eyes on him, I make the courage to move lower and lower until I finally touch that hard part of him that is as fascinating as it is daunting.

Biting my lips, I wrap my fingers around his shaft, surprised to find it so soft and silky despite being so rigid.

"Ah, Sela mina," he throws his head back. "Fuck. I've been imagining your hands on my cock for so long. But nothing does the reality of it justice."

I massage him lightly, and he soon shows me how he likes to be stroked.

"This goes inside of me, doesn't it?" I ask as I swipe my finger over the tip, feeling for the ring attached to it. Theoretically, I understand how it's going to go, but seeing the size of him, I have to wonder if we're anatomically compatible.

He chuckles as he undoubtedly reads my thoughts.

"We're compatible, lass. But don't worry, we're not in a hurry. You're dictating the pace this time. I just want you to be comfortable."

"This time only?" I raise a brow at him as I squeeze his shaft.

"Don't torture me. Not when I'm hanging only by a thread," he says in a strangled tone.

Giving him a playful wink, I lean forward and I swipe my tongue over the bulbous head, his spicy taste hitting me immediately and making me clench my thighs in response. His ring protrudes from a slit at the top, the metal shining even in the darkness of the cave. Clear liquid seeps out, and I tentatively give it a lick. Leaning back, I smack my lips together, swirling my tongue in my mouth to experience the full taste of him.

It's... I must say, I never expected to enjoy it so much. It's a mix of salty and spicy but there's a flavor that is so thoroughly Amon, I can tell it's going to be my next addiction. Especially as I note the immediate effect on my own body, my channel dripping with arousal.

To show him just how much I love this, I bend again, this time capturing the entire head between my lips and sucking, using my tongue to lick him as I would a flavored ice stick.

Placing my hands on the shaft, I move them as he showed me, worshiping his body as he'd worshiped mine.

"Sela," he breathes out my name as he threads his fingers through my hair. "Fuck, lass. You're killing me."

His words are confirmation enough that this act can bring him as much pleasure as it did when he performed it on me, so I continue my efforts, enthusiastically sucking and licking him as he guides me, showing me what he likes and what drives him most mad. His hand in my hair, he massages my scalp lightly as he keeps murmuring words of praise.

"You suck me so well, lass. Your mouth's pure bliss. All wet and hot and fuck..." he trails off as his eyes alternate between open and closed.

I smile as I nuzzle my face against his length, dripping spit all over and stroking him nice and wet.

Just seeing him so lost to pleasure, so out of control because he is under *my* control, and I know this will become a favorite pastime.

"Enough," he suddenly says. "I need to come inside of you, lass," he breathes harshly.

I don't protest as he lifts me up his body, taking my mouth in a savage kiss as he grabs his erection and positions it between my folds. He strokes me softly, the ring touching my sensitive nub and making me shiver from anticipation and the promise of his claiming.

"Slow. We need to go slow," he recites the words like a mantra as he slides the thick head to my entrance.

"Please," I whisper, my gaze connecting with his. My hands on his shoulders, I slowly push myself down, lowering myself on him.

It's...a tight fit to say the least.

My face scrunches in discomfort as I struggle to take more of him inside of me. He's just too big and I'm too...small.

"Can you..." I don't finish the sentence as he reads my mind.

Gripping my hips, he gradually works his length inside me until he's buried to the hilt. His features are tense, his breathing equally so as he holds me tightly to his chest. We both breathe in and out as we try to get used to this new sensation.

Every inch of him is inside of me, and a soft whimper escapes me as I feel him everywhere. He's so big and thick, throbbing against my walls, stretching me and leaving a delicious burn behind.

"Tell me I didn't hurt you," Amon pleads when he feels me tense.

"No," I shake my head. "It wasn't as bad as I thought it would be. In fact... I like it. I like it a lot," I admit as a blush climbs up my cheeks.

"I'm glad to hear that," he chuckles as he licks my lips before kissing me thoroughly. His hands trail up my body, settling on my breasts as he massages my nipples gently, each touch sparking delicious new sensations.

"You're inside me, Amon," I whisper in awe against his lips as I feel him swell even more in size. "We're finally one."

"We...are," he rasps, clenching his jaw as he tries to keep himself still. "Fuck, Sela. I swear to fucking Vessar I never thought anything could be like this... You're so warm and tight and so fucking mine," he groans as he touches his forehead to mine. "So fucking mine."

"Can I...move?"

He smiles in relief when I ask the question.

"A thousand times yes," he answers gruffly.

Raising myself slightly, I move up and down his length—tentatively at first before gaining more speed. His hands are on my ass as he guides me, but he's still respectful of my own pace. This sweet, sweet man is holding himself back just so I'm comfortable.

And that's what I love the most about my Amon. He is the deadliest man in the Empire—mayhap the entire of Arkgor—yet with me he is the gentlest soul.

Generous. Kind. *Soft.*

This infamous general that is reputed to have conquered kingdoms, who led the Vissirian Empire into its age of glory is *soft.*

But only for me.

"You're so beautiful, Sela. The most beautiful thing I've ever laid eyes on," he says on a loud groan. "The first time I saw you I couldn't believe my eyes. You were that stunning. And I was the luckiest male in the entire universe when I realized you were my mate. That you were meant to be mine and mine alone," he rasps, his breath caressing my cheek. "Only ever mine, Sela. This cunt that's gripping me so fucking tight will only ever be filled by my cock, will only ever take my seed and will only ever know my tongue."

"Yes," I whisper, lost in his gaze. His words arouse me to no end as I ride him, my channel squeezing him tightly.

"That's it, love. Fuck yourself on me and take everything you need. Show me how well you take your mate."

I soon get into a steady rhythm, my eyes firmly on his as we stare at each other in this intimate moment. There's always an urgency for more, but there's something utterly hypnotizing about this lovemaking and the way Amon regards me at this moment, his eyes hooded, his mouth slightly parted. His desire for me is written all over his face and I've never felt more powerful than now. Yet it's also clear he's restraining himself for my sake.

"What if I want *you* to fuck *me*?" I lean in to whisper after I've had my time to play.

A growl escapes him, and a couple of *are you sure* later, I find myself on my back as he starts pumping in and out of me, the power of his thrusts making me reel as I see the difference between my shallow motions and his savage strokes.

My back arches with each thrust, and I slide my hands down his back to his ass, feeling for his firm muscles as he pumps in and out of me.

"My beautiful mate. Ah, Sela," he says as he leans back to watch where our bodies are joined. "You take my cock so well, lass," he says as he withdraws all the way until only the tip with the ring is inside me. His thumb is on my bundle of nerves as he strokes me just as he delves forward in one smooth thrust before repeating the process all over again, overstimulating me to no end. "Your body was made for mine," he rasps. "Tell me how good this feels, lass. Tell me how good it feels to have your mate fuck you."

"Yes. Oh, Amon. It's so good," I moan. "You're so big inside me... filling me...making me yours..." I trail off, unable to speak coherently.

"That's it, Sela. Mine. You're so fucking mine, lass. Now and forever."

"Now and forever," I echo.

He licks my neck before kissing me deeply, the combination of his tongue thrusting into my mouth while he's moving inside me making me mindless with pleasure and passion until I become drunk on everything that he is.

Our face paintings have already been wiped off, either on our bodies or on the sheets. We're both a messy whole of tangled limbs and sweaty bodies. But we are one.

Now, at this moment, we are one.

The more he fucks me—the more he thrusts into me in that savage rhythm of his—the more my pleasure soars, my walls gripping him tight. The ring at the end of his cock brushes against a sensitive spot deep within me, making me whimper every time he surges forth.

"Fuck, Sela. I can't hold it in," he rasps as he raises his head. "Have to...bite you."

My eyes widen in confusion.

Bite?

Yet I don't get to voice my question as I feel his mouth open over my neck, his sharp teeth penetrating my flesh and drawing blood.

He sucks on my flesh greedily, and the prick of pain only serves to emphasize the pleasure more.

As he continues to drink from my open wound, I get the inexplicable desire to do the same. Almost as if I'm no longer in control of myself, I bring my hands to his neck, brushing his hair out of the way before laying sloppy kisses all over his skin.

The urge becomes stronger and stronger until my own teeth break through his skin and I taste the sweetness of his blood as it fills my mouth.

There's something utterly intoxicating about the way he tastes, and the more I drink it, the more I find myself getting drunk, my head swimming with an ineffable euphoria.

A tingling glow envelops both our bodies, the bond tying us together. And for a brief moment I can hear his thoughts too, his powerful emotions echoing into my mind and humbling me with the love and desire he feels for me.

Now, more so than ever before, we are one.

Irrevocably bound.

Never to be separated.

The pleasure, too, is intensified tenfold as I wrap my legs around his waist, angling my hips so he can thrust into me deeper, touch every part of me he can.

"My mate," he whispers as he licks at the closing wound. "You're my mate, Sela. Now and forever. "

"Yes," I agree. "Oh, Amon," I whimper as another climax claims me.

His hands go to my hips, holding me tight as he pistons in and out of me chasing his own pleasure. And just as my muscles tense again, his hot seed floods my insides.

He shouts my name with the power of his release. Collapsing on top of me, he rolls us until he's on his back and I'm lying on his chest, our bodies still untied even as he softens inside of me.

"It's done, Sela," he murmurs as he brings his lips to mine, teasing my mouth open with his tongue as we taste each other. "We're mated. Forever."

"Forever."

I sigh contentedly against him, sleep soon claiming me.

We would later realize that our mating hadn't only tied us together for an eternity, but my blood could heal Amon inside out, leaving no scar or mark behind.

Finally, I wouldn't have to worry about him again for my power was now his, too.

A FEW DAYS LATER,

We'd allowed ourselves to spend a mini holiday in bed before starting our new journey. With almost no possessions to our name, we'd simply set out for the first portal we could.

The portal is just a swirling mass of energy located at the edge of a cliff—a precarious location.

"Ready, love?" Amon asks as he squeezes my hand.

I nod.

"Let's do this. It's a fresh start, Amon. *Our* fresh start," I smile at him.

Taking me into his arms, Amon lays a kiss on my forehead as he takes the step inside the portal.

A blinding light surrounds us, but just like his teleportation, one second we're in Arkgor, the next we're in a completely different place.

"Let's find our new home," he states as he looks into the horizon full of possibilities.

Little did we know that our journey in this world would lead us closer than ever to disaster. Especially as my suspicions about my mother's spell turn out to be correct.

Elora *had* cursed me. She'd taken my future away.

Because as the years go by in this new world, as the *thousands* of years pass, we remain childless, and with the passage of time we slowly become...hopeless.

Chapter Twenty-Nine

Spring 536 A.D. Ravenna, Italy

I drop to the ground, the field of wildflowers cushioning my fall, the light scent of grass, moss, and nature filling my nostrils.

"That's absolutely stunning, love," Amon murmurs as he comes closer.

His sketchbook in hand, he lets his eyes roam over my form, my white gown in contrast with the deep purple of the flowers.

"You must join me after you're done," I giggle as I pat the spot next to me.

"Then I must hurry so I can be by your side," he winks playfully at me.

Wielding his pencil with expert precision, he starts sketching me in the field.

The sun is shining bright in the sky, a light breeze brushing my skin as I lay back and pose for him.

It's something I'll never tire of doing, even though our house overflows with all the artworks Amon has produced with me as the main subject.

Since moving to this world, he's taken his interest in art more seriously, always searching to learn and improve himself, just as I've done with medicine and healing plants.

From the beginning, we'd known we couldn't afford to stay in a place for a long time due to the fact that we don't grow old like the people in this world do. So we've taken to moving to a new place every couple decades or so, only returning to the same place after a few generations have passed.

It has been a way for us to escape suspicion with the locals, but also to avoid being tracked by the Empire.

We'd been wrong to think that we wouldn't be followed here or that the Empire will simply let us live our lives in peace.

As we'd found out, time flows differently in the two worlds. Whereas we've been here for a few thousands of years already, in Arkgor, barely a few decades have passed. Certainly not enough for people to forget about Amon.

If anything, his reputation has grown to such an extent that there are now cults worshiping him in the Empire, all because they believe he is still alive and will come back at some point to challenge the Emperor and take the mantle of leadership.

But the more people love Amon and his legacy, the harder it is for the current Emperor to keep his territories under control. Already a few have rebelled, with more fostering the same intention.

Given the state of the Empire, they *need* to show Amon is dead, publicly—as they'd attempted the first time—in order to squash any type of dissenting sentiment from the populace.

My mother had been the only one to know about Amon's Reva heritage and she'd never told anyone about it, most likely hoping for a stupefying surprise during the execution.

We'd only realized that when we first encountered Kress and Finn, Amon's former friends who'd betrayed him, and had been sent over to this world to track him. They had no idea about his heritage, otherwise they would have spread that rumor to squash some of the resistance.

In a way, that is unfortunate for us, since it means they will continually hunt for us and we might never know a moment of peace.

Yet against all odds, we've made a life for ourselves.

Sometimes we work to keep ourselves occupied, though we try to keep interactions with humans to a minimum.

We've messed up too many times by getting involved with humans to know that a close relationship can only result in disaster. Especially since in this world, there aren't many people who possess powers or special abilities. Most are normal. But they all *hunger* for power in a way that we hadn't encountered even in the Empire.

When we arrived in this world, there had been a few established kingdom states. At the time we'd settled in Egypt during the Old Kingdom, enjoying the culture and the freedom of movement.

In the beginning, it had been easy to be ourselves as we hadn't known what the rules of this world were. We continued as before, using our powers indiscriminately. When people noted our abilities, they thought us gods, which in turn made us the central figures of their cults.

It might have been amusing at the start. Particularly for Amon who developed a friendship with quite a few pharaohs and advised them on military issues.

But like all other endeavors, that came to a stop when Kress and Finn discovered us for the first time by tracking our power signatures with sorcery.

Since then, we've become more careful with using our abilities in any way that could draw attention to ourselves and invite Kress and Finn into our lives again.

That isn't to say that we haven't been happy. We have.

We've started to work like regular humans. Amon alternates between using his military knowledge to work as an advisor, and taking commissions for his art—although he only does male figures. He'd told me from the beginning that I would be the only female he'd ever draw, paint or sculpt—not that I'm complaining since I'm a little too possessive of him to share him even for the sake of art.

I usually keep to medicine and healing plants, though depending on the place, being female prevents me from openly practicing my craft.

This world has a great deal of plants that were not available in Arkgor, and I found it absolutely fascinating to travel the world and keep a record of those plants—thus creating my own botanical dictionary.

Yet there's always something missing. Something that's been the source of many contentious arguments between me and Amon.

I can't get pregnant.

We've been together, in this world, for more than two thousand years and I still cannot get pregnant.

We'd suspected my mother had done something to me in our last confrontation, but we'd only realized, years later, that I could not conceive at all. The fact that my monthly courses had stopped altogether should have been our first sign, but we'd continued to be hopeful until we couldn't ignore the truth any longer—I am barren.

Amon, the sweetheart that he is, continues to tell me that it's fine if we never have children. That it will be just the two of us, and for him that is sufficient.

But I know it's not.

I can see the longing in his eyes when we spot a family on a walk out, or when we witness a christening, as is the custom with this new religion everyone's embraced. I can see the desire to be a father in his gaze, and I know it echoes the one I have in my heart.

I've been alone my entire life before he came along, and after I met him, I dared to believe that we would eventually have a family and we'd be blessed with children. Maybe not as many as I would have wished, but at least one or two.

To know that we haven't and that we'll *never* have that causes me unspeakable pain.

More than anything, it hurts to realize that despite not being alone, sometimes I feel...lonely. And that is completely unfair to Amon since he gives me absolutely all of himself.

Yet I can't stop from feeling that—from being unfulfilled despite attempting to live life to the fullest.

Maybe in the first hundred years this issue wasn't as pervasive, as we were still in the effusive honeymoon stage. But slowly, the issue began to pain me so much until it started intervening in our relationship.

Amon tries his best to make me happy and fill the gap of not having a big family. And I love him for that—I *adore* him. And I don't have the heart to tell him that the gap will never be filled—that it's going to grow, increasingly, with each passing year.

And yet...he knows. Of course he knows. After all, sometimes he knows me better than I know myself. At first, he'd tried to make up for it with gifts and other attentions. The field of flowers I'm lying in is a testament of that.

One day, without telling me, he'd faced the dangers of returning to Arkgor to get the purple flower I'd loved so much, and he'd planted it all around Europe in an effort to make me happy.

But he hadn't stopped there.

He'd continued to search for ways to help me, even going as far as infiltrating a group of people with special abilities from the Byzantine Empire, attending their meetings and learning their secrets in an attempt to find a way to help me.

After all, sorcery had caused me to be barren, so sorcery should be the answer.

And as we'd come to realize, the sorcery in this world is compatible with the one in Arkgor. The answer is always in a person's energy. That is the basis of everything. The manifestation of sorcery is simply the intention one has when channeling their energy. Yet despite the simplicity of the concept, there's always a price to be paid, especially for more difficult spells. If you attempt something that's far beyond your capabilities, it could drain your energy and kill you.

With my energy levels, however, I believe that if I learn how to channel my energy to undo the spell, I would be able to do it.

And that is how we've come to be in Ravenna at this time.

Ambrosius, one of the people whom Amon had befriended, had

asked us to come to his residence as he'd promised to look into my problem.

We'd met him around twenty years ago in Rome at a meeting and we'd corresponded throughout the years. Recently, however, he'd announced that he may have a solution and he'd invited us to come over.

In fact, after our little session, we're going to meet with him.

"Done," Amon tells me as he plops down next to me, showing me his sketch.

"I love it," I whisper as I scoot closer to him. "You captured me perfectly. As you always do."

"You're in a good mood today," he raises a brow as he notes my smile.

"I have a good feeling about this, Amon. I don't know why, but I think Ambrosius might be our hope."

"He's the only one powerful enough to attempt it," Amon agrees. "I just... I don't want you to be too disappointed if this doesn't work. We're not going to give up. If I have to go back to Arkgor and find someone to undo the spell, I will do it."

"Ah, Amon, you're too precious," I whisper as I place my head on his chest.

His arms come to rest around my waist as he keeps me close to his body.

"I just hope Kress and Finn won't find us for a while. At least not until we do this."

"If they do, I'll find a way to kill them. Maybe Ambrosius can help me neutralize those damn shields of theirs."

"More and more people are practicing sorcery in Arkgor. Shouldn't that worry us?"

He grunts.

"Under the new Emperor, it's been made completely legal. When I was last there, I heard he planned on creating schools specifically for that."

"But why? Aren't there enough people with innate abilities already? Why support sorcery when you have a much better alternative? Especially since people are giving their lives in search of power."

"You know why," he purses his lips. "The majority of those who have innate abilities are from non-humanoid species. This is the only way the empire could foster more power without compromising their purist values."

"The new Emperor sounds utterly appalling," I grumble.

"They've already imposed new laws on some long-living species, coincidentally also non-humanoid, prohibiting them from having more than one child."

"What? That's preposterous."

He nods.

"He wants to ensure that with each generation, they become fewer and fewer. Either there will be a mass-exodus out of the Empire, or they will rebel."

"The Emperor will never risk them moving away, though. That would mean power in the hands of the enemy."

"Precisely. And I fear that will lead to a third option."

"Genocide," I whisper.

His expression is grim as he agrees.

"Either they are under the Empire's control or not at all. And with how intolerant people have become since all criminal acts are blamed on non-humanoid species, I can see them turning a blind eye if it's happening."

"I'm so happy we're not there anymore."

"If before the Empire could be considered a stratocracy, since the old Emperor was a military man himself and welcomed counsel, now it's become a draconian autocracy under the leadership of a madman."

"Do you wish we'd stayed behind and fought?" I ask tentatively.

We'd discussed this before since I can tell Amon is sympathetic to the cause of the non-humanoid species. Yet every time he'd assured me he was fine as he was with me.

But...

Sometimes I wonder if he's not doing everything for me while neglecting his *own* wants.

What about his purpose? His goals?

I'm always afraid he sacrificed himself for my sake—because he was afraid he'd put me in danger if we stayed behind.

Just like the gap in my heart due to our childlessness, I wonder if there is not one in his heart because he's letting everyone who's putting their hopes in him down.

"Never," he answers immediately, as he usually does. "I would never put you in danger just to fulfill some ego campaign."

"But you know I'm quite invincible," I joke.

"You might not die, Sela. But you can hurt. Even worse. You can hurt *forever*. To imagine you in pain *once* is already too much for my feeble mind. To think that someone could torture you forever?" he shakes his head.

"Wouldn't you wish you were there, though? Offering people direction and helping them escape from under that tyrant? You know they're waiting for you..." I trail off when I feel him stiffen.

It's not the first time he's been made slightly uncomfortable by the topic. Whenever we talk about non-humanoid species or his Reva heritage, I've always had the vague impression that he's been holding back on me. Yes, we might talk about it, but it's never in depth, and he usually brushes off his own struggles in favor of light-hearted banter. And that worries me. Since that time in Arkgor, I've never seen him assume his full Reva form again. He might use some of the complementary abilities at times, but he's never once tried to change again.

Why?

Odd how I've never given that too much thought before, content to accept what he gave me of himself without questioning it.

"When I married you, I told you that I would rather be a husband to you above everything else. Above glory, or power, or my reputation. I renounced everything the moment I made a vow to you, Sela mina. And that is the only vow that matters."

Stubborn male.

He's never going to admit such a thing to me, is he?

I scrunch my nose in annoyance as I nuzzle my face in the material of his tunic.

Well, I guess I will wear him down eventually. I don't want to be the only one to get my wish. Even if it takes us another thousand years, in Arkgor only a handful of years would have passed. He would still be able to act then if he so wishes.

Maybe at some point he will admit that he *does* want all those things.

And I, just like he's done for me from the beginning, will support him wholeheartedly when he decides to pursue them.

My Amon is meant for greatness, and I know he will achieve it in the future.

We stay like that until the weather becomes rather unpleasant and we decide we've had enough for one day. As we get home to our small domus, we take a shower and get ready to pay a visit to Ambrosius.

"Sela, Amon. Welcome," Ambrosius says as he welcomes us to his home, inviting us into his grand hall. "I'm so happy to see you here."

"We thank you for the invitation and for your efforts, Ambrosius," Amon tilts his head in acknowledgement.

"Nonsense. This will be a good learning opportunity for me. Please take a seat while my servant will bring you something to eat and we can discuss further."

"Thank you," I murmur as Amon and I take a seat on one of his plush couches.

Amon's arm is wrapped around my shoulders in a possessive display

—as he usually does whenever there's another male around. I doubt he's going to let go of me the entire night.

Giving him a small smile, I squeeze his hand in a gesture of comfort just as he brings his lips to my temple for a kiss.

Ambrosius takes a seat opposite us as a servant comes in to bring a few trays of food and fresh fruit.

A man in his late fifties, Ambrosius has been learning sorcery since his youth. In this world, however, it's called witchcraft, but humans do not seem to have a solid understanding of how some people can wield it while others cannot.

At the same time, the people who have been studying it for centuries have put together protocols and have compiled lists of spells which, hopefully, might help us too.

"It's been so long since I last saw you two and you look absolutely the same," Ambrosius shakes his head. "Then here I am, a couple of decades later and I have a head full of gray hair. If I hadn't met you before I would have never suspected such a thing was possible."

"I doubt we're the only ones," Amon smiles. "We've met some other people throughout the years who displayed a more than average life span."

"You'll have to teach me your secrets then," he chuckles.

Amon smiles.

"There is no secret. At least not in our case. My kind is known for having an increased lifespan while my wife can regenerate *ab infinitum*," he explains.

We'd had discussions on how much we could share with Ambrosius about our situation, and I'd encouraged Amon to give him as many details as possible since he might be able to help us better if he understands the source of our powers.

After the events in the past, we'd always been worried about sharing too much, but I think Ambrosius is the exception.

"Your kind?" Ambrosius blinks. "I wasn't aware you were a different...kind," he says. His tone, however, is not one of disgust, but one filled with curiosity.

That prompts Amon to smile at him and explain his Reva heritage. And to display it better, he turns his hand into a sword—another perk of his matter manipulation that he'd learned to use.

Being away from the Empire's scrutiny had allowed Amon to explore more of his Reva side and discover all kinds of abilities. I'd repeatedly told him that I still don't think he's reached his peak and that there are plenty more things he can do.

"That is..." Ambrosius trails off, his eyes wide. "Quite spectacular *and* terrifying."

"Amon likes to joke that he is a war machine, but deep down he's just a softie," I wink at my husband.

"What about you then? How is it that you can regenerate like that? Are you a different kind, too?"

"To my knowledge, no. It's been like this since I was born."

"So, you are practically immortal?"

"I think so," I laugh.

If my body regenerates continuously, then it will do so forever.

"But your husband is...not?" He turns to Amon. "I know you said you have an increased life-span, but that doesn't mean forever, does it?"

"In our case it does," he smiles. "We are mated in my tradition, and through blood exchange, her power is mine, too."

Ambrosius nods pensively.

"But you see, despite my healing ability, I was still cursed," I interject. "It's quite paradoxical that I'm able to withstand any type of death and still heal, but I cannot heal from this one spell."

"Tell me more about this curse you speak off."

I swallow hard.

"It was my mother. She...reached inside of me and I could feel her fingers probing in my womb. She took something out too, but I do not know what, only that since then we haven't been able to conceive."

Ambrosius looks pensive for a moment.

"Will you allow me to examine you?"

Sensing Amon tense, I turn to him for approval. He gives me a brisk nod.

"I'll be watching," he murmurs in my ear.

"Do not worry. I do not need to touch her for this," Ambrosius chuckles when he sees Amon's tight expression.

All at once, he relaxes a little.

Silly male.

"If you could stand up," Ambrosius instructs me, taking a book from his collection and searching for something in it.

With his finger on the page, he waves his hand towards me.

"*Revelare.*"

At once, there's a blinding light coming from my lower stomach before I feel a searing pain. Blood oozes through the material of my tunic, and I know that something has appeared on my skin.

"Sela," Amon is immediately to his feet as he comes to my side.

"I think there's something etched in my skin..." I trail off.

"I'll step outside for a moment. Here's ink and paper to write what you see. You might want to do it fast in case it disappears."

"Thank you."

Ambrosius steps outside and Amon lifts my tunic to reveal my stomach.

There are three letters embedded there. *R K W.*

They quickly disappear though as my skin starts to heal, and after I put myself together, we call Ambrosius in the room again, showing him what we'd seen.

He taps his finger against his chin as he studies the letters.

"I'm afraid this will require a very advanced spell."

"What do you mean?" I frown.

"These letters suggest that whatever your mother did to you wasn't a matter of stealing something from your womb. Rather, she blocked a few sources of energy in your body that were instrumental for fertility and conception. I had a feeling it would be this after we corresponded, but this is my confirmation."

"Can you do something about it?" Amon asks, his voice tinged with hope.

"I think so," he nods. "I will need to journey to the Holy See and borrow one of their old books on spell-casting to be able to do it."

"How can we help?" I ask quickly.

"You don't need to do anything. I will get the book and we will perform the ritual at the end of the month. Does that work for you two?"

I stare at him open-mouthed.

That's it? He doesn't need anything?

"Do you not require anything? You need to let us pay you for your services," Amon intervenes. "Tell us what you'd like as payment and you will have it."

"No, really. I do not require anything. Just knowing I can help someone is more than enough. After all, I've dedicated my entire life to the doctrine of Jesus Christ, and that dictates that I help those in need if I can."

"There must be something you could use," Amon insists.

My hand finds his as I show him I'm right by his side with my touch.

"Please, just tell us what you'd like. We have plenty of wealth, or artifacts, or anything you desire. I can make it happen."

Of course my Amon would never feel good being indebted to someone.

"Artifacts?" Ambrosius' eyes suddenly sparkle with greed at that mention.

"We've lived for a long time, so we've amassed quite the collection. I know the Church values Christian artifacts and I have a few that might interest you," Amon explains.

"Can you tell me more?" Ambrosius inquires, his hands fidgeting in his lap.

Somehow, that gesture seems so antithetical to what we know of him—a calm and learned man of letters who's dedicated his entire life to the Church.

"Would you be interested in a cross that belonged to Petros, the first bishop of Antioch. It is my understanding he is a revered figure in your faith?"

There have been times in the past when certain events have tugged at our heartstrings in such a way that we couldn't help ourselves from getting involved. Usually that is when we witness egregious injustices or shameless persecutions such as the one Christians have withstood a few hundred years back.

Whenever we lent a helping hand, we were given a little something in return. Most of the time, it was something materially worthless but entirely too precious for a person.

That is how most of those artifacts had been acquired, including Petros' cross.

Ambrosius blinks in shock.

"You mean St. Peter?"

"The one and the same. We met him once in Asia Minor. He was a very kind man."

"If it's not too much to ask..." he stammers, though his eyes are gleaming with desire.

"It is yours," Amon smiles. "What you're willing to do for us is priceless, Ambrosius. If I can ever help you with anything else, then please let me know."

"That's very thoughtful of you," Ambrosius inclines his head.

"No, on the contrary. You're a good friend for attempting to help us with an advanced spell."

"Yes, thank you so much, Ambrosius."

"What is this book of spells, if I may inquire?"

"It's one of the treasures of the Holy See and it contains the strongest spells inside," Ambrosius relates. "Only high officials have access to it."

"And you're sure you can acquire it?"

"Yes," he confirms.

We set the date of the ritual for the next full moon, which falls at the end of the month. Ambrosius tells us to come back to his house for it.

"Oh, Amon. It's finally happening," I whisper when we finally get back to our house.

"Yes," he nods, though he doesn't seem convinced.

"What is it, love? You're frowning."

"I couldn't read his mind. At all."

"Well, it's bound to happen with these people. They have been training their entire lives," I reply.

"I don't know. Everything seems...too easy," he sighs as he takes a seat. "I'm sorry, I don't want to ruin your happiness, it's just that I'm not convinced."

"Why?"

I take a seat across from him, searching his features.

"How many other such people have we encountered before, Sela? And they've never been able to give us anything. Everyone who examined you said it was beyond their abilities to solve it. They couldn't even recognize the type of spell it was."

"Yes, but maybe Ambrosius is much stronger than that."

"He's still using a spell from the same book that's been gathering dust in the Vatican Library for hundreds of years. You know exactly the one I speak of. We've read it before, together, and we didn't find anything that could help us."

"I think we should trust Ambrosius, Amon. He seems to know exactly what's wrong with me. How many others told us that the issue is with my energy points? That they need to be unblocked."

"No one," he grumbles.

"See. I'm sure he knows what he's about. If it doesn't work, then we'll try something else in the future. But if it does work... If it works," I lick my lips as I look at him, tears accumulating at the corner of my eyes. "We'll have a child, Amon. *Our* child," I whisper.

"Sela," he lets out a pained groan. "My darling Sela," he murmurs as he draws me into his arms. "You're right. I shouldn't question it too much. I apologize. I'm just used to second-guessing everything these days."

"I know. But Ambrosius has been nothing but kind to us."

"So he has," he agrees. "You know I can't help but doubt everyone I can't read. But that is my fault and I accept it. I'll try to not let my worries get in the way of this plan."

"Thank you. I have a really good feeling about this. Here," I say as I bring his hand to my heart. "Something tells me we're going to succeed this time, Amon."

"If you feel so then it must be so. I trust your judgment, Sela."

For the rest of the month, we try to occupy our time as best as we can while trying not to get our hopes up too much. Yet it's hard to do that when my gut feeling tells me this is it.

Ambrosius is going to make my biggest dream come true.

Though Amon persists in being a little skeptical of Ambrosius, he does his best to support me. And a few days before we're due for the ritual, he tells me he has a surprise for me.

"What is it?" I ask, my lips trembling with the urge to smile as he blindfolds me and leads me to one of our storage rooms.

"You'll see. I wanted to apologize for my paranoia and show you that I'm here for you, every step of the way."

"You're keeping me on my toes, Amon. What is it?"

"Come," he chuckles as he closes the door behind us.

Slowly undoing the blindfold, he lets it fall to the ground as I take in the item in front of me.

"You..." my voice breaks as my emotions get the best of me. "You did this?"

He nods, watching me closely to determine my reaction.

"Oh, Amon. I love it," I whisper.

He'd built a baby crib from scratch, and had carved traditional Vissirian figures along the edges.

"It's wonderful."

"If you trust this is going to work, then so do I," he assures me.

"You're the best," I whisper as I turn to him, cupping his face in my hands and rising myself on the tips of my toes to lay a kiss on his lips. "So many years, Amon, and I love you more and more with every day that passes. You know that, don't you?"

He gives me a tight nod.

"Even if we have a child, my love for you will never be less."

"Sela... How could you say that? I would never be jealous of my own child."

"Good," I chuckle. "But I still wanted you to know that no one can replace you in my heart. There is a part that is reserved solely for you, my love."

A day before the ritual my anticipation grows into restlessness and Amon takes me to a market to get some new gowns that I could wear for the ceremony.

We have a wonderful day together as we explore the inner city, eating at a tavern and touring some of the attractions in Ravenna.

And then, before I know it, the day of the full moon is upon us.

"I'm so excited," I whisper to Amon as we make our way to Ambrosius' house.

"I know you are, lass," he chuckles. "It's going to be one of the most memorable moments in our lives."

"It will," I agree.

A tingling surrounds my entire being as I think about the future, renews optimism filling me as I see myself, Amon and our child together. I don't want to get ahead of myself, but maybe...maybe we'll have more than one child.

"Welcome, welcome," Ambrosius invites us into his sitting room. "I've prepared everything for tonight and I have no doubts that it's going to be a complete success," he assures us—exactly what I needed to hear to burst with happiness.

"What does this spell involve?" Amon asks and I give him the side eye.

Ambrosius must know what he's doing. We shouldn't question him too much.

But he doesn't seem to mind as he invites us to take a look at a linen paper.

"This is the ritual," he points out to a passage that looks more or less like gibberish to me. "The Holy See wouldn't allow me to take the book out of the Vatican Library, but I was able to copy the ritual onto this," he explains.

"First, I'm going to tap into all her energy points and activate them to their fullest before I will attempt to awaken the closed ones, too. In essence, I am cleaning and restarting your energy meridians, extracting the bad energy that your mother infused with her spell."

"That sounds logical," I nod, looking at Amon to find him regarding Ambrosius with narrowed eyes.

"Is there any danger to this?" Amon asks.

"No. She might feel a little weak after I perform the ritual, but she should quickly recover."

"Weak? Why?" Amon further probes.

I give him a slight pinch, but he ignores me.

"The restart will likely be a shock to her system," Ambrosius explains. "It will take at least a few days for her system to recover."

"Thank you for explaining. We can go ahead when you're ready. Right, Amon?" I give him a pointed look.

"Yes. We can go forward with it," he strains a smile.

"Excuse us for a moment," I tell Ambrosius as I drag Amon aside.

"What's wrong?" I bite my lip as I ask him.

"I don't like this—that you're going to be weak. That it might harm you."

"He said it won't harm me, Amon. It's just natural that my energy needs to reset after the ritual. What he said makes sense."

"It might, but that doesn't mean I have to like it."

"But you'll take care of me when I'm weak and helpless, won't you?" I bat my lashes at him.

"Of course," he murmurs lovingly. "You know I'd do everything for you, my darling Sela," he whispers as he leans in to kiss my forehead.

His lips linger for a moment too long but I soak in his touch as I try to let go of some of my anxiety.

This is it. This is the moment that will change our lives forever.

"Let's do this," he finally says.

Bringing my hand to his cheek, I stroke him lightly as I take in his beautiful features, made even more so by the love reflected in his eyes.

"Thank you for supporting my decision, Amon. It means the world to me," I confess.

I know how skeptical and scared he is about this. But even though he's been restless all the time leading up to today, he hasn't tried to persuade me off again. He'd simply been by my side regardless of his own doubts. And *that* means more to me than he could ever imagine.

"You don't have to ever thank me for something like this, Sela. As long as it makes you happy, I'm willing to do anything," he gives me another kiss before we return to Ambrosius' side.

"We can proceed," I tell the older man.

"Good," he nods. Turning to address Amon, he continues. "Just like before, I won't have to touch her," he assures him, undoubtedly having noticed how rabid he gets when there's even a hint of someone getting too close to me.

"If you could tell me what I have to do."

"You can lay on the couch there," he points to a seat. "I will simply chant the ritual and use my powers to open your energy meridians at first. Then, I will cleanse the foul spell and I will reset everything. There might be physical residue manifested from the bad energy. If that is the case, please do not be scared."

"That's fine."

"Your husband can sit by your side, but he cannot touch you either, otherwise the spell might fail."

Amon nods.

I take a seat on the couch, laying on my back and placing my hands by my side.

Ambrosius brings two chairs—one for himself, which he positions in front of the couch, and one for Amon, which he places at the end of the couch.

"I'm here all the way, sweet girl," Amon murmurs as he takes his seat.

Knowing he is by my side is all I need to feel fully safe.

"I'll be starting now," Ambrosius announces. "But first. Sela, please give your consent to the ritual. This can only be done with your acquiescence."

"I consent to the ritual," I murmur.

Once that is out of the way, Ambrosius gets to work.

His voice is soft and barely audible as he holds his hand over my body, a bluish glow emanating from his palm. His hand hovers over me, starting with my head and moving down my body all the way down to my feet.

Immediately, I start to feel lightheaded as my body tenses inexplicably.

It's as if something is being forcefully opened inside of me.

Like when I channel my energy for my own use, my body tingles all over as hot points appear at various locations in my body, the heat almost unbearable.

Still, I hold everything in. After all, I am used to pain and can withstand a great deal of it.

"Your meridians have been opened, Sela. Now it is time to cleanse the bad energy. This should be the most painful part. Please bear it for me," Ambrosius instructs.

I give him a tight nod.

"I'm here," Amon whispers, barely holding himself from touching me and ruining the ritual.

As Ambrosius shifts to the second part of the ritual, the pain becomes stronger, and all of it concentrates in my chest, right over my heart. My skin becomes so hot, I feel like I'm going to pass out from it.

I do my best to breathe in and out to withstand it, but it doesn't help much.

The burning sensation increases until it feels like someone is reaching within my body and forcefully pulling my soul out.

A whimper escapes my lips as a small area just above my breast becomes so heated, a shape sears itself on my skin before something attempts to get out of me.

My eyes flare open in shock at the sensation.

Gods, but it really feels as if someone is pulling my heart out of my chest.

Yet I bear it.

"The bad energy is coming to the surface," Ambrosius tells me. "Just a little more and I'll be able to remove it from you," he assures me.

That thought alone is what keeps me going, pushing all the pain down as I focus on the future we will have with our new family.

This pain is nothing compared to the joy we'll know in the future.

My skin breaks as something pops out of me, a loud sound permeating the air before the pain suddenly dulls.

"That's it. I'll now take it," Ambrosius speaks, his eyes on Amon to gauge his reaction.

Amon nods, and Ambrosius reaches out to take something resembling a jewel from my chest.

"This is the bad energy your body has expelled. I will keep it and dispose of it properly," he says in a matter-of-fact tone as he slips the jewel in his pocket. "Now for the reset."

His hand is back to work as he chants the same words of before.

My body is languid, and I can barely feel my strength.

When he is done, I can't even say thank you because the action requires energy that I do not have.

"She needs rest now," he tells Amon. "She should be fine in a week or so. If she is not, come see me. But only after a week."

Amon grits his teeth as he gives a nod of assent.

Gathering me in his arms, he teleports us back to our home.

"Sela..." he breathes out harshly as he strokes my hair. "You look so pale and sickly, my love. How are you feeling?"

"A-alright," I whisper a lie, the word for his benefit alone.

I feel as though I'm dying. I'm cold, tired, and so lightheaded I can barely focus on the shape of Amon in front of me.

"W-water, please," I ask softly.

He immediately procures me a glass of water, helping me drink since I am too weak to hold it for myself.

"Let's get you a hot bath. Maybe that will help?" Amon suggests.

I nod, giving him a small smile.

Carefully, Amon undresses me and takes me to our pool. He takes his own clothes off and with me in his arms, he slowly gets into the water.

"I'm worried," he whispers as he holds me to his chest, keeping my entire body submerged but my head.

He leans in to brush his lips over my forehead, my nose, and then my lips.

"I-I'll b-be f-fine," I stammer.

Despite the hot water, I'm still trembling from the cold.

But Ambrosius had warned me about this side effect. He'd said I would be weak for quite some time and I'd accepted it as the price I have to pay to get my wish. Because of that, there's nothing I can do but bear it in peace.

"We'll h-have a c-child," I whisper, twining my hands around Amon's neck and bringing my lips to his skin as I try to absorb his heat. "I k-know we w-will."

"We will. Of course we will, Sela mina."

"I w-want you to m-make love t-to me t-tonight," I tell him. "T-tonight is the n-night. I k-know it."

"Sela... Can't you see the state you're in? You haven't stopped shaking in my arms and you want me to make love to you? You can't even walk by yourself, lass."

"I c-can. Please, Amon," I plead with him.

And to prove to him that I can, as we exit the bath, I force myself to walk to our bedroom.

"I'm a little tired," I concentrate not to stutter. "But I know this is the moment," I say as I turn my gaze to him, willing him to fulfill this one request of mine.

"Fine," he groans. "But you're not to exert yourself too much, alright?"

I nod.

Still naked, I stretch myself on the bed as I beckon him to me, giving him a brilliant smile to convey all the love I have for him—a love that tonight will conceive a child.

How I know it, I don't know. But I am absolutely certain it will happen.

"Sela, lass. I love you too much to deny you anything," my Amon murmurs as he kisses every inch of my body, slowly arousing me until I'm ready for him. Only then does he sheathe himself into my body, holding me reverently in his arms as we slowly become one with each other.

It's a languid love-making that has little to do with physical pleasure and everything to do with our hearts being in sync—with knowing that I have my male next to me, inside of me. That he's here for me even when I feel like I might shatter in a million pieces if I move just one inch.

"I love you, Amon," I whisper as I thread my fingers through his soft hair.

He's holding himself on his forearms so he won't rest his weight on me, and I make the Herculean effort to lean forward and lay a soft kiss on his lips that soon turns into the sweetest pain as I feel myself explode around him just as something in my body breaks.

The pain is immediate and so intense I'm about to cry.

But I hold it in since the last thing I want is to worry him.

When he finishes, he moves to the side, hugging me and whispering words of love in my ear. I use what little strength I have left to turn over so he can spoon me from behind, but also so he cannot see the tears that fall down my cheeks.

I made this choice. I *chose* to pay this price. And I will bear it until the end.

Unfortunately, it seems that as the days pass, instead of getting better, my body gets worse and worse—to the point that I cannot get out of bed, not even to relieve myself.

Amon, my sweet, sweet Amon, has been helping me with absolutely everything, caring for me as if I were an invalid.

Yet as the symptoms persist and become worse, I start to worry. It's by the fourth day, I realize that something is extremely wrong.

Amon is not home since he's on an errand to buy me some foods I'd been craving.

Taking advantage of the fact that I am alone, I attempt to get out of bed—at least to prove to myself that I can.

The moment I try to swing my legs over the bed, however, I fall. My body connects with the floor, pain flaring everywhere just as a crack resounds in the air.

My breathing intensifies just as horror fills me to the brim. I barely dare look down at my legs, instinctively knowing what awaits me.

Slowly, I move my gaze down my body, my mouth parting in shock as I see my tibia broken in two, one half of the bone sticking out as blood pours from the wound.

It's not only the pain that makes me gasp, but also the fact that seconds pass and it's not healing.

"What happened?" Amon barks as he comes rushing towards me.

"I-I d-don't k-know..." I whisper. Just saying those words and I'm out of breath. "A-Amon...I-I'm s-scared," I confess for the first time.

"Sela, lass no, please. It will be fine, you'll see."

"I don't t-think I-I'm fine."

"I'm going to look for Ambrosius. This isn't right. This..." he trails off as a look of pure anguish washes over his face. "Let me patch you up first," he sighs.

He lifts me carefully on the bed, bending my leg so he can study the wound.

It's been minutes and nothing happened. It's simply...not healing.

Amon brings a cloth as he washes the blood away from my leg before giving me a grim look.

"I'll need to push it back. Maybe it will heal then," he adds hopefully.

"M-maybe," I agree, despite knowing how bad it will hurt to have him push the bone inside.

His own face scrunches up in pain as he touches the location of the wound, one hand on my leg to hold it still while the other is on the bone sticking out.

"Look at me, darlin'. Look into my eyes, alright?"

"A-alright," I whisper, bringing my gaze to his.

Gods, but it's the only thing that's keeping me sane—the love and hope I see in his eyes.

The bone snaps into place, the pain just as bad as I was expecting it to be. Yet as we watch the wound closely, it still does not heal.

"I'll bring some bandages," he mentions quietly, disappearing and reappearing with some white gauze which he uses to wrap my wound tight.

"How are you? In pain?"

I nod.

"Gods, Sela. This is killing me, love. For days... I can't watch you like this anymore. Ambrosius needs to explain what the fuck went wrong."

I nod again. Anything to escape this torment.

I am absolutely useless in this lame body. But more than anything, the ever pervasive pain makes me want to cry out loud and wail.

Yet I can't.

Because that would make my Amon worry even more.

"I'll be back," he whispers, kissing my brow before disappearing from my sight.

It takes him only moments to return, angrier than I've ever seen him before.

"He's gone," he grits out. "There's no trace of him in that house, Sela. He's *gone.*"

"B-but...h-how?"

"I don't know but whatever he did to you... Fuck, Sela. He didn't help you. He *destroyed* you."

Tears coat my lashes before spilling onto my cheeks.

"M-my p-power...is g-gone, isn't it?" I whisper.

He purses his lips as his own eyes turn misty.

"This isn't over," he says just as he disappears once more.

But that's just the thing, isn't it? It *is* over. I feel it everywhere. *I* am over.

Because without my power and in the state I'm in...I know there's only one fate awaiting me.

It takes everything inside of me to bring my hand to my chest and trace the mark left behind by whatever Ambrosius had removed. That hadn't been bad energy, had it? It had been *all* my energy.

Amon had seen through him all along. He'd known to be suspicious where I'd let myself be led by my idiotic dreams.

And now... I'm paying the price.

I can't die.

I *refuse* to die. Not when that means leaving Amon behind. No...I can't do that.

It doesn't take long for my husband to appear again, this time holding a large vellum manuscript in his hands.

"I got the book from the Vatican Library. If there's anything that can help you, it has to be in here. I'll fix this for you, Sela. Please trust me," he says as he comes to my side.

I don't have the heart to tell him I doubt there is any fixing. Not when my body is wasting away one second at a time. I've never seen such rapid decay but I feel it in the way my bones are brittle and easily breakable, my entire body one movement away from being destroyed.

"Amon," I whisper as I reach for him. "Please, hold me," I beg of him.

"Sela..."

"P-please..."

I don't want to die alone.

But I don't tell him that. Because voicing it out loud would be making it seem real. And in my heart I cannot accept that.

I simply cannot die.

He comes behind me as he hugs me to his chest.

My breathing is already shallow, my heart slowing down and making me feel even more lethargic than before.

Every moment that passes is one moment closer to my death. After denying it in my mind too many times, I'm forced to accept it as I barely fill my lungs with air. Each time I try to inhale, it feels as if I'm breathing in shards of glass.

My body is failing me, slowly perishing.

"I l-love you," I wheeze out. "F-forev..."

I can't finish the word as I feel myself growing so weak I cannot move my lips any longer. I am still slightly conscious—enough to hear Amon's desolate cries and the way he tries to shake me back to life.

I'm still there to see the utter devastation on his face when he realizes what's happening—that he's losing me. The entire earth starts shaking and quaking, a black cloud of ash shielding the sun and turning the day into night—all manifestations of his grief.

He's out of his mind with anguish, his eyes wholly black and brimmed with tears.

But I'm also still there for him when he opens that damned book.

"I'm not losing you, Sela," he promises. "I'm not!"

And then he starts chanting from the book.

I don't know what spell he's performing , or what he means to do next.

I only know that my soul is suddenly at peace, a quiet certainty washing over me as death claims me.

This is not the end.

Chapter Thirty

October 1955. Fairydale, Massachusetts

"Darcy! Darcy!" Amon calls my name in a frenzy.

Opening my eyes, I regard him through the lens of our combined history and everything that we've been through. I look at him as the male who's faithfully waited for me, braving any danger in order to bring me back.

But more than anything, I look at him as my greatest love. My mate. The owner of my heart and soul and everything that I am.

Lifting my hand, I focus my energy to the surface as I'd done in the past, feeling my old self back. My palms heat up, light emanating from them as tendrils of electricity coil around me.

"Darcy?" Amon asks in a worried voice.

I shake my head, my lips curling up in a hesitant smile.

"Call me Sela," I whisper.

His eyes widen in shock just as he pulls at the neckline of my shirt, ripping the material.

My birthmark is gone, as is the jewel from the necklace.

"You..."

"I'm back," I confirm. "I'm back for good, my Amon," I say as I reach out to cup his cheek, caressing him gently. "*You* brought me back."

"But...how... It didn't work before."

"Maybe because my powers aren't bound? But this time I remember everything. As Sela and as Elizabeth. I remember absolutely everything, Amon."

"Sela?" he croaks, his voice breaking. "You're back? My Sela?"

Tears trickle down his cheeks before he's on me, pulling me to his chest and hugging me, murmuring sweet words in my ears.

"I didn't dare believe the jewel would fuse with you again. Not after it didn't last time."

"I'm here," I whisper. "I'm here and I'm never leaving you again, Amon. Thank you for fighting for me all this time; for waiting for me. I am humbled to know everything you've been through just to save me."

He shakes his head.

"Never thank me for doing what comes as naturally as breathing. Not when I am not whole without you. Ah, Sela mina, Sela mina. I can't believe you're here," he whispers, drawing back to look at me reverently.

Cupping my cheeks, he lays soft kisses all over my skin.

"My darling girl," he murmurs against my lips.

We hang to each other for what seems like an eternity as we cannot get enough of one another. His body heat transfers to me, that masculine scent that is so thoroughly him enveloping me from head to toe as I get drunk on his very essence.

All my senses are reeling from finally being with him—so close to him. Yet it's because I can experience him through so many mediums that I know this is real. With my combined memories, I love him even more as I see him through the eyes of Darcy, Elizabeth, and ultimately Sela.

I can't imagine what it must have been like for him to know of our history and our love but to try to pretend it wasn't there as he romanced me repeatedly, each time making me fall for him just like the first.

My heart hurts to think of him so lonely and desolate, waiting eons for me to come back, going through life like a shadow of himself because he was missing his mate—the other half of his soul. Our bond goes beyond marriage, maybe even beyond regular mating, for we are truly one—only ever sane when we are together.

Rising from the bed, I move to the middle of the room as I have one more test to perform.

"Sela?" Amon inquires, following behind me.

My lips quirk up as I realize just how panicked he is that something might happen to me again. He's watching me like a hawk to make sure everything is alright.

"There's one more thing I need to try," I say as I take his sword from where he usually stashes it.

"Love, maybe not now..."

I shake my head.

"I need to know that I'm fully myself, Amon."

His mouth set in a grim line, he agrees, though he still hovers around me, his expression one of constant worry.

Withdrawing the sword from its sheath, I'm once more struck by the stunning gleam of the rhodium—how something this beautiful could be the source of pain for so many.

Without hesitating, I bring it over my arm, cutting my inner forearm in a straight, deep line. The pain is immediate as my lip twitches —the only reaction. With my memories as Sela, I also remember what I'd had to withstand in the past, and compared to that, this is but a light caress.

Blood coats the silvery blade, a few drops falling to the ground.

Under our eyes, the wound immediately mends and heals, leaving behind only the faint trace of red sticking to my skin.

My lips tremble with happiness, and I turn to him, a brilliant smile stretching across my face. Amon's expression echoes mine, yet there's still a trace of disbelief, as if he can barely believe this is happening—that I'm actually here in front of him.

Gods, but he's been alone for so long... I can barely stand to think about his fate in this damned prison, let alone the fact that he wandered the Earth for hundreds of years waiting for me to be reborn.

Letting my eyes roam over his figure, I greedily take him in, his beauty never failing to make my heart skip a beat. Yet it's more than that. His beauty is made even more potent by what I know hides within him—the love and compassion, the dedication and sacrifice.

He's Amon d'Artan. The mate of my heart. The only male in existence who's ever going to lay claim to me—body and soul. And this time, I want to give him everything just as he's done to me.

He saved me when it would have been impossible for anyone else to do it.

Now it's my turn to embrace him fully.

"Amon," I softly call his name as I meet his gaze. Taking a step towards him, I remove the shirt off my body until I'm standing naked in front of him. Allowing my energy to surge to the surface, I drape myself in tendrils of electricity, letting my entire body be illuminated by this coveted source of power that lives within me.

"I come before you as my truest self. When all the layers are peeled off, this is the me that loves you more than life itself—your wife, your mate, your eternal companion. This is the me that's been hunted for hundreds of years for this strange ability I possess. Once, you said we are both creatures. Both outsiders. Both hiding in the shadows—whether on Earth, or on Arkgor. So show me, too, my love," I coax slowly. "Show me your truest self."

His eyes widen, and for a moment I doubt he's going to do it.

After all, this is the first time I've requested that of him—the first time I've dared to do so.

In the past, while I'd known everything about his Reva heritage and even witnessed it on occasion, it had been something that seldom made its way into our lives. There had always been a reluctance to Amon when he'd speak about his Reva form, most often simply claiming the powers without bringing up the physical change.

I'd assured him I didn't think him monstrous in the least, but I'm not sure he ever believed me. Certainly, I never pushed when I now realize I should have.

Many things have become crystal clear to me as I've recovered my memories. In more ways than not, I've acquired a new clarity to instances in which I'd been blinded in the past. I can see every mistake and every wrong step I took that brought me closer and closer to my death.

It had been my sheer stubbornness and inane selfishness that had led me to put my faith into Ambrosius—to the point that I'd ignored Amon's instincts and his opinions. I'd been so closed off in my grief and loneliness, that at some point I'd...pushed him away, or, at least, I hadn't paid enough attention to him. Maybe it had not been intentional, but it had happened, nonetheless.

Yet he hadn't budged. Like a steady rock being hit by the strongest torrent, he'd staunchly been by my side in the darkest hours. He'd been most selfless when I'd been at my most selfish.

It's only retrospectively that I see the little signs, his own silent struggles to come to terms with his own dual identity and the fact that he's held that side of himself back. It might not have been a conscious decision as hundreds of years of conditioning, of forcing him to hide and be ashamed of who he really was, have left their mark on him.

Yet it hurts all the same to realize he's been living half a life in order to bury that part of himself that he thinks will not be acceptable to the world.

Not anymore.

We have this precious third chance to do it all over again and I will grasp at it with all I have in me. For the first time, I want to reverse the roles and even the scales.

It's time for him to take and for me to give.

And the first thing I want to offer him is my unwavering acceptance of who he is—*what* he is—of his past, and everything that will dictate the future. But I don't want it to be a fleeting acknowledgement, or a mere verbal affirmation. I don't want him to think that he needs to keep his Reva form hidden when he doesn't have to.

I am his home for a reason—just like he is mine. Because he can truly be himself with me and know there will be no judgment, no reproach and no fear.

"Do you know what you're asking of me, Sela?" he rasps, his voice low and tortured.

I nod.

"I should have asked you eons ago, Amon. In a way, I thought you would show me eventually. But..."

"I never did," he completes my sentence.

"Why?"

"You know why," he slumps his shoulders. "But it doesn't matter. This is who I am and who I've always been."

"You're wrong. This isn't *only* who you are. There's so much more to you, Amon. So much more that even you don't see."

He opens his mouth to reply before closing it, appearing speechless.

"It's enough that you know that side of me exists and accept it."

"No," I shake my head. "It's not enough. You know, before, I never quite realized what your lack of transformation meant. Not until I relived the past again. You told me yourself that once you turned fully, the impulse to do so again would become more and more pronounced. Yet in two millennia, I never once saw you turn like that again. Why?"

He stiffens as a flash of shame crosses his face.

"You changed in secret, did you not?"

"I did," he answers.

I release a relieved sigh. At least he hasn't suppressed himself all this time.

"More so in the last century since there has been no one to see me," he jokes as his shoulders angle up in a lazy shrug.

"Why did you never do it in front of me?" I ask, but at the same time, I ask myself.

Why did I not see this as an issue before? Had I been so egocentric as to not realize what was right in front of me? The quiet struggle he was going through?

That in itself makes me feel like the worst type of mate.

I'd been so lost in my grief because of my infertility that I'd lost track of what was most important in my life.

Him.

My Amon.

The most important person in my life.

"I'm a monster, Sela. One that can't even stand the sight of himself in a mirror. I could never bear to see the same reaction in your eyes."

"Is that how little you think of me?" I whisper, his words hitting me in the chest.

"No, no," he denies vehemently. "It's how *I* see myself," he admits quietly. "*I* am the problem. Not you."

"Show me," I demand again.

If he doesn't trust himself, then I will trust him for the both of us.

He closes his eyes, exhaling in defeat.

"As you wish," he inclines his head.

I swallow hard as I watch the slow transformation.

When he opens his eyes next they are wholly black, his irises a muddy mix of white and red. The blackness bleeds into his skin, his color changing as his body grows in size.

If before he'd been close to seven feet tall, now he is well beyond that. His body mass grows, too, his chest broadening as his muscles ripple with renewed strength. The shirt he'd been wearing tears, the material falling to the ground. The same thing happens with his trousers, the seams bursting as his muscles continue to grow.

Everything about him is bigger, including his cock. Semi-erect and hanging between his legs, it's already almost double the previous size.

Claws protrude from his fingers, long and sharp.

And finally, a tail extends from his back, flailing in the air before it coils around his leg. The tail is long and thick, flaring into a broader ribbed end.

Licking my lips, I look up at him in awe.

When I'd seen him before, it had only been from a distance. I'd seen the distinct features, but I hadn't been able to properly appraise his size.

He is...absolutely magnificent.

Taking a tentative step forward, I lay my palm on top of his chest, a spark of electricity bursting through the surface when we touch.

My eyes widen in surprise.

He senses it, too, because his eyebrows go up as he looks at me curiously.

"Read my mind," I tell him, giving him full access to my thoughts so he can see what I truly think about him.

"Are you sure?"

I nod.

"I want you to see everything, Amon. Everything I feel about you and the fact that your form doesn't scare me, nor disgust me. It does nothing of that nature. On the contrary," I pause as I feel myself redden. "It pleases me immensely."

Maybe it's a side effect of us being mates, or maybe it's just him and the effect he has on my senses, but Gods, he is utterly mesmerizing.

My body reacts to his immediately, desire building inside of me as wetness gushes from my sex. My nipples harden at the thought of those sharp nails touching me, scratching and clawing at me. Strange, but there is not one iota of fear that he might hurt me. In fact, I would rejoice if he did.

"Sela," he growls, his voice deep and thick—a rich bass that rumbles through my entire being.

I open my mind and broadcast all my thoughts to him. I show him the way he makes me feel regardless of his form—that he makes me hot and bothered in such a unique way, as if I would die if he didn't take me right here and now. Yet I also show him the other aspect of my desire—the fact that I want him to take me hard and fast, regardless of the consequences. That I want the pleasure and pain and everything he might give me, for even if he hurts me, I can always heal.

Now, more than ever, we are truly equal just as we are complementary.

He is destruction and I am salvation. He is ruin, but I am the one who can repair.

"Do you see, Amon? Do you see what I think of you?"

His nostrils flare as he undoubtedly scents my arousal, his mouth set in a firm line as he regards me with frightening intensity.

"Sela you... You want me." he states in disbelief. "You don't think me...repugnant?"

My brows furrow together.

"Repugnant? I would never think you repugnant in any shape or form."

"But I'm a monster," he whispers in a hurt tone.

I shake my head as I place my other palm on his chest, touching him gently.

"You're not. To me, you're my Amon. My husband. My mate. My *everything.*"

To show him further that I mean everything, I lean in and press my lips to his skin. His scent is dark and alluring, but so thoroughly him that I would know it anywhere.

It's familiar, and it's home.

It's simply...home.

Moving my lips over his chest, I pepper kisses everywhere, leaving not one inch of skin uncovered.

"Sela," his voice rumbles with pleasure at my touch, a purr-like sound erupting from his chest, the vibrations spreading through my whole body as I glue myself to him.

"You're so handsome," I whisper. "So beautiful, sometimes it hurts to look at you. But like this... Like this you are absolutely stunning, Amon."

His muscles coil under my fingertips as his breathing intensifies.

He hasn't touched me yet, keeping his hands still by his side. I belatedly realize he might be afraid to hurt me with his claws.

Taking hold of his hands, I bring them to my body, wrapping them around me and urging him to touch me.

"Feel how hot I am for you, my love. How much I want you," I murmur.

"I don't want to hurt you," he finally says in a strangled tone.

With our bodies so close like this, I can feel his cock between us, stirring to life and growing larger than ever before. So much so, in fact, that a thrill of anticipation goes down my spine.

"I'm back to my old self, big guy," I let him know. "Nothing can hurt me now. And you might recall that I do like a little bit of pain," I confess, a blush suffusing my cheeks.

His breath hitches just as his claws lightly rake down my back, the effect instantaneous as I moan loudly and arch myself into him. Slowly, he reaches my ass and for a moment I think he's going to stop. But he doesn't. Instead, he surprises me by cupping my ass and raising me to him.

My legs naturally wind around him as I wrap my arms around his neck.

"I can't believe this," he rasps roughly. "You're not...scared."

"You do look quite scary," I add playfully. "And deadly. And if you had horns I don't doubt you would have everyone believe you're a demon. But you're also too goddamn hot. Were I a nun, and I would still want to fuck you, even if I thought you Satan himself."

His lips tug up in an amused smile.

"You would?" he chuckles.

"Of course," I reply seriously. "I'd even sell my soul to have you do wicked, wicked things to me," I wink at him.

"Ah, Sela mina. You really are a treasure, aren't you?" he muses as his eyes sparkle with love and warmth.

As I wrap my legs around him tighter, my center comes into direct contact with the smooth and firm surface of his abdominals. He gives me a mischievous grin before he rubs me up and down his body, coating his skin in my wetness.

The friction makes me gasp, tiny dots of pleasure dancing before my eyes.

"I need you, Amon. I want you like this—the real you. I want to be a Reva mate in truth."

"But you're so small and I'm so..."

"Big?" I raise a brow, my lips trembling with laughter. "I hadn't realized that."

"Sela," he groans, though this time it's clearly in amusement as playful energy emanates from him. "You're killing me, lass. You think I haven't dreamed about this? About fucking you like the beast that I am, stuffing your tight little cunt with my thick cock until you can no longer walk? Until you're so thoroughly fucked you feel me in your body for days after and you remember both the pleasure and the pain? Sometimes I think of little else, Sela, but I fuck you hard enough in my normal form. Like this I would fucking wreak you..."

"What if I want to be wrecked?" I whisper as I grind my pelvis against his rock-hard abs. "I can take it. Stop denying yourself, Amon. Not when I'm right there with you in this madness."

I cup his cheeks as I lean in to kiss him softly on the lips.

"I'm not made of glass."

"I know you're not," he releases a ragged breath.

"Then?"

"You'll tell me to stop if I hurt you, or if it gets too much?" he suddenly asks.

"Yes, although I highly doubt anything you do to me would be *too* much."

He smirks, his lips pulling up against my own.

"Maybe I'll surprise you."

"Now I'm even more intrigued, dear husband, and I fear you'll have quite a lot to live up to."

"Really?" he drawls, his tone changing.

If before it had been sweet and caring, now there's a dangerous lilt to it that makes me shiver in anticipation. My body is already primed for his, ready to welcome his invasion—ready to become his again. But this time, it will be an entirely new experience—the culmination of everything we've been through and all the lessons we've learned.

"I have quite the imagination," I whisper.

Before I know it, my back hits the bed, my breath knocked out of me as my eyes widen in surprise.

He looms over me, his body looking even bigger from this angle. But what captures my attention is his huge cock as it proudly juts out of his body, thick veins covering the entire length. As size of his erection increases, the ring is now a tight fit at the end of it.

"You asked for this, Sela," he warns darkly.

I don't get to ask what he means because he has my legs parted, his mouth already on my sex as he licks every bit of my wetness. My back arches as my hands search for his hair, grabbing on to his scalp as I urge him on. But if this wasn't torture enough, his tail trails up my body, the flared end slapping my nipple before brushing softly against it. He does the same with the other, giving me a tiny dose of pain before soothing it with pleasure.

My eyes snap open as I scream his name, the climax claiming me immediately.

Amon's lips are wrapped around my bundle of nerves as he brings his hands to my thighs, raking his claws on my skin, deep enough to draw blood, but not enough to hurt me. There's only a light sting that makes the pleasure even more potent as he racks another orgasm from me.

I barely catch my breath before he tortures me all over again.

Drawing back, he brings his claws to his lips as he licks the drops of blood from them, his eyes swirling under my very gaze.

"So sweet," he purrs. "So very sweet, Sela."

My gaze is drawn again to his cock, my body instinctively clenching as I imagine how it will feel when he's going to fill me—how full and stretched I will be taking all of him.

The tip is wet, clear liquid seeping from it and leaking down his shaft.

My mouth waters for a taste. Licking my lips, I get to my knees in front of him, moving closer. I swipe the moisture from the tip with my tongue, tasting him and letting out a moan of pure pleasure.

Gods, how long has it been since I've had my mouth on him? Certainly far too long as I lap greedily, loving his male taste and the sounds of rapture that escape him.

He hisses loudly as I wrap my lips around the head, barely able to fit my mouth around it as I give it a good suck.

He doesn't let me continue, though, as I find myself on my back again.

Yet he doesn't move either.

His lips are tipped in a dangerous smile as he watches me, desire dripping from his eyes.

Raising myself on my elbows, I hold his gaze with mine, so entirely enraptured by him, I barely register the feather-like touch against my folds. Looking down, I'm surprised to see his tail between my legs, stroking me softly with the tip.

"Trust me?" Amon asks in a pained voice.

"Always," I nod.

Drenched in my wetness, his tail slides down to my entrance, the ribbed end pushing inside of me.

A gasp escapes me at the foreign sensation as the grungy texture caresses my walls.

"Fuck," Amon tips his head back and lets out a harsh moan.

"You... You can feel it too?" I ask, my voice laced with wonder.

"Yes. The end of my tail is covered in nerve endings. I can feel... everything," he releases a harsh breath as he thrusts it in and out of me.

"Is this what you've been dreaming about? Fucking me with your tail?"

"Oh, Sela, what I dreamed was far, far more depraved," he confesses.

"Show me," I urge him. "Show me everything, Amon."

"Fuck," he curses.

Lifting me by my waist, he continues to fuck me with his tail, rotating it inside of me while he holds me, rocking me back and forth to accentuate the sensation. Though not as thick as his cock, the ribbing enhances my pleasure the more he strokes my inner walls.

My body is glued to his, my lips parting to suck on his skin while my hands hold on to his back, my nails lodged deep into his skin. It doesn't escape me that despite his indestructible armor, he has his guard down with me, allowing me to penetrate his skin and draw blood. And just like he did to me before, I bring my nails down on his back, scratching him.

"Amon," I pant as he thrusts lightly into me.

His breathing intensifies as he shivers from my touch, the effect causing his tail to twitch inside of me. Bringing his mouth to my cheek, he kisses me sloppily before he buries his face in my neck. He licks me leisurely, purring with pleasure every now and then.

Gods, but there's something absolutely magnetic about this Amon. His sensations seem to be intensified in this form, his pleasure much more potent as every inch of his skin serves as a conductor for it.

His teeth bump against my skin, and I note they are much, *much* sharper than before.

"You could rip someone's throat with your teeth, darling," I tease him.

"Maybe I could," he chuckles. "But that doesn't mean I would. Your blood is the only one I'll ever taste," he murmurs.

"Then do it," I urge him. "Bite me. Take my blood. Take everything."

"Not yet," he whispers. He scrapes his teeth against my skin but he doesn't bite, merely teasing me with the option.

I'm about to protest when I find myself flat against the wall, held in the air by his power.

My channel clenches at the sudden emptiness, but I know it's not for long. Not when he strides towards me with such determination, a lopsided smile on his face that speaks of wicked pleasure and sweet retribution.

With only one hand motion, he has my arms and legs spread to form an x.

Stopping in front of me, he takes a moment to let his gaze roam hungrily around my body, taking in my breasts and the way my chest rises and falls with the intensity of my breaths, before going lower to my stomach and the soft hairs of my sex that glisten with arousal—the evidence of my unquenchable desire for him.

"So wet," he murmurs as he brings his tail to my wet folds, the ribbed end brushing softly against my sensitive nub and making me tremble from the onslaught of sensation. "So mine, aren't you, darlin'?"

"Always yours. Even dead and I'm still yours," I whimper, trying to push my hips towards him so he would touch me more.

"No," he rasps, his features hardening. "You'll never die on me again. If anyone attempts to harm you, I will fucking raze their world to the ground. I don't care if you heal. I don't care if you don't mind the pain. And I don't fucking care if you forgive them. *I* won't. If anyone tries to do *anything* to you, they are dead. And so is everyone else who conspires with them," he tells me dangerously.

"I believe you," I whisper. "You're my champion, Amon, and I will never blame you for seeking justice for me."

"Then you won't mind that I went on a little...spree?" he asks in a low voice as he continues to stroke me with his tail.

"What...spree?" I ask, barely able to form the words as he increases his speed.

Wicked, wicked male. He's trying to distract me.

"I may have caused another *plague,*" he adds playfully.

"What did you...do...ah," I trail off on a loud moan.

"Not much, just executed everyone who ever worked with Abel," he shrugs, as if it's nothing.

"How many people are we...talking about?" I ask in between moans as he brings me on the brink of orgasm again.

He's quiet for a moment as he takes my nipple in his mouth, tugging it between his teeth and lavishing it with exquisite tongue strokes that match the rhythm of his tail.

"Half the town," he mentions as he licks his way up my body until we're face to face.

"That's at least a couple thousand."

"Mhm," he purrs. "Maybe a bit more."

"Amon!" I cry out scandalized, but he's quick to fix it by making me climax again.

"I might not be able to kill Kress and Finn because of that damned shield they used to protect themselves. But I can at least do this. I would never leave anything up to chance with you, darlin'. Just like I could never leave anyone go unpunished if they threatened you, in action or in thought."

"But that's a lot of people, Amon," I chide lightly.

"There are two point eight billion people on Earth, darlin'. What's a few thousand," he murmurs as he touches his cheek to mine before taking my lips in a sensual kiss.

He distracts me with his kisses as he replaces his tail with the tip of his cock, swiping the ringed head between my folds.

I moan in his mouth, allowing him to push his tongue in deeper, kiss me with a savageness I'd forgotten he possessed.

Here I am, completely at his mercy as he holds me pinned to a wall with his powers. Never mind the fact that he just told me he's *executed* two thousand people, *or more*. Never mind that he's potentially the most dangerous male to ever live. Yet I could never fear him—not in *that* way, for I know everything he does is for my sake.

If he is the most destructive force, then it is for me.

But if he is the sweetest male, then it is for me, too.

He is so bad, but he is so good.

He is just...mine.

His tongue mates with mine, each stroke more powerful than the last as he tastes me deeply. At the same time, his hands are on my breasts, his claws lightly scraping my nipples and making him thrash against the wall.

His cock is still positioned at my sex, but he doesn't thrust into me. He continues to languidly tease me with it, moving his length between my folds as he lathers himself in my arousal.

"Amon," I moan. "Please."

"Please what, darlin'?" he murmurs seductively, biting my lips until a few drops of blood trickle down my chin.

"Please fuck me. Take me. Mate me. Just...do something," I pant, unable to bear the frustration anymore.

"If you ask me so nicely," he smiles as he draws back. "How can I refuse you anything?"

Fisting his length, he aligns the head to my entrance, slowly pushing in. Already, the difference in size is noticeable as he stretches me.

"That's it, darlin'," he encourages, his eyes glued to our lower bodies. I bring my gaze there, too, just in time to see how his long and thick cock slowly disappears inside of me. The burn is both painful and pleasurable as he pushes into me until he's all the way to the hilt—until I swear I can feel him in my very heart.

I breathe harshly as I accommodate to his size, feeling every pulsation of his cock, every little twitch against my inner walls.

Clenching around him, I hear him groan as he touches his forehead to mine.

"Fuck, Sela. This... I can't believe how well we fit, lass. So good. So fucking tight," he says in a tight voice.

I wiggle around him, urging him to move.

"Show me," I repeat. "I want everything you can give me."

His eyes snap open as he gazes at me intently.

"Oh, Sela mina, there's so much more I have to give you. So much more," he rasps.

Withdrawing all the way, he surges back inside me, the strength of his thrust making me reel, the wall trembling with us.

"More," I encourage him, knowing he's always waiting for my cues.

"More," he echoes as he repeats the motion, every thrust harsher than the previous.

Finding that I can move again, I put my arms around his neck while wrapping my legs around his waist as he bounces me up and down his cock.

I look deep in his eyes so he can see that his appearance doesn't scare me one bit—that I grow hotter just staring into his beautifully odd irises and the swirling flecks of red-silver that mar them.

And as I open my mind for him to see exactly what I want, I see the spark of desire that takes shape in his own gaze.

Bringing his hand to my torso, he trails his fingers on my skin before using his claws to cut a straight line right above my breasts, blood immediately pooling to the surface and spilling down my breasts. He bends down to lap at it, licking every single drop before the cut heals.

But I don't want him to stop.

Time and time again, he cuts me to drink my blood, the slight pain only augmenting the pleasure I get from his wild fucking.

I come too many times to count, and though I think nothing can trump this crazy experience, Amon proves me wrong—that his dreams are, indeed, far more wicked than I would have ever imagined.

His thrusts become frenzied as he spills himself inside of me, his warm seed filling me to the brim and slowly dripping out of me.

He's still hard when he pulls out, but he surprises me when I find out *why* he withdraws.

Swiping his tail along my slit, he gathers our mixed releases, coating the entire surface of the ribbed head. Before I know what he means to do, he pushes his cock back inside me, the sudden thrust making me gasp in surprise.

"A..." I trail off as I feel the end of his tail brushing against my other hole.

"Trust me?" he asks again as he stares deep in my eyes.

The implication finally dawns on me, and I get wetter just thinking about it, never mind actually experiencing it. It wouldn't be the first time he fucked me in the ass. It was something both of us used to enjoy and do quite often. But it would definitely be the first time he fucks me both ways at the same time.

"Always," I whisper.

His tail probes lightly at first, smearing our releases around my tight entrance before he gently pushes inside me.

My mouth forms an o as he breaches me, my muscles clamping down on him.

"Just a little more, darlin'. You can take it," he murmurs in my hair as he pushes the ribbed head of his tail further in my ass. He does it just a little at a time, letting me get used to the intrusion. The combination of my wetness and his seed make it easier for him to slip in, but it's still a tight fit.

The more he advances, though, the indentations on his tail brush against my anal muscles, making me instinctively clench and moan at the foreign sensations.

I'm so full, and getting even fuller as he finally impales me all the way.

His cock twitches inside my channel, swelling even more in size as he releases a loud groan. I'm so tight around him, squeezing him even tighter with every breath as I slowly get used to this foreign sensation.

Gods... His dreams may be wicked, but the reality is much, much more depraved. And I love every single moment of it.

"That's a good girl," he whispers as he tries to stay in control of himself. "We fit so well together, Sela, don't we? Your cunt's stuffed with my cock and your ass with my tail."

He tucks a strand of hair behind my ear as he regards me with a dangerous gleam in his eyes.

"Have I scandalized you yet, darlin'?"

"No," I say, unable to tear my eyes from him as I feel him everywhere. "You're just making me hotter, Amon. You know I'm yours. You can use me as you like."

I wrap my arms tighter around his neck, trying to wiggle my hips so he would move.

"Fucking hell," he groans. "It's been a while since I've fucked your ass, lass. I almost forgot how good it felt."

"I didn't," I whisper. "But this feels better. If only you'd move."

He chuckles, his lips pulling in a lopsided smile.

"You're such a greedy little thing," he coos right before he moves.

His expression matches mine as he grips my hips with the pads of his fingers, thrusting his cock and tail into me at the same time.

"Amon," I whimper. "A-Amon..."

My head falls back as I rest against the wall while he gradually increases his speed. His movements are perfectly in sync as he withdraws almost all the way before pushing back inside to the hilt. I grow so wet and slippery that he has no trouble fitting inside.

"I'm so full. So..."

"You can take it, darlin'. You can take every inch of me."

"Please," I cry out, tears leaking out of my eyes as he starts to *finally* fuck me.

The slow thrusts from before were just the warm-up as he allowed me enough time to get used to having him in both holes.

But now... Now he's pistoning in and out of me to the speed of light, my back hitting against the concrete wall and making it quake, the pain drowned out by too much pleasure.

"Touch yourself," he commands. "I want to see you touch yourself while I fuck you."

I reach between our bodies, finding my nub and rubbing it while he continues to fuck me more out of control than ever.

While his cock moves in and out of me at an incredible speed, his tail starts rotating while thrusting into my ass, the bumps on the surface rubbing against my muscles.

I'm crying and sobbing as I finally reach my climax, the orgasm so powerful, I lose consciousness for a moment.

Amon leans in to lick my tears, swiping his tongue all over my face as he soothes my cries, yet he doesn't stop—and I think he has no intention to do so.

"Beautiful. So fucking beautiful. That's it, Sela. Come for me, lass. Come again," Amon demands harshly as he suddenly changes our positions.

My knees hit the bed as he mounts me from behind. His cock is back inside my sex just as his tail sinks deep in my ass. This time, though, his claws are on my back as he scratches me until he draws blood only to catch every drop with his tongue.

I grab the railing of the bed as he starts fucking me again.

With our size differences, his feet are planted on the ground while I'm fully on the bed, so he doesn't realize that every thrust makes the bed shake and smash against the wall. Yet the sound of it is drowned out by my loud moans and his harsh groans.

"Fuck, Sela. So fucking tight," he growls in my ear as he finally brings his sharp teeth to my neck, biting. Somehow, there is no pain, only an overwhelming pleasure as every single sensation converges in one point.

"Mine," he whispers as he laps at the wound. "Mine. Every single part of you is mine, darlin'."

"Yes," I wheeze out. "Just like you're mine—my mate, my everything."

"Come," he orders again, changing the angles of his thrusts.

Just when I thought I couldn't do it again, he proves me wrong.

He fucks me relentlessly for what feels like hours, delaying his own release so he can rack as much pleasure from my body as he can. Only when he sees me entirely worn out and barely able to vocalize my moans does he finally succumb to his own pleasure.

Pushing into my body with renewed frenzy, he shouts his release, his cock twitching inside of me just as he pumps me full of his cum.

He withdraws his tail from my ass first before he slowly drags his cock out, his seed dripping out of me and staining the sheets.

And as he finally collapses on the bed, his Reva form disappears and he's back to his original appearance.

Oh, and the bed breaks.

We're both staring wildly at each other as a creaking sound erupts in the air before the wooden frame of the bed collapses, and the mattress falls to the ground.

I am the first to laugh and Amon joins in as he somehow still finds the strength to will the wooden pieces away until there's only the mattress left on the floor.

"Come here," he calls, holding his arms open for me.

I purr softly as I cuddle against his chest.

"You were so good," he praises softly. "Thank you."

"Why are you thanking me? There is no wrong in our relationship, Amon. Between the two of us nothing is wrong or taboo. It's just us."

"Exactly that's why. Thank you for opening my eyes and reminding me of that. I'm never going to hide from you again, Sela, and I'm sorry I did in the past."

"You're forgiven," I wink at him as I give him a quick peck.

"Good, now turn around."

I raise my brows in question and he chuckles.

"Nothing is wrong or taboo between us," he repeats my words as he turns me around, grabbing my legs and pulling me towards him until his mouth is on my core.

"I made a mess of you, now I've got to clean you up," he murmurs as he starts licking me.

My wicked male.

I shake my head at him, but I don't let him get away with being the only one participating in this clean-up business. Grabbing his still hard cock, I bring the flat of my tongue against his shaft, licking all his seed and tasting the combination of our releases.

Though I love the feel of his mouth on me, he's not trying to make me come again, merely petting me slowly and affectionately. I do the same to him as I suck him into my mouth, playing with his ring until his cock softens in my mouth.

When Amon is done, he lays a soft kiss to my mound before turning me to him and hugging me to his chest.

"I love you," he whispers, his words dripping with emotion. "I don't think you realize how much, Sela. I'd willingly lay altar at your feet."

His words shock me and fill me with more joy than I'd ever felt possible.

"I love you, too, Amon. More and more every day," I give him the words for the first time as Sela—for the first time in too long.

"Soon we'll be able to put all of this behind us," he murmurs.

"About that," I lick my lips as I turn on my belly, lying on top of his chest with my hands under my chin as I look at him. "Can you tell me what happened in the past? I heard Kress and Finn talking in the library about the spell you performed when I died. Rhiannon said something about it too. Is that how I was reborn?"

He gives me a tight nod.

"I stole the original codex from the Vatican Library. Since we'd already read the codex some centuries before, I knew the spell would be inside."

"But how did you know to do that? That I was..."

"Dying?"

"Yes."

"Because I could hear all your thoughts, Sela. You were so fucking weak you couldn't put up any barriers. I heard everything, lass. Every. Fucking. Thing," he grits out as he remembers. "Hearing you think about not wanting to die alone was quite possibly the single most painful moment in my life. Your heart rate was going down, and I knew something was happening. Since I couldn't find Ambrosius, and there was nothing that could help you, I took the biggest risk."

"You performed the spell," I whisper, blinking back tears as I remember how helpless I'd felt in that moment.

"It was one of their most forbidden spells and it required an enormous amount of energy. The spell was said to be able to preserve a person's essence and nurture it until it became ready to be reborn again. And it worked. After I performed it, your body metamorphosed right before my eyes and it entered a regenerative slumber—similar to the one I undertake when I use up my energy supply."

I blink in surprise.

"What?"

"A metamorphosis to foster your essence. To my understanding, it was some kind of hibernating state to repair the damage that had been done—at least enough so you could be born again. And it happened," he smiles, his eyes misted with tears. "One moment you were in front of me, the next you turned into a small cocoon."

"A cocoon? As in a larva?" I do my best not to laugh despite it being quite funny.

He nods.

"You were like that for over a thousand years. It took you a long time to heal, lass. Alas, it gave me some time to heal too. I might have been a little beat up after all the energy I used for the spell and...my temper got the best of me and I caused a few natural disasters..."

He winces as he explains that he'd immediately gone after Ambrosius and had eventually found him. But not before Ambrosius had spread misinformation about Amon, the codex and the mark that appeared on my skin. In an attempt to paint himself the injured party in case someone looked deeper into the issue, Ambrosius had recorded an erroneous version of the events that happened and accused Amon of being a demon, which Kress and Finn had later helped perpetuate.

After Amon had found Ambrosius, they'd engaged in a few battles over a number of years before Amon used up his last bit of energy to control a mob of people to chase after Ambrosius in an effort to regain control of the jewel. He managed to kill Ambrosius through this tactic, but his strength had been too depleted, causing him to lose track of the jewel in the madness that ensued.

"I was in a deep slumber for a few hundred years. But when I awoke, you were still a little cocoon," he continues, his lips in a perpetual smile when he mentions the cocoon.

While he was waiting for me to emerge from my cocoon, he'd been trying to trace the jewel again, and it had taken him until the year of our marriage as Jeremiah and Elizabeth Creed for him to procure it again.

"That cocoon sounds...a little ridiculous, I'm not going to lie," I admit on a giggle.

"It was magic. You, better than anyone, should know that it exists," he chuckles. "I spoke daily to you. I slept with you by my side. I read to you. I did everything I could think of to help you heal faster so you could be reborn again. And it finally happened. In 1772, you became a beautiful butterfly, and you flew from my side, choosing Fiona as your mother. Against all odds, it happened again when you died in o-five. Lydia was the one who found the cocoon in the church and brought it to me after I'd been imprisoned. I kept you with me until you spread your wings again," he smiles. "And each time, you were stronger than the last. I think all the time you spent as a cocoon helped you heal all the rifts in your essence."

I nod, digesting all the information. Somehow imagining my Amon reading to a small cocoon in hopes I would reemerge from it and turn into a beautiful butterfly threatens to make me devolve into a weeping mess.

If I thought he was cute before, I don't think anything else can trump that.

"I can't believe you did all that for me," I tell him as I wipe at my tears.

"I'd do that and more, lass. You know I'm not whole without you."

"I know," I whisper. "But I still have a question. Why did my abilities only manifest when I arrived in Fairydale?"

The last time I hurt myself was when I'd pricked my finger on that black card Mr. Vaughan had sent me. After that, all my injuries had been able to heal on their own.

"Lydia. I'm sure it must have been Lydia," he answers grimly, his expression shifting as he remembers our beloved daughter. "She was convinced you couldn't know *anything* before you came to Fairydale. She must have ensured that you somehow didn't trigger your abilities until you came to Fairydale."

I squeeze his hand as my expression mirrors his, pain overtaking me as I recall our last interaction.

"She's been doing everything behind the scenes hasn't she? All this time, she took care of every little detail to make sure things went according to plan. She went as far as to let herself be used by the enemy so she could feed him false information. How could she..." my voice breaks. "How could she be so selfless, Amon? She forfeited her own life so that we..."

"We raised a wonderful girl, Sela. But she didn't waste her life. That, I can promise you. She had an incredibly happy life, a loving husband and the best children. I could hear her thoughts before she died and she was completely at peace with everything. More than anything, she had faith that we would succeed."

"Do you think..." I lick my lips as I remember the frightening event from my childhood. "Do you think that shadow watching over me was her?"

"It could be," he nods. "She always said she wanted to know you again when you'd be reborn. And in her own way, I'm certain she did."

"I have an idea," I suddenly say as I pull myself into a seating position. "We should send Lydia and Abraham off with a small ceremony. We've never done anything like that for them and... Maybe it won't help them in the afterlife anymore. But maybe it will help us cope with it better."

His brows go up in surprise but his lips spread into a brilliant smile.

"That's a wonderful idea, darlin'. You know, in the Vissirian way, when a soldier died, we would give him a farewell by sending his body out in the ocean, or river that was closer. I know we don't have their bodies anymore. But what if we penned them a letter and sent it out in the ocean? Who knows, maybe it could reach them at some point, since magic is very much alive."

"I love that," I smile at him as I reach for his hand.

One way or another, I always reach for him, needing his touch more than anything. It's the only thing that can calm me, and I have no clue how I'm going to have to pretend to go along with Rhiannon's plans on my own—not when I'd feel his absence even for a second.

There's also the fact that he has far more information about the witches than I have. Even in the past, he'd always been the one getting more involved and having a knack for them. Besides, he had Lydia to show him the ropes, too.

Suddenly I frown as it dawns on me he suggested a scenario in which he needs to exit his prison.

"But you'd have to come to the surface for that," I bite my nail as I regard him apprehensively. "You'll get hurt, Amon."

"And you can fix me up," he readily replies.

"But the pain...You'll be in pain," I complain, not liking this at all.

"I'll be in pain anyway, darlin'. But I need this just as much as you do."

"We could do something different..." I trail off when his expression falls. "Fine," I sigh. "But you'll drink my blood before, after, and during. Alright?"

"Darlin', I'd drink your blood any time of the day. Just say the word," he drawls smoothly.

"You rogue," I accuse before I launch myself at him.

Unfortunately, it's still me who ends up being tickled until I declare I forfeit.

"I have one more request," I whisper when I finally find my breath after too much laughter.

"What is it?"

"I'll tell you later," I smile sheepishly, knowing he won't be able to refuse me.

It's close to dawn that we decide to hold the ceremony for Lydia and Abraham.

We'd both written the letters together as we'd poured all our love into the words, wishing them only happiness in their future life and apologizing for not being better parents.

Walking hand in hand along the beach in an area that no one would be likely to spot us, we both prepare two bottles in which we sneak in our messages.

Amon uses his power to move the bottles, pushing them towards the horizon line and dropping them in the water somewhere in the middle of nowhere—that way, there's always a chance they might find their targets.

After all, it's magic.

Our entire life has been steeped in magic, and it will always be defined by magic.

And as the sun rises, an orange hue painting the sky, I look up at my husband, watching the beautiful smile that pulls at his lips as he looks into the distance, undoubtedly thinking of Lydia and Abraham and the possibility of them getting our messages.

And that's how I know for sure. Yes, it was magic that they were our children and that we had the blessing to be their parents—that we had even one moment with them.

They might not be among us anymore, but the memories will forever live on. And this time, I will value and defend them whatever the cost.

Amon was right *and* wrong.

Memories might not be the core of a person. But they certainly give you depth of feeling—for you must have loved to know loss and you must have lost to know the fear of loving again. And though the cycle always repeats, it makes us stronger.

One day at a time.

One loved one at a time.

In the end, only memory remains.

So will Lydia and Abraham take their place in the colorful mosaic that is our memory. And even though our time together had been brief on this Earth, every moment had left its mark on us.

We are here because of them.

We are who we are because of them.

"I asked you before," I murmur as the harsh wind of the evening blows in Amon's hair, tendrils of his white locks brushing against my face. "Would you do anything differently? Knowing the outcome as you do now, would you change anything?"

He turns to me as he pulls my jacket tighter around my body, his expression pensive.

"No," he shakes his head.

"Even after everything you endured? All the loss and heartache? Even then?"

"It's *because* of that, Sela. Regardless of all the suffering, it taught me the most important lesson of all."

I raise my brows in curiosity.

"Never take the present for granted; never take even *one* moment for granted. We might be the closest thing to being immortal, but we are not invincible, nor are we infallible. We can't overestimate ourselves or how much time we have left."

I nod slowly.

"Do you?" he fires the question back at me.

"No," I smile. "My road led me to you, Amon. How could I *ever* regret that?"

It might have been a rather windy serpentine, but it had taken me to my ultimate destination. That we're now together is a blessing, but it's by no means the end.

We still have one more battle to face before we can prevail.

One more obstacle.

And in that moment, looking into my mate's eyes and experiencing the most profound type of love there is, an uncharacteristic thirst for revenge blooms inside of me.

Chapter Thirty-One

Turning off the water, I step out of the shower and I dry my body before putting on a purple formal dress and making myself presentable.

"You're staring," I chuckle, finding Amon in his cat form perched on my vanity.

I can't help it, lass. You look spectacular, he speaks in my mind.

"Why, thank you," I flutter my lashes at him before laying a kiss on the white tuft of hair on his head.

Selaaa!

"Please don't tell me you're jealous of a cat now, Amon," I chide softly.

I don't appreciate your lips anywhere but on me, he grumbles, clearly put off.

I shake my head in amusement. Of course he would take issue with that since theoretically it's not his body—he's just borrowing it. Despite being so jealous of Caleb, he'd taken it in stride because it had still been him who'd been by my side and touched me. But now, he's merely inserting his consciousness into Mr. Meow's body.

"You need to behave today. Everyone will be present for the dinner."

The time has come for the entire coven to reunite at the Hale manor to go over the details of the ritual approaching in just a couple of days. And with them here, I will likely have to be more careful about my actions and my words so that we won't be found out—especially now that I am not *just* Darcy.

Since Amon is more knowledgeable about the coven due to Lydia's influence, I'd asked him to become Mr. Meow again temporarily so that we may work together outside of his prison while still making sure he isn't hurt for leaving it.

This has proved to be a good loophole so far. But there is still the matter of all the other coven members that would be present and whose abilities are yet unknown. As such, we must tread very carefully.

I apply some light make-up and perfume, before I head downstairs. Mr. Meow follows behind, but not in a conspicuous manner.

"Darcy! There you are!" Rhiannon exclaims as she sees me come down the stairs. "The dining room has just been finished. Come and take a look."

I give her a bright smile.

"Of course. I know you've been working very hard to give everyone the best welcome."

"Bah," she waves her hand. "We hired a catering firm from Ipswich to do everything. At my age, I can only oversee things now. I'm not quite as sprightly as I was in the past."

"Yes, but you still thought of everything. I'm sure our guests will appreciate everything. Has anyone seen the house before?"

She shakes her head.

"I've met some of the members of the last generation of the six. But this new generation is much younger and more modern. I doubt the house will be to their liking."

"Nonsense. Anyone would be able to appreciate the architectural wonder that is the Hale manor. Especially if they see the gallery with the priceless art works. Even youngsters should be impressed by such a collection."

"They should, shouldn't they?" she nods pensively. "But I'm afraid we'll have little time for an extensive tour of the house or other frivolities, my dear. We'll have dinner, after which we'll all convene to discuss our next steps. Matters have become quite dire," she adds in a severe tone.

"What do you mean?" I frown.

"I know you've been quite cut off from the outside world here, which is for the best. But some...things have happened in town. Terrible things," she purses her lips.

"I don't follow."

"Maybe you felt the earthquake a couple of days ago? It was focused in this region."

Earthquake? I hadn't felt anything of the kind.

Because you were part of it, my love, Amon speaks in my mind. *It must have happened when I fucked you.*

My eyes flare in shock just as my cheeks redden when I realize he is right.

"Oh, *that* earthquake."

"It's not even the worst. We went into town yesterday and it was..." she takes a deep breath as she stops in her tracks. "More than half the town is *dead*, Darcy. When we first discovered the bodies, we went from house to house to check on everyone."

"What? What happened?" I feign shock.

"'Twas just like in eighteen five. The plague is back. Everyone had simply exploded, and only some organic matter remained behind. Horrible. Truly, truly horrible."

"But why didn't you tell me sooner if it's so bad?"

"I didn't want to alarm you. But everyone will find out about it soon enough so I wanted you to hear it from me first.

"I can't believe this," I gasp. "It's him, isn't it? Amon."

She nods grimly.

"I knew the stories from before, but I never quite imagined it would be this bad," she takes a deep breath. "Their bodies had simply liquified into this grime. It was inconceivable, but it opened my eyes to just how strong Amon has grown. If he's able to kill half a town while still being trapped, I can't imagine what he will do if he goes free."

"Does anyone else know? The other residents? The police? What are they saying?" I ask, knowing this would be expected of Darcy to inquire about. She is, after all, not entirely accustomed to the more occult ways of life.

Rhiannon shakes her head.

"Kress and Finn helped us clean the mess. They are both strong telepaths and they erased the memories of the other residents."

"That simple?"

"It's *not* simple. The two of them have been working day and night to do it when they shouldn't have. Just like those people shouldn't have died," she adds vehemently.

"You're right, I'm sorry if I misspoke. It's just that I'm not familiar with the protocol."

"It is what the coven must do to ensure the rest of the world is oblivious to the dangers that loom."

"So whenever you have a...paranormal encounter, you erase people's memories?"

She grunts.

"What about other demons? I'm curious how others have been defeated."

"Via the regular way, which unfortunately did not work on Amon. Kress and Finn were right that he must be a very powerful archdemon to be capable of withstanding the power of six elders and still survive."

Well, considering Amon is *not* actually a demon, of course their tactics would fail.

"Have you personally met other demons?"

"What is with this line of questioning, Darcy?" she comes to a halt as she turns to face me.

I shrug.

"I think it's nerves," I purse my lips as I confess. "The day of the ritual approaches fast and I'm a little afraid if I'm honest. It's a habit of mine to ask for as much information as possible before undertaking a task."

She makes a tsk sound.

"You need to get over your nerves, Darcy. We're dealing with a beast that has no qualms killing thousands of people to make a statement."

"I understand," I nod.

"Of course, sometimes there are *some* good side-effects, too. Archibald has died as well. At least we're quite sure of it. We haven't been able to track him down, but the rest of his friends and relatives are all dead. Vaughan and the Pierces, too."

Of course Amon wouldn't have spared them since he knew they were involved in Abel's schemes. Everyone in his circle must be dead by now.

"How did you track Archibald?"

"With magic," she rolls her eyes, clearly put out with me for asking so many questions.

I nod sympathetically.

"That would be so good. One less danger, no?"

"Precisely."

We head to the dining room, and the doors open to reveal footmen dressed in finery tending to every aspect of the room.

It's almost like going back to my life as Elizabeth and the parties I would attend in England during my season.

"This is wonderful, Rhiannon," I praise, noting the smile that tugs at her lips. "The guests will certainly be impressed."

"Thank you. I rather think the room has never looked more perfect."

Can I kill her, too, darlin'? She ruined our dining room! Amon complains.

You can't kill her, no. That would only raise suspicions since I doubt she would be easy to take down. I tell him.

Finee, he sighs audibly in my head.

Now behave, I warn playfully.

Of course, my love, he immediately acquiesces.

One glance to the corner and I note Mr. Meow hiding under a table as he assesses everything with shrewd eyes.

"There was one more thing I'd like to ask of you, Rhiannon," I smile sweetly.

She raises her brows as she regards me.

"When you have time, could I take a look at the codex? I'd like to read up on some defense spells just in case. You can never be prepared enough, right?"

Rhiannon narrows her eyes at me.

"I suppose you're right," she eventually nods. "I can't have you head blindly into danger like that. Why don't you see me tomorrow morning in my living quarters and I shall let you take a look at it. It's in Latin, of course, but I could help guide you through it."

"That's very generous of you, thank you."

Except I happen to be quite fluent in Latin thanks to my returned memories—different dialects even. I would probably be able to read the codex better than her. But of course I don't say that. For now, I need to embody the vulnerable, at times skittish and confused Darcy.

We discuss the details of the dinner as Rhiannon tells me all about the menu and the rooms she'd opened up for our guests on the first floor.

"Naturally, the Creed is locked so it will only be the other wing."

"That sounds perfect," I murmur.

When the clock strikes one at noon, both Rhiannon and I take our place in the grand hallway, ready to greet everyone who arrives.

Though I would have expected Connor and Thomasa Hale to be present, too, Rhiannon had told me that they would stay out of this since they do not officially belong to the coven, nor do they have any abilities.

It is my understanding that I am quite a big exception to the rule because of my background. Usually, people require an initiation within the coven before they can attend official meetings, take part in discussions pertaining sensitive topics or have any type of access to the codices.

Kress and Finn are the first to arrive. They are both dressed in evening wear as they take their positions by our sides.

"Kress and Finn will be in charge of guarding the codices," Rhiannon explains. "Every family will bring their own codex with them and entrust it to them until the ritual in two days."

"That sounds sensible," I give her a smile.

Of course, I am quite certain they will be taking this chance to look for another spell they could use against Amon. When else would they get access to all six codices at the same time?

Even now, as they stand by our side, I can feel them probing inside my mind, trying to read my thoughts. Kress, in particular, keeps trying to tumble my mental barriers.

Yet he is in for a big surprise. If as Darcy I'd been able to block his attacks, now I can do better.

Pretending that my bracelet falls to the ground, I bend to pick it up and feel his renewed attempt at reading my mind. It's just like feeling his essence trying to pry into mine—something utterly disgusting for anyone but my mate.

I use just a little strength as I hone in on his presence just outside of my consciousness, and I give him a hard kick.

"Agh," he yelps in pain just as my fingers brush over my bracelet.

My lips tremble in amusement but I quickly get a grip on myself.

"Is everything alright?" Rhiannon asks.

"Yes," he croaks, rubbing at his temples.

"Good. Our first guests are here."

Rhiannon and I are standing by one side of the stair case, one next to another, while Kress and Finn are on the other.

A footman opens the front doors, inviting inside an elderly Japanese couple.

"Hana and Kaito Ito," the footman reads their names as they step towards us.

Hana is wearing a sparkling silver long dress while Kaito is dressed in a black tuxedo.

"So good to see you again, Hana," Rhiannon exclaims, greeting the other woman and her husband. "If I may present to you my granddaughter, Darcy."

I pay my respects as we make small talk. Kaito hands Kress a suitcase that contains the codex before the couple are shown to the drawing room for tea while the rest of the guests are still arriving.

Another couple arrives from France, a Mr. and Mrs. Toussaint whom Rhiannon had met before. The Toussaint family is the first one I meet that has magic passed down through the male line.

"Of course the youngsters would be the ones to arrive later," Rhiannon grumbles as she watches the hands of the clock with intense precision.

She's usually a stickler for rules, but she also seems to be quite prejudiced when it comes to things she does not know or understand. The fact that she's never questioned anything she's been told is in itself a red flag.

"Amadi," the footman announces, and a young Ethiopian man comes in.

He hands his suitcase to Kress before coming to our side.

"Good day, Miss Hale," he inclines his head.

"Good day to you, too, Mr. Amadi," Rhiannon greets back. "May I present you my granddaughter, Darcy O'Sullivan?"

"Pleased to meet you, Miss," he takes my hand to lay a kiss on my knuckles. His eyes sparkle at me as he gives me a light wink.

A loud meow echoes in the hall, and I refrain from physically wincing since I know the source of the sound very well.

"The pleasure is all mine, Mr. Amadi."

"Just Amadi," he corrects, still holding my hand.

He continues to look at me even though Rhiannon clears her throat a couple of times.

"The footman will show you to the drawing room where the other arrivals are," she states in a stern tone.

Smiling, he nods at her, following the footman.

"You're not here to flirt with the guests, Darcy," she leans in to whisper in my ear, her tone clearly scandalized.

"I was not flirting," I reply.

"I may be old, dear, but I am not blind. Mr. Amadi was making sweet eyes at you," she continues. "You are not to engage in behavior that would shame our family in any way. Is that understood?"

I don't know why she's so vehement about this when I wasn't doing anything wrong, but I simply agree to appease her.

Isabella Pérez arrives next, looking absolutely stunning in a black velvet gown.

She is around Darcy's age from what I can tell, but she has such beautiful features, I find it hard not to stare.

Curiously enough, Kress and Finn seem to have the same problem as they barely remove their eyes from her. It also doesn't escape me that Kress purposefully brushes his hand against hers when he receives her suitcase with the codex.

Interesting. So they aren't just mindless warriors out to get my Amon. They are still capable of baser emotions.

Isabella greets Rhiannon before she gives me a hug, surprising me with her forwardness.

"I am so happy to meet you, Darcy. I hear we're of the same age so we need to find a moment to chat. I haven't ever had a friend within the coven," she says enthusiastically.

I give her a warm smile, liking her energy.

"Of course. I'd love to do that."

As Isabella is led to the drawing room as well, Rhiannon gives me another warning glance.

It seems that in her view, I am not to interact with any of these people outside of coven business—which is absolutely ludicrous.

Yet as we await for the next guest, it seems he is late.

"Who is the last one?" I ask Rhiannon when I see her get increasingly annoyed with her eyes on the clock.

"A Mr. Aleksander Chernenko. I hope he won't keep us waiting too long."

It's about ten minutes later that the doors open for one last time, and Aleksander Chernenko walks inside the house.

Except that is *not* Aleksander Chernenko.

My eyes narrow at him. It seems my plan has been all in vain if he continues to do things like these, not even caring for his well-being.

He's changed his appearance again, looking as he had when he'd been Caleb, with his dark hair and even darker eyes. He's wearing a tuxedo as well for the occasion, but it's a little too tight on him—*because it's not his.*

A casual smile on his lips, he steps in front of Kress and hands him the suitcase with the codex before coming to our side to greet us.

My eyes are still on Kress and Finn as I track their reactions to him, but so far I don't see anything out of the ordinary. They just seem glad to be done with the entire ordeal.

"We'll go lock the codices before joining you for dinner, Miss Hale," Kress tells Rhiannon, after which they go up the stairs.

I assume the place they will lock the codices in has to be Rhiannon's sleeping quarters.

But I don't get to dwell on that as Amon stops in front of us.

"Miss Hale. You're just as beautiful as I'd heard," he drawls in a seductive voice, his words accented and making seem like the ultimate rogue.

My eyes widen as I note that Rhiannon is *not* chiding him. She's...blushing?

Gods, that is something I'd never thought I'd see.

But then again, this same male charmed Fiona, someone who'd hated him as much as Rhiannon currently hates Amon.

"And Miss Darcy," he murmurs thickly as he kisses my knuckles, his lips lingering a moment too long.

What are you doing here? I demand as I stare in his eyes.

Guarding your virtue, he answers smoothly.

I assure you my virtue is long gone, and you're the one to blame for that, I reply drily. *You're jeopardizing everything.*

I will behave. As long as all those damn men behave, too. Don't think I didn't see that man kiss your hand, he warns lightly.

Amon, Amon, what am I going to do with you?

Let me kill him? he asks hopefully

Behave! No killing anyone until I get my hands on those codices.

Fine, fine. But at least now you have me here, too, he murmurs lovingly just as his eyes turn softer towards me. *I missed you.*

That's all it takes for me to melt.

Three words and his lovesick expression.

I missed you too, I sigh. *Meet me in the bathroom after tea for blood.*

Darlin', you know your way to a man's heart, he groans, almost audibly.

Rhiannon is already watching us like a hawk and I have to pull my hand from his and pretend nothing is wrong while he continues to smile at us.

"Right, let us all head to the drawing room for tea," Rhiannon finally says.

Amon and I walk a distance apart, but his presence is still clogging my senses.

Wicked male. He couldn't sit this one out and let me deal with everything, could he?

As we get inside, tea is served while introductions are being made. Though not everyone has met in person before, they've communicated one way or another, or at least their parents had.

Yet as the topic veers from the mundane to the matter at hand, it's Isabella who speaks first.

"You're all aware that this could end with our deaths, no? The last time the coven attempted something like this, the spell killed the Elders performing it."

"We'll be fine," Amadi replies, stretching in his seat. "The spell feeds on energy. This is just a case of the previous Elders not having enough energy to sustain it until it could actually kill the demon."

"And you're saying we all have more energy than they did?" Isabella raises a brow.

"Miss Pérez is right. The Elders who entrapped Amon were legendary in their own right. What makes us any different from them?" Mrs. Ito intervenes.

"Because we have *her*," Rhiannon intervenes as she points to me. "We have her and they didn't. We already know that my grandmother predicted everything. Trust me that it shall all be fine."

"Lydia Hale was famous for her predictions," Mr. Toussaint mentions. "I met her once, too, in her later years. Wonderful woman."

My smile deepens at his words.

"We've come here because you asked us to, Miss Hale," Isabella continues. "But you've given us little else but Lydia Hale's predictions. Why her? What makes her so special? This is *my* life we're talking about and I'm not about to risk it on an uncertainty."

"Miss Pérez," Rhiannon grits her teeth. "You're a member of the six families, an Elder in your own right despite your...young age. You'd embarrass your family by stepping down when the alternative is letting this demon walk free? Destroy this entire world, perhaps?"

"If I may," Amon interjects, looking quite at home as he leans back in his seat, his legs crossed, his fingers on the cup of tea that he brings to his lips.

Everyone stares at him expectantly.

"Maybe everyone's worries would be more assuaged if Miss Hale and the Holy See explain to us in detail what the plan is for the big day. We have two days to spare until the ritual. Why don't we give her the opportunity to convince us?"

Rhiannon sputters as her eyes widen.

"Convince you?" she repeats in horror. "I shouldn't have to convince you of anything! You're all part of the coven and your duty is to exterminate evil. How could you say that you do not want to do it because you're afraid it's too dangerous? Might I remind you of the oath you all took?"

"Rhiannon," Mr. Toussaint addresses her. "I don't think the issue is that we aren't ready to give our lives to the cause. Rather, it's that we're not sure it's going to work even *if* we do it. Is it worth it for the lives of six Elders *just* to fail?"

"I see that scum of Archibald reached out to you, did he not? He tried to sow distrust."

"That is not what we are discussing. It is true that I'm familiar with Archibald, but at present this has nothing to do with him."

"Well, it should, considering he is dead," Rhiannon says, her lips curling up when four people react with awe—potentially all who'd been in contact with him.

Damn you, Abel, but you really couldn't curb your greed, could you?

"Archibald is dead. As is half of this town."

Everyone gasps.

"By the hands of *that* demon."

"Great," Isabella rolls her eyes. "So you're now telling us he can kill half the town while imprisoned? That certainly bodes well for us."

"And what exactly do you propose we do then, Miss Pérez? Let him escape his prison and kill all of us?"

"Do you think he would?" Amon inquires casually. "I've been studying this demon of yours."

"It's not mine," Rhiannon says through gritted teeth, but Amon ignores her.

"Well, you're certainly the one emotionally involved with this, though I can't quite figure out why."

"Because he is a goddamn demon who's going to destroy the world! It's more alarming you are not involved in this," Rhiannon cries out as she looks around the room, meeting everyone's eyes.

"Regardless of semantics," Amon continues, disregarding Rhiannon's outburst. "I am skeptical about your claims. Mostly because it seems he's been striking out when he was hurt by our people instead of doing it out of pure malice."

Everyone is quiet.

My own eyes widen as I stare at him.

What are you doing?

Sowing dissent, he murmurs in my mind. *And what better way to do it than show everyone the truth?*

But... Are you sure you want to do this?

I'll show them just enough so they question everything. Trust me?

Always.

"Mrs. Ito, I'm told you have a very peculiar gift."

"Define peculiar," she frowns.

"You're able to glean the history of an object with just one touch, are you not?"

"Yes. That is correct," she nods.

"Then could I bother you to read the history of this?" Amon says as he removes the necklace without its jewel from his pocket.

"What is that?" Rhiannon asks.

"It's something I've come into possession of only recently, but something I'm told is priceless. It belonged to Elizabeth Montford."

"Elizabeth Montford, you mean..."

"The lady who was, *allegedly,* killed by the demon. Killed, abused, groomed, raped... he *allegedly* did a lot of things."

"But how..."

"I'll do it," Mrs. Ito nods, taking the necklace from Amon.

Settling back in her seat, she places it within her spread palms as she closes her eyes.

Energy pulsates in the air as a faint light surrounds her.

"So? What do you see?" Isabella asks after a few minutes.

"I see Elizabeth and..." she trails off. "The demon," she clears her throat.

Suddenly, she opens her eyes again, her gaze connecting with Rhiannon's.

"You never told anyone the demon was Mr. Creed, or that Elizabeth and Amon were the adoptive parents of Lydia Hale," she states in a clear voice.

"I..." Rhiannon's eyes widen. "I didn't know..."

"You? *You* didn't know?" Isabella asks. "You're living in their house and you didn't know?"

Rhiannon shakes her head in dismay, looking so thoroughly alarmed it can't be an act. She hadn't known... But how? I had seen Amon's portrait in the Creed suites. Except... Has Rhiannon ever been there? Has anyone?

No, Amon answers in my mind. *No one's been in our rooms but us, darlin'. Do you think I would risk anyone seeing the paintings I did of you —of us? To everyone else, the doors are sealed. Only to you were they open.*

I bite my lip as I give him a small nod, relieved to hear that despite the fact that it might have helped clean his reputation.

"Did you also not know that Amon didn't kill Elizabeth?"

"What?" This time, Rhiannon rises up in indignation, her hand instantly searching for her cane when her legs become wobbly. "Blasphemy. I saw it myself. You, too," she points at Toussaint. "It's been recorded in the collective history."

Mrs. Ito shakes her head.

"It must have been fabricated. This is not at all what I see."

"Then what are you seeing?" Amadi asks.

"Elizabeth was killed by her adoptive son, Abel, Lydia's brother. And he killed his brother, Abraham. He..." her lips tremble. "He stole the necklace. There was a stone here," she points to the empty spot. "He stole that and he gained immense powers."

Everyone is now listening with rapt attention.

"Abel is the man you know as Archibald," she suddenly says.

Rhiannon pales, her wrinkles seemingly more pronounced than ever.

"That... That can't be true..." she croaks.

I almost feel bad for her because she's just now realizing that the person who raped her was related to her.

But right as she's about to say something else, Kress and Finn appear in the doorway, their features darkening as they note what's happening.

"Did you know?" Rhiannon turns to them. "Did you know that the collective memory is fabricated?"

Of course they did. If I'm right, they worked with Abel to fabricate it together.

"What are you talking about?"

"Tell us if you knew," Isabella rises as she pushes her chin up in defiance.

More voices erupt as everyone has questions for the Holy See.

Right at that moment, Amon winks at me before taking his leave as we'd discussed.

I wait for a moment after he exits the room, and when I see that Kress and Finn are entirely too busy being mobbed by angry and confused witches, I leave, too, going straight for the bathroom near the conservatory.

I only just open the door before Amon pulls me inside, caging me in.

The space is crammed as this is a one person bathroom. And with Amon's significant size, we barely have any breathing room.

"I can see why you were such a good general," I murmur when he rests his head in the crook of my neck, breathing harshly.

"Is that so?" he drawls. His lips skim my collarbone as he licks his way up my neck.

"You like strife—confusing your enemy and turning them against each other."

"Mhm... Can we talk about this later? Now I..." he trails off as he sinks his teeth in my neck just as his hand reaches under my dress to touch me.

"Amon I..."

My words are cut off as he makes me come with the minimal touch of his fingers.

"There, that's better," he leans back as he arranges my dress back in place and wipes the blood off his mouth and off my skin.

"You're feeling alright?"

He nods.

"I couldn't let you face this alone," he smiles. "Doesn't matter how strong I *know* you are."

"So, is this really your plan? Confuse them?"

"I've been thinking about the best way to approach this with the minimal damage. Truth to be told, our quarrel isn't with the coven. Especially the younger generation. I'm still half of a mind to cut Rhiannon to pieces for daring to risk your life," he grumbles. "But at the end of the day, our goal is to get me out of my prison, and find a way to neutralize the shield that's protecting Kress and Finn."

"I agree. I quite like the coven," I nod. "I wouldn't want them to be hurt when they're reluctant about this in the first place."

"Precisely my thoughts. If they find out the truth, they are not likely to help Kress and Finn. See, I don't kill indiscriminately as some people say about me," he pouts.

"Only sometimes," I raise a brow.

"Fair enough. I might have been impulsive on occasion. But only when you were harmed, Sela mina," he murmurs. "You're my only limit."

"I know," I sigh. "And I'm actually glad that people are seeing the past for what it was—that they see who was the source of all evil. If only they could see it with Kress and Finn, too..."

"We'd need an object that ties us to them," Amon mentions just as his eyes sparkle with hidden knowledge.

"What is it?"

"The sword," he states. "The rhodium sword they offered to Fiona. If Mrs. Ito can see its history, she will realize it was never sanctified by the pope and will likely find out about Arkgor and the fact that Kress and Finn have been around for centuries."

"But where is the sword?"

Amon smiles.

"In the unlikeliest of places," he chuckles. "Above the fireplace in the dining room."

My eyes widen.

"You're joking," I whisper.

"No," he shakes his head, his lips quirking up. "They offered it to Lydia to safeguard for the future when you would be born, and she placed it in plain sight," he chuckles. "I can wager a guess that Kress would have wanted you to use it against me. Theoretically, it would have been the perfect revenge to have my mate be the one to kill me. Except they didn't count on our resourcefulness."

"They didn't count on many things. Kress might have been a friend to you in the past, Amon, but he never truly knew you."

He grunts, his lips tightening in a firm line.

"And maybe that's my fault too. I didn't know how to open up. I was always hiding for fear someone would find out about my Reva heritage so I barely interacted with people. Kress became my friend because he was also my direct subordinate and right hand."

"Now I can say I'm glad for your trust issues," I chuckle. "Otherwise they would have had a great deal more information to use to their advantage."

"Minx," he leans in to lay a kiss on my lips.

"How come they didn't recognize you when you came in?" I ask what had been baffling me from the beginning.

"A simple spell from our daughter. It masks power signatures. She said I would need it at some point. I think she meant now," he chuckles.

"I'll never stop being in awe of our daughter," I shake my head as I smile. "She really thought of everything, didn't she?"

"She did," he smiles fondly.

I lean into him, taking advantage of this moment to absorb his body heat.

"We need to get a look at the combined codices for a spell. But when?"

"Tonight," Amon states. "During dinner. We'll go there and search for the spell."

"Are you sure you're up for it? You're not too weak, no?"

He shakes his head, a sad smile playing on his lips.

"It's the last stretch, Sela. I can do this."

I purse my lips, unable to *not* worry about him.

"When we find the spell, I can do it by myself," I assure him. "With my energy levels, I should be able to perform any spell."

"See, *that* I don't doubt. As Darcy, I would have been scared to let you do anything on your own because you didn't have your energy back. But now? The stage is yours, Sela mina. And I know you're going to make me the proudest mate."

He kisses me again before he leaves first.

I stay in the bathroom for a while longer to fix my dress and hair, before I join everyone else in the drawing room.

"Then tell us why *she* looks exactly like Elizabeth Montford," Mrs. Ito suddenly points at me when I'm in the doorway.

My eyes widen for a moment, but seeing Amon shake his head, I take a deep breath and focus on what's going on.

"You're all jumping the gun. So what if he didn't kill Elizabeth? He's still a dangerous demon," Kress says through gritted teeth.

"But don't you see? Someone tampered with the collective memory!" Isabella gets to her feet. "How can we trust anything that's happening knowing that someone could do that? It doesn't give us much confidence in the Holy See."

"So you'd rather trust an old lady than the Supreme Authority?" Finn fires.

"You just confirmed he didn't kill Elizabeth, thereby saying *not* to trust the Supreme Authority. Really, Finn?" Amon raises a brow.

Both Kress and Finn look as if they're about to explode. Everyone continues to question them and whether the ritual is truly safe to perform.

"Quiet," Rhiannon screams as she taps her cane to the floor. "I know you all have doubts, but we're talking about someone who caused a plague and killed thousands of people with just the power of his mind. Do we really care about some minor details?"

"Miss Hale, it's clear that we're not going to settle this just yet. We need to know from the Holy See exactly what the spell entails and what will be required of us," Amadi mentions.

"Then let us all head to the dinner and our guests of honor," she motions towards Kress and Finn, "will walk us through everything that will happen."

Kress nods in agreement.

"Shall we?" Rhiannon regards everyone as she nods to the door.

This time, they refrain from commenting as they walk towards the door.

I wait until everyone leaves for the dining hall before I approach Rhiannon.

"This is bad," I whisper. "What if someone pulls out? We won't be able to do the spell."

"We will do it," she grits her teeth. "I don't care what I have to do, but that spell will be performed as we've convened."

My, but she is quite determined.

I have to agree with Amon that she seems too invested in this, and I wonder why.

Because she made it her life's purpose, Amon replies in my mind. *After Abel attacked her, this was the only way she could justify what happened to her. Because if her assault resulted in Lizette, which later resulted in you and you would fulfill the prophecy, then all her pain would not be for nothing. I might not like Rhiannon for her fanaticism, but it makes sense why she would pour all of herself into his mission. For her, there is simply no other way of life.*

My eyes slightly widen at his explanation because it makes too much sense.

I sneak a glance at Rhiannon. Her lips are tight, her features filled with determination.

You're right. I don't know how I didn't see that before. Rhiannon worships Lydia because of her predictions. It makes sense because that's the only thing that gave her purpose. She's been training her entire life for this moment. That is just...sad, and pitiful.

She's yet another victim of Abel's. Gods, I can't believe he was capable of such evil...

But why would Lydia allow it? Surely she could have changed that.

I don't think she could, he adds on a sigh. *I told you before, love. Lydia saw many versions of the future, but only one in which we prevailed. That meant...*

She had to make sacrifices, so I fill in the gaps.

It doesn't escape me that to get to where we are now, people have had to suffer—*innocent* people—and my heart hurts for it. Ultimately, this might make me a bad person, but I do not regret anything.

Not when I'm one step closer to freeing my love.

Not when happiness is within our reach for the first time in forever.

Even in the past, we'd been plagued by too many issues to truly be happy—my infertility, Amon's worries about the Arkgor, and the fact that we've been chased around from one end of this world to the other by the Empire's scouts. There were beautiful years, too, but our happiness was always marred by constant worries.

This time, though, I will make sure things change.

As we enter the dining room, we are all shown to our seats.

To my surprise, I end up seated across from Amon, who gives me a brilliant smile and a wink. Mrs. Ito is seated to my right while Isabel is to my left.

Rhiannon takes her role as hostess seriously, sitting at the end of the table to be able to see everyone. Kress and Finn are by her side, each on one side.

As soon as everyone has taken their seats, she instructs the servers to come in with the food.

The first few courses are served and people eat slowly, without much conflict. That doesn't mean the tension isn't high. Suddenly, it seems that everyone regards everyone with suspicion and animosity.

Amon had certainly succeeded in his goal.

With the way everyone is behaving, I doubt there will be any ritual.

At the first break, Rhiannon rises with a glass of wine, proposing a toast before going into a very odd explanation.

"As you all know, Lydia Hale made a prediction that Darcy O'Sullivan, my granddaughter, would one day either help exterminate the demon or free him. My granddaughter isn't one to go around freeing demons, so that option is out of the question. It can still happen, however, if we fail to perform the spell."

"But why is she so special?" Isabel complains. "You keep telling us she is the key to everything, but you don't tell us *why*."

"Because she is Elizabeth Montford," Rhiannon states.

My eyes flare open in shock—that she would know *and* share it with everyone—while gasps erupt all around the table.

"That can't be..."

"It's why they look the same, is it not?" Mrs. Ito asks.

"Indeed," Rhiannon nods. "And it's her gift and connection to the demon that makes her so special."

"Her gift?" Mr. Toussaint frowns.

It seems to me that Rhiannon hasn't shared *too* much with her coven.

"Show them, Darcy," Rhiannon addresses me. "Show them your gift."

I give her an odd look as I'm trying to piece together what she means to do. But with everyone staring at me, I have no option but to stand up and do a small demonstration.

But before anything, I sneak a glance to Amon to see if he's thinking what I am thinking.

A small smile curves along his lips as he inclines his head at me.

Getting out of my seat, I go to the fireplace, reaching out for the rhodium sword.

Kress makes a choked sound when he realizes what I'm about to do.

"Oh, perfect choice, Darcy!" Rhiannon clasps her hands in happiness.

Giving them a small smile, I bring the sword over my hand, cutting my wrist in one smooth stroke.

"What..."

"What are you doing?"

Everyone is initially baffled until my arm starts to regenerate, the fallen one on the ground disappearing.

"But how? How is that possible?"

"I think Mrs. Ito might be able to tell us that," I murmur as I move forward, laying the sword in front of her.

"What do you think you're doing?" Kress rises from his seat to stop me, Finn closely behind her.

"That sword is priceless and you're letting others handle it?" Finn grits out as he snatches it from before Mrs. Ito.

The elderly woman frowns, narrowing her eyes.

"I did not plan on using it. Only reading its energy," she states slowly —the implication clear.

"This will be instrumental in killing the demon. We can't have you wield it around carelessly."

"But she can?" Isabella fires back. "Or is it that you're hiding something? *Again.*"

They start fighting anew and I note Amon slipping out of the room and heading for the stairs.

Make sure you're not detected when you leave, he whispers in my mind.

I await a few more moments as the arguments become increasingly heated. The coven is pointing fingers at Kress and Finn, demanding to know what they are hiding and becoming increasingly more paranoid about the entire event *and* Rhiannon.

When someone accuses Rhiannon of using the coven's abilities for her own benefit, I use the distraction to get out of the room, too.

Luckily, it seems people are too busy arguing to pay any mind to me, despite being the one who'd started it this time.

Knowing I have no time to waste, I hurry up the stairs to the second floor, heading straight for Rhiannon's living quarters.

Just as I reach the door, Amon opens it for me, a grim expression on his face.

"The codices are in the back. But there is a shield all around them," he says. "We don't have much time, darlin', we need to think of something."

Taking my hand, he leads me to the area where the codices are.

Surprisingly, the suitcases haven't been opened. They are all stacked up one on top of the other.

But there is one other thing.

There are only five of them.

"Rhiannon's isn't here," Amon says.

"It should be," I frown. "Maybe not in plain sight but..."

I pivot, walking around and remembering the last time I was in here. As I reach the middle of the room, I spot an empty table that is nonetheless spotless—no trace of dust or dirt.

Frowning, I reach with my hand, grasping at the empty air.

"Here. I think it's here," I murmur, my eyes narrowed as I study the space.

Before I can overthink it, however, I randomly try something.

"Revelare," I whisper.

Slowly, the codex is revealed. Just as Fiona had kept hers, Rhiannon has a glass case covering it.

"Good job," Amon kisses my cheek. "Now five left."

"Do you think the spell Lydia left us might work?" I ask as we both stare at the five suitcases.

"I'd be willing to bet it would," Amon answers.

"Walk me through it," I give him a smile.

He nods, threading his fingers through mine as we focus on the barrier surrounding the codices.

Amon starts chanting the barrier spell Lydia had left behind and I echo his words, imbuing my energy in my voice.

With our combined energies, the barrier breaks, a whooshing sound reverberating in the room.

Tentatively, I reach out, a big smile spreading across my face when I realize it worked.

"Oh, Amon. We're so close," I whisper as tears of joy stab at my eyes.

It's not the time to be sentimental, though. We both make quick work of opening the suitcases and spreading out the codices on the ground.

"Do you remember how the initial spell went?"

"Yes. Let me see if I can find it," he says as he shifts through each manuscript to find the beginning of the spell.

"This one," he suddenly breathes out, his features shining with excitement.

I look at the page he's pointing out, checking the title and location before going to each codex and turning the page to the spell.

Every codex has a few paragraphs of continuation, and though we have them all open at the same spell, now it's a matter of seeing the order of the verses.

Amon scrunches his face in concentration as he tries hard to remember the spell.

Taking hold of one codex at a time, he orders them around.

"I think this is the order they go in," he tells me, still deep in concentration.

"We can only try and see if it works. At this point, anything is better than waiting around. Every moment is too precious."

"Alright. Let's do this."

I take a deep breath as I go to the beginning of the spell.

Each of the forbidden spells have both an offensive spell and a defensive one—the offensive had been used to trap Amon while the defensive would work to undo the initial spell.

Channeling my energy to the surface, I focus on the words as I say them out loud, following Amon's cue as he points to the next codex, and then the next.

As I say the words, I feel pressure mounting inside of me before being released in the open.

Amon's eyes are wide open as he stretches his arms and legs, his strength slowly coming back

A small whirlpool of energy surrounds him, tearing at his clothes just as his appearance changes back to his original one. His long white hair flows down his back just as his jacket and shirt are ripped to pieces, leaving his torso naked.

More injuries appear on his body, his skin tearing with the power of the currents.

"Amon," I whisper, worried.

"No," he shakes his head. "Keep going," he urges as he grits his teeth in pain.

Trusting him, I continue chanting, moving from codex to codex as the spell uses up more and more of my energy.

Strong winds envelop Amon, the air cutting at his skin and punishing him just as the prison had for his brief escapes.

"Go on," he squeezes his eyes shut.

I focus all the power within me into the spell and as I say the last words, a loud noise resounds in the house just as the ground starts to shake.

"Amon... What's happening?"

Yet as I turn to look at him, I find him fully in his Reva form, his eyes wholly black as he stares at me.

"Did it... Did it work?" I ask as I swallow in uncertainty.

He gives me a brief nod just as he extends his hand towards me.

I take it, catapulted in his arms as he gives me a big hug.

"My strength is coming back," he whispers in my hair. "I can feel it filling every cell of my body. Gods... I haven't felt like this in forever."

"Do you need to heal? The wounds..."

"No," he shakes his head. "I'm perfectly fine."

And to prove to me that he is, he returns to his original form, his skin flawless.

"No wound," I blink in surprise. "But how..."

"I don't know, but it's done, darlin'. You did it," he smiles at me. "You fucking saved me."

Tears pour down my cheeks as I continue to hold onto him.

He's only wearing his pants—or what's left of them. The rest of his clothes have been torn to pieces. But I don't mind it as I take in the warmth of his skin and his sheer presence.

"Can you travel out of Fairydale?" I inquire softly, somehow still skeptical.

I barely ask the question and he disappears from my side only to return a moment later.

"Yes. I can. I was just in England so it's safe to say I'm not a prisoner anymore."

I breathe out in relief.

"We need to search for a spell to neutralize Kress and Finn's shield," I suddenly remember. "While there's time."

I don't wait for him to agree with me as I lower myself to the ground to pore over the manuscripts. Amon helps, too as he flips the pages rapidly, his eyes taking in all the words.

Where I might be a little slow with memorization, he is my opposite, able to retain everything in the blink of an eye.

"Here," he calls out, pointing to the spell.

Yet just as I'm about to align the other manuscripts to the same location, Amon rises to his feet, his eyes narrowing towards the door.

"They're coming," he purses his lips. "I'll hold everyone off while you search for that spell. Until you find it, I doubt I'll be able to lay a blow on them."

I nod just as the door bursts open.

Kress and Finn are the first ones to come inside while the coven is not far behind him.

"Hello to you, too, Kress. Long time no see, no?" Amon clicks his tongue as he regards the two with amusement.

"Darcy! What are you doing?" Rhiannon comes forward, her eyes fluttering between Amon and me. "The demon...he's..."

"He's not a demon, Rhiannon," I tell her. "Just as I am not Darcy."

"W-what?" she sputters.

"I gather you didn't touch the sword, Mrs. Ito?" I call out to the elderly woman in the back.

"I did."

"And what did you see?"

She purses her lips.

"Something that can't possibly be true."

"Ah, so you decided *not* to share that information? Pity," I give her a mocking smile. "You see, for thousands of years your coven has thought itself the ultimate moral authority, but when you take away all the lies, a dire truth remains."

"What are you talking about?" Isabella frowns.

Just at that moment, Amon disappears, with Kress and Finn on his tracks, undoubtedly moving the fight away from here.

Good luck, my mate. I'll find you that spell.

"All the history you know is wrong," I say as I pull down my neckline to reveal my unblemished skin.

Rhiannon gasps.

"The mark..."

"It was never a birthmark. It was an empty spot for something that was stolen from me. Something the Elder Ambrosius took from me, after which he blamed Amon for something that wasn't his fault."

"She's lying," Rhiannon spits at me viciously, already preparing to attack. It seems the coven, too, are calling on to their energies, directing them towards me.

All but Mrs. Ito, who is still trying to make sense of everything.

"You want to fight?" I laugh. "So that's it, only *your* version of the past can be the truth."

"The Supreme Authority would *never* allow something like this," Mr. Toussaint declares.

"Of course. They are oh, so saintly, aren't they?" I roll my eyes. "Fine. If you want to fight, I will fight you. But if you lose..." I trail off as I zero in on Rhiannon. "I want the spell that can neutralize Kress and Finn's shields."

"You dare ask something of me?" Rhiannon bursts out just as she taps her cane to the floor, energy rolling off it.

"If you're as honorable and true as you claim, you will," I state matter-of-factly.

"I won't make any deals with the likes of you," she grits out before she charges at me.

"Then I might have to get it out of you," I release a weary breath, stepping aside to avoid her blast.

But just as she steps forward to deliver more blows, so do the others, each using their abilities and spells to charge at me.

Creating a shield with my energy, I use it to absorb all their blows before hitting back with milder blasts. I don't want them to die, after all.

"It's useless to fight against me," I warn. "And I truly don't want to kill any of you."

I don't get to speak more as Amadi comes forward, his speed similar to Amon's as he aims to lay a blow on my body.

Closing my eyes, I call forth my tendrils of electricity, letting them coil all around the surface of my skin. When he finally hits me, instead of harming me, he harms himself as shocks claim his body.

He falls to the ground, not yet dead, but not far from it.

"Are you really going to keep this up?" I raise a brow as I send the tendrils of electricity towards them, wrapping them around each and everyone. "If I triggered them right now, you'd be fried. Is that what you want?"

"Stop," Mrs. Ito cries out. "I think she's telling the truth."

"Which truth?" Rhiannon asks, her lip twitching in distaste as she finds herself caught.

"Amon isn't a demon. She's not one either. They are...from another world."

"What?" Everyone gasps at the revelation, and I let Mrs. Ito continue.

"I saw it when I touched the sword. I saw their world, Arkgor. Kress and Finn are from there, too. They aren't part of the coven, nor do they work with the Supreme Authority."

"That's preposterous!"

"Is it? I saw them hundreds of years ago and they looked the same. No witch, despite our advanced lifespans, can live that long."

"Then what are they doing here?" Isabella asks.

"They're after Amon. They've been after him from the beginning. And they took advantage of the only weakness he has," she pauses as she raises her eyes at me. "*Her.*"

Mrs. Ito starts to recount everything she's seen when she touched the sword—from Arkgor to what happened in the past and how Kress and Finn had become fanatical in their quest for Amon.

"In their world, Amon was a legendary warrior and an honorable man," she finally says.

"You don't believe that," Mr. Toussaint complains.

"I do," Isabella says. "Why would Mrs. Ito lie? About this?"

"No... That can't be true," Rhiannon mutters, too shocked by what she'd heard.

Seeing that everyone is starting to think about the probability that this could be true, I release them.

"Will you help me?" I ask after a few moments. "I know Kress and Finn are protected by a shield, but I don't know what spell could neutralize it."

No one speaks.

Minutes on end pass as they simply stare at me before Mrs. Ito takes a step forward.

"I'll help."

The others don't speak, merely watching as both Mrs. Ito and I get on our knees on the ground as we sift through the spells.

One by one, the others join us, too—all but Rhiannon.

We look through the codices and we find several spells that could work in this context.

"I guess I'll try all of them," I sigh as I pick up a pencil and a sheet of paper to copy them in their entirety.

There are about five spells, and it takes me a good chunk of time to transfer them onto the new piece of paper.

All the while, loud noises are coming from the outside where the fight is in full swing.

"Can we help?" Mrs. Ito asks as I get up to leave.

"If you want," I shrug.

They can do whatever they want. As long as they aren't my enemies, I no longer care. I can save my mate on my own.

"You're really not Darcy?" Rhiannon finally asks.

I shake my head.

"My name is Sela."

"Sela..." she nods slowly. "Why... How..."

"There was one spell in the original codex that Amon used. I was dying and he managed to save me. I came back as Elizabeth, and now as Darcy. But I'm still...Sela."

"I see," she swallows hard. "Is it really true then? He's not...a demon?"

I give her a tight smile, realizing that all her hopes and dreams are crumbling at this moment. Her entire life's purpose turned out to be one big lie perpetuated for the personal gain of Kress and Finn.

"There are demons in this world, Rhiannon, but my mate is not one. Sometimes, humans can be just as demonic as those biblical hellish creatures. Just look at Ambrosius or Archibald. Just look at everyone who was so ready to crucify us for merely existing or being different."

"But he killed people... He..."

"My Amon has never killed without a reason—without being

provoked. He's never killed out of malice. Yes, he is dangerous, just as he is deadly. But if you are good to him, he will be good to you."

Her lips tremble as she digests my words.

"Then go save your mate," she inclines her head, surprising me with her words.

I nod, hurrying out of the house and to the front lawn where Amon and the other two are engaged in a fierce fight.

Amon is breathing hard, clearly tired, but he is still in his original form. That tells me he still has plenty of strength to spare before tapping into his Reva powers.

Keeping out of sight, I turn my attention to the spells I'd transcribed, focusing my energy on Kress and Finn as I say the words.

The first one doesn't work, as they are still resisting Amon's blows.

On to the second one. And the third.

Yet as I start on the fourth, Kress suddenly sees me, dashing towards me with his sword.

Seeing he's aiming for me, I call on a shield of my own, using pure electricity to keep him out. And as he makes contact with my shield, he reels back, his own protective barriers activated to keep him from getting burned to death.

"You really have no idea who you're dealing with, do you?" I smile as I nod towards Amon.

Just Kress' intention of going after me is enough to make him lose his mind. It doesn't matter that I can take care of myself or that nothing can hurt me.

The intention is more than enough to sign his death sentence.

Amon's muscles ripple as his skin turns black, his white hair a stark contrast to his dark skin. His size is absolutely terrifying and both Kress and Finn pale at the sight.

"That's..." Kress mutters as his eyes widen.

"A Reva," I add from behind him. "And if you've never encountered one before, then I feel sorry for you."

The moment Kress goes after Amon, I continue on with the fifth and last spell, hoping from the bottom of my heart that it will work.

I chant the words fast, all the while imbuing them with all the strength I can muster.

Please work.

As I finish the last word, I look up, afraid this one hadn't worked either.

But as I see Finn try to lay a blow on Amon, my mate swipes his claws at him, tearing off the entire skin off his face.

"It worked," I whisper.

Right at that moment, the coven exits the house too, their eyes bulging in their head as they look upon my deadly mate.

Granted, in his Reva form, I don't doubt anyone would think him a demon from the depths of hell.

Finn falls to the ground, groaning in pain.

Amon doesn't give him a moment to recover before he's on him. His big hand covers Finn's head just as he squeezes tightly, his skull exploding under the immense pressure.

Bits of bone and brain and other bodily fluids paint Amon from head to toe as he drops the dead body at his feet before setting his sights on Kress.

Whereas before he'd been so confident about Amon, now he looks as if he doesn't know whether to keep fighting or simply run.

Well, I guess he chooses the latter as he tries to get away.

I shake my head at him.

In this state, not even a Vissirian army could defeat Amon, and he thinks he stands a chance?

In just a second, Amon is in front of him, his claws sinking deep into his gut before he uses his other hand to decapitate him.

The head falls to the ground just as Amon withdraws his bloody claws.

He's breathing hard, his chest rising and falling with the residual adrenaline. But when he sees me rush towards him, he sheds his Reva form in favor of his humanoid appearance, drawing me to his chest and giving me a tight hug.

"We made it," he whispers. "One hundred and fifty years and I get to hold you in my arms again as a free man. One thousand four hundred and fifteen years and I get to hold you as my Sela again. I love you, darlin'."

Tears course down my cheeks as I tighten my hold on him, burying my face in his chest.

"We made it," I echo. "We're finally free."